THE

RIVAL APPRENTICES,

A TALE OF THE RIOTS OF 1780.

BY THE AUTHOR OF "THE YOUNG APPRENTICE," "NIGHT GUARD," &c.

BEAUTIFULLY ILLUSTRATED.

LONDON :
" BOYS OF ENGLAND" OFFICE, 173, FLEET STREET, E.C
AND ALL BOOKSELLERS.

THE RIVAL APPRENTICES

A TALE OF THE RIOTS OF 1780.

THE FIGHT IN THE OLD RUINS.

PROLOGUE.—THE STORM WAIF.

ALL through the dark hours of that stormy evening in the year 1764 a man's form had hovered round the door of Simon Grandley, the carpenter of East Chepe.

It had been a fearful day—a day of wind and rain—wind that howled like the yells of lost spirits round the chimney-pots, and shrieked up the narrow lanes—rain that beat upon the window-panes as if it would have crashed them in.

Very few pedestrians had ventured out in the streets since about six o'clock, but it seemed truly as if all those who *did* venture out had concentrated themselves in East Chepe for the purpose of watching the movements and thwarting the designs of the tall stranger who had, as I have said, hovered near the carpenter's abode.

He was a tall, military-looking man, apparently about thirty years of age; but he was so wrapped in his heavy cloak, and his hat was so slouched over his face, that little of his form or face could be seen.

He had something beneath his cloak—a bundle of some kind or other—which he clasped often and fondly to his breast, as though he knew that he would soon have to part from it.

At length, as the great clock of St. Paul's boomed out the hour of ten, a party of four men came hurriedly round a corner.

When they beheld the loiterer they uttered an exclamation of satisfaction, and sprang forward.

"Ha! we have him now," said one.

Then, drawing his sword, he sprang upon the stranger.

Before the latter could draw his weapon he was wounded in the arm.

"Mad ruffians!" he cried, "what would you with me? Would you murder me?"

"Aye, if it be murder to kill such as you," replied the other.

The whole four had now drawn, and were pressing on him.

With one convulsive pressure he clasped the bundle to his heart, and then, by a swift movement, glided it down upon the steps of the carpenter's house.

Then his bright sword described a circle in the air, and one of his assailants staggered back badly wounded.

This gave him a chance.

The men had seen nothing of the bundle which he had placed on the steps, and, eager to withdraw their attention from the spot, he took advantage of the diversion caused by the wounding of his foe, and edged rapidly away.

The men were exasperated by the sight of their bleeding comrade.

"Kill him! kill him!" shouted one, regardless of the fact that, in spite of the storm, his words might be wafted to the ears of some one who might rush to the rescue.

And a more savage attack than ever was made upon him.

Gradually yielding ground, walking backwards, and keeping them off by the exercise of the most brilliant swordsmanship, he at length reached the corner of the street, and passed round into the next thoroughfare.

Here he made a stand.

He appeared to have been solely actuated by the desire to draw their attention off that—whatever it might be—which he had placed on the doorstep of Simon Grandley's house.

Having succeeded in this, he cared not, apparently, what became of himself.

The angry blood rose to his cheeks now.

His eyes flashed with fierce pride and resentment.

The fight had a far different character now.

It had been an attack and defence before.

Now it was the single foe who was the assailant.

His sword flashed hither and thither with wondrous celerity, and the combat was certainly in his favour, when his foot slipped, and, as he fell forward, the weapon of one of his antagonists passed right through his shoulder.

One gasping cry he gave.

One wild effort he made to save himself.

Then he fell prone upon the ground.

"At last!" muttered one of the men, as he knelt down and raised his cloak. "But where—where is the child?"

"Is it not there?" asked one of the others, in evident alarm. "I could have sworn that he had it in his arms. Curse the brat! If *he* lives, all is ruined!"

"Perhaps he dropped it in the other street," said another, and they rushed back in a body.

But whatever the bundle was that had been placed on the step of Simon Grandley's house, it was gone now!

The footsteps of the watch, too, warned the assassins to be off, and after a few hurried words they separated, and hastened off in different directions.

*   *   *   *   *   *   *   *   *   *   *   *   *

Simon Grandley, the carpenter, was that evening sitting in his room with his wife.

Simon was then about twenty-five years of age, and had been married to the pretty woman at his side not more than six months.

They had been speaking about their own prospects, and had been discussing, too, the probable fate of a brother of Simon's who had fled from England under peculiarly distressing circumstances.

"What a terrible storm," murmured he, as he rose and glanced out of window. "But hark! that was not the wind."

The wife rose too, and neared the casement.

The shrieks of the blast had completely overcome the sounds of strife.

But now there was a slight lull, and even slighter sounds could be heard.

The combatants had, as I have described, passed round to the other street.

But there was another sound.

A shrill, wailing cry!

"That is the cry of a child, Simon, I am certain," said his wife.

The carpenter laughed.

"A child, Julia?" he said, "a child out in such a storm as this! Who could be so mad as to bring one out?"

Again, as he spoke, a shrill plaint rose up towards heaven.

"Oh, I'm certain of it," answered the young wife. "I'll run down and see."

And before he could make any effort to prevent her, she had rushed from the room down to the street-door.

In a few minutes she returned.

In her arms was a child—a boy not many months old, dressed in elegant clothes, splashed here and there with the blood of the man who now lay upon his face in the street near!

Eagerly both husband and wife searched the clothes of the strangely-left orphan.

All they could find was an initial "G" on one of his clothes, and a letter—half finished.

It read as follows:—

"Christian friends! whoever you may be, into whose hands this poor child may fall, treat him kindly. Bring him up as your own, and you will not lose by your kindness. Those to whom he belongs, and who love him dearly—who part with him as from their own hearts' blood—will some day claim him at your hands. Expect to hear of them on the 15th day of August, in the year——"

Here the letter ended.

No money—no present—accompanied the little foundling; but the kindly hearts of Simon Grandley and his wife could not think of sending him adrift on the world.

And so they took him to their bosoms as their own child, and from the initial "G" on his clothes they christened him "Guy the Foundling."

And so we must allow to drift away sixteen uneventful years, and resume our tale in the year 1780.

THE RIVAL APPRENTICES: A TALE OF THE RIOTS OF 1780.
BOOK I.—UNDER A CLOUD.

CHAPTER I.
THE CHALLENGE.

"I'm not a coward, and I shall not allow you to browbeat me. But I tell you what, Dick Hatherden, you shan't inveigle me into a fight in my master's house!"

The speaker was a fine, handsome lad of some sixteen years, who looked up somewhat angrily from his work at the one who had provoked the remark.

The scene of the altercation was the workshop of a carpenter; not a modern one, be it said, but a rough place, with tools and materials which would scarcely have met the approval of a tradesman in the year of grace 1870.

Three lads were at work upon the tiled floor beneath the skylight, cracked and patched in a hundred places—three lads as dissimilar in appearance as you could easily meet in a day's walk.

The one who had been addressed as Dick Hatherden was about the same age as the speaker, with dark eyes, black hair, and a sallow complexion, with thin lips drawn down at either corner in a vicious and malignant smirk.

He was sinewy and strongly made, with large bony hands, and broad and somewhat stooping shoulders.

The lad from whom he had wrung the retort had dark eyes too, and dark hair; but those eyes were full of a mellow light—the light of honest hope in the future, and resolution to fight the good fight of life.

He, too—Guy the Foundling—was tall and strong, but he was built altogether in a finer and more elegant mould.

The third was somewhere about the same age—rather stout, with a florid complexion, red hair, a wide mouth, always on the grin, and a pair of round blue eyes ever sparkling with mischievous good humour.

"Don't be quarrelling, you two," he cried, as he hammered a nail into a thick plank with a blow that made the place ring again, "or I tell you what, I'll have to pitch into one of you, as sure as my name's Will Lightmore."

Dick Hatherden frowned darkly.

"Don't you interfere, Will," he said, savagely; "it's none of your business. I say again that Guy has proved himself a sneak. He told our master about my being late; he told him that it was I who spoiled the chest that was being made for Colonel Halsted; and then when I tell him he's a pitiful hound, instead of striking me, he only goes on working the faster."

"Yes, that I may be able to keep my hands off you," cried Guy, still going on with his labour. "I'd be sorry to strike you here, and yet I've had enough, heaven knows, to provoke me."

Dick Hatherden laughed sneeringly.

"Provoke you?" he said; "why, it takes a deal to provoke a coward. You haven't the blood in you to fight, or to understand an insult. What can you expect from a fellow that was picked up on a door-step, whose father may have been a beggar and his mother——"

"Stop!" shouted Guy, whose face had now become livid, and whose hand grasped a bright, sharp-edged chisel. "Stop! or I'll not fight you here. I'll kill you. Your insults to me you will have to pay for sooner than you think; but if you mention the name of my unknown mother—who may now be a saint in heaven—I shall forget myself. There, out of the way, Will; I'm quiet now."

This was addressed to the third lad, who, on seeing the dangerous turn affairs were taking, had sprung between the other two, and struck a tragic attitude.

"What, ho! my nobles!" he cried, mockingly, "is it in this way ye would waste your precious blood? Murder is unseemly, my lords; but if ye will be guided by me, both of you, I will suggest a ready way to adjust your differences. Have I said aright?"

Dick Hatherden had been somewhat awed by the desperate manner of Guy.

He had found the latter quiet—not easily angered; and it was astounding to him to behold him standing erect, with cheek pale, eyes flashing, and grasping the chisel with clenching, trembling hands.

"I don't want to provoke him to anything here," he said, sullenly, "but I *do* say that if he is not a coward he will give me a chance of proving myself his master, and letting him have the thrashing I've so long promised him."

"I'm quite ready," began Guy.

But Will, raising his hand in mock majesty, interrupted him.

"Stay!" he cried. "I see a way out of this difficulty, my friends. There is, as you know, not far distant from this house a dark and dismal——"

"There, stop that nonsense, Will," cried Dick Hatherden, with a frown. "Can't you see that I'm in no humour for foolery. Speak plainly, or leave it alone."

"Very well, then," replied Will; "you both know Gorman's Ruins—where the old house was burned. There's a high wall there, which hides everything from passers by. Why not meet there to-night, and have a bout at quarterstaff? I'll be Guy's second, and bring a torch with me; and I dare say, Hatherden, you can find some one among your numerous and choice associates who will do the same for you."

Dick Hatherden was far too greatly pleased by this proposal to observe the sneer conveyed in Will's words.

He knew himself to be a good hand at quarterstaff; and being no coward, although of a dark and vengeful mind, he leaped with delight at the proposal.

"The very thing," he cried; "the very thing! Are you satisfied, Guy?"

"Perfectly."

"But how will you get out? I as an out-door apprentice can do as I please, thank heaven; but you——"

"Oh, I'll find a way to come out," returned Guy. "I'll be there at ten to-night; and if I don't punish you for your insults to-day, and for some time past, may I never see the darling mother whose name your foul mouth would have aspersed!"

There was no chance of further speech on the part of the boys now, for the door of the workshop was thrown open, and Simon Grandley, their master, entered.

He was now a fine, broad-shouldered, ruddy-faced man, of some forty years—a man whose face at once told you of the kindly heart within him.

"Well, boys," he said, "hard at it, I see. There's nothing like work, I say, to make a man happy. Have you finished that job I gave you this morning, Dick?"

"Yes, master, very nearly. I shall be done in a few minutes."

"Good," said his master, "I want you to go out for me to-morrow. Colonel Halsted wants a job done at his house, and I wish you to go round after dinner. I'll give you full instructions before you go."

"Very well, sir," replied the lad, quietly.

But a quick observer would at once have noticed that his calmness was all feigned.

His eyes gleamed at the name, his cheeks flushed, and he sped along with his work twice as quickly as before.

"That makes twice in one week," he murmured to himself; "things are coming to a head quickly!"

So the day passed.

Simon Grandley was in the shop the remainder of the time, and no opportunity was given to either challenger or challenged to speak of the intended bout.

When Dick Hatherden, however, in the evening packed up his tools and quitted the place, the glance he shot from his dark eyes at the one he hated was quite sufficient to remind him of all.

"I'll kill him if I can," he thought, as he went out into the street and hurried homewards. "If I do, I cannot be blamed, as it would be in fair fight."

Supper over, Guy and Will Lightmore repaired to the bedroom they shared together.

"How am I to get out?" said Guy, as he paced his room impatiently. "I would not miss this appointment for the world. Dick Hatherden would deem me a coward, and I should not be able to give him the lie. What is to be done? I can't get over the back wall, it's too high."

"But," interrupted Will, with a roguish smile, "the door in that back wall might be left open by accident."

"Why—how can you manage it?"

"Never mind, Guy, I will manage it," returned the other, gaily. "Now, I tell you what, I couldn't help you to deceive the master if I didn't know you were right. But this sneaking, upstart, treacherous Dick Hatherden *must* be punished; and as you've got the opportunity you must be the one to punish him. Rest yourself till I come back; I won't be long."

CHAPTER II.

THE MEETING AT THE RUINS.

ON quitting the bedroom, Will Lightmore passed on tiptoe down towards the kitchen.

He had discovered that his master had no idea of retiring to rest very early, for he had invited a friend or so to indulge in a friendly glass and a pipe.

He therefore was aware that the house would not be quiet for an hour or so, and that he could easily contrive to slip out with his friend.

The difficulty was, however, how to get in on their return.

This difficulty he had determined that a female hand should solve for him.

"Betty," he said, in a low tone, as he peeped in at the kitchen door; "Betty, are you alone?"

The person whom he addressed was alone, and therefore did not reply.

She was a little, plump, rosy-cheeked damsel of about fifteen, not long fresh from the genial breezes of the country; and truth to tell, she had long ago carried away the heart of the good-natured and susceptible apprentice.

Receiving no reply, Will entered on tiptoe, and, approaching the bright-eyed domestic, slipped his arm round her waist and kissed her.

"Make a noise and slap my face next time, Betty," he said, when he had performed this feat, "to-night no one must know I'm here."

"And pray, sir, why are you here now?" said the young girl, pretending to be indignant.

"I want you to do me a service, Betty," he answered insinuatingly. "There's such a lovely cap with blue ribbons at old Marston's round the corner, I'll buy it for you to-morrow; I will, I swear it," he added, placing his hand upon his heart tragically, "by all the gods!"

"Oh, you get along," answered Betty, considerably mollified and pleased by the mention of the cap, for Will generally kept his promises, "you'd better be quick and be off, for mistress will be down directly. What is it you want?"

"It isn't for myself," whispered the lad, glancing furtively at the door, "it's for Guy; he's going out to-night, and he wants to be let in the back-way about twelve."

Betty held up her hands in horror.

"Oh, Will," she cried, "it's ruin—it's horrible! He'll be turned away, and then——"

"Hush! nonsense, Betty," said Will, coaxingly; "no one will know, because you won't tell. And then remember the blue cap; and Guy—he's promised a pair of earrings too. Now, there's a dear," he added, giving her another kiss, "leave it open, and you can watch from your window and see if anyone comes in."

THE YOUNG GIRL TURNED TO FACE THE INTRUDER.

Betty had no time to answer, for the footstep of Mistress Grandley was heard descending the stairs towards the kitchen.

"I'll leave it open," she said, "and now go."

Will was satisfied.

He waited for no more, but sliding out, hid in a corner till his mistress had passed, and then hurried away to the bedroom, where Guy, as may be imagined, anxiously expected him.

"It's all right, Guy," he said; "now will be let slip the dogs of war. Marry come up, fair coz, your foeman waits, and an he has no broken sconce ere morning then am I no prophet."

"But seriously," he added, quitting the strain of melodrama which he invariably adopted, even on the most solemn occasions, "I have made it all square with Betty. She will see that the gate in the rear of the premises is left open, and so we are safe. I will go first, as I have to procure torches, and a quarter-staff for you. You must follow, and we will meet at Gorman's Ruin."

"Very well," said Guy; "but as for being found out, I am so resolved to punish him after the words he used about my father and mother, that I feel reckless, and hardly care whether I am discovered or not."

"Oh, as for that," said Will, "it's not worth while to be found out when you can avoid it. Now, I'm off. How goes the weather?"

So saying, he approached the window, and glanced out upon the dark street.

"Here, Guy!" he cried, suddenly, "come here."

Guy at once walked to the casement.

"See yonder," said Will, pointing to the dense gloom of an opposite archway; "you can distinguish nothing now in the darkness, but presently you will see two men's forms emerge from yonder archway. I've watched them again and again, and they seem always to meet at this hour. There, look!"

Guy glanced in the direction indicated, and saw gliding from out the gloom two tall figures, wrapped in military cloaks.

They paused for a moment to glance up at the house, seemed satisfied with what they saw, and then walked rapidly away.

"There's some mystery in this," said Guy; "but what it is I can t say. I've often noticed my master speaking to strange-looking men lately—at strange hours, too. But there, it matters not to us. I am impatient to be off. So start, Will, and I'll be after you in a few minutes."

"If I had time," said Will, "I'd follow those men, and see where they go to; but as there's business on hand, why—sharp is the word."

And so, off he went.

The few minutes during which Guy had to wait seemed an age.

There was nothing vindictive in the heart of the lad, but he felt an overwhelming amount of vexation and irritation at the words which Dick Hatherden had used regarding his mother.

The circumstances—the mysterious circumstances—surrounding his introduction into the house of the carpenter, of course placed him in a strange and awkward position.

He was subject to taunts and jeers at the hands of his cowardly rival, to which he found it difficult to reply, and the time had come, therefore, for asserting his ascendancy in a different way.

At last the few moments passed, and with a beating heart he glided down the staircase.

He had reached the back door in safety, and had hoped he had entirely escaped observation, when, as his hand was placed on the handle, a voice said gently—

"Where are you going, Guy?"

He started guiltily.

Standing beside him was a young girl, about fifteen, with a slight, pretty figure, a winning, beautiful face, and bright pleading eyes.

"Where are you going, Guy?" she repeated. "You know how angry my father will be, if you go out without his permission, and I know you've not asked it. Don't go."

"I must go, Minnie—I must, indeed," he said. "It's for no bad purpose, I promise you; but I couldn't explain it to your father. Don't betray me, Minnie."

"Betray you, Guy!" she answered, in a voice that plainly showed how dear to her heart was the handsome apprentice. "You know I would not do that. I'll leave the door open as it is; but don't be late."

The boy would gladly have pressed her to his heart, but the sound of coming footsteps made him dart away through the door, and hurry as fast as he could along the dark street.

Minnie Grandley—born a year after that stormy night when he had been found wailing on the doorstep—had been brought up day by day, hour by hour, with him, and he loved her dearly; but on he hurried, and he forgot her in the whirl of darker thoughts that crowded into his mind.

Gorman's Ruins, where the bout at quarter-staff was to take place, was situated at no great distance from the house of Simon Grandley, the carpenter.

It had been the dwelling of a man who had committed a foul crime, but who, though known well to be guilty, had yet contrived to escape the talons of the law.

People, they said, had taken the law into their own hands.

However this might be, the house was one night found wrapped in flames, and the murderer perished in them.

Since then no attempt had been made to rebuild the place, and there the outer walls stood, gaunt and black, with a dark waste of tangled timber and dank earth enclosed within them.

Into this entrance a passage was effected by an old iron-bound door, which, though somewhat embedded in the soil, could be opened by a gentle pressure.

On arriving at this gloomy spot, Guy found everything still and solemn as the tomb.

A lad less brave than he might have almost doubted the propriety of entering further on the adventure.

But he had inherited a heart that was a stranger to cowardice, and, advancing boldly, he pushed against the rickety door, and passed into the enclosure.

He had no sooner done so than he saw he was not the first comer.

There, sitting on a large beam, with a torch stuck in the old woodwork near him, was Will Lighmore.

"We're first on the field, Guy," cried he. "See here, what a splendid pair of staffs I have here. If you can't crack his sconce with one of them I'd engage to eat them as they are for my supper."

"I hope Dick Hatherden does not mean to shew the white feather," returned Guy, "or I shall have to break my vow after all, and punish him in my master's house; but no, here he comes."

True enough the door was once more pushed open, and Dick Hatherden entered the waste ground, accompanied by a tall boy, whose clothes and general appearance altogether proclaimed him one of the lowest and most degraded classes of society: an "old" young man—one who in his little span of life had seen all the worst doings of the wickedest of God's creatures, and had only profited by the example by becoming one of the worst himself.

No words were exchanged between the chief combatants.

The torch which Dick Hatherden's companion had brought with him was lighted, and placed in a position where it could throw a light over the scene, and in a very few moments the rival apprentices stood face to face, grasping their heavy weapons.

It would have been a good study for an artist, could he have seen them at this moment.

Both were models of strength, as I have said, and both were brave.

But there was a marked difference between them.

Guy the Foundling, with his honest, bold, fearless face, his open brow, his bright eyes, now glittering with excitement, was a far different being from his opponent.

Dick Hatherden stood with his narrow forehead contracted, his angry eyes gleaming, his thin lips compressed, all the evil passions of his vindictive nature thoroughly roused and visible in his features.

He kept his anger, however, sufficiently under control to prevent his acting with rash precipitation, and took his position as calmly as his rival.

One steady look into each other's eyes, one deep-drawn breath, and the fight began.

Both were adepts in the use of the somewhat unwieldy weapon they had chosen, and the quarter-staffs were whirled round with a celerity and judgment which threatened serious consequences.

At length, after several minor blows on either side, Guy brought his weapon down with stunning force on the head of his opponent, who, with a smothered groan, staggered back.

The first bout, therefore, was declared in favour of Guy.

Dick Hatherden, however, though the blow was severe, was not disposed to yield his position at a single blow, and he soon came up again to the fight.

This time, though his blood was boiling, he strove with success to appear calm.

He advanced warily, eyeing his adversary carefully and steadily, and making a feint, avoided a blow from Guy, and brought a tremendous blow down upon his shoulder.

This, had it descended on the head, would have crushed it, and as it was the force was so great that the staff broke in halves.

There was nothing now for it but to abandon the quarterstaff and have recourse to fists.

At this, considering the life which he was reputed to lead among his evil companions, Dick Hatherden ought certainly to have excelled, but somehow or another Guy also had picked up the use of his hands, and Dick soon found that he had met no despicable rival.

His face soon began to show evidences of ill-usage, Guy's features, too, being bruised and swollen.

At length he became savage.

Rushing in at his enemy, he made a feint to strike, and kicked him in the chest.

The next moment a blow in the face sent him sprawling on the ground.

Dick's second knelt down by him and raised him up.

"You'd better give over, Dick," he said; "you've had enough, and I'll teach you a trick or two for next time."

But Dick's heart was swelling now with bitter hate.

He was determined to be even with his enemy one way or another, and to his evil mind the means mattered little.

So, raising himself, he whispered a few words in the ear of his second.

What these words were I need not say, but at any rate they seemed to have an electrical effect upon the hearer.

His eyes sparkled, his mouth lapsed into a mischievous grin, and he raised his friend up.

"Haven't you had enough, Dick?" cried Will Lightmore, laughing.

"No," exclaimed Dick, "I'll have my revenge, or I'll die for it."

And so he squared up again.

But murder gleamed from his glistening eyes—murder lurked in the deadly curl of his lip.

Guy could not observe this in the darkness, for the flickering glow cast upon the face of his adversary by the torches was not sufficient to enable him to see the play of his features.

They advanced—they exchanged blows.

Then Dick rushed in.

A bright gleam shot through the ruddy glow, and the gleam of a knife!

Another instant, and Dick Hatherden would have been a murderer.

But it was not to be.

Will had seen the movement of his hand, and springing forward caught him a blow on the side of the head, which sent him spinning back, and stretched him almost senseless on the ground.

In an instant Dick's second darted at Will Lightmore.

"You're a pretty second," he cried, "to strike my man. Isn't one enough for him?"

"Stand back!" exclaimed Will, as he raised the unbroken quarter-staff from the ground, "stand back! or I'll crush your head in. We were not aware that we had to do with assassins. No more fighting by night. I'll meet you in the daylight when and where you like, but I've seen enough of you!"

Dick now had raised himself, and stood up once more, while Guy surveyed the scene with something like astonishment.

"Never mind, Master Lightmore," cried the discomfited apprentice, as he sheathed his knife, "I'll be even with you yet. We're bound to be together for a long time to come, and we'll see who first repents this night's work."

He had hardly uttered the words when a dark figure loomed up over them.

The figure of a tall man in a large cloak, whose face was nearly concealed by his slouching hat.

He seized Dick angrily by the shoulder.

"What do you here," he cried, "when you are wanted elsewhere for a better purpose? Come with me, and let your vagabond companions remain."

Dick answered nothing.

The presence of the stranger seemed utterly to paralyse him.

He allowed himself, in fact, to be led away without looking at his late antagonist or his second, while the skulking villain who had befriended him followed sheepishly in his wake.

Evidently between these three there was some deep mystery, which had no connection with Guy or Will.

"We will return home," said Guy, as the strange trio quitted the ground; "but I can tell you this, Will, we have not seen the last of Dick Hatherden's attempts at murder."

"You're right there," returned Will. "A man who can slander so with his tongue will not be careful how he acts. We will be careful on our road back."

CHAPTER III.

WHAT MINNIE GRANDLEY SAW FROM THE WINDOW.

THE pretty daughter of Simon Grandley—disturbed greatly by the absence of Guy, whom she loved as much as her little heart was capable of—sought comfort and consolation at once in the room of Betty, and discovered at once, of course, that she also was in the secret.

Their rooms adjoined one another; and for a long hour they chatted away, until, tired out thoroughly, Betty, who had retired to bed, fell asleep.

Then Minnie stole away to her own room, and fastened herself in.

But she could not sleep.

She was, doubtless, the last up in the house; and, if Betty had performed her promise, and left the door unlocked, still Simon Grandley might have taken an over-careful fit, and seen to the doors before retiring.

So the brave little soul resolved to wait up and watch for her lover and his friend, whom she admired also for his courage and his straightforwardness.

She sat at the window there for a long time, looking out.

It was a dreary one in truth.

Simon's house stood at the corner of the street, and from her window she could see into a kind of three-cornered yard, with a little door leading into a back thoroughfare.

This was all the prospect.

The darkness was peopled, truly, by her own imagination.

She could see Guy there, smiling at her; and fashion strange visions for the future.

But it got very dull at last, and she was just nodding off, when her half-closed eyes saw the back door gently opening.

She started up.

"There they are," she hoped.

But her hope was not realised.

Those who entered were two men, wrapped in long cloaks--men who in appearance seemed entirely behind the age.

The maiden's heart leaped wildly.

What could this mysterious entrance by night mean?

Could her father be engaged in any secret conspiracy?

She had heard rumours of strange doings in London. What if Simon Grandley had been seduced into joining them?

She, however, did not allow her thoughts to wander far.

She resolved to watch, and so, gently opening her casement, despite the dull air, she leaned out.

The two men passed in, and closed the door after them.

"Now Guy and Will will be shut out," she thought. "Never mind; these men must go soon, and then I'll reopen the door.

The mysterious objects of her watch passed to the farther end of the yard, and then, suddenly, before her eyes, yet how she knew not, disappeared.

"Am I mad?" she murmured, clasping her hand to her brow.

Then she gazed again.

But there was now but the dark wall and the still yard, and all was silent and gloom!

"I'll not despair!" she thought. "I'll watch on still, and discover this mystery. They were living beings I will swear, and if they return I'll follow them, but I will find out their object here."

Long and weary waiting again, with the cold air chilling her, and the silent night sending a dread to her heart.

But she did not flinch.

She was resolved to discover now, come what might, the meaning of this strange visitation to her father's house.

At length the two figures reappeared in the corner where they had so mysteriously disappeared—gliding out, as it were, from the darkness as if rising from the earth.

She watched their proceedings eagerly.

But what they were doing she could not tell.

They were talking eagerly, when suddenly a gust of wind caught the hat of one of them, and he raised his head as he tried to save it from being blown away.

As he did so his eyes fell upon the young girl leaning from the casement.

An exclamation of anger burst from his lips as he saw her.

In an instant the bright gleam of a pistol-barrel shone in the semi-darkness, and as he presented the weapon at her he said in a clear voice—

"Move one inch, and you die!"

The words were not spoken loudly, but they seemed to ring out distinctly in the still night air.

The girl was paralysed with fear and amazement.

What could they mean?

How long was she to remain stationary?

This latter question was soon answered.

The man who held the pistol presented at her head spoke a few rapid words to his companion and the latter at once approached the door of the house.

"It is open! he will enter! what shall I do!" thought the terrified girl.

Yet she dared not move.

The sight of the pistol held her spellbound.

The time that now elapsed, although but short, seemed an age.

The agony of suspense made it seem doubly as long as it would otherwise have appeared.

But presently the step of a man was heard gently ascending the stairs, and then the door of the room was opened.

The man below now removed his threatening weapon, and the young girl turned to face the intruder.

There was no light in the chamber, and she could see nothing of his face.

"Young girl," he said, "you must descend with me. Come at once, as time is precious."

"Descend!" she repeated, tremblingly. "Whither would you take me?"

And she gazed wistfully at the open door, as if about to cry for help.

The man understood her thoughts.

"You must descend into the courtyard," he said. "Come without delay. Utter one cry, and you shall die by my hand."

"STEALTHILY GUY FOLLOWED THEM AS THEY BORE GRANDLEY TO THE BOAT."

THE RIVAL APPRENTICES

A TALE OF THE RIOTS OF 1780.

"ON THE LIFE OF MY FATHER, I SWEAR," CRIED MINNIE.

As the strange man spoke he grasped her wrist firmly, but not rudely, and prepared to lead her downstairs into the courtyard.

Minnie Grandley was but fifteen, and the idea of resisting, or even disobeying, this strange intruder never once occurred to her.

Spell-bound, amazed, terrified, she descended the stairs gently with him until they reached the court-yard.

Here the second man, who had been lurking in the shadows, stepped eagerly forward.

"It is half an hour beyond midnight now," he said. "We must do what we have to do quickly."

Then he turned to Minnie.

"Young girl," he said, "you have been watching our proceedings from yonder window.

"I was not watching. I saw you by accident," answered Minnie, in a gentle voice.

"No matter! you saw us, and that is sufficient," he replied, sternly. "Our business here is private, and must be known to none. Swear then to reveal to no one that you have seen us, or before the week ends death shall overtake you and all who are dear to you. We do not threaten without knowing our power."

"Does your coming here affect my father's safety?" asked the young girl more boldly.

"It affects him in no way—it is nothing to him. But, come, we cannot delay in trifling with a child. Will you swear, or will you rather risk your father's death—the death of all in this house?"

"I promise," said Minnie, timidly.

The second stranger muttered an oath.

"We cannot waste our time longer," he said. "She must come with us, since she is obstinate."

And he prepared to drag her towards the door.

This settled the matter.

"No, no," cried the terrified girl. "I swear—I swear not to betray you!"

"On the life of your father you swear."

"Yes; on the life of my father I swear," she repeated, tremulously.

"Good. Then you may return to the house; but remember—one word of this—one word even let fall casually, so that our proceedings are known, and within two days not a single soul—man, woman, and child—shall live to say who so well kept his vow of vengeance! You will be watched henceforth each hour in the day, so beware!"

The tone in which these words were uttered left no doubt in the mind of the girl that he meant all he said.

There was a resolute savage tone, and a savage gleam, too, of the eye, which sent a chill and a dread to her heart; and as they passed out of the door and she returned to the house she felt as if a part of her childhood had vanished from her!

And this was Minnie Grandley's first initiation into the most terrible secret of those troublous times.

Scarcely had she crept, with beating heart, up into her room, and resumed her seat at the open window, when the door was again opened, and Guy and Will Lightmore entered the courtyard, and bolted the gate after them.

"They have come in at once," thought she, "and have evidently not seen the strangers. Thank heaven! I shall not be questioned."

But she was wrong.

They *had* seen them, and had wondered too, but the men had darted into a dark thoroughfare and disappeared.

The boys, however, were not able to say a word of their suspicions to Simon Grandley.

They had been absent without leave from the house, and the secret, therefore, was safe also with them.

CHAPTER IV.

COLONEL HALSTED.

HAD Simon Grandley been less perturbed in his mind than he evidently was on the morning following, he would have observed that the faces of both Guy and Dick Hatherden bore distinct signs of a recent combat.

Dick had suffered terribly.

His eyes were black and swollen, his face puffy, and he worked with his back turned to his master when he entered the shop.

Guy looked flushed and strange, but exhibited nothing sufficient to excite any particular suspicion.

Simon Grandley, for the first hours of the morning, scarcely spoke a word to his apprentices, except in the way of simple orders.

And so up to the dinner-hour the boys worked away, Will Lightmore singing over his task, and occasionally exchanging a few words with Guy, while Dick Hatherden sullenly went on with his labour, without speaking or turning his face.

When dinner-time came he plucked up courage and approached his master.

"If you please, sir," he said, "you told me yesterday I was to go to Colonel Halsted's."

"I did," returned his master, starting as from a reverie.

Then he added—

"Why, what on earth is the matter with your face? You can't go to the Colonel's in that state. What have you been doing?"

"That's just what I wanted to say, sir; I think I'd rather not go to-day," replied Dick; "a boy insulted me last night, when I left here, and I tried to thrash him; but he was bigger than I am, and I couldn't."

He knew well that for his own sake Guy would say nothing, and for his own sake too he had no desire to betray his fellow-apprentices.

Betrayal would balk all future attempts at revenge.

"You'll have to go, Guy," said Simon Grandley, turning to the foundling; "I can never permit my name to be disgraced by sending a lad who has been misbehaving himself in such a manner. At two o'clock I'll give you your instructions, Guy, and the address. And as for you, Dick, if I hear of any more of this fighting, I shall punish you severely. I don't believe a word of your story."

When the dinner was over, and the lads returned to their work, Dick Hatherden seemed in a highly nervous and excited state.

He would work away hurriedly for a while; then he would stop, as if to think, and glance furtively over at Guy.

His excitement increased as the time for Guy's departure approached.

Evidently his emotion had some reference to the proposed visit to Colonel Halsted.

At length, as a quarter to two sounded, he seemed worked up into a fit of desperation.

He flung down his tools, set his lips, appeared as if gulping down some unpleasant feeling, and approached the spot where Guy stood.

"Guy," he said, "can I have a word with you?"

Guy looked round somewhat suspiciously.

After the insult on the day before, and what had followed, he was naturally somewhat doubtful as to what the communication might be that Dick desired to make to him.

"What is it?" he said. "Do you want to provoke another quarrel?"

"I do not indeed," returned Dick, in a low tone, as if desirous that Will Lightmore should not hear his words. "I want to tell you something. I want you to do me a service. I must tell you before you go to Colonel Halsted, or it will be too late."

"Very well," said Guy, whose surprise was greatly excited by this extraordinary change in Dick's demeanour. "Very well—I'm listening; and if I can honourably do you good, why I will."

The word "honourably" no doubt rang unpleasantly in the ears of Dick Hatherden.

But he glanced furtively round, knowing there was no time for delay, and said in a whisper—

"It's only this. If Colonel Halsted makes any inquiries, or tells you anything about me, don't tell Mr. Grandley. There's nothing wrong in this mystery, Guy; but I don't want him to know anything."

"This is very strange," said Guy, "very strange. Tell me one thing. Why were you so anxious not to go to the Colonel's with your face knocked about?"

Dick reddened up to the very roots of his hair.

"Oh, if you're going to cross-question me," he said, sullenly, "I won't say any more. I'll chance what comes. It is not much that I have asked you to do; not more than I'd do for *you*, in spite of our quarrel."

Guy thought a moment.

"I'll keep your secret," he said, "if it does not affect our master. But this is the last time I'll have anything to do with your affairs. I don't see my way ——"

"Guy!" cried the voice of his master from upstairs.

And so the conversation was cut short.

As Guy turned to go, Dick's eyes followed him wistfully, and he half drew a packet from his coat pocket.

"Oh!" if I could only trust him!" he muttered; "but no—no, I can't—I dare not."

And so he thrust the packet back into his coat, and renewed his work.

Meanwhile Guy, having received his instructions, sallied forth, and hurried on his way to the house of Colonel Halsted, which stood not far from the gardens of the Temple.

His heart beat high with curiosity.

There was evidently something more in this visit than the mere mending of broken furniture.

A mystery lay concealed somewhere.

Should *he* unravel it?

He hastened on, therefore, with great eagerness, and his heart heaved with anticipative pleasure as at length he arrived at the tall iron gates of Halsted House and pulled timidly at the bell.

This summons was answered by a tall domestic clad in a half military style.

"What is it you want?" he asked, superciliously.

"I'm Simon Grandley's apprentice," said Guy, boldly. "Colonel Halsted sent to say he required a job done."

The man's eyes arched with surprise.

"Another one! What on earth can my master be doing?" he murmured to himself.

"Very well; walk in, my lad," he added, aloud. "I'll tell the Colonel you are here."

Guy accordingly was ushered into a large hall, and up a wide, handsome staircase into a kind of ante-chamber.

Here the servant left him a few moments, when he returned, saying—

"In a few moments the Colonel will see you."

The few moments mentioned by the domestic were somewhat long ones.

Guy was beginning, in fact, to be impatient, when the door opened, and a young girl entered.

She was about sixteen, very dark, with dusky skin, and black, piercing eyes.

Her figure and face were lovely; yet she had in her expression something which repelled while it dazzled you.

She started as her eyes fell on Guy.

Started, as he thought, with surprise and disappointment.

Her eyes softened, however, as they fell upon his handsome features.

"I thought Dick Hatherden, the carpenter's apprentice, was here," she said.

"He was to have come," answered Guy, as he rose from his seat, "but I have come to do the work in his stead."

The girl hesitated a moment, and looked earnestly at him.

Then she said, timidly, but in a manner which plainly showed that she felt deeply interested in the answer—

"Is he ill, then?"

"He is not exactly ill," returned Guy. "He is not well, however."

"Did he send no message?"

"None."

"You are his friend, I suppose?" she added, inquiringly.

Guy's reply was evasive.

"I work at the same shop."

The girl understood the meaning of the words, and pouted her red lips.

Whatever confidence she might have felt inclined to make was at once repelled, and with a shrug of her pretty shoulders she turned and quitted the room.

"This is another small mystery, in its way," thought he.

But he had hardly time to wonder what there could be in common between such a girl as this and Dick Hatherden, when a heavy step was heard.

The servant who had admitted him reappeared, and said—

"Now, then, my lad, Colonel Halsted will see you."

He led the way through the door by which the young girl had disappeared, and after traversing a kind of corridor lined with old portraits, approached another door.

"Open that, and enter," said the man, "the Colonel expects you."

Guy did as directed, and found himself in the midst of a scene which bewildered and surprised him, and, in fact, took away for the moment his power of speech.

Seated in various attitudes round a table in the centre of the room were about a dozen gentlemen, of different ages, each with papers before him.

At the head of the table was a man of about five and forty, who started up in amazement when Guy entered, while every individual at the table glanced at him in wonder, and, as Guy thought, surprise and displeasure.

A look from the one who had risen, however, seemed to repress any exclamations they might have felt inclined to utter.

Advancing towards Guy, he said—

"What is your business with me, my lad?"

"I came here by direction of my master, Simon Grandley," replied Guy. "My fellow apprentice was told to come here to complete some job, but, for some reason or another, he could not come. I was told to ask for Colonel Halsted."

The Colonel smiled.

"Well, well," he said, "I am Colonel Halsted. I had quite forgotten that I had sent to Mr. Grandley. The job has been done by other hands. However, your master and you must not suffer through my forgetfulness."

So saying, he drew from his pocket a purse, and counted out some money.

"Here," he said, as he gave them to Guy, "here is the price of the work, and a piece of silver for yourself. Gentlemen, I will return to you immediately."

He then beckoned Guy to follow him, and led the way out into the corridor.

"Tell me," he said, when they had entered it, "has Dick Hatherden ever made a confidant of you?"

"Never; we are not friends," returned the lad, unhesitatingly.

The Colonel looked relieved.

"Then he never tells you anything?"

"Nothing, sir."

"He's a good lad—tell him he's a good lad. You can go now."

And so Guy went.

He was let out by the same servant, and was soon making his way, lost in wonderment, towards his master's house.

That there was a strange mystery somewhere he was convinced.

Had he been a boy of less intelligence he would have taken, perhaps, no notice of the simple fact that Colonel Halsted had had the job done by some one else.

But he felt convinced there had been no job—at least, none in which the craft of Simon Grandley was concerned.

The manner of the young girl, of the Colonel, of the large conclave of gentlemen, plainly indicated this.

And yet, what could it mean?

What possible position could Dick Hatherden—the uncouth, illiterate apprentice—hold in regard to such people?

The more he puzzled, the more his head ached with the mystery, and he was glad, consequently, when he reached his master's door, and saw Dick Hatherden hurrying to meet him.

"Well," said the latter, eagerly, "did he send any message to me?"

"Yes; he said you were a good lad—that was all."

"Was that all he said? *Did he say it once or twice?* Tell me everything."

"He asked me if you told me your secrets. I answered 'No,' and then he exclaimed, 'He's a good lad—tell him he's a good lad.'"

"Ah! that is right," said Dick, as if he had received most important information.

Then he asked, hesitatingly—

"Did you see anyone else?"

"Yes, a young girl. She seemed to have expected you, and asked if you were ill? I told her you were, and that was the reason you did not come. I know no more, and I daresay you'll soon have a good chance of setting things right there yourself."

"And you'll say nothing to master?"

"I have already given my promise," returned Guy, and passed away.

Dick's eyes gleamed maliciously.

"Ah! ah!" he said, chucklingly, "he's jealous of my position already—jealous of *her* notice of me—jealous that such a man as Colonel Halsted should speak of me. Ah! let him wait awhile. What a little is this to anger him when compared with the disgrace and humiliation I have in store for him in the future!"

So saying, he turned towards the workshop, his heart burning with malignant triumph.

CHAPTER V.

MYSTERY FOLLOWS MYSTERY!

THE account of what happened at Halsted House, as told by Guy to his master, did not seem to the latter in any way extraordinary.

He, of course, had not observed any of the excitement or emotion on the part of Dick Hatherden; and, indeed, it seemed now, that if he *had* observed it, he was too preoccupied by other thoughts to have bestowed more than a passing reflection upon it.

At six o'clock that night Simon Grandley dressed himself and went out, wrapping himself up closely against the sharp March winds; and, for the first time for many a long day, saying nothing to his wife as to what was his destination.

His manner for the past two days had been the subject of great anxiety to her.

During the whole course of their married life he had never, upon any occasion, kept a secret from her.

But it was evident now that something was weighing on his mind.

And this something he resolutely kept to himself, in spite of all her entreaties.

The boys quitted work at six.

Dick Hatherden went home—Will Lightmore went to court Betty—while Guy, sitting in his own room, was reading a favourite book, albeit he was anxiously expecting the hour of supper, which would bring him into the company of Minnie, whom, in his boyish heart, he believed to be the exemplification of all that was good and lovely.

Presently a gentle tap came to the door, and on rising and opening it, Guy saw Minnie herself standing without.

"What do you want, Minnie, dear?" he said, taking her hand affectionately.

"Mamma wants you to step down as quick as you can," she answered. "Bring your hat with you. She is going to send you out on some most special business."

"More mysteries!" thought Guy.

However, he said nothing, but hastily taking his cap from its peg, hurried down the stairs to the room where his mistress was sitting.

Simon Grandley's wife was, as our readers already know, still a young woman.

The bloom of beauty was still upon her cheeks, and her form still was the admiration of all for its rare lovliness —reproduced in a more slight and maidenly degree in Minnie.

GUY THE FOUNDLING.

She was on this evening, however, pale and in sorrow evidently, and her voice trembled as she bade her daughter quit the room for a moment, and beckoned Guy to sit near her.

"What I have got to say, Guy," she began, "may surprise you greatly, more especially as I cannot spare the time to enter into any proper explanations, but another time I will tell you more."

"Never mind the explanations," said Guy, who was anxious to oblige one from whom he had received the kindness of a mother. "Tell me what it is you wish, and it shall be done, even if it imperilled my life."

"You are a good boy, Guy," answered Mrs. Grandley; "but I don't think there will be any necessity to risk your life for me. At least, I hope not. But yet there is peril."

"Your master has all day long been in deep sorrow.

"The reason of this he refuses to tell me.

"Late yesterday he received a letter written is a handwriting I do not know, and when he opened it he appeared terribly distressed.

"He has now gone out without saying a word to me of his destination.

"This bodes no good, and I want you, Guy, to follow him."

A dissatisfied look overspread the face of the apprentice at these words.

She saw in a moment that he had misunderstood her.

"Nay," she said, "I must tell you that I desire to know nothing of his proceedings. I love my husband too much, and trust him too much, to think of prying into any little secret he may have. What I desire is that he shall be watched and aided in case of danger. I am sure some evil threatens us, and I know, Guy, you are brave, and to be trusted. What I want is this. I have discovered that within half an hour from this time he will call at the King's Head in the Strand. I wish you to proceed thither and watch for him Follow him everywhere —see that no one but yourself dogs his footsteps. What he does I desire not to be told. I have full confidence in him, and all I desire in to assure his safety."

"But I am unarmed,' said Guy.

"Heaven grant you may require no weapon," said Mrs. Grandley, fervently; "but it would be wrong to trust yourself in such an adventure without a sword. Wrap yourself in your cloak, and take yonder rapier with you. And now, Heaven bless you, Guy, and send you both home safe to me."

The good woman's heart yearned towards this brave, noble boy almost as much as if he were her own; and her heart throbbed with a kind of motherly pride as, with a glow of eager expectation and courage on his brow, he took down the sword and buckled it on.

When he passed out into the street it may readily be imagined that his heart bounded strangely, and his brain was somewhat confused.

His life, save for the quarrels with Dick Hatherden, had been so uneventful, that he could scarcely comprehend the sudden whirl of events that was now so suddenly surging around him.

But there was something in this which gave him a kind of pleasure.

How this was he could scarcely explain to himself.

But it was so.

He knew, of course, his own strange secret.

He knew that those who had deserted him were coming for him some day, if life and health were spared to them.

He guessed them to stand among the higher classes; and willingly though he worked for those who had saved his life and kept him through so many years, he looked forward with eagerness and hope to the unfolding of a better and grander existence.

Somehow or another this night's adventure, whatever it might be, was connected in his mind with his own secret.

Eagerly, therefore, he hurried on.

The prospect of danger had nothing but a charm for him.

Courage seemed inherent in his veins.

Anyone could see it in his eye—in his walk—in his whole mien.

Wrapped in his cloak, and with his hat pulled down over his face, so that his master might not recognise him, the tall youth looked some mysterious adventurer ready for some daring deed.

Many turned to gaze on him as he passed on.

No one could have dreamed that the form of a young City apprentice was concealed beneath the flowing cloak that was jauntily cast over one shoulder.

He, however, took no notice of anyone.

Keeping as much as possible in the shadow, he pressed on towards the Strand, and at length reached the inn which his mistress had pointed out to him as the King's Head.

It was a strange place.

Improvements have long since removed it; but standing as it did then, with its windows projecting far over the pavement, and its sign flapping in the wind, and its bright lights streaming out over the lampless streets, it had a picturesque as well as a comfortable appearance.

Of this comfort people had evidently availed themselves greatly on this night.

Being rather chilly weather, the glare had attracted a goodly crowd, and the sounds of song and laughter were clearly heard afar.

Guy slackened his pace.

Then he glanced cautiously round.

Very few pedestrians were about.

Now, therefore, was his time.

Cautiously approaching the inn, he peered in at the window of the large room.

Simon Grandley was not there.

No one like him.

Only a drinking, noisy crowd of strangers.

"I must wait outside, then," thought Guy. "Mrs. Grandley was certain he would be here, so I will wait till he does appear."

The next thing to do was to secure a hiding-place, or rather a spot where for the time he could watch without being seen.

This was not difficult to find.

A large archway admitted to the yard of the house of entertainment, and here into the shadow he crept and waited.

He had not long to remain there.

But to him each moment seemed an age, dividing him from some new era of existence.

Presently he became conscious that something unusual was going on.

Several sober, respectable citizens had passed him on their road home.

But none had observed him, or taken any special notice of the old inn.

Presently, however, a man, wrapped in a cloak—a tall, military looking man, with a huge moustache, and wearing a hat jauntily slouched on one side—passed quickly, glanced up at the inn window, and then sauntered on.

But he did not go far.

Three times he passed and repassed.

Then, with an exclamation of annoyance, he hurried up the inn steps.

In a few moments he reappeared with another person.

This was Simon Grandley.

Guy's heart gave a leap.

"Now," he thought, "the mystery is beginning to unfold itself."

Simon and the stranger walked rapidly away in the direction of Blackfriars, and, keeping well in the shadow, Guy followed.

They were evidently anxious to reach some spot where a conference could properly be held, for they exchanged very few words on the road.

In fact, in such a hurry did they seem, that it was a matter of difficulty for the apprentice to keep up with them without running the risk of detection by one or the other.

On reaching Blackfriars Bridge they crossed it rapidly, and arriving on the other side of the river, came upon a piece of wide waste ground.

Here the stranger glanced eagerly from right to left, and then led the way across the darkness.

It was perfectly impossible to see far ahead of you.

Not a light was to be seen anywhere.

But across this desert the stranger seemed able to lead the way unerringly.

A rough footpath—made evidently by the feet of constant passers—ran along the margin of the river, and following this the three came presently in sight of a hut, or small wooden house, in the window of which flickered an uncertain light.

This was evidently their destination, for on nearing it they came to so sudden a stop that Guy's presence was almost discovered.

Only almost, however.

He was just in time to dive down behind a little hillock.

Then he heard the stranger say, as he turned round and peered across the waste land—

"We're in luck, Grandley. Not a soul is in sight."

The carpenter seemed in no humour for much admiration of anything.

"Yes," he said; "I see the place is lonely enough. Let us enter quickly, for the wind is bleak."

He was right here.

The wind was blowing chilly over the river, and howling as if to warn them of some evil overshadowing and threatening them.

Guy felt certain that he was about to witness some crime, or some attempted one; but whether the carpenter was an intended victim, or whether he was an accomplice in some meditated sin, he could not say.

It was soon now to be discovered, however.

The swaggering stranger approached the door, took from his pocket a large key, and opened the lock.

Then the two disappeared within the deserted wooden house.

CHAPTER VI.

LOOKING BACK INTO THE PAST.

GUY raised himself from his hiding place, and gradually approached the window.

He could conceal himself here at the edge of the casement and peer in.

It was a wretched hovel.

An old table and a couple of chairs were all the furniture, while on the hearth smouldered the last remnants of a fire.

The stranger had lit a candle, which flickered to and fro in the wind, and cast weirdlike shadows dancing on the black and grimy walls; and then having flung some wood on the fire, and produced something like a blaze, he sat down at the table with the air of a man who knows he has important business to transact.

There was a wide break in the grimed window, and through this Guy could see all; and he noticed first that the carpenter's face was expressive of deep anxiety.

"Well, Simon Grandley," said the stranger, "this may seem a queer place to transact business in; but I'm no friends with the world, and I don't care even to give anyone a chance of hearing what we say. In the first place, look at this letter—who's writing is it?"

"My father's," said the carpenter. "I know it well; but let me read it."

"Stay; you shall do so presently," said the stranger. "Tell me, first, did you ever know who your father was?"

The carpenter sighed and shook his head.

"No," he said; "I never did."

"Tell me what you knew of him."

Simon Grandley looked searchingly at him.

"Why do you want me to do so?" he asked.

The stranger shrugged his shoulders.

"If you don't our interview is useless, and had better end at once. I must know how far you can go back, or I cannot carry out my mission."

"Well, I will tell you," said the carpenter. "All I can remember is that I used to live with my mother in a little country town, or, rather, village; that now and then a tall, handsome man came to see us, and called himself my father; that he was always kind to me, and brought me presents, and so forth, and then that he suddenly disappeared."

"He was not dead," interrupted the other.

"I know it well," said Simon Grandley. "My mother told me that. She wept long and bitterly at his absence, but she never blamed him for it. She knew well, she always told me, that it was not his fault, and though poverty overtook us, and I had to be apprenticed to a carpenter, instead of being a gentleman, as he always said I should be, nothing but kind words in regard to him ever passed her lips."

"And your mother?" inquired the stranger.

"She is dead," said Simon Grandley, in a voice full of emotion. "And as for my father, he may as well be dead, too, for all that I shall ever see of him again."

The stranger smiled.

"There you are wrong," he said. "This letter, you say, is in your father's writing. It is a mere business one, as you may see at once; but tell me, should you be able to swear to a letter written now by your father to you, when his hand has lost its firmness, when five and twenty years have passed since you have seen his superscription?"

The carpenter grasped his arm firmly, and gazed half angrily in his face.

"Don't jest with me," he said; "I might be dangerous if I were tampered with."

The other laughed.

"I guessed, from all I heard, that you would prove somewhat firey and impatient," he said; "but I am prepared to deal with you fairly, so act fairly by me. I say your father lives, and I wish to know whether there is any sign by which you could be certain that a letter was genuine."

The carpenter pressed his hand to his brow, and seemed for a moment buried in thought.

"This seems like a dream," he said, "yet if what you say be true, I do know a sign by which I should know his letters. This sign I shall keep in my own breast. So, if what you would show me are not from him, stop the jest at once, for they will betray you."

The stranger made no answer to this.

Drawing from his pocket a pocket-book, he took thence two letters, and gave them to Simon Grandly, saying—

"Read, and see for yourself. Take the top one first."

Simon Grandley seized it eagerly, and read.

It was a long letter, speaking of the lapse of years which had passed since they had met—tenderly alluding to the wife whose death-bed he could not attend—speaking of possible rewards, but clearing up no mystery.

In fact, the words with which it wound up only increased the mystery.

They ran thus:—

"Writing, as I do, from such a place as that which now holds me—being what I am—I can say nothing as to time, but that hour of reunion will surely, in Heaven's good pleasure, come at last."

There was no signature.

Only the letters, "L. F." and the faint outline of a crucifix.

"This is my father's letter, I feel sure," said Simon Grandley, "though I would not swear to it."

"And you observe it is dated a year ago," said the other.

"Ah! Then my hopes may even yet be vain," exclaimed Simon, dejectedly.

"No," said the stranger; "no—the other is but three months old. Read that."

Simon had already opened it and began its perusal.

It was as follows:—

"Dear Son,—

"All my yearnings for liberty and reunion may turn out wretched failures, as all my hopes have done before. But if this reaches you, prepare to see me in four months from its date—that is, if you are able, and disposed to aid a father who has so neglected you for twenty-five years. In order to enable me to return from this place to London, it is absolutely necessary that I should have five hundred pounds. If you believe that my neglect is wilful, leave me as I am, and think of me no more. If, on the contrary, you can and will aid me, trust no one but one man, and that is he who brings you this letter, and can whisper in your ear a word that will bring to mind the last time you ever saw me. Save me, my son, from——"

The letter broke off suddenly here again, and then there followed the same marks as on the former one.

"This is strange—most strange," murmured Simon Grandley. "But this *is* my father's writing; I know it by a certain sign, which is known to none else but me. Now, then, for the word."

In eager expectation the carpenter leaned forward, and the stranger whispered.

The effect was electrical.

Simon thrust forth his hand and seized that of his unknown companion.

"Enough," he cried; "I will trust you with all. By what name shall I call you?"

"My name matters little," said the other; "but yet I may as well give it. I am called Alexis Rainsford. And now, since you believe what I have disclosed to you, when and where shall I see you again?"

"On the second night from this, at this spot and hour," said the carpenter; "and now let us go. My head is in such a whirl from these unexpected events that I shall gladly be alone."

"And *I* desire to be away as well," said the other. "I am hungry, and would eat, though I care not much to trust myself among the haunts of men."

In a few moments after this conversation, which was full of complete mystification for Guy the Foundling, who, of course, had not read the letters, the two passed out, and once more began to traverse the gloomy waste land.

They were now engaged in earnest conversation, and though the darkness had somewhat lifted they would not have noticed the presence of Guy even had they glanced in his direction.

He hurried on therefore, and at length reached with them the bridge at Blackfriars.

They crossed it quickly, reached Fleet-street, and had just said "Good night!" when a shrill cry of "Help! help!"—a cry full of pain and horror—attracted their attention.

Guy naturally turned his face in the direction from which the cry proceeded.

When he looked round again the carpenter was gone, and Alexis stood alone.

He now observed Guy for the first time.

"Ha! friend," he cried, "yonder is some one in danger. Draw and follow me!"

Guy was so taken off his guard, and so excited by the sounds of pain, that he lost no time in doing as he was directed.

In an instant his sword had flown from its scabbard, and hurrying after the stranger, he soon found himself running at full speed along a narrow street leading to Whitefriars.

The clashing of swords was heard as they hastened on, and at length, at the corner of a street, they came upon a number of men, who were assailing one gentleman.

He, with his back against a wall, was parrying their strokes with admirable precision.

"Ha! ha! What have we here?" shouted Alexis, as with Guy he dashed into the crowd. "A lot of curs biting at one brave foe! Turn and fall on us."

The astonished crew, though taken aback by so sudden a diversion in favour of their enemy, showed no disposition to fly.

"At them," shouted one who seemed to be their leader; "we are now five to three. If he escapes we are lost."

And so the fight went on with renewed vigour.

The men who had thus assailed one man were all so completely masked that only the gleam of their eyes could be seen.

They fought desperately.

A great stake seemed depending upon the death of their enemy.

Alexis himself was a tower of strength, while Guy, with the activity of youth, flashed hither and thither in a manner that dazzled and defeated the well-aimed strokes of his antagonists.

Presently Alexis flung the sword of his opponent high in the air, and, springing forward, seized him by the throat with a grasp of iron.

It was the leader whom he thus held.

"Stop the fight, and order your men off," shouted Alexis, "or my sword shall be through you like a flash of lightning."

IMPORTANT NOTICE.—This Work will be Published every Wednesday. Two Numbers every week, One Penny the Two. Another Picture Gratis with Nos. 3 and 4.

THE RIVAL APPRENTICES

A TALE OF THE RIOTS OF 1780.

"LAY ON, MACDUFF,' CRIED WILL, SQUARING UP TO HIM.

The man's eyes glanced nervously round. The one whom they had first assailed had pinned a fellow to the wall. Guy was kneeling on the chest of another. The case was hopeless—the leader himself was helpless.

"Desist," he cried, as well as the strong hand of

his assailant permitted him. "Desist and depart; our task must be fulfilled another time."

As he spoke, and as the stranger's enemy dropped dead from the wall to the ground, the loud voice of the watch was heard.

"Twelve o'clock, and a cloudy night."

Clearly the words rang out through the streets. Cloudy indeed!

It was a black leaden sky, without a break anywhere, that hung over London city.

Only a moment the assassins waited to listen.

Then, as their leader was released, they hurried away down a bye-street.

"Which is your way, sir?" asked Alexis.

"The way these villains have gone," said the gentleman who had been attacked, and who was evidently faint from loss of blood. "But it matters not; it is unlikely they will assault me again. Good night, gentlemen, and many thanks to you for your noble aid."

And with the words he turned as if to go.

But they could see his weakness.

"Not so, sir," exclaimed Guy; "we cannot allow you to run the risk of a second cowardly attack. We will accompany you home."

"Well said," put in Alexis, "it is just what I was about to propose. Come, sir, you seem faint; lean on my arm. The watch is now round the corner; and for my own part I have no desire to be mixed up with the finding of dead men in the streets."

From the remarks which Guy had heard him let fall in the old house on the waste lands, it was evident that the mysterious emissary of Simon Grandley's father had no desire to be too particularly intimate with any one.

He was sincerely glad, therefore, when the corner of the street concealed them from the approaching watch.

He could have walked far more quickly, be it said, had it not been that the stranger whom they had saved was wounded and faint—to such a degree, in fact, that Alexis at length drew from his pocket a flask, and gave some of the inspiriting liquid to him.

Then they hastened onward.

Up to this moment neither had been able to see the face of the man they had saved.

Neither, in the excessive darkness, had he been able to distinguish the features of his saviours.

Presently, however, as they came to the corner of the street, they paused.

"Which way now?" asked Alexis.

"Towards the Temple Gardens—to Halsted House," said the stranger.

Alexis started as if struck by an electric shock.

"Halsted House!" he repeated. "You then are——"

"Colonel Halsted," replied the stranger.

Startled enough was Guy the Foundling by this announcement.

But he made no remark.

He saw that by degrees the mysterious circle of events was closing round him.

All he had to do then was to watch and be silent.

Alexis, however, acted far differently.

When he heard the name he leaned forward and whispered a few words in the colonel's ear.

The effect on him was magic.

"Providence has ordained this meeting," he said. "When we reach Halsted House you must be my guest. And your companion here—who is he?"

"I know not," said Alexis; "he heard cries of distress, and rushed with me to your aid. Who are you, my friend?"

"It matters not," said Guy; "and if it did I could not answer you, since I have no name. Maybe we shall meet again. But yonder is Halsted House. You are safe now. Good night."

And with these words he turned away.

"A strange fellow that," murmured Colonel Halsted. "Aye, and brave as he is strange."

"Yes," said Alexis; "and, I may add, discreet as he is brave. I would gladly meet with him again."

"I myself fancy I have heard his voice before," said the colonel, as they passed through the massive gates; "but a truce to him, I am all impatience to have an interview with you, for I feel sure you bring good news from abroad."

And with this the two mysterious men entered the house.

CHAPTER VII.

SIMON TAKES GUY INTO HIS CONFIDENCE.

To do Simon Grandley justice, the cry for help which had so assailed the ears of Alexis Rainsford and Guy the Foundling had not been heard by him at all.

A conflict of strange emotions filled his breast.

To see again the father whom he had so loved in his youth had been the yearning wish of his soul.

Yet, though he had toiled hard, had achieved respectability, and was now what people call well-to-do, five hundred pounds taken out of his savings was to him an immense sum.

Strange doubts, too, still existed in his mind.

He had a kind of fear, in fact, that this re-appearance of his father might threaten evil to him and his.

On opening the door, noiselessly, with his key, he was proceeding to fasten it with the heavy bolts, when his wife rushed out of the front room.

"Oh! that is you, Simon. Thank God you are safe!"

"Safe, my dear, yes—why should I not be?" he said, in surprise, as he proceeded with his fastening up.

"Oh! I have had strange dreams and strange presentiments," she said. "I feared that some evil would overtake you."

Then she hesitated a moment.

Guy had not yet returned.

She would have no opportunity of re-opening the door, and the lad might be out in the streets all night.

She resolved on confession.

"Simon," she said, "let me unbolt the door. Guy is not at home."

The honest carpenter started in amazement.

"Not at home!" he cried. "Why, where on earth is he?"

"He's gone out for me, Simon," said his wife. "Come in, and I'll tell you. He's gone for *me*."

"For you?"

"Yes, I sent him to watch you."

A frown came on the carpenter's brow.

"To watch *me?*" he cried. "Pray since when have you thought——"

His wife interrupted him.

"Stop," said she. "I must speak first. I cannot even for a moment bear to think that you should have a wrong idea of me."

Then, as the still beautiful woman wound her arms round his neck and told him all, the tears stood in his eyes, and he pressed her fondly to his heart.

"You are a silly woman," he said, kissing her, "to be afraid for me. I'll take care of myself, never fear; but what became of the lad? I never saw him. Perhaps he missed me."

"Not he," said Mrs. Grandley; "he's a clever lad, and he loves us both, I am sure. Leave the door unbolted, and he can let himself in with the key I gave him."

"Not so," returned the carpenter, "I wish to speak to him. In such a lad I can place confidence. Retire to rest, dear; while the brave boy is out, I shall fancy he is in danger."

And so, after another embrace, the loving wife retired to her bed.

A long while, as may be imagined, passed before Guy the Foundling returned.

The encounter with the assassins, who would have murdered Colonel Halsted, occupied some time, and the distance from Temple Gardens was considerable.

He discovered also on his road home, what he had not, in the heat of the battle, noticed before, and that was that he was wounded in the arm; and the blood flowing plentifully, he felt faint and weary.

But the worthy carpenter did not tire of waiting.

He was a determined man in his way.

So, having resolved to see Guy before he retired to rest, he smoked his pipe quietly in his sitting-room, and remained up.

Guy could scarcely make out what it meant, when, on approaching the door, he saw a light burning.

But he had nothing to fear.

He had been on no wrong errand, and he advanced therefore boldly.

The key turned in the lock truly.

But the door was bolted.

What should he do?

He feared to betray his mistress by knocking boldly.

"I have half a mind to walk about till morning," thought he.

But he was spared the misfortune of having to put his idea into practice, for in an instant the door was opened and Simon Grandley appeared.

Guy stood dumbfounded.

Simon saved him from embarrassment, however.

"Come in Guy," he said. "I've waited up for you."

Guy stared in surprise at the gentle tone in which this was said.

He said nothing, however, but entering the house waited until his master had refastened the bolts.

Then they entered the front room together.

"Guy," said Simon, "you look faint and ill. Take a drop of that brandy."

"Thank you, sir," said Guy. "I do feel ill. I——"

"You are wounded," cried Simon, kindly. "Why, look at your arm—it is bleeding freely. Let me bind it up."

And the kind-hearted man at once prepared to see to the wound, which he doubted not the brave lad had received in defending him against some unknown enemy.

"I know all," he said, as he was doing this, thinking it best to relieve the youth's mind at once. "Your mistress has told me. You're a good, brave lad, and I'll warrant me, in the end, I'll be able to reward you. But tell me how much have you seen? —how much have you heard?"

Guy told his story unreservedly.

The carpenter listened in something like amazement.

"Well, this is very strange," he said, when the apprentice had explained all; "strange that Alexis should be mixed up with Colonel Halsted. But we must find out what it means. By Heavens, if I thought——"

He stopped and paced the room to and fro for a minute in anger or anxiety.

Then he sat down again.

"No—no!" he said. "I'm worrying myself about nothing. But listen; as you know so much, you had better know the rest. I will tell you what my father said in his letters."

He explained then what the reader already knows.

Then he said, solemnly—

"And now, Guy, since you are in my confidence, I must tell you something more. On no account must my wife know anything of this. It will be of no use to her to know it—its only effect would be to make her unhappy."

"Not a word of what I have seen shall pass my lips," returned Guy. "Mrs. Grandley wished to know nothing, sir. She was only anxious for your safety, that was all."

"I know it, Guy," said Simon, "and so this secret lies between us. I know well that you are to be trusted, and I shall trust you more soon. There are grand things coming. Guy," he added, his hands clenching, and his eyes flashing, "there are grand things coming, and you shall be one to benefit by them. And now, my boy, go to rest. It will soon be morning, and if your wound is no better, a surgeon shall see to it at once."

Then he shook Guy heartily by the hand, and the apprentice, dazed and confounded by the increasing whirl of events, retired to his room, to consider and wonder, until tired nature overcame him, and he lapsed into sleep.

CHAPTER VIII.

THE MEETING OF THE CONSPIRATORS.

WE have now to introduce to our readers a new set of characters.

A strange, wild, lawless, lot!

And a strange wild spot to meet in.

London in 1780, it must be remembered, was not positively Old London.

But it was very much indeed unlike modern London.

There were plenty of houses after the stamp of our old streets of to-day—dull, dreary, comfortless places enough.

But there were intermixed with them queer tenements, lurking away in corners as if ashamed of themselves, and yet hanging over the pavement, with huge, bulging, protruding windows, as if anxious to obtain a glimpse of the world from which they shrank.

It is to one of these that we now introduce our readers.

It was situated not very far from the house of the carpenter in East Chepe, but in a back thoroughfare, where it was unlikely that the watch would keep a very strict look-out.

Certainly, if they had, they would have been somewhat astonished, and not a little upset, in their ordinary calculations by the strange company, which about ten o'clock at night began to arrive in the street.

They were of all ages and styles of dress.

Red-nosed, bloated, Alsatian-looking bullies; sleek, oily-looking citizens; apprentices; men who looked like clerical men in disguise—all were there represented.

About twenty of them arrived by about eleven, and then the door of the old house was closed, and the lights disappeared one by one.

The people who had arrived so mysteriously had not in reality retired to rest, as those in the immediate vicinity might have imagined.

The lights in the front rooms were put out truly.

But in an immense room in the rear all was light and activity.

It was a huge place, like a barn.

In fact, it was not properly a chamber, but an outbuilding, with whitewashed walls and places where windows had been, but where huge planks nailed up now acted in two ways—keeping the light of day from entering, and the light from streaming forth from the lamps.

The place was very rudely furnished. Only a long table of rough wood filled the centre, while round it were long benches similar to those used in common schools.

A cheerful fire, however, blazed on the hearth, and diffused a pleasant warmth, very acceptable on that chill March night.

The table, too, had an abundant supply of glasses full of steaming liquor, and the men, when they had settled themselves, seemed as comfortable as if they had been in a drawing-room.

They talked and laughed, and whispered, and drank their grog for a few minutes, as if that was the entire object of their visit there.

But after these few minutes they became fidgety, and began looking at the door, and sipping their grog nervously as if they expected somebody, from whom something particular was expected.

Their suspense did not last long.

The door opened, and in walked a man of majestic aspect.

He was majestic purely from his height and the nobility of his features.

Otherwise he would have seemed but one of the common herd, for his clothes were poor and threadbare, being black, and patched too.

Nothing looks worse than black when it begins to fade.

There is an air of faded gentility about it—a look as if you had long ago gone into mourning for your own departed comfort, and had never since reason to clothe yourself anew.

This man, however, had a something about him which rescued him from all insult which might otherwise have been attempted to be put upon him by those around.

His features were undoubtedly grand and noble: his eyes shone with a fire which was that of extreme genius or madness.

His hair—white as the driven snow—fell over his broad shoulders, which age had not bent or weakened.

His lips were thin and compressed, his features pinched; but there was that in his appearance altogether which commanded respect—though it was doubtful, indeed, that he should be able to procure any one's love.

A cheer greeted his appearance.

A cheer which brought fresh light into his eyes; and made him walk even more proudly and erectly than before.

He took his seat at the head of the table, and after partaking sparingly of some cold spirits and water rose.

There was a hush immediately.

Everyone's eyes turned towards him.

"Friends," he said, "you all remember what I told you about last meeting.

"I told you that the enemies of our country were at work. I told you that I believed that the enemies of our religion were gaining ground everywhere, and that the Power of Rome was in the ascendant.

"We must awake, brethren, if we do not wish to see our children worshipping idols, and falling on their knees before brazen images."

So he went on, in the strange, half mystical language used by the old Puritans.

It would be idle to give his speech; but we can give its substance.

It traced the history of the indulgences permitted to the Roman Catholics, accused the King of being an enemy to Protestantism, and declared that it was the intention of the Government to subvert the reformed religion and introduce in its stead "the religion of the fire and faggot."

"Wait awhile," he said, solemnly, "and you will see a craven Parliament passing measures to give them more power. Gradually, gradually, Popery is gliding in among us like a serpent. Let us crush it —let us crush it into the dust."

The audience to whom this misguided man spoke these strange and violent words cheered him as he stopped and wiped his brow, where the beads of perspiration had gathered thickly.

He, blinded by his fanatical enthusiasm, saw in

them an assemblage of men earnest and resolute as himself.

His heart therefore glowed with pleasure and enthusiasm as they cheered.

He would have felt no pleasure had he been able to see into their hearts.

Sordid, mean, selfish—all they thought of was the means of self-interest.

They looked forward to the coming of a time—a wild and turbulent time—when they would be able to run riot, and revel in the wealth which hard work had won for others.

What cared they for political rights or religion?

But he, full of his own wild fanaticism, looked upon them as a company of true Protestants and earnest thinkers; as many a good man has been misled before him, who has done all the talking and thinking himself, and imagined that he was understood and believed.

"It shall not be—it shall not be," said one of the roughest and most Alsatian-looking bullies; "we will rise, and put a stop to it!"

He thought it best to say something, as all else were paying more attention to their grog than the speech.

"Aye — rise — rise — that is the word," cried the leader, in a voice full of eager enthusiasm; "let them try to upset by the sword the true religion of the land, and then over the country far and wide there shall glow a red light which shall consume them, and bring desolation upon them for ever.

"And now," he added, after a pause, "now let me tell you that I have secured the services of one of the heads of a noble family. His name I shall not yet disclose; but he will soon be among you. He is even now going from house to house, and from town to town, stirring up in the minds of true believers the courage which is necessary to lead them forth into the combat.

"Now, Hardarker, the blacksmith, what have you to say?"

And the misguided man, true patriot at heart, sank as if exhausted into his chair.

Then there arose a broad-shouldered, bronzed fellow—a thorough man of the people—perhaps the only honest-hearted one among all that assemblage save the white-haired leader.

He, too, blinded by his enthusiasm, saw not what an assembly of reckless desperadoes he had leagued himself with.

WILL LIGHTMORE.

Maddened by religious zeal, like the old Crusaders, he rose, and in a few terse, vigorous, though ungrammatical sentences, told how he had worked night and day for the cause, winding up a speech no less inflammatory than that of the old man, by saying—

"And I tell you what, my friends—what that man standing there tells you is true—what Jonas Barnsdake tells you is true. I know it; and there's not a man in this company as ever knew Gregory Hardarker tell a lie."

There was a great murmur of satisfaction at this, and then the man continued, folding his great brawny arms, and gazing round almost defiantly—

"And now, there's another thing. You all know Simon Grandley, the carpenter?"

There was a murmur of assent.

"Well, now, he don't seem much of a man to be an enemy—he don't seem much of a man to be a friend; but I tell you what, we must have him among us. When I say he don't seem much of a man to be a friend or an enemy, I mean he seems mild and quiet like; but he's got a bold heart and a clear head, and I know he's a good Protestant. If I am given the mission, I will bring him."

"You have the mission," responded Jonas Barnsdake; "but will he betray us if he does not join us?"

"Not he," said the blacksmith. "He'll either join us or hold his tongue, never fear."

The old man seemed much moved at this.

But he said no more.

A quantity of business had to be transacted—such as the counting of their numbers, the discussion of dates, the naming of future days of meeting, and so on.

And thus the night wore on, and the small hours of the morning came.

Then the company broke up after another glass, and separated in different directions.

The leader and the blacksmith walked away for a short time together, when they separated, with a few more earnest words, and the old man went walking on slowly like one in a dream.

His brain was all on fire, his heart swelled with honest pride.

He believed himself to be at the head of a body of honest, earnest men, whereas in his wild enthusiasm he had suffered to be raked together a host of "ne'er-do-wells" from every

hole and corner in London—men whose desperate lives made desperate deeds in the future only so many happy anticipations—whose ideas of a religious rising were confined to visions of rapine and plunder—of fire and violence.

He walked on, however—in his own eyes the leader of a great movement—the chosen apostle of the times! Turning presently into a little, mean-looking house, in a mean-looking bye-street, he entered a a room on the second floor, where he beheld a scene which caused a smile to break over his lips, and a more rational expression altogether to play upon his features.

A child, not more than ten, was sitting on a chair by a table.

On this table were preparations half made, for a rude supper, and the poor little thing (who seemed to have as much strength as the feeble fire that struggled on the hearth) had evidently fallen asleep over her work.

"Poor child, poor child," he murmured. "Amy, Amy wake up. I've come home, and you can go to bed."

The girl, who was evidently used to sudden awakenings, sat bolt upright at once.

Then, after a vigorous application of her knuckles, to her eyes to drive away all sleepy tendencies, she sprang forward and clasped her arms round his neck.

"Dear Grandpa," she said, " I'm so glad you've come back. Now we can have a nice supper together."

And so they sat down together—the young and the old—to their frugal meal.

She, the representative of a coming age, prattling on merrily about nothing.

He, the self-believed prophet and apostle, thinking of far off things; and ever and anon murmuring to himself:

"And in the midst of this I am deceiving *him*—deceiving *him!*"

Who this was whom he was deceiving, and how and why in his religious fanaticism he thought proper to delude any one at all, our story, in its future progress, must show.

CHAPTER IX.

SOME OF DICK HATHERDEN'S FRIENDS.

THERE were two other persons who quitted the old house at the same time as the rest, whom we must follow for a time in furtherance of our plot.

The one was very tall, and the other was short.

The one was broad built, slouching, ill-made, but evidently as strong as a lion, the short one was a lad, ill-made, though strong too.

The lad, in fact, was Dick Hatherden.

His companion was called Bill Hazard; not that, perhaps, the name ever belonged to him, but his many escapes and adventures had entitled him to the cognomen.

"Well, Dick," said he, as they parted from their companions at the corner of the street—"well, Dick, I don't know how you manage it, but most certainly you *do* continue to work matters well. Hang me,

if I don't think you'll be up at the top of the ladder some of these days."

"Don't let's talk till we get home," said Dick; "how do you know who's listening?"

"All right, then, my jewel of prudence," returned the other; "we'll say 'mum,' then."

And so saying, he thrust his hands into the pockets of his breeches, and went forward hastily, with a kind of waddling stride.

They passed on to some considerable distance, and then dived down one of the river alleys, and up a narrow court.

Here they stopped before a house, the staircase of which was outside it, and protruded far out into the thoroughfare.

A long, shrill whistle from Bill Hazard caused a light suddenly to appear at an upper window; then a click was heard; and the door at the top of the staircase was thrown open.

The silent pair then ascended, and, entering a dark passage, closed the door behind them, groping their way upstairs to a top room.

The room was a pretty place to live in—more especially for one who aped to be the respectable apprentice to a respectable man.

Round the cracked and dirty walls were hung all kinds of vulgar pictures; mixed with rusty weapons of various sorts, and clothes, and so forth.

A rough-hewn table was in the centre with some mugs for ale; some dirty eating utensils, and so on.

On one side of the floor was a series of bundles, supposed to represent beds; while on the hearth before the fire—which was the only comfortable thing in the room—lay a huge bloodhound, who raised his head lazily, and growled his satisfaction and approbation as the two entered the room.

"Fill those mugs, and bring out some bread and cheese," said Bill Hazard to a thin scarecrow of a lad, who was none other than Dick's second in the fight with Guy the Foundling. "We're hungry and thirsty—at least, I am."

And so saying, he flung himself into a chair."

As he sat there with the light of the lamp, and the fire full upon his face, you could see what a horrid wretch he was.

His forehead was low, and rendered even lower in appearance by the mass of matted hair that surmounted it.

His eyes were small, deep-set, and twinkling with the cunning of some ferocious animal; his nose was flat; his mouth protruding like that of a negro; his jaws heavy and massive; while again and again over his features crossed scars, caused by blows and burns.

He was the beau ideal of a human brute.

"Well," said he, as Dick Hatherden took a seat also, " I suppose as Tiger here doesn't know what's said, and Quail yonder is too big a fool to understand, I can talk now without having to put up with any of your confounded lectures upon silence."

"You can talk yourself dry, for all I care," said Dick Hatherden, "but as for talking in the street, I've been so followed and hunted about that I'm afraid almost to think."

So he was.

But not for the reason he gave.

In his own evil mind he was tortured continually by the fear lest the game he was playing—a deep, subtle, villanous game—should be thwarted by Guy the Foundling; and as his hate could find no present means of compassing his destruction, he cared not to indulge in useless thoughts.

"Well, you're right enough," said Bill Hazard; "but this is a rare game about your master joining us. Do you think he will?"

"Yes—if they keep the truth from him," said Dick.

Bill Hazard chuckled.

"Oh, no fear," returned he; "old Jonas Barnsdake will only have to preach to him a few times, and he'll become infected to a certainty. There's not a man in London can—Hollo! what are you staring at, booby?"

And with that, turning savagely on Quail, he seized a mug from the table, and dashed the contents full in the boy's face.

Quail made no reply; but placing the mug he had just filled with ale on the table, wiped his face with his sleeve, and then retiring to a corner of the "bed," where the noise of his feet could not be heard, indulged in a kind of grotesque war-dance—flinging out his clenched fists hither and thither as if punching the head of some imaginary foe.

Bill Hazard, having satisfied his brutal propensity, resumed his talk.

"I was speaking," he said, "about Jonas Barnsdake—there's not a man in London that can talk like him; and *I'm* no prophet if he don't bring Simon Grandley round in no time—money and all."

"Very likely," said Dick, abstractedly.

"By the way, *has* he much money?" added Bill.

"What do you want to know for?" asked Dick, looking full in his face; "do you want to rob him?"

"No—no, my cautious friend," said Hazard, chuckling; "I merely asked from curiosity—nothing more. But, come—let's feed."

The meal was taken in silence, almost.

When it had ended, Bill Hazard sidled off, and flung himself in the corner, on a bundle of rags.

Dick waited a moment.

"Here, Bill," he said, "I've forgotten something—Bill, I say!"

No answer.

Save only a significant snore.

"Bill," repeated Dick, in a higher key.

But it was of no avail.

The brute having fed, was asleep already.

"It's all right," muttered the apprentice, "here, Quail."

The wretched boy—half witted evidently—rose from the bundles where he had pretended to sleep, and approached his companion, glidingly.

"Have you got any?" asked Dick, as he approached.

Quail nodded and grinned, and diving into a tear in his coat which did duty as a pocket brought out two gold pieces.

"Here," he said, "I found these in the next room, hidden in a corner. Oh, lad, if he were to wake."

These last words were uttered in consequence of an uneasy movement which Bill Hazard made in his sleep.

But he soon relapsed again.

"Now," said Dick, "crawl back again. I'll change these in the morning and give you some. Perhaps I shall want you to go out with me to-morrow night. I'm not going to be at home all night."

Quail pointed over his shoulder significantly.

"No, no," he said, "he knows nothing of it. There, go to bed now. I'm going to drink another mug of ale, and sit by the fire to think."

Think!

Pretty thoughts, his!

Simon Grandley and his money going to Jonas Barnsdake and his crew!

What if Simon Grandley and his money should go elsewhere—to those who would reward Dick, who would raise him to that ideal position he so coveted?

At any rate, on the next night he resolved to visit Colonel Halsted.

And after making this resolve, and settling his villanous plot to his satisfaction, he crawled into bed between Quail and Bill Hazard.

CHAPTER X.

IN WHICH DICK HATHERDEN FINDS HIS MATCH AGAIN.

"I'M going a little way out to-morrow night," said Simon Grandley to Guy, as they were at work the next morning, "and I want you to come with me."

Dick Hatherden was on the alert.

"Going out to-morrow night, eh?" thought he. "then he is playing into my hands finely."

Simon Grandley knew, of course, that no great friendship existed between Guy the Foundling and Dick Hatherden.

But he had no conception that the evil-minded apprentice was on the watch for anything, and he therefore saw no special call for concealment.

"Yes," he said, "you remember that I have an appointment—you heard me make it. But I don't want you to start from this place with me. You can meet me on Blackfriars Bridge at nine."

"Very well," said Guy, though he knew that Dick's ears were open, and drinking in every word. "I will be there to time, sir."

"And so will we," thought Dick.

His silence was already full of promise.

Gregory Hardarker, the blacksmith, had talked of obtaining the aid of Simon Grandley for their side.

He should disgorge *some* of his money first for the other side, whatever that might be; and he—Dick Hatherden—should partake in the plunder.

Presently, he detected a look which flashed quick as thought from Guy's eyes to the carpenter, which he interpreted at once as advice to say no more.

"There's more in the mind than's on the surface," thought the young villain. "I'll see if making friends with Guy will be any good. Not bad, though. I'll listen and hear a little more."

He felt sure that if he quitted the workshop the conversation would be resumed; and so, leaving his work, he passed out of a side door, which led into the yard and where he could listen.

"I didn't want you to say any more, sir, before Dick," said Guy, advancing to where his master was standing; "he was listening to all; and, as he goes home of a night, I thought he might let slip something. His companions are none of the best, I am afraid, and if you had mentioned anything about money, you might have been waylaid."

"Money," thought Dick, as he kept his ear to the crack of the door. "That is better news still. I wonder how much the old fellow will take with him."

"Well, perhaps your advice is good, my boy," returned the carpenter, "but it never struck me that there was any necessity to suspect Dick Hatherden."

"No, no," exclaimed Guy the Foundling, who was far from anxious to do an injury even to the one whom he knew to be his enemy. "No, no, there is no reason to suspect him. I spoke only of his companions. But are you really going to trust yourself in such a lonely spot with five hundred pounds in your pocket?"

"Yes, no one will suspect such a thing," said the carpenter, "no one will dream that I bear with me such a sum. I shall be safe enough, never fear."

Dick Hatherden re-entered after a few moments, looking as unconcerned as if nothing had happened, and resumed his work.

Will Lightmore meanwhile, who had been working on silently unnoticed, now turned to his master.

"As Guy is going out, Mr. Grandley," he said, "and I shall be left here all alone, may I go out too? I should like to visit my sister, whom I have not seen for so long a time."

"Certainly, Will," exclaimed Mr. Grandley, "you can go as early as you like, but be sure you don't stop out late."

Will took the opportunity to address Guy as soon as Simon Grandley left the workshop.

Advancing to his friend he clapped him on the shoulder, and as Guy glanced round he folded his arms, and surveyed him tragically.

"There *was* a time," he said, "there *was* a time when—but *no* matter!"

"Why, what ails you?" cried Guy, laughing.

"I was about to say," returned the usually light-hearted apprentice, with a serious air, "that something strange has fallen on thee of late. But to be serious. What has changed you? You are going about in most mysterious ways, and I, who have been your friend and confidant, am now discarded entirely. Where were you last night?"

Guy made a gesture expressive of caution.

Then he said, in a whisper—

"Be careful. I will tell you another time. There is a mystery in which much is involved, but I dare not tell all. However, this evening, when we are alone, I will explain all I can."

Dick Hatherden, while this was progressing, was anxious to hear all.

Anything secret had a charm for him.

So, edging nearer by degrees, he at last stood on a half-rounded piece of timber, the other end o which was close to Will Lightmore's feet.

The latter had carefully observed his movements; and, bending down, he whispered something in Guy's ear.

As he did so, Dick Hatherden, on pretence of looking for something, stood with both feet on the end of the wood.

Now was Will's time.

Catching his foot beneath it, he gave a sudden jerk, and in an instant Dick Hatherden measured his length on the floor.

A loud laugh rang through the workshop, as red with anger, and with his mouth half full of shavings, Dick rose, spluttering with rage.

"So much for listeners," said Will.

"And so much—pish!—for cowards," cried Dick Hatherden, advancing threateningly, and spitting out the sawdust and wood shavings at the same time; "I'll teach you to play your silly pranks on me, you grinning ape."

"Come on, Macduff, then," cried Will, squaring up to him: "*I* am not like Guy—I am not so squeamish about having a round or two with you even in my master's workshop; so lay on, I say, and—you know the rest. Come on!"

Guy saw no reason to interfere, so after a few faint expostulations, he stood by while they began their fight.

The first result was a blow from Dick, which brought a crimson flush to Lightmore's cheek.

But merely saying, "Well done, my noble courtier," he remained perfectly calm, until in another moment he saw an opportunity.

Then he dashed in, and, catching Dick a blow that sent him reeling, closed, and began a wrestle in fine style.

To and fro—all over the workshop—the two boys fought and tumbled—the one full of resolution to avenge an insult, the other full of bitter hatred.

Presently they fell, Will being uppermost.

Will, however, took no advantage of his adversary.

Springing to his feet, he aided Dick to rise, saying as he did so—

"A gallant knight never strikes a fallen foe. Stand to it, my friend, and let us finish quickly."

Dick again contrived to get the first blow; but Will Lightmore was very calm, looking straight into his adversary's eyes.

Then suddenly shooting out his fist, he laid Dick Hatherden clean upon his back.

"A hit—a very palpable hit," exclaimed Will, laughing; "but, come! Let there be an end on't. Passion does make thee mad."

Dick, however, rose, furious, and resolved at any cost to have immediate revenge upon his adversary.

THE RIVAL APPRENTICES

A TALE OF THE RIOTS OF 1780.

"'I WILL TELL YOU ALL ON ONE CONDITION,' SAID THE YOUNG TRAITOR."

But as he did so, little Betty, the servant maid, opened the door to call them to dinner.

In an instant the girl saw the aspect of affairs.

Rushing forward, she clasped her arms round Will Lightmore with a tragic air that would have done credit to her youthful lover himself, exclaiming—

"Stand back! you ugly imp. If you strike him again I'll call Mr. Grandley down."

In vain Will protested that it was quite the other way, and that he would rather go on.

Betty wouldn't hear of it, and, in fact, hugged him so closely round the neck, that he was nearly suffocated, when the voice of Simon was heard crying out—

"Now, then, boys."

And so the fight ended.

"Never mind," thought Dick, as he shook off the sawdust and shavings, "we shall have a reckoning soon. As for Guy, perhaps this very night will be the last of *his* triumphs. My blood is on fire, and there's nothing I wouldn't do for revenge."

CHAPTER XI.

BY THE DARK RIVER.

THE evening came at length, and the heart of Dick Hatherden beat high with anticipation.

Just as the time came for their departure, however, a man of most mysterious aspect came to the door with a letter.

It was Guy who opened the door to him, and as his master was busy, asked the stranger what he desired.

"I must speak to Simon Grandley himself," returned he; "my message is for his ear alone."

Guy did not much admire the appearance of the man as he stood there in the shadow.

He was tall, bent as with weakness, and his whole appearance was that of one in ill health.

But yet, as he stood there, he commanded no pity. He was rather one to whom you would at once conceive a natural aversion.

"I don't half like this," thought Guy, as he passed up to his master's room to give him the message. "I shouldn't be at all surprised if there was some evil meant by this fellow. I shall watch."

Simon Grandley made no hesitation in descending.

Though he had no conception whatever who the man was who sought him, still he had made no enemies in his way through life—at any rate, not knowingly or willingly—and he saw no reason therefore to fear any one.

Guy, however, who had become tainted, as it were, with Mrs. Grandley's fears, glided down slowly after him, and concealed himself near the door of the workshop.

There was no need of caution, however.

The man had brought a letter, which Simon Grandley read with much apparent satisfaction.

"Very good," he said; "very good. I will attend to it. You have but come just in time. An hour later, and you would have been too late."

This was said in a cheery, genial tone.

The answer was very different.

"It's nothing to do with me—what do *I* care. I've brought the message—haven't I?".

And with that the fellow walked away.

Simon Grandley laughing loudly at the unmannerly dog, came straight into the workshop.

"Guy," he said, in an undertone, "our plans are altered somewhat. Instead of proceeding to the old hut on the waste land, I have to meet Alexis Rainsford elsewhere. You can meet me therefore at the end of this street and we can proceed together. You had better go at once and dress yourself."

As Guy ascended to his room, Will Lightmore at once followed him.

"Now then, Guy," he said, when they were alone, and began undressing; "now then, Guy, tell me what all this means."

"Well, Will," returned Guy, "I cannot explain to you all. Need I tell you how wrong it would be to divulge my master's secrets—even to you."

"Marry come up, my serious sir," cried Will. "What does Dogberry say? 'I am Sir Oracle, and when I ope my mouth let no dog bark!' Are you going to be a second Dogberry, and preach to me of rights and wrongs? Hast ever found me untrue to a trust, good friend?"

Guy could not help laughing at the mock tragedy of his companion, which was on this occasion, he saw, put on to cover deeper feelings.

"No, Will," said he, "I have always found you good and true, and that is the very reason why you would wish me to be good and true to my master. This is a secret of his, with which I became acquainted accidentally, and I am bound by my honour to keep it sacred."

"'Tis well," said Will, still folding his arms tragically, and forgetting all about his hurry in his wrought-up feelings. "But what am I to think of whisperings between you and Simon Grandley—of secret conferences between you and Mrs. Grandley—of private journeys by night? 'Can such things be, and overcome us like a summer cloud, without our special notice?' Answer me that, sirrah."

"You are not jealous, surely, Will—jealous of your best friend?" exclaimed Guy.

Will relaxed his attitude, and clapped the Foundling on the shoulder.

"The green-eyed monster, Guy," he said, as he struck himself on his breast, "holds no habitation here. No, no. I've an idea, I have a vision—' in my mind's eye, Horatio,' remember—that there is danger afloat; and where there is danger for you, my friend, and for my master—why, there Will Lightmore's place should be. Jealous, my boy? Yes, *I am* jealous, to think that *you* should have all the fun, and wear a sword of a night, when I can only play at cut-and-thrust with my pillow."

"Well, Will," said Guy, grasping him by the hand, and shaking it heartily, "I will see if I cannot induce Mr. Grandley to let you also take part in these adventures. The help of two is better than the help of one any day—if they are both brave. But come, I must dress, or I shall be late."

"Aye, it waxeth late. The clock, even now, is pealing forth the hour of eight," said Will; "you must away."

In a few minutes more Guy was ready, and had descended, leaving Will Lightmore to adorn and disguise himself for the edification of his sister.

First, he placed his hat jauntily and slouchingly on one side of his curly head. Then he darkened his eyebrows with a piece of cork, and placed in his pocket (ready for adjustment in the street) a large

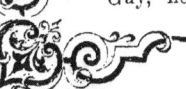

false moustache, which he used on occasions when the London apprentices indulged in a little private theatrical amusements.

Then he took his cloak down, placed it on so that the fastening should come on the top of the right shoulder, and then beneath it buckled on the rapier that he had spoken of as being for playing cut-and-thrust with his pillow.

"Marry come up," said he to himself, as he surveyed himself in the glass, "a very seemly and proper young gentleman, i' faith. Who knows that, like my worthy friend and comrade, Guy, I may not meet some gallant adventure this night?"

With these words he quitted the room, and descending quietly, slipped out of the house without being perceived by any.

Meanwhile, Guy and his master had met at the corner of the street, and were rapidly walking in a direction quite the opposite to that which had been taken by the carpenter on the night of his first interview with Alexis.

"I cannot understand at all the meaning of this change of place, Guy," he said, as they hurried forward. "The other was in a place unknown to any—deserted and quiet, and for a moment I almost feared lest I was being led into some ambuscade."

"And what has changed your opinion now?" asked Guy.

"Simply that this man—this Alexis Rainsford—is the trusted friend of my father; and he would not send to me any one who would betray me."

Talking on and discoursing, they hurried away along the right bank of the river until London was left behind them, and the chill aspect of a March night in the country surrounded them everywhere.

"This is, indeed, a strange place to appoint a meeting," said Guy, as they halted a moment and glanced round them; "it is a spot more fitted for a murder than a business appointment."

Simon Grandley laughed.

"Oh! fear not," he said, "no one has any reason to murder me. But, come, Alexis Rainsford does not know that any one is in my secret. He has no suspicion that any one followed me that night; and I do not wish, in fact, that he should know that I have confided in anyone."

"Very well, sir—am I to remain here?"

"Precisely so," returned Simon. "You see yonder house dimly showing through the trees?"

"Yes."

"Well, remain here. It is there that I have to see him; but I shall not be absent long."

"Very well," said Guy. "I will remain here, concealed among the trees."

And there leaving him, the carpenter walked away, while over the apprentice's heart some dim consciousness of evil seemed to steal as his form disappeared in the gloom.

It was certainly a strange proceeding for Simon Grandley to take him with him as a kind of guard and assistant, and then to leave him amid the dark woods alone.

But Guy was quite willing to act as circumstances dictated.

The man who had saved him from the storm, when he was a weak and friendless child, and who had been his good and kind friend for so many years, had a right to dispose of him as he willed, and so long as his honesty was not concerned, he would have refused him nothing.

The time passed very slowly.

It was about the most dreary place that could possibly have been selected by anyone to wait at night.

Nothing above but a black, leaden sky.

Nothing around but skeleton trees—stripped by bleak March winds; while the river rolled monotonously near, hardly making its presence evident by a sound.

But although he was so eager for action—though his young blood yearned even for danger, rather than a death-like, monotonous stillness, he waited on.

Passing to and fro, engrossed in thoughts of his rapidly changing life, he had almost forgotten the main object of his presence there, when he heard voices, and then the movements of several men among the trees.

Something was about to happen at last.

He at once concealed himself behind a large tree, and watched.

Then he saw approaching through the gloom several men, carrying what seemed to be another in their arms.

This man, as he was borne out into a clearing by the river side, was seen to be bound and gagged, and Guy saw at once that he was none other than Simon Grandley.

The hot blood rushed to the Foundling's face, and his hand involuntarily was placed on his sword handle.

But nothing more.

In an instant the thought entered his mind how utterly useless resistance would be.

Grandley, of course, was helpless, and he—armed though he might be—would be simply of no avail against half a dozen powerful men.

So stealthily he glided after them as they bore his master towards a boat which was moored by the river-side.

It was evident that murder—or, indeed, outrage of any kind—was not their object.

They had a far deeper design; and, as long as they behaved with no actual violence towards his master, Guy deemed it prudent to wait and watch awhile.

The men, who were too eagerly bent upon their business to observe much that passed round them, hurried him into the punt; and began rowing across the stream.

Guy's resolution was at once taken.

There was a smaller boat—a skiff—not far from the spot where the carpenter had been seized, and entering this, he followed in the wake of the masked men.

They did not proceed very far.

If they had they would not have succeeded in tiring Guy out.

The boat which they occupied was a kind of punt, and made very slow progress, while the one in which the pursuer followed was light, and easily propelled.

On reaching a part of the river where there was a slight bend, he observed at no great distance a glimmer of light in the window of a half-ruined house.

Towards this the men directed the punt, and Guy eagerly followed.

Stopping at a spot where a slight creek ran a short way inland, they drew the boat into the shadow, and, leaping out, lifted the carpenter out with some degree of gentleness, and bore him towards the house.

The house had very little in it to recommend it as a habitation.

In fact it was as ruinous and as desolate looking as the place which Alexis Rainsford had chosen for the first meeting.

Notwithstanding this, however, the place was inhabited.

As soon as the four masked men and their burdens had reached the doorway, and knocked, an old man came out, holding a flickering light in his hand.

"What have we here, gentlemen?" said he, in a a cracked voice; "I really——"

"Out of the way, babbler," said one of them, fiercely, as he pushed the old fellow aside, and made way for the others to enter. "We have no time to listen to you. Give me the light, or tell me which is the way to your best room."

The old fellow, who was as nearly a skeleton as a human being could possibly be, was somewhat disturbed in his mind by the somewhat contradictory nature of this remark, but a whisper from one of the other men appeared to set him right.

He shuffled off, leaving them to close the door behind them, and led the way into a large bare room.

This was all Guy could see, for the outer gate was then closed to, and he was left alone in the utter darkness.

CHAPTER XII.

AN OLD FRIEND IN A NEW GUISE.

GUY, as may well be imagined, was in a state of feverish excitement.

What could he do?

To raise an alarm was useless.

No one was near.

To knock at the door and demand admission was utterly useless.

What could he do against so many?

He would, in fact, be only running the risk of endangering his master's life.

So, chafing and burning with excitement, he paced to and fro opposite the door.

Presently, when his excitement had risen to fever pitch, footsteps were heard coming along the road, or, rather, the rutty pathway that skirted the dark river.

Hope once more leaped into Guy's breast.

Whoever this was, he might aid in the rescue of Simon Grandley.

He glanced eagerly through the darkness in the direction of the sound which had just attracted his notice, and saw approaching, after a moment, a shadowy form, wrapped in a cloak.

Guy at once hurried towards him, and impetuously accosted him.

"Sir, pray pardon my addressing you," he cried, "but there is a piece of villany proceeding here, and I claim your aid."

"How now," exclaimed the new-comer, curling fiercely a huge black moustache; "dost think that the sword of a gentleman is at the service of every wanderer?"

"No, no, but I am no wanderer," returned Guy; "and can prove to you my claim to attention. Will you listen to me?"

"Marry come up! Speak on, but hastily, if you please. My time is not my own; an adventure of a far different nature claims my attention. But no matter—I am listening."

There was something very familar in some of the tones of the stranger's gruff voice.

But there was no time for questioning.

Guy quickly told his story—naming even his master.

The stranger's sword instantly flashed from its scabbard.

"Lead on," he cried, "there are two of us now at any rate, and if we can but release this Simon Grandley of yours there will be three. On, on I say! St. George for merry England!"

It was doubtful to Guy whether the loud voice of this stranger would not rouse suspicion in the minds of those within.

But acting on the maxim that "beggars must not be choosers," he accepted the aid thus gallantly proffered, and hurrying to the door of the crazy house knocked loudly.

For a few moments no reply was given.

Then there was heard a scuffling of feet within; and presently the old man made his appearance.

But even then the door was not opened.

A long and heavy chain still confined the door within.

Guy's resolution was at once taken.

He saw, that even with the old man's arm within the aperture, the door could be put to sufficiently to enable the chain to be slipped off.

Seizing him with his left hand, therefore, he put the point of his sword to his shoulder, saying:—

"Utter one cry, and this shall pass through your heart."

The old man shook like an aspen leaf.

"What is it you want?" he asked, in a low tone.

"To enter, and rescue the man who is within there a prisoner," replied the apprentice. "Quick, we have no time to lose."

The old fellow, though his span of life was likely to be so short, had no desire to die with such short shrift.

So as the point of the sword began to prick and sting what little flesh he had left on his tottering frame, he pushed the door partly to, and removed the chain.

In another instant Guy and his strange companion were within the desolate looking hall.

"Say not that I admitted you," said the wretched old man, in a trembling voice, "or I shall be murdered by those men."

These words were whispered lowly.

But there was a world of ghastly horror in them.

"No, villain," said Guy, "we have too much to do to think of you. Which is the room?"

A skeleton hand was pointed towards a door.

In an instant Guy and his companion sprang forward and tried to enter.

In vain!

It was locked on the inside.

A loud knock seemed to rouse those inside, who, if they were conversing at all, were conversing in such low tones as almost to be inaudible to those without.

"Who is there?" cried a voice.

The summons was repeated.

But still no one moved.

"We must force the citadel," cried the stranger, who had so readily accorded his assistance to Guy. "What ho, there! ruffians, since ye will not open the door, we will e'en open it for you!"

And suiting the action to the word he made a dash at the door with his shoulder.

Guy imitated him; and as they both rushed at the somewhat rickety portal the panels shivered from top to bottom.

"One more effort," exclaimed Guy, and with a simultaneous rush they burst through into the room.

Those within were evidently taken utterly by surprise.

At the first sound that indicated a violent assault upon the door they had sprang to their feet, and endeavoured to commence at once the removal of Simon Grandley from the place.

But Simon Grandley was now far too much on the alert.

Bound and gagged though he was, he had immediately felt roused to action by the sounds without.

Whoever it might be who thus violently attacked the door, they were, of course, no friends of his captors, and were therefore friends to him.

So, when Guy and his unknown comrade burst into the room, the masked men had but time to draw their swords, while Simon himself rolled from his chair to the floor.

The stranger at once plunged forward, and with one dexterous cut released the carpenter's hands from their bonds.

Simon himself dragged the gag from his mouth,

IMPETUOUSLY GUY ACCOSTED THE STRANGER.

and seizing a blazing brand from the fire, stood on the defensive.

"What have we here?" cried one of the masked men; "what mad night strollers are these?"

"Ha, ha!" laughed Guy's comrade, as he struck a tragic attitude. "We are obliged to you, most noble captain. Night strollers we are for the nonce, if it so please you; and luckily for our worthy friend we are. You are most beggarly and low assassins, if I am not mistaken. However, surrender your arms, and go with us, and justice can then be had between us."

"This is some fool escaped from a paltry playhouse," said one of the men, addressing his companions. "Our purpose is done—let us away."

"We have not parted yet," replied Guy's companion. "Parting is such sweet sorrow that I could say good-by until to-morrow—Shakespeare. Now, then, Guy, at them."

Before Guy could recover his surprise at these words, which were said in a voice most wonderfully familiar to his ears, the melee and confusion had become general.

The masked men, however, seemed in no hurry to see any absolute bloodshed.

In fact, their attention seemed concentrated upon something behind them, and presently both Guy and his friends saw a dark figure slide away from a corner, and pass through an open door.

Through this the others also were evidently anxious to depart.

But for the present, at any rate, they had no chance.

"Villains!" shouted Simon Grandley, as he flourished his brand, and dashed the flames in the faces of his adversaries, "restore to me my money."

"Madman! we know of no money," cried the one he addressed.

"Why, then, was he brought here?" said Guy, as he wounded his adversary in the arm, and drove him against the wall. "Was it murder, not robbery, you meant?"

"We meant what it matters not to you to know," cried the other, furiously; "our business does not lie with boys."

The business on at present with "the boy," as he termed him, was evidently, however, as much as he could manage, for Guy, who proved himself no mean master of his weapon, soon began to press him hard. There was destined, however, to be no satisfactory conclusion to the contest."

During its progress a form had glided into the room.

The withered skeleton form of the old man.

Suddenly, as the carpenter and his two allies were forcing their antagonists in a corner, the dismal lamp was overturned, and a sudden blow sent the flaming brand flying from the grasp of Simon Grandley.

All was instantly in profound darkness.

"Now, then," cried a voice, "let us avoid bloodshed. One dash, and we are safe."

With these words he made a lunge, which wounded Grandley in the arm, and the captors of the carpenter rushed out into the night.

Then the door was banged to with such violence, that as Guy sprang forward to follow them, he received a violent blow on the head, and was sent reeling back among his friends.

As he stumbled and half fell, he encountered a body, whose skinny contour at once revealed the fact that it was the old man, who had entered and extinguished the light.

Guy grasped him firmly by the arm.

"A light! a light!" he said, "that we may find the door, and pursue them."

"'Tis useless," gasped the terrified old wretch, "their horses are without. Hark! even now they are off!"

These words were said with an evident satisfaction.

And they were true, moreover.

The loud clattering of horses' hoofs was heard, and when lights were procured, and the door opened, all signs of them had disappeared.

When they re-entered the room, another discovery greeted Guy and his master.

During the struggle the moustache of Guy's suddenly found friend had dropped off as well as his hat, and there stood revealed before them, no other than WILL LIGHTMORE—the brave and rollicking Apprentice.

Guy laughed outright as he beheld him, while Simon Grandley stood for a moment wrapped in amazement.

"Why, Will," cried the Foundling, "what masquerade have we here?"

Will eyed his master ruefully, doubting how his pranks would be received.

"That I have erred, I do confess me," he began, in his usual mock heroic strain; then remembering that such was not the way in which to address his master, he added—

"I dressed myself like this to amuse my sister; but I am glad now that I had a sword to defend you."

"My lads," said Simon, taking their hands; "you have behaved like men—like brave men. To you I owe my life, and in the future I shall not forget you. Would, however, that you had come earlier, or that I had taken you with me. The work of years has been undone by the treachery of this one night."

Guy—who even in his excitement knew that he ought not to reveal anything before Will—gazed with eager curiosity at his master.

Simon Grandley understood at once the meaning of the look.

"I have been deceived, trapped."

Then he turned fiercely towards the old man, who was busy endeavouring to rake together a fire from the smouldering embers.

"Tell me, you old villain—you wreck of humanity, strong enough only to harbour the last remnant of an evil mind—who were these men who brought me to this place?"

"Yes," he said, "what I took from home with me is all gone! I have been deceived, trapped."

These words were said fiercely, with no effort at a suppression of passion.

The old man trembled violently, and looked abjectly in the face of the questioner.

"I do not know them—I swear I do not know them," he said.

"Then how came they here?"

"Will you listen if I tell you?" said the old man, "quietly, and without clutching me like that."

The carpenter released his hold of the man's arm.

But at the same time he drew a pistol from his belt, and said:—

"You see this pistol. Death is in it for you if you lie. I can tell it in your face if you do."

The old man was evidently in intense and abject fear.

But he nevertheless told the truth.

The purport of his story was that some hours before the arrival of Simon Gandley and his captors he had been roused from sleep by a loud summons at the door, and on opening it he saw the four masked men.

They made their way into the house, and informed him that they had a friend who was very ill not far off, but who desired for certain reasons to be removed from the spot where he was, and they promised a handsome sum of money if he would allow them to make use of his house.

He swore that he knew nothing of the intentions of the men, or he would never have permitted their entrance.

Who they were he had not the slightest conception.

He had never seen them before.

"Why, then, were you so glad when you heard the sounds that told you they were gone?" asked Simon Grandley, sternly.

"For this reason," said the old man, with less nervousness than before. "I have lived in this desolate house many, many years. This miserable hovel I would wish to be my last resting-place. I desired that nothing should occur to send me again adrift upon the world. A death—a violent death—happening here would have been the means of depriving me, perhaps, of this shelter, which, wretched as it is, is the only one I can afford."

Simon Grandley felt convinced by his manner.

But there was one more question he desired to ask.

"There was a fifth person here, who glided out in the midst of the fight. Who was he?"

"I know not," said the old man. "He seemed a boy—a mere boy; "but I saw not his face."

"What if it were Dick Hatherden?" thought Guy.

But he said nothing, and with this explanation the carpenter was compelled to be content.

It was evident the old man knew no more; and so, quitting the dismal tenement, Simon and the two apprentices hurried away towards London.

At the corner of East Chepe a tall man, dressed in a long cloak, and wearing his hat jauntily on one side, accosted the carpenter.

Guy remembered him at once.

It was Alexis Rainsford.

"You have not kept your appointment," said he. "After waiting on the marshes for an hour, I made my way hither. Wherefore did you not come?"

"Your letter distinctly told me that the place of meeting was changed," began Simon.

Alexis at once interrupted him.

"Letter!" he cried. "I sent no letter."

Simon turned to the two apprentices.

"Go home," he said; "I am safe here, and shall not be long."

So Will Lightmore and Guy quitted him, and within half an hour were fast asleep in bed.

CHAPTER XIII.

STEALTHY STEPS TOWARDS MURDER.

THERE was a shadow over the mind of Dick Hatherden.

He had never been a favourite either with his fellow-apprentices or with his master.

But now affairs had taken even a still worse turn for him.

He knew himself suspected.

Both Will and Guy were of opinion that the dark figure which had glided out of the old house before the masked conspirators had made good their retreat was Dick.

And yet neither one nor the other had spoken of it.

"Curse them!" muttered Dick, on the next evening—the evening of a day during which neither of his comrades in the workshop had seemed disposed to speak with him—"they're in league to drive me away from the place. But they shan't do it. No—no! Guy, too, is jealous of my friendship with Colonel Halsted and his pretty daughter. Never mind—he little knows the plot I am weaving for his destruction!"

With such thoughts as these in his head, he hurried towards the abode of the colonel.

He was admitted at once when he reached the iron gates of the mansion.

How unwelcome would he have been had any within there known the hideous thoughts that filled his breast.

Colonel Halsted was not in.

But he was told to wait.

Ushered into the little ante-chamber where Guy had waited before, it was not long before he was joined by the colonel's daughter.

Her eyes beamed with evident pleasure as she beheld him, and with more pleasure still as he caught her in his arms and kissed her rapturously upon her ripe, red lips.

"I am so glad to see you, Dick," she cried; "it is such a long time since we have had a chance of being together while my father was out."

"Will he be long?" asked the apprentice.

"I do not expect him back for an hour," returned the young girl; "and so now we are alone you can tell me all about the secret of your birth."

Dick smiled.

The time had come now for the disclosure he had longed to make and yet feared to risk.

"Well," he said, as they sat down together on the sofa, and passing his arm round her waist, he drew her towards him so that her head rested on his shoulder; "well, I will tell you—on one condition."

"And that is——"

"That you will not tell the colonel."

"You need not fear that," she said, with a pretty blush, "because he mustn't know yet that I ever spoke to you. He might suspect how much I loved you."

And with that she kissed him fondly, and patted him caressingly on the cheek; and the evil mind of the apprentice bounded with joy.

There was nothing, however bad, that he would not then have done for that young and beautiful creature.

So, after returning her caresses, he told her his story—his lying story—*making himself the hero of Guy's story*—and so representing himself that he seemed in the eyes of Aurora Halsted the hero of a romance.

The bosom of the ambitious girl heaved with pleasure as the story proceeded.

She had hoped for this.

The desire to bear a noble name was a mania with her.

This was her love for Dick.

This was the reason that she caressed and petted him.

For him she had no thought except as being the active means of raising her to a high position.

"I wish my father *could* know of this," she said, looking up lovingly in his eyes, "he might assist you in discovering your friends."

"No—no," cried Dick, hastily, "that would never do. I have not yet told you all. I have an enemy."

"I know it," said Aurora, quietly.

"You know it," exclaimed Dick, in surprise.

"Yes—it is the other apprentice who was sent here. I hate him."

She did not say that her hate was caused by the innate respect she was compelled to feel for him at first sight.

She said "hate," while in her own mind she felt a yearning towards the noble, handsome youth.

"Yes," answered Dick Hatherden, "he *is* my enemy—my bitter enemy—though how *you* knew it I cannot conceive. He has a deep, dark plot against me. He has a plot against his master's life too, which he is already beginning to work out."

The girl shuddered.

Such enormity was horrible in one so young.

"Why, what should he desire his death for?" she asked.

"For a good reason. He knows my story, and being also himself a foundling, he thinks, that if Simon Grandley and his wife were dead, and *I* out

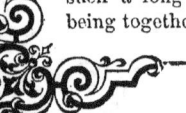

of his way, he would be able to take my place, and pass himself off as the son of the nobleman who left me on that stormy night on the step of the carpenter's house."

"The villain!" murmured Aurora, who, of course, hated anyone who proposed anything to shake the foundation of her prospective greatness; "but you will be able to stop his evil doings, and punish him, I hope, Dick."

"I could—'kill him,'" he was going to say.

But he stopped speaking suddenly.

The steps of some one were heard rapidly approaching.

Aurora at once sprang to her feet.

"Here is my father," she said, and slipped away.

Hardly had she gone a moment, when Colonel Halsted entered.

His features wore a serious, even a stern expression.

They relaxed, however, as he saw Dick Hatherden.

"I am glad you are come," he said; "have you news for me?"

"Yes, colonel," he answered, producing a packet. "This, I believe, contains good news."

The colonel took it eagerly, and opening it, ran his eyes quickly over the documents.

A smile broke over his features as he did so.

"This is good—very good," he murmured; "you are very active and earnest in the cause, Dick; and some of these days may become something better than an apprentice."

"Something better than an apprentice, curse him," thought Dick, bitterly; "and is this all he promises?"

But he merely said—

"I hope so."

"And now," said the colonel, "I want to ask you about some one to whom I owe a debt of gratitude. What is the name of the boy who came hither instead of you one day?"

"Guy the Foundling," replied Dick, who already felt the foundation of his scheme shaking beneath his feet.

"Ah! he's a noble-looking youth—you can see that in one glance—and comes, no doubt, of noble parentage. The other night, when I was attacked in the street, he saved my life. I did not remember his face at the moment, but I did afterwards. I fancy I know something of his secret. When can I see Mr. Grandley?"

"Not to-morrow, colonel," replied Dick, boldly hazarding a lie, "he will be out all day. The day after, however, he will be in. Shall I tell him that you will call on him?"

"No—ask him to call on me," said the colonel; "meanwhile, here is some gold. Keep on the watch, and you need not fear that you will go rewardless in the future."

Dick Hatherden left the colonel's house burning with rage.

He, who had worked so hard, was rewarded by a few gold coins.

Guy—his hated and detested enemy—was thought of by the colonel as a friend; was about to be aided

in his research for his secret, was perhaps about to learn it from the colonel's own lips.

A red mist—a mist of blood—floated before Dick's eyes as he thought of it.

"No, no, it shall never be—it shall never be," he muttered, as he clenched his hands and hurried on more quickly. "He shall die! he shall die! If the colonel lives, Aurora will know all—will learn my imposture—my low birth, and will hate me. No, no, the colonel shall die—and then Guy shall follow him."

And elated with this hideous thought, he hastened on till he reached a low tavern near his squalid home.

Here he invested in a bottle of spirits, and then hurried up to his lodging.

Here he found Bill Hazard sitting dozing by the fire, while Quail was at the table, devouring some coarse food.

"Here, Bill," cried Dick, "wake up—I've got something to tell you."

"Curse it then," said Bill, surlily, "have you got anything to drink? Some one has been and robbed me, and I've not a farthing."

"Oh! that's all right," returned Dick, in a cheery voice, "here's a bottle of brandy; and if you've had no supper, Quail can go out and buy some. But I've news of work to be done, and we must be alone."

"I don't want supper," said Bill; "give me the brandy. Quail, you dolt, you idiot, don't stand gaping there, but take your ugly carcass out into the yard, and stop there till you're called in. Sharp now!"

The wretched boy, who knew well what the result of disobedience would be, instantly obeyed, and sallied forth into the yard, where a drizzling rain was just beginning to fall.

And there he sat at the bottom of the steps in the rain and cold while the two upstairs by the cheery fire plotted murder.

There was just the shadow of revenge expressed in his face as he glanced up at the window; but when, after a while, they called him up again, and—jovial at the prospect of their hideous crime—gave him brandy to cheer him up, he forgot all his feeble hatred, and went to his wretched bed as happy as could be.

CHAPTER XIV.

THE MURDER.

THE next night was fixed for the murder of the Colonel.

Another day, and it would be too late.

THE RIVAL APPRENTICES

A TALE OF THE RIOTS OF 1780.

DICK HATHERDEN, KNIFE IN HAND, GLIDED UP BEHIND THE COLONEL.

On the night fixed for the dreadful crime Colonel Halsted was seated in his room with his daughter, Aurora. She loved him dearly, and anyone could have told it in the glance of her eyes as she sat by his knee, and looked up fondly in his face as he talked to her.

No. 5.

He had been unusually grave and stern during the day.

But now he had unbent.

"Aurora," he said, as he stroked her glossy head; "I fancy I have a surprise for you to-morrow."

"Indeed, what is it?" she asked, eagerly.

Some rich present she imagined, little suspecting what a secret he proposed to unfold.

She little imagined what kind of surprise was intended.

Her father smiled at her question.

"No," he said, "no; I cannot tell you to-night. In the morning I expect to see some one who will tell me whether my surmises are correct. I am morally certain that they are; but, however, I will not compromise myself by a half-explanation till I know."

There is no doubt that the surprise he alluded to had some reference to Guy the Foundling.

But the ideas of the young girl had no reference to him.

She, as I have before said, thought at once of some costly present—some gem, or some present of the kind—or some pleasant jaunt through foreign lands, which she longed so much to see, and which, in the future, she resolved to enjoy in company with her husband.

"Oh, you tantaliser," she cried, "you have set me so longing I shall never sleep all night. You oughtn't to have said anything, if you were not going to tell all."

Colonel Halsted smiled.

"Oh, yes, you will," he said; "you will lie in bed and dream of a happy future and joy unspeakable. And now run away to your room, for I have much to do, and feel that I should like to do it to-night."

The young girl kissed her father, and ran hurriedly away, to conceal her vexation.

"Ah!" thought he, as her pretty little form disappeared from the room, "he would make her a capital husband. Just the age—just the position for her."

But he mentioned no names.

He took to pacing the room now uneasily; and presently, drawing aside the heavy curtains that shaded the window, he gazed out upon the night.

It was a dark, unpleasant night, speaking of storm and unholy doings.

A dismal leaden sky hung like a pall over the city, and the rain fell in a noiseless shower down into the lonely and muddy streets.

Everything was so still and death-like, that the colonel, with a shudder, quitted his post of observation hastily, and drawing the curtains, took up his position again by the fire.

"It is very strange," he murmured, as he passed his hand over his brow, "very strange, indeed, but I feel a presentiment of coming evil. Some undefinable being is warning me of peril; and yet whence can it be? Kirkdale's vagabonds were disposed of so thoroughly the other night that I need surely fear no danger again in *that* quarter."

He paused awhile, and gazed into the decaying fire.

"No," he resumed, as he drew the embers together, "no, I fear nothing of that kind. I fear more some insidious enemy—some villain gliding to his crime."

And as he spoke he glanced round him with a shudder, as if expecting—or, rather, as if he would not have been surprised—to see some half-spectral assassin hovering near him.

After a moment, however, he smiled at his own fears.

"Bah!" he said, rising, and drawing his chair up to the table; "I am a fool. I have got a fit of the blues, and I'm fancying I'm going to die. At any rate I'll finish the work I have begun, and then I shall be prepared for everything."

So saying, he poured himself out a glass of spirits, and drinking it off, set himself to work to examine some papers.

Deep in their perusal, and in certain notes that he now and then added, he did not observe how the storm outside was increasing; but presently, as he paused a moment to rest, he observed that the rain was pattering violently against the panes—that the wind was howling, and shaking the old house to its foundations, and shrieking down the chimneys with strange voices.

"It's the weather that's given me this peculiar feeling," thought the colonel, as he rose and placed his papers in a bureau; "I'm glad there's no meeting to-night, and I can only pity those who are out in the storm. I'll get me to bed now, though scarcely, I fear, to sleep, for until this mystery is cleared up with Simon Grandley I shall feel very anxious."

As he spoke there was a loud ringing at the bell, and a knocking, too, as if someone was without who was eager to escape the storm.

The colonel started.

"Who can it be who comes on such a night as this?" said he; "is this a messenger of evil tidings?"

He was soon satisfied, for at this moment the door was opened; and a servant entered.

"Dick Hatherden, the carpenter's apprentice, is below, and desires to see you, sir," he said.

"Dick Hatherden, and in such a storm as this," exclaimed Colonel Halsted; "then, indeed, my feelings were no superstitious fears. Admit him at once."

The servant at once quitted the room, and in another moment Dick Hatherden entered.

The colonel uttered an exclamation of surprise and fear when he beheld him.

Well he might.

The boy seemed to have grown prematurely old.

His face was pale and thin, his lips white, his eyes wild and bloodshot.

"Why, what ails you, my lad," exclaimed the colonel, "you seem distraught?"

Dick sank as if exhausted into a chair.

The shadow of his crime was already heavy upon him.

Yet, though his physical courage deserted him thus, he was resolved to go through with it.

"I bring a letter," he said, in a hollow voice, "a letter from Alexis Rainsford. Read that, and by the time you have done so, perhaps I shall have recovered strength to speak."

So saying, he drew a note from his pocket.

The colonel poured him out a glass of spirits, gave it to him, and took the letter.

It was written in a straggling, tremulous hand, and ran as follows:—

"Suspected, and at length discovered, I am hiding for my life not many yards from your house. I have been sadly wounded in an affray with some hired assassins; but after I have seen you I shall endeavour to make for the coast and fly to France. Your brave young friend who brings you this encountered me by accident in the street, and saved my life. He can direct you to the place where I am hiding, and will tell you how the affair took place. Hasten to me, for I am faint and in pain.

                    "ALEXIS RAINSFORD."

"Poor fellow!" murmured Colonel Halsted, as he read this epistle (the writing of which had about as much to do with Alexis Rainsford as it had with King George himself). "Poor fellow! I must take some brandy in a flask to him. But tell me, while I buckle on my sword, how did it all happen?"

While the colonel was preparing for his night excursion, the young villain explained in a somewhat disconnected manner how, hurrying from his master's house, where he had been detained somewhat late, he had heard cries of distress resounding amid the wailings of the wind, and how he had at once rushed to the spot.

There he found Alexis Rainsford—whom Dick appeared to know, at any rate, by name—assailed by three ruffians.

A fourth was on the ground dead, and so, as Dick stated, he picked up his sword, ran one of the ruffians through from behind, and fought until the others turned tail.

Then Alexis entreated him to assist him to the ruined house that adjoined the mansion of the colonel.

"And why did he not come to my own house?" asked Halsted.

"I know not," replied Dick. "All he told me was that he dared not. He said that this house was watched by his enemies and yours, and that if he were seen approaching the door, he would be seen, and your fate and his would be sealed."

This, and more, was said while the colonel was getting ready, which he did with as much precision as if he were preparing to start upon a lengthy journey.

Then, as they descended the stairs, he said—

"And now, Dick, you will have to show me the way to the place."

The boy simulated fear and surprise.

"I had hoped, sir," he said, with a pretended tremor of the voice, "that you knew the place yourself. If I am discovered now I should be ruined for ever!"

The colonel smiled.

"Why, what have you to fear," he said; "you who are but an apprentice? What have you to lose? You could get work anywhere. While I—my life, my honour, my position, all are at stake. You need, however, only show me the door of the place, and then you can go home."

These words, simple as they were, served to inflame more than ever the anger of Dick Hatherden against the colonel.

They were not meant to be contemptuous, but they seemed so to his distorted mind, and it served only the more to strengthen his hideous determination for crime.

"I will show you the way," he said, sullenly; "I am but a boy; but I know how to sacrifice myself for a good cause."

And with this righteous reflection he passed on without another word, thoroughly resolved now to go on with his deadly work without pity.

The house of Colonel Halsted was an old one, but it was one which had weathered well the storm.

It had, perhaps, been built before its less fortunate neighbour.

But somehow or another it had a very strong constitution, and its portico was less encroached upon by cracks and green, and its walls were less indented and its windows less bulgy, and its whole appearance more modern and reputable, even setting aside the fact that some sudden decay and ruin had fallen upon its neighbour.

This neighbour had been attacked by fire, and had been saved from utter destruction only at the very moment when the arrest of the devouring element was useless.

It was now almost a ruin—a room here and there having been spared only to become the habitation of rats or other unclean animals.

It was to this spot that Colonel Halsted was inveigled by Dick Hatherden.

Arriving at the door he stopped sullenly.

"This is the place," he said; "I suppose I can go home now?"

"You can," returned Colonel Halsted, contemptuously, "if such is your wish. I have misconceived, however, greatly your character for bravery, as also your affection for me."

"I do not think so," said Dick; "but as no danger threatens you in there, I shall not be wanted, and may as well go home."

"Be it so, then," replied the colonel, and pushing open the door, which for years had boasted no lock or hinge, he disappeared.

Dick tremblingly waited—tremblingly, be it said, not from fear, but from eager excitement lest the colonel should hesitate at last.

Then, after a few moments, he followed.

"Now," he thought, "at length comes the long-desired end—the end that shall make me rich and happy."

Happy!

Wretched deception!

Miserable hallucination of an evil and perverted mind!

The colonel, meanwhile, who had ascertained from Dick that Alexis Rainsford was hiding in a wretched garret on the third floor, entered the house boldly, and ascended—not for the first time—the old and rickety stairs.

It was a ghostly, ghastly place.

Not a single light was there visible now, save what crept through the weird old windows from the riven clouds—riven now by the lightning, which

played, violet and terrible, upon the old oak panelling, and brought out every mark like a blood-stain.

Not a single sound but the booming thunder, which rolled like solemn warnings overhead, and shook the feeble ruin by its reverberations, and called up fearful flutterings—put aside just now—in the old man's heart.

"I am a soldier and a gentleman," thought Colonel Halsted, as he mounted, clutching his sword, "and I must not be afraid; but I would sooner meet a hundred foes upon an honest field of battle than an array of shadows that may hide a hundred assassins."

And all this time the cowardly murderer, that might have stabbed him in the back had he possessed the courage, lurked behind him in the darkness, glided after him noiselessly up the staircase, and clutched his dagger, more because he trembled at the darkness than because he desired to strike.

At length the third floor was reached.

All was very still.

So still, indeed, that for the first time Colonel Halsted began to entertain suspicion.

Not of foul play.

This, indeed, would have been natural.

But he thought not of it.

He merely had a vague idea that he must keep his wits about him.

And so he did—drawing his sword and advancing to the door (beneath the chink of which shone a light) as if he were approaching the citadel of an enemy.

Throwing open a door he beheld a strange scene.

The most wretched of wretched garrets was there before him, and in one corner was the form of a man huddled up in straw and rough cloths.

On the table was a lamp nearly expiring, and by its side a bottle of spirits.

"Are you there, Alexis?" asked the colonel, entering and pushing to the door, through which, however, in another moment glided Dick Hatherden, the young assassin.

"Yes," said a hollow voice, "I am here—here to die, I am afraid. Come near me that I may tell you all."

The colonel unsuspectingly advanced, and knelt down by the side of the huddling form in the corner.

"Give me some brandy again," said the half-smothered voice, "I am faint—see, a glass is near you."

The colonel hurried to pour out the spirits, and in an instant he knew his mistake.

Hardly was his head turned, when a violent blow caught him on the side—the blow of a man in brutal haste, but not steady enough to accomplish his object—the blow of a man only too well primed with drink.

"Murder!" shouted Colonel Halsted, staggering to his feet, and preparing to resist; "I am trapped—deceived! Oh, God! this then was my waking dream!"

Then out from the bed sprang Bill Hazard, his eyes glazed with drink, his cheeks flushed, his hair wild, his mouth contorted into a leer that told of the lust for blood.

In his hand he held a long-handled hammer—a weapon suited to his terrible nature.

Not one word he spoke.

The colonel looked into his face and saw there was no compromise.

He had not come to talk, or to make terms, but to act.

"Villain!" he cried, "what want you with me? Speak—who are you?"

Bill Hazard made no reply.

The great hammer swung round his head, and descended with fearful force on the colonel's shoulder, his shriek of agony being drowned in the solemn roar of Heaven's artillery.

It was the left shoulder upon which the brute's strength had been expended, and the colonel, in spite of the terrible pain, drew back his sword and wounded Bill Hazard in the arm.

Before the latter could revenge himself, the colonel, who was an expert swordsman, again sent his weapon rushing through the villain's arm.

"Death and fury!" shouted Bill, "I'll have your life for this."

And again the long-handled hammer was swung round, and again it descended on the old man's shoulder.

Now was the time for ending the cruel battle, for Dick Hatherden was gliding up behind, waiting for an opportunity to close in and stab the unfortunate victim in the back.

But it was not to be at that moment.

A flash of lightning more vivid than before dashed, as it seemed, through the old garret, and a wailing, shrill, terrible cry, went ringing through the place—

"Murder! Murder!"

Bill Hazard seemed paralysed.

For an instant his long-handled hammer was suspended, as it were, in the air, and then it dropped with a thud as he fled headlong from the room.

Dick Hatherden was now alone with his wretched victim.

But his heart yearned for blood now—his eyes swam in a red mist.

The colonel was leaning against the *débris* of the table, which had been crushed in the fight, and was just gaining breath, in spite of his smashed shoulder, when the young assassin crept behind him and stabbed him in the back.

The blow was not mortal, and as the colonel turned, with the last energy of despair, upon his assailant, he saw who his assassin was.

"Dick Hatherden!" he gasped. "Villain!—wretched murderer! Was it for this——"

He had no time to complete his speech, for Dick Hatherden, roused to murderous desperation by the fear lest even now his victim might escape to denounce him, dashed at the wounded man fiercely.

The colonel, of course, though fifty years had passed over his head, was more than a match for a youth of Dick's age and size.

Under ordinary circumstances, I mean.

As it was, however, the terrible wounds he had received from the long-handled hammer of Bill

Hazard were now telling on him. His left arm, in fact, was utterly useless, and as the young villain rushed at him, he fell heavily to the ground.

Here the crime was soon consummated.

Two stabs from the long knife of the apprentice, and the old man, who had made a last grip at his throat, sank back exhausted.

"Now to dispose of the body," thought Dick, and as the idea flashed through his excited mind his eyes fell upon a half-open cupboard, with a rusty key in its lock.

Seizing the body in his arms, he at once bore it to its place of concealment, the hand of the dead or dying man still grasping his throat.

Just as he placed him on the floor within there echoed through the room a yell of hideous discord—the result of the wind and thunder combined, it might have been.

But to the excited and delirious mind of Dick Hatherden it seemed far different.

It seemed a human voice, raised in warning and anger.

Tearing himself, therefore, convulsively from the grasp of the dead man, he slammed-to the door—turned the key—then, placing it in his pocket, dashed downstairs with headlong speed.

"HEAVEN BE MERCIFUL!" CRIED DICK, DROPPING HIS CARDS.

He opened the street-door hurriedly, scarcely looking to see if he was watched, and then slamming it after him, hurried away through the storm.

The rain was now rapidly descending—the storm still flashed and boomed over the city—and everything was evil and wretched and portentious.

The excitement of the crime was over now, and he crept along with weary heart and shuddering frame.

He saw now the enormity of the crime he had committed—the fearful secret that would weigh upon his heart for ever.

And yet had he not succeeded in his plan?

Whatever secret Colonel Halsted had in common with Guy—whatever he knew in regard to his birth—was it not now set at rest for ever?

However this might be, his success did not seem to bring him any comfort as yet.

Haggard, pale, wet to the skin—shivering as with an ague—he looked the impersonation of horror and despair, as he rushed up the staircase of his lodging and knocked at the door.

Well might Quail start back aghast.

"Why, what ails you, Dick?" he cried, "you look as if you'd been frightened."

"Frightened, fool!" cried Dick, savagely; "why should I be frightened? What have I got to be frightened at? I'm cold—wet through to the skin—that's all. Where's Bill Hazard?"

"In the corner yonder asleep," said the half-witted youth, as he closed the door and followed Hatherden; "he seems half crazed—ha! ha! he's talking in his sleep of murder; and his hands were all red when he came in. But they're clean now, for the hound has licked it off."

And he grinned as if he had said something clever.

Dick's face was averted as Quail spoke, or even he would have noticed the deadly pallor that overspread it.

He was soon convinced of the truth of the boy's words, however, for as he neared the hearth he heard a low growl, and saw Tiger, the bloodhound, busy licking the legs of the sleeping man where the blood of the murdered had splashed over him.

"Give me some brandy," said Dick, as he threw himself into a chair by the fire; and the boy at once brought to him the remains of the spirit which the two wretches had imbibed on the previous evening when planning the murder which they had so brutally carried out.

Glass after glass was poured down his throat until something like insensibility crept over him.

Then he crawled upon the bundles near Bill Hazard, and was soon locked in a heavy slumber.

As soon as he was asleep, Quail rose from the corner by the fire where he had been crouching; and approached Dick, candle in hand.

Kneeling down, he carefully examined his clothes.

"Ah! ah! Blood, too! Blood, too!" he murmured, chuckling, and rubbing his hands. "Quail will watch! Quail will watch!"

And with this he went to bed satisfied, though why it would be difficult to say; for at present, at any rate, nothing more than a vague idea was in his mind that he had discovered something.

Nothing like desire for revenge had yet entered his heart.

————

CHAPTER XV.

A TERRIBLE DISCOVERY.—THE FIRST SHADOW OF THE CLOUD.

WHEN the morning broke, cold and hazy, showing plainly that the storm was only waiting for an opportunity to break out again, Dick sat up on his wretched bed and gazed wildly round him.

His dizzy and aching head plainly told him that what had occurred the night before was no hideous dream, but a more hideous reality, and with his memory came back his disgust and anger for his companion in crime, who, as we have seen, deserted him just at the critical moment.

Rising up, he administered a hearty kick to the sleeping giant, who roused up, uttered a loud oath, and sprang to his feet.

"Oh! it's you, is it? Why the devil didn't you let me be?" he cried, savagely. "Have you only just come home?"

"No; you coward—you miserable traitor," exclaimed Dick, angrily: "you were too dead drunk when I came in last night to speak to. But now you *are* awake, what have you to say for yourself—*you* a man, who could run away and leave a boy like me to finish such a job?"

The big man shuddered.

"Don't talk about it—don't talk about it," he said; "I don't want to speak of it, or think of it. As his eyes glared at me in the darkness, I heard a voice say 'Murder! Murder!' and I fled. Is he dead?"

He added this in a whisper.

"Dead—yes!" returned Dick, "and safely housed, too, if you can only keep a quiet tongue. Our clothes must be burnt, however, for we are smothered in blood. Ha! what is this? Where's my scarf?"

He stood petrified, holding up both his hands.

When he had visited the colonel's house he had worn a scarf with lace ends, given him by Aurora Halsted, and with his own name embroidered in the corner.

Where was it now?

He remembered the clutch which the unfortunate man had made at his throat.

He remembered the death-grasp which he had found it so difficult to release himself from.

He remembered the manner in which he had dragged himself away when the wailing cry had alarmed him into flight as it had done Bill Hazard before.

Where, then, could the tell-tale scarf be, save in the hands of the dead man?

He trembled like an aspen leaf, and turned so pale and horror-stricken that Bill Hazard fairly laughed outright.

"Who's the coward now?" he shouted.

"I am not mad," said Dick, recovering his self-possession in some degree. "I know when danger really threatens us both. I have left my neckerchief, with my name embroidered on it, in the grasp of the dead man. It must be recovered; will you go for it?"

"Not I," returned Bill Hazard, in a surly tone; "do your dirty work yourself."

"Very well; I'll go to-night. Meanwhile, some-thing must be done to avert suspicion. Perhaps," added Dick, "among your other cowardices, you are not afraid to go to Colonel Halsted's door with a letter."

"No. I'll go, if going is any use; but we'll have some breakfast first, and, as you say, we'll get rid of these clothes. Where's Quail?"

"He's gone out to get something for breakfast, I presume," said Dick; "here, let's pile on more wood, and throw these accursed clothes on the flames."

So it was done.

A huge fire was lit beneath the wide, open chimney; and ere Quail returned with the materials for a substantial breakfast, the tell-tale clothes were burned, while an unwholesome smell was diffused through the apartment—a smell which made the bloodhound growl and sniff the air!

When Dick reached the workshop of Simon Grandley that morning he neither felt nor looked the same being that he had been the day before.

Truly discovery was postponed for awhile, at any rate.

By the time he reached the workshop a letter had been placed in the hands of Aurora by Bill Hazard.

This letter, which was an admirable forgery of the colonel's writing, ran as follows:—

"Dearest Aurora,—

"Do not be alarmed. Business has called me away. I shall be absent perhaps a fortnight; but there is no occasion to fear anything. In fact, I would rather that my absence were kept a secret. With best love, your father,

"ARTHUR HALSTED."

Aurora sighed, pouted her lips, thought of the surprise she had been promised, and which had now been put off indefinitely, and then made the best of a bad bargain, and hoped Dick Hatherden would come and see her often.

She little knew the truth.

She would have killed him with her own hand had she known it.

Meanwhile the boy murderer was, as I have said, a different being, both in appearance and in feeling, to the Dick of the day before.

The contemplation of the crime beforehand had not been half so bad as retrospection.

He was haunted now, not only by the terrible scene he had passed through, but by terror lest the tell-tale scarf should be found by some one in the grasp of the dead man.

However, he was determined that he would not sleep on it.

That very night he would revisit the house, which to him now would ever be a haunted one.

He had come to this resolution after a day, which had been doubled in length by his terrors, when Simon Grandley entered the workshop about half an hour before the time for closing.

"Dick," he said, "I want you to remain here all night. I have to be out late, and shall take Guy with me; and there have been so many robberies and crimes of all kinds in this neighbourhood lately, that Mrs. Grandley would not feel herself safe if she were alone with Will."

This communication acted with overwhelming effect upon Dick.

His power of speech seemed gone.

Another night, then, of agonising suspense he would have to undergo—a night when terrible phantoms would hover round his bed, pointing jeeringly in the direction of the room of horror.

But, then, if he refused to stop, what excuse could he make?

His hesitation, his pallor, his inability to frame an excuse, would betray him; and when the disappearance of Colonel Halsted began to be talked of, suspicion might light on him.

So he merely muttered a "Very well, sir," resolving either to escape from the house in the dead of night as soon as Simon Grandley returned, or to postpone the visit to the dead till the next night.

Time went on; and after supper Simon Grandley and Guy went out, and Dick and Will retired to the room of the latter.

CHAPTER XVI.

A LITTLE COMEDY AND A LITTLE TRAGEDY.

WILL LIGHTMORE being placed in such an unpleasant position as regarded a comrade whom he disliked, resolved to make the best of a bad bargain, and proposed a game of cards.

This plan suited Dick very well for a time.

He naturally thought that he would be enabled, in the excitement of the game, to forget the evil spirit that hovered ever near him, so he endeavoured to plunge as heedlessly as he could into the play.

But it was useless.

It was, after all, dull work playing for a few pence in that quiet bed-room; and terrible work, too, at length, when the pale face of Colonel Halsted seemed to the excited imagination of the young murderer to be peering over the shoulder of Will Lightmore.

"Heaven be merciful!" cried Dick, dropping his cards, and starting back, pale and horrorstricken, in his chair.

And there he sat with open mouth, and features working nervously, while the spirit his imagination had conjured up stood pointing at him with bloodstained hand over the shoulder of his companion.

"Why, what ails you?" cried Will Lightmore, with astonishment and some fear; "you look as if you had seen a ghost!"

Dick shuddered, and closed his eyes.

When he opened them again the form was gone, and he sprang up.

"There's some devilry afloat in this house," he exclaimed, as he moved away trembling, and bathed in a profuse perspiration; "if I thought you were tricking me, I should know how to revenge myself."

"So conscience does make cowards of all!" said Will. "Perhaps you have something on your mind. If so, out with it; and though we may have quarrelled, I'll keep your secret, and give you my advice."

Dick Hatherden vouchsafed no reply, but turned towards the window, through which the flashing lightning ever and anon threw lurid flashes over the room.

His mind was wrought up to a pitch of fearful excitement.

Each flash of lightning seemed to bring back to his eyes the scene of the previous night; and the vision he had just beheld appeared a special warning to him to hasten to the ruined house, and secure without further delay the tell-tale scarf.

But how could he effect this.

He was just torturing himself with these ideas when he heard a voice say—

"And he can smile, and murder as he smiles!"

It was but Will Lightmore reading out of his Shakespeare; but his tragic voice, and loud intonation, startled the trembling criminal, and with a sudden resolution he walked back into the centre of the room.

"I can't stop here, Will," he said, in as conciliatory a tone as he could assume; "this place is full of hobgoblins. Besides, this idea of Grandley's about the house being in danger is all nonsense—only nervousness. So I'll slip away, and no one will be any the wiser."

Will Lightmore waved him back majestically.

"What!" he cried, "a soldier, and afraid! You, who talk so much of fighting, fearful of your own shadow. No—no; we are on special duty to-night, and must not desert our posts."

Dick eyed him angrily.

"A plague on your accursed mummery," he said. "I tell you this house is to me like a prison; it is so still one might fancy oneself in a church vault; and more than that, I had promised a dear friend of mine to meet him. I must go. Let me pass."

Will Lightmore placed his back against the door.

"'Most noble, grave, and reverend friend,'" said he, with a provoking smile, "'you have done the "house" some service in your time'; but I tell you plainly, this last service which has been demanded of you *shall* be done as Simon Grandley wishes it, or we'll fight for it."

Dick eyed him savagely a moment.

He meditated, in fact, an onslaught.

But he changed his mind quickly.

Will Lightmore's attitude and whole aspect, in fact, was most determined.

A fight, too, would arouse the house; bring Mrs. Grandley to the room, and only end in disgrace to himself.

So he turned sullenly away.

"Get something to drink, then," he said, "and we will play again."

"'The better part of valour is discretion,'" cried Will, as he turned the key in the lock and placed it in his pocket. "However, as you have surrendered, we will now apply ourselves once more to the game. Open the cupboard behind you, Dick, and you will find a bottle and a glass."

Dick, nothing loth, did as he was directed, and discovered a bottle containing a certain modicum of liquid, which, on tasting it, he discovered to be excellent brandy.

A good glass of this served greatly to restore his humour and courage, and in a few moments the two apprentices were once more deep in a game.

The spirit had imparted to Dick Hatherden a certain recklessness for the time; and under its influence he soon became immersed in play.

So some little time passed.

Then, when they were in the very thick of the game, a knock came at the door, which made Dick start in terror.

Will Lightmore rose, and, proceeding to the door, opened it, to find little Betty, the servant-maid, standing without.

"Here is a letter for Dick Hatherden," she said.

"For me!" exclaimed Dick, in amazement and trepidation; "what can it mean?"

"I should advise you to open it and see," said Will Lightmore, laughing; "people don't put their thoughts on the outside of their letters."

Acting upon this injunction, Dick hurriedly opened the letter.

It was written in a straggling hand, and read as follows:—

"Dear Dick,—

"Be quick and come to me. I have important news. Someone has been to Halsted House and told them that they suspect foul play. Nothing exists to criminate me; but if your scarf with your name on it is in the grasp of the dead man, you should lose no time in getting it away, as the old ruins will be sure to be searched. I would go myself, only as I am out of danger now, I don't see why I should put my head in the noose. I am at the 'Fox and Grapes,' in Gutter Lane.—Yours,
                              "BILL HAZARD.

"P.S.—Quail was very strange this morning in his behaviour; and now has disappeared altogether. This may mean nothing; but it seems curious that he should bolt away just now. Be sure and burn this as soon as read."

Such was the letter, misspelt and ill-written, that Dick held tremblingly in his hand.

His ghastly white visage was totally without expression for a moment, save that of stony horror.

Then suddenly the life leaped back into it.

Holding the paper over the flame of the candle until it was destroyed, he turned to Will, who was indulging in a little amorous play with Betty at the door.

"Will," he said, "a word with you."

Will heaved a tragic sigh.

"The course of true love never *did* run smooth," he said, as he kissed the ruddy lips of the pretty country girl; "but never mind, Betty—we part to meet again."

And so saying, he re-entered the room.

"Now, my most noble gentleman, I am at your service," he said, locking the door, and, as before, keeping the key.

"There, don't get fastening that door again," he said, "I must go, whether Mr. Grandley likes it or not. I've just received a note which tells me that I have been robbed of all my savings by a companion. I know where to find the villain if I go now."

"Spare your breath," said Will, in a more serious tone than usual. "Simon Grandley said that we were, both of us, to remain here to-night, and I'm not going to be left alone if I can help it; so, if

you are going out, as I said before, you'll have to thrash me first."

The idea suddenly flashed into the mind of Dick Hatherden that perhaps he was suspected and a prisoner.

This idea suggested another.

"Curse you for an unmannerly, obstinate, selfish brute," he said, "I'll go to bed, then; but I'll take care that our master knows all in the morning."

So saying, he began to undress.

Will Lightmore was not sufficiently taken off his guard to give up the key.

This he secreted where he was pretty sure that Dick Hatherden could not find it; and then he also undressed, and prepared to lie side by side with the murderer of Colonel Halsted—one whom it would have frozen his very blood to touch had he but known the truth.

He was soon asleep, in spite of the thunder that boomed and the lightning that played without; and as the two lay there side by side, the one with his handsome face placid in sleep seemed the impersonation of goodness and good nature, while the other, dark and scowling, with knit brows, looked like an emissary of the Evil Genius of mankind.

After assuring himself that Will Lightmore slept, Dick Hatherden crept gently from the bed.

Stealthily he resumed his clothes.

Then he drank another draught of brandy, and approached the window.

Running from the window—slanting towards the street—was a wide wall; and along this he had determined to make his way, drop into the thoroughfare, and then trust to chance to favour his re-entering the house.

Will, rocked in the arms of peaceful, happy sleep, heard not the noise that Dick made in gently and slowly opening the window; and very soon the rain was pattering through on to the floor.

In another instant, however, Dick had swung himself out, dropped on the summit of the wall, and drawn the sash down, so as to leave only a few inches open.

Then with a beating heart he made his way along the perilous summit of the wall.

When he reached the end of it he glanced anxiously round.

But no one was in sight; in fact, the storm had driven nearly everyone indoors.

So, dropping carefully into the street, he hurried away—his heart beating, every pulse at work—towards the House of Crime.

CHAPTER XVII.

SHOWING WHAT DICK HATHERDEN SAW IN THE
STORM: AND WHO SAW IT WITH HIM.

THE old ruined house next to the mansion of Colonel Halsted looked gloomy and horrid as Dick Hatherden approached it.

THE RIVAL APPRENTICES

A TALE OF THE RIOTS OF 1780.

GUY DEALT THE GIANT A STAGGERING BLOW ON THE HEAD.

Dick, though trembling and in fear, knew that he must not hesitate, more especially on the very threshold of the place where, even on such a stormy night, he might be perceived by some one. So, though his heart beat fast at the anticipation of the sight he was about to see, he took from his pocket the rusty key, and turned it in the lock. The door opened with a clinking sound, that ran in melancholy cadence through the old house, and awoke echoes that almost made Dick Hatherden rush away again.

But his very fear made him brave.

He knew that if a search were made the damning evidences of his guilt would be patent to all, and for this reason he had more courage to face the Dead Thing that would grin in ghastly mockery at him up stairs, than go away again, with the constant dread of discovery in his heart.

So, having seen that no one watched him, he entered, and closing the door after him, began to grope his way up the old creaking staircase.

The very desperate nature of his undertaking appeared to strengthen his determination as he proceeded, and though the booming of the thunder and the flashing of the lightning startled him as he advanced, he went on steadily, until at length the door of the fatal room was reached.

Here he halted a moment to take breath.

Then, with a sudden jerk, he flung the door open, and plunged into the darkness.

Terrible darkness it was, too.

He had forgotten entirely that he would require a light, or he might have called at his own lodging and brought with him a dark lantern.

As it was, except when the violet lightning darted across the heavens, the place was in total darkness.

Rendered more fearful of everything by this gloom, Dick Hatherden hesitated a moment.

But then, as he stood irresolute, a terrific flash illumined the room, and he saw the door of the cupboard—the mysterious repository of the dead.

Slowly he approached, clenching his teeth, and drawing from his pocket the key, slowly opened the door.

Only a moment he hesitated.

Then he flung it open.

One glance was enough, and with a yell of horror he sprang back.

When, after the last struggle, he had dragged the body of the murdered man into the closet, he had flung it on its back and there left it.

Now it was crouched up in a corner, with its hands drawn up to its chest, as if in a last struggle for life it had huddled itself up there, and the Dread Destroyer had stopped its efforts suddenly.

But there, in its right hand, was the much-coveted scarf.

Recovering his presence of mind, Dick advanced to clutch it.

But at the moment an unearthly laugh was heard, and the lightning ceasing to play left the place in gloom.

Trembling in every limb, he turned towards the spot whence the sound proceeded.

At the window in the grey light he saw the head of a human being—a wild head, with long straggling hair, and eyes that seemed to glitter in the darkness.

"He cannot see me," muttered Dick: "he could never recognise me again, whoever he is. I must end my task now."

And so, resuming his courage, he advanced again.

But, as Fate would have it, the lightning again flashed luridly across the room, and as it did so, a crash was heard, as if the man outside was forcing his way through the shattered casement.

The fear for the future was at once lost in the fear for the present.

Knowing what would be the result of discovery in that room—alone with the dead—he turned away, and leaving the door of the great closet open, with the dead man half falling from it, he dashed out upon the landing and down the stairs.

In his haste he plunged down so far that he found himself among the vaults before he was aware of it, and fell headlong into a pile of old shavings and rubbish which the very solidity of the masonry had preserved somewhat dry.

In an instant an idea suggested itself.

He rose from among the mass and listened.

Not a sound was heard save the storm.

A malicious gleam of satisfaction shot from Dick's eyes.

"I will fire the house," thought he, "and so destroy the dead and the prying fool that startled me from my purpose."

And having so resolved, he seized an armful of the inflammable material, and proceeded to bear it up the staircase, in the direction of what was once the reception-room of the deserted mansion.

The fact that Aurora was next door, and that the flames which destroyed the ruins would destroy the colonel's house too, never once occurred to his over-heated imagination.

CHAPTER XVIII.

IN WHICH GUY MAKES ACQUAINTANCE WITH A VERY PRINCIPAL CHARACTER IN THE STORY.

GUY THE FOUNDLING may well be excused for experiencing surprise at being again taken out on a secret expedition by Simon Grandley, and they had no sooner quitted the house together than he plainly expressed his sentiments.

"Forgive me, sir," he said, "if I am lost in amazement at the mysterious events which have surrounded me for some weeks past. It seems as if the whole current of my life were suddenly being diverted into a new channel."

The worthy carpenter clapped him heartily on the shoulder.

"My lad," he said, "there *is* a change in your life. In that you are right, and I trust that it foreshadows a greater change still. I fancy—but remember, it is only fancy, and you must not suffer your mind to be led away by it—that I have discovered some little clue to your parentage."

Despite of Simon Grandley's admonition, Guy's heart gave a great leap at these words.

His parentage!

What a change did not such a discovery mean for him?

"From whom have you heard this?" asked Guy, in tremulous accents.

"Well, I have heard nothing definite at all,"

replied the carpenter; "but I received a letter yesterday from Colonel Halsted, desiring me to come to his house this evening, as he desired to speak with me about you. I fancy, from the kindly tone of the letter, that he means more than merely rewarding you."

"Rewarding me!" exclaimed Guy. "Why should he think of rewarding me?"

"It seems," said the carpenter, "that he discovered afterwards who it was that aided Alexis Rainsford that night in driving off the villains. But come! I do not intend taking you with me there. I am asked to go alone. I want you to keep an appointment for me which I could not keep with Alexis."

"With Alexis!" repeated the apprentice, in surprise.

"Yes," said Grandley, "you know my secret, and I can trust you. You are aware, of course, that when I was seized by those villains I was robbed of every farthing I had with me."

"Yes."

"Well, I told him, when I met him at the corner that night, that I had been robbed, and could not consequently send the money which I had promised to my father; but he urged me again so piteously on behalf of my unfortunate parent to do all I could to raise it again, that I have spent an anxious day in deliberation, and in running to and from friend to friend. In vain. I find I cannot do it, save by the sale of my home and my business."

These last words were spoken in a voice full of emotion.

"But surely," said Guy, "you would not dream of that?"

"No," said Simon Grandley. "I cannot, at present, bring myself to think of it. But if I could be assured, on better proof, that my father demanded such a sacrifice of me, I would. However, I must give you your directions. You know, maybe, a tavern called the Flying Eagle, in Thames Street."

Guy smiled.

"I have but little opportunity of knowing taverns," he said, "but no doubt I shall be able to find it. Is it there that Alexis Rainsford waits for you?"

"It is. You will find him in the public room. What I desire you to do is to deliver to him this letter, to note how he receives it, and to bring me an answer."

"I am not supposed to be aware of any of your private matters, I presume," said Guy.

The carpenter mused a moment.

"No," he said, "it will be better not to appear so. Unless, indeed, he seems to desire to place confidence in you. Then you may say, 'Do not fear to speak to me—I know all.'"

Simon Grandley then gave him the packet, and, after a few minor directions, despatched him on his errand.

We will leave the carpenter accordingly for the present to proceed to Halsted House, and follow our hero, Guy.

He knew, of course, his way to Thames Street, although he knew nothing of the Flying Eagle,

and after a short, though sharp, walk, he found himself in the "street of fish."

He was about to ask his way, when a swaying sign attracted his attention, and he saw the figure of an eagle flapping to and fro in the wind.

Luck having brought him to the very point he desired, he at once entered and made his way to the public room.

Here he found a number of persons, of various grades of society—seedy professional men, flash bullies, and respectable artisans—hob-nobbing round a blazing fire, and enjoying their beer and their grog.

But no Alexis Rainsford was to be seen.

Either, therefore, Guy was before his time, or the man did not intend to keep his appointment.

Being absent now, however, with the leave of Simon Grandley, Guy had no doubt as to his proper mode of proceeding.

Ordering in some bread and cheese and a tankard of ale, he sat down near the glowing fire, and amused himself in the intervals of eating with taking stock of everybody.

The company was anything but the style of company that he would have chosen had he been able to make a choice.

They were the lowest of the low.

A bousy, greasy crew, redolent of beer and tobacco.

The room itself was warm.

That was its only claim to comfort.

Otherwise it was dirty and grimy, patched and smeared by greasy heads and shoulders.

The floor was sanded, and the only seats were rough forms.

The people did not take much notice of him after his first entrance; they indulged in a few idle stares, and that was all.

Young and old were mingled together in one talking, swearing, gambling crowd, whose eager, dirty faces, were a study to the lad who sat there quietly watching them.

And yet it seemed an age before Alexis Rainsford came in.

When he did he was in no state for much transaction of business.

His hat was perched slouchingly on one side of his head, as it had been on the first occasion that Guy had met him.

His face was red and bloated with drink, and his eyes, too, flashed with evident excitement.

He swaggered in with his hand on the hilt of his sword, and cast his eyes round him with an insolent look of defiance.

"A pretty messenger Simon Grandley's father has chosen, truly," thought Guy.

But he resolved to go through his part quickly.

Just as the bully flung himself down on a bench near the fire, the apprentice rose and approached him.

"Your name is, I believe, Alexis Rainsford?" he said.

The man turned quickly.

A look of supercilious defiance and annoyance was on his face.

"Have a care, young sir," he said, "how you use

the names of people in a place like this. What want you with me?"

Guy drew forth the letter of the carpenter.

"I bring you this," he said, "from Simon Grandley. For my own part, I want nothing from you or with you."

The bully leaned his hand upon his hip and stared at the bold speaker, aghast, as it were, at his daring.

"You are over bold for a youngster, methinks," said Alexis, twirling his huge moustache; "and pray what is to prevent me from chastising you for your insolence when I have read your master's letter?"

"This!" cried Guy, and his bright rapier flashed in an instant from its scabbard. "Take the letter—read it—and let me go. My master simply sent me to you to bring a civil message, and take back a civil answer—not to be browbeaten, or bullied!"

Alexis Rainsford burst into a loud laugh at these words.

A laugh, not of ridicule, but one of real pleasure.

"Before heaven, I admire your pluck, my friend," he cried; "you sustain well the prestige of the brave apprentices of London. Put up your sword; ring the bell yonder, and let us taste their best."

Guy quietly sheathed his rapier, and summoned the attendant, who, at the bidding of Alexis, brought in a foaming tankard of ale.

The countenance of Alexis Rainsford changed at once when he read the letter of Simon Grandley.

First came a look of blank surprise.

Then a look of anger.

Then he dropped the hand that held the letter upon his knee, and glanced into the fire.

"This is false—all false," he muttered, presently, leaning over, and peering, as it were, into Guy's face. "Your master—yet, stay. What know you of this matter?"

The apprentice remembered his master's words.

"'I know all,'" he said.

"Well, well, then," returned Alexis, "then I need not fear to speak. You know that your master was to bring me £500?"

"Yes."

"He has broken his word."

"He has not."

"Not broken it! I swear he has never brought to me one single farthing, and now he says that he came to see me and lost all—that I made a wrong appointment with him, and that now he cannot procure it. His father thought better things of him."

"Mr. Rainsford," said Guy, "you mistake my master entirely. In fact, I heard that you were aware of his loss before to-night. You met him at the corner of the street the very night he was attacked and robbed. He then told you of it—so to night it cannot be a surprise."

Alexis eyed the boy keenly.

"It is a surprise, nevertheless," he said. "I thought that story of his was trumped up because he desired to change his mind. If, however, he was really robbed, and he cannot procure it again, the end will be that his father must remain where he is, and trust in Providence and his own means to contrive an escape."

There was something in the man's manner as he said this that made Guy doubt him.

His glance was furtive.

His eye seemed to question him.

And yet what did it all mean?

Was Alexis Rainsford simply a thief, wishing to procure the money by a false pretence?

This could not be.

The carpenter had unerringly recognised his father's letter by a secret sign.

Then again, if he were one of those who had attacked him and robbed him at the old house by the river, what object had he now in following the matter up, and pestering him for more?

"I'm sorry Grandley did not come himself," said Alexis, finding that Guy did not reply. "I must see him once before I return to France. Tell him that I felt greatly for his loss, and will endeavour to do all I can for his father. I will be here again to-morrow night, at the same hour; and now drink up, and God speed you. I should like to see more of you, I can tell you. You're a brave lad, and may be a nobleman some day. So, if Simon Grandley will bring you, come too—come too."

"I'll tell him what you say," said Guy.

And then he walked out, only saying, "Good night," but never offering his hand.

Alexis Rainsford watched him as he departed—watched him fixedly and anxiously.

"A saucy sprig that," said one of the tipplers near him.

"A brave and honest youth!" cried Alexis, curling his long moustache, and settling his sword, as he glanced fiercely round, "and whoever says aught against him will be no longer my friend."

And with the words he stalked from the room.

"Alexis is out of sorts," said one of the drinkers, in a maudlin tone.

"Aye," said another, with a laugh, "he's gone mad, I think, with religion."

And, after a hearty laugh, they lapsed again into their tippling and their cards, and he was forgotten.

But the word religion had really a peculiar significance.

For when Alexis Rainsford—the friend of Colonel Halsted—quitted the tavern, he took his way hastily and eagerly towards the house of Jonas Barnsdake, the leader of the Protestant Convention.

CHAPTER XIX.

GUY GETS AGAIN INTO TROUBLE, AND OBTAINS A STRANGE COMPANION.

MEANWHILE Guy the Foundling quitted the tavern in a most confused and unpleasant state of mind.

There was something to him most puzzling in the behaviour and the character of Alexis Rainsford.

He liked and yet disliked him.

He was an uncouth, reckless, dare-devil fellow.

And yet there seemed some depth of good in him.

"For my own part, I hope soon to cease from these adventures altogether," thought he, as he hurried home. "I am sure that some evil is brewing somewhere for Simon Grandley, and either for good or evil—I know not which—this Alexis Rainsford is mixed up in it."

And yet, though he thought this, and said the

words half aloud, as if to convince himself of their truth, he had a secret hope that out of the apparent gloom would come the dawning of a better day for himself.

He was thinking thus when a shrill cry rang out upon the night air.

Not such a cry as had attracted his notice before when he had rushed to the assistance of Colonel Halsted.

This was far different.

It seemed the wailing cry of a woman in distress, or a boy in mortal fear or agony.

He stopped and listened.

Again it rang out clearly and distinctly on the night air—this time in more distressing tones than before.

"I'm in for night adventures," thought Guy.

And drawing his rapier, he dashed away towards the scene of the disturbance.

When he came to the spot, however, the brave lad at once sheathed his rapier.

It was not a case of contest such as had engaged his good right arm before.

It was a cruel scene.

A scene of brutal ferocity.

On the pavement was cowering a ragged, wretched boy.

None other than Quail.

He had evidently been subjected to cruel ill-treatment.

He was in tears—his ragged clothes torn into further rags—while Bill Hazard, towering in coward strength over him, kicked him as he sat there helpless, saying at the same time—

"I'll teach you to go spying and watching—I'll teach you to run away. Come back with me, or I'll kill you."

"You'll kill no one here if I know it," rang out a clear, bold voice that made Bill Hazard turn quickly.

And there stood Guy defiantly before him.

The bully gazed in wonder.

Well he might.

The disparity in size was at once apparent.

Bill Hazard, full six feet high, seemed a giant beside the apprentice.

But Guy was nothing daunted by his size.

His conduct had proved him a coward.

"What do you want with me?" shouted Bill. "Do you want me to serve you as I've served him?"

"Please yourself," returned Guy, "but I tell you this much—you shan't strike him again while I am here."

"TAKE THIS LETTER ; READ IT, AND LET ME GO,"
SAID GUY.

"We'll see that," said Hazard, with an oath.

And as he uttered it he advanced with a brutal leer towards Quail.

But Guy was before him.

"Leave him alone," he cried, "or we shall quarrel."

A loud laugh answered him.

Bill Hazard, who had been imbibing copiously the bad ale at the "Fox and Grapes," and who was in a state of excitement and irritation because Dick Hatherden had not kept his appointment, laughed a loud, coarse laugh, and raising his immense fist, brought it down with no small weight on the brow of Guy the Foundling.

The immense force with which the blow was delivered by the giant's brawny arm staggered Guy for a moment.

But he did not yield.

He had given the challenge, and was prepared to abide by it.

So, without a word, he advanced steadily, so as to avoid Quail, who still sat on the ground, cowed and trembling.

Then, as the giant prepared to deal another blow, he sprang lightly aside, and dealt him a blow on the side of his head which sent him reeling against the wall.

A loud curse burst from the fellow's lips as he recovered himself.

A curse wrung from him as much by astonishment as anger.

But he had no time then for revenge.

The sight of the poor, half-witted boy, cowering on the ground, bleeding, and utterly at the mercy of the brutal tyrant, had inflamed the anger of Guy the Foundling, and before Bill Hazard had well assumed the defensive, the brave apprentice rained in upon him such a shower of blows that light seemed to dance everywhere before his eyes.

Bill Hazard had no offensive weapons with him.

Otherwise at this moment some sly stab would have put an end to Guy's life and our history at once.

He saw that nothing but brute force could avail him now.

And so, being no coward, but rather more like a wild beast when roused, he dashed the blood from his eyes, and with a howl, plunged rather than rushed at his antagonist.

Guy was prepared for him.

Anticipating an unusual mode of attack, he lunged out with his right hand just as Bill raised

his huge foot to kick him; and following this up with a side blow with his left, he had the satisfaction of seeing the giant roll over heavily upon the pavement.

He gave him no time to rise.

Springing forward, he knelt upon his chest.

"Give in now," he said; "you've had enough."

The giant was about to reply, but suddenly the idea of being beaten by such a stripling seemed to tickle his fancy.

Dropping his arms, he lay on his back, and burst into a loud laugh, which rang out cheerily in the night air.

"I'm done—I'm done," he said, shaking his huge sides "Let me get up. I give in."

Though not best pleased by a merriment which seemed to cast ridicule upon him, Guy at once jumped up, and Bill Hazard slowly rose to his feet.

"Give us your hand, lad," he said; "you are a brave fellow, and I own myself fairly beaten, though how you did it I cannot well conceive."

Guy, however, did not care to give his hand.

Somehow or another there was an involuntary feeling of dislike in his heart for the man.

"We'll shake hands when we're better acquainted," he said. "Now, then, my boy," he added, addressing Quail, "you come with me. I'll see you right."

This roused Bill Hazard's temper once more.

"Now, don't let us quarrel again," he said; "this boy belongs to me—so he's got to go back to his lodgings. Now, then, Quail—sharp's the word."

But the poor lad had now a dread of his brutal companion.

He cowered away, and came nearer to the side of Guy.

"No, no," he said; "I don't want to go near him —never—never—again."

Guy at once took his resolution.

He drew his sword.

"Now, then, my lad," he said, "come with me. Let that bully approach you any more, if he dares."

Bill Hazard at once saw that any more resistance was useless.

He had no weapon with him.

"Curse you! I'll be even with you ere long," he cried, shaking his huge fist at him. "I know your face well. I've seen you coming out of Simon Grandley's shop. Wait awhile—wait awhile."

And still uttering fearful oaths, he thrust his hands into his breeches'-pocket—as we have described before—and went hurrying away along the dark street, with a long, gliding step.

Guy at once began his way homeward, while Quail came nestling, as it were, to his side, as if afraid that either Bill Hazard, or some shadowy form like him, would rush forth from a dark corner, and carry him bodily away.

He was all confidence and pleasure for a moment.

Then he changed again.

His half-witted brain conceived suddenly a new idea.

He stopped and clutched Guy by the arm.

"Where am I going to?" he said. "Not there— not there!"

And he pointed in the direction of the ruined house of the colonel.

It seemed a strange fatality after the lapse of a few moments.

Guy, of course, who knew nothing of the fact of Dick Hatherden's terrible visit, or of the vision which Quail had seen there in the old garret, thought that the poor creature had feared a return to Bill Hazard's lodgings.

"No, no," he said, "you shall not return there. I will speak to my master, and see if he cannot do something for you at home."

"Good—good!" said Quail, exultingly. "I don't want to go there—there's a mist before my eyes when I think of it. There is death—death—there for everyone who goes. We'll go home."

Even as he spoke there was a red mist in the sky —a red glow that shot up into the sky, and deadened the light of the now unfrequent lightning.

Quail stood gazing in wonder.

Only for an instant, however.

An idea suddenly dawned in his mind, and he clapped his hands together exultingly.

"I thought so—I thought so!" he cried. "A fire —a fire!"

Guy glanced at him in surprise.

"What mean you?" he said.

Quail recoiled at once.

"I like a fire," he said; "let us go and see it."

And then he began walking rapidly in the direction of Colonel Halsted's house.

Guy followed.

There was something in the boy's manner which excited his curiosity.

But never for a moment did he suspect the truth.

Quail went on at a rapid trot till they reached the spot.

A crowd had already collected.

And no wonder.

The fire had got well hold of the old ruins, and was lapping out its red tongues through the broken windows.

Great beams were within there, swaying about in fiery tangles.

Clouds of steam and smoke were intermingled with drifts of fiery particles, like the falling of red snow, which floated out over the crowds of people, and lit up the casements of the houses near.

Quail took one strange wild look at the building, the relics of which were being devoured by the flames.

Then with a sudden gleam of intelligence he turned to Guy—

"I'm not ungrateful. I'll be back to you in a moment."

And then suddenly he dashed away right in among the flames of the burning door.

There was a shriek or two from women in the crowd—a wondering murmur from among the men.

Then in silence all watched.

It was indeed a matter of wonder.

What could he want there?

No one lived there.

That all knew.

But presently, amid the black volumes of smoke that rolled upwards towards the sky, they saw him hurrying along the dangerous parapet towards the house of Colonel Halsted, with some undefined object

in his arms—something that made him stagger and sway to and fro.

The people looked at him awhile.

But presently their attention was withdrawn from him by a sudden rush of flame and smoke from the mansion of Colonel Halsted, which told that that place also was in flames, and that the fire was bursting out from the basement story.

Hardly had this happened, when Quail suddenly appeared in the most mysterious manner behind Guy.

"You see I have come back," he said, with a grin.

"Yes; but where have you been?"

"To save something. But see! the next house is on fire too, and the colonel's daughter is there."

These words, which were spoken with unusual energy by the half-witted boy, at once brought to Guy's mind the existence of Aurora Halsted.

Just as the remembrance flashed through his brain, he saw a white figure appear at a window on the first story.

He was struggling through the crowd when he caught sight of it—he struggled the more when he saw her.

She had retired to rest sulky and angry with everyone.

Her father had disappointed her in the promised revelation, and Dick Hatherden had not made his appearance, and so she had lain in her bed, dreaming of strange things and weird visions, when the smoke and the heat awoke her.

And there she stood now, high above the street, wringing her hands, and screaming for help, while not a soul moved to save her.

The crowd swayed to and fro in intense excitement.

But no one knew what to do.

All seemed confused and mad with horror.

"A ladder—a ladder!" was shouted out by some.

But none ran to get one.

Guy, however, had seen that near at hand was a builder's yard, and at once he rushed across the road, followed by Quail.

He had said nothing to the latter.

And yet, short of wit as he was, he seemed to know that his assistance would be of use.

Others followed too, when they saw their eager movements, guessing that there was some attempt to be made at saving the young girl, who was now joined by a group of terrified domestics; and after a short interval, during which the crowd was roused to a terrific pitch of excitement, the ladders—amid yelling cheers from hoarse throats—were brought through the throng.

Guy was the first to spring up one of them, leaping upon the balcony just as the night-dress of the horrified girl had been caught by a flame.

Quail, roused to frantic energy by the example of his preserver, rushed up another ladder, and seized one of the domestics in his arms.

And in a few moments, amid the shouts and cheers of a hundred people, the brave lads descended with their burdens.

As they did so a heavy hand was placed on Guy's shoulder, and turning, he saw Simon Grandley standing beside him.

"Brave lad—brave lad!" he said. "Let that girl

be placed in the care of a neighbour—yonder, where they are bearing the others. Let Miss Halsted come to our house. See! yonder is a hackney-coach. Call it!"

"I must take that boy with me, Mr. Grandley," said Guy, as the coach came up, and Aurora, now in a dead faint, was placed in it. "I have saved his life to-night, and I am certain that in some way or another he is mixed up in a mystery which concerns us. Here, you lad!" he added, as his master nodded his assent, "jump up here, beside the driver."

Quail (who now that the excitement had evaporated which had prompted him to rush into the ruined house among the roaring, seething flames, was once more fearful lest he should see the giant form of Bill Hazard striding through the throng to seize him) complied eagerly; and in another moment the coachman clacked his whip, the horses, which had pranced uneasily in the glow of the flames, hurried off, and the fire and the hustling, eager, and shouting crowd were left behind.

On reaching Simon Grandley's house, Aurora Halsted was placed under the care of Mrs. Grandley, and Quail was accommodated for that night with a bed in the workshop.

CHAPTER XX.

IN WHICH QUAIL IS INSTALLED IN A SITUATION, AND BILL HAZARD PROPOSES A ROBBERY.

DICK HATHERDEN's escapade of the preceding night was not in any way suspected.

Guy, however, soon put him in a state of confusion and terror, without having the slightest intention of doing so.

"Good morning, Will," said he, as Lightmore entered the workshop, "you should have been with us last night."

"More adventures—more fights, I suppose," said Will, "out of which I am always. My time's to come, however."

Guy smiled.

"Well, you have guessed aright for once," said he; "I have had a fight, and an adventure, too."

And concisely he told the story of the night.

Dick Hatherden listened eagerly to every detail.

He recognised at once in the giant and the ill-used boy Bill Hazard and Quail.

"Well, you acted bravely," said Will; "and where are the boy and the young girl now?"

"They are both here."

At the very moment there was a movement among the shavings in the corner of the workshop, and the ragged and still bloodstained figure of Quail arose.

The eyes of the half-witted boy and Dick Hatherden met, and for a moment not a word was spoken.

Then Quail sprang to the side of his protector.

"You're not going to give me up to him?" said he, in a voice of terror. "Oh! no—no."

"To him," cried Guy, in wonder; "no, what should Dick Hatherden have to do with you? No: you're going to remain here, I hope. Do you know this boy, Dick?"

"Yes," replied Hatherden, sullenly, "you know well I do. Wasn't he my second in the ruins who

I fought you? All I know of him, however, is that he is half-witted; and that he lives in a wretched den with the bully you spoke of. You've brought a pretty fellow into your master's house now—the companion of a thief and a villain."

Quail understood well enough that Dick was disclaiming him.

He had no conception why.

It was enough pleasure for him to know that as Dick declared he did not know him he would not be given up to him.

So he held his peace, and Hatherden, relieved on *his* account, began to fret his evil mind about Aurora.

She saved by Guy—she here in Simon Grandley's house—where she could hear all about Dick Hatherden's imposture—what torture did not these thoughts convey to his mind!

Presently, too, the carpenter came down.

"Guy," he said, " the young lady whose life you saved last night is upstairs, and wishes to speak with you."

"Curse him!" muttered Dick, as the Foundling, with flushed cheek, followed his master.

And then he vented his spleen by leaning over to Quail, saying—

"If you say a word about me and Bill I'll murder you."

"Murder! No, no," whispered Quail in a mysterious whisper, " let me stop here, and don't let Bill see me, and I won't *say a word about the murder of the colonel!*"

"Where are you going, you clumsy brute?" shouted Will, as Dick, in an agony of terror, went spinning back, and fell heavily against him. "Have better manners, or maybe we may come to blows."

"I'm ill—I'm ill," said Dick abjectly, as he staggered to a bench and sat down. "I fell on you by accident. Give me some water."

"There are more things in heaven and earth, Horatio, than are dreamt of in our philosophy," commenced Will to himself, as he good-naturedly fetched his comrade what he asked for. "This behaviour of Dick is strange—most passing strange. If he keeps it up longer I shall say he is mad, though there be some horrid method in his madness. Why, bless me, Dick, you look as tremulous and as pale as if you had been committing a murder and had been found out."

Strange to say, these words, instead of alarming Dick more, appeared to rouse him from his terror.

He took the water, and eyed Will Lightmore steadily.

"Look here," he said, " I don't care about jokes of that kind. You mayn't like me, and I mayn't be good-looking in your eyes; but I tell you what, I won't stand being insulted, and you're a coward if you do it."

The manner in which he said this was so serious and impressive, that Will Lightmore felt, as it were, ashamed of himself.

"If I have wronged you, my friend," he said, " I am sorry. There's my hand."

And he grasped Dick Hatherden's hand, feeling, as he told Guy afterwards, as if he had handled a toad.

Meanwhile, Guy, led into the room by Simon Grandley, had once more been brought face to face with Aurora Halsted.

She smiled graciously, casting upon him the full glory of her beauty; and, indeed, she looked very beautiful, dressed, as she was, in one of the prettiest robes of Minnie Grandley, who stood somewhat nervously near her.

"We have met before," she said, pressing his hand, and looking beamingly into his handsome face; " but I had no idea then, when I received you so coldly, that I should one day owe to you my life."

Guy was dazzled—what boy would not be?—by the beauty of this one, who owned herself so beholden to him—dazzled in spite of the unpleasant smile with which she had once greeted him, and the baleful and evil light there was ever in her eyes.

It is so sweet at all ages to be thanked by beauty!

"I did but my duty, Miss Halsted," he said. "I could not have done less and retained my own self-respect."

"You could not have done more," she answered, " and I shall never, never forget it."

And then she pressed his hand and smiled all the more sweetly on him, because she saw that the eyes of Minnie Grandley were fixed upon both, and that she had already—child as she was in years—made a rival!

Then, full of the enthusiasm of success, she said, with a pretty start—

"But there was another one with you—one who saved my servant-maid. He, too, was a brave fellow. Where is he?"

And so poor Quail—ill-dressed and ragged and trembling—was brought to her, and she took his hand, and thanked him too.

And then, glancing full in Guy's face, though addressing Quail, she said—

"I can reward you, though I could never reward Guy. When my father comes home you shall have a rich recompense for your courage. I could not reward *him* like that."

And having thus praised Guy at poor Quail's expense, and made Minnie's heart leap in her bosom, she sat down.

"I hate her!" thought Minnie.

"What can she mean?" thought Guy. "She is very beautiful!"

Night closed over a strangely unsettled household.

Messages had been sent hither and thither in search of Colonel Halsted, wherever Aurora imagined he might be, and several grand people called in carriages, and offered to take her away with them to their homes.

But she elected to remain with the carpenter and his wife—"if they would keep her!"

And so for awhile she was to stay there!

When night once more fell over the city the evil-minded apprentice sallied forth eagerly.

He had another villanous scheme in his head, to effect which the aid of Bill Hazard would be necessary.

THE RIVAL APPRENTICES

A TALE OF THE RIOTS OF 1780.

![illustration]

AFTER ONE GLANCE ROUND, BILL HAZARD ENTERED.

CHAPTER XXI.

IN WHICH DICK HATHERDEN PROPOSES TO BILL HAZARD AN ACT OF VILLANY.

DICK HATHERDEN, gloomy, dispirited, trembling every shadow, was glad that evening. when he escaped from the workshop of Simon Grandley and made his way towards his own wretched home.

He had certainly no reason for any special terror at this time.

x

x

x

x

The old ruined house being destroyed, and the house, too, of Colonel Halsted having been involved in the general ruin, there was every reason to suppose, of course, that the body and the tell-tale scarf had been consumed together.

Nevertheless, there was in his mind an uncomfortable feeling—a dread of he knew not what.

And so he crawled away along the street like a hangdog, miserable assassin as he was, and flung himself eagerly into his dark garret.

Bill Hazard was not there.

The fire, however, smouldered on the hearth, and the bloodhound lay there.

Dick accordingly roused up the embers, piled on some wood, lit the lamp, and got ready some supper.

Then he fetched a supply of ale and spirits.

He was evidently bent upon putting his fellow-assassin in a good humour.

He took advantage of his absence, however.

It will be remembered by my readers that when Bill was lying in a drunken sleep the apprentice had questioned Quail in regard to money, and that the poor half-witted creature had brought him some gold pieces.

These pieces he had stolen from Bill's pockets.

This system Dick Hatherden had carried on for some time.

He was, in fact, preparing for a rainy day, and had collected a very decent sum.

This, for safety, he kept in a peculiar hiding-place : none other than the old chimney.

Here, then, he removed a brick, and drew forth a little box, which was nearly full of gold and silver pieces.

He looked at the hoard with undisguised satisfaction.

Then he heaved a sigh as he took out a gold piece.

He was a thorough miser at heart, and it grieved him to take instead of adding.

"Never mind," muttered he, as at the sound of approaching footsteps he hurriedly replaced the box in its hiding-place; "never mind! I take this, and by its aid shall replace fifty."

"Ho, ho!" shouted Bill Hazard, as he flung the door open, and entered in a state of semi-intoxication; "ho, ho! a feast, eh? What project have you in view, wherein I am to aid you, that you have prepared this banquet?—a welcome one, be it said, for I have not broken my fast since morning. Thanks to your sleeping out last night, I got very drunk, and have been keeping myself from the tremors by copious potations to-day."

Having delivered himself of this speech—a long one for him—he flung himself into a chair, and took an immense gulp of ale.

Dick Hatherden could not restrain his laughter.

"You're an acute fellow, Will," he said. "I have a new project in view."

"I thought so."

"And yet you are wrong."

"How so?"

"Because you think, as you said before, that I want you to do work that I'm afraid or unwilling to do myself. Now, is it not so?"

"What is it then?"

"Something that without bloodshed will put, perhaps, a hundred pounds in our pockets. Something that I could do without your aid, perhaps, but which would be far more certain with it. Besides, it will give you a chance of revenge."

"Upon whom? Upon that confounded Guy?"

"Aye, curse him!" answered Dick, with a vile oath; "but come, let us eat and drink, and give ourselves courage and sense for our plan."

Bill Hazard had spoken truth when he said he had not broken his fast, and he proved it by the ferocious manner in which he now attacked his victuals.

Dick, who had fed well at the house of Simon Grandley, was, however, far from being as eager, and having soon disposed of what food he required he proceeded to unfold his plan.

"You remember well, Bill," he said, "the five hundred pounds we took from Simon Grandley that night, and what we got for doing the job?"

"I remember it well," returned Bill, "and all I am sorry for is, that instead of handing such a sum as that over to old Jonas Barnsdake, we did not keep it for ourselves."

Dick laughed.

"You're not much of a philosopher," he said.

"Curse your philosophy! Why?"

"Because, don't you see, if we had seized that money, it would have been the end of all our dealings in that way?"

"And what good will it do us giving it to Barnsdake?"

"I will tell you," said Dick, pouring out some spirits; "you see, Dick, Jonas Barnsdake's plan is to rouse the Protestants—to preach a crusade against the Catholics—to arm the citizens, if necessary, and overawe Parliament. There will be rioting and fighting in the streets of London—houses will be sacked, and a rich prize will be his who has pluck and energy."

"How do you know this?" asked Bill Hazard.

"No matter how, but I do," said Dick.

"And yet I thought old Barnsdake was a fanatical sort of a fellow, who would do much for religion, certainly, but who would do nothing wrong, even for that."

"Nor will he."

"How came he to take the money stolen from Simon Grandley then?"

"He thought it was a present from some one in a high position, who desired to be unknown. High people are joining the movement. They reckon on the leadership of Lord George Gordon for one. The more money Jonas Barnsdake obtains, the greater will be the movement, the greater the riot, the more general the sack and pillage."

Bill's eyes glistened.

The prospect well suited his brutal nature.

"I shall have a good hand in that part of the business," said he, with a leer; "but tell me what is this special design you have in hand. You go a very roundabout way to it."

This was true.

But it had been purposely done.

It was necessary, as we have seen, to prime Bill

Hazard before expounding to him any particular design.

Now, however, that he had eaten and drank to his heart's content, Dick said—

"Well, perhaps I have been somewhat roundabout, but now I'll come to the point. I spoke just now of the five hundred pounds we took from Simon Grandley."

"Yes; well."

"That is not all he has got, I can tell you," said Dick; "and at the present moment he has the sum of one hundred pounds in the house. A person who owed him a large sum of money paid him unexpectedly yesterday."

"And this you propose to take?"

"I do."

"Then why don't you do it in the daytime? You're there all day."

Dick smiled.

"I might have done that, and kept it all myself, I know," he said; "but I've good reason for being aware that it is impossible. It is kept in a strong box, which I have no opportunity of opening, as it cannot be opened, except by force. No, I will do my part; and then, as there might be resistance, we must work together."

"All right," responded Bill, well primed by this time; "let us hear the plan."

"I know well the way to enter Will Lightmore's window from the street. I will remove the hasp during the day. We will enter there—creep into the room of the carpenter—take the box, and break it open in the workshop below."

"In order that we may be found out," said Bill Hazard. "Why can't we take it along with us?"

"Because I want to place it in Will Lightmore's box, so as to cast suspicion on him."

"Very good; and if there is any resistance, I'll warrant me Guy the Foundling does not go scot free," said Bill Hazard, savagely; "I'll batter his brains out, if I catch him."

Dick leaned forward and spoke solemnly, as if to enhance the importance of his words.

"If there is resistance," he said, "there is one who ought to be killed before Guy."

"Who is that?"

"Quail."

"That wretched object! Of what earthly use is it to kill him?"

"Because," said Dick, impressively, "*he knows of the murder of Colonel Halsted.*"

Bill Hazard started back, with a furious oath, while a greenish pallor overspread his face.

Then he cried—

"What silly jest is this, Dick? How could he know it, unless you told him?"

Briefly Dick Hatherden told him what the half-witted boy had said to him in the workshop.

The giant listened attentively, though he muttered curses between his teeth.

"Well, if this doesn't beat anything," he said, when Dick finished. "I'll be hanged if I don't always make a mess of things somehow. However, the boy may only have guessed it."

Dick shook his head.

"Not he," he said, "not he. He has not the brains to concoct anything—not the brains to connect Colonel Halsted's disappearance with murder. No, no; he must either have seen the deed done, or he must know some one who *did* see it."

Bill Hazard wiped the heavy drops of sweat from his brow and looked moodily into the fire.

"Well, I can't believe it," he said. "How could he have got there?"

"Well, you see, Bill," said Dick, "I didn't tell you before—because, in fact, I haven't seen you—but I went last night to the old ruins to get back my scarf."

"That accounts, then, for the fire," muttered Bill to himself.

"When I entered the house," continued the carpenter's apprentice, without taking any heed of the interruption, "I saw no one—heard no one—and when I got up into the room and opened the door I saw the colonel sitting up in one corner, with his hands clenched over his chest; so that, you see, he couldn't have been dead when I laid him in. He had the scarf tightly clenched in his hand, and I was just going to take it from him, when I saw a face at the window, and then, in a moment, a man tried to force his way through the glass. This so frightened me, that I took to my heels and fled."

"As I did when you called me a coward," sneered Bill Hazard.

"Not so," replied Dick; "you ran away because you heard a sound—I ran because I saw a face, and knew that my crime was seen and known."

"Then, if you knew it, curse your folly," shouted Bill, bringing his hand down fiercely on the table. "Why didn't you stop there, and kill him there and then—not let him escape, and drivel out his story in the ear of everybody?"

"Don't get in a passion, Bill," returned Dick; "I did not know it was Quail, or I should have remained and settled him. It might have been a strong man, like you, and then what would have been the result? Why, I should have been taken—brought to justice—and *we* should have been discovered."

Bill made no reply.

But he well knew what Dick meant by *we*: that if arrested he would turn king's evidence against his comrade.

"However," said Dick, "whether I have acted rightly or wrongly, I can't say; but there Quail is, at Simon Grandley's house, and if we can get at him we must strangle him. At any rate, we'll go there the night after to-morrow—we'll go there at eleven. We shall then be there when all have retired to rest. Your hand on it, Bill."

And so the two wretches joined hands over the bargain, and drank a glass of steaming grog to its success.

CHAPTER XXII.

DICK HATHERDEN AND BILL HAZARD PROCEED TO CARRY OUT THEIR PLAN.

AURORA HALSTED was treated like a little queen by the Grandleys.

This was exactly what she desired; and she would have been happy indeed if she could have remained

there a longer period, if it was possible. Two things, however, served to disquiet her, and snatch the cup of happiness from her lips.

In the first place, not the slightest tidings could be obtained anywhere of her father's whereabouts, and dismal hints of foul play began to be freely circulated.

Then, again, a few hours had convinced her of the deceit and imposture of Dick Hatherden.

The thought, at first, gave great pain to her mind, which had, as I have said, been most inordinately inflated by the idea that Dick Hatherden, coming into his fortune, would raise her to the position of affluence she so much coveted.

But there was now another notion growing in her bosom.

Guy the Foundling—the real foundling—the one in whom Colonel Halsted had expressed an interest —he was the one against whom the shafts of love must be directed.

He had evidently, at their first meeting, been struck by her beauty, and now that she had turned the full glory of her beauty upon him in his own home, she could not, in her own mind, doubt that she would be able to achieve a conquest.

On the evening fixed for the robbery at Simon Grandley's house, Aurora, on going up to her room, found lying on the table a bouquet of exquisite flowers, that in that cold season must have cost a large sum of money.

By the side of it was a note directed to herself.

It ran thus :—

"DEAREST AURORA,—

"I have not forgotten that to-morrow is your birthday. Accept, therefore, this humble token of my love. You seem cold and strange to me now. What is the reason? You have not spoken a word to me since you have been in this house; nor do you, I fear, desire to speak to me. I know I have enemies here, and doubtless they have lost no opportunities of speaking against me. When you receive this I shall be waiting outside your room. Grant me only one moment's interview.

"DICK HATHERDEN."

We should be wrong if we denied that the young girl's heart took a little leap as she read these words from one to whom she had allowed so many freedoms.

But her love—if, indeed, she had ever felt the faintest degree of love for him—had vanished.

The idea of being deceived was gall and worm-wood to her.

So, crushing the flowers beneath her feet, she stamped upon them.

Then, with bosom heaving with excitement, she turned to quit the room, and hasten down before he could meet her.

But this was not to be.

Dick Hatherden had been engaged in the occupation of removing the hasp from Will Lightmore's window.

He came out on the landing, therefore, just in time to catch her.

He saw she wished to avoid him, but he placed himself in her way.

"One word, Aurora," he cried, "only one word. I will not detain you. Why are you changed?"

"You cannot seriously ask such a question," she replied; "you know the reason—you know you have deceived and imposed upon me."

"In what way?"

"As to your being a foundling. But let us not argue—all is over between us."

"Say not so, Aurora," pleaded Dick. "I can explain all, if I have time."

Aurora laughed mockingly.

"To those inclined to believe you, you might," she said; "but not to me. No, no. I fear me, in the way you use your cleverness, your crest will ever remain an apprentice's club!"

And she strove to pass.

But her jeering jest had roused the blood of the discarded lover.

"An apprentice's club, eh?" he cried loudly, as he grasped her wrist, and gazed malignantly into her face. "You can insult me now then, when before you pretended to love me; but no, you shall not have the triumph you hope for. With that club which you affect so much to despise I will make my way to fortune. Times are coming—stirring times —which will give me the opportunity I seek. Then you will see me rising to distinction, while others still grovel in the dust. And a time may come, too, when those who now are above me will be glad to plead to me for protection which they won't get."

Then he flung her wrist from him, and stood aside for her to pass.

Aurora Halsted was standing there, trembling with passion.

She hated herself now for having in any way placed herself on an equality with this creature.

"Beware!" she said, in a husky voice, "beware how you again molest me in this way, Dick Hatherden. I have persons here to protect me; and re-member, too, that while I have discovered *your* imposture, I have discovered also the worthiness of him whose position you wished to take from him."

"Ah," cried Dick, in a hoarse whisper, "Guy the Foundling is then my rival. I will kill him."

Then he darted away, as if unable further to restrain his rage, and left Aurora to her thoughts.

When he quitted the house of Simon Grandley that night his mind was in a terrible state.

He was a murderer, in spite of his love for Aurora Halsted.

But she might have kept him, perhaps, from a repetition of crime, had she loved him.

Her respect and affection being gone, there was nothing now to keep him from utter shame and ruin.

So, as he hurried away towards his lodgings, his heart was bounding with mad rage.

He felt truly as if his hand was against every man, and every man's hand against him.

He was cheered up, however, a little on reaching home, by finding that Bill Hazard had reciprocated his politeness of the night before, and had got ready a meal preparatory to their jaunt.

"I thought a good bellyfull before we started would not do either of us any harm," he said, "so, as we have not very much time before us, let us

feed. But what is the matter, Dick; you look anything but lively?"

"Well, you see, I feel worried and excited," returned the apprentice; "I'm not such a cool hand as you are. I have done as I said—removed the hasp from the window—but I was nearly caught at it, and this made me nervous. Here, pass the ale."

CHAPTER XXIII.

CONTAINS AN ACCOUNT OF THE ATTEMPTED BURGLARY AND ITS RESULT.

AT eleven o'clock the house of Simon Grandley was dark and silent.

All within were wrapped in slumber—some dreaming, some fast locked in unconsciousness, after hard work.

At this hour Bill Hazard and Dick Hatherden approached the wall by which Dick had made his escape on that night when he had paid his visit to the dead colonel.

Here they took a glance round, to see that no one was observing them, and then made their way over into the courtyard, where there was a ladder.

This they speedily raised, and placed against the house, and Bill Hazard, fixing on a crape-mask, was quickly ascending towards Will Lightmore's window.

Will had been up somewhat later than usual, indulging himself in reading his favourite Shakespeare, and having walked to and fro a considerable time, he was thoroughly tired out when he at length retired to rest.

However, he was a very light sleeper, and when Bill Hazard began raising the window he at once started up and glanced round.

There were curtains to his bed, and through the opening he could see all that passed.

Presently he beheld a masked face and the form of a tall man loom up against the sky.

Then he saw Bill Hazard beginning quietly to raise the sash.

His thoughts became at once in a turmoil of excitement.

What was he to do?

If he tried to raise the alarm now, the robbers might enter and stop him ere he could pass through the door.

Was he then to remain and pretend to sleep?

BILL RAISED THE GLEAMING BLADE.

They certainly could have no reason to desire *his* death.

So, perhaps, for the present, this would be best. Accordingly he watched.

Very gently Bill Hazard raised the sash.

Then, after a glance into the room, he put one leg in.

At this moment one of the spells of the ladder below gave way, and Dick fell, crying out, as he did so, for help.

Bill Hazard, with a curse, at once turned to aid him.

"Now is the very witching time," said Will, and springing from his bed, he dashed to the window, and brought the sash down upon the burglar's leg with a force that made the ruffian roar aloud with pain.

Caught in this novel way, Bill exerted all his strength to extricate himself, and kicked and plunged about to no purpose, while Will, exerting his lungs to their fullest extent, roared out—

"Help!—murder!—help!"

Seeing the danger of being caught in such a position, Bill, finding it beyond his power to raise the window-sash, began kicking violently at Will's bare shins.

In this he would decidedly have had an advantage, had not the apprentice's heavy boots been near at hand.

Seizing one of these, he belaboured the giant's leg so violently as to produce a numbness, and cause him to cease all further efforts at kicking.

Drawing his long knife, he dashed the handle of it through the glass, and crushing away the small pieces of glass, seized Will Lightmore by the throat.

"Now, curse you," he said, "let me go, or I'll throttle you!"

The unfortunate part of the matter was, that Will never slept without locking his door; and when, accordingly, Simon Grandley and Guy answered to his call, they were some time forcing their way in.

They were only just in time.

Will's face was then in dangerous proximity to the glass, and he was nearly choking moreover.

The entrance of Simon and Guy roused Bill to desperation.

Leaving his hold suddenly on the boy's throat, he dashed his clenched fist in his face, and as he staggered back, the ruffian flung up the sash with a

sudden jerk and prepared to descend. Guy, who was half-dressed, was the first to reach the window, and in an instant, reckless of consequences, he leaped out, and rushed after Bill down the ladder.

Dick had long since made good his escape.

Guy was as active as a monkey, and by the time that the burglar had reached the wall he had sprang to his side and closed with him.

"Now then, quick! Come down! I have him!" he shouted.

But it was useless.

In their hurried descent the ladder had slipped and fallen away towards the other side of the court-yard.

To descend as Dick had done was out of Simon Grandley's power, nor could Will Lightmore do anything, lying, as he was, cut and bleeding on the floor of his bedroom.

But there was another who responded at once to the call.

This was Quail.

He had rushed into the room just as the females, who had scrambled on their things anyhow, came trooping in.

He glanced out. He saw that Guy—his preserver, his champion—was in danger, and he hesitated not an instant.

Scrambling out on the window-sill, he dropped, as Dick had done, and was on the wall just as Simon Grandley rushed downstairs towards the street.

The struggle was of very short duration, and Quail, unarmed as he was, useless, from the simple fact that he could not get near the combatants.

Bill Hazard, in a struggle and wrestle of this kind, had, of course, the advantage, and though Guy exerted every sinew in his endeavour to hold his huge adversary until Simon Grandley, or the watch, arrived, he found himself being gradually forced down backwards upon the perilous wall.

Then Bill drew his knife again.

"Curse you! I know you now," he said. "This is the second time we have met. I'll take care we don't meet a third time."

These words were spluttered out disjointedly, as he knelt on his victim's chest, and raised the gleaming blade, at which the women at the window gazed in silent, stony horror.

The knife descended.

But not as Bill Hazard desired.

Ere it reached Guy's chest, it was struck aside by Quail, and as it stuck quivering in the Foundling's shoulder, a second blow from the half-witted lad sent Bill over the perilous edge into the street.

From the pavement he rose with a broken arm, just in time to escape Simon Grandley, who, armed with a pistol, came rushing out of the back gate.

Quickened by fear, his long legs soon carried him out of all fear of pursuit, although it was not long ere the watch, roused by the cries of the carpenter and his family, came rushing up, just in time—to go away again!

Released suddenly from the grasp of the giant, Guy the Foundling was, of course, overbalanced, and fell, in spite of Quail's efforts, into the yard.

Here, after a few minutes, they found him in a dead faint, lying with his head on the shoulder of

the half-witted boy, who was crying over him like a child.

When Guy recovered, which he did to find himself surrounded by an anxious crowd (among whom was Will Lightmore, with his face pale and his head bound up), his first remembrances were of Bill Hazard.

"I know the villain—I remember his face well," he said, in a faint voice, "and Quail, he, too, knows him, and can take us to his haunts."

"Aye, that I *can*," cried Quail, eagerly pressing forward; "let us go now."

"No, no," said the carpenter; "we will do nothing until Guy and Will are well, which will be in a day or two, and then the rascal will be off the scent. Meanwhile, Guy must be kept very quiet—his wound is a bad one."

"Yes: you must not think of exerting yourself," said Aurora, beamingly smiling on him, while Minnie Grandley pressed his hand fondly and said nothing.

She would not—young as she was—share pity with a rival.

And so at last the household retired again to rest, leaving Quail, by his own desire, on the watch.

CHAPTER XXIV.

WHICH TELLS OF TERRIBLE DOINGS, AND INTRO-DUCES THE READER TO THE HOME OF BEN HAR-DARKER, THE BLACKSMITH.

THE failure of the attempt on the house of Simon Grandley put Bill Hazard in no good humour, as may be imagined, though in very truth he and Dick Hatherden ought to have thanked heaven that they were not discovered and punished for their guilt.

In imagination Bill Hazard had already spent the money which he was to acquire.

Villain and depraved wretch that he was, he had still one tender thought in his heart—still one hope that he might have happiness, and forget his evil doings.

In this vain hope, he set out on the third evening after the foolish escapade at the house of the carpenter towards that part of London which is known as Bermondsey.

The house to which he made his way was a small one, only two stories high, with a tiny garden, and a green paling in front—a place which, though humble, spoke of some one who took a pride in it, in spite of its unpretending appearance.

Here he entered boldly, and knocked at the door, which was opened after a moment by a girl of not more than seventeen summers.

She uttered a cry of joyous surprise when she recognised Bill Hazard.

Strange indeed was it that she should experience any pleasure at the appearance of such a man.

But so it is always.

The ugliest, the most ill-favoured, the most evil-minded of men can obtain the love of the prettiest of women.

The exclamation of joy with which she greeted him was changed for one of sorrow and surprise

when he entered the room, and she saw that his left arm was in a sling.

"You have had an accident," exclaimed the blue-eyed, golden-haired creature. "What is it? Have you broken your arm?"

"Yes," said Bill Hazard. "I fell down our stairs in the dark and broke it. But it's getting all right now. Where's your father?"

"He's out, but will soon be in," said Jessie Hardarker, as she ran and fetched some cheese and ale, and then sat down on his knee, and put her arm round his neck. "He's had good luck, Bill, and will be glad enough to see you to tell you about it."

"Can't you tell me, Jessie?" he said, looking admiringly at her.

No wonder.

She was a girl whom anyone would have admired, and she looked specially pretty that night, with her golden hair floating over her bare shoulders, her low bodice just displaying her pretty bosom, and her short skirts allowing a glimpse to be seen of a finely-turned ankle and calf.

"Well, I will, Bill," said the girl, laughing, "only you mustn't let him know I told you first—he'd be angry, you know, for he always likes to tell his own stories."

"No, no; I promise to hold my tongue," said Bill, eagerly.

He was looking forward anxiously to the time when Hardarker *would* come into the good fortune he had heard so much of, and when he could claim Jessie, and a little bit of money—just sufficient to get them into a tavern, for which line of business Bill, in common with all men of his class, had a desperate fancy.

"Well, then, Bill," said Jessie, confidentially, "he's come into all the money he spoke of, and this very night he will bring home with him more than two hundred pounds. He's gone to fetch it at Aiken's, and is at this moment, perhaps, hurrying home the nearest way."

A blood-red mist seemed to float before Bill Hazard's eyes.

"The river-path!" he cried, excitedly, and clutching her wrist.

The girl started and turned pale.

"Why, what ails you, Bill?" she cried.

"Much—much," he answered; "is your father mad, that he ventures along a lonely way like that, with two hundred pounds in his pocket? Why, it is infested with thieves."

Jessie's eyes filled with tears.

"Poor father!" she said, "and perhaps in his joy he's been drinking, and will tell some one. Oh, Bill, hadn't you better go and meet him?"

"No, no," returned he, shaking his head, and drawing her back on his knee; "no, no, I might miss him; and besides, he's perhaps far on his way now, and I should be too late for any good."

He drank some ale, talked away the fears his own strange conduct had aroused, and presently, after looking at the clock, gently put her from his lap and rose.

"I think I'll go now," he said; "it's getting late,

and maybe your father, having been out so long, may come home drunk, and may not like my being here."

There was something in Bill Hazard's manner which alarmed the young girl, and after regarding him for a moment, with her eyes gleaming anxiously and her bosom rising and falling with deep emotion, she said—

"Don't go now, Bill. I feel nervous now you've spoken about father's coming home along that lonely way by himself."

Bill laughed.

A very forced laugh be it said.

"Why, you silly little thing," he said, kissing her, "you've nothing to be alarmed at. Even if your father had told people, he has a bold heart and a strong arm, and there's no fear of his being waylaid without leaving his mark on some one."

The young girl laid her golden head upon his arm and looked up into his face.

"You see it was you, Bill, who frightened me at first," she said. "I should never have thought of the dangers of the river-path if you had not spoken of them. How can you blame *me*, therefore, for speaking of my dread?"

As his lips had met hers a moment before, she had experienced, as it were, a chilling feeling throughout her whole frame.

She thought of this afterwards, with a terrible shudder.

At the moment she ascribed it solely to the cold wind which invaded the room, the fire having waxed low during their love-making.

"I don't blame you," he said; "I only blame myself for my childish folly in alarming you without cause. However, I *must* go now, Jessie; in fact, I ought not to have come, though I promised, for I have work to do to-night. I'll come over again to-morrow, and over a glass of ale your father and I will talk over his good fortune. Good night, Jessie."

This was said as they walked to the door.

His manner seemed changed—the watchful eyes of love saw this at once.

"What is the matter, Bill?" said the poor girl, little divining his awful thoughts. "Have I offended you?"

He took her up in his arms, raising her from the ground like a child.

"Offended me! No, my lass," he said, hoarsely, as he kissed her; "no, no. I hope I may never offend you more."

Then he dropped her down gently from his arms, and hurried away.

"Poor fellow!" thought Jessie; "I know what's the matter with him. He's sorry to hear of father's good fortune; because he's afraid, when I'm rich, he won't get me. Ah, me!"

And so the poor confiding girl closed the door, little recking that behind the corner of the rugged wall Bill Hazard was waiting till she re-entered, that he might return to her father's workshop and choose a weapon suitable for another murder!

CHAPTER XXV.

THE MURDERER CHOOSES HIS WEAPON—THE PATH BY THE DARK RIVER—BILL HAZARD MEETS HIS VICTIM—THE STRUGGLE AND THE ESCAPE.

THE night, dark, and gloomy, and moonless, was just the one suited to the design which Bill Hazard had in hand.

He watched until the young girl had disappeared within the house.

Then he crept back, and skirting the garden, made his way to the back of the premises, where the blacksmith's forge stood.

Here he glided in cautiously, and striking a noiseless match, searched round for some weapon for his deadly purpose.

As luck would have it, he had left his own knife at home, and the first thing that his eyes lighted upon when he entered the workshop was Hardarker's own knife.

This he at once seized, and issuing forth once more into the night, he made his way quietly along the garden, leaped the low fence at the end of it, and was soon hurrying along the river-path.

Until very lately Hazard had not done much in the way of bloodshed.

He had pinked a man many times severely in a brawl, but had not deliberately attempted a murder until he had aided Dick Hatherden in the assassination of Colonel Halsted.

He had grown less scrupulous now, however.

He knew well that Hardarker looked upon his addresses to his daughter in anything but a favourable light, although he permitted him to visit the house, and he felt pretty certain, that now he had come into the money, of which he was always boasting, he would be less inclined than ever to give him Jessie's hand.

He resolved, therefore, upon a very ready way of cutting the knot of the difficulty.

He would meet Hardarker—he would, if he was drunk, rob him of his money; but, if he resisted, he would take it from him by force, and fling his body into the river.

He would then have money to work with, to settle himself in business, and when the period of mourning was over, he would be in a better position to ask Jessie to be his wife.

Thus coolly did the murderer calculate.

He forgot that there are sometimes eyes in the dark watching the guilty.

Hurrying, he reached a little alehouse, the last tenement near the river-path for more than a mile.

Here he drank some strong liquor, to fortify himself, keeping well out of the light, so that he might not be recognised, and then sped on his way.

If Colonel Halsted had not been murdered, Hardarker the blacksmith's life would not have been in danger.

Bill Hazard, however, having once tasted blood, as it were, cared nothing for a second crime.

On, therefore, he sped.

He was absolutely hungering after blood.

It was a lonely way.

For a long time he saw no one.

All was silent, too, as the tomb.

And so dark!

So utterly pitchy dark, that the atmosphere through which he passed seemed to possess a kind of solidity.

Presently, in the distance, he could hear the sound of a man's voice singing.

He paused and listened.

Being so far off, he could not distinguish the voice.

And yet there flashed through his brain an idea that this *was* the blacksmith.

Hurrying on, therefore, he made for a place where there was a ruined wall close to the river's brink.

At this point the blacksmith would have to cross him (if he could conceal himself) along a pathway not many inches wide, and some feet above the river.

Here, then, the murderer waited.

The ruined wall just fitted his purpose.

A kind of ruined buttress formed a screen, from behind which he could watch the proceedings of the man, who, innocent of all wish to harm him, was now his enemy.

The words of the song of the approaching man could now be heard plainly.

And plainly, too, rushed the knowledge to the assassin's brain that Hardarker was not sober.

This rendered his deadly purpose all the more easy to be effected.

Hardarker was bellowing out the refrain of some convivial song about the "forge and hammer," and was apparently stumbling along without taking any heed of where he was going.

But when he neared the ruins he suddenly drew himself up.

"Wo—ho," he cried; "steady, man, steady. Thy foot is scarcely heedful enough to make its way over so narrow a space as that. We must debouch—we must debouch."

Having settled so far his military tactics, he diverged suddenly to the left, thus going round the ruins, and entirely, for the moment, defeating the purpose of his would-be murderer.

"Curse the fellow," muttered Bill Hazard; "he's stolen a march on me truly now. But, no matter; this opportunity must not escape me. I must conceal myself at some other point."

So saying, he made his way from the place where he had hidden himself, and came out once more upon the path at the point where his victim would probably come out.

Here, in the shadow of the trees, he waited.

And now something strange occurred.

Something like the ruling of Fate.

Just as Hardarker came round the corner the whole scene changed.

As if by magic!

The place, as we said before, had been enveloped in utter darkness.

Now the moon, which had so long hidden itself, suddenly burst forth.

THE RIVAL APPRENTICES

A TALE OF THE RIOTS OF 1780.

THE ASSASSIN DEALT HARDARKER A FURIOUS BLOW IN THE FACE.

So, when the unsuspecting man approached, and the murderer glided out of his concealment, a gush of silver light inundated the scene, and the assassin and his victim stood face to face!

Hardarker staggered back.

"What have we here?" cried he, putting his hand to his belt to feel for his knife.

Bill saw he must temporise.

Drunk as he was, the blacksmith was no mean antagonist in a hand-to-hand conflict.

"Why, it's me, Bill Hardarker! Don't you know me?" said the traitor.

"Why, yes, I know your voice now," returned the blacksmith, in a growling tone; "but what are you doing skulking here in the dark? You're enough to frighten a fellow."

"Well, you startled me too," said Bill, putting his knife hastily away. "The truth is, I've been up to your house and had a chat with Jessie. She told me you were coming this way, and so I thought I'd come and meet you."

The blacksmith laughed.

"Don't you think I'm big enough to take care of myself?" he said.

"Yes, yes," returned Bill, as they began to walk slowly back towards the other's house. "You're big enough, generally speaking, but it's not every night that you have a large sum of money in your pocket in such a dark and cut-throat neighbourhood as this. Jessie asked me to come, and so here I am."

Somehow or another the blacksmith did not feel greatly pleased by the prospect of his companionship.

Perhaps some suspicion entered his mind that all was not right.

However this might be, his manner towards Bill Hazard was anything but cordial.

He was gloomy and silent, and seemed anxious to rid himself of Bill's company.

But he saw no way to such an end.

Hazard's spirits seemed to rise as those of his companion became depressed.

"I'm glad I met you to-night," he said. "I told Jessie I would not come, as you might fancy I was interfering. But as we're alone now, I'd like to speak to you about the future."

"Speak away, then," said Hardarker.

"It's about Jessie."

"I thought so."

"Yes," said Bill, pretending to stumble, and managing so as to get the blacksmith between him and the river's steep edge. "Yes, I want to speak with you about a date for our marriage."

The blacksmith laughed.

"Ah! I see," he said; "now I've got a little money you want to get hold of my girl in double quick time."

"Yes," said Bill Hazard, with a forced laugh, as he drew forth his knife; "yes—that's just it."

The moon had now again retreated.

All was once more dark.

Hardarker was near the edge of the quick-flowing river, and Bill's right hand was close to his back.

"Well, then," said the blacksmith, "what have you to say about it?"

"This!" cried Bill, savagely; and the knife was in an instant buried in the back of the unfortunate man.

It was a deadly blow, but not a mortal one.

In an instant, with all the strength of his stentorian lungs, the blacksmith shouted—

"Help!—murder!—help!"

The cry went ringing out loudly over the still river, and in the distance its echoes appeared to be taken up and magnified into the roar of a dozen voices.

This was really no deception.

The cry *had* been heard.

Meanwhile, the blacksmith had turned round upon his adversary and endeavoured to close with him.

But Will Hazard beat him off.

"You murderous, selfish, ungrateful brute," cried Hardarker, as he dealt his adversary a tremendous blow with all his remaining strength, "you shall swing for this! My child, indeed! Why, she'd fit the rope herself round your neck!"

"Where's the money?" cried Bill, in a hoarse tone, as he heard now for the first time the sound of approaching feet and voices; "give it me, and I'll spare your life!"

"Money!" exclaimed Hardarker, who felt sinking fast now, as the blood flowed freely from his wound. "Do you think I'm mad to bring a sum of money like that along a dark river path, with such skulking hounds hovering about as you? No, no—I've no money with me."

"You lie!" shouted Bill, savagely, as he again dashed at him; "quick, now—for your life."

"I have none," yelled the blacksmith, making an unsuccessful attempt to draw his knife; "help!—murder!—murder!"

The voices and feet of an approaching crowd were now plainly heard, and in the distance, too, forms could be seen approaching.

"Ah, ah! I have you now," gasped the blacksmith, as he made a grab at his shoulder; "I'll see you hanged yet for this."

But it was not to be.

The idea of capture made Bill Hazard discard even the desire for the money, for which he had begun his ill-executed crime.

While Hardarker was on the very edge of the river bank the assassin dealt him a furious blow in the face, which sent him reeling back into the deep water, where his body was quickly whirled away by the tide.

The crowd of men were now within a very few yards of him, and Bill, without even glancing behind him, fled off at full speed.

CHAPTER XXVI.

THE FLIGHT — THE PURSUIT ALONG THE RIVER PATH — THE MEETING WITH JESSIE — THE RUN THROUGH THE STREETS — THE ASSASSIN CAGED.

HE knew that resistance would be useless, so he flung the knife into the Thames, and settled himself for a long run."

"After him!"

"Murder!"

"Catch him! Stop him!"

Such were the cries which rung out on the night as the pursued villain dashed by the first of the houses.

Lights came to windows, and half-dressed men and women peered out.

But no one came forth.

So far all went well with the villain.

On he sped, with his heart beating wildly, taking the path direct to the house of Hardarker.

Here he thought he would be enabled to conceal himself, through Jessie's means.

Through the daughter of the man whom he had killed!

He forgot that the first words which would leave the lips of the pursuers would be a denunciation of him as a murderer.

However, on he dashed!

A quarter of an hour at last passed by, and at length, in the distance, appeared the light in the window of the young girl who was waiting for her father.

The father who would never come again.

Another five minutes, and panting, out of breath, he reached the back door.

This was fastened, or had become hitched.

At any rate it would not open, and he was compelled to leap it.

This made a diversion in favour of his pursuers and almost an instant after he had leaped into the garden, the eager hunters of crime came yelling like a pack of hounds to the wall.

This was an impediment they did not expect.

However, after a few moments' consultation, they leaped over, and rushing across the garden, began knocking loudly at the back door.

In an instant Jessie's head was thrust out of a top window.

"What is the matter?" she said.

"The matter is that a man has been murdered."

"Murdered! Where?—who?"

"He has been murdered on the river's brink," said a man, "and the murderer has escaped into this house."

A horrible suspicion entered the girl's mind.

Had her father been killed?

Or had _he_ committed some crime?

The idea never entered her head that Hardarker had fallen a victim to her lover.

Rushing from the window, she came trembling downstairs.

There, in the dark, she met Bill Hazard, who caught her in his arms.

"Stay—stay!" he cried; "don't let them in."

The girl was about to scream.

But he pressed his hand over her mouth.

"For heaven's sake don't ruin me," he said.

A deadly faintness invaded the girl's bosom.

"Oh, Bill!" she said, "what means this?"

And she sank upon the stairs.

"It means that those wretches have pursued me with yells of 'murder,'" he said; "they attacked and killed your father, and——"

"My father! Oh, just heaven!"

This was all.

The shock was too great to allow of further speech.

A great throb seemed to go through her whole being.

Then it was all darkness and oblivion.

This just suited Bill.

Gently he let her lie down on her side on the stairs.

Snatching a kiss—one that he knew would be the last—he rushed along the passage, unbarred the front door, and not even stopping to close it, dashed away along the street.

The result of a conference at the back door had been that, as the murderer had made good his escape into the house, he would effectually bar their entrance that way.

Leaving two of their number, therefore, in the rear of the premises, the other pursuers made their way to the front, and there, of course, they were assembled when Bill Hazard came dashing furiously through them.

Guessing that an opposition would be made to his progress, he had drawn his knife, and brandishing this above his head, he made a dash at the foremost man, and sent him wounded and yelling among his comrades.

This temporary confusion enabled him to get a fresh start, and away he rushed at a furious speed, with oaths bursting every moment from between his foaming lips.

Soon the pursuers gathered numbers.

"Murder! murder! stop the villain!" was the cry that echoed along the streets of the quiet metropolis.

People heard it, and came dashing out of side streets to join in the chase.

Men whose own hands, perhaps, were by no means free from blood-stains joined in the chase from mere love of excitement.

The watch, too, presently began to gather, and before Bill Hazard had reached the neighbourhood of his own home, a crowd of at least fifty people were at his heels.

He was now rapidly succumbing.

His brain, after the terrible race he had had, began to whirl.

Red lights danced before his eyes.

Maddening feelings invaded his breast.

Had, indeed, such not been the case, he would never have dreamed of making for his own home.

He would be certain to be captured there.

However, so his fate led him.

Putting on an extra rush, he dashed into the dark archway and up the staircase.

His only hope of escape now was, that he could enter his room, and, getting Dick Hatherden to barricade the door, make his escape through the roof.

As it happened, the loud yells of the rushing mob had roused Dick from slumber.

The door, therefore, was ajar, and ere Dick knew what it meant, Bill Hazard had rushed in and bolted it.

Seeing him thus, with bloodshot eyes, with pale face, and lips covered with a bloody foam, the lad saw at once that something terrible was the matter.

"What ails you, Bill?" he cried; "are you pursued?"

"Yes, pursued by men as if I were a wild beast; but I have no time for words. I must escape by the roof, while you and Tiger keep the door. To the door, good dog!"

The bloodhound at once sprung up and stood by the door, with his red eyes gleaming, ready to seize the first comer.

Bill Hazard rushed to the table, and raised a bottle of spirits to his lips.

Then, after a hearty draught of the raw liquid, he seized a rapier from the wall, and rushed up the ladder-like stairs that led to the roof.

Here, however, he was again foiled.

Somehow or another the trap-door was fixed.

"Curse it," he cried, as he heard a rush of feet outside, and the loud groaning noise of a number of angry men. "What have you been doing to the trap, Dick? I can't move it."

"It can only have stuck; push it hard," cried Dick Hatherden.

But it was of no use giving advice.

Move it would not.

It had evidently been fastened down on the *outside*.

CHAPTER XXVII.

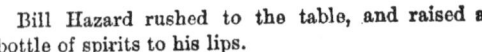

THE ASSAULT ON THE OLD HOUSE—TIGER ON THE WATCH—THE ASSAILANTS FORCE THEIR WAY—THE BLOODHOUND AND THE FAT WATCHMAN—THE CONFERENCE—THE CONFLICT, AND ARREST OF BILL HAZARD.

THE door now began to be assailed by violent blows and pushes from strong shoulders, while loud and vehement were the exclamations of anger and disappointment when they found it would not easily yield.

The bloodhound watched his master at one moment, and then cast his gaze upon the creaking door whose panels were gradually yielding.

He was evidently somewhat puzzled.

Bill, meanwhile, had given up the attack on the trap-door as useless.

It was evidently fastened down in no light manner from above.

In fact, it did not yield half an inch to the pressure of his brawny arm.

"I wish we had a rope," he said; "I would chance a descent from the window into the back yard; but it would be death to jump out."

He had scarcely formed the idea when the door gave way, and a crowd of men of all grades and ages almost fell into the room.

The bloodhound at once fastened upon the first, who, being a portly watchman, lay wriggling at the feet of the others, and caused several to fall sprawling over the savage animal.

Bill Hazard stood back, pale and ghastly, but with set lips, his great chest heaving and his right hand grasping his long sword.

"Well, my masters," he cried, "what means this? You have given me a fine chase. What is it for?"

"Villain!—murderer!" shouted a chorus of cries at once. "Seize him!"

However, though all agreed as to the appellations which were justly due to him, no one seemed eager to be the first in the seizing part of the matter.

He looked a tower of brute strength as he stood there before them.

Dick Hatherden interposed at this moment.

"Pray, gentlemen," he said, as he dragged Tiger from off the fat watchman, and held him by the collar, let *me* demand some little explanation. This is *my* room, and——"

"Your friend, too, I suppose," sneered one of the men.

"Yes; and I want to know," pursued Dick, "by what right, and for what purpose, you have thus burst into this room at this late hour?"

"Well, then," said the man, "if you *must* know, this *friend* of yours has murdered a man, and flung his body into the river, and we've come to take him to prison."

These words sent a thrill through the heart of Dick Hatherden.

He was afraid to turn towards Bill Hazard.

His satisfaction would have been too apparent to all.

He made sure, in fact, that it was Guy the Foundling who had fallen a victim to Bill's revenge.

"And, pray, whom do you accuse him of murdering?" asked Dick.

"We believe it to be Hardarker, the blacksmith," said one of the men who had pursued him at first, "but we are not sure."

"Are you sure he killed any one?" asked Dick, with a sneer; "or has one of your comrades committed the crime himself, and desires now to put it upon his shoulders?"

The man took no notice of these jeering words.

"Sure—we saw him push him into the river," said he; "there's no doubt about it. But I, for one, won't stop here all night. If that fellow's going to prison, let's take him."

A hurried conference then took place among the crowd at the door.

Bill took advantage of this.

Taking Tiger's collar out of Dick's hand, he suddenly cried—

"At them, good dog!"

The bloodhound at once, with a growl, leaped into the midst of the throng, and dragged one of the foremost to the ground, while Bill dashed in, sword in hand, at the same moment.

It was a mad effort.

Had the men wished to turn and fly they could not have done so, for they were firmly wedged in on the stairs and on the landing, and ere Bill had made his way more than a yard, he was seized from behind by two powerful men, and forced back into the room.

One moment he eyed them defiantly.

His heart was good, at that moment, to have murdered them all.

But he saw the utter folly now of further resistance.

So he flung his sword down.

"I give in," he said. "Come off, Tiger, and leave that poor devil some little breath to swear my life away with. I'll go quietly, but I know nothing of Hardarker's murder. I am the intended husband of his daughter, and it's not likely I'd kill him just as he's come into some money, before he's made a will in our favour."

This sudden quietude on Bill Hazard's part so far roused the suspicions of the watch, that they all the more hurriedly fastened on the handcuffs, and in a moment he stood a prisoner.

"Good bye, Dick," he said; "this foolish matter will soon be settled. Come and see me when I'm in Newgate."

And so, with a jaunty air, he walked away with his captors.

In half an hour he was the inmate of a stone cell, where he was destined to hear and see some of the most extraordinary things recorded in the history of those times.

CHAPTER XXVIII.

AURORA QUITS HER NEW FRIENDS—BILL HAZARD BEFORE THE MAGISTRATES—JESSIE HARDARKER IN COURT—SIMON GRANDLEY'S SUSPICIONS OF DICK HATHERDEN — THE PROGRESS OF JONAS BARNSDAKE AND HIS FRIENDS—THE PREPARATIONS FOR THE RISING—THE APPRENTICES' LODGE.

No news whatever being heard of Colonel Halsted, Aurora began naturally to feel alarmed.

Her friends came to see her repeatedly, and begged her to quit the carpenter's house, and at length, yielding to the solicitations of a rich uncle, one Sir Lascelles Royston, she quitted the place, and retired to his mansion.

This was somewhere about three weeks after her first arrival.

During this time events of some importance had taken place.

Among these events were two which affect our story greatly.

Bill Hazard was examined before the magistrates on a charge of murder, and committed for trial.

The body of Hardarker, the blacksmith, had been found floating in the river.

It had been stopped by some wooden piles, driven into the bed of the stream near the bank, and in the pockets was discovered the money which he had told Hazard he had not got with him, and which had been the cause of his death.

In the court poor Jessie had sat, white and trembling, hardly able to cast a glance from her tearless, burning eyes upon the man whom she felt to be guilty of the base and cruel murder of her unfortunate father.

And amid general execration the murderer—already, as it may be said, convicted—was hurried back to his cell, where (for the convenience of the governor of the gaol, who was beautifying his own residence, and restoring some portions of the other part of the prison) three other prisoners were also confined.

The news of this murder and trial being brought to Simon Grandley's house, and the fact being now made absolutely public that Dick Hatherden, the apprentice, was Bill's companion, the carpenter began to have serious suspicions of his honesty.

Dick knew what kind of ordeal he would have to undergo, and he went through it boldly.

So boldly indeed he fenced the questions put to him, that there was no possibility of bringing any guilty knowledge home to him.

"I am thoroughly disgusted at the idea of your being the companion of such a man," said his master. "Such association *must* tend to lower and disgrace you, even if you are not absolutely guilty of any acts of theft or deeper crime. You had better at once remove to a different lodging. It must be a perfect den of filth and iniquity.

"I will do so at once, sir," replied Dick. "But, you see, I never knew that Bill Hazard was anything like what they've made him out to be on his trial. He tells me very differently."

"Have you seen him, then, in private?" asked the carpenter, in surprise.

"Yes; he sent for me to Newgate."

"And you went there?"

"I did, and he swore to me that he was walking by the river, when he met a man whom he did not know to be Hardarker; that the man tumbled up against him; that they then quarrelled; and that after this they fought, and entirely by accident the man fell into the river."

"But how about the stab in the back?"

"That was given in self-defence," said Dick, "at least so he says; but, of course, I know nothing of it, and I am sorry I ever went now, as it has displeased you.

"You ought never to return to your lodgings, even to fetch your things away," said the carpenter. "I will send for them for you."

Dick Hatherden trembled at the very thought of such a proceeding.

Little did Simon Grandley know about his secret hoard of gold.

"No," said Dick, "there are things that must be got there that cannot be got by any one but myself. *I* will go once again, and then I am done with Bill and the neighbourhood for ever."

And so it passed off.

Though feeling an unpleasant doubt in regard to Dick's intimacy with Bill Hazard, the carpenter felt no more concern about it.

Dick Hatherden took possession of his hoard, and concealed it in the workshop.

He resisted all offers on the part of Simon Grandley to come into the house, but he did go so far as to take up his home as far as possible from his old haunts.

His only fear now was that Bill Hazard, to save himself from trouble, would tell the whole secret, and involve him—if only for spite's sake—in his own ruin.

How far he was right in this respect the future will show.

The second event was more directly concerning Simon Grandley.

Jonas Barnsdake, at the suggestion of Hardarker, the unfortunate blacksmith, had resolved upon obtaining for the Protestant Association the aid, personal and monetary, of the stout-hearted carpenter.

He had met him on many occasions, and had had slight conversation with him.

On these occasions he had let fall many expressions which had roused Simon Grandley's curiosity, and made his heart leap, moreover.

But he had explained nothing.

It must be remembered that Simon Grandley was a superstitious man.

A man of strong good feelings, and especially on the subject of religion.

Jonas Barnsdake was, as Bill Hazard had said, a man who could talk another into anything; and the words he used, simple as they were, made Simon Grandley's heart swell, and produced a glow throughout his frame which made him fancy himself at once one of the chosen saviours and leaders of his native land.

From the moment that this conversation took place, to which Simon Grandley had been invited specially by Jonas Barnsdake, the carpenter began to feel restless and uneasy at home.

He was no bigot, and yet so did the infatuated old leader work upon his feelings, that he felt that England was being ruined because Catholics were to be treated in future like human beings.

And so he became an enrolled member of the Secret Protestant Association, and would have gone out, and buckled on his sword, and fought with the best of them, at the first intimation from Barnsdake that his services were wanted.

Everything was now arranged for action.

As soon as the question of Catholic Emancipation was mooted in Parliament, then was to be the signal for a general uprising.

Petitions were to be poured in, strikes to be organised, and trade stopped.

And hearing this, the riff-raff and scum rubbed their hands and chuckled.

Theirs was to be the harvest of crime.

So matters went on, and the month of May—the ever-memorable month of May—approached.

CHAPTER XXIX.

THE BEGINNING OF THE TUMULTS.

I HAVE said that Aurora Halsted's uncle succeeded at last in persuading her to leave the Grandleys, and take up her abode with him.

She had cried at parting, and looked wondrously sentimental at Guy the Foundling, and clasped his hand, and called him her preserver, till she had made *him* awkward and Minnie angry.

But when she reached Sir Lascelles Royston's house she soon found other things to think of.

Sir Lascelles was not, as his name would seem to imply, a sprig of nobility.

He was an uncle on her mother's side—a man who had risen from nothing, and consequently was more overbearing, and obnoxious, and detestable in his manners, than anyone could be who has wondrous notions of blue blood and aristocratic descent.

It is always your self-made man who is the most arrogant, tyrannical, and uncompromising.

Sir Lascelles employed nearly two hundred hands in a factory near Lambeth.

And over these two hundred hands one man presided—a man who received a good salary, yet who was always poor, and lived in a small garret with his only child, as we have seen.

None other, in fact, than Jonas Barnsdake.

Over these two hundred men he had a wonderful power.

They revered him as a second Cromwell.

They listened to him as to an apostle.

There were young and old, it must be remembered, among those employed at the factory.

Old fellows, with grey hair, worked side by side with fresh-cheeked young apprentices.

And young and old believed in old Jonas; and among the societies into which the City lads had enrolled themselves his name was respected as if he had been the richest man in London.

He had the power, therefore, at the time we speak of, of turning out into the streets of the City a large, well-armed, and dangerous army, of whom the London apprentices were not the least formidable members.

Will Lightmore and Guy belonged naturally to an apprentice society, and one evening—ever to be remembered by them—they issued forth together, with the special permission of Simon Grandley, to visit what they termed their lodge.

This "lodge" was held at a tavern—not one of the low places which were the delight of Bill Hazard and his set.

It was, on the contrary, a very model of neatness and comfort. Kept by an old couple who had entered it on the very morning of their marriage, and never ceased proprietorship, the Yellow Ensign was well known and respected in the neighbourhood, and for this very reason the parents of the apprentices felt little or no annoyance when they knew that the lads congregated there.

On the occasions of their meeting, which were not very often, they had a large and commodious room placed entirely at their service.

On this evening the meeting presented an appearance of uninterrupted jollity and pleasure.

Will Lightmore was the president of the night.

Guy the Foundling, as great a favourite as Will, was vice-president.

At one end of the room was a kind of stage, arranged ready for a performance, for at nine that night a theatrical representation was to take place, in which Will was to enact a fierce outlaw—just the sort of character he approved—since it gave him an opportunity of displaying the gruff voice he imitated so well, and for quoting certain scraps of Shakespeare, which had no reference whatever to the piece, but which, as he expressed it, "rolled out well."

During the little business and conviviality which always preceded any affair of this kind, the room, it must be understood, was entirely closed against strangers.

The proceedings had been going on some little time, however, when a loud riot was heard outside the door, and ere the apprentices knew well what was happening, it was thrown violently open, and a throng of redfaced excited men burst in.

Will Lightmore and Guy the Foundling started up and faced the intruders angrily.

"What is the meaning of this?" cried the former. "Do you think, gentlemen, that we are children, that we shall suffer quietly such an insult to be put upon us?"

One of the men—a burly, red-faced bully—burst into a coarse laugh.

"Why, what young lion's cub have we got here?

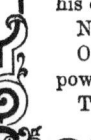

—a regular fire-eater, by his words and manner," he cried; "these rooms are public——"

A tall man, with a long, wiry moustache, better dressed than the others, and who had evidently not been indulging in such frequent and deep potations stepped forward at this moment and interposed.

"Stay, Richborne," he cried, placing his hand on the shoulder of the bully; " we must have no noise and fighting here. Young gentlemen," he added, turning with respect towards the assembled apprentices, "if it will not be considered by you too great a disturbance, *we* should consider it a favour if you would allow us to occupy one corner of your room. We will not interfere with you, and when you commence your performances will be happy to listen and applaud."

These words were said with so much real courtesy that, though our hero and his friends could not but regard their intrusion as ill-timed and perplexing, they had no course left to them but submission.

Permission having, therefore, been accorded, the leader of the strange party, after casting a meaning glance at Dick Hatherden, who sat at the table near Guy, passed to one corner of the room, where they ranged themselves in as small a space as possible, and were soon engaged in earnest conversation.

Dick took the earliest opportunity to slip out of the room.

He knew well the man who had glanced at him— knew him as one of the most resolute and dangerous followers of Jonas Barnsdake—and what could be the meaning of their sudden irruption into the room he could not imagine.

On proceeding downstairs he made his way at once into the little parlour, where the old man and his wife were sitting.

He made a peculiar sign to Ezekiel Lambert—the Boniface—and then said, in a low tone—

" Why are the men here to-night?"

" That is more than I can tell," replied Ezekiel.

"But why have they burst into our room? They surely have nothing to suspect us; for they cannot suppose that the apprentices know anything of their plots; or, if they did, would do anything to prevent them."

"The truth is," replied Ezekiel, in a low tone, " they are suspected to be here."

" By whom?"

" That I know nothing about."

" Then who told you?"

"Captain Almer. He says that they had no sooner seated themselves in the public room than some fellows came in whom he knew to be spies."

" Well?"

" Having decided this in his own mind, he led all his men out into the stables, and as soon as the spies were gone he asked you and your friends to let them remain in your room."

"And why so if it disturbs all our evening?" asked Dick Hatherden.

"Because they will be safe there," replied Boniface, "for, unless the watch demand an entrance, I will allow no one to enter the private room of the apprentices."

"Very good," said Dick, "but is a meeting so absolutely necessary to-night."

"I believe so; in fact, I fancy from all I have heard that strange things will happen ere many hours are over."

Dick waited to hear no more.

He guessed, indeed, what was coming; and—resolved as he was not to compromise himself too far —he thanked Ezekiel Lambert and hurried back to the "lodge" room.

Here he found that preparations were in active progress for the representation, which was a kind of rehearsal for a better performance, which was to take place before friends, and in which the lads took female as well as male parts.

The lights in front of the stage were lit.

The musicians were beginning to tune up.

The conspirators over in the corner—for such they really were—were evidently neglecting their business to watch the proceedings.

In the space of ten minutes Dick had dressed for his part, and the curtain rose presently and disclosed the first scene of the grand play of "Roland the Outcast; or, the Perjured Lord and the Fair Maid of Arlenstone."

Dick acted the Perjured Lord; Guy the Foundling was the Lover of the Fair Maid; and Roland the Outcast, who turned out to be the father, long since considered to be dead by the hand of the Perjured Lord, was performed with true dramatic force by Will Lightmore.

He strutted the stage like a lion seeking for its prey, and caused abundant applause among the assembly by the way he jingled his spurs and curled his ferocious moustache, and uttered wild and ferocious speeches about his " che—ild," and the " purr—jered villain" who had stolen her from her home.

And then, when he at last seized Dick Hatherden by the throat, and shouted—

"There's blood upon thy hands—there is no speculation in those eyes that I do gaze upon. Have at thee, thou murderer and traitor, or I will let slip the little blood that still runs in thy coward veins."

The audience were so taken by his manner that they did not observe he was mixing up Shakespeare with the author of the play; nor did they see that Dick was white, and trembling and gasping from no assumed emotion.

Now Will Lightmore never intended any allusion to the subject of Dick's crime.

Of course, he was not aware of it.

Had he been, or had he had the slightest suspicion in regard to it, he would have revolted at the bare idea of speaking to him.

And yet, seeing him now, with his face white and ghastly—his eyes sunken in his head and rolling wildly—he could not place it down to good acting, but some feeling of hideous guilt.

" 'What rogue and coward slave have we here?'" cried he. " 'Is it, then, a truth that you confess to murder?'"

Dick Hatherden sprang to his feet.

"You lie!—you lie!" he shouted. "It was not I that killed him."

Then, by a superhuman effort, he recovered himself, and, with a forced laugh, cried—

"Bah! I have forgotten my part. We shall have to have another rehearsal."

"Rehearsal!" muttered Richborne; "if that was acting, I'll be hanged. If that was not the real terror of a bloodstained villain, I'll be hanged twice."

Hatherden's manner truly disconcerted all present.

But, fortunately for him, something occurred which put an end for the moment to his fears.

Something strangely mysterious it was.

A roar, as of hundreds of voices, was heard without, in the street, which until this moment had been so wrapped in quiet.

Then a second roar, and a flash of light in the windows.

Then a pistol-shot, and the crashing of the panes of glass.

Richborne, and the one who had been spoken of as Captain Almer, sprang excitedly to their feet, the former appearing suddenly to lose all traces of his drunkenness.

"This is most strange and unaccountable," exclaimed Almer. "What means the signal, when the time is not yet come?"

"Something unexpected has happened," said the other; "that is the only thing I can suppose."

And he, too, hurried to the casement.

Reaching there, what they heard and saw seemed to corroborate their words.

A red glow, as from a great fire, was seen in the distance.

And as they watched the fading and brightening of the sky, the roar of hundreds of human voices could be heard in the far distance.

"Well, we're wanted, I suppose," said Captain Almer; "and so we had best begone. Come, my friends, let us——"

His words were interrupted.

The door flung open hurriedly, admitted a pale, excited man, with white hair streaming over his shoulders.

None other than Jonas Barnsdake.

"Quick! my friends," he cried, in a voice hoarse and thick with excitement; "quick!—we are wanted—the work is begun!"

Captain Almer and his followers waited for no more.

They at once quitted the room, and, as may be imagined, the apprentices did not remain behind.

All thoughts of proceeding with the play were at an end.

They knew that strange and desperate doings were progressing somewhere.

There then was their duty perhaps, and away they went,—Guy the Foundling and Will Lightmore leading the way, while Dick Hatherden at once quitted their ranks and joined those of the conspirators.

We must not accompany them now.

We must retrograde a little while, and show what was going on while the apprentices and the conspirators were collected at the Yellow Ensign.

CHAPTER XXX.

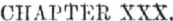

THE SIGN OF THE LAMB AND FLEECE—DEVIL'S ALLEY —THE CROWD OF DISCONTENTED WITHOUT AND THE CROWD OF CONSPIRATORS WITHIN—THE SIGNS OF A STORM—THE SUDDEN OUTBURST—THE ATTACK ON THE TAVERN — THE DEFENCE — THE ARRIVAL OF THE SOLDIERS—APPRENTICES TO THE RESCUE—ALEXIS RAINSFORD IN A NEW CHARACTER.

AT the corner of a narrow alley, which led into a broader thoroughfare, about a mile and a half distant from the Yellow Ensign, stood a tavern, which rejoiced in the appellation of the Lamb and Fleece.

At this place there was assembled a company of persons of a far different character to what were gathered together in the other.

They were a mingled company.

Some were English, some Irish, some French and German.

All were excited, and evidently full of stern emotion.

The fact was that, as is usual at such times, evil-minded agitators had seized the opportunity to inflame the minds of the Catholics against the Protestants; to persuade them that a chance was come to revive old dissensions with a better prospect of success.

In fact they were endeavouring, by misrepresentations, by promises of aid from abroad, and other means, to persuade the English and Irish Catholics to rise and make the Catholic Emancipation Bill a pretext for a religious warfare.

Thus we see existing in London at this time a secret Protestant Association and a secret Catholic Association—the existence of one being as useless and as mischievous as that of the other.

As is generally the case, the Catholic party, being the weaker, had spies among its ranks.

On this evening these traitors had been at work; and as their fiendish labours had been principally employed among a set of men who were the sworn followers of Jonas Barnsdake, it may be imagined that the crowd that began to hover at an early hour round the Lamb and Fleece was not composed of any tame elements.

Knots of men and women gathered there, glancing up ever and anon at the brilliantly lighted windows, and then turning to converse in eager and angry whispers.

Mischief was evidently brewing.

But it required time and drink to rouse their passions fully.

As they passed in and out of the tavern, and the spirits began to mount to their brains, they began to speak louder, and shake their fists at the windows, as if in warning of what was to come.

At length, a tall and brawny fellow, in a fustian jacket, entered the bar with two or three companions, and loudly demanded some spirits.

THE RIVAL APPRENTICES

A TALE OF THE RIOTS OF 1780.

THE ATTACK ON THE TAVERN BY THE RIOTERS.

Their eyes, red and bleary, their pallid faces and hoarse voices, told how they were affected with drink and excitement, and this, added to the in- solent tone with which they demanded refresh- ment, caused the landlord to refuse them what they desired.

"There—be off with you!" he cried; "you have had quite enough."

Some of the men round burst out in a loud, coarse laugh.

"Enough, eh?" he cried, "enough! I suppose you want all you've got for the Popish conspirators upstairs. Come—no nonsense—let's have some drink; we're thirsty."

These words quickly inflamed the fury of the landlord.

"Come, none of your insolence—none of your insults here," he shouted, red with anger. "You can't be served—that's enough! and so bundle off, or you'll be put out."

"Oh, we shall, shall we!" said the man, drawing a great bludgeon from beneath his coat. "But I should like to see the man that can do it."

In an instant his wish was gratified.

The landlord whispered a few words to a man behind the bar, and then leaped over into the open space, crying—

"Now then, those who want comfort and quietness, follow my example."

And he seized the leading ruffian by the throat, avoiding a tremendous blow aimed at him with the bludgeon.

Most of the customers were Catholics, and they at once, therefore, took part with the landlord.

A rapid, but fierce, conflict accordingly ensued.

Desperately and furiously the drunken ruffians resisted.

But in vain.

The force to oppose them was too powerful, and after a quick contest, which was brutal in its savage intensity, the man and his followers were hurled, bruised and bleeding, into the street.

This was the signal for uproar.

Crowds of excited men and women thronged round them.

A hundred eager questions were asked on all sides at once.

Then came a hush for a moment, succeeded by a terrific roar.

"No Popery!—down with the Catholics!"

"Pull down the tavern!"

"Down with it about their ears."

And with the words a shower of missiles of every kind was poured in upon the building, while yells of approbation resounded from every side.

And so began the riot.

It is well known that the sight of the first blood always succeeds in exasperating a man, even if he begins a contest in the calmest of moods.

While nothing had been done but gathering round and staring at the well-lit windows, and muttering threats at the assembled "conspirators," as they chose to call the Catholics, all went quietly enough.

But when, in an ill-advised moment, the landlord hurled the angry rioters—bleeding and bruised—in among the crowd, the whole crew of them—women as well as men—took common cause with them.

A few hurried whispers passed, as I have said.

Whispers so low that a hush appeared to have fallen upon the scene.

Then a change!

Missiles were chosen anywhere.

Stones from the road were hurled at the windows.

Clubs and staves were taken from beneath coats—pistols and swords made their appearance as if by magic.

Those who had weapons remained and forced their way to the front.

Those who had none with them rushed away in the direction of their homes in search of them.

And in the minds of all there was but one feeling, and that was that a terrible struggle of *some* kind had begun.

CHAPTER XXXI.

THE PREPARATIONS FOR DEFENCE—THE BARRICADE
—THE LANDLORD ADDRESSES THE MOB—THE
BLOW AND THE PISTOL-SHOT—THE ATTACK COM-
MENCES WITH A VENGEANCE—THE BREAKING-IN
OF THE DOORS—THE RESISTANCE—THE FLIGHT—
THE INCENDIARY.

MEANWHILE, it must not be supposed that those within the "Lamb and Fleece" were idle.

They saw at once that the feelings of the mob were aroused, and they at once, therefore, made preparations for defence.

The doors were closed with a rush, barricaded strongly, furniture being dragged out and piled against them.

All was excitement.

Every heart beat wildly.

For everyone knew his own life to be in immediate jeopardy.

The Catholics in the room above were soon apprised of the state of affairs.

Generously, at once they offered to quit the house and face the mob.

It was a tall, handsome man who came to Boniface with this proposition.

None other than Alexis Rainsford.

The bosom friend of Simon Grandley's father—the friend of Colonel Halsted *and* of Jonas Barnsdake—of Catholics and Protestants as well!

"Let us go out and face them," he said; "they will not dare maltreat us, and you will by these means save your house."

As he spoke, a roar of execration—a howl of revenge—filled the street.

The landlord grimly smiled.

"You talk of daring to maltreat you," he said; "what would they *not* dare? No, no. It never shall be said that I betrayed my guests into the hands of a diabolical gang, who would murder them. Ha! now they begin. They shall have as good a reception as possible."

These last words were in answer to an assault upon the door.

"Out with them!"

"Down with the conspirators!"

"No Popery!"

"Pull the place down about their ears!"

The same cries again.

Then more yells and blows.

"There's no sign of compromise here," said the landlord. "Joe," he added, turning to one of his

men, "go to my room, and bring out the muskets you will find there. We shall have to defend this house pretty stiffly."

The man at once obeyed.

Then Alexis again said to the gentlemen who crowded the bar—

"Again I say let us leave this place. I do not wish to hazard the ruin of this worthy man. Let us open the door, and demand of these howling demons what they desire."

"No, no," said the landlord; "I cannot permit it. Besides, if nothing else will move you, let me tell you that I require and claim your protection."

The arrival of Joe with the firearms, and a second and more savage assault on the door, closed this conversation.

They proceeded at once to dispose their forces as best they could.

A large body remained in the bar, ready to repair any breach in the defences, as well as to repel attacks, while a second body, armed with muskets, proceeded once more upstairs, to fire upon the mob from the windows.

The landlord ascended with these, and boldly passed out upon the balcony.

Standing there calmly, despite the yells which greeted him on all sides, he raised his hand to intimate that he desired to address them.

For a moment there was a confused murmuring.

Then silence.

The mob began to see their power.

It was in deference to them that he stood there.

So they resolved to listen.

"My friends," he said, "your conduct surprises me. I have always endeavoured to do my best for you; and during all the years I have been in this house I have always treated you with civility. But now you are attacking my house, destroying my property, and trying to bring ruin on me. Tell me why—tell me what you want."

"Give us the conspirators!"

"No Popery!"

"Fling the Catholics out of the window that we may hang 'em!"

And all these cries from men, and women too, who, perhaps in all their lives had never seen the inside of a chapel.

Cries addressed to a set of men who had assembled to prevent disorder—to concert means for preserving the public safety.

"I won't give them up," cried Boniface, stoutly; "they are my guests, and I won't betray them if I die for it."

"Ho, ho! you refuse then?" cried a stalwart fellow, who towered a full head above those near him.

"I do," said the landlord.

"Then take that!" cried the brute.

And with a huge flint stone he took sure aim, and the stout-hearted landlord of the "Lamb and Fleece" went staggering back, bleeding and half stunned, right through the half-open window.

The fellow soon repented his temerity.

There was a sharp report from the casement, and with one wild yell he fell back, shot through the head.

It was a rash shot.

Yet who can blame him who fired it?

In such a scene of fearful exasperation, punishment upon the instant for such disgusting brutality would be the first thought to spring to a man's mind.

However, the effect of the pistol-shot was at once seen.

Hardly had the dead man sunk among the throng, when a howl arose as from a thousand loosened wild beasts.

Pistols and muskets were discharged at the windows.

Bricks, and stones, and chumps of wood, were hurled through the shivering glass.

And then, amid deafening cheers, a body of men struggled through the crowd, and with huge axes began to demolish the door.

The battle now was no longer one-sided.

The gentlemen in the room above began firing rapidly.

Every time one fellow made himself too conspicuous among the crowd he was popped off neatly, while on the other hand the firing by the mob at unseen foes took but little effect.

For this, however, they cared not.

When one of their own number fell they howled truly.

But that was all.

They were licking their lips already over their anticipated vengeance.

The besieged laboured under one terrible disadvantage.

The men who were battering down the door were comparatively out of harm's way, for, in order to fire upon them, the besiegers would have had to expose themselves at the windows, and court certain death.

So it seemed evident that unless assistance arrived in time, the place would certainly be broken into, and all within it massacred.

Half-an-hour passed.

Half-an-hour of furious firing and fighting, and yet no soldiers to the rescue!

The authorities had heard of the riot, and knew its cause.

For this very reason they desired not to be too hasty.

"Perhaps it will pass over," they thought.

Vain hope!

The blood of the mob was up.

Murder was before their eyes.

Their fingers itched to clutch the throats of those whom their disordered fancies had fashioned into enemies.

And so at length, when the door began to yield to the furious blows of the hatchets, a wild cheer rang along the thronged streets.

Another blow! The door yields more—the third hinge is off—it sways and falls outwards!

The way is open now, save for the barricade of furniture.

"Hurrah!" shouts the foremost man, leaping forward.

It was his last word in this world.

From among the interstices of the barricade a

deadly volley poured, and he, with four of his comrades, fell, shot through the heart.

The people cared not for death now, however.

Eager hands soon again caught up the hatchets, and to work the maddened rioters went with a will once more.

The battle now became most desperate.

Many fell outside, and those within began to feel the effects of shots fired by a kind of forlorn hope that advanced behind the axe-bearers, and fired over their shoulders as they worked.

Such desperate courage—if so such madness could be named—necessarily had its effect.

The frail barrier, composed of chairs and tables, was soon broken to pieces by the steady blows of the hatchet-bearers, whose ranks were continually reinforced by volunteers, as fast as any retired wounded; and at length, with a loud shout of triumph, the foremost of the crowd burst through the barricade into the bar.

Resistance here was simply madness.

As I have said, both the landlord and his guests had only kept up the defence in the hope that aid would arrive.

Now further fight was useless.

All had therefore been arranged before hand.

When, consequently, the rioters had burst in and imagined themselves to have achieved a glorious victory, a voice shouted—

"Now then for your lives!"

And in an instant all was in total darkness.

Then, as the landlord and his band of supporters dashed through the inner door by which it had been settled to make their retreat, a volley of firearms was poured suddenly in upon the crowd from the stairs, killing many, and illumining the place momentarily with hideous, lurid flames.

That volley, of course, staggered them, and enabled the besieged to make good their escape to the back door, and fly into the street at the rear of the building.

To save the place by their own hands was now impossible.

The only chance now was to insist upon the prompt action of the authorities.

Off they, therefore, scattered in various directions through the city.

Meanwhile, a man sprang through the crowd with a blazing torch.

"Ho, ho! they have put us in darkness, have they? We'll soon have a light."

And he flung the blazing brand into the bar, among the ruins of the furniture!

CHAPTER XXXII.

THE CONFLAGRATION—THE RUSH FOR DRINK—JONAS BARNSDAKE IN HIS ELEMENT—HORRIBLE FATE OF THE MADDENED RIOTERS—GUY AND WILL LIGHTMORE TO THE RESCUE—THE CONFLICT—THE SURPRISE—THE MAD PREACHER—SIMON GRANDLEY APPEARS IN A STRANGE CHARACTER.

IN the heat of the struggle—the confusion—the carrying away of wounded men—the terror of the females—the inexpressible surprise and horror of the whole situation—but little notice had been taken of the contents of the bar.

The tired and excited men had been invited by the landlord to drink whatever they chose, and although they had not availed themselves of this to any inordinate extent, they had placed half-filled glasses here and bottles there, and in the rush and hurry they had been overturned.

The floor of the bar, therefore, was full of inflammable materials, and when the burning brand was cast into it the result may be imagined.

A fiery glow spread through the place.

A heat overcame all.

Then lurid flames sprang up, and the bar was on fire.

The madcap ruffian who had done this deed laughed loudly, and the crowd, inebriated with excitement, laughed loudly too.

"Let's broach the spirits," shouted one.

The words acted like magic.

All thoughts of pursuit at once were dispelled.

The ruffians had the chance now of robbery, and pillage, and drunkenness without disturbance.

"Aye, aye! the spirits!" shouted many voices.

And then, regardless of the fact that the place was on fire, they lit the lamps and rushed hither and thither—some down into the cellars—some upstairs into the private rooms.

The question of religion was for the moment merged in one of self-gratification.

The demon Drink had possession of their faculties, and all they desired was to glut their senses with the fine old spirits kept at the "Lamb and Fleece" without the annoyance of paying for it.

A different turn was, however, given suddenly to their ideas.

Jonas Barnsdake, just as the flames began to leap through the windows of the old building, arrived at the spot, together with Richborne and his men, while Will Lightmore, Guy the Foundling, and Dick Hatherden led the way with the band of excited apprentices.

"The sacred work has begun then," cried the infatuated old man, as he elbowed his way through the crowd; "where are our enemies?"

"What's the old fool mumbling about?" said a man, shoving him on one side, as he tried to force his way towards the scene of action.

"Hush!" said a woman; "that's Jonas Barnsdake."

The name acted like a talisman.

In an instant all was changed.

"Jonas Barnsdake! Ha, ha! Here's our leader just come in time," said the man.

Then he turned respectfully to the old man.

"I mistook you, sir," he said. "You see the boys are at it. We've been tumbling out some cursed Catholic conspirators."

"Good!—good!" said Jonas Barnsdake, still hustling his way through the crowd. "The Lord will reward you for it."

How little the Lord had to do with such a conflict he might surely have understood, had he chosen to interpret rightly the sounds which issued from the burning building.

Already drunkenness was in the ascendant.

Yells and execrations of the most hideous nature resounded in the air.

Wild curses—laughter—songs—were heard everywhere, while ever and anon some terrible shriek burst forth from the lips of some wretch whose helpless limbs the fire began to lap.

Too overcome by drink to move, they were burnt there as they lay, while their companions raged round them, as if to covet the same fate.

Jonas, however, only saw in the fire—in the blood that had been spilled—the indications of the beginning of a glorious warfare in the sacred cause of religion; and as if to aid him in his mad purpose, a band of resolute and brave hearts now appeared upon the scene, determined to do what they could to save the building, and take vengeance on the reckless marauders.

Of these some, of course, were Catholics.

A great number of them, however, and among them the apprentices, had entered into the struggle for no other reason than because they desired to restore order, to save property, and to punish reckless villany.

Now a fearful fight ensued.

The men who remained outside — only because they were unable to enter through the thronging of drunken rioters within — turned at once savagely on their assailants.

Again the insane watch-cries were repeated—

"No Popery!"

"Down with the Romish conspirators!"

"Hang them up!"

When, after all, every trace of religious contest had disappeared, to give place to a drunken riot!

"See that old, bareheaded maniac," said Guy the Foundling, as, with Will Lightmore and Dick Hatherden, who dared not openly desert them, they forced their way towards Jonas Barnsdale; "a tap on the head would do him no real harm, and might save many a life."

"Would it so, young fellow!" cried a voice, and turning he saw a huge bully coming towards him, club in hand.

"It would," replied Guy, stoutly, and still pushed on.

But the big man barred his passage.

"Know you not that is our leader?" said the man. "He is as good a Protestant as ever drew breath, and as honest a man in everything as ever lived. Do you think he'd tell us wrong?"

"I don't care whether he's Protestant or Catholic,"

"A FIERCE CONFLICT ENSUED" (see p. 66).

replied Guy; "he's mad now, and he's causing people to be murdered. So, come on, lads!—follow me."

"That's right, boys," shouted Will Lightmore; "stand not upon the order of your going, but go at once."

And he began forcing his way more violently than before.

"Ho, ho! We have Catholics among our City apprentices, have we?" exclaimed the man. "So, young fellow, you talk of tapping the old man on the skull. Mayhap your own stands a good chance of being broken first."

"As yours may also, my worthy friend," said Guy the Foundling, as he aimed a blow at him with his club.

Both he and Will Lightmore wore swords.

But, unless obliged, they determined not to use them.

The blow did not reach the tall man, but it was almost as useful, inasmuch as it knocked down a man in front of him, and cleared the way, so that Guy and his strange antagonist were brought face to face.

Clubs were no longer of any use.

The fellow drew his sword, and the contest began fiercely.

Dick Hatherden, being wedged in among the other apprentices, was compelled to fight on Guy's side, and the crowd taking part against them, a pitched battle commenced.

Our readers have doubtless not forgotten that a small body of Catholics were striving, on the other side of this strange battle-field, to force their way into the tavern, and eject the drunken crew before all chance of saving the place was gone.

It was Guy's desire, therefore, to make his way to them.

"Let us join our unknown friends yonder," cried the Foundling to Will Lightmore; "and we can then keep these mad devils at bay until the military arrive."

"Lead on, then, most noble chieftain," said Will Lightmore, who even in the midst of danger did not forget his usual style of speech; "though methinks it will be no easy matter."

"You are right," said the tall man, aiming a left-handed blow at him.

"And you wrong," cried Guy.

And in an instant his sword-blade ran through the fellow's shoulder.

As he fell, with a loud cry, they dashed forward. "Now, then, for the old leader," said Guy. "We must knock him over, or carry him away, or this carnage will go on until morning."

So saying, they dashed onwards towards Jonas Barnsdake.

He was standing on a slightly rising point of ground, and urging the crowd on to fresh exertions.

It was a piteous sight to see him.

His face was deadly pale from intense inward excitement.

His eyes glared fiercely.

His long white hair, streaming in the wind, was the only thing in him at this moment which seemed to claim respect.

All things else—his attitude, his manner, his words—were uncompromising.

"On there—on there, my friends!" he shouted! "strike for the good cause! The Lord is with you; You fight on Heaven's side!"

And so the misguided men fought on to annihilate the small band opposed to them, never remembering their comrades who were frizzling and dying amid the flames of the burning tavern.

Guy's plan of securing the person of Jonas Barnsdake was the correct one.

Without his presence—without his mad exhortations—the crowd would not have been roused to deeds of violence.

So he fought his way desperately.

At length he reached the spot.

"Desist, old man!" he cried, as he seized him by the arm, "nor urge your fellow-creatures to slay one another. Desist, or my sword ends for ever your maniacal preachings."

"Hold, Guy—he is *my* friend," cried a voice.

And as the words were spoken, Simon Grandley, the carpenter, his master, stood before him.

Horror-stricken, amazed, Guy the Foundling dropped his sword and fell back, just as the gallop of cavalry was heard, and the people shouted—

"The soldiers! The soldiers are on us!"

CHAPTER XXXIII.

THE ARRIVAL OF THE SOLDIERS—THE BURNING OF THE TAVERN—THE ATTACK ON THE CROWD—GUY THE FOUNDLING DETERMINES TO SAVE THE PEOPLE—HIS PERILOUS PLAN—HIS SCENE WITH THE COLONEL—THE PLAN SUCCEEDS—THE DISPERSION OF THE CROWD—A FORCED TRANQUILLITY.

JUST as the soldiers galloped up, trampling down those in their way, and sending the others scampering in every direction, the most lamentable scene of all occurred.

The flames had now full sway in the old tavern, and the spirits caused them to shoot upwards with terrific fury.

The casements were now, of course, entirely gone, and within, among the smoke and flame, could be seen suffering human beings, staggering in drunkenness, mad with pain, but senseless, not knowing which way to escape from the torment they had created for themselves.

One after another they fell down into the fierce fire—men and women together—and in a few moments their charred corpses were undistinguishable from the surrounding beams and other falling *débris*.

All attempts at saving the building had long since been abandoned.

Even to save life had been found impossible, and the crowd, whom the advent of the soldiers had considerably cooled, began to think already of the dear friends and relations who had met with a hideous death in the flames.

They mingled now in one confused mass—Catholics and Protestants together—and, borne up against the burning house by the pressure from behind, implored uselessly for mercy.

Soldiers, when brought in contact with their own brothers, as it were, in civil tumults, seem always inspired with a spirit of unnecessary brutality.

So, though the crowd was only a helpless, struggling mass before them, they struck at them with the flat of their swords, and forced their horses brutally against the front ranks.

This was quite unnecessary.

The foremost—or, rather, the hindmost—of the crowd struggled truly, but it was but a struggle to get away.

If they turned to face the soldiers, it was but to watch for a chance of safety.

These movements the soldiers chose to regard as a show of resistance.

And they acted accordingly.

The ground was soon a mass of trampled, writhing human beings.

It was this, perhaps—this useless and shameful cruelty—that roused the people to resentment.

Guy the Foundling, as we have seen, was utterly amazed and astounded by the sight of Simon Grandley, his master, defending old Jonas Barnsdake, the leader of the tumult—the evil spirit of the hour.

He had, as I have said, dropped his sword and fallen back, almost into the arms of his friend, Will Lightmore.

"What!" cried he, "*you*, master!—you here among these men, defending him who has been the first cause of all this tumult? I am bewildered."

"Well may you be, young man," said Jonas Barnsdake, solemnly; "it is not given to such as you to understand——"

"There's your sword," cried Will Lightmore, interrupting the speech of the old man; "you'll want it. See, the soldiers are here, and ten to one if they don't attack friends and foes alike."

As we have seen, his prophesy was quite a correct one.

"Something must be done quickly," said Guy, as he saw the huddling together of the people, and beheld one after another forced into the flames of the burning tavern.

Something must be done!

Yes, truly; but what?

There seemed no way of getting to the front.

Yet there alone could any good be done.

He turned to Will Lightmore.

"If something is not thought of and carried out

immediately," he said, "there will be wholesale murder here. Can you suggest anything?"

Will thought a moment.

As a rule his brain was remarkably clear.

But the whirl of events, and the terrible nature of the scene, somewhat bewildered him.

At length he said—

"Perhaps the officer might listen to reason, if any-one has the pluck to face him."

"Show me how to get there, and I'll do it," said Guy.

"We must walk on the people's shoulders," said Will.

No sooner said than done.

"Help me up," said Guy to a stalwart man standing by; "I'm going to speak to the officer. Let me pass on, good people. I am not very heavy Help me, and I'll save you."

"Be quick then," said a man somewhat in advance. "See, the cavalry have wheeled round for another charge."

This was too true.

The lad redoubled his exertions, and followed, by Will Lightmore, he was not long before he reached the front.

The people aided him, imagining he knew the officer.

If they had known the simple truth, they would have imagined that he was merely bent on securing his own safety.

On reaching the point he desired, he saw, by the light of the still burning house, the officer on horse-back on one side, giving orders to his men, who had retired to some distance.

"Give me your pistol," he said to a man who was holding it irresolutely.

And taking it from his hands before the man well knew what he meant, he rushed away, and boldly seized the reins of the colonel's horse.

"Stop, sir," he cried; "call off your men—this bloodshed is unnecessary."

"Let go my bridle, boy, or I will cut you down," cried the officer, savagely. "Let go, I say, and quickly!"

Guy raised his pistol till it was within a foot of the colonel's head.

"Try to carry out your threat, and this bullet shall end your career for ever," said he, in a resolute voice. "I wish but to speak to you, and I *will* be heard."

The colonel was amazed.

"You are a bold lad," he said. "Speak!"

"If your soldiers charge now," returned Guy, "it will be nothing but murder. The people have no means of escape."

"But they face us even now," said the colonel.

"Because they cannot retreat," answered the apprentice. "On one side is the blazing tavern; on the other a blank wall; on the other the fallen timbers and brickwork choke up the lane. Give them time and opportunity, and all they desire is escape."

The colonel fiercely twirled his long moustache.

"You're a strange sort of boy, in very truth. Tell me, who are you?"

"We shall meet again probably," said Guy, somewhat contemptuously, "This is no time for talking. Give your orders, and let these poor people go their way in peace."

He let go his hold on the bridle as he spoke.

The colonel seized him by the arm.

"Stay one moment," he said.

"Well?"

"You are a brave lad."

"You said that before. See, the crowd is swaying to and fro."

"Yes, yes; but since you kn•w so much, tell me more."

"What mean you?"

"Who is the ringleader of this riot, and where is he?" asked the colonel, eagerly.

Guy shook his head, and wrested himself from the officer's grasp.

"I know nothing of him;" he said, "and more than that, I told you before this is no time for talk. If you let these people have time to recover them-selves, I should doubt much whether you or your men would reach the barracks in safety."

This enraged the colonel.

"What," he cried, "do you threaten?"

"No—I want justice done quickly."

"Curse you, leave my bridle," replied the officer, whose good sense was again overcome with anger at the idea of being dictated to by a boy; "or I will order my men to charge."

The pistol was again levelled.

"Beware," said Guy, "recollect my words."

The colonel gazed into his face.

In every feature determination was written.

"Bah! well, have it your way."

Then he waved his men back, and advanced towards the crowd.

"You have assembled here," he said, as the men scowled upon him fiercely, "in a riotous manner, and attacked the house of a peaceable citizen. But there may be many amongst you who are innocent of any desire to participate in these proceedings. There-fore, I call upon you to disperse quietly. My men shall have orders to remain quiet as long as you do. Disperse quietly, therefore, to your homes, and I shall leave till to-morrow the discovery of the mad and guilty men who have urged you on to these deeds of violence."

The crowd needed no further telling.

They felt crushed for the time.

Their hearts were swelling with desire for revenge.

But they knew this was not the time to secure it.

Against the well-equipped and heavy cavalry what could they do?

And even if they *did* succeed in harassing them for a time, would not infantry, and artillery too, be brought up at a moment's notice?

So sullenly they turned away.

Dead and wounded were lifted from the ground and borne off; and in the course of half an hour the open space before what had once been the "Lamb and Fleece" was as empty as a desert.

The inn itself was now no more.

Built of wood, it had burnt like tinder; and a heap of blackened ashes was all that remained of it.

More terrible fact still.

It was all that remained of sixty-five men and women, whose mad thirst for strong drink had led them into the devouring flames!

CHAPTER XXXIV.

GUY THE FOUNDLING AND WILL LIGHTMORE MEET WITH AN ADVENTURE ON THE ROAD HOME—THE APPEARANCE AND EXTRAORDINARY DISAPPEARANCE OF QUAIL—THE VAIN SEARCH—THE ATTEMPTED MURDER—THE STRANGE SAVIOUR—THE VOW OF VENGEANCE.

As may be conceived, Guy and his companions had had enough of hard work and excitement for that night.

Gladly, therefore, they made their way from the scene of disaster.

They separated, of course, in different directions, and at length Guy and Will Lightmore were left to pursue their way home together.

As for Dick Hatherden, he had disappeared.

And so, indeed, had Simon Grandley.

He had gone as mysteriously as he had come.

"This has been a strange night, Will," said Guy, with a sigh.

"Bah! sigh not," cried Will Lightmore; "sighs were for women made. But as for this riot, there are more things in heaven and earth, Horatio, than are dreamed of in *our* philosophy."

"At your quotations again, eh?"

"Yes; and again," said the other, "these tumults prove to me that 'there's something rotten in the state of Denmark.' There'll be more blood-letting yet, or *I'm* no prophet."

"Let's hope not," said Guy; "the scene of to-night was truly horrible. People rushing, for drink's sake, into the very jaws of death—setting up the banner of religion that they may attack offenceless men, and satiate their lust for strong liquor. I hope to see no more of it."

"If there be more of it, 'twill be good for you in one way," said Will.

"How so?"

"'Twill give you a chance of displaying again that courage and address by which you saved a thousand lives this night. Nay, interrupt me not, for I will have my say. With *such* courage and address you ought to be taken notice of by those who could place you at the summit of the ladder."

Guy laughed merrily.

"Surely you don't want to make me conceited,' he said.

"There's no fear of that."

"I don't know so much about that," replied the Foundling; "the best of us are liable to have our heads turned by too much praise. But what think you of the presence of Simon Grandley here? Is it not surprising and unaccountable?"

Will Lightmore shrugged his shoulders.

"I have begun to give up surprise as a bad job," he said; "otherwise it would certainly seem to me a perfect riddle why Simon Grandley should be here; and, secondly——"

"Why he should befriend that old madman, Jonas Barnsdake."

"Just so; but what's that?"

A dark shadow as they stopped fell across their path, and even in the uncertain light they recognised the shambling gait of Quail, the half-witted apprentice.

"What do you here?" cried Guy, somewhat sternly. "I care not to be watched. Who has sent you here to act the spy upon my actions?"

In an instant the idea flashed across his brain that he had been sent by Simon Grandley to observe his actions.

Had he been able to observe it in the darkness, he would have seen that a tear glistened in Quail's eyes as he listened.

"No," he said, in a tone broken by emotion; "no, I do not come to act as a spy upon you. I came to warn you—to save you."

"To save *me?* From what—from whom?"

"From Dick Hatherden!"

"He has not been near me," said Guy, "except when he was assisting me against the lawless mob. He had no evil designs against me this night, I think. Your fears have deceived you, Quail."

The half-witted boy laughed.

"You know him not," said he, "He would have destroyed you just now without being seen had there been a conflict in the streets. But you stopped the riot, and he was foiled. I come now to save you from the same fate as——"

Whoever it was whom he desired to name, he had no chance giving him then of naming him.

Suddenly his voice failed him, and he appeared to stagger back.

Then as if by magic he disappeared!

"Why, he has gone like a spirit," said Guy, glancing everywhere around him in complete bewilderment.

"'Be he a spirit of earth or goblin damned,' I'll seek him!" exclaimed Will.

And whipping out his light rapier, he dashed one way, while Guy dashed another.

The mystery, however, was complete.

Quail had utterly disappeared.

For some time they continued the search.

But they had at length to give it up as an utter failure.

Spirit or not, Quail had vanished absolutely from the spot.

Nor, indeed, was there any apparent space where he could be concealed from view.

"This is a strange mystery, indeed," murmured Guy the Foundling, as they quitted the dark and and narrow thoroughfare; "it perplexes me."

"Well it may, indeed," said Will Lightmore. "If I were inclined to superstition, I might well be forgiven now if I imagined that evil agency had been at work. But as it is, I suppose the poor, half-witted being was on the verge of some confession, and that the very idea of the disclosure turned his brain, and he fled as it were from himself."

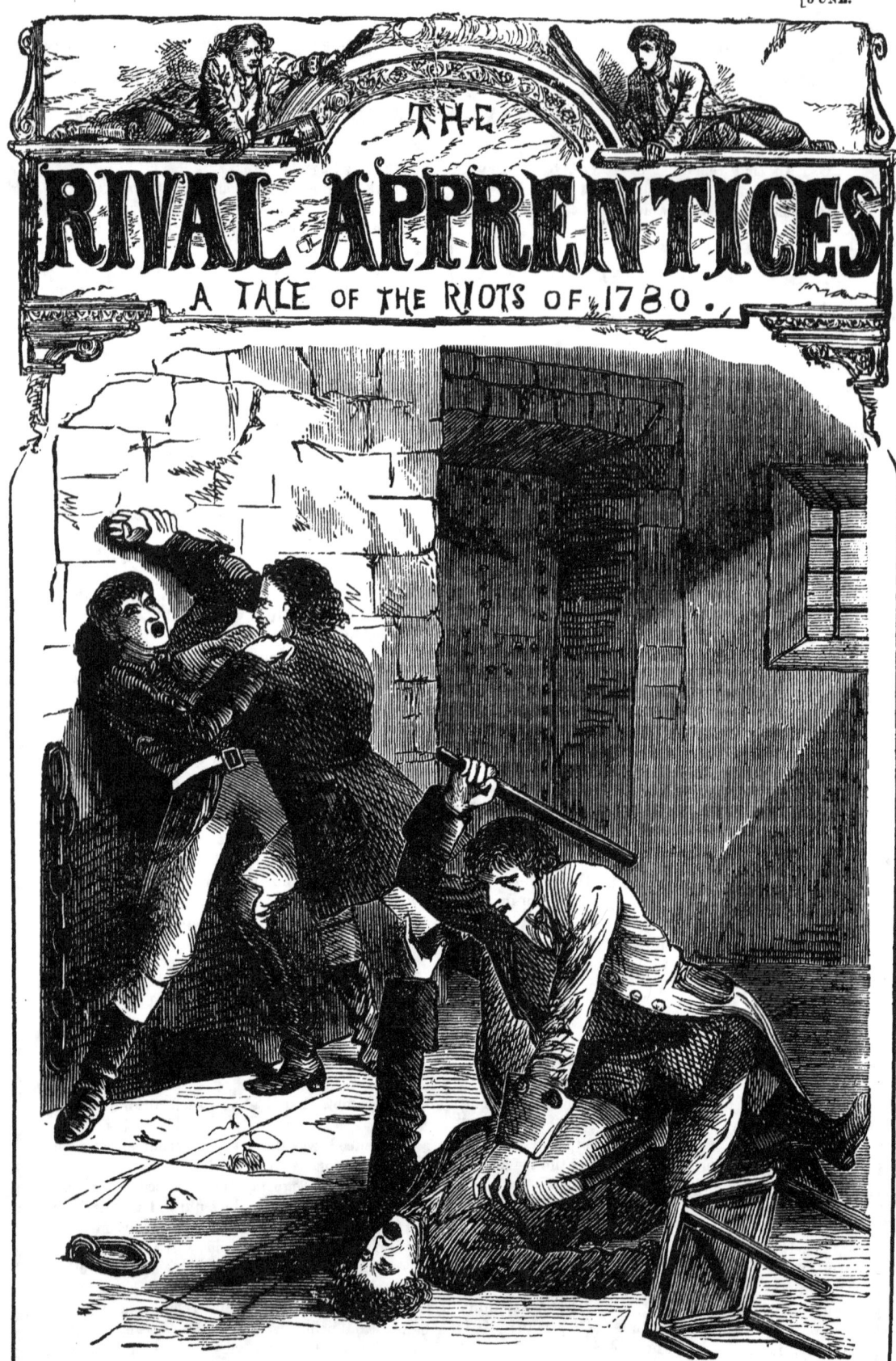

THE RIVAL APPRENTICES

A TALE OF THE RIOTS OF 1780.

THE FIGHT IN THE PRISON CELL.

"We will question him when we reach home," said Guy; "but come, I'm tired—let us hurry away."

My readers, of course, are prepared to believe that no supernatural agency was at work in the disappearance of Quail.

The truth was that Dick Hatherden *had* been looking out for an opportunity to wreak his vengeance on Guy the Foundling in the crowd, as in the *mêlée*, of course, it would have been impossible for any one to have noticed whence the shot came.

Defeated in this, he was sullenly wending his way homewards, when he heard footsteps following him.

He listened, and at once recognised the voices of Guy and Will.

He was in no humour just then for their company.

"I will wait up here and let them pass," he said to himself. "It is no use attempting anything now, when both are together—so I'll not join them. I've no inclination for talking."

The lane, as I have said, was very dark and narrow, and just at the point where Dick Hatherden stood, there was a door slightly on the jar—a door leading, apparently, into a kind of yard.

Here he ensconsed himself.

Here he saw them joined by Quail, and heard the half-made confession.

Fear has a strange effect sometimes—fear, at least, of the future.

It gives strength and courage.

His fingers seemed suddenly endowed with supernatural strength, and stretching forth his arm he clutched the throat of the unfortunate Quail with such a grip that all power of speech instantaneously left him. The blood flew to his head; his eyeballs protruded from their sockets; and when Dick Hatherden drew him through the door and flung him to the ground, he was nearly senseless.

Having disposed of his victim for the moment, he immediately commenced guarding against difficulties.

Rushing to the door, he shot the rusty bolts, and listened.

No one attempted to effect an entrance.

This was not surprising.

The door when shut was flush with the brickwork, and, more than this, the proprietor of the place had, in accordance with some freak of fancy, caused it to be painted so as to resemble as nearly as possible the wall itself.

So when Will Lightmore and Guy the Foundling began their search for Quail, they could distinguish no possible outlet by which he could have escaped them, and, as we have seen, after the lapse of a few minutes they went their way.

Dick quietly waited until they had disappeared.

I say quietly.

By this word I mean to convey the idea that he did not commence any active attack.

However, seeing that Quail showed signs of entirely recovering from his insensibility, he rushed to the spot where he lay, and knelt down by his side.

He was prepared as he did so for any act of brutality and violence.

But somehow or another the sight of the wretched being as he lay there unnerved him.

Lucky this was for Quail.

If it had not been so, his career would have been ended there and then.

Not that I mean to imply that Dick Hatherden had any intention of letting him off scot-free.

He only hesitated.

It was this moment of hesitation that saved the half-witted lad.

"So you were following and spying on my actions, were you?" he said, savagely, as he clutched again the wretched boy's throat.

There was no answer—only a faint gurgle, and Dick, seeing that the boy could not speak unless he loosened his hold on his windpipe, relaxed his grip for a time.

"Answer me," he said, savagely; "who sent you?"

"No one," tremulously ejaculated Quail.

"You lie—you would not have come into that crowd, that danger, for nothing. Quick—tell me, or I'll throttle you."

He had no conception of the true affection which might spring up in the heart of a poor, half-brained creature such as Quail.

He, having no idea of the meaning of the word gratitude, could not imagine that a lad such as he could remember how Guy the Foundling had saved his life.

In Quail's mind, meanwhile, strangely constituted as it was, the idea occurred to him—

"He says he will kill me if I do not tell him. He will kill me all the same if I do."

Not that he even for a moment thought of treachery.

Nothing was further from his thoughts.

"No one sent me, I tell you," he said, with a certain doggedness. "I can't tell anything I don't know."

During this little delay an event occurred, which materially altered things, and which somewhat influenced Dick Hatherden's future, moreover; as well as that of Quail.

As the young murderer was feeling for his knife to put a quick end to the one whom he regarded as a dangerous enemy, the door at the top of a little flight of steps leading to the house opened, and a figure appeared bearing a light.

It was the figure of a young girl about sixteen, plump, full formed, and with wavy dark hair falling over her shoulders.

She was dressed in a somewhat fantastic garb—a parti-coloured bodice and a blue skirt, reaching not much below her knees, and showing therefore a considerable portion of a well-formed leg.

"What is the matter?" she cried boldly as she caught sight of the two figures on the ground.

Dick Hatherden's ready wit soon invented an excuse.

"I was afraid you were all in bed," he said. "This lad had been set upon by some ruffians in the street, and I dragged him in here for safety. Deny this not, or woe to you to-morrow," he added, in a hoarse, threatening whisper.

"Bring him in, then," said the girl, in a tone which Dick at once saw was that of a foreigner. "Bring him in, and we will give him some refreshment."

This was not at all consonant with his ideas.

"Thank you, no," he said, "I need not bring

him in now: but if you will bring him a little spirit out here I would be glad."

The girl turned to comply with this request.

Dick watched her eagerly.

Murder was still in his heart.

In fact, he deemed it necessary for his safety that he should get rid of one who knew of the murder of Colonel Halsted.

This, moreover, might be his last chance.

So as the light of the lamp faded away along the passage he raised his knife and sent it quivering into the body of the wretched lad.

"Help, murder," shrieked Quail, in a shrill tone of agony.

"Curse it! I have struck him in the wrong place now," said Dick.

And indeed in the darkness he *had* done so.

Instead of burying the sharp steel as he had thought in the heart of the lad, he had sent it into the shoulder blade, and there it stuck, resisting all efforts of the assassin to remove it.

There was now no time to be lost.

The cry which the half-witted boy had uttered in his agony quickly brought the young girl back to the scene of action, accompanied by her father.

There was nothing for it, therefore, for Dick Hatherden, but flight.

With fury in his heart, to think that after risking so much his enemy should escape him, he leaped up from the ground just as the light reappeared, and dashing through the doorway, rushed at mad speed down the road.

When, therefore, the girl and her father entered the courtyard they found Quail alone, and nearly senseless.

Such is the frailty of human nature, that probably if they had discovered him dirty, and ragged, and wretched, as he had been when he had been a kind of servant to Dick Hatherden and Bill Hazard, they would have taken no interest in him, but regarded him as simply some vagabond who had fallen a victim to the bad passions of his evil companions.

As it happened, however, poor Quail, as soon as he had entered the service of Simon Grandley, as he had done at once when he had been brought home by Guy the Foundling, had been dressed in a new suit of clothes by the kind-hearted carpenter.

In the eyes of the young girl and her father, therefore, he took a different position altogether.

"Poor lad!" murmured the girl, as she knelt down by his side; "poor lad! Oh! how I do blame myself for not having insisted upon his entering the house at once. I caught the glance of his evil eye as he asked me to bring him the brandy."

"Him! whom?" asked her father, as he poured some spirit between the lips of the now fainting lad.

"The one who was with him," returned the young girl. "He said he had dragged the poor fellow out of the street from some ruffians, who had assaulted him, and at the very moment he was speaking he was murdering him!"

"Let us bear him into the house," said the father; "see, the knife of the assassin is still sticking in his shoulder. It would be dangerous to extract it here, and he will remain in a fainting state until we do something for him."

So they bore him into the house.

When Quail opened his eyes he found himself in bed in a very peculiar domicile.

It was a long room and very narrow.

At the farther end was a man of about fifty years of age, dressed in a parti-coloured dressing gown, and a red cap of the kind called *fez*.

He was smoking his pipe and looking intently into the fire, while at his feet, reading to him, was a beautiful young girl—the girl whose coming into the yard had proved Quail's salvation.

The place was furnished and appointed in a most peculiar style.

Bottles, skins, skeletons of animals, were placed on shelves, or hung on the walls side by side with old books, and dresses, and knives, and daggers, and pistols, and here and there a helmet or a mailed glove or a breastplate.

It seemed, indeed, like an old curiosity shop; for when you turned your head in another direction you saw hideous images of all kinds ranged on shelves, and side-boards, grinning mandarins, horrible Indian gods, and exaggerated representations of animals in china and painted wood.

To Quail's disordered mind, disordered and agonised now all the more by the scenes he had just passed through, the place had a weird look, which it might not have worn at any other time.

"Where am I?" he wailed out.

The young girl, who had taken at once a strange interest in him, immediately sprang up, and putting down her book, seized a lamp from the table and ran to him.

"Did you ask for anything?" she said.

"I asked where I was," he answered, in a faint voice, "but now I see your face, I remember. I hope I'm well enough to go home now."

The girl smiled.

"You'll be some time yet before you'll be well enough to go home," she said; "at least, so my father says. You have been very badly wounded and will have to take rest. Do you know the man who attacked you?"

Quail hesitated.

For an instant the idea occurred to him that by telling the truth—by explaining all Dick Hatherden's villany—he might rid himself of a deadly enemy, and secure, too, to Guy, and Will, and Simon Grandley an immunity from all treachery in the future.

But then the cunning which always seem inseparable from half-witted people suggested another plan.

If he gave Dick Hatherden up to justice he would most certainly be hanged.

This was not punishment enough.

Not return enough for the long hours of misery and privation and tyranny which he had been subjected to by Dick Hatherden and Bill Hazard.

No.

He would not betray him now.

He would wait till the summer of success was upon him—wait till everything appeared to smile upon him—and then, when he imagined that happiness was his, he would intervene to spoil his plans

—to upset his dreamings—to bring misery upon him just as he imagined happiness to be within his grasp.

So he resolved to be silent.

"No," he said, feebly; "it was too dark to see anyone's face. I suppose it was one of the ruffians who attacked me in the street."

"But he said he had saved you from them," returned the girl.

"Did he? Very likely," said Quail.

Then he lapsed into silence.

"Father," said the young girl, who seemed to have taken a wonderful interest in their unexpected patient, "I think you are wanted here."

The old man rose, and approached the bed solemnly.

"Why am I wanted?" he said.

"See how pale he looks—how ghastly, and yet he talks of wanting to go home," she answered. "Why, I should think it would about kill him to move him."

"It would, indeed," he said, significantly; "but I will provide against anything of that kind."

Then he leaned over the bed.

"My boy," he said, "you have been severely injured. Don't you know that?"

"Yes," groaned Quail, "I do, indeed. I'm in dreadful pain."

"Then you must not think of moving yet. To-morrow, or the next day, perhaps, you may be able to get about; but meanwhile you must remain here, or inflammation might set in, and then, you know, you would die. No, no. You can send for any friend you please; but as for moving, we can't allow it."

He then quitted the bedside, raked about among a number of bottles, and presently returned with some medicine, which he made the patient swallow.

"There," he said, nodding meaningly at his daughter, "you'll find there'll be no more home-sickness now, Alva."

And he was right.

With the young girl seated by his side he dozed off into dreams of paradise and houris, and was soon wrapped in a profound and peaceful slumber.

CHAPTER XXXV.

WITHIN THE WALLS OF OLD NEWGATE.

WE must now quit Quail and his newly-found friends, and request our readers to accompany us inside the walls of Old Newgate.

The prison in the days of which we write had a far different kind of government to what it has now.

Prisoners, if uncondemned, were allowed to roam about its dismal inner yards, and indulge in all kinds of boisterous games.

They were certainly unable to drink, but they made up for this by the noise and tumult they made, substituting a kind of mental for physical drunkenness.

Some week or so after the first entrance of Bill Hazard into the gloomy precincts of the "stone jug," as it was facetiously named by the footpads

of the day (from which, be it said, he could scarcely hope to issue with life), he was in the yard with several others, when a quarrel arose among the prisoners.

One of them had struck another an unfair blow, or he had cheated at some game.

However this might be, a fight commenced, and in a few moments it became general.

The governor of the gaol, who was seated in his room with two gentlemen, heard the tumult, and started from his chair in alarm.

They had been, were even then, engaged in discussing the events which had lately occurred at the "Lamb and Fleece," and the probable fate of those rioters who had been arrested already, and were confined in the strongest cells in the prison.

A murderer like Bill Hatherden might have liberty to roam the yard.

Not so one guilty of high treason.

"See," cried one of the gentlemen, pointing to the window; "see the yard is full of rioters. The prisoners have risen."

The governor turned pale.

Not that he was a coward.

Not so.

He merely had a kind of foreshadowing of what was coming in the future.

"This is really very shocking," he said, "very shocking. What is to be done?"

"Throw open the window," said the first speaker, "and let us all threaten to fire upon them if they do not desist."

And without even waiting for the governor's permission he threw open the window.

The governor advanced at once and leaned out.

He was a brave man, in fact, was this Captain Desford, and could have faced all the howling raging crew undauntedly.

"Hold there! What means this?" he shouted in a stentorian voice; "have ye all gone mad? Or do ye want me and my friends here to fire a shot or two amongst ye to keep ye civil? Stop that riot there, or by Heavens I fire."

The sound of the loud and well-known voice had the desired effect.

All desisted and glanced up at the window.

Among those who looked most earnestly, and kept their eyes fixed there the longest, was Bill Hazard.

Why, we will explain by-and-bye.

The others huddling together, and muttering hideous curses and blasphemies, listened for some more.

"The next time I find such a disturbance as this," proceeded the captain, "I'll make a representation to the authorities, and I'll stop this yard exercise altogether. Ye shall all be confined to your cells. Mark my words—you know I don't talk for amusement."

They knew it too.

They remembered well how grimly the old fellow had stood by at execution after execution.

So he had no need to say more.

The grumbling crowd—all but Bill Hazard—separated into various groups, and commenced their amusements again.

He, for his part, stood with folded arms gazing up at the governor's house.

There he remained full half an hour, apparently deep in thought.

What he was thinking of the next chapter will show.

CHAPTER XXXVI.

BILL HAZARD'S COMPANION, FLAXMAN, TELLS HIS STORY—THE DISCARDED SON—THE LIFE OF CRIME—THE RICH BRIDE—THE LONE HOUSE—THE ATTEMPTED BURGLARY—THE MURDER AND THE CAPTURE.

IT so happened that one of the men who had been the chief instigators of the disturbance in the prison-yard was the companion of Bill Hazard in his cell.

He was in a most moody state that evening when they were locked up together; and until the turnkeys had brought them their last meal, Bill did not attempt to disturb him.

When they were alone, however, he spoke.

"I say, Bob Flaxman," he said, "what ails you?"

"Oh, the devil ails me," growled the other; "I don't want to talk."

"I dare say not," returned Bill; "nor should *I* care to talk, if I hadn't something particular to say. I want to help you—so, no flam."

"Help me," said the other, with an oath; "I wish you'd help me to crack that fellow's skull that cheated me—that cursed Bob White—the sneak! the coward!"

"How did he cheat you?"

"Why, my Madge," said the man, who, in spite of his statement that he didn't want to talk, was evidently glad to get the matter off his mind, "my Madge brought me a guinea yesterday—poor girl! it's all she was able to scrape together for me—and that cursed White, he knew it, and when we were out in the yard we were 'dicing,' and he cheated me. I was going to take up my money again, but he was too quick for me. That's why I struck him."

"Well, maybe you'll soon be able to pay him out," said Bill, "when you both get out again."

The man shook his head.

"I don't know what Bob White's in for," he said, "and so I can't tell what chance he has of getting out. But as for me, unless I get through the stone walls against the governor's wish, I don't go till I go to be stretched."

"This is my man," thought Bill, and his evil heart gave a thump.

"Tell us," he said, "what you're in for."

"Well," said the other, sententiously, "I don't mind if I do. Mind, I'm not one of that lot that's so innocent—that never did anything. I don't pretend to be a lamb. I *did* my bit, and if I hadn't been found out, I'd a' been a member of a haristocratic club, and driven my pair as well as any of the nobs. Oh, I've been a bit of a dandy in *my* time, I can tell you. I've been dressed up to that 'ere style of gentility that you'd a' taken me for a prince."

"Well, well," said Bill Hazard, impatiently, as he glanced at his companion's well-formed person, and contrasted it with his own long and shambling limbs; "never mind what you *have* been—think of what you *may* be."

"May be!" laughed the other; "perhaps what I *may* be will be a cold body in Dr. Corpus's dissecting room. But come! as I see you are impatient for my little story, I'll begin. I shan't make it long, for I'm rather anxious to know what you're in such a cursed fidget about."

"Something for the good of both of us," said Bill Hazard.

"I dare say," returned Flaxman. "Well, you must know, in the first place, that I'm a discarded son. I was brought up pretty decent until I was about ten years of age, when my mother married again. My stepfather was a great brute, and used to pitch into me so much that at last I flung a knife at him. He beat me frightfully for that, and when I complained of it to my mother, she told me to 'go to the devil.' I think I've done exactly what she told me.

"Well, I ran away, and got among the street boys, who soon taught me how to steal, and for years I did nothing but live on handkerchief-lifting and so. Then I took to higher branches of the profession—did a little highway robbery and so forth—and got in 'quod' many a time. And so time passed away till I met Madge, and she came to live with me.

"She was always begging and praying of me to live an honest life, and I resolved to make one grand sweep, and then quit the road for ever.

"I laid in wait for bankers, for lawyers, for

"THE GOVERNOR STARTED TO THE WINDOW IN ALARM."

farmers; but, as luck would have it, they seemed to be afraid to take any money out with them. And so I kept on, as if Fate was cutting out for me the job which has brought me here.

"I was sitting—down in the dumps enough, I can tell you—in the taproom of an inn, a little way westward of London, one evening, when I heard a man say—

"'Have you heard about the good fortune of the mistress up at the Holly House?'

"'No,' said the chap he addressed; 'no, I haven't.'

"And then they went on to tell how this lady had been lately married to a Captain Barfoot, who had not long been home from India; and that whereas she was but a poor woman before, her house now was full of wealth, and not only wealth in coin, but in golden ornaments.

"You can think how my heart bounded at this. Here was my golden dream about to be realised. I would rob this house, where wealth could so easily be spared, and I would then quit the road for ever, and retire in peace to the arms of my Madge.

"The very next night I resolved to put this scheme into execution, and as if to hurry me on to it, it came in as black as ink, and with a gloomy wind howling about, so that my doings could not be heard.

"I had made a number of inquiries in the neighbourhood during the day, and the result of these was that the captain had gone to London, to make some purchases for his newly-married wife, and would not be back for two days.

"The house was only guarded by two female servants, and a gardener who slept in the stable-loft.

"So far all seemed to promise favourably.

"At length night came, and with its arrival off I was in the direction of the rear of the premises.

"The neighbourhood was, as you have already understood, a very quiet one, and I met no one on my road.

"So far so good.

"All was going well with me.

"I could not be recognised, even if the robbery should be discovered, and I should be accused of it.

"So on I went, light-hearted enough, I can tell you, already counting my golden eggs.

"The garden at the back was only fenced.

"It was no difficult matter for me, therefore, to make my way into the garden, and I then saw, to my unspeakable joy, that the stable (in the loft of which the old gardener slept) was quite disconnected from the house, and that it would be next to an impossibility that he could hear any cries that arose from the house.

"I need not bother you with any details.

"I soon stood within one of the bed-chambers—luxuriously furnished, and seeming to me like a promise of the wealth I should find in other parts of the building.

"For some moments I imagined that the place was uninhabited; but when I closed the window, the warmth of the atmosphere told me that some one was sleeping there.

"Rendered more cautious by this discovery, I advanced on tiptoe, intending to make my way out of this room and proceed to those that were untenanted.

"But as my ill-luck would have it, just as I had half crossed the room I caught sight of a box—a likely-looking box—which seemed to tell of golden treasures within.

"Accordingly, I made my way to the table where it lay.

"Its key was lying by its side.

"I seized it eagerly.

"But, as bad fortune would have it, I knocked something over, which fell with a heavy thud to the ground.

"I glanced round at once.

"The sleeper had not moved.

"'So far so good,' thought I, and at once, with renewed courage, proceeded to make my search for the golden treasure.

"The key was turned in the lock, the glittering sovereigns were before me, when my throat was seized by a strong hand.

"'I have been deceived. The captain is here,' thought I.

"But I was wrong.

"When I turned round, eager to face the man who was robbing me of my booty, I saw, to my utter amazement, a woman, standing in her night-dress, her dishevelled hair falling over her shoulders—her eyes gleaming brightly through the darkness.

"'Villain!' she cried, 'what do you here?'

"As you may guess," said Flaxman, with a hideous smile, "I wasn't very anxious to give any explanations, or enter into any special conversation with the lady.

"So I just aimed a blow at her, which staggered her a bit, but didn't make her let go her hold.

"Instead of doing this she screamed with all her might, and with a violent effort dragged me to the window.

"There the moonlight streamed in full upon her, and I saw who it was.

"It was my mother!

"She, then, was the one who had suddenly come into so much riches by marrying a third time.

"The recognition was mutual.

"It flashed from our eyes before it was spoken of by our tongues.

"'Villain,' she cried, 'I know you—you are my son Robert. This then is what you have come to.'

"'Sweet mother,' said I, pressing her throat so that she could shriek no more; 'sweet mother, you bade me go to the devil, and I have been going there my own way; and now, dearest parent, I am going to send you there before me.'

"While I had been talking, I had drawn my knife, and in another moment I had plunged it into her breast.

"She gave one gasping cry, and fell down with such a look in her eyes as I shan't easily forget; and then I thought all my troubles were over, and I should be able to go on with my work in peace.

"But this was not to be.

"Her screeching had aroused the place, and the women came yelling into the room, followed by the

gardener, who, for reasons best known to himself, had slept in the house that night.

"They all laid on me like a lot of devils, and before I could well make any attempt at escape I was knocked on the floor, bruised and battered by sticks and pokers.

"When I came to my senses I was here; and that's the end of my story."

There was something inexpressibly horrible about the cool manner in which the ruffian had told his story—something so coldblooded, so hideously and outrageously brutal, that even Bill Hazard regarded him with a kind of a disgusted wonder.

He took care, however, that Flaxman did not perceive this, for brute beast as he was, he was just the one for the job he proposed.

So, repressing the disgust, which even he, assassin as he was, felt for the man who could thus coolly tell of the murder of his own mother, he said—

"Well, then, if that's been your game, you've no chance of escape."

"No, indeed—I told you that my next appearance on any stage would be on a dissecting room table," laughed the other.

"Well, I'll change your ideas of that," said Bill Hazard; "I mean to make my escape."

"Your escape?"

Then a loud laugh followed expressions of utter ridicule and disdain of the idea.

"You can laugh and jeer as much as you please," growled Bill, "but what I say I mean, and before a week's gone I'll be a free man. If you don't care to help, stop where you are, and be hanged, as you most certainly will be. If you like to help me, and get out of this den, why then I'll tell you my plan."

There was something so resolute and determined in the manner of the speaker that the matricide began to be convinced that he had really some definite idea.

"Speak on then," he said. "I thought you were only having the laugh of me: but if you really mean what you say, I'm your man. It can but get us shot, and that's better than being hangèd any day of the week."

"Well, then," said Bill Hazard, "the fact is that when you and your companion made that disturbance in the yard, the governor opened his window and said he would fire on us."

"Yes—I heard him."

"Well, then, as I wasn't one of the chaps as was making the noise, I wasn't going to stop there and be shot, and so I slides away, and puts my back up against the wall, where I could look on. Then, as I looks up at the governor's window, I sees that his house is the lowest part of the whole prison, and that if a fellow could get on top of his roof he can climb along and make his way to the top of the outer wall. It's as easy as boiling eggs."

"Yes," said Flaxman, "when you're once on the roof; but you've to get there."

"Why, that's easier still," said Bill Hazard. "There's a big water-pipe running up from the yard to the very top of his house. We can climb up this, and if we break our necks in trying, why, as you

say, it's better to die like that than be hanged. The real difficulty is how to get out of this 'ere cell, and that we must do together."

"And how?"

"Wait till the warders come for their last round to-morrow night, and then overpower them. Take their keys—get out into the yard—you know the rest."

"Why not to-night?" asked Flaxman, who was now becoming excited.

"We have no weapons. See here," said Bill Hazard, and with the words he rose, and approaching his bed, showed his companion a long piece of iron, which had been used to mend the bedstead, and was now fastened to it by screws.

"Here's a weapon for both of us," he said; "and this," he added, producing two long nails, "is all we have to work with to detach it."

"No matter," said Flaxman; "we must do our best."

And so they began.

All through that night, except when the warders came for their last round, those two hardened villains worked in the darkness, with the two long nails, whose points they had sharpened into miniature chisels on the stone floor.

The early morning light enabled them to labour more surely, and ere breakfast-time came they were enabled to desist awhile and sleep, certain that, as soon as they required the implements, a few minutes would place them ready to hand.

At length evening once more came, and the two desperadoes—one now as thoroughly roused as the other—awaited eagerly the time when their deliverance from confinement—and, in fact, from certain death—should arrive.

By supper-time the implements were ready.

But at the meal-time any attempt would have been extremely dangerous, as the last visit would take place within a quarter of an hour afterwards.

The time between supper-time and the last visit was occupied in crushing up the two tin plates on which their food was placed into a roll, with a point, so as to form a kind of dagger; and in forming out of the bedclothes two tolerably strong ropes, which they rolled round their bodies.

Then they waited patiently.

Presently the unsuspecting warders entered the cell.

The two ruffians remained still until their intended victims had advanced into the centre of the cell.

Then one rushed towards the door and closed it with a clang.

He could have escaped then.

But of what use would it have been without the keys?

So, having shut it, he sprang upon one of the men, while Bill Hazard, with half the iron from the bedstead, dashed upon the other.

The men were so taken aback by the suddenness of the assault, that they were unable to cry out, and, indeed, if they had done so, their shout would have been heard but a little way from the cell.

"Give us the keys quickly, and let us bind you," said Bill Hazard, as he held one of the warders by

the throat, "and we won't harm you. Refuse, and you'll find that we are awkward people to trifle with."

Flaxman, who was holding the other warder by the throat against the wall, and was jobbing his head against the stone wall, paused for a moment for the answer to Bill Hazard's question.

Not that he shrank from another deed of blood.

Not at all.

But the time necessary to kill these two strong men would be considerable, and during the delay other warders might arrive to know the reason of their comrades' absence.

"I will *not* give the keys," replied the turnkey steadily; "and the best advice I can give you is to loose your hold of me, or you may find yourself in the wrong box."

This was enough.

With a savage curse Bill Hazard raised his iron and struck him on the head.

Flaxman followed his example, and in an instant all four were struggling for life or death.

It was a silent, murderous fight.

No mercy was now to be expected on either side, and to call out was useless.

The keepers truly were strong men.

But they fought at a disadvantage.

They had not the vision before them of a shameful and public death, even though now they were in great peril.

Bill Hazard and Robert Flaxman, of course, were roused to a fiendish state of brutality.

And by this they conquered at length.

While Flaxman held his man by the throat and throttled him against the wall, Bill Hazard got his antagonist on the ground, and was beating him on the head with the heavy iron.

"Mercy!" at length groaned the wretched man, in a dying voice.

"You'll get a lot of mercy now," cried Bill, with a fearful oath; "you should have given in before.

"We've no time to waste on you now."

And with the words another terrible blow ended the poor wretch's career for ever.

Then Bill hurried to aid his companion.

The warder was a far more powerful man than the prisoner, and had the other been able to hold his own against Hazard the tide of affairs would most certainly have turned in favour of justice.

As it was, however, Hazard having disposed of his own enemy, came up behind the warder and dealt him a terrible blow on the top of the head.

A blow which at once settled the matter, for without even a groan he fell to the floor dead.

"Ugh!" said Bill, wiping his face, "this has been a long and a tough job. Let's get the keys and be off."

A search of the bodies of the two unfortunate men soon brought to light the keys.

The next thing was to assume the uniforms of the men, and perfect the disguise.

This they were not long in doing, and though the fit of the clothes was anything but exact, the ruffians hoped that in the semi-darkness they would pass unchallenged.

Issuing from the cell where the two victims of

their brutal violence lay still and cold in the light of the dismal lamp, the two men hurried off along the corridor, until they reached an iron-bound door.

This they unlocked with trembling hands, and found themselves in a kind of hall.

On one side was the room in which the turnkeys sat, and on the other was the entrance to the yard.

As ill-luck would have it, everything seemed to favour the two villains.

The turnkeys were all on their duties, and so, without interruption, the prisoners unlocked the door and found themselves in the open air.

"It isn't so close here as in the cell, is it?" said Bill Hazard, with a laugh.

"It'll be better still outside," growled Flaxman. "Let's be quick. All the time I'm out here I feel as if I were being pursued."

They hurried on now to the governor's house, where lights were still to be seen in the windows.

The water-pipe was soon found, and Bill Hazard first began the ascent.

He soon found, however, that in his eagerness he had made a miscalculation.

The water pipe was a strong one, and was easily climbed.

But it did not reach the roof.

About three yards from it, it passed *into* the wall, and ascended within the brickwork to an inner gutter.

This was an impediment upon which he had not reckoned.

However, having succeeded so far, he was resolved not to be beaten in the end, and he at once cast about him for another mode of retreat.

Near the spot where he hung was a window partially open, and from the pipe to this ran a narrow coping, not more than six inches wide.

This to an ordinary individual, not impressed, as *he* was now, with the certainty of a shameful death, would have seemed an insurmountable obstacle.

To Bill Hazard, however, it was nothing.

He had hazarded worse than this before, and accordingly he gently stepped on the coping, pressing his body up against the brickwork and clutching at it with his fingers.

With a very slow progression, he at length made his way to the window and passed his arm in at the opening.

Then he peered in.

The room was empty; and so, without wasting a thought on his companion, who was waiting and wondering below in the yard, he threw up the sash and entered.

No one was in the room.

It was, in fact, a kind of ante-chamber, and as the door of communication was open, he passed through, and found himself in a bedroom, where a pretty girl, about eighteen, was just setting her lamp on the table, preparatory to undressing for bed.

On seeing him she uttered a wild shriek of terror.

THE RIVAL APPRENTICES

A TALE OF THE RIOTS OF 1780.

"OUY RUSHED FORWARD AND SEIZED DICK BY THE THROAT."

It was not a loud shriek, but a kind of smothered cry of horror.

When the ruffian approached nearer to her she seemed struck dumb.

There she stood, glancing at the ruffian as he neared her with upraised fist, her eyes gleaming wildly, her pretty bosom heaving tumultuously with emotion, as if it would burst from the bonds which held its exquisite roundness, her hands clenching, and her every limb quivering with terror.

She seemed as it were fascinated by the sight of the villain who had so unexpectedly made his entrance.

"What do you here?" she contrived to murmur, in a quavering, uncertain voice.

"I am not here to harm you," said Bill Hazard, who had, indeed, no desire to be delayed by another crime; "all I wish for is that you will be silent and let me pass."

At this moment the girl started again into a fresh attitude of terror, and turning round Bill Hazard saw that Flaxman had followed his example and entered the room.

"Oh! what means this?" murmured the young girl. "Oh! say—you do not mean harm to my father?"

"Your father, girl," said Bill, gruffly. "Who's he?"

"Captain Desford, the governor."

"The governor—whew!" exclaimed Bill, as he shut the window, and pushed the door to also. "That makes a little difference. I was going out of the room without more to do, but now I can't. If you're the governor's daughter why I know well that you won't allow us to do what *we* want quietly. So here goes."

With these words he took from his pocket a portion of the rope which they had constructed out of the bedclothes, and seizing her wrist, added—

"Now then, young girl, look here. We don't want to harm you, but we must bind and gag you for our own safety's sake."

She sank on her knees.

Her bosom heaved violently, and she glanced up at the men in a kind of agony.

"My father—my father!" she murmured, clasping her hands, "you would not injure him!"

"No—no," said Bill Hazard, "we merely desire to make our escape, and to hurt no one."

As he said this he drew her arms behind her with a twist and proceeded to bind them together, while Flaxman busied himself in undoing a piece of stuff ready for a gag.

She would have submitted to all this quietly—have calmly allowed them to bind and silence her, since they had promised not to harm her father.

But suddenly her eyes rested upon stains, the meaning of which she could not mistake.

Stains of blood!

She knew they must be human!

These convicts, fresh from their cells, must also be fresh from murder!

The thought maddened her.

She forgot her own danger.

She forgot that prudence dictated silence.

Horror over-mastered every other feeling.

One stony look she cast upon them.

Then her terror gave itself vent in a wild agonised cry.

This sealed her fate.

In an instant she saw it.

"Oh! that's your game, is it?" said Bill Hazard, furiously.

And drawing out one of the sharp-pointed instruments which he had fashioned out of the tin plates, he seized her by the back of her hair, drew her head back, and drove it into her bosom, where it quivered between the snowy breasts, as if terrified by being brutally driven into that soft abode of purity and beauty.

One horrified glance she cast at her murderers.

Once the now freed hands were raised, and pressed in agony over the bosom, where the blood now streamed over the white flesh.

Then all was over.

"'Twas a pity," said Bill, as she fell back dead; "but there, it's no use talking about it. We were bound to look to ourselves."

"Yes," returned Flaxman, with an oath, "and so we shall have to with a vengeance."

"What mean you?" cried Hazard, turning quickly to the other, who had approached the door and opened it.

"Why, I hear footsteps coming up. Put out the light—quick."

Hazard lost no time in following his friend's injunction.

Only just in time, too, was he.

Hardly had the room been enveloped in darkness when the door was flung open, and three persons rushed in, and fell headlong over the body of the governor's daughter as it lay on its back bathed in blood.

This was the time for the convicts.

In an instant they rushed out, and fled headlong down the stairs.

In the darkness the governor and his two friends knew nothing, of course, of the murder, but the cry which had escaped the lips of the young girl, and the flight now of the two men, told them at once that some villany had been at work.

Rushing out of the room, therefore, and shouting for help, the two friends dashed after the convicts, leaving Captain Desford to see to the young girl, whom they supposed to be in a dead faint.

He, however, as his hand came in contact with her still warm bosom, and felt the instrument of murder still sticking between her breasts, saw at once how matters stood; and wild with fury—utterly unable to conceive a reason for the murder of his innocent child—he left her where she was, and followed his friends.

Bill Hazard and his companion, however, were now beyond reach.

Hearing the shout and the footsteps they had come to a standstill on the staircase, knowing that to proceed farther would be madness, if they were to be taken front and rear as well. As soon as their pursuers came up to them they made a sudden dash, and striking them with their clenched fists in the face, hurled them backwards on the stairs.

Then they once more descended at a run, just as Captain Desford, plunging down, went sprawling over the bodies of his friends.

Their progress to the front door was now unimpeded, and in a few moments they were in the street.

"I'm off to Carlton's!" cried Bill, and away he rushed; while Flaxman took another direction.

Stopping a moment in a dark street to tear off some of the evidences of murder that still disfigured him, Bill hurried into a tavern and swallowed some brandy.

Then he hurried off again.

At the corner of the street he saw a carriage, and as it slowly passed him he caught sight of two faces he knew well.

The one was the face of Guy the Foundling.

The other was that of Jessie Hardarker, the daughter of the murdered blacksmith.

Bill Hazard stood in amazement looking after the coach.

What could it mean?

What was Guy the Foundling doing with Jessie?

How came they together?

Jessie's face was as pale as marble, and her whole expression was one of agony.

He had it.

He would follow the carriage.

Circumstances aided him well.

A hackney coach came by at this moment, and he at once hailed it.

"Follow that carriage for me," he said to the man, "and wherever it stops, stop a few yards off."

He then jumped in, and keeping his head out of window, he watched the carriage as they rattled on.

Presently it seemed as if a struggle or commotion of some kind was going on in the carriage.

Then a man, or a very large bundle, was tossed from it, and he heard the cry of a human voice, or the scream or yell of a wounded beast.

But the clatter and rattle of the cab wheels upon the road, and the distance between the two vehicles, made the ear of Bill Hatherden uncertain in this matter; and, indeed, he was not sure that his eyes had not deceived him in the obscurity of the night light.

Presently the carriage stopped at the door of a large house.

Guy the Foundling descended, and helping Jessie Hardarker to alight also led her into the house.

The cab containing Bill Hazard stopped some yards off.

The pavement before the house being brilliantly illuminated by two ornamental lamps near the kerbstone, it was easy for Bill Hazard to discern the departure of those in the carriage, and their entrance into any of the houses near it.

"They have gone into the house, have they not?' said he to the driver.

"Yes, into the house of Ephraim Carter, the lawyer."

"Are you sure at this distance? Had we not better go nearer?"

"No, I can trust my sight. I can see well at this distance. He has taken the young girl into Ephraim Carter's. He's a cute man that Carter. I know him well."

"What can she be doing?" said Hazard to himself.

"What you will never guess," answered the voice of one who seemed to rise from the very ground.

He came up from the earth as it were, a shadow within a shadow, and grasped the edge of the cab window with both hands, as Bill jerked his head back from the window.

CHAPTER XXXVII.

BILL HAZARD MEETS AN OLD FRIEND—THE RIVALS —THE CHIEF OF THE BOW-STREET RUNNERS — THE ATTACK — THE COMPACT — THE CAB APPROACHES NEWGATE—THE PROCLAMATION— THE OWL CONCEIVES A PLAN OF TREACHERY.

IT was too dark in that deep shade to discern features, yet the man who had thus suddenly risen from the ground thrust his head in at the cab window, saying, in a low voice—

"Bill Hazard."

Instantly after, just in time to escape the thrust of a knife then being drawn to strike him, he imitated with his lips the shrill sound of a night bird—a sound indeed very much like the sharp song of the locust.

Bill Hazard at once dropped the hand which held the knife.

He evidently knew the newcomer.

"Ah!" he said; "it is The Owl, is it?"

"Yes; I am The Owl."

"I thought you were dead."

"And I had the same idea as regards you, my friend," replied The Owl; "at least, if not dead, I thought you were safely caged in the stone jug. But it matters not. It seems we are both alive, and in pursuit of the same purpose."

These words stung Bill Hazard to the quick.

To enable the reader to understand the reason why we must ask him to accompany us back for a few moments.

For "the same purpose" meant to ascertain why Guy the Foundling was with Jessie Hardarker, and for what purpose she was visiting the house of the lawyer with him.

The fact was that Alec Redford—(known always as "The Owl," because of his being so awake to his knaveries in the dark, when others could not see)— was a lover of Jessie Hardarker.

The lovely girl had had the misfortune to win the affections of two of the greatest ruffians that could in those days be found in London.

Consequently Bill Hazard and The Owl were rivals.

They knew it.

They hated one another for that reason.

But now?

Both were in uncertainty.

Jessie, knowing the hideous crime of which Bill Hazard had been guilty, loved him, of course, no longer.

But, of course, The Owl knew nothing of this.

He was aware that Hazard had been committed to Newgate, and, though Jessie had on a former occasion refused to listen to him, and though now she was overwhelmed with grief, he had gone on this very evening to her father's house, hoping that while he consoled her he might urge once more the love suit he had once thought hopeless.

It was a strange thing, indeed, that he or Bill Hazard should have loved Jessie Hardarker.

She was so entirely opposed in every respect to their brutal natures.

Coming of a healthy and sturdy stock she was plump and well formed, with strong, well-made limbs, and a form altogether calculated to rouse the admiration of any man.

But then, on the other hand, this voluptuous exterior concealed a heart which was one of purity, innocence, and goodness.

On this evening, when The Owl made his way to her father's house, he was surprised by seeing her issue forth, clad in the deepest black, which spoke of her recent sorrow, and enter a hackney coach.

His jealous heart at once prevented his addressing her.

"I will watch," he thought.

And he *did* watch.

What did he discover?

He saw her drive to the house of Simon Grandley, and issue forth again, accompanied by Guy the Foundling.

But he knew not what had transpired within.

He knew not that Jessie had been there to plead with the carpenter to aid her in investigating the crime of which her lover was accused.

He knew not that Bill Hazard was still, in her mind, a being incapable of a cool and deliberate murder.

She clung to the hope, faint as it was, that there had been a quarrel—that Bill Hazard had proved superior to the blacksmith in strength—that what was now termed a murder was only a fight.

Simon Grandley, though holding a far different opinion, consented to aid her, and—unable himself to accompany her—sent Guy the Foundling in his place.

And so we return to the moment when The Owl had stated that they were there for the same purpose.

"Then it was you that I saw tossed out of the carriage not fifteen minutes ago?" said Bill Hazard.

"Yes," said The Owl. "When I saw the hackney carriage waiting at the door of Simon Grandley the carpenter, I crept into it, and hid myself under the seat. Their conversation aroused me into fury, and I discovered myself. Then the fellow who was with her seized me by the throat and hurled me from the coach. Oh, what pain I am in! I have lost an eye, and had my teeth knocked down my throat. Curses on him who struck me. But let me get in there with you. Since we are both alive we must renew our old friendship and our old alliance."

This did not exactly suit Bill Hazard.

"Get in here," he growled, as he opened the door; "but I do not know yet that we are to be allies."

"Ah, you are in a rage," said The Owl, pausing with one foot in the cab; "you are meditating an assault upon me."

"No; I am not in a rage."

"Bah! I have but one eye left, and in this darkness, if I had a hundred, I could not see your face, my friend; but I have ears to hear, and your voice tells me that mischief is brewing. Take care, however; remember, The Owl has talons."

"Get in, fool!" said Bill Hazard; "I was excited by your unexpected appearance. I shall be in a rage, perhaps, if you insult me. Get in! perhaps it will be best for us both to be allies again."

"I think so," said The Owl, as he sprang into the cab.

It contained two seats—a back and a front.

Bill Hazard sat on the former.

The Owl seated himself upon the latter.

"I have my knife in my hand, Bill Hazard, remember that!" said The Owl.

"Good!" said Bill; "and I also. Remember that!"

"A scratch from mine makes an end of you."

"I should live two seconds after the scratch, friend. In half that time I could split you as a fisherman does a mullet."

It was in this amiable manner that these two "friends" met and settled matters after a separation of nearly six months.

While this was passing two vehicles, coming from different directions, were nearing the cab.

One of them was the one which had conveyed Guy the Foundling and Jessie Hardarker to the house of the lawyer.

The driver was now driving slowly, casting his eyes about in search of the body of the man whom he had seen flung out.

"Ha!" he said, presently; "is not that a cab I see in the shade there?"

He halted his horses abruptly.

The light of the carriage lamps had revealed the vicinity of the cab, and at the same instant the vehicle which was driving slowly from the other end of the street also halted.

"Ah, ah!" said he; "it appears this street is not so deserted after all. It must have been somewhere about here that my fare pitched his friend out."

"Hallo, there!" shouted the driver of the third vehicle at this moment. "Why don't you drive on?"

"Because I am not sure of places here about. It is seldom I have business here about. This is Redford Street, is it not?"

"Yes; of course it is. Cannot you see the name of the street yonder?"

The driver was silent a moment.

He was again looking for the body.

"Whom have you got in there?" asked the cabman.

"Lieutenant Halmer, the chief of the Bow Street runners."

"Do you hear that?" growled Bill Hazard to The Owl.

"Yes; wait a moment. He arrived a few days since from the country," said The Owl; "but hush. Let us hear what these cabmen are chattering about."

Accordingly they listened.

But the conversation of the cabmen soon lapsed into mere gossip, and impatient of the delay, Lieut. Halmer thrust his head out of window and bawled out—

"Will you never be done with your abominable gabble? Drive on, rascal."

"It *is* Halmer, as I live," exclaimed The Owl, in a whisper, and with difficulty, for his mouth and gums were terribly bruised.

"I wonder where he can be going to," said Bill Hazard; "but, after all, it's most likely he's going to the lawyer's. He has, no doubt, heard something in regard to the riots, and is about to begin weaving a web around the Protestant Association. Ha, ha!"

"Bah! no such thing," said The Owl, spitting out another tooth. "There, that makes five teeth in all I have lost, and an eye."

"Curses on your teeth and your eyes," cried Bill Hazard, savagely. "That is certainly Lieutenant Halmer."

"Of course it was. He is in that cab."

"He must know then that I have escaped, and perhaps——"

His speech was cut short by a loud cry from the other vehicle.

"Here," roared the lieutenant of police, dashing open the door of the hackney coach, and scrambling to the ground; "I go no further with such an ignorant fool for a driver. I paid you in advance, curse you! or I would not have given you a halfpenny. But, mark me! I'll prosecute you for this. Here, you other fellow," he added, addressing the man who drove Hazard's vehicle, "can I have a seat in your carriage as far as Newgate?"

"Certainly. Get in, sir," said Bill Hazard, answering for the cabman, and in a gentle voice, the voice of a very old man, "we are going in that direction, I and my friend."

It was too dark to distinguish features.

Lieutenant Halmer could hardly make out that two persons were in the cab, and he scrambled in, groaning, and saying—

"Thank you, gentlemen, whoever you are. I have the misfortune to be very sore and bruised. I was thrown from my horse this morning. It is not far, I believe, to Newgate?"

"No, sir," said Bill Hazard, who would not have seen the man for a sack of gold.

Then he leaned forward, and as the cab began to move, whispered in his ear—

"I am Bill Hazard, the murderer, escaped from Newgate, and if you so much as squeak you are a dead man."

"Bill Hazard!" echoed the lieutenant, with a chill of terror invading his very bones as he heard the words.

"And I am The Owl," whispered the man at his side; "you know how he punishes those whom he suspects to be traitors."

"Good Lord deliver me!"

"You may well say that," growled Bill Hazard; "you had discovered something about us, and were on your way to Newgate to inform."

"No—on my life no!"

"Then you have discovered something about the Protestant rising."

To this the lieutenant made no reply.

In fact he was unable to.

His tongue was powerless, from the consternation of his mind.

To have blindly stepped into a cab already occupied by two men of whom he stood in such dread—to be shut up with the ferocious Bill Hazard and the terrible Owl—to discover that they guessed his purpose in going to Newgate, made him quiver with terror from the crown of his head to the sole of his foot.

"Ha!" continued Bill Hazard, giving the arm of the trembling man a sharp pinch; "it is true, then, that you have discovered or else have suspected something."

"Discovered! Yes—I have made a charming discovery."

"Good; let us hear it."

"My charming discovery is, that my dear friends Bill Hazard and The Owl are alive, and in my company."

"Yes, in your company," said Bill Hazard, "in the company of a lieutenant of police,* who would at the first chance say to the authorities, 'Here are two great rascals, give them to the hangman without delay.' What then if you are Lieutenant Halmer, you will find I am Bill Hazard."

And with that the speaker seized him by the throat with both hands as if about to strangle him.

"Oh!" gasped Halmer, "I am a dead man!"

Quivering with his throat in the fierce grasp of Bill Hazard, and imagining that the poisoned knife which The Owl always carried with him was bared and raised to finish him, the unfortunate man was ready to give up the ghost in sheer terror.

Just then a flood of light poured into the cab through the window, and the cabman halted.

They were close to Newgate; and on the wall was a proclamation, hastily written out in large letters, telling of the murders, and the escape of the two men, and offering £100 for the capture of the two villains.

"If you say a word, or utter a cry, you are a dead man," said Bill Hazard in the ear of the lieutenant.

Then thrusting his head from the window, he exclaimed to the cabman—

"The gentleman has changed his mind. Drive on till I tell you to stop."

The cabman cared little how far or how long he drove, providing he was paid his fare, and not knowing or even suspecting what was going on in the cab, went on.

Lieutenant Halmer had been a sad rogue in his time, and while Bill Hazard and The Owl had kept their hands from murder had been a friend to them.

"Let us be allies and comrades as formerly," he said, finding that the grasp on his throat did not in any degree relax or grow tighter.

"Now you speak sensibly," said Bill Hazard, taking his hands from the neck of his captive; "tell us what brings you to London."

"Answer me first one question."

"It depends on what the question is."

At this point of the conversation it was interrupted by The Owl, who pretended to fall on one side.

His real object was to whisper in the ear of Lieutenant Halmer.

What he said—not even a whisper of what he said—reached Bill Hazard, or in spite of the fact that

---

* We use the word "police" here for convenience, although, of course, the force was not then in existence under that title.

they were two to one he would have dashed in upon them.

"We'll talk when we get out of this infernal close cab," said Lieutenant Halmer; "we don't want to be riding like this all night without a purpose. Stop at some inn if there is one open."

Bill growled his assent, and poking his head out of the carriage window stopped the vehicle

He was in no good humour, as may be easily imagined.

When he saw Jessie Hardarker sitting in the hackney coach with Guy the Foundling his first resolve was to wait their departure from the lawyer's house and attempt the murder of Guy.

Now his thoughts had been turned into a different channel by the extraordinary meeting which had taken place between him and the chief of the police.

He must first dispose of him.

Then with the aid of The Owl, and one or two other ruffians of his stamp, he would proceed to the house of the murdered blacksmith, see Jessie, carry her off, and compel her to become his wife.

CHAPTER XXXVIII.

THE TAVERN—THE TREACHERY OF THE OWL—THE ATTACK ON HIM BY BILL HAZARD—ALONE ONCE MORE IN NEWGATE.

THERE was a tavern close by where they had halted, and the three entered after dismissing the cab.

"This is not a very pleasant looking place," said the lieutenant; "I suppose, however, that you know it, Hazard?"

"I do," said The Owl; "there are plenty of *my* friends here."

These words, accompanied by a sly sidelong glance at the lieutenant, appeared thoroughly to satisfy that worthy, and the trio accordingly passed into the tap-room.

The hour was, as my readers are aware, a very late one.

The taproom consequently contained no one.

The last loungers were collected round the bar.

"Bring in some brandy—plenty of it," said Lieutenant Halmer; "our meeting at first was far from a pleasant one, and my nerves were sorely shaken."

The Owl at once volunteered.

He was absent about five minutes only

But while he had been away something had evidently happened to please him.

His face, always ugly, and now rendered thoroughly hideous by the blow which had deprived him of an eye and swollen up the parts, was illumined by a broad grin—a grin of evident malignity.

Bill Hazard began all at once to suspect something.

He knew not what it was, but there seemed in his mind a presentiment of evil.

However, he seized the brandy and drank eagerly.

While he did so some of the loungers came in and joined them.

Whether his own fears magnified matters it was impossible for him to say.

But he fancied that even they seemed suspicious in their movements.

Presently he understood all.

The conversation, now carried on by Lieutenant Halmer and himself, had become of a desultory character, and the former was evidently labouring under some suppressed excitement.

Suddenly the door opened and admitted three men.

Their costume at once proclaimed who they were.

They were Bow Street runners.

"Sold, by G——!" shouted Bill, as he sprang up.

One look at the face of The Owl was enough to tell him all.

The Owl had seen the reward, and had sold him to Lieutenant Halmer.

The thought maddened him.

He saw himself once more in Newgate—he saw The Owl left free to pursue Jessie with his attentions.

All this flashed across his mind in an instant, and leaping up, he seized The Owl by the throat.

"Villain!—traitor!" he cried, "it is you who have done this! Curse you—you shall die for it!"

And before anyone could prevent him he had grasped The Owl by the throat, and dashed him with such force against the stone chimney-piece that he fell bathed in blood on the floor.

His head had suffered severely when he had been flung by Guy out of the carriage, and this second assault rendered him utterly senseless.

Bill Hazard would have proceeded further, but he was prevented.

Otherwise The Owl would never have arisen from the ground alive.

The three Bow Street runners, however, assisted by the ruffians in the room, soon overpowered Bill, and in a few minutes he was standing handcuffed and helpless.

"You may stand grinning there, if you like," he said to Lieut. Halmer, who, in fact, showed every disposition to be merry at the turn affairs had taken; "but if you only knew what I felt in my heart you'd tremble."

"Why should I tremble?" asked the lieutenant, speaking more boldly now that his enemy was powerless to attack him; "you cannot harm me."

"No; but I'm not dead yet. Before I *am*, mark me, you'll be."

There was something so ferocious, so desperate, so prophetic, in the way the man said this that Halmer felt the same chill in the blood which he had experienced when riding with him in the cab.

"Away with him!" he said to the Bow Street runners, turning his back, and approaching the prostrate form of The Owl. "There is no occasion to waste time in listening to his mad words."

Bill Hazard saw there was no use in attempting resistance.

Not only were his wrists fastened with gyves, but a rope had been so secured round both ankles as to render quick locomotion impossible.

So he made no answer to the words of Lieutenant Halmer, but quietly passed out with the constables.

Within half-an-hour he was once more in a cell

—a strange cell—in Newgate, chained to the wall by wrists and ankles.

CHAPTER XXXIX.

JESSIE HARDARKER'S LOVE—THE MYSTERIOUS LADY —GUY GOES IN FOR A NEW ADVENTURE — AN UNEXPECTED MEETING — THE CONFLICT — THE TRAP—A HAZARDOUS TRIAL.

HAD Jessie Hardarker known the further terrible crimes of which Bill Hazard had been guilty there is no doubt that she would have at once dismissed from her mind all idea of assisting in saving him from death.

But, of course, she knew nothing of what had transpired at Newgate.

The escape of the convicts, and the murder of the warders and the governor's daughter, had occurred, as we have seen, just before her arrival with Guy the Foundling at the house of the lawyer, and ignorant, consequently, of how thoroughly depraved and horribly bloodstained the man whose cause she was pleading was, she appealed most earnestly to the advocate to save him.

In obedience to the kind dictates of his own warm heart, Simon Grandley had, as I have before mentioned, consented to aid her, for her own sweet sake, not for her ruffianly lover's.

And so, as she possessed money wherewith to pay, the lawyer agreed to do all he could—promised to employ able counsel, and gave great hopes of success.

On leaving the house Guy saw her to her door, and then hurried homewards.

He had to pass Newgate on his way, and there, staring him in the face, was the proclamation, telling of three fresh murders, and offering a reward for the capture of William Hazard and Robert Flaxman.

"Good heavens!" exclaimed Guy, as he shudderingly passed, "and it is for such a man that that gentle girl is exerting herself. Let us hope that when she hears of this she will discard him altogether."

He was hurrying home, passing round the corner of a narrow, low street, when he saw a young girl hurrying along by the side of a lad of his own age.

He could not in the semi-darkness distinguish the features of either.

His curiosity, however, was roused.

What was a girl of her years, and dressed elegantly, as she seemed to be, doing at such an hour in such a place?

He resolved to follow them, and discover, if he could, the mystery.

Perhaps under ordinary circumstances he would not have been induced to do this.

The peculiar events, however, which had crowded upon his young life of late caused his mind to be somewhat prone to suspicion, and to magnify things which would at any other time have seemed unimportant.

So he followed them.

Presently they turned down a still darker passage, but which had at its corner a bright lamp.

As Guy passed this the lad stopped the girl a moment, and he saw them pass.

They were the faces of Aurora Halsted and Dick Hatherden.

For an instant Guy could hardly believe the evidence of his senses.

But so it was.

He had heard from Quail, who was now somewhat recovered, that he had been attacked by Dick.

Quail had told this to Guy in confidence.

Otherwise, Hatherden would certainly have been expelled from the carpenter's house.

Feeling sure, now, however, that he was in the act of planning some fresh villany, Guy resolved to be on the watch, and as the two once more moved on he crept after them, and as they again stopped, pressed himself up into a doorway to listen.

"Let me advance first, Aurora," said Dick, "I must be careful, or we shall never be permitted to see your father. No one in the house knows that I am bringing you here. I only wish you had taken my advice and assumed boy's clothes."

"Never mind that now," returned Aurora, impatiently, as if annoyed at Dick Hatherden for holding back at the last moment. "I am here; and since my father has sent for me, let us hasten. I will not return now without seeing him."

The look which passed over Dick's face at this was seen by Guy alone. He understood its significance at once.

It was a look of triumph—of craft—of gratified malice.

He felt confident that he was leading the young girl into some trap, and he resolved to save her.

Dick now turned from Aurora, and approaching a door, pushed it slightly.

It opened at once, revealing a dark passage, into which Dick passed and gave a peculiar whistle.

This was answered from above, and then he emerged once more.

"Now then, Aurora," he said, "enter. It is very dark, but don't be afraid."

The young girl sprang forward eagerly.

She might be cool and calculating in other things, but she loved her father.

Guy the Foundling dashed forward just in time to prevent her entering.

"What are you doing here, Miss Halsted?" he said. "Excuse my interference, because I feel sure you are being deceived."

"I am here for the purpose of seeing my father," she began.

But Dick Hatherden interrupted her.

"Stay, Aurora," he said; "give him no satisfaction. What right has he to interfere with you in the performance of a sacred duty?"

Aurora Halsted, had it been a stranger who interrupted her, would certainly have haughtily demanded his reason for interference, and insisted upon his departing.

But as we have seen, her heart had been touched in its most tender point by the noble bearing and manner of Guy the Foundling, and now his strange and sudden appearance, and his evident eagerness

to prevent her entrance into the house, struck her so forcibly that she hesitated and trembled.

"Guy," she said, "tell me! Why do you not wish me to enter that house?"

"Because, Miss Halsted——. You will excuse my speaking openly and boldly?"

"Yes, yes! Speak out."

"Because, then, I believe that your father is dead—that he was the victim of foul play—and that you are being led into this place for some purpose known best to Dick Hatherden and his friends."

"You lie!" cried Dick, advancing threateningly towards him.

Guy rushed forward and seized him by the throat, while with his left hand he prevented Aurora's approach.

"Have a care," he cried; "have a care what words you use to me. I am no weak, wretched creature, like Quail, whom you can beat and ill use at your pleasure. Be civil, or you may find that I shall give you a thrashing which you may remember a long time."

As Dick made no pretence of resistance, Guy released him and turned to Aurora.

"What do you wish to do now, Miss Halsted?" he said.

"I think I must enter," she said, hesitatingly. "My father has sent for me, and if he is really there, what would he think of me were I to refuse to go?"

"Shall I enter with you then?" said Guy.

Aurora placed her hand on his arm appealingly, and looked up into his face.

"Oh! yes," she said, in a whisper, "if he will let you."

"He shall!" returned Guy.

Then approaching Dick Hatherden, he said—

"If no foul play is intended here, I also can enter and see the colonel."

Dick was in the shadow.

His face, therefore, could not be seen.

If Guy had but seen it he would have turned away, and compelled Aurora to leave the place with him and have taken her home.

As it was Dick answered promptly—

"Certainly, there can be no objection to that. But remember, if the colonel's whereabouts is betrayed to any one, we shall know who was the spy."

"I am no spy," said Guy the Foundling. "Now, Miss Halsted, since you wish it, let us enter together."

They accordingly entered the dark passage, and the door was closed behind them.

"Now then," said Dick Hatherden, in a whisper, "you must preserve silence while you are here. Follow me as softly as you can, for if I am found bringing you into this place, without first asking permission, something serious might happen."

He said this in such a manner as entirely to put Aurora Halsted off her guard, though Guy the Foundling had such an opinion of him that he suspected him always.

Along the dark passage they went—up a dark and narrow staircase, and then along an upper corridor.

At the extremity of this a faint light was visible, and towards this Dick Hatherden led them.

The light issued from a very small chamber, furnished in a style which seemed in no way consistent with the general appearance of the house.

It was indeed furnished in a style of the utmost luxury.

The carpet was soft and springy, the ottomans were of the most finished pattern, and replete with easy elegance; beautiful pictures and mirrors adorned the walls, and the window was shaded with crimson curtains.

Guy's heart misgave him.

Why had Aurora been brought here?

What manner of house was this whose exterior was so poor and even infamous, and whose interior was so grand?

"Remain here a moment," said Dick Hatherden, in a whisper, "and I will go and explain to the colonel the reason of your being here."

Then he hastily quitted the room, and in an instant there was heard the click of the key in the lock.

"You are caged now, Master Guy," cried Dick, in a loud voice, expressive of triumph and derision. "I have you, however, and since you have driven me to this you may expect the consequences."

There was no doubt in the mind of either Guy the Foundling or Aurora Halsted that they were trapped.

What, however, could be the fate which Dick Hatherden designed for her she could not conceive.

That he was angry and exasperated with her she had known when she had turned the cold shoulder upon him at Simon Grandley's.

But this evening he had more than renewed his vows of love.

He had declared himself as entirely forgiving her past scorn.

He had sworn that time would prove his utter innocence of all attempt at deluding her in regard to his birth and position, and without mentioning the names of any one person in particular he implied that all she had heard at the house of Simon Grandley was false.

"Now," he said, "I am going to take you to your father. He, at least, has not been turned from me by any calumnies."

It required truly a strong nerve to be able thus to speak of one who had been murdered by him in cold blood.

But Dick Hatherden was hardened in crime, and would have risked anything to secure to himself the prize he had sought so long.

Not that his passion for Aurora could rightly be called love.

It was unworthy the name.

It was, however, a passion as strong as could be expected in one so destitute of proper human feeling.

Then again, even if he did not love her, there was another incentive.

She was possessed of money.

THE RIVAL APPRENTICES

A TALE OF THE RIOTS OF 1780.

THE RIOT OUTSIDE THE "RED EAGLE."

As far as he was aware, there was no will left by her father, so that there was nothing which bound her to any particular course in regard to marriage.

While she was in the power of her guardians, however, his suit was simply an absurd one. He had resolved, therefore, no matter how, to take

her from them, trusting to time and persuasion to induce her to become his.

He had succeeded so far beyond his best hopes.

Not only was she in his power, but Guy also—his special, his hated foe.

The one, therefore, he would destroy.

"What can this mean, Guy?" cried Aurora, clasping her hands in terror. "Oh! I hope—I pray I may not have been deceived."

She clung to Guy's arm as she spoke, and looked in earnest appeal into his face, as if in it she could read her fate.

"I fear much," returned the Foundling, "that you have been most cruelly deceived. My belief is that your poor father is dead, and that whatever letter you received from him is but a forgery. If it were not so, why are we captive here? How could Dick Hatherden have the power to do us harm were the colonel here?"

"Alas!" murmured Aurora, "you take from me now all hope. See, here is the letter."

Guy took it and read it.

"DEAREST AURORA,

"I am concealed in a house whither Dick Hatherden can lead you. I dare not send before, or you should have long since heard from me. Tell no one of this letter, because, were my place of hiding once known, I should be arrested and cast into prison. Hasten, dear child, as I leave soon for France, and wish to see you and embrace you ere I go.

"Your affectionate but wretched father,

"ARTHUR HALSTED."

"Do you know his handwriting well?" asked Guy, when he had finished its perusal.

"No," returned Aurora; "I have seen but little of it. What I *have* seen of it, however, has been like this."

"Well, there is certainly some strange mystery in all this," said Guy. "I have most certainly a presentiment that all is not right here. However, time will soon show. If the colonel is here, we shall not be detained long."

"But remember Dick's words," said Aurora; "'you have driven me to this, and must take the consequences.' What does that mean?"

"Danger to me, but not to you," returned Guy. "He loves you—he hates me. This is the difference."

"He has, I fancy, made an absurd mistake," said Aurora, with a blush; "but it matters not. No harm shall befall you while *I* am here. Where *you* go I go."

Guy gazed in surprise at the young girl as she spoke thus boldly.

He had before imagined that Aurora Halsted had taken somewhat of a liking to him, when she first made her appearance at the house of Simon Grandley, after he had saved her at the peril of his life.

But he had no conception that any such strong feeling had arisen in her mind as would make her dream of aiding him at the peril of her life or liberty.

He was about to remonstrate with her, when a new terror arose for her.

There was a loud roar of laughter, a wild discordant peal, as of a number of persons half inebriated.

It proceeded evidently from some room in the house in which they were.

What could it mean?

Aurora glanced at Guy in terror.

In his face she saw nothing to reassure her.

"Oh, Guy!" she cried, bursting into tears, "where am I? What does it all mean?"

"Indeed, I know not," he said; "I fear to think. Let me try yonder window."

He pushed aside the red curtains which hung over it, and peered out.

A bright moon was shining, but its rays were slanting, and only the upper part of the open space at the back of the premises was lit by it.

He tried the casement, and finding it yield easily he threw it up.

"See here, Aurora," he said; "there are no bars —there is no impediment to my ascent. There is a water-pipe here. I can descend by that, and see if there is any mode of escape from below."

Aurora leaned out and glanced downwards as Guy impetuously leaped upon the window sill.

It was a good depth down even to the point where *she* could see.

How much farther it was below that point she could not tell.

All else was enveloped in utter darkness.

"Be careful, Guy," she said, as he swung himself off the sill, and grasped the water-pipe lightly; "it is a dangerous experiment. The depth is greater than you think."

Guy did not wait to listen for other words.

Sliding down without once looking below him, he at length passed from the moonlight into the darkness, and after a few moments touched the hard surface of the courtyard.

Naturally, when he had reached this point, he imagined that he would be able to find some outlet into the dark network of streets wherein the mysterious house was situated.

But he was disappointed.

He could walk round and round; but that was all.

For a long time neither a door nor a window was visible.

But just as he was about to reascend in despair to the room where he had left Aurora Halsted, he saw in one corner of the courtyard a faint glimmer of light, which seemed to proceed from the wall itself.

Rushing towards it, he perceived that it came from a small ventilator, through which could be obtained a view of an immense room, beautifully illuminated and luxuriously furnished, in which were to be seen in various attitudes nearly a hundred men and women.

The instant that Guy beheld them he understood the character of the house into which he and Aurora had been led.

Throughout the immense apartment were dispersed in every direction tables of wood and marble,

where men and women in every stage of intoxication were playing cards or dice. In the centre were two immense tables, used for the sole purpose of *rouge et noir*.

Guy gazed at the scene in a kind of horror.

He saw at once what kind of house Aurora had been inveigled into, but how to save her was beyond his power to imagine.

Again around the courtyard he sought everywhere in search of an outlet.

Finding, however, that all his endeavours were in vain, he ascended with some difficulty towards the room where Aurora Halsted was waiting for him in terror and suspense.

When he entered the room Aurora met him, with starting eyes and clenched hands.

"Is there a chance of escape?" she said.

Guy shook his head.

"No," he said, in a low tone; "and since there is not, let us not be heard plotting. We must abide the issue together, and depend upon me, they shall never harm you whilst life is left me."

No sooner had the words left his lips than the door was burst open, and Dick Hatherden entered the room, followed by six masked ruffians.

It was easy for Aurora Halsted to see, at her first glance at Dick's face, that she had no mercy to expect from him.

His features were set into a look of fierce determination, and as he came into the apartment he glanced at Guy, and resolutely refused to look at the one whom a few minutes before he had sworn to be his only hope in life.

"These are your prisoners, gentlemen," he said. "I must leave it to you to determine their fate. I know neither the one nor the other, but I think that the lad yonder is the more dangerous of the two."

During this speech, Aurora Halsted, as may well be imagined, was lost in bewilderment.

She looked from one to the other of those who were present, as if doubting the evidence of her own senses.

She saw now that a decisive crisis had arrived.

BOOK THE SECOND.—THE STORM BREAKS.

CHAPTER I.

WILL LIGHTMORE ON THE TRACK.

FOR three days after the evening on which Guy the Foundling had started with Jessie Hardarker for the lawyer's, the house of Simon Grandley had been in a state of great excitement; both Dick Hatherden and Guy the Foundling had disappeared without giving him the slightest clue to their whereabouts.

Strange to say, the worthy carpenter did not feel the same anxiety about Guy that he did about Dick Hatherden.

He had sufficient faith in Guy to believe whatever time he absented himself from his house was spent in his interest, or the interest of his friends.

But as regarded Dick Hatherden it was different.

Ever since the evening when he had discovered the brutal treatment to which Dick had subjected the unfortunate apprentice, Quail, he had regarded him with suspicion.

In fact, he began to believe what Guy the Foundling had believed all along, that Dick had been the prime mover in the burglary which had nearly proved fatal to two of them.

When, therefore, the three days had passed, Simon Grandley began to feel nervous.

Both he and his wife and little Minnie thought of the most impossible plans for rescuing Guy from unknown enemies, while Will Lightmore was every evening on the watch at every most impossible spot in the neighbourhood.

On the fourth evening, Will, having asked leave of his master to visit his aunt as before, sallied forth, not to see the aforesaid aunt, but simply to take a round of the places he knew, in search of his friend and fellow-apprentice.

He knew from description the place where Quail

had been so cowardly assaulted by Dick Hatherden, and starting from this point, he made his way to the tavern which had been burnt by the rioters on that same evening.

Not a vestige of this, of course, was to be seen, except blackened bricks and timber; but near it was another tavern, whose landlord had kindly and gratefully taken the custom of the Lamb and Fleece, and here Will Lightmore heard the whereabouts of Dick Hatherden.

Boniface, being in a state of pleasant excitement, was very anxious to give information.

"You see, sir," he said, "one of the fellows who was in the row the other night came in here with a broken pate, and while he was telling others how he got it I heard him say his name was Hatherden. If that's the chap that you mean, I know where he hangs out."

Will, although bursting with impatience, was, of course, afraid to appear too anxious.

But in the course of a conversation, during which several sixpennyworths of strong drink passed from one to the other, he discovered that the place to which Dick Hatherden had betaken himself was known by the sign of the Red Eagle.

It was situated at the corner of Water Lane, and was known to be one of the most disreputable houses for miles round.

The character which the landlord gave it, however, was not sufficient to deter Will Lightmore from proceeding in search of Dick Hatherden, who, he was confident, was well aware of the whereabouts of Guy the Foundling.

Hastening thither, therefore, he found himself opposite an old and gloomy house, without a single light in any of its windows.

There happened, as luck would have it, to be an old woman standing at the door of an adjoining tenement.

On seeing Will she at once accosted him.

"What are you seeking for, young gentleman?" she said.

"The Red Eagle," replied Will Lightmore. "There is some likeness of a bird over yonder door, but it is so discoloured and knocked about by time that one cannot recognise it."

"Nevertheless, young gentleman," replied the old woman, "that is the place you seek, and if you knock at the door, old Burly will answer you."

There must have been some presentiment in the mind of Will Lightmore, or he would never have asked the old woman to remain at the door while he knocked.

The instant afterwards, he saw that he had acted rightly.

No sooner had his knock echoed through the street than one of the large windows that protruded over the narrow door was thrown open, and a voice cried,

"What the devil are you doing here at this time of night, disturbing peaceable people from their beds?"

As if to give the lie to his words, a roar of drunken laughter resounded through the house, and some loud roysterer coming to the casement, cried—

"What are you doing here, old peach blossom? Don't you know that we have been shouting for wine this last half-hour, while you have been courting out of window one of the doubtful maids of the city?"

"You are wrong, my lord," cried the landlord; "there is some drunken knave without that demands admittance. Let me know from him what he wants."

Suiting the action to the word, he leaned farther out, crying—

"What want you there? The house is closed for the night."

"I want Dick Hatherden," cried Will Lightmore. "I wish to speak with him for a moment."

"I know him not. The house is closed, I say. We want no late stragglers here. Be off, or I will call the watch."

"I come with a special message," cried Will Lightmore. "I am a friend—a fellow-apprentice of his."

There was a pause and a hush now, as if some one from within was giving directions.

Then, before Will Lightmore was aware of it, or before even, indeed, a suspicion was awakened in his mind, a hand was extended from the window and a pistol fired.

"We want no thieves here," was the excuse.

Will Lightmore knew well that murder was intended.

The shot, however, did not reach him, and springing aside he at once made for the doorway, where the old woman still watched these proceedings.

"I have five pounds here," said Will; "they are yours if you will admit me, and allow me to do as I wish."

Five pounds was a thing which to the old woman represented a fortune, and though in mortal fear of a crusty husband, she invited him to step in and state his desire.

Will Lightmore's plan was soon explained.

Dick Hatherden and Guy the Foundling having disappeared at the same moment, and Dick having been proved to have been in the house next door, he was certain, he said, that his friend was somewhere confined against his will.

This, though it was but a guess, was, as our readers well know, about as shrewd a one as he could have made.

It would have been much the same to the woman whatever he said.

She was so overwhelmed at the idea of the five pounds that she kept counting what she could do with it more than listening to what he was describing in regard to his friends.

She heard enough of it, however, to understand that his purpose was far from a bad one, if she had chosen so to think.

But her head was an obstinate one, and very thick apparently, and the words of Will Lightmore appeared to reverberate.

"We're old people, and don't care to disturb ourselves by moving," she said, as she led the way upstairs, "or we'd long ago have left this place, for what with the noise, and the frequent visits of the watch, we've never any peace; and now you've come to worry us."

To this polite speech Will Lightmore thought it most prudent not to reply, but simply followed her in silence.

On entering the room into which the old woman ushered him he saw that all attempts were useless for that night.

Looking out of the window, he could see the back of the house in which he supposed Guy the Foundling to be imprisoned, but not a single light was to be seen in any of the windows.

Everything, in fact, was enveloped in darkness.

The old woman, who had followed him into the room, seemed even now doubtful whether she had acted properly in admitting him.

"I know well, young man," she said, "that the house next door there contains all kinds of bad characters, but still that is no reason why I should assist anyone in robbing it. If I thought that you had got any design of that kind I should call the watch."

"I can say no more than I have done," replied Will Lightmore. "I repeat that I have a friend within there who is detained against his will, and my sole object is to save him."

"Then why do you not call in the aid of the watch?"

"That is my own business," cried Will; "if I cannot save him myself, I have hundreds at my back to help me. Fear not! you shall not be harmed; but as I am here, and shall remain till morning, let me have a light, and I'll retire to bed."

In the course of another quarter of an hour the brave lad was wrapped in a deep slumber, and all was again quiet in the house.

CHAPTER II.

THE MYSTERY OF THE UNDERGROUND CELLAR—THE MEETING OF GUY AND AURORA.

MEANWHILE we must return to Aurora and Guy the Foundling.

It will be remembered that our hero had only just ascended into the room where he and Aurora were confined when Dick Hatherden entered, followed by a number of men in masks.

Against such odds it would have been madness for him to have striven, and he could, therefore, do nothing but expostulate.

"What means my detention here?" he cried, addressing Dick. "I demand the immediate release of myself and Miss Halsted."

Dick regarded him with a triumphant leer.

"Who entered the house with her own free will," he said. "It was not my wish that you should see Colonel Halsted, but your own. If you did not wish it, why should you force yourself into the house?"

"If he is here, let me see him instantly," replied Guy.

"Follow me then," replied Dick; "it is his wish to see you even before his daughter."

Aurora sprang forward and seized Guy by the arm.

"Oh, do not blame me," she cried, "I know there is some base and cruel design against you. Gentlemen," she added, turning to the masked men, "if you have a spark of humanity left in you let me quit this place. I am sure—I can swear—my father is not in this house."

The men made no reply.

At a sign, however, from Dick Hatherden they rushed in between Guy and Aurora, and in less time than it takes to describe it our hero was dragged out into the dark passage.

The wild cry which escaped Aurora Halsted's lips as he disappeared made him at first inclined to make a desperate resistance.

From this act of folly, however, a second thought saved him.

To resist was simply to give them an excuse for using violence, and thus deprive him entirely of all chance of aiding Aurora.

He permitted them, therefore, to lead him along the corridor down a narrow stone staircase, which wound round for some distance, till it reached a series of subterranean vaults.

Throughout the entire time that he had been in the house he had known perfectly well that the name of Colonel Halsted had been used purely as a blind, and he was not therefore at all surprised when instead of being ushered into his presence, he was flung rather than pushed into a dark cellar.

The door was too quickly closed to allow him to ask the cause of their violence, or the probable duration of his captivity, and not a single ray of light entering the place, he was perfectly unable to discern the size or nature of his prison.

He could not know, of course, but that there might be some pitfall designed purposely for the destruction of captives, and therefore he determined to be very careful how he moved to and fro.

Nevertheless, his state of mind would not permit him to remain still.

Pressing slowly along by the wall, he soon found that the circumference of the cell was very small, and that his fears in regard to pitfalls were vain.

A new cause of disquietude, however, soon arose.

In going the round of the place he stumbled, and as his hands touched the floor he found that what had caused his fall was a mass of human bones.

He had scarcely recovered from the consternation into which this discovery had thrown him, when a noise above his head attracted his attention.

Then there was a sudden light, the fall of some heavy body, and then all was quiet and darkness again.

A low groaning noise near him, however, soon told him he was no longer alone.

The sound evidently proceeded from a human being in agony, and approaching the spot from whence it proceeded, Guy discovered that a man was lying bruised and senseless on the ground.

The idea that he had a fellow prisoner of any kind, although a stranger, was so pleasing to Guy, that drawing from the breast of his coat a flask containing some brandy he poured a few drops into the mouth of the unconscious stranger.

In a few moments he had the satisfaction of seeing he was reviving.

He was astonished, however, at the result that followed.

Starting to his feet, the stranger staggered to and fro, tossing his arms wildly, and shouting—

"Back, robbers and murderers! You have taken all! Let me go—let me quit this place of infamy."

Then, overcome by weakness, he fell back again upon the ground.

Guy at once hurried to the spot.

"You are mistaken, my friend," he said; "you have fallen in some mysterious manner through the roof of this vault, where I, like you, am a prisoner."

"Ah! I remember now," said the man, in a faint voice, for he had received great injuries in his descent. "There was a fight in the gambling room, a rush of thieves upon me to secure my money, and then a rapid fall, and I recollect no more. Have you also been the victim of their iniquities?"

"Yes, in a different way," said Guy; "but I fear, for whatever reason we are here, we are destined to remain here for ever. We have nothing for it, however, but to wait upon events, and see what will turn up by the morning."

The morning came and went, however, the next day passed, and the next night, and yet another day and another night, and another, and another, but no one entered the cell. The third night brings us to that on which Will Lightmore made his appearance at the front door.

To him, therefore, we will return, and see what measures he took to secure the safety of his friends.

It was on the morning of the fourth day that he woke early, and dressing himself quickly, glanced out of the little window of his room.

He was most agreeably surprised to find that from his casement he could see all that passed in the chamber opposite.

As our readers are aware, Will Lightmore knew

nothing of the presence of Aurora Halsted in the gambling house, and he was astounded, therefore, when, on looking out, he beheld her face at the window.

Always beautiful, she looked specially so now, with the glory of the early morning's sun surrounding her head like a halo.

Knowing well that she and Dick Hatherden had been such great friends, he was for the moment inclined to believe that she might have something to do with the disappearance of Guy the Foundling.

But the remembrance of the night on which Guy had saved her from the burning house at once banished this idea from his brain.

If, indeed, he had conceived the idea, one look at her agonised face would have been enough to dispel it.

The thought in a moment occurred to him, Was she a prisoner also?

As for Aurora herself, she had no sooner beheld the features of the apprentice at the window than she threw hers open, and made signs for him to lean out further.

"What is the matter?" he cried.

"We are both prisoners here," replied Aurora; "I and Guy."

"But Guy—where is he?" cried Will.

"I know not," said Aurora. "For three days I have not seen him. They forced him away from me, and I believe him to be, if still alive, in some miserable dungeon."

"Are there many men in the house?" asked Will.

"That I cannot answer; I have seen only Dick Hatherden and six others. But it is not safe to talk here any longer. If you can bring help, do so, in heaven's name."

"Fear not," said Will; "I will not delay, now that I know you are here. I will lose not a single moment in bringing aid to you. Keep up your courage, but do not let them suspect that you have seen a friend."

Then he at once closed the window and hurried down the stairs.

Will Lightmore had resolved that, come what might, he would not return to the house of Simon Grandley without either bringing Guy with him, or, at any rate, certain news of his death.

Instead, therefore, of proceeding to the house of the carpenter, he hurried towards the City Arms, a house which was well known as the head-quarters of the oldest and strongest of the City apprentices.

He knew well that they would not desert him in such a time as this, and he was aware also, that no matter what amount of riot and disturbance took place, the watch would be powerless to prevent it.

To attack the gambling-house in the day would, of course, be a matter of impossibility, as all the apprentices would have been at work.

It was necessary, however, to procure the services of one or two to act as recruiting agents, and at the City Arms he soon found one or two willing spirits to assist him.

The time of meeting was fixed for nine o'clock, and the place of rendezvous a large waste piece of ground, known as Godding's Fields, and situated not far from the gambling-house.

CHAPTER III.

THE BEGINNING OF THE RIOTS.

WHEN Guy the Foundling had been dragged from the side of Aurora Halsted by the six masked men, Dick Hatherden remained with her in the room.

"Well, Mr. Hatherden," she said, standing haughtily and defiantly before him, "and what now have you to say for yourself?"

Dick approached her gently, with what he intended to be a winning smile.

"Dearest Aurora," he said, "all is fair in love and war. I knew well that your affection for me had suffered at any rate a temporary eclipse. I knew that you, while at your friend's, would be surrounded by every luxury—by friends whose presence would steal from you all remembrance of one so lowly as myself; and so I framed, for the sake of seeing you thus alone, this——"

"Infamous lie," said Aurora Halsted, finishing the sentence for him.

Dick reddened, and bit his lip.

He saw how matters stood.

"You speak harshly," he said.

"Not so harshly as you deserve," she cried. "Tell me, where is my father?"

"Alas! I know not."

"Then the letter I received was a forgery? Oh heavens, that I should have been so deceived!"

And clasping her hands, she burst into tears, and sank down upon the rich ottoman.

Dick Hatherden gazed at her a moment ere he approached her.

She was indeed a girl to raise the admiration of any man, especially in her sorrow.

Her light tresses, as she leaned forward, coiled over her bare shoulders, and the white bosom now tremulous with emotion.

Her white, round, gold-clasped arms rested on her lap; her bright blue eyes gleamed with tears; her pretty lips quivered with agitation.

Dick gently drew near her, and passed his arm around her waist.

She sprang from him as from a toad.

"Back," she cried, "touch me not!"

He detained her forcibly.

"You *shall* hear me," he cried, passionately. "Do you think that I am now going at a moment's notice to cast aside the dream of my youth? Did you not lead me on with golden promises of love and wealth? Did you not promise to be mine? Did you not swear never to love another? and then, did you not, when Guy the Foundling saved you from the flames, cast your glamour upon him? I will not, I cannot, give up my old visions. Oh! Aurora," he added, adopting a more tender tone, and casting himself upon his knees before her, "say that you love me— *do* say that you love me, and I will forsake all in the world for you!"

She gazed at him with contempt as he spoke, and sprang from him again, now that her hand was released.

"Leave me," she said; "I hate you. If I am compelled to remain here, let me at least be rid of your odious presence."

There was no use in pleading more.

Dick saw this.

There was no mistaking her manner.

No mistaking the flash of her eyes—the bitter scorn of her voice.

He leaped to his feet and stood before her, pale, angry, defiant.

"Good then, madam," he said, "good. I shall know now how to act. Learn from my words now what your position here is. Your father, to the best of my belief, is dead—not a soul in the world knows that you are here, except Guy the Foundling, who is safely beyond human aid."

"Oh! you would not murder him?" cried Aurora, clasping her hands in agony.

"Not if *you* are gentle towards me," replied Dick. "His fate depends on your conduct towards me. If you consent to become mine, he shall be set free—if you refuse, he dies."

Aurora gazed at him in wonder.

It was indeed a change.

An inconceivable change.

Could this be the one whom she had once loved—loved in spite of all her ideas of earthly advancement.

"Refuse or consent to be yours. What mean you?" cried she. "Would you have me marry you in such a place as this?"

"Why not?—every place is the same. We can have a priest and witnesses, and depend upon it it is *my* interest to make the union as binding as it can be."

"I refuse then, once and for ever," said Aurora. "Come what may, I will never be yours."

Dick Hatherden turned towards the door.

"Very well, then," he said, "I will leave you. Perhaps to-morrow you may be in a better humour."

Then without another word, he quitted the room, locking the door carefully after him.

Three times during each day Dick Hatherden paid a visit to Aurora's lonely room.

But there was no change in her demeanour towards him.

Her answer, in spite of continued threats against the life of Guy, was always the same, and Dick began to fear that even a continuance of imprisonment would have no effect upon her resolution.

And so time went on until the evening of the fourth day arrived.

Punctually to their time the apprentices assembled in Godding's Fields.

Such an immense assemblage, for there were nearly one hundred of them, naturally attracted the attention of the watch, who, of course, at once conceived the idea that a recommencement of the riots was threatened.

A few words of explanation, however, from Will Lightmore proved enough to prevent any attempt on the part of the authorities to put a stop to the proceedings, and full of excitement the apprentices hurried, six a-breast, along the now quiet streets.

Their progress, as may be imagined, excited no ordinary curiosity among the few passers-by, and the inhabitants of the houses.

But, in spite of all questions, they refused to give any information, but pressed on towards the point of attack.

On reaching the Red Eagle Will Lightmore at once advanced to the door.

A head was protruded as before from the window, and a voice demanded angrily what was the meaning of such a concourse of people before the inn.

"We have come to demand the instant surrender of a friend whom you are keeping here against his will."

"We know nothing of you or your friend either," replied the voice; "and if you do not clear off quickly I shall shout for the watch."

Of this, of course, Will Lightmore took no notice.

"You refuse then to open your doors?" cried he.

"I do," replied the voice; "we keep no accommodation for such a crew of vagabonds as you have here."

"If the Red Eagle were what it pretended to be —a house of entertainment—it must be open at this early hour. Come, boys, we must not stop loitering here, but set to work at once."

The apprentices wanted no further reminding.

Under Lightmore's directions they at once attacked the door with fury.

Some were armed with heavy bludgeons, and with these they soon succeeded in splitting the panels of the doors.

But the besieged had no conception of being thus easily hoisted from their quarters.

The temporary lull which had enabled the apprentices to make good their first attack had only been caused by the rush of the gamblers to seize their firearms, or any weapons which came to their hand, and in the space of a few minutes a sharp volley rang out through the still air. Aimed at haphazard in the darkness, and from windows which, as I have said before, protruded some distance beyond the doorway, the shots took little effect, but they caused such universal consternation throughout the street that the inhabitants came rushing out like mad people from their houses.

If, however, the people at the Red Eagle imagined that any good would accrue to them from this they were mistaken.

The Red Eagle was like a haunted house in the neighbourhood.

It was avoided by everyone, except, indeed, those who were of the same calibre and stamp as the landlord.

The intelligence that the apprentices had collected together for the purpose of forcing an entrance into the place seemed to spread delight through the gathering throng.

In a few moments many had rushed away, and returned, bearing crowbars and implements necessary for forcing open the door of the house.

The frequenters of the gambling house had every reason to make a strenuous defence.

They were not all the low *habitués* of the quarter.

On the contrary, there were many there whose noble names would have astonished many of their companions.

Seeing the increasing crowd, therefore, they begged the landlord to deliver up the person, whoever it was, for whose sake all this disturbance had arisen.

But the landlord upon this point was resolute.

Somehow or another Dick Hatherden had more influence in the house than the whole of the rest of the guests put together.

"Shall I give them up?" he said to Dick.

"No," was the answer.

And it was a sufficient one.

"You hear, gentlemen," said the landlord, "I cannot. This person I dare not disobey."

A hurried consultation took place among the guests.

"We will release them ourselves," cried one of them, "in a few moments."

Dick Hatherden burst into a scornful laugh.

"Do as you please," he said; "but you have fired upon them, and they will have their revenge."

These words would probably have taken no effect whatever upon the minds of those present, had not at this moment the front door given way, and a loud roar of anger resounded through the building.

"There, you see," said Dick, "those are the men from whom you expect mercy."

The guests at once rushed to the door of the room, prepared to fight for dear life.

"On, gentlemen, on!" cried Dick, "you see that my words were correct. The release of the persons in this house is but an excuse for robbery and murder."

The battle on the top of the stairs soon became furious.

The apprentices were in greater numbers than the gamblers.

But the latter had the advantage of knowing their ground, and for some time contrived to keep their assailants in check.

Not for long, however.

The apprentices, roused by the cheers of those without, and the bold example of Will Lightmore, burst at length the opposing ranks, and forced their way into the large room, from the window of which the landlord had addressed the crowd.

Once here, the work of demolition commenced.

Those who were not engaged in attacking the gamblers seized hold of articles of furniture, smashed them into pieces, and flung them from the window.

The crowd below received this part of the performance with delight.

A number of those present were mad fanatics.

Not a few of them wore the ribbon which had been issued by the Protestant Association.

But a few days—in fact, indeed, we may say a few hours—were to elapse before Lord George Gordon, that well-meaning madman, was to present to the Houses of Parliament a petition, signed by one hundred thousand persons, the whole of whom he had begged to accompany him to the House with their colours pinned to their breasts.

Those, therefore, who were really interested in the question, as well as those who hoped to find benefit for themselves in a period of rapine and disaster, had eagerly got ready the ribbons which were to show them one of the chosen.

The riot, which had had its initiative in the attack on the gambling-house, seemed a commencement of the revolution impending.

The hearts of both true and false religionists beat as the firing was heard and the shouts of the angry men.

The broken furniture cast from the windows was siezed at once and piled in the first open space that could be found.

Here torches were applied to it; spirits brought from the Red Eagle were poured on it, and soon a good flame arose.

Then came a scene droll in its very grotesque horror.

The men who seized on the spirits soon became inebriated, and, joining hands round the bonfire, began to dance wildly round it, while some here and there falling from among the rest, plunged head-foremost among the flames.

It was while they were dancing thus that Dick Hatherden rushed wildly from the house.

A demoniacal leer was upon his face, and he glanced rapidly round him in search of a passage for escape.

This was vain, however.

One of the apprentices had seen him, and as he stood undecided he was seized from behind and flung to the ground.

Here at dagger's point, he was compelled to surrender; and borne away by a guard of six, he was carried to a quieter spot, to await the decision of Will Lightmore.

The cause of his attempted escape is readily explained.

Finding that his old comrades, the apprentices, were rapidly gaining the upper hand, he ascended to the room where Aurora Halsted was kneeling by the side of the ottoman in prayer.

She had guessed when she heard the first shot fired that friends were coming to the rescue.

But still the peril was no less.

No woman cares to be in the midst of a scene of carnage and confusion.

Such she knew *must* be in case of resistance.

And so there she knelt and prayed.

It was in this posture that Dick Hatherden found her.

"Aurora!" he cried, "I am here to save you."

For an instant she believed him.

Springing up, she clutched his arm.

"Oh, yes—yes. Let me fly with you from this place; anywhere—anywhere out of such a scene as this!"

Dick smiled.

"You have come to reason then," he said, "I was sure that you would."

This spoiled all for him.

Had he been silent she might have fled with him.

But these words brought to mind the hatred she entertained for him—the fact that her friends were there to save her, and she flung his arm away.

"Leave me," she cried, "I forgot myself. No—no! I will rather perish in this scene of horror than owe my life to you."

THE RIVAL APPRENTICES

A TALE OF THE RIOTS OF 1780.

THE SOLDIERS NOW FIRED ON THE MOB.

At this moment a cheer arose from the apprentices below.

It spoke of renewed victory.
There was danger for him in more delay.

No. 13.

"Curse you for these insults," he cried, "you shall not live to scorn me more. Die then in the flames that will soon encompass this house. They know not where you are, and in the din of battle your shrieks will be unheard."

Before she well understood the terrific significance of his words, he had sprung from her side and passed from the room.

The turning of the key in the lock told her that Dick Hatherden really meant what he said, and overcome with horror, she once more sank upon her knees.

It was after this scene, as I have before stated, that Dick Hatherden had rushed wildly from the house, resolved to leave it and its inmates to the terrible fate that threatened them.

As yet, of course, the flames had not reached the house, but the wind was already blowing clouds of sparks from the bonfire in at the open windows.

It could not be doubted therefore that his prophecy would soon prove true.

Will Lightmore saw the danger, and while he urged some of his companions to search the upper rooms, endeavoured to force his way down into the subterranean vaults, where Aurora had declared that the Foundling was hidden.

The resistance of the landlord and his guests to the inroad of the apprentices was kept up with unabated vigour.

The proprietor of the Red Eagle, in fact, was utterly ignorant of Dick's flight.

He imagined that his absence was simply owing to his having been parted from his friends in the mélée, and Boniface accordingly urged his friends by every means in his power to save him from his resolute and unexpected enemies.

Another quarter of an hour passed.

Still neither Aurora nor Guy the Foundling had been discovered.

Within the building the battle raged fiercely.

Every landing place, every door in every corridor, had its own set of combatants.

Outside in the street the maddened people, excited continually more and more by the spirits which they had stolen from the Red Eagle, were still dancing and shouting round their bonfire.

Suddenly a cry of fire arose.

It was too true.

The showers of sparks had at length accomplished what Dick Hatherden had expected, and tongues of red flames soon began to leap out of the large windows.

The sight of this mutual foe roused both besieged and besiegers to renewed exertions, and a terrible rush was made on both sides.

The one side was endeavouring to force its way into the street, whilst the other was striving to reach the rooms where they supposed Aurora and Guy to be confined.

It fell to the lot of Hugh Marling, one of Guy's particular friends, to discover and save Aurora Halsted from her impending danger.

He found her still upon her knees.

She had never moved since Dick's departure.

In fact, she had given up all hope.

When, therefore, she heard the door open, she did not even turn her head, expecting that if she did so, her eyes would light upon the hated features of her enemy.

The voice of the newcomer soon disabused her mind of this terror.

She sprang to her feet at once and confronted him.

"Quick," said he, "the house is on fire; there is no time to be lost."

She hesitated a moment.

In spite of the ingenuousness of the young stranger, there was a lingering suspicion in her breast that he might be an emissary of Dick Hatherden.

"I would rather remain here and face my death," she said, "than pass again into the power of that villain Hatherden. Assure me that you do not come from him, or I shall remain where I am."

The young fellow advanced toward her somewhat impatiently.

He felt almost angry at her doubting him.

"No, no," he said, "I come from Guy the Foundling and Will Lightmore, sworn enemies of Dick Hatherden. If we remain here another minute all retreat will be cut off, and you will destroy yourself and me for no purpose."

As he said these words he seized her by the wrist, and drew her with a kind of gentle force towards the door.

As they passed through it the din of battle had nearly ceased.

It was easy to see the reason why.

Dense columns of black smoke began to wreathe and curl up the stairs.

The fire, in fact, had begun to take a hold upon its victim with a vengeance.

They were but just in time.

One other moment's delay would have sufficed to cut of all chance off retreat.

On reaching the lower passage they came upon a dense crowd of struggling persons.

All fighting had now ceased, and the efforts of every one were now directed to clearing out of the burning edifice as soon as possible.

Victims of this useless battle lay strewn here and there across their path; but the horror which would at any other time have been roused in the breast of the young girl by such a sight was now swallowed up in the eager desire for flight.

Stepping over them as if they had been mere logs of wood, Aurora Halsted hurried along with her preserver until they reached the street.

Here she glanced round her eagerly.

Where was Guy?

At any other time she would scarcely have liked to ask.

Their mutual danger, however, did away with this feeling.

"Where is he?" she asked, stopping and looking round her anxiously, instead of hurrying, as her companion expected, from the tumultuous scene.

"Whom mean you?"

"Guy the Foundling."

"I know not," said Hugh Marling. "Will Lightmore has gone to save him, but how far he has succeeded I know not."

"Leave me, then, and return to aid him," cried Aurora, earnestly.

"What! leave you in this crowd?"

"No one will harm me."

Hugh Marling shook his head.

No! no!" he cried, "Will Lightmore bade me not leave you, even for a moment. He has good friends to aid him besides me. Let us hasten hence."

"Whither would you take me?"

"Yonder—not many yards hence," said Hugh. "You need fear nothing, for Dick Hatherden is a prisoner, and will, no doubt, ere many hours are over, swing for this evening's job."

Aurora, however, did not move.

She was resolved to face the danger.

The unfortunate girl—truly unfortunate in her adventures, in her former misplaced love for Dick, and in the murder of her father—had conceived, as we have seen, a hopeless affection for Guy, which now had ripened into love, through companionship in danger.

So she was determined to be close at hand to aid him, if he required aid, and no entreaties upon Hugh Marling's part would move her.

CHAPTER IV.

THE BATTLE IN THE STREETS.

MEANWHILE, we must return to Will Lightmore who, fighting his way through the crowd with some of his friends, made for the vaults.

The atmosphere of the subterranean part of the house now was stifling.

The vaults truly were not on fire; but there being no means of ventilation the heat of the burning house alone soon stagnated the air.

Even in the cell where Guy and his companion were confined the heat had already made itself felt.

During the three days that they had been immured a terrible time had been passed.

Not a living soul had visited them.

Indeed not a human voice had been heard.

Guy had heard a murmur and a rumble now and then, which indicated that living beings were near.

But that was all.

Not even a ray of light illumined the utter darkness.

The story of his companion was soon told.

He was the son of a person of respectability, residing in the neighbourhood, and having lately come into a little property he had been inveigled by one of his companions into the Red Eagle.

Here the spirit of gambling got tightly hold of him.

Night after night was spent there in fast and furious play.

At length on that night, when he came tumbling through the trap-door in the ceiling of the vault, he had discovered some of the *habitués* cheating.

Exasperated, he sprang up and threatened to denounce them.

This was enough.

He was at once set upon furiously, and having been wounded repeatedly, was driven to the fatal trap-door, and hurled into the vault beneath.

Wounded as he was, there was, as my readers may conceive, but little hope of recovery for him.

Guy tried all he could to alleviate his sufferings. But in vain.

Wounded before, and crushed by the fall, he never rallied much, and on the third night he expired in terrible agony.

And so during the fourth day, and up to the time of the attack, Guy was alone with the dead!

This silent companionship, in such a place of gloom, was, as may be conceived, immeasurably horrid, combined as it was with the absence of all food.

His thirst was more terrible, however, than his hunger.

His parched mouth seemed to burn with fire.

His blood ran like liquid metal through his veins.

Again and again during the still hours he shouted aloud for water.

But in vain.

No sound—not even a mocking laugh—answered him.

The noise of the attack upon the Red Eagle by the apprentices and the others who had joined them, was so great that it, of course, reached the ears of Guy the Foundling, sick and faint as he was.

But he could not understand it.

Neither could he imagine that (whatever it might be) it could have any advantageous meaning to himself.

So he sat down listlessly. Listening and waiting on events.

When Will and his friends thundered at the door, he knew that human beings—friends or foes, which ever they might be—were near him, and he consequently shouted aloud for help.

His voice—feeble as it was—was still easily recognisable.

"Hurrah!" cried Will, "we have found him—safe and alive! Cheer up, Guy, we are here to save you!"

Guy made no answer.

He was overwhelmed.

The surprise seemed hardly real.

During the moment's lull that followed he scarcely believed that he had heard aright.

He rather inclined to the idea that he had been the victim of some delusion—that, in fact, he had been the sport of some mad dream, induced by want of food and confinement in his dark and lonely cell.

He listened eagerly for a repetition of the sound.

He had not long to wait.

"Now then, boys," exclaimed Will Lightmore; "now then, let us assault it with a will. We have no time to lose."

And accordingly, with their clubs and their feet and their shoulders, they battered away at it resolutely.

It was not long before it yielded, and a number of the excited besiegers rushed in.

As they did so they found Guy stretched senseless with excitement on the dead body of his unfortunate companion in misfortune.

A few minutes sufficed to bear him out into the fresh air, where with the assistance of stimulants he was soon called back to life.

Aurora was among the first to greet him.

He woke to find her bending over him with a countenance full of love and anxiety.

A smile broke over her sunny face as he opened his eyes.

"Ah, he lives! he lives! thank Heaven!" she cried.

"You then also are saved, Aurora," he said, faintly, "and how has it all been done—what means this riot."

"Your brave and noble friend, Will Lightmore, has been the author of our safety," said Aurora.

And then in a few words she told him all that had happened.

"That villain Hatherden, then, has been captured," he said.

"Yes, he is not far distant," said Will, whose hand Guy had taken and pressed warmly. "This time he shall not escape punishment; but, hark, what is that?"

A loud rumbling sound, a roar from numerous voices, and then the sharp rattle of musketry, was heard.

To explain this we must for a moment retrace our steps.

When the maddened mob broke into the spirit vaults of the Red Eagle, and once felt their power in their drunken sort of way, they began to lose all command over themselves.

Fire having cut them off from the supplies which they were drawing so liberally from the gambling house, they turned and looked for it elsewhere.

Not far from the Red Eagle stood a tavern, rejoicing in the sign of the Puritan's Head.

Towards this at once they flocked eagerly, and without apprising the landlord in any way of their kindly intentions, burst into the premises, and commenced helping themselves to anything they could lay hands on.

And, having been shown the example at the other place, they flung out the furniture as before, and constructed a huge bonfire, that they might see how thoroughly to make beasts of themselves.

The news flew like lightning.

As long as such a notorious and infamous place as the Red Eagle was the victim of the mob's wrath the authorities felt inclined to wink at the matter.

Not so when the rioting and plundering became more general.

They knew well the movements of the Protestant Association.

They anticipated the glow of party spite which would soon madden the public mind, and they cared not to give the populace beforehand a feeling of security in evil doing.

When intelligence came, therefore, that indiscriminate rioting had commenced, the watch was sent towards the spot in great numbers.

They were utterly useless.

The mob tossed them about like so many toys.

In fact, the watch was never of any use against any organised or a rabid throng.

Their very appearance at any period of difficulty was the signal for laughter.

On this occasion there was no distinction.

They were hooted and jeered, and one of them who made himself somewhat too officious was cast headlong into the flames of the huge bonfire, and severely burnt.

Hearing this the authorities at once adopted other measures.

A regiment of the line was called out, and ordered to proceed against the rioters without delay, and to take measures, no matter how stringent, to put a stop to the riots.

The command could not have been given to a better man than it was.

This was one named Colonel Wood.

He was well known in the service.

More known than liked.

He was what may truly be called a bloodthirsty man.

He was brave as a lion in battle.

This no one sought to deny.

But being now at home, and not in active service, he sought the opportunity of seeing blood flow anywhere where there was a chance.

He took the present command with pleasure.

There was a chance of a formidable disturbance.

Danger also there would be.

But for this he cared not.

There would be excitement at any rate.

And this was what he fed on.

"Soldiers," he cried, as they hurriedly marshalled themselves; "you must forget when you enter upon this service that you are proceeding against your fellow citizens—you must remember only that they are men who are seeking to undermine your peaceful homes—to destroy the Constitution—to turn London into a scene of murder and rapine. It is your duty to forget who those men are—and if you see a friend among the mob shoot him the first, lest the sight of him should turn you from your duty."

The soldiers, who were for the most part veterans who had served with him in many a campaign abroad, did not much enjoy the idea of firing upon peaceful citizens.

But still they had been lazy for a long time.

And, more than this, they had in view a share of the very plunder they were to be sent to put a stop to.

So they simply cheered his words, and marched off with the bloodthirsty old fellow at their head.

On arriving in the neighbourhood of the riot they found a number of persons beginning to break into a private house.

These, on being summoned to desist, refused.

And so, Colonel Wood immediately gave the order—

"Fire!"

This was the sound which Guy and Aurora had heard, and which brought them running full speed to the spot.

CHAPTER V.

THE DEFEAT.

DICK HATHERDEN, helpless and a prisoner, among those whose interest he knew it to be to destroy him, gazed round at the tumultuous assemblage with almost listless eyes.

He would have cried out for help, but he dared not.

Instant death would have followed.

So he looked on, as I have said, with utter indifference, while the flames sported with the houses, and the bonfire flashed in the centre of the street—while men and women, mad with drink, hurried hither and thither, and roared out loud songs, or yelled out in pain, as they rolled accidentally into the fire.

But when he heard the cry—

"The soldiers are coming!"

Then hope once more revived in his breast.

Eagerly he watched for them.

In the *mêlée* that would be certain to ensue there would be a splendid chance for him of escape.

Those with him understood this too.

They were told not to quit that spot until Guy the Foundling made his appearance.

But, as yet, they saw nothing of him.

And still the sound of the approaching military was heard!

On reaching the large open space at the corner of the narrow street where the Red Eagle was situated the soldiers halted.

The colonel advanced to the front.

"Now then!" he cried, in a stentorian voice, which was heard high above the din; "now then, good people, this cannot be permitted. Disperse at once, and nothing more will be done. If you persist, however, in this disgraceful conduct, I have full authority to order my soldiers to fire upon you."

The blood of the mob was up.

They cared not for his words.

Only a volley of abuse and a significant hustling together was the answer.

The colonel turned towards his men.

"Present," he cried.

Then, as the muskets were levelled, he once more appealed to the crowd.

"I give you five minutes more to consider," he said; "you see (pointing to the soldiers)—you see I am determined."

The crowd only made another movement, which was to get the best armed in front.

Then loud shouts rent the air.

"Down with the soldiers!"

"Hurrah for the people!"

"Down with the friends of the Catholics!"

Again the insensate cries which had no reference to the action of the moment.

The time passed rapidly.

The colonel saw that the mob meant resistance.

But he would not, bloodthirsty though he was, break his word.

The full five minutes were allowed.

Then, placing in his pocket the watch he had calmly looked at, he shouted—

"Fire!"

In an instant a murderous volley was poured in upon the people.

There was momentary huddling together of the crowd; a few rapid words passed.

Then in one mass they dashed against the soldiers.

The second rank immediately delivered a volley.

But this did not have the desired effect.

It only enraged the crowd still more.

With terrible curses they rushed forward.

"Charge!" cried the inflexible colonel.

And the glittering bayonets were brought down to the charging point, and the soldiers dashed forward to meet the mob.

A horrible scene ensued.

The maddened rioters appeared to court their doom.

Some sprang as if purposely on the points of the bayonets.

Some seized them in their bare hands, in a frantic endeavour to wrest them from the soldiers.

But they were soon borne down.

While they struggled, the rear ranks of the troops closed in and fired over their comrades' shoulders.

Shrieks of women and groans of men rent the night air.

Curses, yells of agony, shouts for mercy!

All were now strangely mingled.

Still the old colonel urged his men on.

He was inflexible truly now.

He had scented blood, and like the wild beast he craved for more.

So, while the infuriated people refused to surrender, he gave out with cool voice the orders to mow them down.

In the whirl of the mob at the rear, Aurora and Guy were soon involved with their friends.

A third charge with the bayonet sent the people helter skelter in all directions, and away with them were borne Dick Hatherden and his captors.

Now was his chance.

And he was not slow to perceive and take advantage of it.

Bound as he was, he made a rush towards the advancing throng; and was in an instant, as it were, caught up and incorporated with it.

It would have been utterly vain for his captors to attempt any re-capture.

Indeed, amid the whirling crowd, they could not see him; and had in fact more than enough to do to save themselves from being trampled to death.

Away along the by-streets the now alarmed mob went helter-skelter, never once looking behind, trampling heedlessly on those who fell.

And so, in the course of half an hour, the space near the Red Eagle was cleared, and nothing remained to show what had passed but the remains of the bonfire, the still burning gambling house, and the dead bodies of the mad victims of folly.

CHAPTER VI.

A STRANGE LOVE.

GUY THE FOUNDLING, though so weakened by his long sojourn in the cell without food, was now so far recovered in consequence of the inhalation of fresh air and the administration of brandy, that he was enabled to walk without help.

The excitement of the moment, moreover, seemed to enable him to perform prodigies.

When the tide of human beings had surged towards him and Aurora, who stood by his side, holding his hand in terror, he glanced round him almost wildly in search of a shelter for both of them.

As good fortune would have it, there was a door-

way near, which was just large enough to hold them, and into this he at once drew her.

In spite of all his trials she was by far the weaker of the two, and as he stood there supporting her by holding her round the waist, all sense of weakness appeared to have left him.

Again and again the swaying crowd surged up against them.

Aurora was in terrible fear.

She crept closer still to her preserver.

Her head rested on his breast, her warm breath fanned his cheek.

The old suspicion entered his heart.

Did this girl love him?

Had some evil genius thrown them unkindly together?

Again and again had Guy to exert the fullest of his strength to keep back the mob.

The pressure was at times so great that Aurora trembled for her life.

"Oh! Guy," she murmured, "it would be terrible to die thus."

"Talk not of dying," he said, as she pressed closer to him, "you have, I hope, a long, long life yet before you."

There was in his voice as he spoke a kind of tenderness which was not the tenderness of affection, but of pity.

She misunderstood it.

Her tearful eyes gazed up into his—her lips trembled—her warm breast throbbed against his.

"Oh! in this hour of danger," she murmured, "I feel how I love you for all the peril you have gone through for me. This is the second time you have risked your life to save mine. I only hope that I *may* have long years to live that I may prove my gratitude to you."

Guy may be excused if, with this lovely creature nestling in his arms, he knew not what to do.

He hastily kissed the quivering lips, which were upturned as if asking for an embrace, and pressed her more closely to him.

But even as he did so, a cold chill seemed to invade his heart.

He could not love this girl.

Admire her, he of course, did.

No one gazing upon her beauty could avoid doing so.

But Minnie—sweet Minnie Grandley—had absolute possession of his affections.

What, meanwhile, could he do?

What, indeed, could he answer?

Under other circumstances he might have called her his sister, and used expressions which would have chilled at once her misplaced affection.

But no opportunity was given to him.

While his kiss still trembled on her lips she was driven farther back by the rushing crowd until, in spite of Guy's protection, she fainted in his arms.

The position now was a terrible one.

He felt his own strength rapidly giving way.

He could sustain her sufficiently to prevent her falling to the ground, but that was all.

He could not keep from her the cruel, murderous pressure of the crowd.

Ten minutes of indescribable agony of mind went by.

He felt fainting.

A cold sweat invaded his limbs.

The whole scene of riot and confusion appeared to swim round him.

Then suddenly a rush of blessed air swept across his forehead—the crowd broke and fled another way.

They were saved!

Guy did not wait to make any effort to rouse the fainting girl.

He was glad to seize upon the chance of effecting his escape.

So, gathering together all the strength that was left to him, he raised her in his arms, and staggering from the doorway, rushed down a narrow street, and reaching a little tavern, hurried in.

Here he had just time to stagger to a seat with his fair burden, when a strange weakness overcame him, and he sank back in a faint.

CHAPTER VII.

THE OLD LOVE AGAIN.

WHEN our hero awoke, he found himself lying upon a couch, in a private room in the tavern, with several persons round him.

With the exception of Aurora, all those present were strangers.

She was sitting near him, chafing his hands, and looking all that a pretty girl can look when she is in love and in sorrow.

The others were a stout elderly gentleman, an elderly lady, and a gentleman who was, evidently, a doctor.

Guy sat up and glanced round him in astonishment.

"Why, what does all this mean—where am I?" he cried.

"This is my uncle, Guy," said Aurora, gently, "and this is my aunt. I sent for them. This gentleman is Dr. Scarfely. I have told them all."

"Yes," added Colonel Halsted's brother-in-law, Robert Hallwyn. "Yes, Aurora has told us of your gallant conduct, which we really cannot sufficiently admire. As for reward, it would be absurd to dream of it. There is no reward sufficient for such bravery."

"Unless," said Mrs. Hallwyn, with an arch smile, and a look at Aurora, "unless indeed——"

"Ah! yes, unless," replied Hallwyn, significantly; "but of that by-and-bye."

"Let us hope so," thought Guy, who began to feel extremely uncomfortable—criminal in fact—when he remembered the kiss he pressed upon her lips.

"How do you feel now?" asked the doctor, fortunately giving a turn to the conversation.

"Very ill—very weak," said Guy. "Let me have some wine."

Wine being brought, he was advised when he had drank it to go to bed.

This he refused to do.

If it *was* his fate to be ill, he preferred to be so at the house of Simon Grandley, where he should be among friends, where Minnie could smooth his

pillow; where, in fact, he should feel himself at home.

Besides, he wished truly to be away from the influence of Aurora.

Not that he feared least his love for Minnie should be undermined.

Far from it.

It was too deeply rooted for that.

But, as most young men would have been under the circumstances, when a pretty girl's feelings were concerned, he felt awkward.

"I would rather at once proceed to Simon Grandley's," he said; "they will be most anxious to see me. Besides, that is my home, and I should feel ill at ease in a strange place like this."

"My house is at your service," said Mr. Hallwyn, cordially.

"I thank you, sir," said Guy, "but I would much rather return to my master's. I know well how anxious all there are to see me after my being absent four days."

During this conversation the eyes of Aurora Halsted were turned upon him more than once with an expression of reproach.

Could she not tend him?

Such was her first thought.

The second thought was more galling.

He would be tended by Minnie Grandley.

The fierce demon of jealousy at once invaded her bosom.

But, though Guy noticed the colour rise and then fade, she said nothing.

Had she been less conscious of her own beauty she could have felt thrown back upon herself by such a desire of the Foundling's to hurry home.

She, however, took it in another sense.

He desired to return to the house of Simon Grandley, no doubt.

That was but natural.

Simon Grandley was his master—his benefactor and friend.

As such Guy owed him, of course, the first duty; but as for Minnie——

She must have cast a web over him—must have influenced him by some strange glamour—or Guy would never even have dreamed of her.

Perhaps he *did not* think of her.

There was joy to her in this thought.

Perhaps Simon Grandley knew that Guy the Foundling was the heir to a fine property, and so desired him as a husband for his daughter.

These ideas flashed quickly through the young girl's brain while Guy the Foundling was preparing to depart.

Mr. Hallwyn, however, would not suffer him to go before he had partaken of a substantial meal.

"Wine, my boy," he said, "may give you strength for a time, but it is only a false strength. After your long fast you require food."

Having acceded to this request the hero took his leave.

He had seen enough now to know Aurora's feelings towards him.

"Now or never," he thought, "is the time to end this for ever."

She gave him a chance, as if on purpose.

"Good bye, dear Guy," she said, as she stood in the doorway apart from her friends, "I shall never forget your devoted courage, and I shall come and see you."

"Do," returned Guy, "do. I shall always be glad to see you. I shall look upon you for ever as a dear sister!"

He pressed her hand as he said this, and quitted her side.

He did not glance round.

Had he done so he would scarcely have been astonished.

The words he had uttered seemed to have turned her into stone.

She stood there, gazing after him with a still, unmoving stare.

Sister!

That was all then!

After all her yearnings—the unconquerable love that was welling up in her maiden bosom—the heart-burnings—the eager desire that their lives should be linked together!

Sister!

The word was so cold, so chilling—so utterly repugnant to the feelings of one whose nature was all fire—that she could scarcely at first give credit to her senses.

When she had somewhat recovered she gave a shudder, and, rushing away from the spot, threw herself into the arms of her aunt, and wept bitterly.

In vain was she asked to render an explanation of her grief.

She said it arose from excitement—from—in fact she didn't know.

And that was all she would say.

Her heart was full of more than sorrow, be it added.

It was full of plotting now—plotting to upset all Minnie's plans of happiness.

Guy, meanwhile, when he had quitted Aurora, eagerly hurried homewards.

Loving Minnie as he did, he knew how anxious she would be to see him, and how full of alarm, moreover, Simon and his wife would be at his unaccountable absence.

He did not find them as he expected, however, plunged in consternation.

Will Lightmore had not long arrived and told of his deliverance.

Their only fear now, therefore, was that he might be imperilled by the riots.

There was no reserve in this meeting.

Minnie Grandley flung her arms round his neck and wept her joy out there, while Simon and his wife looked on with tears in their eyes.

Dick Hatherden was for the time forgotten in the general joy—a joy in which, be it said, Betty, the servant girl, joined, heartily hugging and kissing Will Lightmore to her heart's content, in spite of the presence of her master and mistress.

When, however, Dick was thought of, it was settled to be a matter of difficulty what could be done in regard to him.

To punish him Simon had all the will.

Yet how?

Would it be prudent or serviceable to himself to assert his power over him as a master?

He decided at length that it would not be judicious.

More than one thing led him to arrive at this conclusion.

Main of all reasons, however, was the fact that Dick Hatherden knew all his connection with the Protestant Association—a matter which he desired to be kept secret.

"Let him be, and go his own way to the devil," said Simon, when Guy asked him what he had resolved to do; "we can drive him there no sooner than he can go himself."

———

CHAPTER VIII.

THE CONSPIRATORS MEET ONCE MORE — JONAS BARNSDAKE'S ELOQUENCE — DICK HATHERDEN ADDRESSES THE MEETING—HE PROPOSES TO AID THEM—THE STORY HE TOLD—THE OWL AND THE TREASURE—A SCHEME OF VILLAINY.

WE must now turn for a time to some personages whom we have neglected.

Jonas Barnsdake and his friends.

They were, as may be imagined, well pleased with the course events were taking.

Jonas, especially, persisted in regarding the riots as produced entirely by religious zeal.

"The good work has begun in earnest," he said to the man who brought him the news of the riot at the Red Eagle; "and soon the enthusiasm will spread more and more. But a few hours now have we to wait before our great leader will enter the Commons at the head of an army against which no fanatics dare try to stand."

On the evening of the day of the riots near the Red Eagle, Jonas and a large party of friends were assembled in the room where we first met them.

The faces of all were pale and anxious.

Even those whose hearts were not in the cause, knew now that something definite and desperate was about to happen.

Jonas Barnsdake himself wore a look as if he felt inspired, and when he rose to address the assemblage he poured forth such a torrent of eloquence that he surprised even himself.

Among those present were, as may be guessed, Dick Hatherden and some of his worthy companions.

When Jonas Barnsdake had finished speaking he rose to his feet.

"Gentlemen," he said, "I'm only a poor apprentice, and therefore it may appear presumptuous to address you; but as I and my friends have found out something of importance perhaps you will give me leave to speak."

"Certainly," said Jonas Barnsdake; "in such a good cause as this there should be no distinction of persons."

A loud murmur of assent followed these words.

Accordingly Dick Hatherden began.

"Well then, gentlemen," he said; "we all know that in two days there is to be a great gathering in London.

"Our chief here has spoken to you of it.

"It is a time to which we are all looking forward with anxiety.

"We know that those hours will be fraught with danger.

"But even *you* do not know to what extent that danger will surround you.

"What I have to tell you is a strange story, and will take some little time.

"But, as it will show you how—through traitors or some such agency—our doings are well known to the authorities, I beg you will grant me time."

Permission was at once accorded, and Dick Hatherden began.

But as it would be tedious to give his own words we will narrate it in our own.

When Dick Hatherden escaped from the hands of those who had captured him on the occasion of the riot, he rushed away at once from that neighbourhood, and making for a low house of entertainment which he knew in Westminster, slept there for the night.

Not knowing who might have been watching him he kept within all day.

Towards night, however, he ventured out.

He had not gone many yards from the door when a hand was placed on his shoulder.

As may be supposed he started in some alarm.

But though he glanced round at once, he did not in the semi-darkness recognise the person who had thus accosted him.

"Who are you, and what do you want with me?" he said.

The other laughed.

"What," he cried, "don't you know me?"

The voice seemed familiar.

"Are you The Owl?" he asked.

"That's the name, my lad," replied the other. "Bill Hazard, you know, is still in prison, while I am free. I know what position you hold among the fellows who are going to turn out in a day or two, so I've come here to tell you something important."

"What is it, then?"

The Owl laughed.

"There's a condition attached to it."

"And what's that?"

"Well, it is money that will open all secrets," said the Owl; "and money is the condition now. But, come, let's go in and have a drink, and I will tell you all about it."

They adjourned accordingly into the tap-room of the Five Bells, where there were very few people, and seated themselves by the fire.

"In the first place," said Dick Hatherden, "tell me how you found out that I was here."

The Owl clapped him on the back and leaned forward confidentially.

"That's one of the secrets," he said; "you see *you* slept in a kind of back kitchen."

"I did."

THE RIVAL APPRENTICES

A TALE OF THE RIOTS OF 1780.

"THEY SHALL BE BURNT!" CRIED ALEXIS. "THEY WOULD RUIN US!"

"Well, *I* was iu the rat-hole."

"The rat-hole—what is that?"

"Why, you see, it's a deserted vault beneath the kitchen. It's right against the beer cellar; but it's never used, and, in fact, it's been forgotten, I think. That's were I live."

"Not a very comfortable lodging," said Dick. "What makes you go there?"

"Why I am on the track of a mystery," replied The Owl, "and that's what I am going to explain. I think it will be a grand thing for you and for me; but, meanwhile, you must understand that I am in immediate want of money, and I want you to aid me in getting it."

Dick's eyes glistened.

His companion's thoughts were just consonant with his own.

He had decided not to return to his master.

Money, therefore, was the first thing that was necessary.

"I will, willingly," he said; "if you only tell me how it is to be managed."

"That I will at once," returned The Owl.

Then he drew his chair closer to Dick Hatherden, and lowered his voice.

"You see, old Gramstay, that keeps this house, is a bit of a miser, and I have found out that he keeps his money here. I know where it is concealed, and I thought, at one time, that I could succeed in doing the job myself, but I find I can't."

"Why not? Is the treasure box so heavy that you can't carry it?" returned Dick, with a smile.

"No, it isn't that. But the old fellow not only sleeps with loaded weapons beneath his pillow, but he has taught a huge and savage mastiff to sleep on the treasure box."

"The attempt will never succeed, then," cried Dick. "The dog will wake on the first alarm."

"Ah! that is where *you* will aid me."

"How so?"

"Easily. Your back kitchen is by no means comfortable, is it?"

"It might be better."

"Well, then, you must tell your landlord that you will rent one of his rooms."

"I see—one near his bedroom?"

"Exactly. Well, then, when night comes, you must coax the dog out and give him a piece of poisoned meat, which will be prepared by me. He will be dead in a couple of hours, and then we can proceed to our work."

"Why not give it to him in the day-time?"

"Why, if the dog died in the day, suspicion would at once be excited. No! no! I am an older hand at such things than you, and I understand them better."

"And when are we to do this?"

"To-morrow night."

"Very well, I will be ready; but do not forget one thing."

"What is that?"

"To get a room from an old miser requires money. I have none."

"Very good; then I will give you some. I have but a few shillings, but to those you are welcome. It wont take much. I'll be here to-morrow and bring with me the prepared meat."

"But the secret?"

The Owl grinned.

"Ah," he said; "wait till we've done this job.

The first great secret for you will be to catch hold of a lump of money. Will it not?"

"Yes," said Dick; "but you swear you are not deceiving me?"

If he had known that he had betrayed Bill Hazard into the hands of justice he would have fled from him at once.

But the Bow Street runners were not men to prattle about their business.

"Deceiving you—why should I?" asked The Owl. "It will be for my good as well as yours if I do not deceive you. No—no, when we've got the old man's gold we'll be more able to achieve what is the great desire of your heart."

"Does old Gramstay know that you live in what you call the rat-hole?"

"Not he."

"Then how do you get to it?"

"Ah! that is part of my secret," cried The Owl; "let's have some drink now, for I must be going. Here is the silver you want, and mind the first thing in the morning you make terms with the old man."

And so they parted.

CHAPTER IX.

DICK HATHERDEN ACTS ON THE OWL'S ADVICE—HE OBTAINS THE ROOM AND LOOKS ABOUT HIM—HIS ADVENTURE WITH THE PRETTY SERVING-MAID—THE MASTIFF AND THE POISONED MEAT—THE LOVE ADVENTURE OF THE TRAITOR—NIGHT APPROACHES.

ON the following morning Dick Hatherden lost no time in acting upon the advice of The Owl.

He entered the bar early, called for some of the best ale, asked the landlord to join him, and said—

"I say, Mr. Gramstay, I shall never be able to sleep in your back kitchen there."

The old miser looked at him in pretended astonishment—

"Not in that beautiful room?"

Dick laughed.

"Beautiful room," cried he, "and beautiful company."

"Company! Why, what company?"

"Rats and mice. I wonder I've a bit of toe left, the way they were nibbling at me. Haven't you a room upstairs?"

"Yes; but it's more money—much more money," said Gramstay.

"That doesn't matter," said Dick; "I am going out this morning, and I shall get some and pay you."

"Very well," said the miser at once. "Will you have a look at it now?"

"No; not now. I will wait till evening. It's sure to suit me. I'm in a hurry now. Good morning."

And so he hastily quitted the place.

As may be imagined, both he and The Owl, intent on their villanous purpose, were eager for evening to arrive.

They both arrived nearly at the same time.

The prepared meat was ready, and with eager haste Dick asked to see his room.

The old man at once despatched the servant to show it to him.

Nothing could have happened better for Dick than this.

He saw his way at once.

He saw the bed-chamber—a little murky place, with which, however, he expressed every satisfaction.

Then, as they were preparing to leave it, he started suddenly.

"What's that?" he cried.

"What's what?" asked the girl, who was one of the pert and pretty sort.

"I thought I heard a noise, like that of a dog howling, that's all."

"A dog?"

"Yes; I didn't know you had one."

"We have one, but he sleeps in master's room. He's generally so quiet that no one thinks we have one. There must be something wrong going on to make him growl. I will go and see. You stop here."

"No; I may as well come," said Dick.

"Master will be cross if he knows it."

"But then he won't. There may be some one in there. See, then, what danger you would be in."

The girl herself was apprehensive of some peril.

So, though she had objected, she was really glad of his aid and company.

They approached the door together, therefore, and the girl cautiously opened it.

It was not far from his own bedroom.

This Dick at once noticed.

All was quiet within.

"There's nothing here wrong," cried Dick, as he held the candle up and glanced round, while the mastiff, with a slight growl, left his post on the chest and approached.

"Oh! if master were to know this," said the girl; "quick—let us go."

Dick's chance was now or never.

He flung his arm round the girl's waist and kissed her, while, at the same time, he dropped the prepared meat on the floor.

"I'll scream if you do that again," cried the girl, blushing and laughing.

"That's an invitation," thought Dick.

And so again their lips met in a thrilling kiss.

"If you were to scream, the old man would be up," he said as, casting a sly glance downwards, he saw that the mastiff had eaten the meat. "We'll go now, though, or we may be found out."

And then he kissed her again, pulled to the door and went down.

"The fool just played into my hands," thought Dick.

"A very nice young man, and I hope he'll stop here," said the girl to herself.

The Owl was waiting anxiously in the taproom.

"Is all well?" he asked, as Dick entered.

"All correct," said Dick; "we've nothing to do now but to wait. But I do not yet see how you are to join me upstairs."

"Oh, never fear," returned The Owl, "I know the place well, and everything that goes on in it, or I should not have been able to tell you all I have. At one o'clock I'll be standing at your bedside."

"But you don't know the room."

"Don't I. Well, we'll see when the time comes."

The Owl now, although knowing perfectly well that the robbery would be likely to end in bloodshed, became quite jovial, and after partaking of and paying for a sumptuous supper, he called for some strong drink, and produced some cards.

"This will pass away the time," he said.   "I'm impatient, I can tell you, and if I hadn't got something to do the time would never seem to pass."

It passed quickly, however.

At length the time for closing came.

Lighted to his room by the pretty servant, Dick eagerly locked the door and threw himself on his bed, dressed as he was, to sleep off some of the fumes of drink.

The young girl had evidently hoped and imagined that there would be some repetition of the love-making of a few hours before.

But in this she was mistaken.

Dick was in no humour for that.

All he desired was that the inmates of the house would retire as soon as possible to rest.

So he kissed her, pretended to be more drunk than he really was, and stumbled in.

"Well, a drunken man is a beast," said the girl.

And with that she dismissed him from her thoughts till the morrow.

Then, however, she resolved to renew her fascinations.

Dick was not badly dressed considering his station; and she had seen him flashing about some money.

So she was determined, if possible, to pin him safely to her apron.

The drink which Dick Hatherden had imbibed soon took effect upon him, and in a few moments he had lapsed into a dead slumber.

CHAPTER X.

NIGHT COMES — THE DREAM OF THE PAST — THE FRIGHT OF THE YOUNG ASSASSIN — THE OWL ROUSES HIM TO LIFE—THE MURDERERS PREPARE FOR THE DEED — THE MONEY-CHEST — THE OLD MAN IS ROUSED—THE MURDER—THE ALARM IS GIVEN — THE ATTACK ON THE DOOR—ANOTHER DOUBLE MURDER—HOW THE BODIES WERE DISPOSED OF.

THREE o'clock struck by the clock of St. Stephens.

Loudly, solemnly, it chimed over the still and sleeping city.

Strange noises had been heard around the Five Bells.

Yet all slept.

Suddenly Dick Hatherden sprang up in the darkness like one demented.

"No, no," he cried, in wild accents, and flinging his arms about in the air. "No, no. It was not I who killed him, no——"

Then he was flung back on the bed, and a heavy hand was placed over his mouth.

"Curse you," said a voice, "would you rouse up the whole house?"

It was The Owl who spoke.

But for a few moments Dick could not recognise him.

He kept kicking and trying to cry out; and it was not until The Owl had shook him violently for some minutes that he subsided.

"Well you're a nice sort of fellow to help any one, *you* are," said The Owl, as he sat down on the bed and wiped the beads of perspiration off his forehead. "I wonder the whole cursed house isn't swarming about us."

"How could I know it was you? I was dreaming," said Dick.

His voice was still doleful, and his limbs shivering as with ague.

No wonder.

He had had a horrible vision.

He had dreamed over again the murder of old Colonel Halsted.

Then he had seen once more the chamber where the assassination had been committed—he had seen the confusion and broken furniture, which told of the deadly struggle, and the corpse sitting up in the cupboard in an attitude as if of life.

He could not, at this moment, throw off the dream of horror.

But presently came another vision!

It was no longer the chamber of crime.

It was a court, and the judge was passing sentence.

He heard the awful condemnation—

"Death."

Then he was fighting with half-a-dozen powerful constables, and was dragged shrieking from the dock.

It was at this moment that he had been found by The Owl.

"Strike a light," he said. "There's some brandy on the table. We require some of it—at any rate, *I* do, after my dream."

The light having been procured, Dick took a deep draught of the ardent spirit, and his courage having thus been artificially renewed, he was prepared for work.

"Now, then," he said to The Owl, "what is your programme of operations?"

"We must enter the room together," said the other. "You must stand by the bedside of old Gramstay while I pick the lock of the chest. If he wakes and observes us you must kill him."

Dick shuddered.

He was in no mood for blood-shedding.

His dream had spoiled him for murder—at any rate, for the time.

"I would rather *you* did it," he said.

"Why?—are you afraid?"

"Not I. But the old man is strong and powerful, and could master me. At any rate, I could not overpower him quickly enough to prevent him crying out."

"And you," sneered The Owl, "because you're overcome with some squeamishness, want me to leave in your hands the task of opening the treasure chest, when you don't understand how to pick a lock."

"I do," replied Dick; "try me."

The Owl, however, was resolute.

"If you're going to cry off," he said, "tell me so. All I know is that I am not going to alter my plan. You'll have the full share of swag, and to-morrow night I'll explain to you the mystery I promised. Come—no lagging. Time is passing, and old people wake early."

Dick saw there was no getting out of it.

Further refusal would make The Owl angry.

Then he knew the consequence.

So he opened the door and listened.

All was still.

The strange noises had been caused by The Owl forcing an entrance.

But neither they nor the mad cries of Dick Hatherden had roused any one.

"Everything favours us," whispered The Owl, "come, along."

He passed on as quickly and as easily as if he had known the way from one room to another all his life.

In a few moments the old man's door was opened and shut, and they stood within the bed chamber.

All was hushed.

The business had been done well.

The faithful guardian of his master's gold was long since dead.

The Owl crept on all fours towards the chest, and dragging the cold body of the dog off it, placed it on the floor, while Dick gliding to the bedside of the old man stood ready, knife in hand.

The Owl was an adept at his work.

It was not long before the much coveted gold lay exposed to view in the light of the dark lantern which he had brought with him.

"See here," he whispered, exultingly, as he clutched a handful, and before putting it in his pocket showed it to Dick.

In an instant he repented it.

Two of the coins fell with a rattle on the floor; and in an instant the old man started up.

The rattle of his favourite gold was quite enough to rouse him.

Had thunder boomed around his bed, and lightning flashed in upon him, they would have had no greater effect.

Dick, whose attention had for a moment been distracted, turned at once towards him, knife in hand.

But he was too late to prevent the old miser's shouting at the top of his voice—

"Ah! thieves—villains—murderers! Help here—help!"

In another instant Dick's knife descended.

But in his nervousness he only stabbed the old fellow through the shoulder.

This maddened him, without taking from him his power of speech.

More stoutly still rose the cry.

"Help! help!"

The Owl was exasperated.

All the time he had been shovelling the gold into his pockets.

"Curse you," he cried; "can't you quiet him—we'll have all the house upon us in a moment.

Smother him in the bedclothes if you can't do anything else."

This time Dick obeyed.

Raising the knife once more, he plunged it in the old man's chest.

This was enough.

He uttered one shrill cry.

Then a groan gurgled as it were upon his lips.

And then—

Death claimed him.

Again Dick Hatherden was a murderer.

Just as the deed was completed there was a loud noise at the door.

There were no other persons in the house, save the servant whom we have already described, and a man who assisted behind the bar.

Both slept on the same floor of the old tavern, and both had heard the cries of the old fellow and hurried from their beds.

"What is the matter? Open the door, here," cried the man.

"Quick," said The Owl; "cover up the body in the bedclothes and then open the door."

Dick turned to him in amazement.

"What! and admit them? Are you mad?" said he.

"There is no other means of exit."

"The window."

"No, no, there is a sheer fall of twenty feet. Throw open the door and then lie down, they will fall over you, and we will dash down the stairs and escape."

The Owl knew more of the place than Dick, so he simply did as directed.

Creeping along as noiselessly as he could, he opened the door and then lay down.

It happened just as The Owl had said.

The man and the girl, who stood there in their nightdresses, came plunging in, and both fell headlong over the prostrate form of Dick.

But they did not remain so an instant.

When Dick tried to spring up, the agile girl was up, too, and had him by the throat.

"Villain," she said, "I know you. So you've been robbing master."

One gleam of moonlight had told all.

It had revealed to the horror-stricken maid the features of him whom she had hoped to have secured to herself as a husband.

Dick had a weakness of a decided nature in favour of the fair sex.

He felt loath to kill the unfortunate creature before him.

But seeing that The Owl had quite his match in the stalwart barman, he said, as he grasped the wrist of the hand which had seized his throat and with his knife-hand pushed her from him—

"Unhand me, girl, and promise to be quiet, or I must kill you."

The cool and cruel way in which these words were said was sufficient to convince her that he meant all he said.

But she was a courageous girl.

And, moreover, she had confidence in the strength of her robust arms, and large, muscular limbs.

"No, no," she cried, working her lithe body from his grasp, and seizing him more firmly with both hands, "I am not afraid, and will hold you till help comes."

And then exerting all her strength she forced him back against the wall.

Dick felt now that she must die.

She knew him—she could bear witness against him, and be his death.

That was enough.

Firmly clutching his knife, he suddenly drove it into her back between her shoulders.

She had not expected this.

In fact, she had not seen the knife.

With one gasping cry, one murmured word, "Villain," she sank down—her hold relaxed and with a thud she fell on the floor.

Dick knelt down, and placed his hand over her heart.

It still beat.

"She lives," he cried, and ruthlessly again the knife was buried in the fair body, from whose white bosom one long sigh came shuddering forth and all was over.

Then he turned to aid The Owl.

Another crime yet had to be accomplished, for the man knew them both, and was aware that Dick was a lodger.

He found The Owl struggling violently, and evidently at a disadvantage.

The brave barman's efforts, however, were now entirely unavailing.

Dick Hatherden glided up behind, and in an instant the knife, still reeking with the blood of the murdered girl, was plunged into his back.

He fell heavily to the ground, and in a moment the murder was completed by The Owl.

"Well," said the latter, as he came out into the passage, "we've had a tidy fight for it. That girl nearly settled *you*; and as for me, if she had kept you much longer, I should have been done for altogether. Well, there's no hurry now. All seems quiet in the neighbourhood, and we're alone in the house, so we'd better go down to the bar and have something to drink."

Dick Hatherden, who was trembling with excitement, gladly acquiesced in this arrangement; and in a very short time the two villains were regaling themselves with some ardent spirits.

Day was fully breaking ere they were ready to start.

Before going they changed their clothes for some belonging to the barman, as their own were smothered in blood.

"And now," said Dick, "I tell you my advice."

"And what is that?"

"That we fire the house."

The Owl thought a moment.

"Well," he said, "there's just a chance of its interfering with the unravelling of the secret I mentioned to you."

"Don't let it do that!"

"And yet," continued The Owl, "if we don't do as you say, this house will be broken into, and my rat-hole will be explored, and then it's all up with our work for to-night. Yes, we'll do it. Follow me."

So saying, he hurried up the stairs; and making for the landing where the body of the murdered girl lay, threw open the window shutters and admitted the light of day.

To any persons less hardened in sin than Dick Hatherden and The Owl, the sight of the wretched girl as she lay there with her night-clothes and her white limbs dabbled in blood, would have caused a feeling of sickening horror.

But with them it was different.

They were used to sights of the kind.

Taking up the body, therefore, by the head and feet, so as not to stain the clothes they wore, they carried it into the bed-room of the old man.

Here they dragged the bed into the centre of the room, and placed on it the bodies of the girl and the dog beside the murdered landlord.

Then they took the corpse of the barman, and carried it into the room which had been occupied by Dick Hatherden, so that it might be supposed that he, too, had perished in the fire.

Then Dick went down into the bar and brought up two gallons of spirits.

This was poured over the dead bodies, the floors, and over the heap of broken furniture which The Owl had made.

This was then set fire to, and the doors closed; after which they slunk down and let themselves into the parlours.

These and the bar were quickly drenched in spirits and fired; and when they at length passed out into the street they left behind them a perfect sea of flame.

"Now then," said The Owl, as they reached the corner of the street, "we must separate. I found five hundred pounds in gold, and I have given you half, have I not?"

"Yes."

"Well, that is proof I am not deceiving you. So meet me to-night at eight (it will be dark then) at this corner, and I will tell you the secret."

Then they parted, and hurried away in different directions.

CHAPTER XI.

THE VAULT—THE STORY OF THE STRANGE DUEL—THE BURNING PAPERS—THE FIGHT AND THE RESULT—THE ALARM—THE CONSPIRATORS ENTER THE CELLAR—THE PLANS OF THE CATHOLICS—THE EAVESDROPPERS.

NIGHT came, and at the appointed hour Dick and The Owl met.

It was a part of Dick's programme, on coming into a sum of money almost fabulous to him, to dress himself in the height of the fashion, to throw himself once more in the path of Aurora Halsted, and, while begging her pardon for all that had occurred at the Red Eagle, endeavour to persuade her that he had at length discovered his friends, and was now about to realise a splendid fortune.

But for the present he had satisfied himself with buying some new clothes of an ordinary shape and texture, and casting the tell-tale garments of the murdered barman into the river Thames.

Both he and The Owl were eager to see what had happened.

When they neared the spot an immense crowd was assembled.

In the darkness there was nothing to fear.

So they mingled freely with the crowd.

What a change was there.

The Genius of Evil seemed to have specially favoured his disciples.

The tavern was absolutely gone.

Where it had stood there was but an empty space —a smoking ruin.

Many were the remarks made by the crowd, and from them the murderers at once gathered that the general belief was that the whole household had perished in the flames.

There had been no need of the precautions they had taken in removing the bodies.

Not a vestige of them had been seen.

They had disappeared among the terrific conflagration of the old wooden house.

The Owl hurried Dick away towards a spot at the back of the ruins.

Here by the side of a wall he slung himself down into a ditch, and so reached a window, if a grated hole can be so called.

This he pushed open, and Dick, who had followed him, found that they were standing in a vaulted chamber or cellar beneath the Five Bells.

"I see where we are," he said.

"Yes; but you can't *guess* what you are *going* to see."

And so saying The Owl who, like his namesake, seemed able to see in the dark, led him across the vault, and pushed open a door which seemed in somewhat better repair than the window by which they had entered.

He halted as he pushed it.

"Be silent," he said, "for a moment. I do not think that anyone has yet arrived, but they may have assembled earlier."

Dick was lost in astonishment.

What could he mean?

What strange company had he come to see?

However he resolved to do as he was bid.

In the hideous tragedy of the preceding night The Owl had acted as he had promised.

So he could trust him now.

Having entered and closed the door behind them, The Owl hurried across the murky chamber, and glanced through an aperture in the wall, which in the darkness was quite invisible to Dick Hatherden.

The scrutiny seemed to satisfy him.

"It's all right," he said, returning, "so we can have a drink and a smoke before they come."

So saying he struck a light and lighted a murky lantern, that stood on a kind of extempore shelf in the corner.

This showed what kind of place it was.

It was as black, cobwebby, chill, wretched a place as could be.

Yet there was a table, a chair, and a kind of extemporised bed.

The Owl had made it his home.

And here he was with two hundred and fifty pounds in his pocket still remaining there.

Of necessity, there was some mysterious reason for this.

It soon came out what it was.

"You seem surprised at my home," he said, as he seated himself on the table.

"Well, it's not a luxurious one, you must admit," said Dick Hatherden.

"No, you're right; but I have a purpose in it," said The Owl; "I'll tell you what.

"One night I was hiding away from the Bow Street runners in this crib (which I found quite by accident) when I heard a noise in the adjoining vault.

"As you may fancy, I listened eagerly.

"I thought, of course, that they were after me.

"I was soon undeceived.

"I saw a number of men in a cellar, which had been so draped and disguised as to look like a room of elegant appearance.

"They were evidently excited, and one of them was burning some papers at a lamp, while at his sword's point he was keeping back a man who would have withheld his arm.

"'They must be burnt,' he cried, 'or they would ruin us if found by any one.'

"And in a few moments they were ashes.

"The man whom he had pushed back, and evidently wounded, was now in a state of great exasperation.

"'This insult cannot be borne,' he cried; 'defend yourself.'

"And he drew and placed himself in front of the other.

"He was nothing loth.

"He put himself at once into position, and waved back the others, who I could see were anxious to interfere.

"'No, no, friends,' he cried, 'let this madman have his own way—I will soon teach him his folly.'

"The battle was short and fierce.

"Both were good swordsmen.

"Both, moreover, seemed determined to fight it out to the death.

"The man who had burned the papers was the better man, however.

"And he had the sympathy, evidently, of all those round him.

"Every time he made a successful thrust or parry there was suppressed cheering.

"Whether this disheartened his opponent, or whether he was angry at his own shortcomings, I cannot say.

"At any rate, his strokes became very wild and furious.

"The other remained quite quiet.

"Every thrust told now.

"After a while, indeed, his adversary was compelled to give ground.

"He was severely wounded, and the blood was trickling down his fine clothes.

"His face was deadly pale.

"There was on his face, too, a look as if he plainly saw the fate threatening him.

"At length the other assumed a different course of action.

"He appeared to rouse himself to more rapid exertion.

"This quite upset the other's plans.

"He seemed faint and weary, and became still wilder.

"The end came soon now.

"Suddenly the conqueror's sword gleamed like a flash of light.

"So quick was it that I scarcely saw it strike; but there was a groan and a heavy fall, and the challenger was dead.

"The other wiped his sword, returned it to its scabbard, and turned to the company—

"'Have I done right, gentlemen?' he said, bowing respectfully.

"'Yes, Alexis Rainsford.'"

"Alexis Rainsford," interrupted Dick Hatherden, in surprise.

"Do you know him then?" asked The Owl.

"Yes, I do indeed. He was a friend of poor Colonel Halsted, who was such a friend to me."

"Well, let me finish, for I have no doubt they will soon be here.

"'Yes, Alexis Rainsford,' said one of the assemblage; 'yes, you have done right. Indeed, you could have done no other; but explain more fully your reasons for burning those papers.'

"'I will,' said Alexis Rainsford. 'You must know that Reuben Arkwright, then, who has fallen now a victim to his own folly, entrusted me with certain papers connected with our movements, and the action we were to take to stop the excitement which will take place against us if this Protestant demonstration takes place.

"'They were entrusted to me, you must understand, for the purpose of showing them to our leader, whose name I need not mention.

"'They were shown and returned to me.

"'I was told to read them.

"'I did so; and told Reuben Arkwright so.

"'He then desired to take them again.

"'This I refused to allow.

"'*Why* I refused is readily explained.

"'I was told by our chief to destroy them when I had read them, for the simple reason that he has no faith in Reuben Arkwright's honesty.

"'That is all my explanation.'

"His words were received with enthusiasm, and the body being placed on one side beneath a cloak they sat down round the table.

"They then went into a lot of minute details in regard to their plan.

"These I could not follow, but I knew that, as you are a member of the Protestant Association, you would gladly discover this secret."

"And will they be sure to be here again to-night?" asked Dick Hatherden.

"Yes, certain. I heard them make arrangements to do so, but they did not name the hour. You will get rewarded for this discovery, and, of course, you will share the gain with me."

"Depend upon it I will," said Dick Hatherden; "but hark, put out the light, I hear some one approaching."

The Owl sprang up.

In an instant the place was again in utter darkness.

"Where is the part where we can see them?" asked Dick, eagerly.

"This way; take my hand," said The Owl, and led him to the side of the vault.

Here there were two loopholes, through which, as some people entered bearing lights, he could see the room which The Owl had described.

About twenty men filed into the place one after another.

For some time Dick Hatherden saw no one whose face was familiar.

Presently, however, he started.

"Ha!" he said; "there is Alexis Rainsford, and by the Lord, there is walking by his side one of our men—Oldham, the joiner. We have traitors in the camp."

CHAPTER XII.

THE FATE OF CONSPIRACIES — THE PLANS OF THE CATHOLICS TO STAY THE PROCESSION—THE OWL AND DICK HATHERDEN OVERHEAR THEIR SCHEMES — THEY RESOLVE TO TELL JONAS BARNSDAKE — THE PROTESTANT CONSPIRATORS TAKE MEASURES ACCORDINGLY—THE ATTACK AND SURPRISE.

THIS is, alas, the evil of all conspiracies.

It has been so from the beginning.

No matter in what country, a conspiracy—however successfully it may have carried out its business in the first instance—has always at some time or another had to combat the acts of a traitor.

Abundant instances could be cited.

In this case—excepting so far as it tended to bloodshed—it mattered little.

But so it was.

By the side of Alexis Rainsford walked Oldham, who had pretended to be one of the staunchest of the friends of the Protestant Association.

It is always your traitor who is so impetuously enthusiastic.

It is he always who tries to impress upon you his fidelity.

A man who has independence in him (which means, after all, only a proper knowledge of his own abilities) will be sure to let out this feeling now and then.

He is your best servant—your best friend.

Oldham, on the contrary, was a conspirator of that sort that a far-seeing tyrant would have used as a tool in any dirty work.

He was a specious-looking wretch.

He had a high forehead—one of those benevolent-looking brows that one sees on fraudulent managers of companies, and chairmen of bubble companies.

He spoke with a bland mellifluence; he was a martyr to his love of religion; he idolised the Protestant faith and was a Catholic at heart!

"We shall hear some pretty things now," said the Owl; "but I thought he was a Protestant and a friend of your master's."

"I thought he was a friend to Simon Grandley," whispered Oldham; "I know nothing of his faith. He was a friend, however, to Colonel Halsted, who was a Catholic. But hush! they are going to begin!"

To give my readers a full account of their proceedings would be tedious.

The details would possess no interest.

They began by detailing what had been done, and then proceeded to detail what was yet to be done.

The treachery of Oldham was undoubted.

And all, after all, that his treachery tended to do was to place money in his own pocket, and cause a collision between the people in the streets.

The opponents of the movement, however, of which Lord George Gordon had foolishly suffered himself to be named head, had a more Jesuitical policy really in view.

They desired to gain the names of those who were the chiefs of the subdivisions of the vast multitude which was expected to assemble, and either spirit them away, or reduce them to such an abject state of drunkenness that they would be unable to appear at the time agreed upon.

Thus, they wished so to confuse the whole affair that it would take the form of a mere disorderly mob, and not an organised and well-conducted procession.

Dick Hatherden heard enough, however, to make his heart leap.

He heard enough to take to the leaders of the Protestant Association, and procure for himself the thanks of all.

This would be the first step towards the grandeur to which he aspired.

So, on the evening we named some little time back, he told all.

That is to say, in regard to Oldham, the joiner.

The means which had led to the discovery, he, of course, concealed.

His words were listened to with deep attention.

When he had concluded he was received with loud applause.

As may well be imagined, he did not, in giving details of the affair, forget to magnify the perils he had undergone.

He was regarded, therefore, as a prodigy of valour.

When the applause had subsided, Jonas Barnsdake rose.

Immediate steps must be taken, he said, to counteract the Jesuitical influence of their enemies.

A consultation consequently was at once held upon the subject.

The details of this I need not give.

Suffice it that on the following night it was resolved to proceed to the ruined tavern and attack and make prisoners the whole of the conspirators.

An hour was named, and, as may be imagined, few were absent.

All had come armed.

To Dick Hatherden was assigned the part of leader on this occasion.

This was exactly what he had been craving for.

It seemed the commencement of what was now his sole aim and ambition—to attain a position in which he could appear to advantage before Aurora Halsted.

All was very quiet as they approached the spot near the ruins of the Five Bells, where The Owl was ready to receive them.

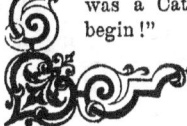

THE RIVAL APPRENTICES

A TALE OF THE RIOTS OF 1780.

A DOZEN BRUTAL HANDS FELLED HIM TO THE EARTH.

They were in great numbers, and their appearance consequently might have excited suspicion in the neighbourhood.

They were therefore told off in parties of six. The importance of the task assigned to him was not lost upon Dick Hatherden.

It was just the beginning of all he had wished and hoped for.

So it was, as may be imagined, with a beating heart that he took his way into the vaults beneath the ruins of the Five Bells, and waited in the largest one of all until the arrival of the main body of the conspirators.

At length all were assembled.

Every heart beat high with excitement, while old Jonas Barnsdake seemed beside himself with eagerness.

"Now," said Dick Hatherden, turning to The Owl, whose services (knowing, as he did, every intricacy of the place) he could not have dispensed with; "now, tell me what are the best means to use for surrounding them."

"Well," said The Owl, "*I* can tell you what to do —and none better. The ground about here is regularly honeycombed, and when they least expect it we can pour into their council chamber. Now let us consult as to which parties are to take the different positions."

A hurried and whispered conference took place.

Then Jonas Barnsdake and about twenty others, headed by Dick Hatherden, made their way through a narrow passage pointed out by The Owl, and thus got round to the further entrance of the furnished vault.

As they approached, The Owl suddenly halted.

"Wait a moment," he whispered; "there are sentinels posted here, I see."

He was right.

All along the dark underground corridor men were walking to and fro.

"We shall have difficulty here," said he. "Let half a dozen of the boldest follow me. These men must be silenced."

Drenched in blood as Dick Hatherden was, so to speak, the suggestion of The Owl had, of course, no terror for him.

He knew his meaning at once, and his knife was drawn ready from his belt.

It was different with others.

More especially with Jonas Barnsdake.

I have, I think, before sufficiently indicated his character to show that he was not a man of really bloodthirsty feelings.

When he saw the riots in the open streets, he and the soldiers advancing to the attack, he was aware, of course, that blood would be shed.

But this was in the open thoroughfare.

It was, in fact, the kind of *émeute* to which he had looked so enthusiastically forward as the commencement of a great movement.

But sly murder was a thing he could not in any way countenance.

His heart leaped, therefore, with no pleasant emotion when he heard what The Owl proposed.

That if the sentinels gave the alarm there would be wholesale bloodshed he could not doubt.

Yet this did not seem to authorise murder in his eyes.

"Stay," he said, in a low, tremulous voice, as he placed his hand on the arm of The Owl; "it will be possible to seize and bind them, will it not?"

The Owl chuckled.

A horrid chuckle that angered the old fanatic.

"There is no reason for that," he said; "we can dispose of them."

"It shall not be!" exclaimed Jonas Barnsdake, in a voice which might have betrayed them all. "No, no. Murder shall not lie on the souls of those who are engaged in promoting the sacred cause of religion. Harm them unnecessarily, and I will myself give the alarm."

The Owl turned to Dick Hatherden.

"Curse him!" he said. "Is this the man for a leader?"

"He is so now, at any rate," replied Dick; "and were you to attempt anything against him you would see how the men would rally round him. We must obey him now. I will speak to him."

He turned to Jonas Barnsdake.

"We are losing valuable time," he said, in a whisper; "if we do not silence these men we can do nothing. We shall, in fact, fall into our own trap. For what purpose are we here but to destroy them?"

Jonas Barnsdake shuddered.

"Heaven forbid!" he said; "we came for no such purpose. We came hither to let them know how we have discovered their plans, and to take them prisoners. We can hold them captive until they are no longer objects of fear, and then release them."

"Very well," growled The Owl, who was disgusted now at having anything to do with the affair; "we must be careful, then, how we act. We must glide along the ground and throw ourselves suddenly upon them."

So saying, he prepared to act upon his own suggestion.

Crawling along, followed by Dick Hatherden and some of the others, who by no means shared Jonas Barnsdake's scruples, he made his way along by the wall, and was soon standing behind one of the men.

Each of those who followed acted likewise.

Then, at a preconcerted signal, all sprang up, and before the astonished sentinels knew what was the matter, a gleaming knife pointed at the throat of each showed that death would follow the giving of an alarm.

"Now then! cords, cords," said Dick Hatherden to the others, who now came crowding noiselessly up. "Bind them quickly, or even this slight disturbance may reach the ears of those within."

The conspirators, delighted with the result of their first attempt, at once complied.

In a few minutes all those who had been stationed as sentinels were prisoners.

Blood, consequently, had not been shed as yet.

"Now," said Jonas Barnsdake, in a tone of exultation, "we will advance on the others. Let me proceed to the door and summon them to surrender."

A loud knock at the door of the vault startled the assembled conspirators.

"Who is there?" cried a voice.

"Those who demand your instant surrender," cried Jonas Barnsdake, in a loud voice.

There followed a few moments of silence.

Then the voice again spoke.

"You have made some mistake. To whom are we to surrender? We are doing no wrong."

"Unfasten the door, then," said Jonas Barnsdake, "and we will explain."

Again a few moments of whispered conference; after which the door was flung open, and Jonas Barnsdake and his friends found themselves confronted by a goodly array of gentlemen and others, who had stationed themselves, sword in hand, to defend the entrance.

"Now, sir," said Alexis Rainsford, confronting Jonas Barnsdake, "what is it you want?"

For an instant Jonas Barnsdake was so astounded at the verification of Dick Hatherden's words, that he could scarcely speak.

However, he recovered himself after a moment.

"Sir," he said, "I demand the unconditional surrender of yourself and friends into our hands."

"A modest request, truly," returned Alexis Rainsford. "And to whom then should we have the honour of surrendering?"

"To Jonas Barnsdake," replied the old man, proudly, "president of the Protestant Association."

"Well," said Alexis Rainsford, who evidently had some difficulty in retaining his composure; "well, this is altogether a most extraordinary proceeding. What have we to do with Protestant Associations? We know nothing of what you mean. How can our doings affect you? You have made a mistake; therefore, retire now, and leave us to ourselves."

Jonas Barnsdake assumed an air of sternness.

"You do not understand," he said; "then will I explain to you my meaning. You have been overheard—the object of your councils is known. But it is not by such as you that the good cause will be undone. No; no rabble rout shall make its way to the doors of St. Stephen's through Catholic interference. Until the glorious day is over you remain prisoners in our hands."

Alexis Rainsford uttered a sneering laugh.

This was to cover his real emotion.

But it failed.

All could see how agitated he was.

And no wonder was it.

He was well aware that now all would recognise the double game he had been playing.

Recognise it, too, before he had the chance of explaining his reason.

"And pray what else do you demand?" he asked, with a jeer.

"Oldham the joiner!"

"Oldham the joiner!"

"Pitch him out to us!"

"Let us have the traitor!"

"They answer for me," said Jonas Barnsdake, as these cries were shouted out simultaneously by the excited throng behind him; "you see the villain even now slinking away. But he cannot escape—the place is surrounded!"

Jonas Barnsdake was right.

As soon as the traitor had heard the cries of the mob, he had endeavoured, as the saying is, to make himself as small as he could, and to slink away into a corner.

But in vain.

The keen eyes of the old man had seen him, and the words fell upon his ear that told him the place was surrounded, and all hope of escape gone; he trembled, turned pale, and sat down.

Alexis Rainsford who, in spite of his natural bravery, experienced a strange and unaccountable emotion within his breast, now whispered a few words to two or three of the gentlemen by whom he was surrounded.

Then he once more turned to Jonas Barnsdake.

"Sir," he said, "these proceedings on your part are either the acts of a madman, or they are the result of mistake. As the fairest thing under the circumstances, therefore, we suggest that you and I shall select six each of our followers and dismiss the rest to their homes. Then we can remain here and enter into full explanations, which will, I am sure, be the best for all."

This was received with loud cries of "No, no."

The throng behind, as well as Jonas Barnsdake, had no faith in such an arrangement.

They knew it was nothing but a compromise.

Besides they wanted Oldham.

Jonas Barnsdake shook his head.

"No—no," he said, "that will not suit us. The time is approaching now for our great movement. Do you think us mad enough to let loose now those who can thwart all our plans? No, gentlemen, you must either surrender quietly or take the consequences. I again warn you that you are surrounded on all sides."

"We care not for that," said Alexis. "Gentlemen, we must do our duty."

Then waving his sword around his head, he added, boldly—

"Now, then, since we are to be your prisoners, take us."

Jonas Barnsdake drew his sword and sprang forward.

His enthusiasm gave to him something of the agility of youth.

The others quickly followed, The Owl and Dick Hatherden being the foremost.

A struggle had all along been imminent.

No one, therefore, was taken by surprise.

The clash of arms was here and there drowned in the discharge of pistols where any one saw the chance of discharging one in the mêlée without injuring a friend.

Oldham, the joiner, meanwhile was palpitating with fear.

He knew well how little mercy he could expect.

His object, therefore, was rather to escape than to defend his liberty.

Crawling along, therefore, beneath the feet of the combatants, regardless of kicks and cuffs, he made for the door.

But in vain.

Jonas Barnsdake, as we know, had but told the truth when he had said they were surrounded.

As soon as the struggle commenced, the others who had been left behind in the first vault broke through the doorway, and in a few minutes the Catholics were exposed to a cross attack.

Alexis soon saw the case was hopeless.

He had indulged in the illusion that his enemies knew nothing of the outer vault.

This illusion being dispelled there was nothing for it but submission.

Bloodshed was useless when escape was out of the question.

"Stop the fight, my friends," cried Alexis, in a loud voice. "We must yield to an inevitable fate. We are surrounded and helpless, and I for one desire no useless slaughter."

The battle was soon over.

And it was a singularly bloodless one.

Excepting a few wounds on either side no harm had been done.

Very gladly Jonas Barnsdake saw the delivery of the arms.

"And now, gentlemen," he said, "we shall leave you. You have acted as brave men, and have yielded only to absolute necessity. No slur, therefore, can rest upon your names. You will be treated here with all possible respect, and though captive will receive every comfort you may deem necessary."

The words had scarcely left his lips, when a shout of derision and pleasure was raised behind him.

Oldham, the joiner, who had betrayed the doings of Jonas Barnsdake and his friends, had, as we have seen, endeavoured to make good his escape, and had positively risked being trampled to death in endeavouring to avoid the fate which he felt now threatened him at the hands of the mob.

But in vain.

One or two among Jonas Barnsdake's band had contrived to keep their eyes upon him, and, seeing him sneaking towards the door just as the swords were being delivered over, they pounced upon him and dragged him away to the outer vault, where they bound him and flung him in a corner.

The arrangements were soon completed.

Alexis and his friends were locked in the council chamber, and a sufficient guard having been placed over them, Jonas Barnsdake and the rest withdrew.

CHAPTER XIII.

THE FATE OF A TRAITOR.

IN regard to Oldham silence was kept.

They knew well that the old man, fanatic as he was, would not be the one to counsel violence to one man by many.

They waited, therefore, until he had departed, after he had given them directions as to their next place of meeting, before they proceeded to any active demonstrations against their wretched prisoner.

He himself, as he lay there gagged and helpless, was more dead than alive.

He guessed that some terrible fate awaited him. What it was, however, he knew not.

While the conspirators had been talking to Jonas Barnsdake they had left the traitor where they had flung him.

He hoped, in fact, at one time that they were going to leave him there till day broke.

But as to this he was soon undeceived.

In a few minutes a low confused murmur told that the men were coming back, and then he saw them crowding into the vault.

At least thirty of them returned to have a share in what they deemed sport.

Among them, as may be imagined, were The Owl and Dick Hatherden.

"Let's have a good drink, all of us, before we go," said the former. "Let some of you go and fetch it in here; I and Dick Hatherden will pay the score. If we go to a tavern in such numbers we shall be suspected."

"And where are we going to take Oldham?"

"We'll take him to Denham Wood and have a good game with him," said The Owl. "He'll have a treat that he never had before, and he can't have a second time."

These words sounded, as may be imagined, ominously in the ears of Oldham as he lay bruised and aching on the floor of the murky cellar.

But he was helpless; and so there he lay, uttering now and then a moan of pain, which obtained for him a kick from one of his brutal captors.

The drink having been obtained in unlimited quantities, the men, having indulged till their leaders thought it unsafe to give them more, seized the unhappy traitor and dragged him away.

Denham's wood was some distance to the East of London.

But they did not care for trouble.

The treat they had in store fully, in their eyes, compensated for that.

So on they went, through a foul and densely populated neighbourhood, until they reached the open country.

Denham Wood was soon reached.

It was a place somewhat after the style of Epping Forest.

All traces of it now, however, have disappeared, and modern London houses occupy the site.

The trees grew literally matted together, more especially on the skirts of the high road, and it was exactly, therefore, the kind of place which was suited to the deed which was proposed to be accomplished by The Owl and his companions.

Making their way through the dense foliage, the men at length reached what could not be called a clearing, but a spot where the trees were not so dense as elsewhere.

Here they halted, first flinging their prisoner down like a sack on the ground.

They removed now the gag from his mouth.

There was no fear of his cries being heard here.

So they proposed to amuse themselves at his expense by listening to his entreaties for mercy.

After the first gasp which the poor wretch made for fresh air he roared out—

"Release me from these bonds; they cut into my flesh."

A loud laugh answered him.

He gazed in helpless agony from one to the other of his captors.

In search of what there was no trace of.

Not a look of compassion was on the face of one of them.

They had come there for a feast of blood, and they were resolved to enjoy it.

Their helpless victim rolled and writhed on the floor in complete desperation.

He was still bound, and, seeing that his helplessness spoiled part of the amusement, one of the men advanced and cut his bonds.

The wretched man sprang to his feet with a wild, defiant look.

"Now," he cried, "tell me what is it you want with me?"

"Lie down, dog!" exclaimed one.

A shout of derisive laughter followed, and a dozen brutal hands felled him to the earth.

"Your crime you know well," said The Owl, with drunken solemnity; "it remains only to punish you."

"Punish me! I swear I know not my crime!" exclaimed the miserable man.

"You have been a traitor to the Protestant Association."

"Never!"

"You were found with its enemies."

"So was Alexis Rainsford."

"Why were you there?"

"To watch the proceedings, and report them to Jonas Barnsdake."

A laugh followed these words.

In a more justly constituted tribunal it would have caused merriment to hear such a justification.

"Ah, very likely," said Dick Hatherden, who was seated near The Owl on the trunk of a fallen tree; "but the worst part of it for *you* is that we don't believe you. Now, boys, if you are ready."

During this colloquy one of the two men had been manipulating the rope with which the prisoner had been bound, making a noose, and otherwise preparing for the execution.

This was done behind the back of the wretched prisoner.

When, therefore, he heard the words, "Now, boys, if you are ready," he started round in evident surprise and terror.

He had feared only before.

He felt certain now.

He flung himself upon his knees.

"Oh! spare me—spare me," he cried, "I swear I am innocent. I swear I am no traitor. Oh! for the love of Heaven, do not murder me."

A loud chorus of derisive yells followed this sally.

He saw his case was hopeless.

And yet he clung to life madly.

"If you will spare me," he cried, "I will betray to you all the secrets of the Catholics. I will tell you such things as will ruin all their plans. Only give me life, and I will tell you where they keep their treasure—the money they expected to expend in thwarting the plans of the Protestant Association."

The Owl laughed loudly.

"Ha! ha!" he cried, "I can tell you that. In their pockets. Here, waste no more time. If he wants to mumble a prayer or two let him."

The throng advanced upon him in a body, seized him, pinioned him, in spite of his frantic struggles,

and then stood him on the back of a man, who bowed down his body for the purpose.

Then the rope was adjusted round his neck, and secured by the other end to a stout branch of a tree.

"Now, then," said The Owl, "we give you five minutes. At the end of that time Jack Ranford will fall upon his face and you will be dead. So, if you want to say anything, say it."

No prayer left the man's lips.

His face was convulsed with hideous rage, and passion, and dread.

A volley of awful curses burst from his lips.

He cursed them all; he invoked the horrors of hell upon their heads.

And in the midst of all this the time was up.

Jack Ranford, the man upon whose bent back he stood, flung himself suddenly upon his face, and the wretched prisoner fell with a thud.

If the crowd who were round him imagined that they would see a long, cruel scene of kicking and yelling they were wrong.

The rope was a stout one, the fall long, and Jack Ranford fell with the suddenness and precision of a drop.

Consequently, the wretched man died instantaneously.

A yell of brutal satisfaction greeted his fall.

Then the crowd dispersed, after pinning to his body a paper, with the word "Traitor" written upon it.

In a few minutes the wood had reassumed its old quiet aspect, save that the miserable man hung there to the bough of the tree alone!

CHAPTER XIV.

A SECRET MISSION.

As we have before intimated, Guy the Foundling was now as much mixed up in the Protestant Association as Dick Hatherden.

Simon Grandley had entered into it from purely good motives, and had so far an influence over Guy the Foundling as to induce him to become one of them.

And yet, strange to say, in all this they neither of them had the remotest conception that their enemy was in any way connected with the same conspiracy.

Dick himself was well aware that it was the intention of Jonas Barnsdake to appeal to Simon Grandley.

It had been proposed to the meeting publicly by Hardarker, the blacksmith.

But in regard to Guy it was different.

Dick had not the remotest conception that his fellow-apprentice and enemy were mixed up in the same matters as himself.

It was on the evening after the capture of Alexis Rainsford and his friends that Simon Grandley took Guy the Foundling into his private room.

Minnie and her mother were sent to the other room, and after locking the door Simon produced a decanter of wine, and poured some out for himself and Guy.

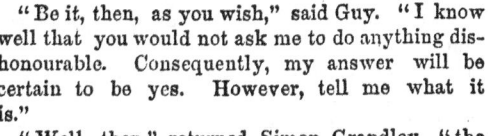

"After all that has happened, Guy," said the carpenter, evidently by way of preface to something else, "I look upon you as a son, and I fancy I treat you as one. Do I, or do I not?"

"You do, indeed, sir," said Guy, earnestly.

The carpenter smiled.

"And you would like, doubtless, to be still more a son, eh? Well—well, we must wait awhile, and if when you discover the secret of your birth you still love Minnie she is yours, with my blessing."

Guy the Foundling flushed with unexpected pleasure.

"To possess Minnie," he said, "is the dearest wish of my heart. Do not fancy that *I* shall ever change, no matter *what* good fortune awaits me in the future. All *I* need fear is that if I find that my origin, after all, is poor and humble, *you* may perhaps despise me."

"My lad," said the carpenter earnestly, "do not for one moment judge me so ill. No matter what your position might be as long as you could work to keep her, Minnie should be yours. So on that point make yourself easy. And now let us talk of another thing. This strange movement of which Lord George Gordon is the head."

"Ah!" cried Guy, "the time approaches quickly now. To-morrow is the day for the demonstration —is it not?"

"It was to have been, but it has been put off," said Simon Grandley; "it will not now take place until the 10th of this month (May). Meanwhile, there is much to be done to prevent the whole affair becoming confusion and disorder."

"And what good will come from it, after all?" asked Guy.

This was somewhat of a poser.

"Well," said Simon Grandley, who, infected with the fanaticism of the time, was somewhat ignorant, be it remembered, of the real objects of the whole affair, "it will save us from being overridden by the Catholics."

And—having satisfied himself with the utterance of this very vague reply—he proceeded—

"Yes; chiefs have yet to be appointed in several districts. Many have been appointed already; but at the last moment faint hearts have been found to back out of all kind of action. Now, you I desire to be in the position of a chief. But first I must tell you that there is peculiar work to be done."

"I fear no danger."

"I know it, Guy," replied his master; "but it is not exactly danger that I speak of. There is diplomatic work to be done."

Guy smiled.

"I fear I am not fitted for that," he said.

"Oh, yes—you *can* do what I mean. The question simply is—will you?"

"If *you* tell me I *will*," replied our hero with earnestness.

Simon Grandley poured out some more wine.

"Yes—yes; I know all that, my boy," he cried, clapping him on the shoulder; "I know all that, but I will not take you at a disadvantage. If you passed me your word you would not break it, I know; but I will not not ask you to do so until you understand what it is I require."

"Be it, then, as you wish," said Guy. "I know well that you would not ask me to do anything dishonourable. Consequently, my answer will be certain to be yes. However, tell me what it is."

"Well, then," returned Simon Grandley, "the fact is that we suspect the uncle of Aurora Halsted to have invested himself, as it were, in the mantle of the colonel, and to have become one of our most inveterate opponents."

"He was probably always on the same side as the colonel," said Guy.

"Yes; but we never heard of his interfering actively," replied Grandley. "Now it is with him that your duty lies."

Guy started.

This was far from being what he could wish.

He had no desire to be again brought into contact with Aurora.

"What am I to do with him?" he asked.

"I will tell you," said his master. "He has retired, it seems, to his country house, which is situated near Richmond."

"Yes."

"There are congregated every night numberless chiefs of the Catholic party, who are devising plans, not, mind you, for bloodshed, but for so upsetting the entire system of our great demonstration that it will lose all its force upon the Government, turn us into ridicule, and, in fact, be a weapon in the hands of our enemies."

"Well," said Guy.

He did not yet see what possible good *he* could do in the matter.

"Jonas Barnsdake," continued the carpenter, "stole a march upon some of these fellows last night, caught them in their place of meeting, and holds them even now prisoners. Now, what you are to do is this. You must take a good horse and start towards Richmond."

"I begin to see," said Guy.

"Oh! you will understand it all soon enough," said the carpenter, smiling. "Well you must arrive late and thoroughly wearied at the door of Hallwyn House.

"You must knock, give your name, and ask to be allowed to rest till morning.

"You will certainly be admitted, and as the the saviour of Aurora Halsted will be treated with every distinction.

"While there you must endeavour to discover how matters stand. Do you understand me?"

"Yes," said Guy, slowly, "I think I do."

"You do not seem to approve of the task."

"Well," returned the apprentice, "I do not as I see it now. It appears that I am to act the part of a spy."

"Not so."

"It is nothing else."

"You look at the affair with a jaundiced eye," said Simon Grandley.

"Well, if I do, let us argue the point."

And so they did.

It ended by Guy yielding.

The carpenter, in fact, put the matter in such a light—made, indeed, such an entire affair of religion

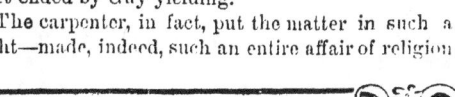

of it—that our hero became infected with the same enthusiasm.

He saw, in fact, that it would be doing no injury to *one* person, whereas it would be doing good, as Simon Grandley persuaded him, to the Protestant cause.

So at length he consented.

Simon Grandley grasped him heartily by the hand when he said " Yes."

"I knew you would do it," he said. " To-morrow night you can make your report to the meeting, and I will get you appointed to a responsible post. Meanwhile, I will see that Mrs. Grandley gets you a good supper, while *I* procure you a good horse."

An hour after this, having taken leave of all, and specially of Minnie, Guy was on horseback, and speeding away as hard as his horse would carry him towards Richmond.

CHAPTER XV.

GUY'S ADVENTURES ON THE ROAD.

HE had not observed, as he issued forth from the street in which his master's house was situated, that a horseman enveloped in a long cloak was drinking some ale out of a tankard at the corner of the street, and that as soon as our hero passed he followed at some little distance.

His mind was too occupied to observe this.

At least while he was in London.

As he left the busy city behind him, however, it was different.

The slightest sound could then be distinguished, and hearing the regular beatings of a horse's feet he slackened his pace.

He had no desire to have a man of whom he knew nothing following him mysteriously.

However, there seemed no cause for fear.

The other traveller came riding on at the same rate as before, until he reached Guy's side.

" Going to Richmond, sir," he said, inquiringly.

"No; beyond it," replied Guy.

"I am glad to hear it," returned the other, " for along this road on such dark nights as these company is always agreeable."

Guy laughed.

"Well, as for me," he said, " I like company, but I have nothing to fear, no matter how dark the night may be, for I carry no more than enough to pay for baiting my horse and getting a meal for myself."

" You are fortunate," replied the stranger. "I am far differently situated, for I bear with me the worth of five hundred pounds."

" Well, there are two of us now," said Guy, " and it is improbable, therefore, that we shall be attacked."

" On this part of the road certainly not," returned the other; " this is not deserted enough for the footpads. It is further on towards Richmond that my gentlemen begin *their* sport."

And so, chatting pleasantly and familiarly, they rode along.

At the first inn they stopped and partook of some refreshment.

Here they had a chance of looking at one another.

The man who had been so far Guy's companion was dressed in the garb of a gentleman of quality.

Beyond this little could be said.

His face was by no means attractive.

In fact, it was repulsive in the extreme.

His eyes were small, round, and cunning.

His long hooked nose hung over an extremely uncouth mouth.

His complexion was sallow, wrinkled, and unnatural.

Yet withal he could put on a genial smile, and had a pleasant, even a winning voice, and manner.

He seemed much taken with Guy at once.

" Well," he said, as they prepared to remount, " I had a good look at you before I went farther, for, to tell you the truth, I have not been altogether comfortable in your company."

Guy laughed aloud.

" And pray, why not ? " he asked.

" Because I might have been deceived in your manner," replied the other, as they trotted off. " You see, your footpads are so gentlemanly, and so civil-spoken. However, you're too young for that kind of thing."

And so they jogged on once more.

Soon the country began to become lonely and desolate.

Scarcely a house could be seen across the dark country.

Only a twinkle here and there was to be seen among far-off trees.

A kind of dread came over Guy.

Not a dread of death.

He had in him too much life, and health, and spirits for that.

It was only a dread of some unknown evil impending.

An idea that soon he would have to battle for life and liberty.

This had no reference whatever to his quondam companion.

It had reference to the manner in which he was about to be introduced into the house of Aurora Halsted's uncle.

Suddenly, however, when he had lapsed almost into a reverie on horseback, he was startled by a sudden action on the part of the stranger.

The latter suddenly pulled his horse almost upon his, seized his bridle, and drawing a pistol from his belt, cried—

" Now then, my young jeweller, I want your money at once."

Guy laughed.

" You're trying my courage, I suppose," he exclaimed, in a voice which he intended to be unconcerned, although in reality he was drawing out his pistol. " Come, we have no time for fooling. I am no jeweller, and I must get on my way."

The other still kept hold of the bridle.

" Now, look here, my young friend," he said, " I don't want to kill you, because you're a decent sort of fellow : but I know who you are, and I want the money, or, rather, the jewels that you're taking to Lady Haxfield's."

All this was so much Greek to Guy the Foundling.

"I don't in the least know," he said, "what you mean. In the first place, who is Lady Haxfield?"

The man, who was evidently a highwayman of the most approved order, laughed loudly.

"You keep it up well, my lad," he said, "but it won't do—it really won't do. In the first place, you're old Gawthorne's apprentice, aren't you?"

"Gawthorne! who is he?" asked Guy.

"Good—good. Who is he? Why, the goldsmith in Eastchepe."

"Then you are immensely wrong," returned Guy, "and as soon as you put yourself right the better. I am not the apprentice to a jeweller, but to a carpenter, and my master's name is not Gawthorne, but Simon Grandley."

He had no sooner said these words than he repented them.

What if this man was a spy, and had only got up this attempt at robbery as a blind?

He was soon undeceived, however, on this point.

"You are lying to me," cried the man. "I know you well."

And as he spoke he levelled a pistol at Guy's head.

Guy had his also in his hand.

But he saw at once that to present it at his assailant would be his death warrant.

So he temporised for a moment.

Getting his feet out of the stirrups as he spoke, he said—

"Well, if you *know* me, I suppose I had better find the jewels."

And then suddenly, before the man was aware of what he meant, he flung himself from his horse, and fired his weapon as he reached the ground.

The pistol-shot, however, instead of wounding the rider, shot the horse dead, and with a yell of pain, the animal fell to the ground, the highwayman being pitched almost on the top of Guy the Foundling, and his pistol being flung from his grasp.

A struggle was now, of course, inevitable.

Guy braced all his nerves to their strongest, and as the other endeavoured to draw his sword, he struck him a blow with his fist which numbed for the moment the muscles of his right arm.

Quick as lightning he drew his weapon, and when the highwayman at length dashed at him he was on guard.

A rapid contest ensued.

The robber, finding himself thus prevented from getting rid of his enemy by a cowardly *coup*, was somewhat taken aback by the new aspect of affairs.

But, nevertheless, he was no coward, and resolved to pay his enemy out for making so unexpected a stand.

Being no mean swordsman, he succeeded, by his superior length and strength of arm, in driving Guy back towards a ditch that yawned behind him.

Our hero, however, saw his danger in time, and nerving himself for a desperate effort, rushed in upon his adversary.

The other, stepping back to avoid a rapid blow, lost his advantage.

In an instant Guy the Foundling saw his chance, and quick as lightning his sword flashed in the semi-darkness, and was plunged in the shoulder of the robber.

The latter uttered a howl of rage and agony.

But he was not entirely disabled.

It was the left shoulder upon which Guy's sword had taken effect, and his right arm, therefore, was still free.

With furious dashes he endeavoured now to confuse his enemy.

But to no purpose.

Guy, having been the first to wound his adversary, saw that he had the game in his own hands, and rushed upon his foe as he had done before.

A slight skirmish—a slight wound in Guy's arm.

And then—the end came.

Our hero's sword this time passed clean through the robber's heart.

Only one gurgle followed; no cry.

Then the highwayman fell a senseless, lifeless lump of clay on the road.

Guy was about to remount his horse, when an idea occurred to him.

"This fellow said he had five hundred pounds," thought he; "if he has them with him, they have been stolen from some one who can ill afford the loss. I'll make myself master of them, and give them to Simon Grandley to use for the good cause."

No sooner did the idea flash into his mind than it was acted upon.

Tying his horse up to a tree, to make sure that he could not escape, he knelt down by the side of the dead highwayman, and began turning out his pockets.

He had no conception, of course, of securing such an amount as five hundred pounds.

But he had no doubt that the thief was in possession of *some* amount of stolen property.

He had made an unsuccessful attempt on several pockets, when, just as he clutched a heavy purse, a hand was placed upon his shoulder.

Starting round, he saw that he was surrounded by a number of constables.

"Ho! ho, my fine fellow," cried one, "we've found you in the very act, have we?"

"What do you mean?" cried Guy, indignantly.

Yet as he spoke the truth flashed across him.

He was really in an awkward predicament.

Here was he found by the side of a dead man, absolutely in the act of rifling his pockets.

He sprang up as he uttered the words.

Yet there was dread in his heart.

"Mean! What do I mean?" said the constable who had addressed him. "Well, my friends, what do you think of that?"

A roar of laughter greeted these words.

"It's about the coolest thing I've heard," exclaimed one.

"Perhaps the gentleman really doesn't know," sneered another.

"Well, we'll soon explain," said the first speaker. "Come, young fellow, you must come with us."

"With you! Whither?" asked Guy.

"First to the round-house, and then, in the morning, to the magistrates."

THE RIVAL APPRENTICES

A TALE OF THE RIOTS OF 1780.

WITH A LOUD CRY HE FELL BACKWARDS.

"And pray why am I to go with you?" asked Guy the Foundling.

"Oh! there, don't waste time," said the constable, "it ain't worth while. We've found you

robbing this man, whom you've just murdered. That's enough, ain't it? Come; no nonsense, or we must force you."

Guy pressed his hand wildly to his brow.

"Why, you are mad," he said. "I was on my way to Hallwyn House when I was attacked here by this man, who pretended to be a friend. He told me on the road he had a quantity of money, and while he was beguiling me with this tale he suddenly demanded my money. I resisted, and a struggle ensued——"

He could say no more.

Another roar of laughter greeted him.

Not one of them believed a word he said.

"Here, tell that to the magistrate," said the first constable; "it doesn't suit us. Are you coming quietly?"

"Yes, yes. I'll come," said Guy; "but I can tell you I feel quite confused. You will see to-morrow that I tell the right story; but I give in that appearances are sadly against me."

The constables accordingly surrounded him; and —his horse being led after him—he was conveyed about a mile along the road, past the door of Aurora's uncle's house, until at length they arrived at a round-house at the edge of the road.

Those of my readers who have walked along the road to Harrow remember, no doubt, the little building of brick and mortar which was celebrated as the place in which Jack Sheppard was once confined, and from which he made his escape during the night.

I have seen it myself, and I am not at all surprised that any one possessing the daring and ingenuity of Jack Sheppard should have been able to get away from it.

It was quite round, with a peaked tiled roof, and a small opening (what the French call a *Judas*) in the door-way.

It was built of ordinary bricks and mortar, and the soil round it was soft and easily moved.

Just such another one was the place in which they confined Guy the Foundling.

"You'll not find any great luxury in here," said the constable, through the grating, as he locked him in, "but you won't be there many hours."

Guy did not answer.

A hurried consultation, however, took place among the men outside.

Then one approached.

"I say, my friend?" he said.

"Well?" answered Guy, in a voice by no means expressive of good nature.

"You'll be here some hours; would you like some refreshment?"

Guy the Foundling saw their drift—saw that it was more for their own good than his; but still the idea was by no means displeasing.

"Yes," he said, "I should; but there's one condition I must insist on. I suppose I have to pay beforehand."

"Precisely."

"Then, as I have no guarantee that if I give you the money you'll come back, one of you must remain behind as a security."

The men laughed.

As it happened on this particular occasion the idea had not occurred to them.

"Very well," said one of the constables, "I will remain. Open the door, Bill."

The door was accordingly opened, and the man entered.

In a short space of time the beer was brought and disposed of, the man released, and Guy the Foundling was left to himself.

He threw himself at first on the murky straw in his cell and tried to sleep.

But in vain.

His thoughts were too busy for that.

He could think of nothing else but the failure of his enterprise, and the anger and surprise of Simon Grandley when he did not return.

Of his own danger he did not think at all.

Presently, as he was cogitating, and wondering how, with such evidence against him, he could escape, he heard the sound of horses' feet, and loud laughter, as from several persons approaching.

He listened eagerly.

Why he knew not.

Some presentiment, however, told him that the coming of these people would be of advantage to him.

His heart beat wildly.

They came nearer.

Then, as they approached the round-house, they halted.

The night was a very clear one.

Their voices, therefore, could easily be distinguished.

"Let's look in the round-house," cried one; "may be some of our pals have been lagged."

"Aye—aye!" exclaimed several.

Then there was a rush of feet towards the door.

A loud knocking followed.

"Who is there?" cried Guy the Foundling.

"Friends; what are you here for?" asked a voice.

"By mistake entirely."

A laugh followed this.

"That is generally the case," said the unknown speaker; "how did it happen?"

Guy the Foundling told his story as he had told it to the constables.

Roars of hearty laughter greeted him as he ingenuously narrated how he had turned the tables on the highwayman.

He saw the reason at once.

They believed him to be romancing.

Footpads themselves, they were not likely to believe such a story.

"Well done—well done," cried they, when he had finished speaking; "a clever fellow—a clever fellow. He'd make a good lawyer—that he would. Come, let's give him his liberty, he deserves it."

Naturally annoyed as he was at the disbelief of the men in his innocence he was too sensible to permit his annoyance to be seen.

"I can't help you much," he cried, "for there are no bolts or bars within."

"Never mind," said the stranger, "we'll open the door from without."

And so they began the attack.

But the task was more difficult than they had imagined.

The door, though to all outward appearance old and shaky, was of good sound material, and their blows fell on it for a long time quite harmlessly.

They did not despair, however.

Stalwart shoulders pushed and fell against the panelling, and at length a breach was made.

They had just succeeded in this, when the sound of horses' feet was heard.

The riders were rapidly approaching.

"Ten to one it's the mounted patrol," exclaimed one of the men. "Quick! let's have him out."

In spite of the prospect of a sharp skirmish, they never once thought of abandoning him.

Guy the Foundling could now, of course, aid them.

Tearing away the woodwork with his hands where it had been splintered, he just contrived to wriggle out through the hole as the horsemen came riding quickly up.

CHAPTER XVI.

THE ADVENTURES OF GUY THE FOUNDLING CONTINUED.

"WHAT have we here?" cried the leader of the patrol, in a loud voice. "What means this attack on the roundhouse?"

The patrol leapt from their horses and drew their swords as their chief spoke.

"A friend of ours was unjustly confined in it," exclaimed one of the highwaymen, "and so we released him. Now you have the truth."

"Ah! I know you, Tom Fielding," cried the constable. "Come on, my brave fellows," he added to his men; "two hundred pounds reward is ours if we seize him and his gang!"

"Fly," said one of the robbers, turning to Guy the Foundling; "take a horse and go."

But Guy shook his head.

He knew now who his companions were.

But still they had released him and got into trouble through doing so.

He could not, therefore, desert them.

"No, no," he said; "I will fight with the rest."

"No surrender," shouted the one whom the patrol had addressed as Tom Fielding; "let's show them what stuff we are made of."

The battle, therefore, began fiercely.

The fact of Guy the Foundling making common cause with those who had released him from durance vile rendered the numbers even.

It was well for the highwaymen it was so.

The patrol was chosen from among the bravest and most powerful men among the constabulary; and, used to constant conflicts and dangers, they thought nothing of risking their lives to bring offenders to justice.

Tom Fielding, who seemed the special object of their attack, was by no means, however, one of those bloodthirsty wretches who were the terror of the road.

He was more of the Claude Duval stamp.

Evil as was his course of life, he had never been known to shed blood.

Except, be it added, in a fair conflict.

Murder was forbidden in his band.

A terror to rich old ladies and venturesome riders on the dark highway, he was still spoken of even by those he had robbed as behaving in as gentlemanly and quiet a manner as a man pursuing such a calling could do.

So, after all, Guy had not mixed himself up with a bloodstained crew.

They fought like lions.

All knew the consequences of capture.

In those days it did not require murder to cause a man to be hung.

Robbing another of sixpence on the high road was sufficient.

For a long time the issue of the conflict was doubtful.

But at length fortune seemed to declare for the "gentlemen of the road."

In this case the general order of things was reversed.

The constables were fighting for money while the highwaymen were fighting for dear life.

Urging each other on with shouts of encouragement, the latter at last began to gain ground.

This first sign of yielding was greeted with loud shouts by the highwaymen.

"Now, my lads," shouted Tom Fielding, "drive these fellows into yonder horsepond and then mount."

Several of the constables and also of the highwaymen were wounded—the former most severely.

The defenders of the public peace, therefore, were gradually forced towards the water's edge.

Bravely they struggled to redeem their failing fortunes.

But in vain.

Their antagonists were now flushed and excited with victory.

At length the edge of the horsepond was reached by the struggling throng.

The water here was not deep.

But the bank at this point was high.

A plunge, therefore, into the muddy water on such a night was by no means a pleasant prospect.

A desperate stand was made here, therefore, for a minute.

"Yield," shouted Tom Fielding; "throw down your arms and we will molest you no further."

But this did not in any way suit the ideas of the patrol.

They preferred a ducking to such a confession of weakness.

About two minutes only this last assault and defence lasted.

"Now, then, boys, all together," shouted Tom Fielding.

Then a succession of splashes was heard, mingled with loud cries.

The defenders of the law had suffered an ignominious defeat.

The highwaymen had adopted a strange mode of tactics.

A mode which showed that they had been in a very similar predicament before.

Instead of driving their enemies into the water at the point of the sword, they suddenly lowered their weapons and rushed in at them headforemost.

The patrol consequently were literally sent flying over the brink into the pond of water.

Not a moment now was lost.

A shout of derisive laughter certainly arose from the lips of even the wounded robbers.

But they did not pause even an instant to glance at their discomfited foes.

Following Tom Fielding, they rushed away to the spot where the horses of the constables and all were mingled confusedly, and in the space of a minute they were mounted and away.

As they dashed along in the direction of Hallwyn House, Tom Fielding brought his horse close up to that of Guy the Foundling.

"Young fellow," he said, "you are a brave man, and I am proud to have released you. But now you are free, confess your story to have been an invention."

"Indeed no," said Guy, "I will even tell you who I am."

Briefly, as far as he could without betraying the interests and secrets of others, he told Fielding the story of his midnight ride.

"Well then," replied the highwayman, when the apprentice had finished speaking, "all I can say is that I am proud to have been the means of saving you. Had you been of less worthy metal you would have made your escape from such as we are when we were attacked by the patrol. However, yonder is Hallwyn House, and I can promise you that you will henceforward be free of this road."

Guy smiled.

"By what token?" he asked.

"Simply your name," said Tom Fielding. "Tell me—what is it?"

"Guy the Foundling. I have no other," replied our hero.

"Good, then," returned the highwayman. "Guy the Foundling and all his friends will be free of this road as long as Tom Fielding and his friends hold it. Friend—your hand. It is one unstained by brutal crime, and you need not fear to shake it."

Guy took his hand and pressed it warmly.

"I can say, without the fear of insulting you, that I hope soon to see you in a better position—following a more respectable profession. Meanwhile, accept my gratitude and this purse. It is the one I took from the highwayman whom I killed. You have earned both by your bravery. Good night."

"I will accept it," said Tom Fielding, "for we have made but a bad trade of late. But, as for a better position, I fear I can say little in regard to that. Disappointed in love—ruined in fortune—the only place where I am free from insult is the high road. Adieu; we may meet again."

And so they parted, Guy making the best of his way towards Hallwyn House, upon a horse that had belonged to one of the patrol.

There was not a light to be seen anywhere, as, pushing open the rusty iron gate, he cantered along the softly-gravelled avenue in front of the old building.

Every one apparently had retired to rest.

Nevertheless Guy was not disheartened.

He felt that, having overcome so many difficulties,

there was all the more reason why he should accomplish his mission.

So he boldly knocked at the door.

A long silence ensued.

Then a head was poked out of a window, and in the moonlight he could distinguish the gleam of a gun or a pistol.

"Who's there?" shouted a man's voice.

"I come to see Mr. Hallwyn."

"What's your name?"

"Guy the Foundling."

"That's a good name to travel with," growled the man. "I don't know you; go away!"

"But I must see Mr. Hallwyn."

"Then you must come again in the morning. Be off or I'll fire."

Guy drew forth a pistol.

"I am armed as well as you," he said, "so no trifling. Go and tell your master that I want to see him."

"Master, eh?" growled the man. "Well, well; I'll tell Mr. Hallwyn. Wait awhile; and none of your footpad games here, mind ye. If you've got companions to back ye, so have we. There's plenty of people here to——"

The old man—for such he was evidently by his voice—was suddenly interrupted in his talk by a hand being pressed over his mouth.

Then an interval of silence ensued.

Guy was becoming impatient, when he heard the rattling of chains and bolts, and the door was opened.

"Come in," said the old man; "I'll see to your horse. Tie him to that iron bolt there."

Guy the Foundling followed his instructions, and in a few moments found himself standing in a large room in the presence of Mr. Hallwyn.

The latter was fully dressed.

This, when coupled with the extreme quiet of the house, and the words of the old man—"There's plenty of people here"—told that something peculiar was going on.

The suspicions of Simon Grandley, therefore, were not wrong.

There would have been an evident shade of annoyance on the face of Robert Hallwyn, had the person who disturbed him been anyone else but Guy the Foundling.

But though he was disturbed in his mind by his arrival at such an unseasonable hour, he was, notwithstanding, influenced by no feeling of anger.

No wonder.

Guy the Foundling had saved the life and honour of Aurora Halsted at the peril of his own.

He had proved himself in many ways a hero of no common order.

How, then, could he be anything but welcome to Hallwyn House?

"Well, my lad," said Robert Hallwyn, "and what brings you here at this hour? Nothing wrong I hope."

Guy smiled as he pressed his host's hand.

"Very wrong, indeed," he said; "I have been arrested as a highwayman."

"A highwayman!"

Guy quickly explained himself.

Mr. Hallwyn listened attentively.

"Did you give them any clue to your destination?" he said.

"No—none at all."

Guy forgot he had named Hallwyn House.

"And what brought you into this neighbourhood?" asked Mr. Hallwyn.

"I was on a private mission for my master," replied the apprentice, who, though not minding speaking evasively, still resolved to speak the truth; "but now, if you can spare me a bed, I would crave permission to remain here to-night and proceed on my journey in the morning. I shall even then have to disguise myself, or I shall be in danger of being again captured."

"Certainly, you are most welcome here," said Mr. Hallwyn, his desire to act hospitably overcoming everything else. "You are, no doubt, tired, and would be glad to retire at once."

"I should," returned Guy. "I have had enough adventures for one night."

"You have, indeed," said Mr. Hallwyn, as he opened the door and summoned the servant. "Here, George, see this gentleman to his room."

In a few minutes Guy had taken leave of Mr. Hallwyn for the night and retired to his room.

Here the servant, George, brought him presently some refreshment, and then all was quiet once more.

Guy the Foundling eagerly partook of some wine and some light food.

His adventures on the highway had whet his appetite, and, moreover, he anticipated being up for hours still.

Presently he cautiously opened his door and listened.

Not a sound was to be heard.

"Simon Grandley has chosen a bad spy," he said, as he once more closed the door. "I can't go wandering about the house like a ghost. Hark! What is that?"

He ran to the window and threw it up as noiselessly as he could.

What he had heard was the rush of many horsemen up the avenue.

What did this signify?

To him only one thing.

Recapture, disgrace, and an ignominious death on the scaffold.

Such seemed the truly unavoidable result of such an adventure as he had been engaged in.

He leaned out, after first extinguishing his lamp, and listened eagerly.

He was enabled to do this better, as his window, though high from the ground, was just above the front entrance.

As he took this position, the newcomers knocked loudly and peremptorily at the door.

Again the old man poked his head out of the casement.

"Why, dear me, here is a posse of people," Guy could hear him grumbling to himself just below. "What can it all mean? What do you want, gentlemen?"

This was, of course, said in a louder tone.

"We are constables, and we demand the person of a young fellow who has just taken refuge in this house," returned a voice.

Guy recognised it.

It was that of the constable who had roused his followers by the promise of a reward for the capture of Tom Fielding.

"I am lost," he said, as he closed the window and saw to the priming of his pistols.

CHAPTER XVII.

DICK HATHERDEN'S NEW SCHEME OF REVENGE.

WE must leave Guy the Foundling for a time in this unpleasant and dangerous predicament while we return to London.

I have described already how, as Guy passed the corner of the street in which Simon Grandley resided, he was followed by a man on horseback, and I have described, too, the adventures that resulted from this encounter.

But this man was not the only one who had observed him.

As he rode round two men were sauntering along, and as the horsemen passed them they saw both their faces in the flashing light of a tavern lamp.

One of them started as he saw them.

Then he clutched his companion by the arm.

"Did you observe these men?" asked he.

"Yes."

"Did you not recognise one?"

"No: I never saw them before."

"You think not. That's where you are wrong. One of them we neither of us know; the other you have seen often—in the shop, in the streets at night, in the riots."

"And who is it?"

"Guy the Foundling, the apprentice of Simon Grandley, the carpenter. Come in here with me," he added, drawing his companion into the tavern; "I will tell you something."

As they passed in, the light revealed the features of Dick Hatherden and The Owl.

Some new villany, then, was afloat.

The two worthies passed into a private room, and ordered refreshment.

Dick Hatherden had followed the example of nearly all criminals.

He drowned his cares and his horrid thoughts in strong drink.

"Now then," said The Owl, who, with the generosity of a man who was spending money lightly earned, paid for the drink without being asked; "now then, what are you going to propose— something by which we're to make some more money?"

"You're a greedy fellow," said Dick.

"There's a good pair of us then, when we're together," replied The Owl, laughing. "But come, you helped me, so I'll help you. Tell me what it is you require."

"Well," said Dick, "it is simply this. You saw Guy the apprentice go by?"

"Yes."

"Well, that is one absent from the house. Will Lightmore is out as well; while Simon Grandley himself, I know, has a particular mission to-night."

"I follow you."

"Consequently, if any one were to break into the house, there would be no one to oppose them but women."

"I see."

"Well, then the inference is clear. I propose to enter the place this very night."

"And rob it?"

"Yes, of two things—one money; the other a girl."

The Owl laughed.

"What, in love?"

Dick Hatherden's brow contracted.

"No," he said; "it is hate which impels me—not love."

"Hate!" echoed The Owl; "if I hated a girl I should kill her, not carry her off!"

Dick smiled.

"There are worse punishments than killing," he said; "I might kill her, and she might die without knowing who struck the blow. No, no, that won't suit me."

"And who is the girl?"

"She is my master's daughter—or, rather, the daughter of him who *was* my master, for he will never see me again in *his* workshop. It is Minnie Grandley."

"And what's she done that you hate her so?" asked The Owl, who, having plenty of ale before him, was in no hurry to move, and wished to waste, therefore, as much time as possible.

"You mistake me entirely," said Dick Hatherden. "I don't hate *her*. She never gave me much cause for that. It's because she loves Guy the Foundling that I wish to carry her off. I want to wound him through her: to take her from him, force her to marry me, and thus ruin his dream of love for ever. Quick, drink up, and let's be going."

The Owl laughed.

"Well, you're in a wonderful hurry," he said.

"Yes; my blood is on fire!"

"Well, that's all very right, I daresay; but I think you're in a confounded hurry. We've got no tools to work with. I don't know anything about the house; and if we go helter skelter at it, without any preparation, it's ten to one if we are not trapped in the act."

Dick uttered a fierce oath.

"I know best what I am doing and what I want," he said; "you can give it up if you like, but *I* don't. I've made my mind up to do it to-night, and if you don't want to help me, all you've got to do is to say so, and I'll look for some one else."

The Owl laughed.

"Well," he cried, "you said your blood was on fire. I must believe you now. We'll drink up, then go and fetch tools, and then return and commence work."

Speedily disposing of their ale, and having a "topper" of ardent spirits at the bar, the two ruffians made their way to the low neighbourhood, where Dick Hatherden had formerly lived with Bill Hazard.

He had returned to this den immediately after the riots, as being the best place he could choose for the purposes of concealment.

The Owl, too, had taken up his quarters there, in the same house, so that there was not much trouble in obtaining the means of breaking into the carpenter's house.

The outer part of the building we have already described, as well as the manner in which Dick Hatherden and Bill Hazard endeavoured to force their way in on a former occasion, when Quail saved Guy the Foundling's life.

Dick now proceeded to describe to The Owl the construction of the interior of the house.

It seemed that in the room in which the little servant girl Betty slept was a trap-door, communicating with the lower part of the house.

It was proposed, therefore, that they should enter the workshop, and, taking one of the short ladders, make their way, first into the young girl's bed-chamber, and then thence into Minnie Grandley's.

Having secured her, and effectually prevented her from crying out, they would then proceed to Simon Grandley's chamber, and steal all they could lay hands on, issuing forth from the place by the front door, with their booty and the young girl also.

Having explained thus much, and arranged everything in order, the two ruffians quitted the den of infamy and hurried off.

The night, as may be imagined, was now pretty far advanced.

Everything was very quiet in the old city.

Darkness hung over it like a pall.

"This is just the night for our work," exclaimed Dick as they hastened along. "Old Grandley is by this time in the thick of some political mystery, and all his people are asleep."

The Owl made no answer.

He was watching something which Dick Hatherden had not perceived.

He was more used to this night work than the apprentice.

An old hand in crime, he feared and watched every shadow.

What he saw now was something which roused fear in his mind.

Creeping along the wall opposite was something which every now and then assumed the figure of a man, but which at intervals was lost entirely in the shade.

He felt sure they were the objects of some suspicion.

So he kept silence and watched.

"Are you asleep?" cried Dick Hatherden, finding his companion made no reply.

"No," said The Owl, in a low voice, "I'm awake, as you'll see presently. Don't speak, but keep on."

Dick made no answer.

He had great faith in the criminal cunning of his companion, and was content to leave him to himself.

Presently they reached the corner of the street.

The mysterious shadow was then before them.

"Wait here," cried The Owl.

And he darted across the road.

But the object of his concern was gone.

It had vanished as if by magic.

"Curse me if I understand this," cried he, as, after searching everywhere, he returned to Dick.

"Why, what is the matter?"

"Well, that's what I don't know."

"What made you rush away in such a hurry just now?"

The Owl explained all.

"You're nervous," said Dick; "that's about it. There's not a soul about, and unless it was the devil we should have heard footsteps. Let's hurry on."

On again they went.

This time no shadow appeared.

But had they but known what this meant, it would have given them still greater concern.

The shadow, which was none other than a human being on the watch, was now following them closely.

CHAPTER XVIII.
THE RESULT OF THE CONSPIRACY.

SIMON GRANDLEY'S house, when the two ruffians approached it, was buried, indeed, in silence and darkness.

In fact not a soul was up.

Will Lightmore, as Dick had said, was out as well as the carpenter.

But Quail?

Where was he?

We shall see presently.

Dick had completely forgotten him, or he had ignored his existence.

"Well," said The Owl, as they arrived opposite the building and looked up at it, "there's no doubting it. Everything is as silent as death. Where are we to begin?"

"At the yard gate. We can pick the lock. Here, this way," said Dick.

And with the words he led The Owl round to the yard door, through which it will be remembered the two masked men entered in the commencement of my story, when Minnie Grandley saw them from her window.

The lock did not require to be tampered with.

The gate, in fact, was open.

"We're in luck's way to-night," said The Owl.

"We are indeed, it seems to me," replied Dick. "But let's push on. The door being open may mean that somebody's about."

So saying, he led the way towards a doorway at the other end of the yard.

This, as my readers are aware, led into the workshop.

The old lock was soon picked, and the two thieves stood within the house.

The door was then refastened as well as it could be, and they commenced proceedings.

"Betty's a light sleeper," whispered Dick, as he fixed a ladder against the trap-door, "so mind what you're up to."

"Never fear," replied The Owl, "I'll go up like a mouse."

So saying he crept up.

Dick anxiously waited below.

The trap-door had not been made use of for a long time.

The bolts, therefore, were somewhat stiff; but The Owl, with the patience of an old burglar, went quietly to work, and, though it took him a full quarter of an hour to remove them, he succeeded in doing so noiselessly.

"It's all right, Dick," he whispered. "Follow me as quickly as you can."

Then he pulled down the trap, which was one that opened downwards, and proceeded to enter the bed-chamber.

On this evening it had happened that Will Lightmore had been with Betty rather later than usual.

I must explain this in order that my readers may understand what follows.

Simon Grandley and Guy the Foundling being out, the apprentice had deemed it a most convenient time to have a private talk with Betty.

When it was really bed-time, therefore, he had entered her room with her, and there the two had sat for a full hour at the open window indulging in their youthful love dreams, until it was time for Will Lightmore to go upon the business he had laid out for himself for that night.

When he had kissed and bade her adieu, therefore, it was more than an hour after Guy the Foundling had passed the corner of the street, and only a few minutes before the two villains arrived at the yard gate.

She undressed herself very slowly.

Will Lightmore had that night unveiled his heart thoroughly to her.

The poor girl had long loved him.

Loved him, perhaps, with all the more intensity and purity and truth because she was beneath him; because she looked up to him; because she had been so doubtful whether, after all, his was but a passing fancy, which would vanish with age and good fortune.

She undressed slowly, therefore, and dreamily, stopping every now and then to smile and think, and press her hand over her pretty bosom, as if to keep down the beatings of her excited heart.

Thus it was that, as Dick Hatherden and The Owl entered the workshop, she was but just about entering her bed.

She was very quick of hearing, however.

Even the slight noise made by The Owl in removing the bolts caught her ear.

She knew at once that something wrong was going on.

So she remained still and listened, only placing her hand beneath her pillow and drawing something thence.

When The Owl therefore emerged from the dark mouth of the trap she saw him at once.

But she raised no alarm.

She saw at the first glance that he had not any weapon in his hands, although heavily armed.

So she resolved to wait, and, if possible, capture him.

This was a brave idea truly.

But though she was a strong girl it was a mad one.

She trusted too much to the strength of her well-formed limbs, which had been rendered fleshy and muscular by hard work.

So she waited.

When the Owl had raised himself nearly to the summit of the steps, and was, in fact, in the room, she raised her pistol.

"Back, or you die!" she cried.

The Owl started.

He had heard nothing or seen nothing before.

Now he beheld something white standing by the side of the bed.

"Ah!" he cried; "who is there?"

And then he saw by the light of the moon the gleam of a pistol.

"Back, or you die!" cried the brave girl.

But the Owl only laughed.

He was not one to be alarmed by a woman's threats.

"I'll soon silence you, my pretty one," he cried, and advanced towards her.

But he was wrong.

She was determined; and as brave as determined, moreover.

So, as he made a step towards her, she took aim and fired.

The Owl uttered a cry, and fell backwards on the edge of the trap-door.

But she had not effected her purpose.

Her hand had trembled as she fired, and instead of the bullet passing through his head, it had only wounded him slightly.

So he quickly recovered, and with an oath sprang up and rushed at her.

The girl uttered a scream.

But she had no occasion to fear for her life.

The Owl was always prepared for emergencies, and had adopted another plan entirely.

He knew well that the pistol-shot would alarm the house, and he would be discovered if he was not quick.

He seized the girl by the throat, therefore, and with his other hand tore the sheet from the bed.

In this he enveloped her head, and tied it so closely round her mouth as to prevent her crying out. Then he bound her ankles and wrists, and her legs also above the knees, with the other sheet, and placed her within the bed, drawing the clothes over her helpless form, so as to make it appear that she was fast asleep.

He then rushed to the trap-door, through which the head of Dick Hatherden appeared.

"Hurry down into the workshop, Dick," said The Owl; "all the women in the house will be in the room directly."

They at once redescended and the trap was closed after them.

They had scarcely had time to conceal themselves among some of the heaps of things in the workshop when the sound of footsteps above told them that the alarmed inmates of the house had entered the servant girl's bedroom.

"Now," whispered The Owl; "now is our fate to be decided."

"Why?" asked Dick, impatiently.

He cared not for the gold.

He would have liked to have rushed up in the midst of the women, and killed those who resisted the abduction of Minnie.

"I will tell you," said The Owl. "The servant is lying silent and helpless in bed. If they do not examine her too closely they will imagine that she sleeps. Then they will imagine that the sound came from the street, and retire again to their rooms. If they do discover what condition she is in, why then it will be time enough to make an open attack upon them."

So they waited.

It happened exactly as The Owl had predicted that it would.

Minnie and Mrs. Grandley entered the room gently and listened.

Not a sound—not even the breathing of Betty—was to be heard.

They approached the bed and looked at her.

She looked merely as if she was lying there with the clothes drawn over her head for warmth.

"It could not have been discharged here," said Minnie. "It is only fancy; it must have been in the street."

Betty heard her speaking, and longed to speak or make some motion to attract their notice.

But in vain.

Her arms and her legs were so firmly bound together, that except movements which were quite compatible with a person's being asleep, she could make none.

So Minnie and her mother passed out, and the poor girl was again alone.

A few minutes passed.

Then she heard the trap-door opened once more—this time without any pretence of noiselessness.

"Ha! ha! my fine young lady," said The Owl, approaching the bed, and patting Betty on the shoulder—"ha! ha! your little plan failed, you see. I'm much obliged for your attempt to kill me, and I won't forget you for it! I've got something better to do to-night, but I'll remember this night, and I'll pay you for it, mark me."

The young girl knew not what the ruffian meant.

But somehow or another his words made her shudder.

A cold perspiration broke out on every limb.

And yet there she was, helpless to aid herself or those dear to her.

Oh, how she prayed then that Will Lightmore might return in time.

Passing from her room, The Owl and Dick Hatherden entered the passage.

Here they removed their boots, and placed on crape masks, and walked along noiseless and stealthy, like bloodthirsty wretches as they were.

Their point of destination was the bedchamber of Minnie Grandley.

The girl first, the money second.

Dick cared little for gold, if its pursuit spoiled his revenge.

Reaching the door of the young girl's room, they tried the lock.

It was fastened within.

"This is a cursed job," said The Owl, in a growling whisper.

"Why?"

THE RIVAL APPRENTICES

A TALE OF THE RIOTS OF 1780.

"HE'S GIVEN US THE SLIP, AND NO MISTAKE," CRIED ONE OF THE CONSTABLES.

"While we're nabbing the girl we might be taking the gold; whereas, it she's awake, she'll hear us, and then we'll be arrested."

"Leave me, and let me do it alone then," cried Dick, "if you're afraid."

A chuckle was the only answer.

The Owl considered it his special privilege to do a little grumbling.

Therefore Dick Hatherden's objections to it only served to amuse him.

He knelt down, took out his wires and other tools, and in a very short space of time the lock yielded.

"Now," muttered Dick Hatherden, exultingly—"now for my revenge!"

They cautiously entered the room.

Minnie Grandley was once more wrapped in the sweet embraces of slumber.

Youth soon lapses into forgetfulness in spite of unusual disturbances, and there she lay with one white arm thrown over her head, and the other resting on her snowy bosom.

"Guard the door," said Dick Hatherden; and he approached the bed.

"Wake!" he cried, bending down and shaking her by the shoulder—"wake!"

The young girl woke at once, and sprang up in terror.

She would have shrieked aloud for help, but the cry seemed frozen on her lips when she beheld the masked man holding a gleaming knife.

"Oh! what do you want with me?" she cried, tremulously. "Spare me—spare me!"

"If you utter one cry," said Dick Hatherden, "I will plunge this knife into your bosom. Dress yourself quickly and come with us."

So saying he took her clothes, flung them on the bed, and drew the curtains of the couch, saying—

"Five minutes—I give you no longer."

What was the unfortunate girl to do?

The love of life is strong in the breasts of the young.

She knew well that the ruffians she had seen were not to be trifled with.

So, trusting in providence to release her from them, and to save her from any hideous outrage at their hands, she dressed herself in all haste.

As soon as she had done so, and had stepped out upon the floor, they made her don her walking habit, and then seat herself upon a chair.

To this they bound her tightly, and gagged her as they had done Betty.

"Now, then, for the old girl herself," said Dick. "It's in her room that the money is, and if *she* squeals I'll pay her out for old scores by scragging her."

So saying the ruffians hurried from the room towards the other.

If they wished to do all before the return of Simon Grandley they must hasten.

They found Mrs. Grandley's room open, or, at least, on the jar.

They crept in stealthily.

"All's very quiet," whispered Dick. "Follow me this way. I've seen him hide it."

He made his way to a bureau that stood close by the window.

In the lock of the door of this was a bunch of keys ready for their use.

Such ease as this in all they were seeking might have aroused suspicion.

But it did not.

They well knew, by former experience, how careless people were.

Turning the key in the lock, Dick, with trembling hands, took forth from the bureau a small brown box, which felt very heavy.

Intimating to The Owl by a gesture that all was right, Dick rose and neared the bed.

As he did so he started back with an exclamation of genuine surprise.

"Why, she's not here," he cried. "Where can she be? Let's hurry away."

"Yes, without the girl," thought The Owl, but he did not give vent to his wish.

He only led the way out of the room and towards Minnie Grandley's chamber.

On reaching this everything seemed enveloped in unnatural darkness.

"The moon's taken it into its head not to shine," said The Owl, with an oath. "It's as dark as pitch. But there's one thing, we can find the girl easy enough."

And, with Dick, he began groping his way to the middle of the room.

As they reached it the door was heard to close suddenly behind them; the window shutters, which had excluded the light, were thrown open, and a sight met their eyes which fairly bewildered them.

Standing round them, armed and free, were Mrs. Grandley, Minnie, Betty, and Quail.

For a few moments no one spoke.

Then Mrs. Grandley said, in a tremulous voice—

"Pray, gentlemen, what do you want here in my house?"

It was rather a posing question.

Both The Owl and Dick Hatherden felt it to be very much so.

But they soon recovered self-possession.

"Well, madam," said The Owl, in a sneering, mock-respectful tone, "I haven't had the great pleasure of being introduced to you, but I believe you're Mrs. Grandley. If so, you know the box that my friend yonder has got in his hand. It contains your husband's money. We came for that, and we came also for your daughter. We're going to take both with us."

"Villain!" exclaimed Mrs. Grandley, fiercely, "do you dare say this to my face?"

"Yes, I dare," said The Owl, coolly, as he drew his long knife.

Then he turned to Dick Hatherden.

"I'm the strongest," he said; "I'll walk off the girl; you take the box."

In spite of the unpleasant aspect of affairs, Dick Hatherden felt no inclination to fly

His blood was up.

He seemed caged, as it were; but nothing could be done without bold action.

"Come on, then," he said; and seizing the box, which The Owl had in his hand, he rushed towards the door, so as to have it open by the time that his companion was ready to carry off the girl.

But he was resisted in a manner he had little expected.

Quail was there before him—his strange, wild features pale, even livid, with excitement.

"Back! back!" shouted he, as he drew from his

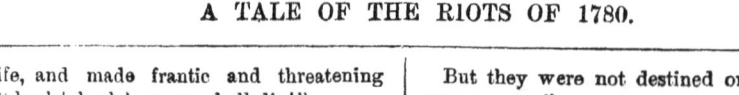

belt a knife, and made frantic and threatening gestures—"back! back! or you shall die!"

Dick uttered a scornful laugh, and made a fierce rush at him.

But he had miscalculated the force of Quail's strength and resolution.

He found himself so fiercely assailed that he was compelled to drop the box and defend himself.

The Owl, meanwhile, made a rush at the group of women to seize Minnie Grandley.

But strong as he was, he found that he had met his match.

Minnie herself, had she been alone, would have been utterly powerless to save herself from being carried off, but Mrs. Grandley now aided her with all her strength, and Betty, throwing up the window, shouted lustily for help.

While the fight was going on, therefore, a strange event happened.

From the wall, as it seemed, but really, of course, from a door dexterously concealed, emerged several men.

Among them Simon Grandley.

"Hark!" cried one, as they poured in the court-yard—"hark! there is a cry of distress."

Clearly it rang out again.

"Help! help!"

And Betty's voice, be it said, was by no means a weak one when she chose to exert herself to the utmost.

"By heavens it is in *my* house!" cried the carpenter. "Gentlemen, let me beg your aid."

And with the words he rushed towards the door, which had been left partially open by the two ruffians.

Betty clapped her hands delightedly together as she saw the approach of aid.

"Ha!" she cried, "they are coming to save us: here is master and ever so many friends."

The Owl turned to Dick with a fierce oath.

"We must make our escape," he said; "it's no use stopping here to be nabbed."

And with that he hurled Minnie Grandley from him with such force that, being dashed against her mother, she fell with her on the bed.

He then flew to the door and opened it.

This Dick Hatherden had been entirely unable to accomplish.

Quail seemed for the moment to be endowed with superhuman strength.

Why he should have been so willing upon this occasion to incur death the sequel will show.

The Owl saw at once how affairs stood.

He saw that the boy's hands were closely encircling Dick Hatherden's throat.

He saw that his guilty companion, in fact, was fast getting the worst of it.

With one drive of his knife, therefore, he freed him from Quail's grasp; and with a yell of rage and agony the latter fell back, wounded desperately in the chest.

"Now," cried The Owl, seizing the box as Dick sprang to his feet; "now let us fly for our lives!"

In another moment they had opened the door and began hurrying down the stairs.

But they were not destined on this occasion to escape so easily.

All I have described did not occupy many minutes; and when, therefore, the two ruffians rushed down the stairs they were met by Simon Grandley and his friends.

"Curses on the whole affair!" cried The Owl. "I wish I had had nothing to do with it. Now we shall be nabbed, and no mistake. We must try a rush."

To retreat was impossible.

The women stood at the top of the stairs, and weak as they might be, would have the power of precipitating them among the others as they advanced.

So a rush for it was the only chance.

And this failed.

The new-comers were far too numerous for them, and though they fought violently, they, in the course of a few minutes, were prisoners.

In half an hour more they were occupying a cell close to that in which Bill Hazard was in chains.

Here we must leave them for awhile (as we must leave poor wounded Quail also) while we return to Guy the Foundling.

CHAPTER XIX.

GUY MAKES A STRANGE DISCOVERY.

"I AM lost!" he had said, as he closed his window, on hearing the constables demanding an entrance to Hallwyn House.

Yet though he uttered the words, he did not believe them.

Otherwise he would not have carefully seen to the priming of his pistols.

Hope is always strong in the breasts of the young, and it could not seem to Guy the Foundling that all his bright hopes would be thus rudely dashed to the ground.

So he waited, pistol in hand, and his eyes fixed on the door.

Presently a gentle tap was heard.

He made no sign.

Perhaps it might be a ruse.

Then the tapping was renewed, and a voice spoke quickly.

Evidently it was that of a female.

He approached the door and listened.

"Quick! open the door!" cried the voice of Aurora Halsted.

He sprang forward at once, and obeyed her.

He knew well that she would not betray him.

She was standing there in a loose robe, looking very white and agitated.

"You must fly!" she said. "No time must be lost. Oh! why came you here to-night?"

"How can I fly?" returned Guy: "the place appears surrounded!"

"Follow me," said Aurora: "you saved *my* life once—I will save yours now!"

She gave him her hand, and led him out into the dark corridor.

The sounds of angry voices could be heard plainly below.

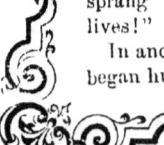

But she passed down by another way.

The house was a strange old place, and full of winding staircases, and down one of these she led him, until they reached a door which opened into the garden.

This she unlocked.

"There," she said, "these are the grounds. Be very careful even now. Do not show yourself in the road, as you do not know how many may be watching for you. Conceal yourself among the bushes; and in the morning at dawn meet me by yonder elm tree. Quick now! I hear voices coming."

She pressed his hand, and, closing the door, left him to himself.

Love had again conquered the feeling of pique and hate engendered by his eagerness to rush to the arms of Minnie Grandley after the riots.

This thought, however, did not occur to Guy the Foundling.

He thanked her for her aid.

And that was all.

His own position was far too critical to allow of much thought for her.

He looked round him for a place of concealment.

Around him was a dense mass of trees, and flowers, and small bushes; but he was at present too near the house to be safe.

Making his way at random, therefore, and as gently and noiselessly as he could, through the foliage, he arrived at length at a place where some ruins were visible even in the dark night.

Here he halted, and seating himself upon some fallen brickwork, waited.

Presently he heard voices not very far off, accompanied by breaking of boughs.

The constables were evidently searching the grounds.

At least, so it appeared to him.

What was to be done?

To attempt to fly would be to throw himself into the arms of his enemies.

So quitting his seat, he crept down beneath some bushes and waited.

It was not long before he clearly distinguished approaching footsteps crashing through the boughs.

Then voices.

Then the flash of lanterns held in the hands of constables.

"Well, he's given us the slip, and no mistake, this time," cried one of them, as they stopped at the end of the ruined wall to rest. "I'm hanged if I care about this job at all. We may be making fools of ourselves after all."

"How so?"

"Because he mayn't turn out to be a highwayman."

"But he killed the man."

"So he tells us himself; but I'm beginning to be doubtful about his criminality. He may explain it all away, and then we'll have had all our trouble for nothing, and look fools in the bargain."

"No, no! we're only doing our duty," said one of the others. "Let's have another beat up."

And so they once more started in pursuit of their "game."

The mind of Guy the Foundling was, as may be imagined, greatly perplexed.

The natural impulse of his youthful heart when he found a chance of escape had been to embrace it.

But *now* he regretted the step.

There was a kind of admission of guilt in the very fact of his attempting to elude justice.

But now a plan suggested itself to his mind, and he resolved, if possible, to avoid capture at any price until the morning.

So he dragged himself beneath the bushes as far as he could in spite of the tangles, and there lay.

The constables were very determined in their search.

But failure will cause any one to become disheartened.

At length, therefore, they gave up the search, and having warned Mr. Hallwyn that they should hold him responsible for aiding and abetting the flight of a criminal they departed.

Of course, Guy the Foundling did not know the exact moment of their leaving.

He, therefore, was in his place of concealment long after they left the vicinity.

At length he had just made up his mind to creep from his cramped position and make his way to some point nearer the house when a sound close by his ear startled him.

Had it been merely the movement of a twig or a stone it would not have startled him.

But it was nothing of the kind.

It was a human voice.

A voice issuing, as it were, from the bowels of the earth.

What could it mean?

He listened eagerly.

Not that he for the moment connected the sound with the mission which Simon Grandley had given him.

He was merely stirred up by curiosity.

At length the voices seemed to rise above the level of his head, and they then became intelligible.

"Do you think all is safe?" asked a strange voice.

"Yes," replied another, whom Guy the Foundling recognised as that of Mr. Hallwyn.

"But the young stranger from London, where is he?" said the other.

"I know not," replied Mr. Hallwyn, "he is not now in the house. I assure you all is safe. Let us return."

"I see no necessity," said the stranger, who spoke with a slightly foreign accent, "we have decided now pretty well what to do, and what part we are to assume if there is any riot. As for the disappearance of Alexis Rainsford and our other friends, that is a mystery which I feel myself quite unable to solve; but let us hope they will show themselves before the time of action arrives. There is but little interval yet. So now we may safely go."

"If such be your wish, go by all means," said Mr. Hallwyn, evidently somewhat nettled; "what say *you*, my friends?"

"We agree with Colonel Damas," replied several voices at once.

"Very well, so be it, then; and when are we to meet again?"

"On the third night from this, in these ruins," said the colonel.

"Let it be so settled, then," said Mr. Hallwyn; "and since you *will* go—good night, and a safe journey."

"Let us hope so," said the colonel; "when next we meet, if we can't settle anything else, we shall, at least, be able to discuss the news I shall receive from France, which, I hope, will be of great importance."

Then there was the sound of ascending footsteps, a rustling among the trees, and the old ruins resumed their former quiet.

"Strange things come to pass," murmured Guy the Foundling, as he raised himself from his recumbent position; "here I have absolutely discovered all that Simon Grandley wished to discover by accident, without willingly playing the spy at all."

This was just what he could have wished it to be.

As we had seen, he had not relished the plan at first.

Now, as the knowledge had been, as it were, forced upon him, he saw no reason why he should not give information to Simon Grandley.

But as to one thing he was determined.

He would give no information, even to the master whom he loved so well, until he had assured himself of one thing.

This was, that—beyond the frustration of the designs of the Catholics—no harm should come to Mr. Hallwyn or his friends.

CHAPTER XX.

THE VEILED WOMAN.

MORNING at length dawned.

Guy the Foundling, as may be imagined, was delighted when he beheld the first gleam of sunlight, and hurried eagerly towards the place which Aurora had appointed as their place of meeting.

He saw at once by her altered look that matters were brighter.

"I am so glad, Guy," she said, holding both her hands out to him; "all is clear now—the men have gone, and you can hasten freely to London."

"I have work to do ere I can return thither," he said, with a smile, as he drew her arm into his, and walked towards the house.

"What may that be?"

"I have decided upon giving myself up."

"What!—to the authorities?"

"Yes. It is the best proof I can give of my innocence."

He could feel the little warm arm tremble as it lay within his.

"Oh, Guy! you must be mad. Of what avail have been all our efforts to save you," cried Aurora, "if you thus wilfully throw yourself again into danger?"

"I assure you," replied Guy, "it will not be running into danger, but quite the reverse."

Aurora shook her head.

"I will prove it, then," said the Foundling, "if you will listen. The very fact of my escaping forcibly from the round-house is a kind of evidence of guilt?"

"That may be; but——"

"Nay—hear me. That act was done under the impulse of the moment. When I reflected on it I saw its folly. I must now say that I fled because I had most important work to perform; and to show that I was assured of my innocence, and do not fear the proper administration of justice, I will walk into court in the morning, when the inquiry is going on, and deliver myself up."

"You are wrong," said Aurora; "you do not know what these country justices are?"

"I will trust in Heaven and my innocence," he said.

They had by this time reached the house, where they found Mr. Hallwyn awaiting them.

There was a slight feeling of compunction in the mind of Guy the Foundling as they met.

He felt almost like a culprit.

He could not bring himself at first to take the position of a spy, and now he was face to face with the man whom, in a certain sense, he was called upon to betray. He made an inward resolve that he would never again engage in such a business.

A hearty breakfast and some of Mr. Hallwyn's good old wine made Guy the Foundling all the more energetic in his resolve to show himself in court, and his host finding him so determined offered to accompany him.

The heart of the apprentice beat high as he neared the place.

His visit was, of course, accompanied with peril.

But he preferred this to continued uncertainty.

The judge might prefer to take the view of the constables, and then what evidence could he offer in proof of his own words?

On the other hand, if he made off now, and succeeded in reaching London in safety, he would always be in a state of nervousness as to the result of future meetings with the constables.

Perhaps in the midst of his happiest moments he might be seized and carried away to prison—at a time when he would not be able to prove his innocence.

When they neared the precincts of the court they found an immense concourse of people assembled.

Elbowing through these they reached the passage, and were pressing forward with the rest when a constable darting forward seized Guy the Foundling by the shoulder.

"Here's the one we want," cried he.

The next moment he regretted his words.

A well-directed blow catching him in the face sent him staggering back among his fellow constables.

Then Mr. Hallwyn and Guy, amid the laughter of those around, pressed into the court-house, where an examination was taking place.

The constable who had received the blow, however, was in no humour to put up with it quietly.

So he hurriedly made his way into the room, hoping to be able to be the first to inform the justices of the fact that the prisoner was there ready for arrest.

Guy the Foundling, however, did not give him the chance he sought.

He quickly approached one of the other constables and whispered to him.

In another moment a communication had been made to the chief judge.

Surprise was most evidently depicted on his countenance, and he turned at once to consult those who sat with him.

The result was that the examination was stopped for a few moments, and then Guy was placed in the dock.

"We are glad, both for your own sake, and for the sake of all concerned," said one of the justices, "that you have presented yourself here to-day. We have discovered that the man killed is a notorious character—both a robber and a murderer; and you have only done society a service in ridding it of him. But you must admit yourself that you have acted most imprudently."

"How so, sir?" asked Guy.

"In taking from his pockets a purse of money, and in associating yourself after with a band of marauders. How can you explain this?"

The constable who had seized Guy in the passage was very crestfallen on seeing the friendly manner in which the magistrate addressed Guy.

He resolved to keep very quiet.

"Well, sir," answered Guy, "I thought, and naturally enough I think, that I might as well have the money he had with him as the next footpad that passed that way, or any patrol that might find his body in the road."

"But, knowing your innocence, why did you make your escape, and accept the assistance of such a set of ruffians?" asked the magistrate.

"I had a commission to do for my master," said Guy, "and I was resolved, if possible, to perform it ere morning. I own my folly in this respect; but I have willingly come forward now to yield myself for examination."

The judge nodded, and a consultation between the three on the bench ensued.

It lasted but a short time.

Then one of those who had not as yet spoken turned to him, gave him a severe castigation and a long series of directions for his future conduct, and finally discharged him without any stain upon his character.

So far so good.

But that examination had not as yet borne all its fruits.

Guy the Foundling, in fact, had been too taken up with his own position to observe all that was passing in the court-room.

During the whole of the examination into the robber's death a woman closely veiled had been seated in the court apart—sitting very still, but eagerly taking in all the details of the death of the strange man.

When, however, Guy the Foundling rose up and was examined by the judge, her head was raised at once.

From that moment she had eyes for no one but him.

Her gaze was riveted upon him.

When he left the court she quitted too, glided through the crowd, and when Guy and Mr. Hallwyn were some distance from the court-house, she tapped the Foundling on the shoulder.

He turned round, and on seeing the veiled woman started in surprise.

She threw up her veil, and he started again.

No wonder was it.

Her face was one which one seldom sees in a life-time.

It was beautiful, but pale as marble, the eyes glancing out strangely and wistfully from their white setting.

The mouth was delicately chiselled; but the lips now were livid, and so set as to have the appearance of being thin.

Evidently past the term of extreme youth, she was yet formed in a mould of exquisite symmetry.

"Look at me," she said to Guy the Foundling, "and mark me well."

The words were said in an odd, almost a cruel, voice.

Guy the Foundling knew not what to say or to think.

Had he been unfortunate enough to fall in with a madwoman?

"I look at you, madam," he said, with a respectful bow, "and I shall not easily forget so beautiful a face."

The fair one seemed by no means pleased with his compliment.

"No empty flatteries for me," she cried; "I care not for them. I wish you but to remember my face, that it may haunt you day and night. I am your avenging demon, and in your brightest, happiest moments I will come to destroy you!"

Guy the Foundling and Mr. Hallwyn gazed at her in bewilderment.

"You have mistaken my young friend here for some one else," said the latter.

The woman laughed bitterly.

"Mistaken him!" she cried. "I cannot well do that, when I take him at his own word. Did I not hear him say that he had slain on the highway the man who lies dead in yonder court-room?"

"Yes."

"Know, then, that with that one dies all the pleasure of life. He was the only one I ever loved, and now he has been cruelly murdered! Standing by his dead body, holding his cold hand in mine, I swore to avenge him; and here, in the very face of his murderer, I renew the vow!"

She raised her hand towards heaven as she said these words.

There was something very solemn in her attitude and manner.

Both Guy the Foundling and Robert Hallwyn were moved with pity towards her.

But what could be done, what could be said, under such circumstances?

"Madam," said Guy, "I sincerely grieve for your position; but what can I say? Your lover or husband, whichever he may have been, attacked me on the road, and in self-defence I slew him. It was his life or mine—and I preferred to save my own. Believe me——"

The strange woman waved him away with a scornful gesture.

"Say no more," she said; "say no more! When

the time comes you will see how much I put faith in your sorrow."

Then she turned away.

Robert Hallwyn shuddered as they resumed their walk.

"You have made an enemy in her," said he, "that I should be sorry to have myself, Guy. There is something about her eyes which chilled my blood."

"Yes, there is indeed a cruel determination in them. But I may never see her again."

"Depend upon it she will make every effort to discover you."

"But she knows not even my name or my address in London."

"That says nothing," said Robert Hallwyn. "Take my advice: be on your guard. That woman is one who will discover you, no matter where you may be concealed. She did not even ask to know your whereabouts or your name. She feels convinced that when she desires to do so she can find you."

Guy the Foundling laughed.

"Well," he said, "I fancy you have a disposition to frighten me. But never fear—I will take your advice. But in my opinion the woman is mad, and is as likely to forget all about me as not. But here is my road: I had better hurry back to London."

"How about your business for Simon Grandley?" said Robert.

For the moment Guy the Foundling had forgotten this.

But he was not taken off his guard.

"That must be postponed," he said; "I should not find now the person I require."

"But you have no horse, and you have not said good-bye to Aurora."

"I cannot wait now to do so," returned Guy; "you must do so for me. Bid her believe that I regret sincerely being obliged to go, but I will see her soon again, and thank her myself for her kind assistance in saving my life."

Then he shook Mr. Hallwyn heartily by the hand and departed.

CHAPTER XXI.

THE END OF A SAD LIFE.

WE must now return to Simon Grandley and his friends.

Quail, it will be remembered, when the two ruffians left the room where the struggle had commenced, lay on his back severely wounded.

When, therefore, Simon and the others had gone with their prisoners to the lock-up, the women carried the unfortunate lad to the bed, and laid him upon it.

Betty then was despatched for a surgeon.

On arriving he found Quail very unwell—in fact, helpless and speechless.

A little restorative, however, enabled him to speak; though the leech shook his head gravely, and when he departed said—

"A bad case—a bad case! I fear it is all up with him."

It seemed, indeed, plain enough to all that the hand of death was upon the unfortunate boy.

Revive he certainly did under the hands of the doctor.

But to him and to others it was but too evident that this revival was but the last flicker of the flame.

"Can I do anything for you?" said Minnie Grandley, as, with tears in her eyes, she sat by the bedside of the unfortunate boy.

"Yes," was the feeble reply.

"Oh! tell me, then. I will do anything to please you."

"You can do two things to please me. It will be the last time now, for I know that death is coming. Stoop down, kiss my forehead, and bless me; and then stop with me till all is over."

The approach of the Great Enemy seemed to have cleared his brain, and he spoke with a clearness and an emotion which was quite foreign to his usual style.

Need we say that Minnie Grandley complied with his request.

Thankful she was that she did so.

The gratitude that beamed from his eyes was payment enough.

The pressure of the hand which he gave her afterwards, the tears which started, told her more.

She saw now the meaning of many things which had been mysterious before.

She understood now the stolen glances, the flushing cheeks, the devotion at last of his life.

The wild, half-idiotic boy loved her!

He had been ashamed, knowing his own infirmities, to confess this before.

Now, however, with the shadow of death hanging over him, he was quite willing that she should know all; and afford to him the pleasure of her presence till the latest breath should take from him all power of love or hate.

Noon on the following day brought with it Guy the Foundling.

Eager to tell Simon Grandley the wonderful occurrences which had befallen him, he rushed into the workshop, where Simon Grandley and Will Lightmore were discussing the attempted robbery and abduction of the night before.

"Ha! ha! what have we here?" cried Will as Guy entered; "talk of a certain person, and lo! he will appear. You look wan and weary, Sir Traveller, as if the news of last night's misdoings had already reached your ears."

Guy started.

"Last night's misdoings!"

Had the words any possible reference to his odd adventures of the past night.

"What misdoings?" he asked, in surprise.

Simon Grandley quickly narrated to him the events of the dark hours.

"Curse him," cried Guy, as he heard of the attempt of Dick Hatherden to carry off Minnie Grandley. "I am glad, indeed, to hear that he is caged. Now, perhaps, he will obtain his deserts. But poor Quail—I must hasten to see him."

Poor Quail, indeed!

He was gradually but surely sinking.

Memories of the past crowded into his brain as he faded away.

He could not babble of green fields, or fashion into words the sweet memories of a mother's love, for he had never known them.

His were indeed hard lessons of life.

What *he* could remember were cruel passages of life—dark arches near the river, harsh words, abuse, unkindness—horrors of no mean character.

These he spoke of, mingling them here and there with words indicative of the kindness now shown him.

Then, as the long night drew nearer, he spoke of Minnie in sorrowing accents that made their hearts bleed.

Such love, such devotion, seemed too great to be contained in such a body!

Just as his last breath was leaving him, however, the poor lad seemed to recover consciousness.

"Bend down," he said, quietly.

And Minnie leaned over him.

"I have been so weak and ill," he said, "that I had nearly forgotten. I have a great secret to tell. When I am dead—oh, do not start, but listen to me, for that I am dying I know too well. When I am dead, look in my old coat, and you will find sewn in the breast pocket a letter. Give it to Guy. It will clear up what is now a great mystery."

That night saw the last of him.

He was quite unable to speak; but though this power had left him, his last pressure of the hand was for Minnie, and the last look of his eyes.

And such was the end of the poor orphan waif.

As soon as the poor spirit had fled Minnie Grandley told to Guy the last injunctions she had received from Quail.

The coat—the old ragged coat—which the wretched lad had worn when living with Bill Hazard and Dick Hatherden, was found in his room, carefully hidden away in a cupboard.

Sure enough, too, on examining it there was found the letter sewn in the breast.

It ran thus:—

"Dear Guy,—

"I did not wish to say a word in regard to this matter while I was alive. I shall not long be in this world. I feel it. I have too many enemies and no one to care for me, while the one I love is as immeasurably beyond my reach as if she were already in heaven! Minnie Grandley! oh! you will know my love only when the grave has received me, and I cannot be ashamed of my confession.

"But to my secret—

"Colonel Halsted is, indeed, dead—murdered by Dick Hatherden and Bill Hazard.

(Then followed an account of the murder.)

"I was afraid (continued the letter) to tell of this while I lived, though I often wished that I could see those villains punished; but I was afraid of being in some way implicated, and did not like to tell. Of Bill Hazard's part in the murder there is no proof except my word, but in regard to Dick Hatherden there is. When the murder was done the dying man clutched a piece of Dick's handkerchief from his throat. This is still in his skeleton

hand, for on the night of the fire I dragged the corpse from the closet where it was concealed, and where Dick hoped it would be burned, and placed it beneath some projecting wood-work on the roof of the third house from the colonel's. You will find it there, with the handkerchief bearing embroidered on it Dick Hatherden's name.

"And now Heaven bless you all.

"Tell Minnie how I loved her. You, Guy, will not be jealous of, or offended with a poor, wretched, witless creature such as I am. Again, God bless you all. Good-bye,

"QUAIL."

"Poor fellow," murmured Guy, as he finished reading this letter, which was, of course, ill spelt and strangely scrawled, "he was worthy of a better fate. Aurora must know this—the murderers of her father shall yet be punished."

He knew not then how strangely the tide of events would turn.

CHAPTER XXII.

THE CAPTURE OF THE CONSPIRATORS.

SIMON GRANDLEY was delighted, as may be imagined, at the information which Guy the Foundling gave him—the result of no definite plan of action but the mere chance of the moment.

"Ah!" he said, rubbing his hands, "they will make but a bad show when the great day arrives. We must proceed thither as quickly as possible and be ready for the time of their meeting."

"There is no hurry," said Guy the Foundling; "and, besides, you forget one thing."

"What is that?"

"I cannot be one of the party."

The carpenter gazed at him—not angrily, but in sorrowful surprise.

"I should be sorry, indeed," he said, "not to have you in my company. Why cannot you join us?"

"I should appear what I almost feel now—a traitor," said Guy, vehemently. "I have already told secrets which I only discovered through the kindness of Aurora in saving me from the constables. I cannot and will not appear openly in the matter."

"Without your aid how can we discover the place?" said Simon Grandley.

He resolved to try his utmost to obtain the aid of the brave apprentice.

"I can describe it so accurately that you cannot miss it," said Guy; "there will, however, be no necessity for me to be seen in the neighbourhood that they may recognise me. On the eve of your departure I'll warrant you shall have such instructions that you will be able to reach the spot as easily as if I were guiding you."

Persuasion was useless.

Guy the Foundling was fully determined not to be of the party.

And Simon Grandley, remembering the many services he had rendered him, forebore to press him.

So, on the appointed evening, having received full information from Guy, the party of adventurers set out.

THE RIVAL APPRENTICES

A TALE OF THE RIOTS OF 1780.

"HARK! WHAT IS THAT NOISE?" CRIED MISTRESS CALLENDAR.

There were fully a hundred of them, and all full of zeal and courage.

It was a strange, disconnected style of proceeding, this action on the part of the Protestants.

But, nevertheless, their movements, though apparently secret, were well known and watched by the authorities.

Any large movements of this kind, no matter how cleverly conducted, are dangerous.

And so, while the Protestants and the Catholics were preparing for a riot such as would ring throughout the whole world, the Government were taking measures to prevent it.

The movement of so many as a hundred men at once would, of course, have excited suspicion.

So they divided themselves into a number of small bands, and having settled the hour and place of rendezvous, started, as I have said, full of zeal.

The information given to them by Guy the Foundling had been so precise that they had no difficulty in finding the spot; and long before the hour arranged for the assembling of Mr. Hallwyn and his friends, Simon Grandley and his followers were in the grounds.

The ruins where Guy had heard the mysterious voices were the most prominent objects in the grounds, and it being a bright moonlight night they experienced no difficulty in finding them.

Then came a halt and a conference.

How best should they entrap the Catholic conspirators?

After various schemes had been proposed, the plan of Simon Grandley was adopted.

This was to discover the entrance to the subterranean cavern, and then send half the men down, leaving the other fifty scattered in the underwood.

When Mr. Hallwyn and his friends had descended a shrill whistle was to be given by those below.

Then Simon Grandley and his men were to close round the entrance; and caught thus between two fires, the Catholics would, of course, surrender.

Such, at least, was the programme.

It was not long before, with dark lanterns, the first body of besiegers had made their way down into the subterranean place of meeting, which they found far larger and far more convenient for their purpose than they had anticipated.

It was an immense succession of vaults, the walls of which had been broken down so as to form it into one large chamber.

At one end there was a large pile of stones and rubbish, and from the appearance of this part of the place it was evident that it was not used.

Here, then, the men scrambled up, and compressing themselves into as small a space as possible, waited for the coming of the conspirators.

It was not long before the tramp of men was heard, and then footsteps descended the staircase—or, rather, stone steps.

There were about twenty of them.

Among them were Mr. Hallwyn and—to Simon Grandley's utter surprise—Alexis Rainsford.

How had he escaped?

How had he contrived to elude his guards, and make his way from out of the bowels of the earth? This was a mystery he could not fathom.

There was no time now, however, for thinking upon this.

They must be made prisoners, and explanation would follow.

Eagerly Simon Grandley waited for the sound of the expected signal.

Presently it rang out with a muffled sound, coming as if from far beneath the earth.

"Now, my men," cried Simon.

And in another moment they had rushed down the steps and closed up in a compact body at the summit.

The scene below was pre-eminently picturesque.

The conspirators had lit a number of torches, which were stuck round the vault in numerous places, and shed a flickering, lurid light upon all.

They were huddled now into a compact group.

They were, in fact, utterly taken by surprise.

Robert Hallwyn was the first to recover, and he advanced towards Simon Grandley just as the latter was about to speak.

"Pray permit me to ask," he said, "what does all this mean?"

Simon smiled.

He saw at a glance the entire success of his plan.

"The explanation is self-evident I should imagine," he said, quietly.

"Do not trifle with us," said Alexis Rainsford, coming forward: "with me at any rate."

Simon Grandley knew the significance of these words and the emphasis upon them.

Alexis held his secret.

But this did not cause him to lose his dignity.

"I trifle with no one," he said; "I have no cause to do so. You are Catholics, who are conspiring to turn into a riot and a revolt that which, conducted as we desire it, will be a peaceful demonstration of the people of England. We are Protestants, and we are resolved to prevent disturbance. Therefore, gentlemen, you are our prisoners."

Then he added—

"As for you, Alexis Rainsford, I am astounded and bewildered to see you here, when——"

"Stay," interrupted Alexis, hurriedly; "at the proper time I will explain all."

These words, accompanied by a look, silenced Simon on this point.

"Well, gentlemen, I agree with Mr. Rainsford," he said. "This is no time or place for explanations. The question is, do you surrender yourselves? There are a hundred brave and willing hearts here; and though doubtless you are also brave and zealous, you are but twenty, and a conflict can but end in useless bloodshed. What say you?"

A hurried and whispered consultation took place among the conspirators.

The result could not be doubtful.

"Well," said Robert Hallwyn, "there is no use in denying that we are fairly captured. What is it you propose?"

"That you and three others, as the principals in this matter, adjourn to your house with four of us, and there settle upon terms," said Simon Grandley.

This was at once agreed to.

Robert Hallwyn, Alexis Rainsford, and two others accompanied Simon Grandley, who, with Jonas Barnsdale and two other friends, at once set out across the dark plantation towards Hallwyn House.

"This is the doing of Guy the Foundling, I feel assured," said Hallwyn, bitterly, to the carpenter,

as they went along. "This, then, was his mission —to betray me!"

"Guy was never a traitor," returned Simon Grandley; "he only acts where he thinks himself right."

With this remark Robert Hallwyn by no means coincided.

But he said nothing.

In his own heart, however, he made one firm resolve.

He had observed the intense love which Aurora had for Guy, and he could not for one moment doubt that it was reciprocated.

"He shall never possess my niece," he cried; "that I will make certain."

He need not have made that resolve.

But he knew nothing of the true state of affairs, as I have said.

So it relieved his heart for a time.

On reaching the house he entered a private room, for the purpose of discussing preliminaries.

"I will not put you to the pain, gentlemen," said Simon Grandley, "of denying that your meetings have reference to the upsetting of the arrangements of the Protestant Association, because it is always painful to have to deny for a purpose what you know to be true. Granted that you were conspiring to upset our arrangements and stir up disorder, can we now, if we release your friends, depend upon you abstaining from any action in the matter?"

Silence followed this speech for a few moments.

Then a hurried conference took place.

During this, of course, Simon Grandley and his friends did not interfere.

They retired to a different part of the room, and there remained until Alexis Rainsford called to them to come back.

"Gentlemen," said he, when they were once more seated, "we have considered your proposition, and in reply to it can only say that to make any such promise as you propose would be breaking the vows we have made."

"We cannot release you without the promise is made," replied Simon Grandley; "on that point we are resolved."

"We thoroughly understand that," said Robert Hallwyn. "What we mean is, that rather than give the promise you require of us, we will continue prisoners in your hands."

"So be it then," replied Simon Grandley; "on no other condition can we permit you to quit the place. Therefore, we must beg of you to return with us. All your comforts shall be attended to, but——"

"You will permit me to see my niece?" said Robert Hallwyn.

"That I cannot," said Grandley, "unless, indeed, it be in my presence."

Robert Hallwyn's brow grew dark.

"That is useless," he said, in a tone of anger; "quite useless."

Simon smiled.

"Certainly it would be useless, if your object is to tell her where you are going, and how to affect your deliverance. But, come, gentlemen—

come, time flies—let us return, since you so will it."

Another short and secret conference now took place among the prisoners.

But it brought no further result.

"We have sworn to perform certain things, and we will perform them, unless we are captives," said Alexis.

And so they returned to the underground cellars in the ruins.

It was an uncomfortable, damp, unhealthy place to choose as a place of confinement.

But there were two things to be said.

It was not for long.

And, besides, there was a chance that the very nature of the place might cause a desire on the part of the captives to obtain liberty at any price.

A good guard was left behind.

The necessary provisions were procured, and then the rest of the successful captors made their way back to London.

CHAPTER XXIII.

A MYSTERIOUS STORY, AND HOW IT WAS PUT TO GOOD USE.

NATURALLY, Simon Grandley was delighted by the success of his stratagem.

But he was wrong in his elation.

He had not been so successful as he thought.

Throughout the conversation between him and the conspirators which I have but hinted at there had been a listener.

A light form had been concealed behind the hangings of the window.

This was Aurora Halsted.

She had seen the eight men approaching the house, and had recognised Simon Grandley.

It at once occurred to her, why was he at her uncle's house?

Guy had appeared mysteriously, and disappeared again without an adieu.

There was evidently a mystery somewhere.

Women love mystery.

So she determined to fathom it.

Hastily entering the room where she deemed most probable they would enter, she concealed herself behind the heavy curtains of the window.

Here she heard all.

Not only the discussion between both sides, but also the whispered conference.

Her quick apprehension caused her to see all at a glance.

When they were gone her brain felt in a whirl of excitement.

What was to be done?

She was grateful to Simon Grandley.

Grateful also, and more than so, to Guy the Foundling.

But she loved her uncle also.

Naturally, then, she found herself in a complete dilemma.

If she made a public affair of it, it would not only expose Mr. Hallwyn to severe consequences, but entirely mar all his plans.

The thing to be done, then, was to effect his escape in secret.

This was a weighty undertaking.

And yet she must do it alone, she thought.

Yet no!

There was a possibility yet of obtaining aid.

A bright idea occurred to her, in fact.

There was an old housekeeper at Hallwyn House, named Mistress Lucy Callendar.

This woman was a devoted servant of the Hallwyn family.

In fact, from time immemorial she had been with them, and there could not be the slightest fear that she would do anything to betray them.

She had always been a kind of fixture in the house—felt herself a part of it—and to betray any one of the name of Hallwyn would be like betraying herself.

So she was the very one to apply to.

She knew the inns and outs of the place: was acquainted, no doubt, with all the secrets of the old ruins, and would, doubtless, know some way of reaching it.

So at least thought Aurora.

The wish in her was father to the thought.

She hurried at once to the room of the old woman, who had just completed her morning's toilet.

Mistress Callendar had taken a great fancy to the pretty young girl, and would, she knew, be happy to do her a service.

"I've come to ask you a strange thing," said Aurora; "I'm full of curiosity, and I want you to satisfy it."

The old woman smiled.

She liked to be quoted as an authority.

"Well," she said, graciously, "if it's anything I can tell ye, I will."

Aurora looked round her mysteriously.

She knew that the greater the mystery the greater pleasure there would be in unravelling it.

"It is about the ruins," she said, in a whisper; "tell me all you know about them, and then I have something strange to tell you."

"Well, you see, there are a great many stories connected with those ruins," said Mrs. Callendar; "they say they're haunted."

"I'm sure they are," said Aurora.

"What—have you seen anything?"

"I have; but tell me first all you know," replied the girl, with an arch smile.

"Well," replied the old woman (and you may be sure Aurora listened with her ears strained), "you see this house and the ruins were formerly joined by a subterranean passage.

"This was in the time of the Civil Wars.

"The ruins were not then such ruins as they are now.

"A hundred years make a wonderful deal of difference in places.

"It was a ruin, but there were habitable rooms in it, and many's the strange things that have gone on within them.

"Robert Hallwyn, the ancestor of my dear master, your uncle, was a staunch Royalist, and when the King's cause had become hopeless, he took refuge here.

"His father, George Hallwyn, was an old man, and held different opinions to his son.

"Not that he was a Puritan.

"But he thought the King had deserved his fate, and was sorry, and angry too, to see his son take part in the struggle in his favour.

"But when Robert came, weary and wounded, and flying from his enemies, he gave him shelter at once, although doing so put his own life in jeopardy.

"For a little while he was safe.

"But only for awhile.

"The Puritans discovered his place of concealment, and one evening the house was surrounded by soldiers.

"The old man was well nigh distracted.

"'There is only one thing for it, Robert,' he said; 'you must fly by the secret way.'

"'But my wife and child?' he cried, in agonised accents; 'what of them?'

"'They can remain,' said George Hallwyn; 'there is no danger for them. Quick! they are beating at the door more savagely. Fly—fly!'

"A fearful scene of sorrow and weeping—a scene the less harrowing because so short a time was allowed for it—took place between husband and wife and child.

"Then the old man led him into a certain room in the house, from which a spiral staircase conducted them to a cellar.

"This cellar was boarded, and in the centre was an immense trap-door.

"This was opened, and a dark staircase was revealed.

"'Now, my son,' said the old man. 'I must leave you.'

"'But I know not my way.'

"'If I delay and remain here,' said George Hallwyn, 'of course the Puritan soldiers when they break in here will suspect I have been aiding your escape. They will kill your wife and child, and myself also. This will in no wise advantage you.'

"'No—no!' exclaimed Robert. 'Tell me, which way shall I go?'

"'Descend this staircase,' said his father, 'and go straight on until you reach a doorway; push this open, and you will find another staircase, still leading downwards; then you will find a gradual ascent into the cellars of the old ruins.'

"'But it is pitch dark.'

"'Here, take the lantern—quick! They are breaking down the doors!'

"The lantern was taken, the trap-door lowered, and the old man hurried down to the other part of the house, flinging aside his coat and waistcoat as he went, and drawing his sword.

"The Puritan soldiers had already burst into the passage.

"George Hallwyn confronted them, angrily and haughtily.

"'What means this intrusion, gentlemen?' he said. 'Are you disposed to rob me?'

"The leader—a thin, sallow-faced man—approached him.

"'We well understand,' he said, 'your love for the Puritan cause; but we know, also, you have another love.'

" ' And that is ?'

" ' Your son.'

" ' I acknowledge it.   Well ?'

" ' You know he is a Royalist, and is now flying from justice ?'

" ' I know it not.'

" ' Well then take my word, for it is so,' said the Puritan leader.   ' He was discovered to be not only a Royalist, but one of the most bigoted of them. He had a hand in the execution, or rather the murder, of our respected leader, Colonel Armstrong, whom, in their retreat after the battle of Marston Moor, they hung to a tree.   So, sir, though you are his father, we tell you it is death for him if we find him, and death to those who conceal him.'

" ' I am fully aware,' said George Hallwyn, in as unmoved a voice and manner as he could assume, ' I am fully aware that no mercy is to be expected for him and for me if I had hidden him from you. But I can tell you this.   Much as I coincide in your measures against the King, I should conceal my son were he in peril.'

" ' Then maybe he is here," exclaimed the Puritan leader, eyeing him sternly.

" ' Search and see for yourselves,' replied George Hallwyn ; ' if he is here you will find him.'

" A search, of course, was at once instituted.

" But it failed.

" Not a sign of flight was anywhere discoverable in the house.

" The servants, in fact, knew nothing of the arrival or departure of their master's son.

" The Puritans, however, though unable to obtain any satisfactory answers from anyone, resolved not to be so easily baffled.

" They had been deceived by George Hallwyn's manner at first.

" But after the search it was far different.

" His manner then—his evident triumph and pleasure at their non-success—was enough to tell them that he had in some way outwitted them.

" ' Master George Hallwyn,' said Captain Pleadwell, the leader of the Puritan host, ' we know your love for our cause, as I said before ; but as affection for your offspring may prove a greater incentive than that, we must put in force the entire order we have.'

" ' And that is ?' asked the old man, eagerly, expecting some new peril for Robert.

" ' To take possession of this house for a time, to keep strict watch on its occupants, and to make sure that the one we seek can neither enter nor depart.'

" The old man answered him cheerfully.

" He naturally thought that his son had long ago made his escape.

" ' Very well,' he said, ' you are but fulfilling your orders.   I do not complain."

" And so the soldiers stopped.

" A week passed.

" George Hallwyn treated them with the utmost kindness and hospitality.

" ' Robert has long ago discovered you are here, and would as soon dream of entering a lion's den as of coming while you are present.   But remain as long as you please.'

" Such was the answer he invariably gave, if questioned in regard to his son.

" Of course, he troubled not about him.

" He imagined him to be miles away.

" At length the Puritans were about to take their leave, when one of the men—who had been carefully employed in searching the place ever since they had been there—rushed eagerly into the leader's presence—

" ' I have made a discovery,' he cried.

" George Hallwyn, who was present, turned deadly pale at this.

" He feared some calamity.

" Yet what could it be ?

" His son had fled long since.

" So he assumed a smile.

" ' And pray, may I ask, what great discovery is it you have made ?' he said.

" ' A great one, truly,' replied the trooper, with a ghastly grin.   I have discovered a secret door leading to a subterranean passage.   Come, captain, with me.'

" With a kind of strange presentiment weighing upon his mind, George Hallwyn followed the men.

" They had, indeed, discovered the door by which his son had descended.

" The trooper led them to the trap-door, and opened it at once.

" ' I went no further than this,' he said, ' but now bring lights and follow me.'

" Four of them, including the old man, at once descended, and passed along the corridor.

" For some distance they found nothing.

" The first door was passed—they reached the second.

" Here they stumbled over something.

" In an instant lights were held over the spot ; and a ghastly scene presented itself.

" There, extended on the floor, quite dead, with the bricks of a fallen wall lying heavy on him, was Robert Hallwyn.

" He had been killed in trying to effect his escape.

" ' Oh! my son—my son,' exclaimed the old man, and fell upon the body.

" When they raised him, he, too, was dead !

" And they do say," continued Mistress Lucy Callendar, " that ever since then on All Hallows Eve (when they found the body) the father and son can be seen walking round and round the ruins, pale and ghastly, and stained with blood."

The old woman paused.

Aurora listened intently.

She had not thought it wise to make any interruption.

She knew there was no reason for immediate hurry.

" Well, you have kept this secret a long time," she said, in a sort of pretended reproach ; " the idea, now, of you never having told me this before."

" The fact is, Mistress Halsted," returned the old woman, " I never thought of it."

" Well, now, I am different," said Aurora, " Now, I only found out my secret this very morning, and I'm going to tell it you now."

The old lady was all ears at once.

She loved to hear as well as to tell a mystery.

Aurora told her story quickly.

"Well," said Mistress Callendar, when she had finished, "it is quite a revival of the old story. But never mind, what is it you wish to do?"

"We must release them."

"But how?"

"By your aid, dear Mistress Callendar," said Aurora, with a sweet smile.

The old lady bridled up.

"By *my* aid!" she said, "I don't pretend to understand such things."

And yet all the time she was hoping that she would have the guidance of the affair.

"In the first place," said Aurora, "you must show me the trap-door."

"Very good; but I don't see how we are to contrive it," said Mrs. Callendar.

"Leave that to me," replied Aurora; "are you willing to aid me?"

"I am."

"Then to-night at nine o'clock," said the resolute girl, "I will come to your room again, and we will try what we can do."

Then she went away.

Her bosom was now, as may be imagined, full of contending emotions.

If Guy the Foundling had in any way responded to her love she would have been willing to have sacrificed her uncle at once for him.

Now, however, circumstances were very greatly different.

She took a delight in the idea that in saving Robert Hallwyn she would be thwarting the plans of the one who did not reciprocate her affections.

Very eagerly, therefore, the young girl waited until the evening.

At the hour of nine precisely she entered the old housekeeper's room.

"Now, Mistress Callendar, I am ready," she said. "Have you a lantern?"

"I know where we can get one," replied she; "but what are those for?"

She pointed as she spoke to a pair of pistols that were sticking in Aurora's belt.

"They are for our protection," said the young girl; "and now let us hasten. We know not what we may have to contend with. Perhaps Simon Grandley and his friends may return before we are aware of it, for a relay or some such thing, and then we should be lost."

"We have a very ready excuse to offer," said Mistress Callendar.

"And what is that?"

"You can say that I have been telling you the story of the ruins, and that I brought you here to show you the mysteries."

Aurora smiled.

"You would not deceive such men as Simon Grandley and his companions," she said; "but come, I have no fear in the matter. I love my uncle, and *will* save him in spite of them, even if in so doing I peril my life."

To reach the room in which was the trap-door was easy.

To raise the trap was easy.

But this done, a new difficulty presented itself unexpectedly.

The old woman was afraid to proceed any further in the adventure.

Aurora, who saw her hesitation and nervousness long before words were spoken on the subject, began at once to descend.

She imagined that if she set an example old Lucy would follow.

She was wrong.

"Hark! What is that noise?" cried Mistress Callendar, as the young girl was half through the trap.

She trembled so as she spoke that she almost dropped upon Aurora the large lantern which she was holding over the dark entrance of the secret staircase.

"I hear no sound," said Aurora.

There was, in fact, nothing to be heard but the whistling of the wind.

The old woman was superstitious.

The story she had herself told produced in her a horror.

"I can go no farther," she said.

"Coward!" exclaimed the young girl, "are you, then, going to desert me?"

"I cannot—I dare not proceed," said Mrs. Callendar; "we may see them."

"Them! Whom?"

"The spirits."

"Nonsense!" said Aurora, rising from the entrance and dropping down the trap again. "What spirits would come where there are fifty armed men? Tell me once for all, are you afraid to join me in my adventure this night?"

The old woman was evidently so terrified that all her desire was to fly.

"I cannot—I dare not," she said; "but if you *will* go, I will wait here for you."

"Then you do not mind committing *me* to the spirits," said Aurora.

"You do not believe in them, and do not, therefore, fear them," said the old woman; "besides, those whom *I* should fear are your friends. If you are rash enough to go, go and chance it. I will remain here and watch."

Aurora was a brave girl.

We have seen that on more than one occasion in our tale.

"Very well," she said, "give me the lantern, and I will descend alone."

She took the lantern, and, having descended the stairs, loosened her pistols, partially obscured the light, and rapidly passed away.

The old woman had not bargained for anything like this.

She had never dreamed of being left in utter darkness.

When, therefore, she saw the last twinkle of the lantern disappear she crawled away, and, finding the door, fled into the inhabited part of the house.

Meanwhile, Aurora advanced boldly, though her fair breast trembled with emotion.

She had made up her mind for the deed, and she would go through it bravely.

Her resolution was made up as much of innate

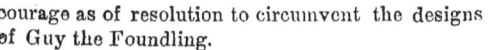

courage as of resolution to circumvent the designs of Guy the Foundling.

Her love was gradually turning, as it does often, to hate.

Not that she hated him yet.

But she desired to show him her power—to—in fact, *shall* we confess it—to bring herself once more into his notice.

She advanced until she arrived at the first door.

Here she listened as she pushed it slightly open.

But not a sound was heard.

"I must go on now in the darkness," she murmured, forgetting the fate of her uncle's ancestor, "else I shall betray myself long ere I reach the vaults."

So she sped on in the darkness until she reached the second door.

Here, as she pushed it gently open, she could hear the sound of voices.

Her heart at once bounded wildly in her bosom.

"Now, at length," she thought, "I am approaching the consummation."

She advanced still farther.

Then suddenly she came full butt against a wall.

It was with difficulty, as she did this, that she could repress a cry.

But, though the blow was a heavy one, she uttered no sound.

She turned instead to ascertain the cause of this sudden stoppage, and, in doing so, saw a brilliant light just ahead of her.

She saw at once how matters stood.

She had, without being aware of it, come to a turn in the subterranean passage which led directly into that part of the vaults which was occupied by Simon Grandley's friends and their prisoners.

It was fortunate for her that the wall was composed only of earth.

Otherwise she would have fallen senseless upon the ground, and her fate might have been similar to that of poor Robert Hallwyn, the Royalist.

As it was, she soon recovered, and, with beating heart, hurried onwards.

At length she reached the spot where the light was to be seen.

It turned out to be neither a corridor nor a door, as she had imagined.

It was simply a hole broken through the brick-work of the vault.

It had evidently not long been made

It had, in fact, been blocked up as long ago as the time when the body of Robert Hallwyn had been discovered, and had been only broken down by the present conspirators.

The brave girl drew her fair head slightly above the edge of it and looked in.

She saw she was as yet too early to take any decisive step.

So she sat down and waited patiently until they had retired to rest.

At present all was life and activity within the great vault.

The prisoners, finding that it was useless to attempt an escape, or trusting to put their captors

off their guard, were giving themselves up to jollity, enjoying a glass of strong ale, and playing a variety of games.

They little knew how near was someone whose sole object was to aid their escape.

So they played and drank on, and the time passed quickly enough.

For them at least.

For the one who waited, it appeared to roll on leaden wings.

She thought the hours would never pass.

However, after her patience was nearly exhausted, Robert Hallwyn rose.

"It's getting very late," he said, "and I'm tired, so I'll turn in."

His example was followed by all the others, and they began at once to take up positions on the ground, covering themselves over with the blankets which had been brought from Hallwyn House.

Aurora watched their proceedings with intense eagerness.

She was hoping that her uncle would take up his position near the gap.

But in this she was destined to be disappointed.

He came near it, then complained of the draught and walked away.

Some of the prisoners, however, lay down near it, and among them Alexis Rainsford.

Aurora saw his face plainly as he laid himself down.

It seemed familiar to her.

But where she had seen it she could not remember.

Had she but brought to her recollection the fact that she had seen him in company with her own father, and at her father's house, she would then have been all the more inclined to trust him.

As it was, he had a handsome face, and that goes a great way with the ladies.

Taking off his coat and waistcoat, he formed of them a pillow, which raised his head to within a few inches of the gap where Aurora waited so eagerly.

The guard lighted their pipes and sat round among the prisoners.

Aurora's bosom was beating with intense emotion.

But she was still resolved to spoil nothing by rash eagerness.

Laying down upon her face, with her head not many inches from that of Alexis Rainsford, she waited.

A quarter of an hour passed.

The guard was half asleep.

They knew nothing of the subterranean subway, and the sentinels at the staircase on the other side were wide awake.

Naturally, therefore, they imagined there was not much necessity for caution.

Aurora raised her head, and seeing how matters stood, put out her hand and touched Alexis lightly on the head.

Alexis moved uneasily.

But being in a deep sleep, he did not raise himself.

A second time she touched his head—this time more forcibly.

As he raised it, she bent her lips down to his ear, and whispered—

"Hush! I come to save you!"

Alexis Rainsford had gone through many a strange adventure.

He was, of course, therefore, prepared for most emergencies.

"Aurora Halsted!" he murmured, in astonishment, as he saw the pretty face.

But he uttered no cry.

"Keep still," whispered Aurora, keeping her face close to his. "If you escape, can you bring friends to rescue my uncle and the rest?"

"Yes, in two hours," was the reply, given in a low voice also.

"Then do as I bid you. I will retire into the darkness; do you then gradually draw yourself through the opening and follow me."

"Whither?"

"Ask not now, but come if you trust me," and with the words she drew back.

It was by no means devoid of peril, this secret flight.

If one of the guards had been roused from sleep he would certainly have fired.

Every man, in fact, was furnished with pistols for this purpose.

Death was to be the reward of attempted flight.

However, Alexis determined to make the attempt at all risks.

Gradually he worked his body so that it was half through the opening.

Then he paused and glanced round the dimly-lighted vault.

All was very still.

Another strenuous effort, and he rolled noiselessly on to the floor of the subway.

Then, crawling along until he had passed from the light, he rose.

He found himself now standing side by side with Aurora Halsted.

"Now," she said, in a voice tremulous with joyful excitement, "take my hand and come."

Alexis Rainsford at once obeyed the mandate of his fair conductress.

He took the plump little hand in his, feeling as he did so a sensation as if he should have liked to have pressed it to his lips.

If he had done so, seeing that she was compassing his escape, it would not have been surprising.

But, somehow or another, a strange emotion had filled his breast.

The fair face of Aurora Halsted coming to him, as it had done, in a vision, as it were, had raised in him feelings to which he had long been a stranger; and when he held her little, warm, plump hand in his he began thinking that he would not mind how long he should be compelled to go on wandering and wandering in such company.

But their wandering thus on this occasion was not destined to be a long one.

As soon as they reached the first door Aurora closed it firmly behind her and lit her lantern.

"Now," she said, "they can no longer hear or see us. We are safe."

Alexis felt completely bewildered by the strange events of the night.

"If such a way as this was known to your uncle," he said, "why is it that he did not make use of it to escape?"

Aurora smiled.

"He did not know that I should be there to open the door for him," she said; "that door which we have just passed is always kept bolted, and he knew that, except by violence, which would arouse your guards, it was impossible to pass through. Now, however, all will be well, since, as you say, you can procure assistance."

"That I can and will," replied Alexis; "and I will see that those who will be benefited by this night's work shall know the friend to whom they owe it."

They had by this time climbed the ladder and passed through the trap.

In a few moments they had quitted this portion of the house, and stood in the drawing-room.

And thus Alexis Rainsford accomplished an escape which, like that he had effected when held a prisoner by The Owl and his companions, caused him to be regarded almost as a worker of miracles.

Old Mistress Callendar was waiting there in anxiety and terror.

She had given Aurora up for lost after all this delay.

Superstitious as she was, she had regarded it as something like tempting Providence to venture down into the dark subterranean way, and she had begun to imagine that the fate of the Royalist ancestor had befallen her.

She welcomed them, therefore, with a cry of joy as they entered.

"I am safe, you see, Lucy," said Aurora, with a smile, "in spite of all your fears; and what is more, I have succeeded in my mission. Give me some wine—I am faint."

Both she and her companion were faint and weary with excitement.

A little wine, however, sufficed to restore them to their spirits.

And then while they talked Alexis had time to observe his companion.

She had been pale when he saw her first in the vault.

Now, however, her colour had come back to her cheeks and the light to her eyes.

His eyes wandered delightedly over her pretty features, her delicately rounded form, and his heart bounded excitedly in his breast.

He had never really loved before.

He felt now, however, that he had met the being that would rule his heart.

"Miss Halsted," he said, however, rising, after a short time, for duty told him to go, "you have proved yourself this night to possess a brave heart. I shall never, no matter what may happen, forget you."

The pressure of the hand which accompanied these words caused the rich blood to overspread the features of Aurora Halsted.

THE RIVAL APPRENTICES

A TALE OF THE RIOTS OF 1780.

IN ANOTHER INSTANT A BULLET WENT CRASHING THROUGH HIS BRAIN.

She, too, had remarked upon the handsome face of Alexis, and had felt an electric thrill pass through her form as he held her hand in his.

"My duty and affection to my uncle bade me do as I have done," she said, with a lovely smile; "I only hope that success will crown your efforts."

"They *shall* if I live," replied Alexis; "and you may depend upon it I shall hasten back."

These words were accompanied by a look and another pressure of the hand, which set her heart beating more wildly than ever, and when she went to bed that night she sighed deeply in spite of success, and murmured—

"This man is very handsome. I wonder when he will return."

So in doing an action which she rejoiced in because it annoyed Guy the Foundling she positively did him a service.

She had unconsciously released him from *her* thraldom, and fallen in love with Alexis.

When the escape of the latter, be it said, was discovered by Robert Hallwyn and his friends and their guards, it was regarded as a miracle.

Every spot was searched by Simon Grandley's partizans, even the subway.

But not a trace of anything was found to indicate a flight; and a search above in the plantation, of course ended in similar discomfiture.

So they could only watch and prepare for any rescue that might be attempted.

CHAPTER XXIV.

CHAINED!

It may well be imagined that Dick Hatherden and The Owl, when they found themselves within the walls of Newgate, were in a state of mental exasperation which is not easy to be described.

The turnkeys of that part of the prison had, of course, been used to hideous language, but I doubt if they in the course of their long experience ever heard more horrible and blasphemous oaths than were uttered by these two ruffians when they were placed, chained, in the cell.

"This is all through you, curse you!" exclaimed The Owl, menacing his companion with his clenched fist, though he was too far off to do him any injury, or, indeed, to touch him. "I told you at the time that the girl would ruin all. Why could you not have been content to have robbed the old man without hindering time and risking our liberty by attempting to carry off his minx of a daughter?"

Dick Hatherden, being far out of his reach, laughed in his face.

"No wonder you curse at the girls," he said; "you are so accursedly ugly that not one of them will speak to you. Even Jessie Hardarker turned you up for Bill Hazard."

"Who mentioned my name?" growled a voice from a corner.

Both started, and glanced with some fear in the direction of the sound.

It was a very large cell, but they had imagined themselves to be alone.

In this idea they were wrong.

In the dark gloom of the corner a form was crouching.

What it was it would have been difficult to tell.

The voice only betrayed it to be a human being.

"Who spoke then?" cried The Owl.

"I," growled the voice again.

"Then be silent, since you cannot give a name," said Dick Hatherden.

A fearful oath was at once heard.

"Curse you! Do you pretend not to know Bill Hazard?" cried the man.

"Bill Hazard," echoed both the other villains in one breath.

A loud laugh answered them.

"Aye, Bill Hazard," answered he; "what then? There should be no reason why you should fear me, either of you? We've been good friends together, and we ought to have kept so. As for Dick Hatherden, I don't see that he's been a bad sort of fellow. He never betrayed me; but as for you, curse you," he added, shaking his chained foot at The Owl, "you are a sneak—a traitor—a——hang you, there's no name bad enough for you. But wait a bit—wait till I'm free, and then——"

A loud roar of merriment burst from the lips of The Owl.

"Free—free! that is good. When you're free you'll be no use to anyone," he cried.

"No use to anyone? Why not?"

"For a very good reason?"

"Give it—give it—curse ye!"

"Because when you're next introduced into the fresh air, you'll dance a jig at Tyburn!"

The curses and the language which accompanied their remarks, and the volley of verbal horror which · ·s roared out at the allusion to Tyburn Tree, I will not repeat.

It can only be imagined.

And even then only a faint conception can be attained.

It was as if a number of wild beasts, instinct with the most ferocious passions, had been let loose, and suddenly granted the power of speech.

At length The Owl broke out again against Dick Hatherden.

"D—— you," he shouted, "I say again it's your fault we're here. What did you want better? We had the swag, and no one had seen us, and yet you must needs risk everything by waiting to carry off that girl. Curse the girls, I say."

Dick laughed heartily.

"If you're so devilish uncivil," he cried, "I won't help you to escape."

The Owl cursed again.

"Escape," he cried, "yes. I know how much escaping there is from here. Don't try to catch old birds."

"Catch you! Why should I try? It's no advantage to me for you to escape," replied Dick. "If you're in such a pleasant temper, why you'd better stop where you are and let the hangman get you into a better humour."

The words were said with an earnestness which brought a kind of conviction even to the sullen mind of The Owl that Dick Hatherden had really in his mind a plan of escape.

Yet he would not yield to such a thought, at any rate would not allow Dick to suppose that he entertained such a one.

He merely laughed a scornful laugh, while Bill Hazard, who had escaped only to be brought back and sentenced to death (he was to suffer in three days), slunk further into his corner, and indulged in useless blasphemy.

"Laugh away, my friendly Owl," cried Dick Hatherden, making himself as comfortable as his chains would allow him; "but let those enjoy the laugh who win. I mean to escape, and since you will not believe me, good night. By the way, you Owl, you were cursing the girls again just now."

"Well!"

"You said it was through them we were here!"

"Yes—the devil fly away with them—so it is," growled he.

"Then they will be the means of saving *me*. Good night again."

And so he coiled himself up, nor could any howlings on the part of his companions rouse him into conversation again.

It must be here told that the gaoler had a pretty daughter.

In regard to her it will be necessary for me to digress a little, as upon her depends this portion of my tale.

She was a very pretty girl, was this Rosa Morley.

When I say pretty, I mean none of your milk-and-water prettiness.

She was a nice, rosy-cheeked, plump, fresh-looking beauty, with well-made limbs and nicely-rounded shoulders, and a full bust, which with two sparkling eyes, with a spice of wickedness in them, make up a very tempting portrait for any admirer of the female sex.

She was well aware that she was an object of masculine admiration.

Else she would not have worn such short dresses to display her pretty ankle, or such low-cut boddices to show her milk-white bosom.

Else she would not have laughed so, or simpered so, or blushed so.

In fact, she would not have been such a coquette.

A coquette was all she was.

She was a good girl, this Rose Morley.

She was pretty and knew it, and showed certain of her lovely points a little, though modestly.

But in her heart she was as pure as an angel.

Upon this girl Dick Hatherden depended for his escape.

This may seem absurd.

But it was so.

And why?

That is the secret which our next chapter must show.

CHAPTER XXV.

THE MURDER AT THE TOLL-GATE HOUSE.

ABOUT three years before the time which saw Dick Hatherden and The Owl immured in the cells of Newgate, a man with his cloak wrapped round him tightly, to keep out the chilly blast, was plodding along the road from London to Uxbridge.

His hat was so slouched over his face that it was difficult to discern his features; but it was easy to see that his mind was full of dark thoughts.

Every now and then he uttered some fierce exclamation, and his gaze was cast upon the ground.

It was a bleak part of the country he was now traversing.

Not a house was to be seen for miles around.

A broad, dusty road wound through the dark country like a snake.

But where it led to it was not easy to see.

The moon had long since hidden itself.

The stars were far away behind banks of leaden clouds.

But the man knew his way.

Hugging his thoughts to himself he pressed on eagerly, and at length in the distance a dim light was visible.

A grunt of satisfaction escaped him.

"At last," he said.

That was all.

It meant a great deal to him, however, for if you could have peered beneath that broad slouched hat you would have seen a gleam of light in his eyes and a smile illumine his rugged visage.

On, on, he went.

At length he could see the form of the habitation where the light was visible.

It was simply the toll-gate house.

A little wooden edifice standing on the edge of the dusty road.

But it meant a great deal to him.

He gathered his cloak round him so that it should not impede his movements, and then lapsed into a run.

It was not long before the old toll-house was reached.

The gate was closed.

Evidently the old man who kept it did not expect any great traffic on the road, and had thrown himself on his bed to rest.

The stranger hurried on and knocked loudly at the door, leaping over the gate as if he could not wait for it to be opened; for it must be understood there was a toll for passengers as well as carts and beasts.

The old toll-gate keeper was not long in opening the door.

"Good evening, or rather good night, sir," he said. "With what can I serve you?"

He soon saw it was no ordinary traveller that stood before him, for the stranger walked into the little room.

"You can do much," replied the latter. "In the first place, you can give me shelter awhile from the bitter blast; you can give me refreshment, for which I can pay; and you can listen to my story, which will amuse you."

The manner in which these words were uttered was jeering and unpleasant, and the toll-gate keeper could not help observing it.

He looked at the stranger very sharply.

He was a sinister looking man, this toll-gate keeper.

In fact, though both he and his guest were rugged-looking men, there could not have been two persons of more opposite character of face.

Both were rugged and weather-beaten.

Both were lined and wrinkled.

Both seemed as if they had gone through an immense variety of troubles.

But while the one appeared to have been seared and inhumanised by the progress of time, the other appeared only weighed down by sorrow and disappointment.

Taking no verbal notice of the manner of the stranger, the old toll-gate keeper busied himself in rousing up the fire and preparing the table for his guest.

It was by no means an uncommon thing for him to do.

It was a particularly lonely part of the country, and travellers who knew not the neighbourhood very often applied to the old man to give them rest and refreshment, for which they paid well.

The supper—consisting of homely materials, though there was plenty of it—was soon laid on the table, and the two sat down.

"It is very late, and I've had a good meal before this," said the toll-gate keeper, "but I may as well join you. It will do for my breakfast."

The stranger smiled.

"You always were a good trencherman, Mr. Morley," he said.

The old man started.

"You know my name?" he cried.

"Aye, and what then?"

"It seems strange, that is all," replied Morley; "there's not many people that *do* about here."

"Ah! But, you see, I'm not one about here," said the other, as he quaffed a glass of strong ale; "besides, all people have not such bad memories as *you* seem to have. Don't you know *me?*"

The toll-gate keeper eyed him intently for a moment.

"Know you," he cried, "no; that, I must confess, I do not."

"You do not! Then I will enlighten you on the subject. My name's Alexander Otterly, at your service."

"Alexander Otterly!"

The echoed words showed how much the other was astounded.

Had one risen from the dead he could not have produced a more tremendous effect upon him than did this man's words.

And why?

That is the secret we must tell presently.

"Well, you seem surprised!" cried the stranger, with a frown.

"Surprised!" exclaimed Morley. "Why, I should think it is enough to make anyone surprised. I thought you were dead."

"Dead! and why should you think that?" exclaimed Otterly.

"Because I have never seen you or heard from you for five years."

Otterly laughed bitterly.

"Not heard from me!" he cried; "how should you? I left you a treasure, but I did not say when I was coming to claim it."

"No; that is true."

"Well, when I gave into your hand those five hundred pounds I said to you, 'I have a daughter for whose sake I am saving this treasure, but I do not wish to give it her yet,' did I not?"

"Yes."

"Well now I'll tell you why I said that. That money I gave you to take charge of for me was stolen."

"Stolen!"

That was all that the toll-gate keeper said in answer.

But the one word appeared to have an extraordinary effect upon him.

His eyes glistened and a brighter colour came into his cheek.

"Aye, what of that?" cried Otterly. "That word is not so new to you. I don't suppose that all your transactions would bear the exact scrutiny of daylight. That money I stole, and I stole it in order that I might give it to a daughter who was innocent as the day—who knew nothing of her father's crime. I had a reason which I shall keep a secret why I did not wish to bestow this upon her until a certain period had elapsed, and I had a fear also of being arrested and placed in prison. I *was* arrested. I have been four years in prison; and I find on coming from it that my child is dead. I come now to recover my treasure, that with it I may depart from England, and bury my sorrows and my crimes in another land."

A stranger might not have noticed the strange workings of the old toll-keeper's face as Otterly spoke these words.

But Otterly knew him well.

He knew at once that some screw was loose somewhere.

Where he could not guess.

He imagined that the old man desired to stick to the money, and was angry at the idea of his returning to claim it.

He was wrong.

The man was angry; but it was not avarice that made him desire the absence of Otterly.

It was fear.

"You don't seem to be very glad to see me, Morley," said Otterly. "Surely you don't mind my having my own?"

"No, no!" said the toll-keeper, hastily—"no, no! I've taken good care of your money, and I'll show you where I have kept it presently. But when you told me the money was stolen, why it made me tremble to think what a risk I had run by keeping stolen property in my place so long. But come, if you are ready I will conduct you to the spot where I have kept it."

Otterly seemed anxious now to secure his treasure, and rose up.

"I'm ready," he said; "I'll have a better appetite when I've heard the chink of the coin."

"Good! then I'll get the key," returned Morley, turning round and making his way towards a cupboard.

Had Otterly seen now his face and the weapon he held in his hand, he would have had great doubts as to the common-sense of trusting himself to such a leader.

However, he did *not* see him.

He was busy quaffing the remainder of his beer.

The toll-keeper now took up the candle, lit a lantern, and, going to a corner of the old room, pulled up a trap-door.

"This is a secret I would not tell all people," he said. "I've kept many a thing down here that I would not care for people to see."

"You needn't be afraid of *my* telling tales," said Otterly; "all *I* want is to get my money and hasten from the country."

The old toll-keeper descended first.

When he reached the bottom he waited for the other to descend.

Then he drew a string and the trap closed above.

"No one will interrupt us, even if they enter my cottage, now," he said.

"This is a strange place," said Otterly, as he glanced round him.

Old Morley took advantage of this moment.

Drawing a pistol from his belt he fired, and with a loud cry Otterly fell to the ground.

But he was not dead.

He was only terribly wounded—too terribly to rise.

"What mean you by this?" he cried, feebly, "would you murder me? Take half my money—and let me go."

Morley laughed aloud.

"Half the money," he said, jeeringly, "why it's all spent long ago. Do you think I could bear to know it was here and not take it? Do you think I could look at it and hear its chink and not use it? No, no, Simon Morley knows better how to contrive than that."

"Let me go, then," cried Otterly, raising himself slightly, in spite of his deadly faintness. "I have no more to be robbed of, and you have taken my treasure. Leave me at least life."

All this time the old toll-gate keeper had been reloading.

"Leave you life," said he, "in order that you may have your revenge and bring the constables down upon me? No, no, Otterly, I want peace and quiet in my old age."

And so saying he took fair aim, holding the lantern so that its light was full upon the face of his victim.

Otterly, with the instinct of preservation which remains to the last, tried to rise, and actually *did* rise on his elbow.

But his strength was now rapidly failing, and in another instant a bullet went crashing through his skull.

Only one groan escaped him, and he was dead.

The old man gazed at the body with a ghastly—a horrid grin.

He had told the truth.

The money which had been left in his charge by the robber had all been spent—squandered in low vice and debauchery.

What he had feared had been Otterly's terrible revenge when he discovered his loss, and he had hoped that on the body of his murdered guest he would discover some more cash.

To discover this was his next task.

Laying down his light he searched the still warm body well, and discovered, to his delight, the sum of twenty sovereigns.

"Now," he cried, "now I shall be able to quit this place of which I have such a horror, and accept that situation in London which my daughter has so long wished me to take!"

Poor Rosa Morley!

Little did she dream what a hideous character her father was, or she would never have thought of bringing him from his house of murder.

As her father, she might have saved him by her silence.

As it was, Rosa Morley held the position of lady's-maid to the family of the governor of Newgate prison, and had been the trusted companion of the unfortunate girl who had been stabbed by Bill Hazard on the night of his escape.

Since then she had still retained a situation in the family, being a great favourite with them, and through her interest the murderous keeper of the toll-gate obtained a situation as warder in the prison.

It was strange, indeed, that he should have selected a place connected so intimately with punishment and death.

But he felt secure.

He had buried the body of the unfortunate Otterly, and had so disposed of everything that no one could have suspected that any secret was there hidden.

He had taken a long time in concealing his crime.

Being so far from any habitable spot, he had no fear of being seen.

He had, therefore, brought barrows full of earth from the neighbouring wood, and by these means raised the flooring of the cellar a foot all over.

Then he scattered chalk and stones over it after stamping it down.

And so his fearful secret was hidden, and unsuspected by the new-comers.

CHAPTER XXVI.

THE MYSTERIOUS LETTER.

ROSA MORLEY was seated in a little room sewing, on the night after the capture of The Owl and Dick Hatherden.

Her rosy features were illumined by a smile, and her plump little bosom rose and fell every now and then as a deep sigh escaped her.

She was thinking of her lover.

He was a warder—a young, handsome fellow, who had a prospect of doing well in the world—and she had that evening given her consent to marry him in three months.

Her reverie was suddenly cut short, however, by the entrance of one of her fellow-servants.

"Here, Rosa," she said, "here's a letter for you. Joe brought it."

Joe was the lover.

The girl laughed.

"Oh, it's some of his fun. I shan't open it at all!" she cried.

"No," she said, "he told me it was from one of the convicts, and he looked cross to me at the idea of one of the convicts writing to you."

"Then I'd better not read it, had I?" asked Rose, turning pale.

"I should," replied the other, who was really bursting with curiosity to hear what it all meant, "depend upon it, it's particular."

The first glance which Rosa Morley cast upon the contents of the missive which had so strangely been sent to her caused her the utmost astonishment.

Not unmixed with fear, be it said, as was very natural.

The letter began—

"On your life be silent when you receive this!"

She let it half drop from her grasp.

Her cheek grew pale, and she looked uneasily at her companion.

"Sophie," she said. "let me be alone. This letter has unnerved me, and I must have time to think."

The girl looked disappointed.

She was a good-natured creature, but she had a great amount of that truly female quality—curiosity.

"Cannot I help you, and give you advice?" she said, with a smile.

"Thank you, Sophie," replied Rosa, "I fear that in *this* you cannot, it is so *very* private; but if I *do* need any advice depend upon it I will seek yours."

The young girl, finding that persuasion was of no avail, accordingly quitted the room, with a pout on her lips and a resolution in her heart to discover all she could.

Rosa then locked the door and resumed the reading of her letter.

"On your life be silent when you receive this. If anyone is with you, dismiss them ere you peruse it.

"I wish to see you. It may seem strange, but it is a matter of life or death.

"It concerns the life of one whom you love dearly —your father.

"I wish you to ask permission to see a prisoner now in chains called Richard Hatherden.

"You are liked by the governor's family, and have a certain interest with them, and this request will not be refused to you.

"If you refuse to see me and grant me the request I shall make, I am bound to inform you that I have the power of destroying your father, and shall do so.

"On no account let your father know of this. Burn it as soon as read.   "D. HATHERDEN."

Truly this was a mysterious epistle.

What was she to do?

To her old Morley was an object of veneration and love.

She, of course, knew nothing of his crimes.

She only regarded him as her father—one whom it was her duty to defend in danger.

Her first act was to re-read the letter.

Then she burnt it.

Dick Hatherden's threats were already having their due effect.

She had commenced by obeying the injunctions he had laid down.

In fact, the letter was so ingeniously worded as to be eminently calculated to produce the effect which the ruffian desired.

There was no vile language in it—no hideous threat of violence.

It was a calm, cool, calculating affair, although written in a hurry.

It stated simply that the writer desired a certain thing done, and that if it were not done he would be the cause of her father's death.

For a little while only she sat still to consider her course of action.

Then she rose decided.

There was no way out of the dilemma.

If she consulted her father or told any one, the intention of the writer was certain.

He would compass her father's death.

"I will see him," she murmured, as she approached the door; "there can be no harm, at all events, in that. He's chained, and can't do me any injury."

With a beating heart she made her way to the room of the governor's wife.

The lady opened her eyes with astonishment when she preferred her request.

She knew Rosa Morley always as such a good, well-behaved, modest girl.

What could she want to see a prisoner who was in chains on a charge of murder?

"Why, my dear child," said the worthy dame, "what *do* you mean?"

Rosa flushed.

She knew how thoroughly unexplainable was her conduct.

"I mean really what I say, madam," she said; "I wish to see him."

"And for what purpose?"

Rose shook her head.

"That question I regret I cannot answer," said she, sorrowfully; "but oh! madam, believe me it is for a worthy object! Oh! I entreat you, madam, do obtain for me this favour, and I shall be ever grateful."

"Well," said the governor's lady, "you take me so entirely by surprise by so strange a request, that I know not what to say or do. What will Captain Desford say when I tell him what you have asked me, and request him to grant such a favour? He will think you mad, and blame me for aiding you in such a foolish matter. But tell me—is it your lover who is in custody, or a brother, or what?"

"Madam, you are aware I have long been engaged to Joe," replied the girl, ingenuously; "this person I desire to see is an utter stranger— one whom I have never beheld—one whose name I never heard till to-night. It is Richard Hatherden."

The captain's wife turned deadly pale.

"The greatest villain yet unhung," she said, "the friend of him who murdered my dear daughter. Oh! he wants to see you for some dreadful purpose. Take my advice in time, my girl, and go not near him."

Rosa shook her head, and felt impatient at these words.

If he was so great a villain, and could injure her father, there was, of course, all the more reason why she should see him quickly.

"Madam," said she, firmly, though respectfully, "I wish to see this man. My reasons, though I keep them so secret, are honest ones, and if *you* will not aid me I must go to the governor of the prison and ask him myself."

The captain's wife rose from her chair in bewilderment.

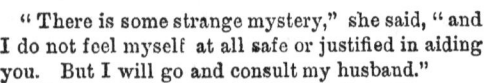

"There is some strange mystery," she said, "and I do not feel myself at all safe or justified in aiding you. But I will go and consult my husband."

"Tell me, is this interview to be alone?"

Dick Hatherden had not spoken of this in his letter to her.

But that was unnecessary.

Her own common sense told her that if this ruffian had a secret which affected her father's life the interview must be a private one.

"Yes," she said, "the meeting must take place in private."

The governor's lady raised her hands aloft in astonishment.

"Well," she said, as she quitted the room, "you are indeed a courageous girl!"

It was about half an hour ere the lady returned to the room.

During this time Rosa Morley had been a prey to violent emotion.

"Oh, madam!" she cried, as her mistress entered, "have you succeeded?"

Her mistress saw at once at what a pitch of mental excitement she had arrived.

"I have, my girl," she said, "and you can see this ruffian alone. But as the captain is very doubtful as to what purpose Hatherden can possibly have in desiring a private interview with a young girl whom he has never seen, he has ordered him to be removed from the cell where he is now chained up with others and chained in a cell alone; you will thus be able to speak to him in safety."

"And when—when shall I see him?" cried Rosa, clasping her hands.

Her mistress eyed her with a glance almost of suspicion.

"One would almost fancy you had been deceiving me, and that you *do* know this person," she said, "are you quite sure he is a stranger to you?"

"Oh! yes—yes!" cried the girl, "I swear I know him not! But he has a secret."

"Why not let my husband wring it from him by fear?"

"No—no!" exclaimed the girl, "no, no. I must go through this trial myself."

She uttered these words mechanically, as it were.

She seemed, in fact, to be under the influence of some overwhelming—some inconceivable and invisible power.

There was a presentiment in her mind that she was about to hear some revelation which would influence her life and that of her father for ever.

Her mistress tried no further persuasion to deter her from her purpose.

Her curiosity was roused, it is true, as greatly as that of Sophie.

But she, too, hoped that when the interview had taken place it would be satisfied.

Half an hour more passed.

It was now near midnight.

All the prison was very quiet, when the captain suddenly entered.

"Now, you foolish girl," he said, addressing Rosa, "now you can go. There is a warder without who will take you. But once more I warn you—do not go at all."

"A chained man can do me but little hurt," said Rosa Morley.

"True, true; and since I have consented, for the sake of your kindness to my poor murdered child, why go, and be careful how near you approach the ruffian. A strong guard is at the door, however, and at the first cry for help they will enter."

So, with a beating heart, the young girl followed her conductor, and in a few minutes was in the cell of Dick Hatherden.

CHAPTER XXVII.
THE SECRET DIVULGED.

WHEN they were left alone both the prisoner and his visitor scrutinised each other carefully for a moment by the light of the lamp which was left to them.

Naturally, from what Rosa Morley had heard about Dick Hatherden, she had expected to find a being of brutal and loathsome appearance.

Now all my readers are aware that Dick Hatherden, except in the leering and malicious look of his eyes, was not particularly bad-looking.

Otherwise he would not have attracted the attention of such a girl as Aurora Halsted.

Confinement and anxiety had done much, moreover, towards taking from him his coarse and bloated appearance.

He was, in fact, very pale and careworn, and having put on a sanctified look for the occasion, he succeeded in completely for the moment appeasing her fears.

"You are Rosa Morley?" he said, eagerly; "the daughter of old Morley, the warder?"

"I am," said Rosa, trembling, she knew not why, as he spoke.

"You are not betraying me—we cannot be overheard?" he said, inquiringly.

"No, no! I am not," she cried. "Keep me no longer in suspense: tell me all."

"Sit down on the bench near me. They may be listening at the keyhole," said Dick Hatherden. "There, don't be afraid," he added, as he saw her hesitation, "no doubt they are near enough to aid you if you cry for help. Besides, you may take your oath *I* don't want to hurt you: I want you to aid me."

Rosa Morley plucked up her courage and sat on the bench nearly beside him.

"Now," he said, in a low voice, as he leaned towards her, "all I'm going to tell you is sacred truth; so listen, and don't cry out, as you may feel inclined to."

Rosa trembled violently.

The horrid presentiments were, then, coming true after all.

Very slowly and deliberately Dick Hatherden told his awful story.

The girl listened with all her mind, trembling and starting every moment with nervous starts.

She looked like one who was petrified with terror.

She could scarcely, indeed, believe what she heard.

And yet she could not help listening greedily to every word he uttered.

At length Dick Hatherden stopped suddenly as he spoke of the burial of the body.

The young girl stopped a moment, and then turned her eyes on him.

"This—this—is some horrid dream!" she cried, passing her hand over her brow, as if to collect her thoughts. "Say—say all you have been saying is not true!"

"It is too true—too true," he said. "And now," he added, "*you* must save him."

"*I* save him?—how can I?" asked the trembling girl.

"I can tell you," he cried, in a resolute, almost fierce tone. "*I* must escape from this place, and you must assist me."

"I assist you?"

"Aye! I am innocent of the charge against me, but if I stand my trial my life will be sworn away. Now if you refuse I shall give your father up to justice. The body, remember, is still there, and no further proof will be required against him."

The girl felt half mad.

What could *she* do? How aid this man's escape from prison?

And then might not his story be a horrid invention?

She resolved to ascertain this ere she said more, or thought more of aiding him.

"How am I to know," said she, "that what you have told me is true?"

Dick Hatherden laughed grimly.

"You need not go far to learn that," he said.

"What mean you?"

"Ask your father—you will need no further proof of what I say."

The girl glanced at him as if to seek the truth in his expression.

She needed no more proof if she had chosen to accept it.

The expression she caught there was one of evident triumph.

It plainly said—

"Ask, and you will find I am right."

It had a certain determinate effect upon her agitated mind.

It made her resolve to temporise with the villain until she had seen her father.

"Very well," she said, in a low, crushed voice, which plainly told Dick Hatherden what effect his communication had produced within—"very well. Keep silent as to this matter, and I will see my father. If what you say is true I will do as you wish; for not only you, but both I and he also, must fly from this place."

Dick Hatherden caught her by the arm as she rose to leave the place.

"Remember," he cried, "no flitting without me. I shall give you an hour—no more. When that has elapsed I shall call in the warders and disclose all."

"I will not fly," said Rosa—"let me go. I feel faint and ill."

As she quitted the cell the warders at the door stopped her.

"The interview is over?" said one, inquiringly, "and the prisoner can return to his old quarters?"

"No," said Rosa, summoning all her presence of mind—"no. He has asked me a question I cannot answer. I am going to my father, and will return in a few moments if you will continue your watch awhile."

The men, who, sitting out there on a bench, were in the middle of an animated conversation, were nothing loth to take advantage of the opportunity thus afforded them, and consequently the real duration of her absence was not observed.

She hurried away with all speed to the room where her father was sitting with some of the other warders.

She was so excited as she entered the room that she never for one moment paused to see who was present.

"Father," she said, approaching him, "I wish to speak to you immediately."

Her pale face and trembling form excited his astonishment, and he rose and followed her at once.

The sight of his face, also, had a strange effect upon Rosa's mind.

Before this she had simply regarded him as her father, and had never, therefore, criticised his appearance.

Now, to her mind, there seemed something horrible in his aspect.

This only proved how very strongly Dick's words had affected her.

They passed in silence to their own rooms, old Morley feeling convinced that something strange and horrible was about to happen.

As soon as they entered, the old man proceeded to the fireplace and began stirring the embers, keeping his face averted from her guiltily, although in very truth he had not the slightest reason to suppose that she knew of his crime.

"Well?" he said, "what is the matter? what has so scared you?"

"Father," she answered solemnly, though her voice trembled violently, "I have an awful question to ask you. Did you know a man of the name of John Otterly?"

The effect was instantaneous.

The poker fell from his hands and he staggered back to a chair.

Rosa seized the lamp from the table and held it near to his face.

It was ashen, hideously contorted, full of evidences of horror.

There needed no further proof of the shame that had fallen on her.

With palsied hand she replaced the lamp on the table whence she had taken it.

"Enough—enough," she said. "I wish for no confession or denial of your guilt. It is all written plainly on your face. Were you a stranger to me you should be given up instantly to justice; but you are my father! and, crime-stained as you are, I will not deliver you to the hangman. No—you must save yourself and me!"

The old man had, while she was speaking, bowed his head upon his hands and avoided her gaze.

His crime had truly come home to him now.

To hear his little Rosa speaking to him such hard, such terrible words!

THE RIVAL APPRENTICES

A TALE OF THE RIOTS OF 1780.

THE DISCOVERY OF THE BODY OF MORLEY.

He could not face her even when she spoke of escape.

He feared to gaze into her innocent eyes—the reflex of eyes that had loved him years ago.

"How," he murmured—"how can we escape if all is known?"

"All is not known."

"How else, then, did you learn it?" asked the wretched man.

The young girl quickly told him of the mysterious letter, and the interview she had just had with Dick Hatherden.

The murderer listened with all his senses deadened, as it were, by the blow.

It seemed to deprive him of all power of thought and action.

When she had finished speaking he said, still not looking up—

"And what is to be done? How can he escape? *I* cannot do anything."

"He wishes to see *you*," returned Rosa.

"Then why did he not see me first?" replied Morley—"the villain!"

"Because he knew well he could better work on *my* feelings," said Rosa; "and besides, perhaps, he feared you might serve him as you did John Otterley."

"Enough," said Morley, waving her back with one hand, as he rose and approached the door: "*I* will see the wretch this time, and make terms with him."

CHAPTER XXVIII.

THE PLAN OF ESCAPE.

ROSA gladly heard her father's words.

She desired no further talk with such a criminal as Dick Hatherden.

Morley, therefore, at once made his way towards the cell.

Once out of the presence of Rosa his natural ferocity returned.

How he longed for an opportunity to murder his new enemy.

But he knew such a desire as that would be utterly futile.

He was in Hatherden's power now, and he must temporise.

So, hurrying towards the cell, he was soon in the presence of his enemy.

An enemy he had never seen before!

"Now," said he, sitting down near the chained man, and speaking in a quick, stern voice—"now, what is this cock-and-bull story you have been telling my girl?"

Dick smiled.

"Is that the style you're going to treat the matter, eh?" he asked.

There was such a wicked leer in his eye, that Morley at once deemed it better to change his tactics.

"Tell me where did you get hold of this tale, then?" he said. "You've not got the rights of it."

"Oh, no, of course not," said Dick. "People are never guilty. They never give in till they 'drop,' and then they're thought guilty and *feel* guilty too. Mark me, Master Morley—I'm a desperate man. I'm in here for a thing that'll hang me as sure as I'm here on the right day. I'm in for murder.

And so shall *you* be, side by side with me, if you don't consent to aid my escape."

Morley trembled.

He feared being overheard.

"Hush!" he said. "Be not so excited. I have come to talk of that."

"You confess, then."

"Yes, yes. But what matters that so that I do as you desire? Now, tell me, when do you desire to fly?"

"To-morrow night."

"Good. I will procure you the files, and so on, and a suit of my daughter's clothes, and——"

"Stay. You have no idea of what to do," said Dick Hatherden. "*I* will explain to you all that is to be done. I have a better notion of how to fly from stone walls than ever you would have with your guilty tremblings. Listen to me."

"I will; only speak low and quickly," said the murderer.

"To-night you must give me the files," said Dick; "to-morrow you must take a letter, which I will give you before you go."

"It is an invitation to a friend of mine to assist me in my escape. He will enter the prison dressed in two suits of clothes, one of which will be for me. He must be supposed to be a friend of yours, and when you have brought me my suit and made all ready, you and I and Rosa will make good our escape, and he will remain for a time in your rooms. When he knows all is safe he will make a fuss about being kept so long, and will express his indignation at being made a fool of when he finds you have fled. Do you understand me."

"I do," said the old man, grimly. "There'll be no need of Rosa's running any risk, however, for she can go to-night."

"Let that be as you like," said Dick; "here is the letter."

Morley laughed.

"You're a clever hand," he said, "and yet you've forgotten something."

"What is that?"

"How are you to stop the row of your fellow-convicts when they find that you are making good your escape?"

Dick grinned hideously.

"That I leave to you."

"To me?"

"Aye; their drink must be drugged, as must also that of the turnkeys."

Old Morley breathed more freely.

He saw now that the enterprise was not so dangerous as he had feared.

It had never occurred to him to drug the turnkeys' food.

This done, the prison was as easily opened to Dick as could be.

"You are an old hand at it, I see, though you *are* so young," he said. "Good; I'll take your advice. I see now what the clothes are wanted for. I mustn't drug the warder at the door, or his drowsiness would excite suspicion—eh?"

"Just so," said Dick; "I see you are no fool. Be quick now; send me back to my own cell; have me chained up again, and then bring me the files under

pretence of seeing that all is right. Mind, no tricks, or I will tell all. You may think you can escape me, but you are wrong. I have those watching without the prison who would pounce upon you directly you quitted the gate."

This was not true.

But Dick Hatherden had a wonderful knack of appearing serious.

And old Morley believed him.

In fact, so great was his terror of discovery that he never once dreamed of acting a deceitful part.

All he wished was, to get away from the prison in safety, and make his way to some place where he was unknown.

CHAPTER XXIX.

THE ESCAPE.

As may be imagined, the next day was one of intense excitement to all concerned.

To Rosa the few hours during which she remained in Newgate were replete with misery.

The wife of Captain Desford, the governor, inundated her with questions.

This was but natural.

The whole affair was such a mystery

But what could Rosa answer?

All she could do was to weep and say she had been entrusted with a great secret.

"What that is, madam, I dare not, on my life, tell," she said, sobbingly.

And that was all they could get from her.

At mid-day she asked leave to visit her friends.

This leave given, she quitted the place, and fled in all haste to the spot where she was to meet her criminal father.

She took no adieu of her lover.

She had given him up for ever.

She could not (so her pure little heart argued) ever bring the one she loved to shame.

Dick Hatherden, meanwhile, had been busy all night, and ere morning was free.

Except that purposely a thin link of iron was left here and there to keep his chains together.

Old Morley was, perhaps, the most nervously agitated of all.

He had no more in reality to risk than Dick Hatherden.

But he had not the nerve of that younger villain, nor had he been apprenticed, as it were, to a course of villany.

The murder of John Otterly had been the unplanned work of a moment.

The crimes of Dick Hatherden were links in a long chain of villany.

Old Morley, therefore, less hardened than the younger rogue, trembled as night approached.

However, he need not have done so.

The measures suggested by Dick had been faithfully carried out.

The warders were rapidly succumbing to the effects of the drug as nine o'clock at night came, and a loud ring was heard at the large gate.

This was Dick's friend.

He was a rough-looking, villanous-faced individual, about Dick's size.

"Can I see Mr. Morley?" he asked of the warder at the gate.

"It's rather late."

The man laughed.

"Oh, it's not about any business," he said. "It's only in reply to a private letter of his that I'm here. I'm an old friend of his not long returned to London, and he's asked me to come and see him this evening."

"Indeed!" thought the warder of the gate—"indeed! You are an old friend, eh? Well it matters not to me what companions old Morley keeps, but I will swear I've had that fellow here under lock and key."

"All right," he said aloud. "Come in. Do you know your way?"

This was said with a meaning which the stranger seemed to take quickly.

"No," he said; "you had better guide me to him, or go and tell him that John Aversham wants to see him."

The warder closed the gate carefully.

"The men are all mad to-night, I think," said he; "they seem not to understand a word that is said to them; so come on, I will show you your bedroom."

Had it not all been satisfactorily arranged beforehand, the meeting of Morley and Aversham would have been very awkward.

Neither had seen the other before: but, as it was, they greeted each other with extended hands; and the warder almost convinced now that his suspicions were wrong left them alone.

No sooner had he done so than the door was locked and the preparations commenced.

Aversham divested himself of his outer suit, which was of exactly the same material as the under one, and the old warder hurried away to Dick Hatherden's cell, carrying with him also a large mug of beer containing a quantity of soporific stuff sufficient to make them sleepy at once.

"Here's some beer," said Morley, as he entered; "be quick and drink it, for if I'm caught I should be quodded at once."

"Ha! ha!" laughed Dick Hatherden, as he raised the mug to his lips and pretended to drink; "ha! ha! he talks about being quodded and he's in quod now. What do you think of this, boys?" added the treacherous villain, as he turned to his companions. "See what it is to be friendly with the warder."

"You don't deceive me," cried The Owl, as he took a deep draught of the drugged liquid, "you've been blabbing; that's how you've done it. Never mind, a man can but die once, and while we are here we may as well enjoy ourselves."

So both he and Bill Hazard drank deeply.

"There," cried the Owl, as he emptied the mug and returned it to Old Morley; "Dick can get plenty more, but we can't."

In a few moments the drug began to have its effect.

The Owl and Bill Hazard looked at each other in anger and surprise.

They felt something to be wrong.

"What's this?" cried Hazard as he pressed his

hand to his brow. "Have we been poisoned. What—villains —ah !—Dick, this is your work."

Dick laughed.

"No, no," he said ; "there is no poison in the cup you have drunk, only something to make you sleep a little while I make good my escape. I thought you might be jealous, and by your outcry spoil all. Never fear, I will return and save you in good time."

The last words were lost upon those to whom they were addressed.

They had fallen down helplessly.

Dick now broke away the slight links which still remained.

Then he hurried off his own clothes, and donned those brought by Aversham.

All was now ready.

The hearts of both beat high.

Escape was near—nay, it might even be considered assured.

Carefully and slowly they quitted the cell containing the sleeping criminals.

All was quiet without.

Newgate was more like a huge sepulchre than a prison full of rogues.

A grand idea entered the mind of Dick Hatherden as they stepped out into the still, stone corridor.

" I say, Morley, what think you ?" he said.

" I know not."

" I have a splendid idea."

" Keep it, then, until we get outside," said the old tollgate-keeper. " I shall never feel safe until I am miles away from this place."

" It's no use saying anything about it when we're outside," said Dick Hatherden. " It's simply this. All the warders are asleep. Let's set all the prisoners free."

Old Morley uttered a curse.

" You're mad," he cried,—" quite mad ! No, no ! I'll not help in anything of the kind. If you attempt such a thing, I'll rouse the warder, and the governor will soon put a stop to such a movement. Think of ourselves—that's enough."

Dick Hatherden's burst of unselfish enthusiasm soon evaporated.

" All right," he said, " let's get out of this ; the sooner the better."

The warder of the gate made no objection.

How could he ?

Old Morley was going out with the friend whom he had invited to see him.

Nothing could be more simple.

So the great gates of Newgate were opened for them, and clanged to behind them.

And they were free

CHAPTER XXX.

THE OLD TAVERN BY THE RIVER—THE BENEVOLENT LANDLORD AND HIS WIFE—THE MEETING IN THE PARLOUR—PLANS OF ESCAPE—THE CONVERSATION AFTER SUPPER—MORE CRIME—THE SORROWING DAUGHTER SEES HER FATHER IN HIS TRUE CHARACTER.

THE place to which Rosa Morley had been de-spatched by her father was a tavern kept by an old friend of his.

It was called the Ship and Turtle, and was situated upon the banks of the river, in one of the lowest spots imaginable.

The man who kept it had secured to himself the title of undoubted respectability.

He had kept the house for many years, and nothing could be said against it.

No disturbances had occurred.

No fights.

No mysterious deaths had been chronicled as having there happened.

So Master Brasser had become wealthy and fat, in spite of the fact that he was as big a rogue as ever escaped a cell in Newgate.

Dark deeds were in reality perpetrated there which would have made the hair of any respectable citizen of London stand on end, and would have brought Brasser to the hangman long ago.

But they were carefully concealed.

They were done in midnight hours, and the corpses of victims were carried far away.

To such a place Morley had sent his young and innocent daughter.

His intention was to leave the country that very night.

Here every convenience for such a purpose could be obtained.

A boat could be put off in the middle of the night, and Rose and he taken on board one of the many vessels which, below London Bridge, were waiting to receive contraband goods.

Such was his plan.

He little knew what strange events would happen to put a stop to all his plans.

Towards this place, then, Rosa hastened when she hurried away from the prison, heartbroken, and weary of life.

She knew not to what a place she was making her way.

Else probably she would rather have flung herself from the bridge than have placed her life and honour in such frail keeping as that of Brasser.

However, when she reached the Ship and Turtle nothing occurred to offend her.

Brasser was by no means a man whose character you could read by his looks.

He was a villain.

That we have already demonstrated expressively enough.

Further than this we could not say.

To appearance he was a far from ill-looking—in fact, he was a benevolent-looking old man.

Just the model of a well-to-do tradesman of that time.

He smiled kindly upon Rosa as she delivered her father's message.

He understood from the wording of the note and he also thought that all was not right.

But he did not allow her to observe any change in his countenance.

He was too old an adept in crime to do anything so foolish.

" I see, my dear, your father wishes you to remain here a few hours until he comes."

"Yes."

"Very well, my wife shall see to your comforts," he said. "Come this way."

And so saying, he led her into an inner room, far away from the bustle and noise of the bar and introduced her to a comely matronly woman, who was evidently by no means of the same style and temperament as himself.

She, in fact, knew nothing of her husband's transactions.

He had contrived during a long life of infamy to conceal his character.

From her as from others.

She, therefore, looked upon him as the best and kindest of men.

And not wrongly.

To her he was; though to others he was of a notoriously brutal reputation.

With this woman Rosa remained in conversation all day, keeping herself as quiet as she could, though in reality in a turmoil of excitement.

When night came she became so excited that she could scarcely endure herself.

Well she might.

She pictured to herself the horrible result of exposure to her father and herself.

She kept her head out of the window, straining her eyes in the direction he would come, often not hearing the words of Mistress Brasser, who, of course, was quite unable to understand the reason of the young girl's unaccountable agitation.

At length her father's form and that of Dick Hatherden came in view.

After waiting so eagerly did any pleasure invade her heart?

No.

A cold chill ran through every fibre of her trembling body.

While he was away she had thought, not of his guilt, but of his escape.

Now, as her eyes once more fell upon him, she realised again the crime for which he was in gaol—saw his victim, and went through again the scene in the prison.

She realised, in fact, how thoroughly hopeless and terrible her life was for ever!

"I will retire to rest, now," she said, turning suddenly to Dame Brasser.

The woman was astounded at such a speech at such a moment.

"I thought you said your father was coming, my dear," she said.

"Yes; he is coming."

"Then, will you not see him to-night? I thought he had just escaped a great danger."

Rosa put her little hands in the large plump ones of the worthy dame.

"Yes, yes," she said, looking up into her face appealingly; "I know he has; but I would rather not see him to-night. If he asks for me, tell him I am not well: as I have my reasons, but pray don't ask them."

Fortunately for Rosa, Mrs. Brasser was not of an inquisitive turn of mind.

A strange thing for a woman.

A very lucky thing for her husband.

Else would all his villanies and crimes have long ago been known.

"Very well, my dear," said Mrs. Brasser, "have it your own way. I'll show you to a nice little room, and, as you've eaten nothing this whole blessed day, why, I'll insist upon you just picking a little bit of something nice by way of a change."

And so she conducted Rosa Morley to a pleasant little room on the same floor.

"Poor girl!" she said, as she left her, "no doubt her feelings are too much for her, knowing that her poor dear father has been in danger, and she away from him. No doubt she didn't wish to let him see how agitated she was. Ah! I know what feelings is!"

And with a deep sigh from her plenteous bosom, she proceeded downstairs to prepare the "something nice" which she had promised her new *protegée*.

Meanwhile the three villains had retired into a private room behind the bar.

Here they locked themselves in, and consulted, safe in the knowledge that no sound could issue from the chamber, with its double doors and thick brick walls.

"Morley," cried Brasser, smacking him on the shoulder, "you're an unlucky cove!"

"Unlucky! Well, I don't know how you can say that," replied the old tollgate-keeper.

"But I do say it," replied the other, quaffing some ale, "and I can prove it."

"Very well—prove away. I'm more in the humour for listening than talking."

"Look here, then. I've been the landlord of this house for twenty-five years, haven't I?"

"Yes."

"Do I do much business—you know what I mean—on the square?"

"No."

"Well, then, how do I live? Just explain to me that!" he cried, chucklingly.

"You know best," said Morley. "We humble people can only guess."

"Guess! Well, you might keep at that, and *then* go wrong. Shall I tell you?"

"Please yourself," said Morley, who was getting annoyed at his roundabout fashion.

"Well, then, I will. I make my living—aye, and a good one it is!—the same as you began to when you took John Otterly into your cellar and scragged him."

Had he struck Morley an unexpected and violent blow on the head, he could not have so staggered him as these words did.

The old man half rose from his chair, gasping for breath.

Both Brasser and Dick Hatherden burst out into an uproarious laugh.

"Why, what the deuce ails you?" cried Brasser. "Are you mad?"

"I begin to think I am," said Morley, sinking down again. "What does it mean? Everyone seems to know all; and I so careful to preserve it as a secret. I—who—"

"Thought yourself so clever," interrupted Dick Hatherden. "But no matter, your friend will not

betray you; that would be of no advantage to him. Let him prove his case."

"Yes, I was going to show our friend here why he is unlucky," said Brasser, still laughing. "Now, he kills a man whose money he has spent beforehand, and, having taken a few pounds from his pocket, runs away from the scene of the disaster, and becomes warder in a prison. Was ever such folly heard of?"

"What would you have had me do?" asked Morley, in a tone of irritation.

"Well, answer me. This was the first man that you ever killed?"

"Yes."

"And it is the last?"

"Yes."

"There lies your mistake then," said the landlord, coolly; "and I can prove it to you. You killed him, you hid him away, and unless you had blabbed to a pal in a drunken fit you would never have been suspected of being able to commit such a crime. And then you run away with a few paltry pounds. Why, if I'd had *your* chances at that tollgate I'd have made thousands, and no one would ever have been the wiser."

"I dare say this is all very well," said Morley; "but it's not what I want to talk about. I want to get away from this place to-night. What I wish for is to know how I'm to go."

"That's easy enough—the going is," said the landlord; "but not to-night."

"Not to-night!" Morley gasped out. "I dare not remain longer."

Brasser laughed.

"Dare not!" he cried; "why, who knows you're here. You're a poor coward after all."

"I'm no coward; but I see no use in remaining if I can go."

"Well, then, I'll tell you plainly. You can't go to-night. I'll keep you safe and sound until to-morrow night. Then you can go, and welcome, and I'll charge you nothing for board and lodging. The truth is the *Espagnol* does not lie down where you think until twenty-four hours hence, and, more than that, old Santa Puerta, the captain, would think nothing of bundling you overboard if you came there without proper credentials. I must let him know first. Meanwhile eat, drink, and be merry, and be certain that while Dick Brasser's got a yellow coin in his pocket the watch never show their noses on the inner side of his threshold. Now, then, let's have some supper, and then to bed. But stay, your silent friend here," he added, pointing to Dick, who was paying more attention to his pipe and his ale than to their conversation, "is he going to accompany you on your trip to Antwerp?"

Dick shook his head.

"No, no," he said, "none of your foreign countries for me. I mean to stick to England, in spite of its having behaved so ungratefully, and in spite of the dangers surrounding me. I'll stop and see our friend here off, and then—hey for my old quarters!"

"I admire your pluck!" exclaimed Brasser. "You're a lad of my own sort, and anything I can do for you in the future I will. Now, then, I'll see to the supper."

By this time Rosa had retired to her room, and Mrs. Brasser had taken up the supper she had spoken of.

So she was ready to attend upon her husband's two guests.

"Well," she said, as she retired to the bar, after carrying in the necessaries—"well, I don't like to say such a thing to the poor young thing upstairs, but this I *do* know. If that was my father, the less I saw of him the better I should like it."

Supper over, Dick Hatherden and Morley retired to their chamber.

This happened to be next that in which poor Rosa had been placed.

It was separated from hers only by a thin wooden partition.

Every word, they said, therefore, was plainly audible to her.

"I wonder," said old Morley, as they retired to their respective beds, "that you like to stop in London when you have a chance of quitting this cursed country for ever."

"Ah! you don't understand me," said Dick Hatherden; "in fact, I don't think you ever would. I am young. Whatever hopes I have left me in life are concentrated in London; there live those I care for and those I hate. I have vengeance to take on my enemies, and until I have done so there will be no more happiness for me. So I shall wait till you are in safety, and then I shall go back to my old haunts. Meanwhile have you any money?"

"None—absolutely none, beyond a paltry sum of five pounds," said Morley.

Dick Hatherden laughed aloud.

"Five pounds!—why that will not be enough to bribe the Spanish captain."

"No, I leave that to our friend, Brasser, here," returned the old man.

"But how about you and—and Rosa, when you land at Antwerp?" suggested Dick.

"We must do the best we can. If we starve there it will be a better fate for her than if I were taken to the scaffold, and—and she were pointed at as the daughter of a murderer."

"Well perhaps you're right there," said Dick. "But come, I've a suggestion to make."

"Make it then."

"In the first place, if you thought Rosa were settled—settled happily and comfortably I mean—you'd rather go away from England alone. Now say—would you not?"

The old man raised his hands.

He never for a moment fathomed the meaning of his companion.

"Aye, that I would—that I would!" he cried with earnestness.

"I thought so," said Dick. "Well, now then, what do you say? She's a pretty girl, and would make a man a good wife. I've got some money hidden away, and after the famous riots that will begin before a few hours are over, I'll have plenty more. I like her; let's see if she could like me. Leave her with me. I'll marry her. And some of these days, when you feel inclined to slip home again, you'll find us comfortably installed in a fine business. That's not so bad a prospect, is it, eh?"

The eyes of Old Morley glared and dilated as Dick Hatherden spoke.

If there was one thing more than another that was a redeeming point in his otherwise black character, it was his pure and unselfish love for his child.

"Madman!" he cried, half rising from his bed, and clenching his fists—"madman! What are you saying? You marry my child!—you, whose blood-stained hands——"

"Hold there!—no compliments," exclaimed Dick Hatherden, with a laugh which in no way covered his bitter feeling of resentment. "Talk not of blood-stained hands, else you, perhaps, might come off second best. A murderer's daughter may well mate with a murderer. But there, you see, is the difference between us. *You* murdered John Otterly in cold blood; *I* have never killed anyone except to ensure my escape."

"I care not. Talk no more of it," cried Morley; "you shall not have her."

"Very well—I care not," said Dick Hatherden. "Take her with you, then, and mate her with some German thief. Your delicacy will be rewarded. And so, that being settled, let me ask you another question, which in your present humour is more to the point."

"Well, what is it? If it does not affect Rosa I am quite willing."

"It *does* affect her, inasmuch as by following my instructions you may have the chance of giving her something to eat. I propose to speak of how to get some money."

The eyes of old Morley glistened immoderately at this.

He forgot at once the proposition which he had considered an insult to Rosa.

"Aye, that is common sense—that is good sense," he said. "Say, how can we get some?—a good round sum I mean. I will risk anything—everything—to aid you!"

"Spoken bravely!" cried Dick Hatherden. "It would be of no use if you were not willing to risk something. Tell me, in the first place, has old Brasser much money?"

"He is rolling in wealth, I believe," returned Morley. "But what of him?"

"Very much. We must possess ourselves of his money," said Dick.

Morley trembled.

"Hush!" he said—"you are imprudent. Speak not so loud—we may be overheard. Brasser is a suspicious fellow, and may be on the watch for us."

"Not he," said Dick Hatherden; "and if he is we can readily pass things off. He's as sound as a church by this time. Now the question is, shall we do the deed to-night or to-morrow night?"

"The deed!" replied Morley, shudderingly—"why, you talk as if of deeds of blood!"

"Bah! that is your murderous fancy," said Dick Hatherden. "We'll drug him and take his money, and be off in his boat before he's aware of anything wrong. But come, you don't seem quite up to the mark now, so we'll sleep on it, and talk in the morning."

In a very short time the two murderers had lapsed into slumber.

A slumber as peaceful and sweet as that of a new-born babe.

And the words of these two callous-minded miscreants had been heard distinctly, and thoroughly understood, by the poor horror-stricken girl in the adjoining chamber.

CHAPTER XXXI.

ANOTHER MURDER.

ON the next morning Rosa Morley felt herself in a state of mind not easily described.

She knew not what to do.

What she had heard convinced her that some evil of no small extent was intended to Brasser.

She, of course, had not heard the conversation between the villanous landlord and her father.

She was unable, therefore, to judge of his real character.

Had she known him to be the villain he was, she would still have set her wits to work to prevent his murder, but she would not have stirred her hands to prevent his being robbed.

To give notice to the authorities would be to implicate her father.

This she was resolved not to do.

There was time yet for him to repent.

And of this she would not deprive him.

Innocent child!

Hers truly was hoping against hope after hearing the words that had passed between him and Dick Hatherden.

But filial affection is like other love—in too many instances blind.

Yet what was she to do?

A thought struck her.

An appeal to her father was the only thing she could reasonably fix upon.

She would even threaten him with exposure if he persisted in his scheme.

As for his anger, she feared it not.

Immediately after she learned, therefore, that her father had arisen she sent for him.

He came at once.

He would have avoided the interview, but somehow he dared not.

He feared the gentle girl now.

She was to his dark mind a kind of superior being, and when she began to detail to him all she had heard, and threatened him with exposure, he fairly was conquered, and she saw it.

Yet what could he do?

He must have money, and the only way to get it was to rob Brasser.

He must rid himself of Rosa's presence, therefore, by a ruse.

"Well, my dear child," he said, "for your sake I will desist from the attempt; but I must tell you this—we *must* have money."

"We need not rob to get it."

"No; but it is dangerous for me to be seen out now that the escape of Dick Hatherden from Newgate is known to be my doing. I tell you what you

must do. To-night, when it is dark, you must take a note to a friend of mine, who will lend you twenty pounds. This will be sufficient for us for a while. You must go disguised. Mistress Brasser will arrange that for you. Will you go?

"I will do anything rather than you should commit the robbery," said Rosa.

Accordingly, as soon as the shades of night had fallen, Rosa was dispatched on an errand to a part of the town from which it was certain she would be unable to return until the lapse of several hours.

Then Dick Hatherden and Morley retired to their rooms.

They had been for some time in company with old Brasser, and had seen his money.

Morley had obtained a view of it in a way which preved his artfulness and deceit.

He had appealed to the landlord to lend him a few sovereigns.

"Lightly come—lightly go" is an old and recognised motto everywhere.

So Brasser, who, villain as he was, was always known to be generous to friends, at once consented not only to lend the money but to give it at any rate for an indefinite period.

Then, taking it from his hoard, he incautiously permitted both Dick Hatherden and the murderous toll-gate keeper to see the quantity of gold coins, and also their repository.

"It is all right," said Morley, as they entered their chamber, "the gold is ours."

A peculiar smile flitted over the features of Dick Hatherden.

"Yes," he said, "no doubt. But at what hour are you supposed to quit this?"

"In about two hours' time. No delay, therefore, must be permitted, else Rosa will be back and all will be lost."

"Never fear," said Dick, "we will arrange all satisfactorily."

And as he spoke, the back of the old man being turned towards him, he struck him suddenly on the back of his head with the butt-end of a pistol.

His murderous aim well regulated the strength of the blow.

It did not kill—it brought no blood—it simply stunned the victim.

Dick had apparently prepared everything properly for his villanous purpose.

The sight of the gold had been far too great a temptation for his nerves.

He had resolved to possess all, and the girl too if he could get her.

The latter was but a secondary consideration; but still her beauty had pleased him.

Taking now from his pocket some rope, he proceeded to pass it round the senseless man's body, and having arranged it to his satisfaction he threw open the casement.

All was very still out there.

Very few lights varied the monotony of the banks of the old Thames.

The rushing of the stream against the piles, and the occasional challenge of one boatman to another, alone broke the silence which hung over the dark ｈaters.

Seeing that it was almost a certainty that he would not be disturbed, Dick raised the body in his arms and thrust it through the window.

The use of the rope was now easily understood.

If he had flung the body out, the splash would have attracted the notice of all within the house, whereas now he could lower it slowly—gently—treacherously into the stream!

The body of the wretched old man was soon let down, and floated away towards the ocean, until near London Bridge it was whirled aside, and driven upon some stone steps beneath an archway leading to what now is known as Thames Street.

Here it was found at early dawn by a gentleman seeking a boatman, and conveyed to a neighbouring tavern.

What discoveries were made in consequence I shall not pause here to tell.

For the moment I must return to the Ship and Turtle, and Dick Hatherden and Rosa,

The old man being disposed of, and the window once more closed, the young villain proceeded to consummate the plans of robbery for which he had added one more to his long list of crimes.

Going rapidly downstairs, he asked eagerly and excitedly for Morley.

"Are you gone mad, my friend?" asked Brasser. "He this moment, or at least only a few minutes ago, ascended with you. He must be there still."

"He is not then," said Dick Hatherden. "I turned round suddenly, as I was about to undress, and found him gone. The door was closed, and I sought in every room, every nook and corner, without success. And what is more extraordinary, there was not a sound anywhere to tell me he was going."

"I saw a dark shadow across my window," said Brasser. "Perhaps he has thrown himself out."

"No, no!" cried Dick, "that cannot be! He had not the pluck. Besides, his escape was assured."

"Nevertheless he is a precious old fool sometimes," replied Brasser. "We may as well see."

And so, lighting a lamp, he led the way down a stone staircase until they reached a door leading out upon the shingly bank of the river.

"It's rather dark here," cried Dick Hatherden. "If you know it better than I, show a light."

He went on ahead, and did as he was asked, raising the lamp aloft.

This was exactly what the designing young thief desired.

Quick as lightning he closed the door and shot the bolts.

Then he turned back up the stairs and rushed into the landlord's room.

A bright lamp was burning there, and in an instant the expert young robber had seized the small box containing Brasser's savings, and fled through the bar into the street.

The outcry made by the landlord when he found himself thus thrust out of his own house may well be conceived; and it was, of course, soon heard and responded to by his wife.

But it was then too late to prevent the robbery, even if it had been known.

As it was, Brasser never suspected anything of the kind, and never looked for his money.

THE RIVAL APPRENTICES

A TALE OF THE RIOTS OF 1780.

THE FATE OF THE TRAITOR.

All he could guess was that an attempt had been made upon his life and that some villainy was on foot. But of what nature or with what design he could not for a moment conceive.

He sought everywhere for D   Hatherden, but naturally in vain.

And then at last, seeing that bot' he and Morley had vanished, he set them down as a couple of madmen, and troubled himself no further about them, until weeks after he discovered to his horror the loss of all his villanously acquired gains.

Meanwhile, Dick Hatherden, who, as usual, cared not what danger he risked so that he arrived at the desired point, did not fly headlong from the street, as many would have done.

On quitting the house he only passed to the opposite side of the way, and concealed himself beneath a dark archway, from which he could command a view of the whole street.

His object was to intercept Rosa on her return, and beguile her away by an artfully told tale.

It was not long before, even in the semi-darkness, he saw her approaching at a rapid pace.

Leaving his place of concealment, he at once hastened towards her.

Rendered nervous and excited by recent horrid events, the young girl could scarcely restrain a cry as she beheld him approaching her, but a gleam from a lamp hard by in a moment revealed his features and dispelled her fear.

"Stop here," he cried. "Nay, be not afraid; no evil has happened. Your father has been in danger but he has escaped."

Rosa clasped her hands.

"Have they been in pursuit of him, then?" she cried, in a tone of agony.

"Yes; they are even now in the Ship and Turtle, and, indeed, I have had to conceal myself at great risk without to meet you here. Your father——"

"Where is he? Oh! tell me where is he? Take me to him!" exclaimed Rosa.

"That's exactly what I'm going to *do*," said Dick. "There, don't distress yourself, he's safe enough now."

And, speaking to her in the soft and insinuating voice he could so well assume, he drew her arm in his.

The trembling and sorrow-stricken girl made no resistance.

She was so overcome by faintness, indeed, that she could scarcely walk alone; and she forgot in her whirl of thought that she was in the company of one who was as great a criminal as her father, if not a greater than he.

Dick hurried her on in the direction of his old haunts, where he was sure of being able to obtain safe concealment for the night both for her and him.

It was not long before he and Rosa were standing in the very room where we first introduced our readers to Hatherden, Bill Hazard, and Quail.

Once here, he locked the door and proceeded to business.

He had long since seen the folly of beating about the bush.

"Rosa Morley," he said, "I have somewhat deceived you—but I have done so in kindness. Your father is dead."

Rosa staggered back.

"Dead!" she shrieked.

"Aye, dead. He flung himself this evening, in a fit of madness, from the window of his bedroom in the Ship and Turtle, when he found the officers were after him, and I had the greatest difficulty in saving myself. I have saved you from shame and ruin by bringing you here."

Rosa did not hear his last words.

"Poor father!" she cried again—"gone to his account with all his sins upon his soul!"

"Aye, better so, perhaps, for all," said Dick, sententiously. "But come, Rosa, there's a room in there for you. Go and rest for the night. In the morning I have something to speak to you about."

"I would rather not remain here," said Rosa, pleadingly.

"You *must* remain," said Dick, in a voice which admitted of no denial; and taking her hand, he led her forcibly in, gave her a lamp and went out, locking the door behind him.

Here we must leave her awhile to her sad and terrible thoughts, while we return to other characters in our varied and eventful story.

CHAPTER XXXII.

THE END OF A TRAITOR.

ALEXIS RAINSFORD lost no time, as may be imagined, in securing means for the release of his friends immured by Simon Grandley in the subterranean vaults near Hallwyn House.

There was but little time to work.

Very few hours, in fact.

No great space was to elapse before the commencement of the movement which they imagined was to convulse society.

So when he left Aurora Halsted, not without regret, as I have said, he never pulled rein until he reached London.

Arrived here, he partook of some refreshment, and then proceeded to a house situated no great distance from that of the carpenter.

Here he passed in by a back-door, and proceeding to a room on the highest floor of the house, locked himself in, and began making a complete transformation of himself.

He placed on a suit of ragged clothes.

Then he put on a wig of grey hair, and a huge beard of a similar colour.

Thus disguised, he was utterly unrecognisable.

"Ha!" he said, chucklingly, as he surveyed himself in the glass, "now I shall be able to go into the lion's den even unrecognised."

It may appear strange that such a course was in any way necessary.

But it was so.

He had to go a long round of visits to all parts of London.

And in doing this he stood the chance of being watched.

Completing his attire by placing on him a large cloak and a broad slouched hat, he quitted the house, and issued forth into the street.

To follow all his movements would be tedious.

Suffice it to say that he visited a number of

houses, proceeding about his business in a most mysterious manner—knocking at the doors, whispering a few words only, and then going his way again.

At last, when it had waxed very late, he made his way to a part of the town which many men, even a courageous one, would have hesitated to enter.

Entering a narrow and ill-looking lane, he knocked a peculiar knock at the door, and in a few moments stood in the presence of a tall man, with a face of unusually fierce expression.

Scarcely a brutal face.

More the face of a man who had made his mind up for terrible doings.

"You are late, Master Rainsford," he said, addressing Alexis.

"I am; but *you* are wanted."

These words, significantly said, seemed thoroughly understood by the man.

"This is a strange hour for the executioner's work," he said. "Where is the deed to be done?"

"In an hour's time at the old place of meeting," replied Alexis. "You will not fail?"

"I will not."

"Till then, adieu."

And the two parted.

It had soon been arranged.

The fate of a fellow being had been settled in those few words.

Quitting this place, Alexis Rainsford once more hurried on.

This time the neighbourhood he entered was by no means so low or so full of intricacies.

The house at which he stopped, however, was a poor one, and the person who opened the door was by no means the sort of being that one would have imagined to be the friend, or even associate, of Alexis.

It was a young man, short, thick-set, and bullet-headed.

He was evidently an artisan.

"What want you with me?" he said, in a surly tone.

Evidently the visit of Alexis Rainsford was by no means welcome.

"You are summoned to the meeting-house," said Alexis.

"To-night?"

"Yes—now. Strange events have happened; and all are expected."

"Good!" replied the man. "I will be there."

"I shall be there before you," replied Alexis.

And he turned to go.

But when the door closed he did not hurry away.

Instead of doing so he concealed himself in a doorway near.

Evidently he suspected this man.

In this case, however, he was wrong.

Within a few moments the man came out, cloaked like Alexis, and took his way towards the place of meeting.

"He thinks he is not suspected—the villain!" said Alexis to himself, as he hurried off. "Did he suspect, London would hold him no longer."

Alexis, hurrying on by a nearer route, arrived, in the course of a quarter of an hour, at a house on the margin of the river.

A strange old place.

Apparently uninhabited, in fact.

But only apparently.

A gentle knock brought a man to the door, and, having given a kind of password, Alexis passed in.

When the door was closed, he placed on his face a mask, and, ascending a staircase, found himself in a few minutes in the presence of a number of men similarly attired to himself.

He was made way for directly he appeared.

He was recognised apparently by those present, by some sign which would have been unnoticed by a stranger, as being the leader of the movement, or the head of the proceedings for that night, at any rate.

Going to the farther end of the room, he sat down on a raised chair.

"Gentlemen," he said, "let the door be locked. We have most important, nay, even most terrible, business to transact this evening. Milrose is below, and you know, therefore, that a traitor is among us."

The name seemed to produce an electrifying effect.

It was well known.

And universally dreaded.

He was the private executioner of this Inquisition.

No wonder there were so many leaping hearts.

No wonder was it that the eyes of all turned to the masked faces of their companions.

Only *one* traitor was there.

For all they knew they might be unjustly accused.

They knew, too, the terrible, severe, and swift nature of the tribunal before which they stood, or rather of which they formed a part.

The ensuing words of Alexis Rainsford, therefore, were listened to eagerly.

He began by telling them of the capture of their friends at the ruins near Hallwyn House.

Then he added—

"While lying down, when they imagined me asleep, the men left in charge of us began talking freely.

"They began by speaking of treachery in general, and then the name of John Eldroyd was mentioned.

"'He is the man who told us where to discover the haunt of the Catholic conspirators,' said the man.

"'And is he a Catholic himself?' asked the other.

"'Ah! a pretended one,' said the first speaker. 'He is in reality no more a Catholic than I am. But he went among them on purpose to discover their plans, and he has betrayed them for money.'

"Now then," said Alexis Rainsford, "this is the last time that we can meet here.

"It was dangerous to come at all.

"But as there was no spot better than this for carrying out that act of justice which we are now called upon to perform, I thought it best to ask you hither.

"Now, then, I call upon John Eldroyd to unmask.

" I know he is here.

" If, therefore, he can defend himself, he should have no fear.

" If, on the other hand, he refuses to unmask, it is some proof that my words are correct, and I shall demand that all present shall reveal themselves."

A pause ensued.

A very short one.

Then one of the masked men rose, and threw off his domino.

" Here is John Eldroyd," he said.

He was the man upon whom Alexis Rainsford had called last.

A murmur ran through the assemblage.

Every eye was upon him.

" Well ? " asked Alexis, " and what have you to say in defence ? "

" I deny all you have said," returned the man, doggedly.

" Denial is of no use.   We must have proofs."

" *You* only have assertions to prove my guilt with," replied Eldroyd, boldly.

Alexis smiled, grimly.

" You persist, then, in denying your guilt ? "

" I do."

" Do you know your own handwriting ? "

" I do, of course."

" Good ! " said Alexis, emphatically.

Then he put his hand into the breast pocket of his coat, and drew out some papers.

" Here is a letter," he said, showing one to the accused.   " Is it in your writing ? "

John Eldroyd was about to take it from his hand.

But Alexis stopped him.

" Now," he said, " this is the proof that will convict you—this is what will bring your head to the block ! "

John Eldroyd turned pale.

" If it isn't my writing, it's a very good imitation of it," he said, doggedly.

" It is yours," said Alexis, " and is signed with your name.   It gives your address ; it gives the password ; it describes this place ; and it describes little particulars which could only come from you."

He then read it.

It exactly bore out his words.

The letter was then passed round, and a unanimous feeling of fury seemed at once to pervade the assemblage.

" Well, gentlemen," cried Alexis, appealing to the excited throng before him, " what is your verdict ?—is he guilty or not guilty ? "

" Guilty."

There was not a dissentient voice.

In fact, there was no doubt of his guilt.

I have not thought it necessary to give the entire chain of circumstances which led to the belief in his guilt.

But the story that Alexis Rainsford told, the letter he read, and the interpretation he gave of the meaning, plainly convinced them that he, and no other, was the traitor.

Eldroyd himself stood with folded arms, eyeing his judges.

His face was very pale.

But he was, nevertheless, firm.

He knew well that, whatever doom they might decide upon, resistance was useless.

He resolved, consequently, to face it out.

" The executioner is waiting below," said Alexis Rainsford ; " here in the vaults. No time had better be lost.   This will be our last meeting here.   And when they search the place let the headless body of this traitor tell them how we punish such villains ! "

" Away with him at once," cried the conspirators.

" This is quick judgment," said the prisoner. " Surely you will give me time to prepare myself ? "

" A few minutes only."

" It is murder then—not an execution."

" You should be prepared now," said Alexis. " Knowing yourself to be a traitor, you should always have considered yourself on the point of death.   Those who wilfully merit death should never leave it to the last moment to make their peace with heaven.   Gentlemen, I will now ask another question.   It is not necessary for all to be present.   Let three of us accompany the condemned. Choose among yourselves."

This took but little discussion.

Then the culprit was bound, and Alexis and two others descended with him to a cellar.

Here everything was duly arranged.

The executioner—habited all in black, with masked face—looked like the old headsman of London.

On one side was a block, with a place for the neck to fit into.

In fact, everything was properly designed for the ghastly ceremony.

Eldroyd's heart beat violently.

His face was as pale as death, and his limbs shook.

Still, however, he did not show fear.

He knew that death was imminent.

But as he also knew that nothing could save him, he resolved to die game.

And so he did very soon.

Ten minutes were given him to think and pray.

Then his eyes were bandaged, his head placed on the block, and in an instant the axe was raised.   A dull thud was heard, and the head of the condemned rolled into the basket which was there to receive it.

The body was then raised, and flung through a window into the river ; and after a rapid consultation as to the time and place of the next meeting, the conspirators separated.

Alexis Rainsford was the last to go ; and on quitting his companions, he passed along the river bank lost in thought.

He had proceeded some little distance when a cry reached him from the water.

He listened, and it was again repeated.

Then, as he peered out into the darkness, he saw something white flutter for a moment, and then disappear.

A boat was near at hand.

He rushed towards it, and pulled off.

" There is some villany afloat here," he cried, and with a vigorous pull he began making his way towards the spot where he had seen the disappearance of the white form.

———

CHAPTER XXXIII.

THE SCENE ON THE THAMES AT NIGHT.

In order to explain this scene, we must beg our readers to accompany us to a little house situated about midway in a narrow street leading from the river.

The little house in question was situated between two large ones, and was occupied by but one family.

It was a dram-shop, and was renowned among a certain class of persons as affording a very good glass of brandy at a cheap rate.

The police themselves liked the brandy, and drank it, but they had grave suspicions as to whence it was obtained.

However, as nothing had been proved, or seemed capable of being proved, against the landlord, they continued to frequent his house and drink his brandy—first, because they liked it, and secondly, because they could watch him the better.

Giles Roper and his wife were oddities—not oddities in the pleasant use of the word, not oddities which one could laugh at, but oddities because they were hideous.

Roper was a tall man, with a face so unearthly and pale that he had won the appellation of " The Spectre."

His teeth shone horribly and unevenly in a wide and grinning mouth, his eyes were round as a ball, his nose thin and sharp, his whole body angular and long.

His wife was as bad as himself, both in words and appearance.

Her face had been destroyed in early life by vitriol, and her countenance was horrible to look upon.

Between them, this husband and wife seemed to have monopolised all the ugliness of the neighbourhood.

There was one other inmate of the house, who was very rarely seen by the customers.

This one was Alice, as those who knew her had named her.

She was between sixteen and seventeen years of age—an age when in all countries women are most fresh and charming.

Her hair was dark brown, but her skin was as fair and white as if her locks had been golden.

Her figure was finely developed, her bust being fully formed, her limbs rounded and graceful, and her waist slender and lissom.

Very few of those—as I have said—who frequented the Bull's Head had seen this girl, and none knew her except as Alice.

There was apparently some secret as regarded her existence, which old Roper took good care to guard jealously from everybody.

He would answer no inquiries regarding her; he would take up anyone very short who ventured to be inquisitive on her account; and even went the length once of telling a young aristocrat who had discovered her by accident that he would give him into custody if he interfered with her.

Alice was not the child of "The Spectre" and his wife, and very, very rarely was treated as such.

Food of a certain kind they were apparently compelled to give her, but clothes she was ill provided with.

Her usual dress was a coloured petticoat, reaching a little below her knees, a black bodice cut low, white stockings, and black boots.

These she always kept in good order.

The one she washed and mended herself, the latter she bought with what little money she could spare from the odd pence given her by the privileged customers who saw her.

There was but one room to which she attended solely.

This was a little room on the first floor, where upon certain occasions many odd characters assembled—characters who seemed lawless and reckless enough, but who always behaved with respect to the friendless girl, and generally gave her money.

On the evening on which we introduce them to our readers, Roper and his wife, having sent Alice to bed, sat down in their bar together.

There were but few persons in the wine-shop, and those few were located at the farther extremity of the large room, quite beyond listening distance.

"Madge," said Roper, to his fair wife, " Turner has seen me to-day."

" Well ?"

" You say well. It is not well. We have been deceived, grossly deceived, and I will not be deceived any longer."

" How deceived?"

" He told us that we were to keep her existence a secret, adding, ' As long as she lives I will pay you one hundred pounds a year for her support.' Well, I think it profitable to keep her, and have done so for ten years, and received my money to-day; and Turner comes to me and says, ' I shall pay no more money for Alice—it would be better for me if she were to die.'"

" This is strange."

" Yes, I told him so. He merely laughed, saying, ' Time has altered the case. Adieu.' And without another word he went."

" And what are you going to do? We can't afford to keep the girl idle."

Roper grinned horribly.

" Do you think I am foolish enough to think of it? No. That girl is no use to us in our business; more than that, she knows too many of my secrets, and the fact of her being here may some day destroy us. I will put her where I put Ronald."

The wife laughed.

" She'll be safe there," she said; " but killing ain't very profitable work. Wouldn't that young aristocrat buy her?"

Roper shook his sconce deprecatingly.

" He might," he said; " but that game won't pay. He'd get fond of her, and then she'll tell him everything. Where should we be then? No, no. I'll take her out with me to-night and finish the job right off."

" Well, well," returned Madge, methodically knitting a stocking, " I'll leave it all to you; no doubt you know best. It 'll be one mouth less to feed."

" Yes, I have a good chance to-night; the brandy

is getting low, so I am going on a boating excursion. She won't suspect anything."

That night the customers at the sign of the Bull's Head were turned out early.

Alice had retired to her room some quarter of an hour when a knock came at her door.

She had half undressed herself, and was doing her hair, when she rose to undo the bolt and let in the landlady.

The hideous woman cast an envious look at the white skin and the delicate breast of the young girl, over which the dark, dishevelled locks fell in glorious abundance, and a feeling of hateful jealousy invaded her heart.

"Better dead than in my house to tempt my husband," she said, inwardly.

But the evil thoughts which filled her heart made no impression on her features.

She smiled what was intended to be a benevolent smile on the young girl as she said—

"Alice, my husband has to go and procure some brandy to-night, and Bill is too drunk to be trusted. He wants you to go down to the river with him and keep watch."

Alice was so used to obedience that she simply said yes, and began to re-dress herself.

The idea of the possibility of saying no never once entered her head.

In a few minutes she was walking down the road with Roper quite unsuspectingly; though, had she seen Bill at the door of the next house, making desperate love to the servant, she would have regarded it as a significant fact.

When they arrived on the margin of the river, Roper said—

"We must cross over to the other side, my little one. My brandy is over there."

He pointed to a large mass on the opposite side of the river, which was nothing more nor less than a barge piled with casks.

Perhaps it is needless to say that this brandy did not belong to Roper, nor did he intend to purchase it.

He never paid for his commodities. The river supplied him with everything necessary for his shop.

Wines of every description, spirits of every description, were in turn stolen by the worthy proprietor of the Bull's Head, and until now he had escaped scot free.

His movements were peculiar.

Opposite the end of the street were moored several boats.

Into any one of these he would slip, run across the river to a well-laden barge, seize a barrel or a casket of spirit bottles, and return homewards.

At the landing-place Bill would watch, having a truck at hand for transporting the stolen goods.

This truck the man would wheel home and back again while Roper went after another cargo.

These robberies were audaciously impudent, but it was their very impudence which established their success.

The girl glanced at the river, and said the boats were far from shore.

"I cannot wade out to them through the water," she said.

"I will carry you," returned Roper, promptly.

He raised the girl in his arms.

He had intended to seize this opportunity and throw her into the mid-stream, where, without help, she must certainly have perished.

But no sooner had he raised her in his powerful arms than a new feeling took possession of him.

The contact with her soft, warm form—a form glowing with the pure, ripe beauty of maidenhood—sent the blood thrilling through his veins, and made him carry her out in safety to the boat.

This thought was—

"I never knew till now how lovely Alice is. If she will be mine, I will save her. Madge is old and ugly—I want a change."

When they were out in mid-stream he put his arm round her waist.

Alice made no resistance.

She looked upon him as a father, though a very odd and harsh one, be it said.

"Alice," he said, kissing her, "I have got something to tell you. I have been paid by a man to bring you out on the river to-night to kill you, that you may never trouble him again."

The girl shuddered and drew back.

"I don't understand you," she said, in a whisper of horror. "I have troubled no one."

"Yes, there is one who would give a thousand pounds to hear you were dead. But I offer you life. All I ask is that you will love me. My wife is getting old and ugly—you are young and beautiful. Be mine, and I will keep you like a queen."

He pressed her soft form to him, and kissed her ardently.

Alice recoiled from him.

"You are mad, sir! let me go!" she said, trembling. "You know there is only one I love, and——"

"He is dead."

The girl smiled.

"No, he is not dead," she said. "I know it—I feel it—I shall see him again."

"Never! But come, tell me, will you consent to be mine?"

He pulled her roughly towards him.

She sprang up.

"Touch me not!" she cried; "for I will choose death in preference to your insults."

He stood up also, steadying the boat, like an experienced boatman, and seized her round the waist, while she struggled violently to get away.

"You shall not die!" he cried. "You shall live to be mine!"

A sudden idea flashed across her mind.

"I will be yours," she said, "if you will let me. Sit down quietly—the rocking of the boat alarms me."

The man kissed her fervently, and released her.

In an instant she had sprang from the boat, and was hurrying away with the fast flowing tide.

In vain Roper rowed eagerly after her, in vain he searched the banks.

Nowhere could a trace of the body be found.

"Well, well," he said, as he pulled towards a barge, and prepared to extract a keg of brandy, "the deed is done, as it was intended to be done. But she was too beautiful to die."

When he had secured his prize, he took it ashore, and hid it beneath the wall of the house, ready for Gilbert to fetch.

Then he made towards home.

CHAPTER XXXIV.

ALEXIS RAINSFORD SPEAKS HIS MIND.

THE death of his victim—for naturally Giles Roper considered the girl dead—did not in the least affect the equanimity of this man of hot passions.

For the moment he had liked her.

He had considered it probable that she would have ministered to his enjoyment.

But the instant she had gone—cast herself thus recklessly into the bosom of the waters—he had cast her from his mind, and gone about his ordinary proceedings as if nothing had occurred.

He was soon, however, roused from his torpor.

Events had not delayed themselves for him.

He had delayed to see to his thefts and secure himself against discovery, and when he reached home some two hours had passed.

Knowing well what had proceeded on the river, he might have felt a little compunction, or, rather, fear, in addressing his Madge.

But he did not.

In fact, he had almost forgotten his Madge.

No wonder was it.

He had done a wonderful stroke of business.

So women were out of the question.

When he entered, however, he was startled.

He saw something was wrong.

Madge was as pale as death.

Some customers were about.

But these were talking by themselves.

She was sitting gazing into the fire.

He entered hastily.

"What ails you, Madge?" he cried.

She started as from a dream.

Then she sprang up, and drew him aside.

"Much," she said. "Turner is upstairs."

"Turner? Well?"

"Well? Are you mad? Don't you know what you've been doing?"

"I *do*; but was it not by his orders?"

The woman shrugged her shoulders.

"All right then," she said. "Go upstairs and see for yourself."

Giles Roper had been tasting a good drop of un-adulterated spirit.

He, therefore, had plenty of what is called "pot courage."

"Curse you for a fool!" he cried; and plunged up the narrow staircase.

Turning into a room on the first floor, he found himself in the presence of a man, who was walking to and fro with rapid strides, evidently under the influence of great excitement.

He stopped and faced round as Giles Roper entered the chamber.

Giles had called him Turner.

He was no other than Alexis Rainsford.

Giles bowed deeply.

"Your visit is an unexpected pleasure," he said.

"No doubt," returned Turner. "I come in regard to Alice."

The landlord turned pale.

"Yes?" he said. "What of her?"

"I wish to see her."

"To see her? Why, Master Turner, you surely forget!"

"I forget nothing. Where is she?"

Giles Roper shrugged his shoulders.

"I know not—you must ask the river," he said.

Alexis strode forward and seized him by the collar.

"Giles Roper," he said, "you are a villain!"

Roper smiled in a sickly manner.

"You have always thought so," he answered, "and now you tell me. If you had not thought me so you would not have asked me to act as I have done towards Alice."

"As you have done? What mean you, ruffian?" shouted Alexis.

Giles Roper began to get angry, and in conse-quence to regain courage.

He wrenched himself free of Alexis Rainsford's strong grasp.

"Hands off, Mr. Turner," he said. "I understand your game."

Alexis smiled grimly.

"Do you?" he said. "I doubt it. In the first place, I say, where is Alice?"

"Dead!"

"Dead? And you have murdered her?"

"By your directions."

"You lie, villain!"

"Do you deny, then, that you came to me, saying, 'Keep this girl, and you shall have so much for doing so?'"

"I do not."

"Do you deny to have come to me yesterday, saying, 'I no longer desire the girl to live. I would give a thousand pounds if I could be assured she was dead?'"

Giles Roper demanded this with a fierce shake of the fist.

But he soon changed his manner.

Something about Alexis Rainsford told him he had made some grievous error.

Alexis smiled.

"Be not excited, Master Roper," he said; "I deny nothing of all this."

"Then, are you mad? or—what does it all mean?"

"Simply this," replied Alexis, severely. "I gave this girl into your charge, and I did not tell you who she was. You discovered it—nay, deny it not. You found out that she was heiress to a large sum of money if Guy the Foundling were dead. You formed a plan to murder her and him. You have a niece whom you intended to pass off upon the world as Alice. And then, when you thought you had matured your plans, I discovered your design—your rascally, your cowardly, design! Good! I came to you. 'Get rid of the girl,' I said, to try you. I never dreamed that you would so soon attempt to carry your threat into execution. I should have

watched you had it been in my mind that you would so soon have tried to put into practice your brutal attempt. But I *have* foiled you, nevertheless."

Giles Roper turned whiter than before.

What was coming next?

He feared to think.

"How have you foiled me?" he said. "You told me to kill her, and I have."

"She is not dead—I saved her," returned Rainsford, sternly. "I tell you what I am about to do," said Alexis; "I am about to send her back here."

"Here!"

Giles Roper said this delightedly.

He saw a chance now of safety.

He had imagined, before this, rightly enough that Alexis Rainsford might be induced to take condign vengeance upon him; and though Giles was not absolutely a coward, he was much subject to that peculiar and salutary kind of fear for which criminals are noted.

He feared to set wrong against right.

"Yes," said Alexis; "but there is no reason for you to rejoice. You had better by far be without such a load upon your mind."

"Then send her elsewhere."

"That I refuse to do," replied Alexis. "I shall send her here because you will be compelled to see to her welfare. You will be watched at all hours, and at the first attempt to injure her death will be your portion."

"And how am I to be paid for this?"

"The money which you have received, and which you have *not* spent upon her, would be sufficient to enable you to act as you should towards her. But,

as you shall have no excuse for using her badly, I will pay you as before. Only remember this: I expect when I see her again that she will be better cared for and dressed than she is now."

"How know you how she is dressed? You have not seen her."

"Madman, did I not tell you I had saved her life this night?"

"And where is she now?"

"Here," cried Alexis.

And opening a door behind him, he disclosed a bedchamber, in which the unfortunate young girl lay sleeping in bed.

Giles started back in wonder.

"Ah! you may well smile," said Alexis; "I saw her jump from your boat—*why* she has told me—and swimming to her aid I saved her, and brought her here ere you returned. Mark me—guard her well, or you may meet death sooner than you dream."

With these words he turned to go.

Giles Roper clutched his arm and stayed him as he went.

"One word," he said; "one word ere you go."

"What is that?"

"Tell me—who is this Guy the Foundling? Where is he? and what is he to Alice?"

Alexis turned upon him sternly.

"Have a care of your tongue, man," he said; "my secrets are not for such as *you*."

And with the words he strode down the stairs and out of the house.

"Curse him," muttered Giles Roper, as he went, "I will be even with him yet."

END OF BOOK THE SECOND.

BOOK THE THIRD.

THE STORM BREAKS AT LAST.

CHAPTER I.

WHICH TELLS OF A LITTLE LOVE PASSAGE BETWEEN A LONG NEGLECTED HERO AND HEROINE.

IN the face of the events which were now looming in the distance, or, rather, which were pressing forward with unabated vigour, Simon Grandley did not consider London a proper place for the residence of his wife and child.

There had already been disturbances.

But these were nothing to what was to be expected every hour.

When once the grand petition—signed by one hundred thousand people — was rejected by the Commons, as the carpenter had reason to fear it would be, he knew well that London would, as it were, be delivered up to mad devilment and riot.

He—determined as he was to take a leading part in the great demonstration—was aware that if his family were still in London his mind would be distraught by the fact, and he would be unable to think undividedly of his friends.

His mind would be constantly reverting to the dear ones who would be in danger.

He therefore set himself to the task of finding for them a home, and without much difficulty found a pleasant little spot some four miles from London, where they could remain secluded during the turbulent times.

Guy the Foundling was the one to whom he would have wished to have left the guardianship of his family.

But this he knew to be impossible.

Or rather he chose to think it impossible.

The truth was that in all his great speculations he had associated the name of Guy.

In fact, so thoroughly done so that it seemed he could not move in this great crisis without the aid of his apprentice.

Simon, therefore, to a certain extent was compelled to trust to chance. The third day after the arrival of the family in their new home was that on which the disturbances were expected in London.

THE RIVAL APPRENTICES

A TALE OF THE RIOTS OF 1780.

STEALTHILY THE VILLAIN GLIDED AFTER THE YOUNG GIRL.

On the evening of this day Minnie and her mother were seated in the balcony of the little house, while Will Lightmore and Betty the serving maid were below in the grounds.

To explain what followed we must describe the place slightly.

It was situated on the margin of the river, with its grounds running down to the water's edge, whence the vilest characters could reach it by only crawling through a low hedge.

The grounds themselves were more like a forest than the ordinary gardens of a gentleman's house.

It was, in fact, more like what we should call a hunting box in the present day.

The house itself was situated some distance from the water's edge, and faced the other way, between it and the river being the densest part of the wooded gardens.

"Betty," said Will, as they passed along towards the margin of the stream, and he glided his arm round her lissom waist, "I have a secret to confide to thee—a secret most astounding and confounding! One that will chill the marrow of your bones!"

"Then don't tell it me," said Betty; "I shan't like to hear it."

Will laughed.

"I must! I will! 'Tis not my will but fate that guides my tongue."

"Don't be a fool, then, if you can help it," returned Betty, who never liked to see her lover in one of his poetical moods.

She didn't understand his quotations half her time.

And not understanding them she, of course, considered them nonsense.

"Well, I won't, then, if you don't like it," he said. "The truth is I am going away."

"Going away?"

The girl's heart sank within her; and she turned pale.

"Yes! this very night."

Betty made no reply—only clung more closely to his arm.

"And now, Betty, I want you to do me a favour."

"I will if I can."

"Mrs. Grandley must not know of it."

"She cannot help knowing it," said Betty; "you have been left here in charge of all of us."

They had now come to a part of the wood where some trees had been felled.

He drew her to one of these, and they sat down side by side.

"Betty," he said, "I've just got half an hour to spare, and I've a deal to say."

He said this in a wavering kind of voice, and his manner imparted a kind of nervousness to her.

Her heart leaped wildly in her bosom.

She felt, in fact, he was going to say something very important.

"Well, Betty, as you don't answer me, I must explain," said Will Lightmore, with a kind of determined boldness, which came very much against the grain. "I love you—I do, indeed, Betty; and I want you to be my wife."

Betty saw a loophole here for a word or two.

"Oh! Will," she cried, with a little laugh; "and you only an apprentice."

"Ah! but I don't mean now, you provoking little witch. I mean a long time yet."

"Ah! that's another thing," said Betty, demurely, looking down.

"Yes, I want you to promise that you will be my wife some of these days. I'm going away for a little while, Betty—only to London—but it's into great danger; and while I'm there I want to know that I have some one to love me and care for me, and be sorry if I'm—if I'm——"

He could not finish the sentence, which he was unwillingly framing.

Two warm arms were slid round his neck, and a weeping face crept down upon his shoulder.

"You can't love me," sobbed the girl, "or you would not be so cruel."

We need say little after this.

The love which Will offered was freely accepted, and when the end of the prescribed half hour had come they were sitting hand in hand, happy and betrothed.

Scarcely happy in one way, however, because they had so soon to part.

"You see, now," said Will, "I couldn't well keep away. There's Guy gone up to London with Mr. Grandley, and I'm to watch a place which doesn't want watching. It isn't likely I'd stop here with nothing to do while I know what danger they're running into. You wouldn't have me do it, now, would you, Betty?"

"No, Will, I shouldn't like you to seem a coward," said the girl.

No girl does.

The best way to win a girl's heart is to show pluck.

"Then, you see, I must go," said her lover; "and that being so, I don't want Mrs. Grandley to know anything about it. Let her think I've run away. Let her say so, Betty, and don't deny it."

"Why? I can't see why?"

"Because, if she knew where I was gone, she'd be sending after me to London, and Simon Grandley would send me back again."

"Then you're not going to tell him that you're there?"

"No, I'm only going to watch. When I'm wanted I shall be there."

In a few minutes after this the two young lovers parted, with many a kiss and many a fond and passionate embrace.

Somehow or another Betty felt all her sadness lifted from her heart.

Will's manner was so confident, that it was impossible to believe that any real harm was about to befall him.

She knew him to be brave, she knew him to be strong, she knew that he loved her.

How, then, could fortune be so unkind as to suffer any evil to befall him?

So they parted—Will Lightmore going off quickly towards the stream, and Betty returning slowly through the woods towards the house.

———

CHAPTER II.

IN WHICH A RUFFIAN UNEXPECTEDLY GETS HIS DESERTS.

DURING the little love-making scene there had been an unseen spectator.

Every word had been heard, and every action seen, by a third party.

This third party was one who would have roused the utmost alarm in the mind of a strong man, had he been there unarmed amid those lonely glades.

How much more so, then, was he calculated to cause terror in the heart of a feeble girl!

He was a short, thick-set, bull-necked fellow, with a red, bloated face, bleary eyes, and altogether a villanous looking appearance.

He wore a slouched hat, high boots, and had a villanous smile upon his face which told of any amount of devilry.

Just after Betty had promised to be the wife of the carpenter's young apprentice, Will had taken from his pocket a gold brooch, and presented it to his sweetheart.

The villain had seen the glitter of the jewel, and in an instant he formed a plan.

Concealed as he was behind a tree, he heard, as I have said, all the conversation, and knew that he had only to wait awhile and the young girl would be alone.

As soon, therefore, as Will Lightmore had gone, he crept slowly after the young girl, like a serpent after its prey.

She—thinking only of the one who had just left her—heard not the slight rustling of the branches which the stealthy ruffian made.

He was used to mean and paltry ways of earning his living.

That even his manner of walking would have told anyone, even if his villanous appearance were disregarded.

As soon as he imagined that she had proceeded far enough away from Will Lightmore, he hurried forward, and gliding behind the unsuspecting girl, seized her by the wrist with one hand, while with the other he prevented her crying out.

"Be quiet, or I'll kill you," he said, releasing his hold, and drawing a knife.

Betty was by no means a coward, that is as girls go.

But the sight of this villain—coming upon her as he did after a scene of such excitement—completely upset her.

She leaned against a tree for support.

"What want you with me?" she cried.

"In the first place, that gold brooch you have just stuck in your bosom," he said, savagely. "Quick! out with it."

The girl glanced round her, as if in hope that help was near.

But all was still and deserted.

To cry out was to court death.

The ruffian laughed brutally as he saw her evident distress.

"You see you can't help yourself, my pretty one," he said; "so off with the brooch, and out with all the money you have about you, or I'll bury this knife in your breast."

The manner in which the words were said left no doubt upon the mind of Betty that the cold-blooded villain would carry out his murderous resolve in case of refusal.

With a heavy heart, therefore, she took off the brooch, and withdrawing from her pocket what little silver she possessed, gave them all into the hands of her tormentor.

The man pocketed them eagerly.

Then he turned to her again.

"You're a devilish pretty girl," he said, "and before we part I mean to have a nice kiss."

"That you won't, then," she cried, as she fled from him; "you've got my money and the brooch. Be satisfied."

"But I'm not," cried the ruffian, whose passions were inflamed by the sight of her pretty face and form. "I mean to have a kiss ere I go, or I'll know why."

And so saying he darted forward, seized her by one arm, and passed the other round her waist.

But she was not destined to submit to any insult that evening.

Hardly had his lips approached hers when a stunning blow stretched him senseless on the ground, and Guy the Foundling springing forward, caught Betty in his arms as she reeled back, half-fainting.

"Why, Betty!" exclaimed Guy, in surprise, "what on earth ails you? What has this ruffian been doing?"

A few words explained all.

"The villain!" exclaimed Guy. "Well, run along home and tell them I am coming. I'll see to him."

The young girl, glad enough to escape from the place, then rushed off, and Guy, kneeling down by the side of the now reviving villain, deprived him of all his ill-gotten gains and his weapons.

Then he waited for him to recover.

It was not long ere he did.

Then he looked round him wildly as he half sat up.

Guy prevented his rising.

"One moment!" he cried; "you have not an unfortunate girl to deal with, but a man. What are you doing here?"

The ruffian was completely cowed.

He saw he was in Guy's power.

"What do you want with me?" he said, sullenly.

"You reply to my question by another," responded Guy the Foundling; "that will not do. Tell me at once why you are here, or, perchance, a bullet from my pistol there may put a stop to your chance of replying."

The man scowled terribly.

Yet he saw it was useless to resist.

He knew, in fact, he had been disarmed.

"I came here for the purpose of robbery," he said, fiercely. "The girl's told you that, so you know it, and needn't ask me."

"That is not all," said the apprentice.

The look which Guy cast on the ruffian made him quail.

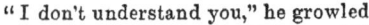

"I don't understand you," he growled.

"Then I'll make you," said Guy. "You see this pistol. Tell me at once why you were found skulking in these private grounds or I fire. You have already given sufficient cause, and no one will trouble himself about the carcase of such a worthless wretch as you. Quick! Speak!"

The fellow saw at once now that prevarication was useless.

"I came here to see if Simon Grandley and you were here," he said.

"And pray what know you of me?"

"Simply that you are Guy the Foundling, that you are the apprentice of Grandley the carpenter, and that you are aiding him in——"

He hesitated.

"In what?" demanded Guy.

"In the Protestant movement."

"And pray why did you, or rather those who sent you, desire to know if we were here or not? Did you come to murder us?"

"No. Merely to report to them—my masters—whether you were here, as you could not be found at the carpenter's house."

"And, pray, who sent you?"

"Alexis Rainsford."

Guy started.

"Alexis Rainsford!" he cried "Why, he is a prisoner."

"No," replied the man, "he has long since escaped. How I know not. I am certain, however, that he is free, and in London, as I have not long left him."

"And how knew he that we were here—or rather that Simon Grandley had removed his family hither?"

"I know not that," replied the man. "You are asking me now for his private thoughts, which I cannot by any possibility know. And now, since you have learned all, and taken from me, moreover, what you want, let me go."

"Not at all," said Guy the Foundling; "not at all."

"Why, what more do you require?"

"I require nothing of you, so to speak," replied the apprentice; "but I should be acting the part of a madman were I to permit you to return to my enemies and inform them of our proceedings."

"Then what are you about to do with me?" asked the man.

"You will have to remain here," replied Guy the Foundling; "no harm will be done you if you only remain quiet. Come, follow me, or, rather, precede me along yonder avenue. I trust not cowards like yourself. Remember, if you attempt flight, death will be your portion."

The man saw no use in refusing.

He had done his best.

And more than this, he had been paid for it beforehand.

So he went on contentedly.

"I may have a chance of escape," thought he, "or if not, why, I shall have a lodging and good living."

It was not long before he was placed in a cellar beneath the old house, where some food and ale were given him, and the bed made up to render him as comfortable as possible.

Guy's visit to the place was only for the purpose of obtaining something which Simon considered necessary.

He stopped but a few hours, gave instructions to them how to treat their unexpected prisoner, and then, after a tender farewell of Minnie, he took his leave.

"There is little of carpentering doing now," said Mrs. Grandley, as she saw him hurrying away from the house. "Someone has completely turned the head of my husband, and he thinks of nothing now but politics."

"And Guy, too," said Minnie; "he is no longer the simple, loving, hardworking apprentice, but has his head full of martial notions. I almost wish that if this convulsion is to take place it would take place at once. Anything is to be preferred to the horror of suspense."

"Ah!" thought Betty, who had heard it all as she was preparing the evening meal, "and my Will is as mad as any of the others, and yet I mustn't speak!"

CHAPTER III.

AN ADVENTURE ON THE ROAD, AND WHAT CAME OF IT.

WILL LIGHTMORE, on leaving the side of his beloved Betty, hurried away so quickly that he had no chance of hearing any of the disturbance in the wood between her and the villanous robber.

A bright idea had entered his brain.

Not an unusual thing.

Will was by no means a dullard.

He was quick to conceive, and, as we have already seen, quicker to execute.

He was bold enough, too, to face any danger that presented itself.

In the present instance he had by no means a pleasant task before him.

He had, unjustifiably, as he imagined, been left out of the danger, whatever it might be, to which his master and his fellow-apprentice were about to be exposed.

Determined, therefore, to seek an opportunity of showing his zeal, he had quitted the old house, never dreaming that, amid all the turmoil and excitement, any danger would threaten his mistress or her daughter in that remote place.

He had not proceeded far before, as he entered a house to obtain a little refreshment, he came bolt against an old man in the costume of a beggar.

There seemed no doubting his vocation.

He was bent, wrinkled, gray-headed, ragged—overcome, in all seeming, with poverty and wretchedness.

He bowed to Will Lightmore as he passed in, and apologised in a low tone for his rudeness; and as Will turned to him, and dropped a coin into his extended hat, the apprentice caught a gleam in his eye which was far more like the gleam of a young man than that of an old one.

But he thought no more of it.

If it was so, it was but one of the usual impostures of that day, as of this, and he was content to let it pass.

The only idea which the rencontre and the look caused to arise in his mind was this—

"Was it prudent for him to travel on foot so far?"

He might meet all manner of characters, some of whom might ease him of his life for the sake of even the small sum he carried.

He was known at the inn sufficiently as the apprentice of Simon Grandley to enable him to hire a horse for a small amount of money, and this, accordingly, he resolved upon doing.

So he told the landlord his requirements.

"How far do you travel?" asked Boniface.

"To London—to the Bull's Head, near Thames Street," said Will Lightmore. "It is not far."

"The Bull's Head! I know it well," replied the landlord. "It is kept by one Giles Roper. It is not a long journey, and my black mare will take you there well."

And with that he bustled off, leaving Will in the room.

Within ten minutes the latter was mounted and off.

Then a strange thing happened.

The beggar who had fallen against him in the entry had watched him from a shadowy corner, and now, as the apprentice rode off, he darted out from his place of concealment and rushed into the tavern.

But his appearance was now completely changed. His rags were gone; his whole seeming now was that of a well-to-do farmer.

"Landlord," he said, "I want a good horse."

Boniface rubbed his hands.

"I'm doing a good trade in hiring," thought he.

"Yes, sir," he said aloud; "how far do you wish to go?"

"To the Bull's Head, near Thames-street."

The landlord started.

"The Bull's Head! That is strange," he said.

"Strange!" echoed the stranger. "Why so?"

"The very last traveller that started hence was going to the Bull's Head."

The man laughed.

"Why is that odd?" he said. "Why should not two men go to the same place on the same night? Perhaps we are going on the same business. But come—can I have the horse?"

"Oh yes, yes, of course," replied the landlord, rubbing his hands; "yes, yes: I was only thinking it was odd, that was all."

And so in a few minutes the strange beggar was mounted, and away he was riding after Will Lightmore.

There was some common land lying by the side of the road to London some distance from the roadside inn, and the strange man was not slow to take advantage of the circumstance.

Forcing his horse into a quiet trot, as soon as he saw the form of Will Lightmore on his steed not far in front of him, he edged him off the road upon the velvety turf, and so prevented the sound of his progress from reaching the ears of the one whom he was evidently following.

As soon as the grass effectually deadened the sound of the horse's hoofs, he went at a more rapid pace, and at last burst out upon the highway just at the side of Will Lightmore.

The latter started back, and placed his hand upon his pistols.

"What have we here," he cried; "highwaymen?"

"No, not highwaymen, my friend," responded the whilom beggar, "but a road companion."

The voice, in spite of the different tone now adopted, seemed somehow to have a familiar twang about it.

But that was all Will could say.

He knew not where he had heard it.

"Very well," he said; "very well! I am glad of company. I am well armed; yet, even if armed the best, one knows not how or when one may meet with dangerous folk."

There seemed very little danger, however, likely to accrue from the stranger's companionship.

They chatted on pleasantly and comfortably enough upon various topics, more especially dwelling upon the convulsed state of society, and the dread prospects in view, until at length London came in sight, and Will began to blame himself for the evil thoughts which had entered his head in regard to the stranger.

"We seem to be going the same way all through," he said, at length.

"I travel to the Bull's Head, near Thames-street corner," replied the other.

"And I, too," replied Will; "it is strange, indeed."

"Scarcely strange if we both know Giles Roper," returned the man.

Will felt uneasy.

His visit to the Bull's Head was connected with private, nay, secret business.

What if this man knew his intentions?

But yet it was scarcely likely.

"I know him well," said Will. "He lets a good bed when one is in search of one, and I coming up to London so late to see my friends am always glad to secure a home for the while in his hospitable house."

The stranger smiled to himself but said nothing.

His thoughts, however, evidently did not in any way coincide with Will's words.

"We shall see," he murmured to himself.

And for the rest of the way they rode in complete silence.

When, at length, however, they reached the Bull's Head, and Bill (Giles Roper's groom) had taken care of their horses, the "beggar" whispered in the apprentice's ear—

"Be more discreet, Will Lightmore, the next time you ride."

Will sprang round to resent the words.

But in vain.

The mysterious speaker had vanished.

Who he was he could not by any process of reasoning divine.

Nor, apparently, were there any means of ascertaining the fact from anyone.

No one appeared to know anything whatever in regard to him.

Nor, in fact, except **when** delivering over his horse to the ostler, had anyone seen anything of him.

One thing, however, acted as a consolation to Will Lightmore.

He had disclosed to the stranger nothing of his business, and so he, without fear of any after consequences, called for supper and a bed, and was soon fast asleep within a few feet of the couch where slept the fair object of Alexis Rainsford's care and Giles Roper's guilty passion.

CHAPTER IV.

HOW THE CAPTIVES FARED AT HALLWYN HOUSE.

As soon as the dread ordeal had been gone through in the old house by the river, and the traitor had been sent to his death, Alexis Rainsford set to work to arrange for the release of the captives at Hallwyn House.

Without them he knew well that all hopes of staying the efforts of the Protestant Association were at an end.

Although they were not overwhelming in numbers, still they represented numbers.

Each man had a number of friends, who would not move in the matter until the word of command was given by the head of what they called the sections.

Eagerly, therefore, Alexis Rainsford took his way towards the house of Robert Hallwyn.

He had with him only a few men.

Sufficient, however, as he imagined, to succeed in rescuing the prisoners, if acting in a proper manner.

They arrived at Hallwyn House in the small hours of the morning, and, after giving the password which had been agreed upon by Aurora and Alexis, they were at once admitted.

The plan arranged upon was simple.

Half the men, headed by Alexis, were to pass through the secret door along the subterranean passage, and the other half were to proceed to the gate upon the outer part of the ruins, and demand an entrance.

Thus, taken between two fires as it were, it was rightly supposed that the captors would be compelled to yield, more especially as, of course, the besiegers would be reinforced by the captives.

It happened exactly as Alexis Rainsford had predicted.

Those whom he headed, of course, entered by the unsuspected subterranean way, and burst upon the astonished guards just as the loud knocking at the doorway on the summit of the stone steps proclaimed an accession of forces.

"We come to save you, my friends," cried Alexis, addressing the captives; "here are arms in plenty."

Then, addressing Simon Grandley's adherents, he added—

"Resistance is useless. You see we far outnumber you—so yield."

He had not to do with cowards, however.

The Protestants, fully believing they were aiding a good cause, had already made enormous sacrifices to back it.

They were not composed of the scum of the population.

Nearly every man there was a shopkeeper or an artisan.

To these time was everything.

And yet they had given up their hours freely to guard those whom they imagined would be the instigators of riot.

So when Alexis Rainsford demanded a surrender they sprang to arms.

Each man there was resolute.

"No surrender."

"Down with them."

"Guard well the door!"

Such were the cries which resounded through the vaults.

And then a fierce conflict ensued.

Alexis Rainsford, however, had resolved upon a method to put an end to a bloodthirsty and wholly unnecessary combat.

A combat, in its small way, as cruel, as unjustifiable, and as reckless, as the great war now initiated by the vengeful passions and gross ambition of a French tyrant against a peaceful and great nation.

The prisoners were the persons whose departure Simon Grandley's men were directed to prevent.

Those whom Alexis had with him were strangers to them.

The captives once removed, therefore, there would be no cause for the further proceeding of hostilities.

Directions to this effect were in an instant spread among the captives, and Robert Hallwyn led the way for them to enter the subterranean passage.

As this countermarch was made the guard was attacked fiercely by Alexis and his followers, as they strove to dash forward and stop the flight of the prisoners; while ere the struggle had well begun the door was burst open, and the second detachment of deliverers caught the Protestants on the rear.

The conflict was now at an end.

Resistance was useless.

Simon Grandley's men were overpowered.

Not without bloodshed, be it said.

But yet without absolute loss of life.

"The prisoners have fled, and are now beyond your reach," shouted Alexis, dashing into the middle of the combatants. "Stop this useless fight."

A few more little skirmishes.

Then all desisted.

In fact, to fight now was wanton.

The Protestants retired sullenly into the grounds, and Alexis, having given directions to his men, proceeded to the house.

He was anxious, truly, to see Robert Hallwyn, and congratulate him.

But—shall we confess it?

Yes; this was not the only inducement to a visit there.

He had not forgotten the bright eyes of Aurora Halsted.

Love had never yet truly taken possession of his soul.

Now even political fame and triumph was secondary to it.

He found Robert Hallwyn and his niece anxiously awaiting him, and his heart leaped with unusual sensations as Aurora pressed his hand and thanked him for his bravery.

That pressure made him forget, or, rather, not even hear the words of gratitude spoken to him by Robert Hallwyn.

And how was it with Aurora?

We must speak truly. She was far from being indifferent to the handsome face, the manners, the courage of her new friend, Alexis Rainsford.

Yet she could not be said to love him.

She had in the first instance been moved by Dick Hatherden.

In the days when he was less criminal he had appeared before her in the light of a hero.

He was young—not ill-looking.

In fact, in spite of certain defects, he had a manly appearance.

And then—

Was he not her worshipper?

Was he not oppressed too?

Was he not, according to his own showing, the rightful heir to great property, kept from him by the machinations of Guy the Foundling and Simon Grandley?

All these points were sufficient to create an interest—an overwhelming interest—in the mind of an enthusiastic girl.

It did in hers.

And with her he for a long time remained a hero of romance.

When he disclosed the cloven hoof, even then it seemed most difficult for her to believe in his perfidy.

And then—

There came a revulsion.

She met Guy the Foundling.

She admired him; she saw his resolution, his manly courage, and she threw her whole passionate being into her love for him.

And this was repulsed.

Most decidedly and unequivocally repulsed by Guy, because of former love.

Hate, they say, is most akin to love.

And in her case it seemed so.

Yet only for awhile.

The interest she had conceived in Guy the Foundling scarcely admitted it.

She hated him for the moment.

Hated him because he was so handsome and yet so cold — hated him because he loved Minnie Grandley—but hated her more than all.

She was the rival and the stumbling-block in her path.

No wonder was it, then, that she detested her very name.

She had used all her endeavours to secure the love of Guy.

She had even lately saved his life, only, as she thought, to be betrayed.

What, then, must her feelings have been towards him at the moment that Alexis Rainsford appeared upon the scene?

Alexis Rainsford would hardly have been complimented had he known.

She saw in him a handsome, and a bold, courageous man.

But she also saw something beyond.

Something more consonant with her private feelings.

The enemy of Guy the Foundling.

One who would assist her in compassing any punishment which she thought it necessary to inflict upon the one who had rejected her advances.

Had she known all she would have seen how foolish this was.

One visit to the house of the villain Giles Roper would have told her that Alexis Rainsford was preserving and shielding with his life from harm the one who was mysteriously co-heiress with Guy the Foundling in a large fortune.

Knowing nothing of this, however, she permitted her feelings to have full sway; and when, early on the following morning, Alexis Rainsford left her, it was almost a lover-like parting that took place.

CHAPTER V.

IN WHICH DICK HATHERDEN TRIES TO REINSTATE HIMSELF IN THE AFFECTIONS OF AN OLD SWEET-HEART, AND FINDS A NEW ONE.

AURORA was left once more to herself on the day after Alexis' departure.

Robert Hallwyn was wanted in London.

His duty called him to the same spot as it called Alexis Rainsford.

On that evening—a pleasant evening in early summer—she wandered out in the grounds towards the ruins which had of late been the scene of so many strange events.

It was nearly dusk.

She had not, therefore, wandered out to enjoy reading in solitude, but simply amid the silent greenery to think upon events.

So, near the ruins she sat herself down upon some fallen trees, and lapsed into memories of the past and readings of the future.

She was dreaming thus, lost to all outward things, when a voice startled her.

It was close beside her, and seemed wondrously familiar.

"Well met, Miss Halsted," it said; "and how fare things with you?"

She started round, and as she did so uttered a cry of surprise.

Surprise not unmingled with anger and alarm, be it said.

The man who stood beside her was none other than Dick Hatherden.

But how changed!

He was nothing like the apprentice of old.

He was dressed in the height of fashion, and, in fact, in some way or another had contrived to do away with all the appearances of low and vulgar life, which had, as it were, been his disfigurement hitherto.

Aurora was so astounded that for a moment she could not speak.

When, however, she found her voice, she said, as she rose up—

"And pray, sir, what do you here?"

Dick bowed lowly.

"I came to see you," he said.

"And what want you with me?" she demanded, scanning his altered appearance with much amazement.

Dick laid his hand upon his heart in the most approved style.

"Can you doubt what I desire?" he said.

"I *do* doubt," replied Aurora. "I cannot for the life of me conceive!"

The tone irritated Dick Hatherden.

It was cold and chilling.

Evidently the old dream had passed utterly away here.

"You cannot conceive!" he cried. "Aurora, can you say this to me—to me, who was once all in all to you—to me, to whom you once promised eternal love? I come to ask you for a renewal of your love —to let me explain all: to let me do away with all those wrong impressions which——"

Aurora waved her hand to ask him to stop speaking.

"Say no more," she said, "it would be but waste of breath."

Dick scowled upon her.

But in an instant a bright smile was woven on his lips.

He must dissemble.

He had good reason to do so.

We will explain why.

On the day after his murder of old Morley, and his seizure of his daughter, great news had come to him.

Going into a public-house, where he had been known long before his departure from the service of the carpenter, he met one of his old companions.

He was greeted with acclamation.

More enthusiastically than he expected it would be.

"Why, my old friend," cried his former companion, "you are quite a stranger."

Dick laughed.

"So would you be," he said, "if you had gone through all the adventures I've been through, setting aside being in the stone jug, as I have been."

The fellow whom he was addressing laughed at this.

He was one of those who delighted in the commission of crime, and who, if he could not commit it himself, was pleased to hear of its successful commission by others.

"Well, perhaps I should be the same as you," he said; "but I'd have had a powerful desire to get out again if I'd had the chance before me that you had."

"What do you mean?" asked Dick, abruptly.

He began to be nettled.

He fancied almost that the man was amusing himself at his expense.

"Why, do you really mean you don't know it?"

The man spoke incredulously.

Dick saw at once there was some real meaning in his words.

So he sat down near him.

"Now, look here," he said, "don't be trying to make a fool of me, because I can tell you this—it doesn't pay."

"I'm making no fool of you."

"Out with it, then."

"Good. Send for some drink," replied the other, "and if you're really as ignorant as you pretend to be, why, I'll tell you something that'll right down surprise you."

Dick saw by the manner of his companion that he really meant what he said; and, accordingly, having ordered the drink required, he set himself to listen.

It was a strange history he heard.

But it was a stranger thing still that it should be told by the lips of such a man as now narrated to him.

He seemed quite *au fait* as regarded Aurora Halsted and her story.

"You remember Miss Halsted?" he said.

Dick flushed crimson.

"Of course I do," he said. "What's that got to do with it?"

"Everything. In the first place, it's true that you and she were once on good terms, so much so, in fact, that you thought you were going to marry her?"

"Yes."

"Well, you quarrelled?"

"Yes—yes."

Dick was getting impatient.

And angry too.

He never liked to appear small.

And not knowing his companion's drift, he certainly imagined he was looking small now.

"Well, all I can say is, you must make it up as soon as you can and how you can."

"Why now of all other times?"

"Because it's come to my ears that she's just got twenty thousand pounds left to her."

Dick looked at him incredulously.

"You're romancing," he said.

"Not I," replied the other; "I know it—I know it! There, I can't say any more. She was worth having before; but now—oh, if I *had* such a chance!"

Dick banged the table savagely.

He knew how Aurora had treated him.

The thing to him was not so easy as it seemed to the other.

"Well, it's provoking," he said.

"*I* call it devilish nice."

"No, no! you don't understand me," said Dick. "You see, on the last occasion that we met we parted deadly enemies."

"All the better. Lovers always quarrel."

The speaker apparently had resolved to see everything in a favourable light.

"I don't see what's to be done," mused Dick. "I know nothing that will bring her to a different frame of mind. She's dead set against me, and, perhaps, if I were to approach her, would order me from her presence."

The other clapped him on the shoulder.

"Will you be guided by me?"

"Yes: if there seems a chance."

"Very well, there *is* a chance, and a good one," continued the more jovial ruffian. "You must dress yourself up in the extreme of fashion, and go to the

THE RIVAL APPRENTICES

A TALE OF THE RIOTS OF 1780.

THE ESCAPE.

place where she is, pretend great contrition, and then, after you have persuaded her to listen, tell her of this accession of fortune."

"Which she will not believe."

"She will.   I will give you the name of the person to whom she is to apply.   I will give you on paper the name of the lawyer who holds the property, as also the name of the person who has left it to her. She will recognise the latter, and can inquire of the former. So how can she disbelieve you?"

In the face of such statements as these, how could Dick Hatherden refuse to believe his newly-found friend?

Instead of discrediting him, he became enthusiastic, and grasped his hand.

"Excuse my want of belief," he said; "you will see that I will follow out your plan, exactly."

"And we will share the plunder?"

Dick Hatherden did not exactly like this expression.

He had still a sneaking liking for Aurora Halsted. In fact, as far as his nature was capable of it, he loved her.

So that really any scheme which had for its object his marriage with her satisfied his passions as well as his greed for money.

"Doubt not that you shall have a good share, friend Ordin," he said; "but we won't call it plunder—it's legitimate gain, as long as she is willing to have me."

Ordin laughed.

Well he might.

It seemed to him that his friend was becoming far too squeamish.

"Have it your own way," he said; "but come, let me give you the names, &c."

And so, having arranged preliminaries, and drunk deeply to the success of the scheme, the villains separated.

And thus came it that we find Dick Hatherden by the side of Aurora Halsted pleading his cause once more.

She knew not how much more villany she could rouse in his mind, or she would never have refused him.

She would have preferred temporising.

For even if she gave in afterwards, the first refusal would be enough to rouse him to anger and to inextinguishable spite.

"I wonder you say such words to me, Master Hatherden," she said.

"Why wonder?" he asked, allowing his voice to sink to as gentle a pitch as possible. "Have you forgotten all my old devotion—my unconquerable devotion to you?"

"I have forgotten nothing," she said, "not even your infamous behaviour to me in the old tavern which the rioters dragged to pieces. I have not forgotten that you then intended to dishonour or to murder me. Let me pass, sir, and never let me see your face again."

This was almost too much for Dick Hatherden's temper.

But he curbed it as well as he could.

"Be not hasty," he said, gently opposing her flight; "pray let me explain."

Aurora eyed him fiercely.

"Speak, then, and quickly," she said.

Dick Hatherden saw that he must put on a different style of address.

"Miss Halsted," he said, in a voice full of pretended respect, "in order to understand what I say you must listen patiently. I have much to tell you, and it is but fair that I should have a patient hearing."

"I listen," said Aurora, haughtily.

He was quite wrong if he imagined that his specious words or his clothes had made any impression upon Aurora.

She resumed her seat, and tapped the ground impatiently with her foot.

"In the first place, you speak of my deceiving you, and taking you to the tavern that night under pretence of seeing your father.

"Believe me, it was but because of my great love for you. I could not bear the idea of another supplanting me in your love, and more especially when that other was that designing villain, Guy the Foundling.

"I knew how constantly he was endeavouring to injure me in your eyes.

"I knew that I, too, had deceived you somewhat, and I was afraid that unless I took strong measures I should lose you for ever.

"The desperate idea then entered my brain—I would force you into a marriage.

"For your love afterwards I trusted to old associations."

"Which have gone for ever from my mind," said Aurora, coldly.

Dick paid no heed to this.

"Now, Aurora," he proceeded, "I bring you not only my renewed protestations of love, but news of good fortune.

"I have never cast my eyes upon another, therefore you cannot refuse to believe that my heart is still yours.

"I need say no more of that.

"I will give you a proof that I am telling nothing but the truth. Your father died, leaving you poor."

Aurora's eyes flashed, and her bosom heaved violently as he said this.

"What matters it to you if he did?" she cried; "he has left me beyond want."

"Yes," replied Dick Hatherden, pursuing what he imagined to be an advantage, "but what he *has* left is nothing to one who, like you, has been fed in the lap of luxury. Did I cease my attentions to you after his death? Did fortune make any difference in my affection?"

He paused.

Aurora remained silent.

"I answer for you, then," he said; "it made *no* difference. But now I bring you wealth and fortune—nay, curl not your lip in disdain, I have proofs or I would not assert this to you. Take this letter and read it."

So saying, he drew forth the note which Ordin had given him.

This was but one of the documents in regard to the property.

Aurora took it and prepared to treat it with utter incredulity.

But the first glance told her differently.

Her colour came and went, and her breast heaved with emotion.

"Well," she said, "and is this your only proof?"

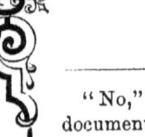

"No," he said, producing the other parts of the documents, "here are other things in regard to it."

Aurora took them and read them through.

There was no doubting the truth of his words.

She knew the names; she expected, in fact, the legacy.

The only mystery to her was how did Dick Hatherden discover the secret.

She could not, of course, guess that he had heard it from Ordin, and that Ordin had obtained his information and stolen the documents from a drunken lawyer's clerk.

"This is certainly correct," replied Aurora, stiffly. "I am obliged to you for the knowledge you have given me, and shall be glad to reward you."

Dick flushed.

His vanity caused him to imagine that she meant to reward him in the only way he desired to be rewarded.

He flung himself on one knee before her.

"Oh! you *can* reward me, Aurora," he said; "you know well how. Be mine, dearest, and——"

She sprang up indignantly.

"Madman! villain!" she cried, her eyes ablaze with anger. "Do you suppose because I have preserved my calmness I do not despise and hate you? Do you imagine that I would suffer myself to marry such a thing as *you* are? to be caressed by hands that for aught I know may have been dyed in my father's blood? Leave my sight, fool and ruffian, and let me see you no more."

Dick Hatherden staggered to his feet, stunned and stupefied.

For an instant he could scarcely believe his ears.

When he recovered himself he saw her walking quickly from him.

His evil passions were roused now to the extremest pitch of fury.

He saw himself duped and defeated.

All chance of obtaining possession of Aurora was now vanished.

He had, moreover, given her the means of obtaining riches.

And all for nothing!

He felt now the consequences of his crimes coming crushingly upon him.

Roused, therefore, to a terrible pitch of anger, he sprang after her.

She felt him coming.

She heard the crackling of boughs beneath his rapid feet and she knew her danger.

Facing about, she saw him hastening towards her with red, gleaming eyes, and white face full of vengeful hate, and her heart leaped wildly with a sense of unknown danger.

Circumstances had, however, taught her to be prepared.

Just as he advanced towards her, menacingly shouting—

"The papers—the papers! Give them back to me."

She drew from her bosom a tiny pistol—quite a bijou in its way—and presented it at his head.

"Back, villain!" she cried; "back, or I will send the contents of this through your skull. With all I

suspect and all I know, be thankful for your life and leave me."

Dick Hatherden literally writhed at being thus outwitted.

But what could he do?

The beautiful girl stood there before him determinedly: her eyes full of resolute courage—the pistol pointed steadily at his head.

Then a sudden rash idea occurred to him.

"Bah!" he said, with a forced laugh; "the pistol is not loaded."

And he made a feint to advance.

In an instant there was a report and a flash, and he fell wounded and bleeding to the ground, while Aurora fled hurriedly away towards Hallwyn House, not even looking back to see what had been the effect of her shot.

CHAPTER VI.

NEARLY DEAD—WILL LIGHTMORE'S NEW PROTEGEE.

HAD Dick Hatherden been but a foot or two nearer, or had Aurora taken better aim, he would certainly have never risen from the earth alive.

As it was, however, the shot fired from the little silver-mounted pistol missed its aim, and struck him on the right ear, completely cutting it from his head, disfiguring him terribly, and smothering him in blood.

Stunned, in fact, by the blow, he remained for a while on the ground where he had fallen.

When he did rise—feeling faint and sick—he hastily bound up his wound. With a curse loud and terrible upon her who had thus attacked him, he slowly made his way towards the high-road, and, refreshing himself at the nearest inn, hurried off towards London.

His destination was the Bull's Head, the house kept by Giles Roper.

But, before describing what happened to him there, we must retrace our steps for awhile, and ask our readers to remember that Will Lightmore, on his secret mission to London, arrived in company with a mysterious stranger, who, after whispering in his ear some unintelligible words, fled, and left him to wonder.

Will was by no means nervous.

Yet he felt unpleasantly influenced by the strange rencontre.

It showed that he was watched.

This was bad enough, when he desired all his actions to be unknown, even to his friends.

But there was not much use talking of it or thinking of it.

All he could do was to be discreet.

In spite of the upset consequent upon the discovery that he had been in company of a spy, he sat down to a good supper, and disposed of it, and retired at a somewhat late hour to rest.

As Giles Roper was showing him to his room, he fancied that he saw something more substantial than a shadow lurking near on the watch.

He took no cognisance of this, however.

Something seemed to tell him to remain quiet, and glad he soon was that he had done so.

He had scarcely turned the key in the lock when there came a tapping at the door.

The sound was so slight at first that he thought he was mistaken.

But it was again repeated, and he at once opened the door.

His surprise may be imagined when he saw a young girl standing there.

"Strange, this!" he thought.

But he said aloud—

"Well, my fair mistress, how can I serve you?"

"By granting me an interview for five minutes," returned the young girl, in a trembling voice, and with a hurried look round her.

Will opened wide the door.

"Enter," he said.

Alice—for it was she—the *protégée* of Alexis Rainsford, entered hastily.

"Lock the door," she said; "they would kill me if they found me here."

More and more puzzled, Will obeyed.

Alice, beautiful as she was, looked very wild.

Was it a mad girl before him?

He was soon disabused of this idea.

"You're a stranger; no friend, I am sure, to the villain who keeps this house," she said.

"I am quite a stranger."

"I knew it, and therefore I am resolved to trust you. I am in dreadful peril here, and you can save me."

Then, ere Will Lightmore could utter any words of deprecation, she told the story of the insults to which she had been subject from Giles Roper, the journey on the river, and his brutal offers.

She knew nothing, of course, of the visit which Alexis Rainsford had paid to the Bull's Head.

She knew not he had been her saviour from the turbulent river; she knew not, therefore, that she had been so left under the charge of Giles Roper that he dared not, for his own sake, treat her otherwise than with respect.

He had been very quiet and respectful, truly, in his manner towards her since that time.

But she attributed that only to some deeper and more villanous design on his part.

Not certainly to his own feelings.

Now, therefore, if it *could* be so, she was more frightened of him than ever.

On account of this very pretension of kindness.

"I know not how I came back here," she said; "I leaped into the water to avoid the ruffian, and I suppose he leaped after me."

"But he wished your death, you say; or, rather, another wished it."

"So he said," replied Alice; "but I trust that was but one of his wicked inventions. He threatened to kill me, I believe, simply because I would not consent to his villanous proposals; and he saved me merely for his own purpose. Oh, sir, save me from him!"

Will Lightmore felt himself in an awkward position.

"Well," he said, "you take me so by surprise that I know not what to do. Have you any friends in London; because, if so, why do you not fly to them?"

The girl smiled.

"You little understand my position," she said. "Fly to them! Why, I cannot even escape from my room, or, rather, from beyond this passage."

"How is that?"

"Simply because I, in common with all who sleep in this corridor, am locked in. There is a common door leading from this to the large staircase, and that door Giles Roper takes care to keep closed at night."

Will Lightmore looked angry.

"It is a great liberty," he said. "How knows he that his guests would agree to such an arrangement?"

Alice approached nearer.

Placing her hand on his arm, she looked up pleadingly into his face.

"Sir," she said, "you will not betray me if I tell you more?"

"Betray you? No!"

"I will tell you why Giles Roper closes these rooms in, then," she said. "Very few travellers who come to this place ever make their way out again."

"They are murdered?"

Alice shuddered.

"Yes, I have seen it," she said.

"Then I, too, must beware," said Will Lightmore. "But, come, you have not told me—have you any friends in London?"

"No friends—no real friends," said Alice; "but I know the names of some people who will, I know, befriend me."

"Tell me their names, then, and where they live, and I will take you to them," said Will Lightmore.

"Their name is Grandley," said Alice; "he is a carpenter—the head of the family."

"Grandley!" exclaimed Will Lightmore, in astonishment.

"What, do you know them?"

"Simon Grandley, the carpenter, is my master," said Will Lightmore. "If he is your friend, fear not. To-morrow we will proceed to his house."

"It must be by stealth; we must escape in the middle of the night."

"Why not in the face of day?" said the bold apprentice.

The girl shuddered, as with horror.

"Oh, no, no!" she cried; "I could not stand that. I could not stand the terrible words he would use; no, no. I must go by stealth and in the night, or I should fear to go at all."

The young girl was evidently in earnest.

Yet she raised a difficulty.

In face of bolted doors, how could anything be done?

"Have you *any* friend in the house?" asked Will Lightmore.

"The landlady would aid me to escape simply because she is jealous of me. But she dare not."

"And is she the only one?"

Alice mused.

"No, no. There is Harriet—the servant next door. She assists Mistress Roper sometimes, and comes for that purpose to-morrow. She is a brave girl, and will aid me."

"Does she sleep here to-morrow night?" asked Will, excitedly.

He saw a way out of the difficulty.

"No; but she stops very late."

"That will do," said Will; "I can see my way clearly now, if others will but act with me. She must wait until I and the others who sleep in this corridor retire to rest; she must then slip out and open the door yonder. Then you and I must slip into the back yard of the inn, and remain there while she brings my horse out of the stable. Then we will get over the wall, and we will be with Simon Grandley, or rather with Mistress Grandley, in the twinkling of an eye."

Alice looked at him in bewilderment and joy.

"Oh! how shall I ever reward you!" she cried, clasping her hands.

"Easily," said the gallant apprentice. "Bid me good night, now; let me take one kiss of those cherry lips, and go and sleep in security, for to-morrow night you shall be free."

The young girl innocently and trustfully held her lips up to be kissed by Will Lightmore, then, bidding him good night, she glided away to her own room, leaving him to dream that he was the hero of some fairy tale.

CHAPTER VII.

THE ESCAPE.

WHEN Will Lightmore awoke on the following morning, it is not surprising that the events of the preceding evening seemed to him like a dream.

He soon woke, however, to the reality of them, for on quitting his room to proceed to breakfast, a pretty hand wafted to him a kiss from a pretty pair of lips.

Will went down after this with a pleasant fluttering at his heart.

Like all young fellows of his age, he was somewhat vain.

Or, rather, he was flattered by attentions from the other sex.

"She is very pretty," he thought; "and if it were not for Betty—but there, Betty's worth a hundred."

That breakfast was by no means a pleasant one.

Opposite to him in the little room was a man who kept a constant watch upon him.

Who he was he could not tell.

At any rate for a long time.

Then he fancied he knew the voice.

He determined to be satisfied.

"You seem to know my face, my friend," he said.

The other smiled.

"We have been fellow travellers," returned the other.

"When?"

"Last night."

"Then what mean you by your mysterious words to me at the door?"

The other shook his head.

"I know not what you mean," he said. "I parted with you, certainly, near the door, but whatever words were said to you were not spoken by me, but someone else. If I had wished to have spoken I could have done so on the road."

Although he said these words his manner was far from convincing.

Will Lightmore felt for an instant a strong desire to give him the lie.

But he resisted it.

The sweet, pleading face of Alice would come before him and stay his tongue.

No.

He must save her first.

It was not likely that this stranger had anything to do with her.

He, therefore, must be disposed of after.

"Ah! I must have been mistaken," said Will Lightmore.

Then came forth from his lips words which scarcely seemed framed by his own will.

"If I were not convinced beforehand of my mistake, I should say that you were last night disguised as a beggar, and that I met you on the road to London."

The stranger flushed, yet burst into a loud laugh.

"Bless me, sir!" he cried, "ye are given somewhat to romancing this morning."

"Indeed I but repeat my impressions," replied Will.

"They are grossly wrong, then," said the other, "and might lead you into serious trouble. As it is, I simply listen, am amused, and shall think no more of it."

Will was certain, however, that he had made some sort of discovery.

He felt sure that this man *was* a spy.

On the preceding night it had not once occurred to him that the beggar and the man who had ridden after him were the same person.

It was a peculiar intonation of the voice, and a peculiar look in the eyes, which had changed his opinion.

However, he was satisfied.

He had been already taught the necessity of caution.

Now there was a greater reason than ever for it.

One thing pleased him, however.

He saw that the stranger and Giles Roper were not friends.

In fact, the former seemed to avoid the landlord's eye.

That was most satisfactory.

It proved that there was no connivance between him and the villanous landlord of the Bull's Head.

Breakfast over, Will Lightmore strolled into the street.

He desired to proceed to Simon Grandley's workshop and have "a look round," to observe if anything was going on.

Under original circumstances he would not have wished to meet either Simon Grandley or Guy the Foundling at all.

Now, however, it was different.

If he required any aid in rescuing Alice, they were the persons to afford it to him.

So, after breakfast, he made his way towards the old workshop.

But no one was there.

The shop was closed, and all seemed deserted.

Will Lightmore now saw how well he had acted.

Both Simon Grandley and Guy the Foundling had allowed him to think before starting from the country house that nothing particular was to happen to interfere with the regular routine business.

It was evident now they had been deceiving him, Mrs. Grandley, and Minnie.

Angry as he was at not having been included in the carpenter's plans, he sought everywhere in the neighbourhood to discover if he had been seen by any of his friends.

Uselessly, however.

Someone had come in the middle of the night, removed some things from the house, and disappeared before any one observed who they were.

With this information Will had to be satisfied.

Had he been entirely dependent upon himself, he would, of course, have expended his time in finding out the whereabouts of his master.

For this reason he had come to London, but now Alice had given a new direction to his thoughts.

He had promised to befriend her—to save her from a fate worse than death—and he was determined to keep his promise.

To her, of course, was left the task of arranging with Harriet, the friendly servant girl in the neighbouring house.

She found it no difficult matter to do this.

The girl hated Giles Roper as cordially as ever Alice did.

Cordially, then, she joined in the plan.

She would come to the house, purposely be late with her work, and when the lodgers had retired to rest she would open the secret door.

Evening came at length.

Will Lightmore's heart beat high.

He felt as excited as if it was for himself or for some old friend that he was working.

He went early to bed.

He had a reason for this.

Giles Roper, as we have said, always locked the door of communication.

He would now be able to demand the reason.

He remained in his room therefore for some time without undressing himself.

Then he rose, and proceeding along the corridor, knocked loudly at the door.

For a few moments there was no answer.

Then the voice of Giles Roper was heard.

"Here, what's all this row about?"

Will Lightmore knocked loudly again at the door.

"Now I should think it was time to kick up a row when the door of the passage is closed upon a man at ten o'clock at night."

"It was a mistake," growled Giles; "we thought it was later. What is it you want?"

"I am ill," said Will; "I want spirits."

The door was immediately opened.

"We always keep this door locked," said Roper, in a maudlin voice, which showed he was drunk. "To-morrow night we will get you a different place to sleep in."

And, with these words, he led the way downstairs.

"Oh, as for that," said Will, who had no desire to be removed to another room, "I am comfortable enough; but I don't like being locked in. However, if it's your rule, I sha'n't complain of it."

The spirits, which had been the pretext of his making the disturbance at the door, were soon disposed of.

Then he turned suddenly to Giles Roper.

"That's a curious fashion you have of locking that door of a night," he said; "it's not many people could stand such a thing. Suppose for a moment there was a fire."

Giles was too drunk to be suspicious.

Besides, there seemed no cause why Will Lightmore should be asking these questions more than for the very reasons he gave.

So, instead of staving off Will's suspicions, Roper became communicative.

"You see," he said, in an undertone, "I've got a niece up there that's not quite right in her head, and, if she were to escape, she'd get me into no end of trouble. Her head's full of all kinds of strange stories. She's an heiress, I'm a villain; and, there——"

Giles Roper then drew himself up with a kind of solemnity.

He began to think he was saying too much.

"Well, Will," he added, "*you* don't want to hear all this. It's of no interest to you; so I'll show you the way up again if you like."

"There's no necessity," said Will Lightmore, carelessly, "I can find my way readily enough."

"Ah! but the door's locked; don't forget that," returned Giles, with a drunken laugh.

As soon as Will had re-entered the corridor he heard the key again turned in the lock.

His ruse, therefore, had failed.

However, there was still the young servant-maid to depend on.

It must be confessed that just one suspicion crossed the mind of the apprentice that he might be making a fool of himself.

The strange way in which Alice had made herself known; the manner in which she had entered his bedroom, and appealed to him, was enough in some minds to create an idea of madness.

But he dismissed it at once.

He would never have entertained it had he known the service he was doing to Guy the Foundling in befriending her.

Strange this!

For as yet Guy the Foundling knew not of her existence.

Her beauty, her innocence were enough, compared with the villany of Giles Roper, to show that there must be some right on her side.

The unworthy thought, therefore, being dismissed, he proceeded to her door, and gently knocked.

The young girl sprang out delightedly.

"Is the time come?" she said, while her eyes sparkled with pleasure.

"No; but all will be well, I hope," returned Will.

And then in a few words he told her of the result of his interview with Giles Roper.

The young girl shook her head.

"Ah!" she said, "you don't know him, or you

would never have tried to deceive him. He is a perfect demon of suspicion."

"Do you hope that your servant-girl friend will aid you ?"

"Yes, I am sure. Hark ! there is the key in the lock. See—see, the door opens. It is she."

Alice was right.

The head of a young girl was seen at the door-way, and Will at once sprang forward.

"Here is the key," she said. "Lock it on the inside, and then Roper won't suspect."

"And the horse ?"

"Will be ready, saddled, outside the garden wall, at one in the morning precisely."

"Brave girl!" thought Will Lightmore, as he locked the door. "Against such, a cowardly old villian like Giles Roper is powerless."

Eagerly they waited till the appointed time.

Every sound in the house fell with painful distinctness on their ears.

At last, however, they became fainter. Then they heard the shutters being put up, and the old tavern lapsed into quietude.

At one in the morning all there was as still as death.

As the clock struck Will Lightmore proceeded to Alice's room.

"Now," he said, as the young girl appeared, "the time is come."

The door was soon opened, and led now by the trembling and excited girl, Will descended the stairs, and proceeding through the bar of the tavern, entered the garden.

It was a farce to call it a garden, growing as it did down a street in the city leading to the foul banks of the river.

But, in spite of time, and neglect, and smoke, one or two trees grew towards its farther end, and over-shadowed the road.

This was a fortunate circumstance, as it enabled Will Lightmore to easily reach the top of the wall, and then draw Alice after him.

The young servant girl had kept her word to the letter.

There she stood with the horse ready saddled and bridled.

Jumping down, therefore, while Alice sat on the wall, Will soon received her in his arms, and drew her to the ground.

"Now, then," he said, as he prepared to lift her on the horse's back, "let us hope your troubles are over."

The word scarcely left his lips when the whole scene changed.

Three men rushed forward, sword in hand.

Their leader was readily recognised.

It was Giles Roper.

CHAPTER VIII.

THE FIGHT IN THE STREET.

"Curse you !" shouted the infuriated landlord, who was sobered by the discovery of Alice's attempted escape. "I'll have your life, you sneaking, under-handed villain."

And he dashed at Will Lightmore so quickly that the apprentice had no time to see that one of those who accompanied his assailant was Dick Hatherden.

The third, of course, was Ordin.

Will at once placed the rescued girl behind him, and, drawing his sword, sheltered himself as far as possible behind his horse, and resisted the attack.

The three, be it said, did not assail him at once.

Dick Hatherden and Giles Roper were the attacking party, while Ordin, acting under previous instructions, sought to seize and carry away towards the house the two girls.

He did not know one from the other, so he resolved to take both.

But he found more than his match.

Alice, though naturally weak and fragile, was roused now to unusual strength and courage by the fact of her escape so far from the tyranny and licentious advances of Giles Roper, and she had no conception of allowing herself to be captured again so easily, and dragged back to the old tavern.

Harriet, on the other hand, was a strong, stoutly made girl, with fine, compactly made arms and legs, used to hard work, and not at all inclined to suffer rude mauling at the hands of any man.

So when Ordin tried to seize her, he received such a stunning blow in the face that he fell reeling back, and taking advantage of his temporary discomfiture, the two girls darted away towards the end of the street.

Not that their object was to fly and leave their brave protector in the lurch.

They were far from being so ungrateful.

Their object was to go in search of assistance.

As it happened, they were just in time.

Hardly had they reached the end of the thoroughfare when the watch came in sight.

Eagerly and quickly the two girls told their story, and rather pleased than otherwise at being the momentary protectors of two such pretty damsels, the constables hurried to the scene of conflict.

Will Lightmore had by this time discovered the surprising fact that one of his assailants was none other than Dick Hatherden.

Dick, in fact, had arrived just as the Bull's Head was closing.

Being late in his room, which was in the rear of the premises, he saw the escape of Will and Alice over the wall, and he at once hastened to inform Ordin and Giles Roper.

The discovery of Dick by Will Lightmore caused a most desperate determination to arise in the mind of the latter.

He no longer sheltered himself behind his faithful steed.

No longer, in fact, acted upon the defensive.

Inspired with hatred and revenge by the sight of one whom he regarded as nothing but a thief and a murderer, he sprang forward, and attacked his assailants with fierce ardour.

For a moment they yielded.

Surprise made them do so.

They had anticipated an easy victory.

In fact, they had conceived it possible to disarm or disable Will Lightmore, and then force Alice to return to the house, within a few minutes.

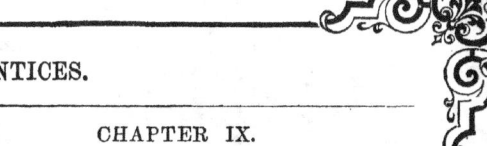

They never for a moment anticipated such a repulse as Ordin had suffered.

That one instant of yielding gave Will Lightmore the advantage.

He wounded Dick Hatherden by a rapid thrust, and then turned upon Ordin, who had not yet recovered complete possession of his senses, and, just as the watch came running up to the rescue, he had struck him senseless on the earth.

There remained now only Giles Roper and Dick Hatherden.

The former still fought angrily.

In fact, he thought that he had a case to make out.

The latter seemed wavering.

He soon wavered no longer.

"Seize that one!" shouted Will Lightmore to the watch; "he is a thief and a murderer!"

Dick waited for no more.

With one bound he dashed away, and before any one was able to follow him he had disappeared amid the shadows of the end of the street where it sloped down to the river-bank.

A portion of the watch surrounded Giles Roper, while some went in useless pursuit of Dick Hatherden.

Giles at once commenced a vehement attack on Will Lightmore, declaring that he had stolen his niece, and crying out very loudly that he would have the law upon him.

The watch, however, knew pretty well what kind of man they had to deal with.

They recognised Giles Roper, and, on hearing the declaration of Alice that she was not his niece, and that he had been detaining her by force, they advised him somewhat roughly to be off.

"At least tell me," said the baffled ruffian, turning to Will Lightmore ; "at least tell me where you are going to take the girl to."

Alice clung appealingly to Will.

"Oh, no, no!" she cried ; "do not tell him—do not tell him ! Let us hurry away, and never let me see his hateful face again !"

Will Lightmore deigned no reply to the old villain's request.

He simply turned to where his horse stood, and leaping into the saddle, he helped Alice, with the aid of Harriet, to mount behind him.

They were soon ready, and after Will Lightmore had shaken hands with the brave girl who had aided them, and Alice had embraced her, they started rapidly.

"Whither are you taking me ?" asked she, as he left London behind him and passed out into the green fields. "Not, surely, to Simon Grandley's house this way."

"Not to his town house, but to his wife and daughter in the country," said Will. "You will be doubly safe there."

And on they went, the apprentice feeling by the trembling of the girl's bosom as she clung to him how full of emotion she was at her escape.

CHAPTER IX.

HOW THE RIOTS BEGAN.

AND now, at length, we come to the period of the riots—a period only separated from our present time by ninety years.

We shall have to recount scenes happily unparalleled in any civilised city, save Paris, for many a long day.

The workings of the Protestant Association had hitherto been conducted in secret.

Except in Scotland.

The Act passed in 1778 in favour of the oppressed Roman Catholics did not extend to Scotland.

But, as the Catholics in that country were far more persecuted than their co-religionists in England, as they had great claims upon the Government for their legal, peaceable, and exemplary behaviour, it was most wisely determined to bring about their admission into the benefits of the repealing Act.

At once a cry of horror and alarm was raised.

Popery was about to be re-established.

A dissenting clergyman in Edinburgh took the lead in a fiery pamphlet, which was published at the expense of a society calling itself "A Society for the Propagation of Christian Knowledge."

This was printed by tens of thousands and distributed.

Branch societies were formed, and other pamphlets, hotter than the fires of Smithfield, were printed and distributed.

At length the popular feeling was fanned into a flame.

On the night of the 29th of January, 1779, copies of the following letter were dropped in the streets, lanes, and closes of Edinburgh :—

"MEN AND BRETHREN,

"Whoever shall find this letter will take it as a warning to meet at Leith Wynd on Wednesday next in the evening, to pull down that pillar of Popery erected there.

(Signed) "A PROTESTANT.

"P.S.—Please to read this carefully, keep it clean, and drop it somewhere else. For King and country. Unity."

The summons was obeyed.

At the time appointed all the rabble of that ancient city assembled at the "Pillar of Popery," which was the house of a Catholic priest, with a chapel attached to it.

They broke all the windows first.

Then they burst open the doors, and, in spite of magistrates and others, the furniture and everything in the place was demolished and the house set fire to.

Next morning a party of the same religionists repaired to another chapel, in what is called the Black Friars Wynd, and there broke everything to pieces, and destroyed or carried off a valuable collection of books.

This over, they paraded through the streets, breaking the windows of every house that harboured, or was supposed to harbour, a Papist or a friend to Papists.

THE RIVAL APPRENTICES

A TALE OF THE RIOTS OF 1780.

THE ATTACK ON NEWGATE.

In the evening the maddened rioters assembled to destroy the house of a Mr. Robertson. But, fortunately, a party of dragoons arrived in time to save his house and its contents.

A declaration that the English Parliament had abandoned the bill at length quelled the riots.

But even then Catholics had to skulk and hide themselves.

At length, as we have before intimated, Charles Fox and other liberal-minded men declared it quite time that there should be complete religious toleration.

This once more fanned the flame.

Eighty-five Christian corresponding societies affiliated to that of Edinburgh were formed in different parts of England, and Lord George Gordon (brother to the Duke of Gordon) was chief of the movement in London.

Lord George Gordon was at this time in his twenty-ninth year.

It has been the custom with some historians to call him a madman.

It was not so.

He was simply overloaded with religious zeal.

In fact, a fanatic.

He was eccentric in his habits, somewhat careless in his style of dress, but he was full of oratorical inspiration.

The Protestant Association chose him as their president, and fierce were the speeches which he made from his seat in Parliament against Sir George Saville, the original mover of the toleration bill.

"Every man in Scotland," he declared, "except a few Papists, were ripe for rebellion, and would die rather than submit."

He would come to the House of Commons, he declared, backed by 150,000 men, with a petition so long that it would reach from the Speaker's chair to the centre window of Whitehall, out of which Charles I. walked to his execution.

Aided by Jonas Barnsdake, Simon Grandley, and others, he canvassed the capital and the neighbourhood, and, as president and champion, advertised in the papers for signatures.

St. George's Fields was to be the chief starting place, and every man was to wear a blue cockade, and if less than 20,000 came, he declared he would not start.

And so far we come to the eve of the riots.

CHAPTER X.

THE RIOTS BEGIN.

On the appointed day—the 2nd of June—sixty thousand, or, according to some accounts, a hundred thousand petitioners and associators met in St. George's Fields, and ranged themselves in four separate bodies, one of which was entirely composed of Scotsmen.

After a stirring harangue from Lord George, the several columns struck off by different roads for Westminster, the largest one marching through Newington Butts and the Borough to London Bridge, and thence through the heart of the City, walking six abreast, and preceded by Jonas Barnsdake, carrying in his hand the anti-Popery petition, said to be signed by 120,000 names and marks.

As pre-arranged, the columns concentrated near the Houses of Parliament, and filled and blocked up all the streets and avenues leading to them.

It was an imposing sight.

Yet one thing marred all.

The honest fanatics were by this time joined by all the knaves and cut-purses in London, and while the members of the Protestant Association shouted "No Popery! No Popery!" the members of the fraternity of thieves picked pockets and did all they could to create a profitable riot.

As the Peers and the members of the House of Commons came down they were compelled to assume blue cockades and to join in the cry of "No Popery."

Many of them were not let off so easily.

The Archbishop of York and sundry bishops, the Duke of Northumberland and various temporal peers, were treated with great indignity.

The Bishop of Lichfield had his gown torn from his back.

The Bishop of Lincoln, after having his carriage demolished, fled into a house, and, being pursued, though only perhaps by his own fears, went out of the garret window (some say disguised as a woman) and over the roof into another house.

Others fared quite as badly.

And, yet, at this very moment, the Duke of Richmond, in the House of Lords, was introducing a motion for annual Parliaments, and something very like universal suffrage.

The rabble—roused to greater fury—then threatened to rush into the House.

But the doorkeepers shut them out.

A motion was made by Lord Townshend that the peers should issue forth in a body to rescue their brethren outside.

But thereupon there arose a debate whether the mace should go with them or not, and it was determined in the negative, for fear it should be broken or stolen.

Next their lordships indulged in accusations and recriminations.

The Opposition charged the Ministers with being the original cause of all the mischief by their scandalous and cowardly concessions to the No Popery rioters in Scotland.

And so—to make this necessary part of our story short—time was wasted in talk, and nothing done to quell the disturbance outside.

In the Commons the excitement was far greater.

For Lord George Gordon went in as a member to present the petition, while his followers outside the House tore the coats off those who had voted for the obnoxious bill.

A deafening roar was meanwhile kept up incessantly of—

"Repeal the Bill! Repeal!"

"No Popery!"

"No Popery!"

"Lord George Gordon!"

"Lord George!"

Some time passed by.

Lord George was still in the House.

This delay enraged them, and they began to thunder at the doors, and threatened to break them open.

Meanwhile, his own position was a truly perilous one.

Several of the members threatened him with instant death if the sanctity of the House should be thus violated.

In fact, Henry Herbert, afterwards Earl of Carnarvon, followed him closely about with that determination.

General Muir, brother to the Duke of Athol, who was a relation of Lord George, held his sword ready to pass it through him on the first irruption of the populace.

General Conway, too, declared he would die defending the doorway with his sword sooner than the rioters should enter.

Lord George behaved with much presence of mind.

Order being in some measure restored, Lord George moved for bringing up and immediately considering the petition, and this being seconded, it was proposed to put off the discussion for three days.

This gave rise to a fierce debate.

During the progress of this, Lord George Gordon went more than once into the lobby to harangue the mob, and encourage them to persevere, inasmuch as terror would be sure to induce the King and Ministers to grant the prayer of the petition.

He also told them who were speaking for and who against the petition.

When he returned into the House, Colonel Herbert took hold of his lordship.

"I imputed this conduct of yours," he said, "to madness before, but now I find there is more of malice than of madness in it."

"I regret," replied Lord George, "that one for whom I entertain so high a respect should have such an opinion of me."

"That may be," said the colonel; "but if you repeat your proceedings, I shall move for your commitment to Newgate."

Lord George upon this went no more into the lobby, but addressed the people from the top of the gallery stairs.

His denunciations of Burke and others roused the crowd to fury.

Destruction was threatened to all who opposed their will and the Protestant interest.

The House, however, was full of courage.

Undeterred by these menaces, they adopted the amendment, and only six voted with Lord George Gordon.

About nine in the evening, Mr. Addington, a magistrate, arrived in Palace Yard, with a party of horse and foot-guards, who were hissed and hooted by the mob.

Undismayed, however, he addressed them—told them he would send the soldiers away if they would promise to be quiet, and actually sent the cavalry off at a gallop.

The mob at this immediately gave him three cheers, and began to disperse.

As the members of the Protestant Association returned to their homes, one division of them passed by the chapel of the Bavarian Ambassador in Warwick Street, Golden Square, broke it open, destroyed what was in it, and set fire to it.

Another body did the same to the chapel of the Sardinian Ambassador in Lincoln's-Inn-Fields.

Then there was a lull.

All these matters went on quietly enough till Saturday night.

Then, when they had received their weekly pay, and had roused themselves to a pitch of unnatural excitement through drink, a mob assembled in Moorfields, and did some mischief to the poor Catholics in the neighbourhood.

On Sunday morning soldiers were sent to the spot, with special orders not to fire.

Their efforts to seize the ringleaders were badly seconded by the civic authorities, who, in fact, were either afraid of the tumult, or partook of the general fanaticism.

Catholic chapels, and several houses occupied by Catholics, were completely destroyed.

While the fanatics were demolishing altars and crosses, and the thieves were picking pockets, the more decent kind of zealots looked on.

The mob knew the military dared not fire without the command of the civil authority.

The soldiers, consequently—seeing that they were not going to be used effectually—did all they could to keep on good terms with the mob, who positively in some instances pulled their noses and spat in their faces!*

A single charge by one troop of horse and a few broken heads might at this stage of the business have scattered the people, and prevented further mischief.

But there seemed no one there to command.

On Monday morning, June 5th, three of the rioters who had been apprehended were committed to Newgate.

A party of the guards who escorted them to prison were pelted by the mob.

At an early hour, too, the house of Sir George Savile, in Leicester Fields, was attacked and stripped.

Part of the furniture was burned before the door; the more valuable portion was carried off by the thieves, and then fire was set to the building.

Meanwhile, some of the rioters went to the house of Lord George Gordon, in Welbeck Street, and regaled him with a bonfire made of things brought from Catholic houses in Moorfields.

Others went to Virginia Lane, Wapping, and others to Smithfield, and destroyed chapels, and committed other outrages.

Tradesmen who aided in the arrest of rioters experienced to the full the vindictiveness of the mob.

Their houses and shops were broken open and stripped, and such parts of their property as were not stolen were committed to the flames.

The whole of that night London was in the hands of an excited and maddened populace.

On Tuesday, however, two hundred members of the House of Commons had the courage to attend their parliamentary duties, notwithstanding the

---

* See "Knight's History of England," and "Fanaticism and Treason," a volume published at the time.

threats of the crowd through which they had to pass.

Westminster Hall and the avenues to the Houses were lined with military, horse and foot.

Some of the Lords also met.

Lord Sandwich, in attempting to reach the House, was dragged out of his carriage, which was broken to pieces, and was then almost torn to pieces himself.

Mr. Hyde, a justice of the peace, hastened to his rescue with a small party of light horse.

He found him at the end of Parliament-street, in the hands of the mob, and severely wounded on the head.

There was one resolute, insolent fellow with a bludgeon in his hand, who shouted—

"If I don't murder him now I'll murder him before I'm done with him."

This was none other than Ordin.

He had been in the hands of the justice more than once, and had now a chance of revenge.

Most of the rabble now had oaken sticks in their hands, as well as blue cockades in their hats.

Here and there floated a banner with the motto— "No Popery!"

These words, too, were chalked on the carriages of all the lords and members that went to the House.

Justice Hyde, having rescued Lord Sandwich, attempted to disperse the mob by riding among them, but the light horse did not even strike with the flats of their sabres.

As the crowd was giving way, Ordin hoisted a flag and shouted—

"To Hyde's house a-hoy!"

The cry was re-echoed by a hundred hoarse throats.

Like a living stream the crowd hurried off, and in an incredibly short space of time the house was pulled down.

CHAPTER XI.

THE RIOTS (CONTINUED).

LORD GEORGE GORDON, meanwhile, was at length alarmed at the effects of his own fanaticism.

He issued a handbill, consequently, disavowing, in the name of the Protestant Association, all desire to foment the riots, and then went down to the House of Commons with a blue cockade in his hat.

Colonel Herbert bade him take off that badge of sedition, and threatened to do it himself if he refused.

Lord Gordon instantly obeyed, and put the cockade in his pocket.

But, though Lord George might disavow participation or a wish to foment the rioting, he had already done too much towards it.

His ill-directed zeal had roused a terrible conflagration.

The decent part of the members of the Protestant Association were wringing their hands at the mischief they had caused, and were doing all they could to repress the mob.

Jonas Barnsdake and Simon Grandley and their friends, however, were nowhere now.

They hated themselves almost for being part of such a disorderly scene.

But they were powerless now to avert the tumult.

The worst spirits among the worst of London's populace were stirred up to deeds of villany.

And, as may be imagined, among those who incited them to greater ruffianism than others were Dick Hatherden and his gang.

Alexis Rainsford, strange to say, had made no appearance in the matter.

Nor as yet had the Catholics offered any combined resistance to the fury of the mob.

They thought probably that the Protestants were doing sufficient injury to their own cause.

Dick Hatherden, meanwhile, who had only joined either side from the love of gain, had collected round him as villanous a gang as could be well imagined.

Among these were Ordin and Giles Roper, together with a number of blear-eyed ragged ruffians, who seemed to have been raked together from all the hells in the metropolis.

To them the work which Dick Hatherden had proposed was, indeed, congenial.

It was that they should march to Newgate, and release their brother rioters.

At the mere whisper of such a daring deed shouts of joy arose.

Dick Hatherden was elevated to a position on a tub, and by the expiring light of a bonfire harangued the multitude.

It was a picturesque scene this, as the flickering flames fell on the swarthy, excited faces of thousands, and Dick felt the full influence of the scene.

He was not deficient in a rude kind of eloquence.

He had attained, moreover, almost the pinnacle of his ambition.

He had triumphed over his enemies and the law.

Simon Grandley and his Protestants had merely formed the pretext.

Mob law now held sway, and *he* was the acknowledged leader of thousands.

No wonder then was it that he launched forth in fiery language.

Shouts of approval rent the air.

Hats were waved; sticks, knives, crowbars, huge hammers were brandished.

Yells were raised for the signal to advance.

Dick Hatherden kept them there till he had worked them up to fever heat.

Then theatrically shouting out, and waving his hat aloft, he sprang from his rostrum, and amid deafening cheers rushed to the front.

In the dusk of that memorable evening of June 6th, the immense multitude made its way down Holborn to Newgate.

They halted in a huge, tumultuous mass in front of the prison.

Then Dick Hatherden and his friends advanced to the door and knocked loudly.

Of course, they did not anticipate that it would be opened.

But, at any rate, it would bring some one to the

windows, and they hoped that the sight of the vile, drunken, madly impassioned multitude would have the effect of intimidating them.

It was not so, as it proved.

When the loud knocking was heard at the gate, Mr. Akerman, the keeper, put his head out of a window above the portal.

"What want you, gentlemen?" he cried.

"Our friends and comrades," exclaimed Dick Hatherden. "Release them at once!"

And the cry was re-echoed wildly through the place.

"Give us our friends!"

"Quick—release them!"

But they had miscalculated.

Akerman was not a man to be intimidated.

"No—no!" he cried, firmly. "They are in my charge, and there they shall remain till they are torn from me!"

"Take that, then!" cried Dick Hatherden.

And drawing a pistol from his belt, he fired at the keeper, who, having fortunately seen the movement of his hand, drew in his head just as the shot sped, and thus saved himself.

Yells of execration rent the air, and the window was crashed to.

"Pull it down!"

"Have him out and hang him!"

"Burn the place about his ears!"

Not only cries, however, told the temper of the mob.

Sledge hammers, pickaxes, crowbars, were brought into use; and some were so eager to have a share in the attack that they madly struck at the stone walls with their clubs.

A house near at hand happened to be undergoing repairs, and in an incredibly short space of time some of the crowd had seized the loose timbers lying about, and had brought them to bear as battering rams against the iron-bound door.

It must not be supposed that the paid guardians of the prison remained idle during all this commotion.

From every window and barred loophole, and even from the summit of the building, shots were fired, and stones and other missiles flung down, upon the excited crowd below.

Directly the news had arrived at the jail that the rioters were marching towards it, due precautions had been taken to prevent any outbreak among the prisoners.

They had at once been placed in the cells and doubly secured with chains.

Arrangements in those days, however, were far different to what they are now, and the news soon spread rapidly amongst the prisoners that the rioters were there to release them.

There were more than three hundred prisoners in the gaol, four of whom (among them being Bill Hazard and The Owl) were under sentence of death, and ordered for execution on the following Thursday.

The shouts and yells of these men could be heard far above the noise of the rabble without.

It was very slow work attacking an immense building formed of stone and iron, and the mob soon got weary of it.

Dick Hatherden and his immediate companions appeared suddenly with firebrands and other combustibles, which they flung into the keeper's dwelling-house.

Their example was soon followed by the crowd, who, amidst cheers and shouts, fed the rapidly spreading flames.

The yelling of the mob without the prison was now joined by the maddening cries of the felons within, who were agitated by the hope of escape and liberty, and the dread, moreover, of being burnt to death.

The fire soon spread from the keeper's house to the chapel, and from this to some of the doors and passages leading to the wards and cells.

The crowd now rushed in, and by the ready way in which they discovered the different parts of the prison, they showed that they were no strangers to it.

Their activity was wonderful.

They dragged the prisoners out by the hair of their heads, by their legs or arms, or any part they could catch hold of, and not one of the hundreds confined was killed, or even injured.

The conflagration, however, was rapid and tremendous.

After the lapse of a few hours nothing was left of the strongest prison in England, which had been rebuilt at a cost of a hundred and forty thousand pounds, but a few bare stone walls, too massive to be destroyed by fire.

Dick Hatherden and Ordin were the ones who rushed first into the prison, and they were not long in discovering the cell in which the Owl and Bill Hazard were confined.

They were shrieking and yelling at one another with all their might, every now and then mingling the most hideous curses with their cries.

They seemed struck dumb when they beheld the face of Dick Hatherden amidst the glow of the ruddy flames.

"You may well be silent," cried Dick; "the last time that you saw me you were cursing me for escaping. I promised to come back to release you, and here I am to do it."

"Then, curse you, be quick and do what you are going to do," cried Bill Hazard, "for I don't want to run the risk of being burnt alive while I am chained up to the wall."

A few moments more, and The Owl and his companions, together with the rest of the prisoners, had passed out of the gaol and mingled with the crowd.

By these they were welcomed, murderers and all, as if they were saints, hoisted on the shoulders of the people, and treated to unlimited drink.

Having succeeded so well in destroying the prison at Newgate, the mob thought they would let a few more villains out on society.

They proceeded, accordingly, to the new prison at Clerkenwell, which they broke open, and set free all the felons and other prisoners.

The decent members of the Protestant Association were by this time, as I have said, fairly wringing their hands at the mischief caused by their mistaken zeal.

The rioters were now composed of the lowest rabble in London and its populous neighbourhood, who cared more for a pot of beer or a glass of gin than for the whole Protestant interest.

But when these fellows were joined by all the highwaymen and footpads, cutpurses and professional housebreakers, their excesses became far more frightful.

The felons first proceeded to the house of Sir John Fielding, the police magistrate, who had committed many of them to the cells from which they had just escaped, and destroyed or stole furniture, books, papers, and everything in it.

At about twelve o'clock at night, another desperate gang attacked the house of Lord Mansfield, the Lord Chief Justice, in Bloomsbury-square.

Having broken open the doors and windows, they flung the superb furniture into the street, and kindled fires to destroy it.

They then went to his library and destroyed thousands of volumes, together with many valuable manuscripts, papers, and deeds.

The rich wearing apparel and splendid pictures they wantonly burnt.

As for the wine in the cellars, they drank till they were nearly raving mad.

Lord and Lady Mansfield had no means of defending themselves against such a mob of dissolute maniacs.

They made their escape, therefore, through a back door a few minutes before the rioters broke in, and were admitted by a gentleman to his house in Lincoln's Inn.

On this gentleman's return to Bloomsbury Square, and when nearly all the mischief had been done, he found a detachment of foot soldiers had arrived.

"Thank Heaven, they have come at last!" he murmured, as he made his way through the crowd.

"Your congratulation is premature," said the voice of a man near him.

He turned hastily, expecting to see a sneering smile on the face of the speaker.

It was not so.

He saw the face of an earnest man of middle age, whose expression was one of sorrow at what was going forward.

It was none other than Simon Grandley who had spoken.

"Why am I premature?" asked the gentleman.

"You will see that if you ask the commander of the men," replied Simon Grandley.

"I will do so at once," said the gentleman, who, being an intimate friend of the Lord Chief Justice, considered himself naturally in a position to act with a little authority.

Elbowing his way to the side of the officer in command, he accordingly urged him to cause his men to enter the house.

The reply was that the magistrates had all fled, and that consequently it was quite impossible for the military to act.

It was, in fact, some hours after this before a magistrate could be found, and during the time that was thus lost the fury of the mob was increased to such a pitch by the liquor they had drunk, that when the soldiers at length fired, even the sight of

their companions falling dead beside them produced little or no effect.[*]

CHAPTER XII.
STILL MORE HORROR.

On the following day—Wednesday the 7th of June—the scenes were still more dreadful.

All the shops were shut, and at most of the houses bits of blue silk, by way of flags, were hung out, and the words "No Popery" chalked on the doors and window-shutters, with the view of deprecating the fury of the mob, who now, however, plundered and ill-treated all classes, only giving the Catholics the preference.

Ruffians, armed with iron bars torn from the railings in front of Lord Mansfield's house, went through the town extorting money from all they met, and shouting—

"No Popery!"

One ruffian in particular—none other than Bill Hazard—was mounted on horseback, and refused to take anything but gold.

At Caen Wood, Highgate, Lord Mansfield had a country house, and towards this the drunken rabble were proceeding, when they were met by another crowd coming another way.

The Protestants, who had innocently enough been the cause of delivering London over to a rabble rout, had at length roused themselves to action.

The riot they had raised they had resolved to assist in quelling.

During the previous night large meetings had been held in the haunts where the secret conclaves had been held before.

The meetings which had previously to this taken place in so stealthy a manner were now held publicly.

Had it been otherwise, and had traitors been at work, it would have resulted to all intents and purposes in the same manner.

In fact, no one would have troubled himself to interfere with them.

However, as it was, they had in view now the

---

[*] "The scene here altogether appears to have been terrific in the extreme. The violence and ferocity of the ruffians—armed with sledge hammers and other instruments of destruction—who burst into the house; the savage shouts of the surrounding multitude; the wholesale desolation; the row of bonfires playing in the street, heaped with the contents of the sacked mansion—with splendid furniture, books, pictures, and manuscripts, the loss of which was irreparable; the drunken wretches staggering over each other, or rolling on the ground; the pealing of the musketry, followed the next instant by the screams of the wounded and the dying and the roar of vengeance from ten thousand throats; soon after this, the fires lighted in every room; and finally, the flames rushing upwards from windows and roofs in one magnificent conflagration—all these horrors may well be conceived to have formed a picture, or, rather, a succession of pictures, which, thus exhibited under the dark sky of midnight, would seem hardly of this world. The inhabitants thronged from every part of the town to the spot; and during this night, indeed, all London was awake, the houses in many parts being lighted up as in a general illumination."—We quote this from "Sketches of Popular Tumults Illustrative of the Evils of Social Ignorance." London. 1887.

pulling down of the unwieldy monster they had stirred into action, and were practically, therefore, aiding a timid and wavering Government.

Among those engaged in this laudable work there were none more ready or eager than Simon Grandley and Jonas Barnsdake.

They had awakened from their dream.

They saw now, in fact, their folly.

Not that they disapproved of the agitation for the Protestant cause.

But saw in how different a style it should have been done.

Measures were at once concerted in order, as far as possible, to correct the mischief.

London was, in fact, in a state of anarchy and revolution.

No man's life was safe, no woman's honour secure.

What they had to do, therefore, was to risk their lives in defence of the innocent people who were in greatest danger.

Four bands of determined men were soon formed, and the command of one was assigned to Simon Grandley and Guy the Foundling.

This was the party that met the rioters as they went singing, shouting, and swearing, towards Lord Mansfield's house at Highgate.

Dick Hatherden, The Owl, and Bill Hazard were on the opposite side, and as the Protestants issued hurriedly and in good array from the side lanes, these three—excited almost to madness by excess of drink—advanced insolently to the front.

"What want you, my friends?" cried Dick, with a swagger; "are you bound upon the same errand as ourselves? We are on our road to my Lord Mansfield's house, prepared to attack and sack it, as we did that in Bloomsbury-square."

Simon Grandley stepped forward and confronted him suddenly.

"Dick Hatherden!" he exclaimed, in a voice of utter surprise.

"Aye, what then, old master?" said Dick, swaying his sword to and fro.

"What then? Why, what do you here?"

The villanous apprentice burst into a loud laugh.

"Ha! ha!" he cried; "what do I here? Rather, say I, what do *you* here? What does my old friend, Guy the Foundling, here? There, stand aside, old man!" he added, with a scowl. "I wish you no harm, and have, indeed, no time now for private quarrels. But I am leader here, and must beg you will not attempt to bar our progress."

"Dick Hatherden," said Simon Grandley, solemnly, "I and my men here are come to turn the tide of this most infamous rabble back upon London, and to aid in protecting peaceable people. Retire, therefore, or blood will be shed."

Dick laughed brutally.

Then he waved his sword aloft, turning towards his men.

"Come on, my friends," he shouted; "here are some Catholics to oppose us!"

The mob never waited to discover the truth of these words.

They only took it as a double reason for more riot.

"Down with them!"

"No Popery!"

"Cut them down!"

And, without allowing Simon Grandley the slightest chance of explaining the falsehood uttered by their leader, the rabble dashed upon the Protestant host.

In an instant Simon Grandley found himself engaged with Bill Hazard, while Dick Hatherden (in spite of his declaration that he had no time to think of private quarrels) singled out Guy the Foundling.

The contest was a most severe one.

On both sides there was an excess of resolution and anger.

The friends of Simon Grandley looked upon their foes as a rabble that was for wilful evil creating this disturbance in the heart of a peaceful community, and as the cause, too, why the Protestant Association had been brought into such disrepute.

On the other hand, the rioters were disgusted at the unexpected interruption to their march, which might so delay them as to give time to the authorities to stop their intended raid upon Lord Mansfield's house.

Loud cries resounded on all sides, and on each side the utmost bravery was shown.

In the midst of such a press of opposing foemen it was difficult, as may be imagined, for any set of combatants to keep long together.

Nevertheless, Dick Hatherden and Bill Hazard kept up their attack upon Simon Grandley and Guy the Foundling.

Guy and Dick—old enemies met once more—fought with more than their former ardour.

Dick had never been a coward.

Nor had he been at any time at all an indifferent swordsman.

For a length of time now, however, he had had a wide experience.

Villain as he was, he was familiar with scenes of bloodshed; and the many adventures which he had passed through of all kinds had made him an excellent swordsman.

Guy was also an adept with his weapon, and a contest, therefore, of no ordinary interest ensued between them.

In the peculiar condition of affairs it was, of course, impossible for anyone to pause and observe them.

Otherwise it would have been an interesting sight to have watched their movements.

Right at length began to prevail.

Dick Hatherden found himself **wounded**, and began to give ground.

He no sooner saw this than he uttered at the top of his voice a shrill cry.

The cry of a night bird.

In an instant The Owl responded.

Dashing down those who opposed his progress, the huge ruffian made his way to Dick Hatherden's side.

He looked upon it as his duty to protect him.

He had kept his word and saved his life and the life of Bill Hazard, and the two villains were bound by their peculiar code of honour to risk their lives in future for him.

Things looked serious now for Guy the Foundling.

For he had to encounter them both at once.

Simon Grandley saw what was going on.

But though his heart leaped excitedly he could do nothing.

The unequal combat, however, did not last for long.

Leaping, struggling, out of the crowd came a form which both Guy the Foundling and the carpenter well knew.

That of Will Lightmore.

He was bronzed with constant exposure to all weathers during the last few days, and a sword cut hardly healed on his forehead told of recent strife.

There was no time for the expression of surprise at this moment.

Will, whirling his sword round his head, attacked The Owl fiercely.

With curses the ruffian left off his attack upon Guy the Foundling, and turned to face his new and unfatigued antagonist.

He found it no light work.

Animated by a resolution to conquer, the friends of Simon Grandley watched eagerly the movements of the leaders, and seeing Dick and his immediate companions yielding, they pressed on still more fiercely.

But the crowd at the back of Dick Hatherden was by far the greatest.

They were excited by drink. They were utterly reckless of consequences; and those in the extreme rear pressed on those in front, notwithstanding the endeavours of some to struggle behind. ·

There was every probability, therefore, that sheer despair would be the means of turning the tide in favour of the rabble, when suddenly there was heard the sound of approaching horsemen.

"Retreat, my friends," shouted Will Lightmore, as he ran his sword clean through the breast of The Owl; "the dragoons are here to aid us!"

There was no time to ask what he meant.

The Protestants, however, at once made a retrograde movement of a few yards, and then, as they left open the mouth of the lane through which they had come upon the scene of action, a large body of cavalry came dashing up, and charged upon the rioters.

They acted with all moderation, wheeling round and returning after they had trampled down the first row.

Then the commander shouted to them in a loud voice to disperse, and ordered his men to unsling their short carbines and present.

This had at once the desired effect.

An English mob, even with right on its side, is never equal to an encounter with soldiers."

In vain, therefore, Dick Hatherden stormed and cursed at them.

In vain he and Bill Hazard raised the dead body of The Owl on their shoulders, and invoked in their hearts the spirit of vengeance.

These men, partially sobered by their march, by the recent fight, and by the formidable aspect of the troops, came suddenly to the recollection that they had *not* got right on their side.

They had not only the fear of being seized upon and hurried away as rioters.

They had the prospect of being seized as malefactors.

Consequently, none of Dick Hatherden's inflammatory speeches were heeded in the least.

In fact, he soon saw the prudence of hurrying away himself, and with the body of The Owl in their midst, the huge multitude went hurrying back towards London, while the dragoons followed with carbines unslung, ready at any moment to pour in a deadly volley, should the rioters show any disposition to rally, or attempt any further depredations on their way.

Dick Hatherden showed his prudence in causing to be carried off the field such an apparently useless piece of lumber as the body of The Owl.

It was not from any feeling of old friendship that he acted.

It was purely because he did not desire him to be recognized.

Had he been so, it might have aroused in the minds of the authorities an anxious desire to seek for his friends, whereas in the present turmoil and confusion they were forgotten.

CHAPTER XIII.

THE BITTEREST SCENE OF ALL.

MEANWHILE the rioting had not ceased in London itself.

The King's Bench prison, the new gaol, the Borough Clink, the Surrey Bridewell were all burned during the day.

Not a prison, in fact, was left in London but the Poultry, Compter, and the Fleet, which shared the same fate in the night.

The Bank of England offered naturally a tempting bait to such a set of ruthless and scurvy vagabonds.

Two attempts were made upon it, but the assailants were repulsed by a strong body of soldiers, who had now orders to use thier arms, and at this point killed and wounded a great many.

The Mansion-House, the British Museum, the Royal Exchange, and the Tower, were all destined to destruction, and written lists were circulated through the mob.

Mob law, however, was not destined to reign long.

Things had begun to assume a slightly different aspect.

Counting regulars and militia, there were now in all in London 25,000 men under arms.

The King, too, had given orders for the military to act where necessary, in spite of the absence of magistrates.

Some of the first to act were a party of militia, who had marched twenty-five miles during the heat of the day.

It was in Holborn, towards which these soldiers directed their steps, that one of the most awful scenes in the whole riots occurred.

THE RIVAL APPRENTICES

A TALE OF THE RIOTS OF 1780.

A TRAITOR'S DEATH.

On Holborn Bridge stood the house of a Mr. Langdale, a distiller of great wealth.

Being a Catholic, of course there was an excuse for the infuriated mob, who were drunk with excitement and success, and thirsting for drink, and in the dusk of the evening they began surrounding the house.

Mr. Langdale resided in the front part of the premises, and a large assemblage of ladies and gentlemen were gathered in the spacious drawing-rooms.

All present were Catholics, who had been invited there by Mr. Langdale for protection, some of their number being unfortunate persons who had been turned out of their homes.

To distract the minds of his disturbed and anxious guests, Mr. Langdale had given directions for some music to strike up, when a loud roar without was heard.

Then a pistol-shot came crashing through a window-pane.

This foolish act of a maddened rioter probably saved many lives.

Mr. Langdale and his friends rushed to the window and gazed out upon the night.

A sight met their eyes which infuriated the gentlemen, and raised a chilling feeling of horror in the fair breasts of the women.

Across the street, crowding up even against the opposite houses, was one seething mass of infuriate humanity.

Not, perhaps, so terribly bloodthirsty as those throngs of demons who gathered in the streets of Paris in the days of the great revolution, some twelve years after; but still there were quite enough elements of horror and anticipatory strife.

Women, half mad, danced grotesque dances and brandished knives.

Men sang, and swore, and shouted to intimidate their enemies, before commencing their actual work of villanous outrage.

The old cries were raised again—

"No Popery!"

"Down with the Catholics!"

"String them up to the lamps!"

And—worse luck for the infatuated man who had begun all—

"Lord George Gordon for ever!"

Mr. Langdale drew his guests from the window to the rear of the room.

The men hurriedly consulted together.

The women clustered round them with clasped hands and eyes, from which tears fell upon their heaving bosoms.

What was to be done?

Well might that question be asked.

They were but a handful as it were.

What could they do against so many?

"We must escape by the back," said Mr. Langdale, after a moment's consultation, "and leave them to do as they please with my house. I see no help for it."

But this was not to be.

The rioters had resolved, as I have said, upon surrounding the place, and so not leaving the inmates the slightest chance of escape.

They knew well that in bursting into such a place they would have feast enough of spirits.

When they had finished one feast they had resolved to have a feast of blood.

Mr. Langdale and his friends had scarcely decided upon making their way out of the rear of the premises, when several of the servants rushed unsummoned into the room.

"The rioters! the rioters!" they cried.

"Well, well! what of them?" exclaimed Mr. Langdale. "Have you come here to warn us now that we have seen them from the window?"

He said this severely.

He had had reasons before this to dilate upon their laziness.

He knew well that while his guests had been earnestly talking upstairs they had been carousing in the kitchen.

The old butler—who was really a well meaning man, although in very truth he was a little too much addicted to the pleasures of the bottle—advanced towards his master.

His air was full of respect, and his pale face told of his trouble.

"Sir," he said, "we knew of the rioters being here as soon as you."

"Then why did you remain below, Symons?"

"In the first place, sir, you did not summon us; and in the second place, we were trying to close up the rear of the premises."

"Why so?"

"The place is surrounded on all sides, sir," replied Symons. "They are swarming up to the doors of the distillery."

Mr. Langdale turned very pale, and his heart beat violently.

But he did not desire to alarm his guests, more especially the women.

Once set them into a state of alarm, and all chance of the men making themselves useful is gone.

"Well, gentlemen," he said, "I don't know what to propose now."

"Why so?" asked his wife, clinging to him eagerly.

"Why, you see, these fellows are all round the place, and it won't be safe to try and get out into the back streets. We must, I suppose, go up to the roof and escape to the next houses."

"But why talk of escape at all?" asked one of the gentlemen.

Mr. Langdale raised his hand and pointed towards the window through which the pistol shot had come.

"Do you wish to remain?" said he. "For my part, I intend to save my wife and these ladies. When we have done that, you can join me if you please in firing upon the ruffians from the roof."

Mr. Langdale—considering that the property which the mad rioters were threatening with destruction was worth more than one hundred thousand pounds—was very cool and collected.

In a few minutes he had led the way up towards the roof, from which the ladies, even in their anxiety to fly, could not help looking down in wonder at the excited crowd below.

I have said that all was at present quiet.

I mean, of course, comparatively quiet.

There was, of course, the same yelling and shouting and mad dancing.

But that was all.

There seemed not the slightest preparation for an attack.

"Perhaps, after all," said Mrs. Langdale, "you have made a mistake; these men seem congregated round yonder tavern. They may be only halting on their road elsewhere."

Mr. Langdale shook his head.

"No, no, my dear," he answered; "if I were anything but a distiller, I might believe it, but they are mad for drink, and will have it; see, see, am I not right? They are beginning already."

He was right.

During the apparent lull those among the crowd who were less under the influence of drink had brought from a neighbouring building some huge pieces of timber, as they had done at Newgate, to form battering rams for the destruction of the door.

However, in this instance they had gone more systematically to work.

They had balanced one immense beam between three uprights by means of strong ropes, so with comparatively little force it could be sent with tremendous effect into the very centre of the house door.

It was this engine of destruction which Mr. Langdale had seen on the roof of his house.

The sight of it told him at once how little mercy he had to expect from the mob.

Had they shouted and yelled, and demanded entrance, he might have had something to hope.

But now it was evident that cold-blooded murder was all they intended.

Just as Mr. Langdale had succeeded in leading his guests to the roof of the adjoining house, the first assault was made upon the door.

And with the assault rose again the cries into the air—

"Out with him!"

"No Popery!"

"Pull down the house about his ears."

"Lord George for ever!"

"Curse the vagabonds," cried Mr. Langdale; "they care not whether we are Catholics or Protestants. If I were a Protestant they would hate me all the more for taking away their excuse for attacking me. Come, let us be quick; there is no time to be lost."

In such circumstances as these there was no room for ceremony.

On reaching the roof of the second house they found a skylight, and without a moment's delay broke it open.

Of course there was an instant rush to the spot of all the inmates to resent the unexpected attack upon the premises.

But a few words explained all.

It mattered not whether they were Catholics or Protestants.

One and all sympathised with them when opposed to such a devilish rabble as then filled the streets.

The women having been safely disposed of, and the way being left open for the men when they chose to return, Mr. Langdale and his friends made their way back to the distillery.

In the upper rooms of his house he had a goodly stock of arms.

With these it was his intention to fire upon the mob below, and endeavour to intimidate them, as well as attract the attention of the authorities.

I have said before that it was the design of the rioters to surround the place.

This they could not do effectually.

They could surround the basement of the building, because an immense archway ran from Holborn to the rear of the premises.

But, of course, the house was continued over this archway, and consequently the house was joined to the next one.

In their mad and venomous fury the crowd did not perceive this, and, consequently, Mr. Langdale was not suspected of having the means of escape so ready.

At any time, however, when the battle waged too high, he and his friends could retire.

Poor satisfaction this!

Poor, indeed, when retiring meant the loss to him of property worth, as I have said, over a hundred thousand pounds.

As soon as Langdale and his friends had armed themselves they leaned over the parapet of the house, and fired a volley upon the crowd, who were now assaulting the house with double fury.

The men servants, after the first alarm, had hidden themselves behind doors and in dark corners, ready at the first opportunity to mingle with the crowd when it burst in, and so effect their escape.

With the exception of the old butler, whom I have before mentioned.

He was an old servant of the family, and was besides a man of pluck and energy.

Finding, therefore that all attempts at defending the basement story were useless, he ascended to the roof and joined his master.

"Mr. Langdale," he said, "if you take my advice, you will cease firing upon the mob."

"Why?" cried his master, almost angrily.

He imagined that the man was influenced by fear.

"Simply for this reason," replied the old domestic; "you are unable now to injure those who are foremost in the attack. You cannot fire point-blank downwards, and so you only reach those who are in the centre of the crowd."

"What, then, do you propose?" said Mr. Langdale.

"That we should all descend on to the second floor, break up the heavier articles of furniture, and drop them upon the people below."

The plan was eagerly adopted.

Four of the gentlemen were posted upon the balcony with muskets to cover the proceedings of the others, while Mr. Langdale and six assistants began breaking up the chairs and tables.

If the plan suggested by the butler had been adopted earlier, there is no doubt that such diversion would have been caused by the mob that considerable delay would have been occasioned in the formation of the battering ram we have before described.

Now, however, too much progress had been made.

Just as a heavy sideboard, hurled over the balcony with the united strength of all Langdale's friends, had fallen upon and crushed half a dozen of the maddened crowd, two ominous crashes were heard.

Mr. Langdale knew well what they meant.

They told him as plainly as words could have spoken that all efforts were in vain—that he must yield to what seemed an inevitable fate—that he must, in fact, quit his house without any further attempt of protecting it, and leave the whole of a splendid property in the hands of a set of ungovernable madmen.

"Come, my friends," he said; "I will submit you to no further danger. We can defend the place no longer, and must fly."

Within a few moments the house of Mr. Langdale was deserted, while around the building swarmed the maddened beings who risked their lives for drink.

It was not long before the stores of spirits were broken into.

Barrels were staved in, and the liquor drank out of the hats or the hands of the people.

Hogsheads of spirits were rolled out into the street, and there burst, the men and women, and even children, kneeling down and drinking it out of the gutters.

At first it was merely a drunken orgie.

It soon became worse.

The place, of course, was involved in perfect darkness, and in order to see their way it was necessary for the rioters to carry flambeaux.

As they became insensible with the strong liquor, they, of course, became careless, and dropped the flaming brands.

Some fell where there was nothing to ignite, or where they were soon trampled under foot.

But it was not so with others.

They fell hissing into the streams of spirits which now ran everywhere, and a hideous scene of horror resulted.

Lurid flames shot upwards to the sky.

Long tongues of fire rushed from room to room; barrels burst with terrific explosions, causing death and destruction everywhere around.

Shrieks of agony rent the air.

But these were from the wounded, and those who, at any rate, resisted.

There were many who resisted not at all.

They were so thoroughly, in fact, soaked in drink that all resistance was utterly impossible.

And so some groaned and gave up the ghost.

Others did not feel the pain.

For a good reason.

They were dead before the flames touched them. Dead simply with the drink!

The fire soon told upon the building.

The men, maddened as they were by strong spirit, wanted still more, and continued to roll the barrels out into the street.

But they were soon stopped at it.

The flames ran along the ground and drove them from the building, and King Fire had it all to himself.

It was a grand yet awful sight.

Tongues of flame were rushing out of windows and licking along the walls.

Great beams went swaying to and fro in fiery tangles.

Ceilings kept falling in, with myriads of red sparks and flakes floating through the hot air.

Sparks and flakes that floated down upon the shouting, yelling people like a fall of red snow.

In the midst of this fearful uproar—this scene, fit only to represent a scene from hell itself, where men and women were lying in a flaming gutter—a running stream of fire—men dead and charred, or cursing with their last breath—women either dead, or drinking in a last draught of spirit, with tiny babes burnt to cinders on their breasts; people still dancing elsewhere, and yelling, singing, and blaspheming—in the midst of this there was a shout that the soldiers were coming.

But who cared?

The news only produced a kind of jibbering laughter.

Let the soldiers come!

Let the soldiers fire!

Let them kill when they pleased!

What mattered it!

They would die drinking!

To remonstrate with such a set would have been simply absurd.

Many would not hear it.

The others were too excited to care.

So the stern order was given—

"Fire!"

The troops at once obeyed.

It was cruel work, truly—this firing against Englishmen.

But how could they regard such a mob as fellow-creatures.

They were more like infuriated demons than human beings.

The first volley had no effect, save to kill and wound many.

The mad riot went on as before!

Again the order was given—

"Fire!"

This time with more effect.

Twenty of the least intoxicated of the rabble fell dead or in agony on the ground.

This brought the people to their senses, and a huddling together began.

This might have meant resistance.

Whatever it meant, however, it was not given time to become formidable.

"Charge!" shouted the commanding officer.

And with their glittering bayonets the compact line of redcoats dashed in upon the mob.

It was all over now.

Those of the rioters who could escape fled in all directions from the scene.

Those who lay drunk and incapable of moving were left to sleep off their horrid sleep, while the military watched the place till morning.

There was no use in attempting to stay the progress of the flames now.

All was destroyed.

The fire, in fact, mounted into the air like the eruption of a volcano.

Six and thirty great fires were blazing in different quarters of the town, and nothing but the serenity of the night saved the whole of London from destruction.

In streets where there were no fires, persons were seen hurriedly removing their goods and effects at midnight.

Universal panic prevailed.

No man knew, indeed, how long the merciful wind would be still, or to what point the mob would next carry their fury.

At one moment was heard the tremendous shouting of the rabble.

At the next instant the dreadful report of musketry firing in platoons.

Everything seemed, indeed, to threaten anarchy and desolation.

Sleep or rest were things not thought of.

The streets everywhere swarmed with people, and uproar, confusion, and terror reigned in every part.

Some of the respectable inhabitants, however, as I have before shown, had recovered from their strange consternation, and formed themselves into armed associations which acted with the regular troops and militia.

In some instances the mob had obtained arms, and the fire of the troops was returned.

But nowhere was anything like a resolute resistance made.

A detachment of the Guards soon beat them from Blackfriars Bridge, where they had set fire to the toll-gates.

Several were here killed by musketry, and others were thrown over into the river.

The Fleet Prison was set fire to in the course of the night, but the fire was not extinguished, nor, in fact, was the mob dispersed, until the following morning, when the troops discharged their muskets right into the crowd.

Among those who were here shot was a young chimney sweeper who had forty guineas in his pocket!

We come now to Thursday, June 8th.

Various encounters occurred during the day.

But towards night a mournful tranquillity prevailed.

The immense rabble which had recently appeared so irresistible, was now scattered like chaff before the wind, and those who when they first appeared wondered whence they came, were now equally astounded, and wondered where they could have gone!

The return of killed returned to Lord Amherst, the commander-in-chief, was two hundred and ten, and of wounded two hundred and forty-eight.

This account was, of course, defective, as many of both dead and wounded were removed by their friends, and no list could be taken of those who perished in the fire, or by the excessive use of ardent spirits.

Powder and ball do not seem to have been so fatal as their own inordinate appetites.

And so we close the story of the riots, drawing the veil over a city which looked as if it had been stormed and sacked: but with the people once more

in tranquillity, and Lord George Gordon, the leader of the riots, in prison.

CHAPTER XIV.

DICK HATHERDEN BEGINS PLOTTING AGAIN.

IN a garret in one of the lowest parts of the city were two men.

One was lying on a bed, with his arm bandaged and slung.

The other was sitting by his side.

The wounded man was Dick Hatherden.

The other was Ordin.

In the last affair with the troops, Dick had been wounded by a shot in the arm, and as he lay on his bed he groaned and cursed in a manner frightful to hear.

Ordin at length got out of patience.

"Haven't you anything better to do than to make that row?" said he.

"If you were in the same pain as I am, you'd do the same," growled Dick.

Ordin laughed.

"Well," cried he, "it's all very well to make that row and disturbance, but I tell you what it is—you've lost all your pluck, or else you've forgotten what you said to me before you were shot, just when you'd collared all those shiners from the dead body of the old merchant?"

Dick's eyes glistened.

He had evidently not forgotten.

"No, no," he said, "I remember well. Give me some of that brandy and I'll tell you."

Dick, like the rest, had drank deeply.

But not to the enormous extent that the others had done.

Now, however, a draught of the reviving liquid was specially grateful.

When he had drank it he said—

"In the plan I've got before me, Ordin, I shall want your assistance."

"Which I will freely give."

"Give," said Dick Hatherden, petulantly, wilfully, as it were, misinterpreting his companion's words; "I don't want anyone to give me anything. I mean simply that I want you to help me, and I'll pay well—you know I can."

"I do. I suppose you hauled a good bit out of that old fellow."

Dick grinned in spite of his pain.

"Aye!" he said, "that I did. Nearly a thousand pounds in gold and notes."

The words thrilled through Ordin's frame.

He had, to his own mind, been most unfortunate.

Throughout the riots he had not succeeded in securing more than twenty pounds.

This to a professed thief was nothing.

"That's a good bit," he said. "Well, tell me what do you want me to do."

"It's about that girl again."

"What, Aurora Halsted?"

"The same."

"Why, she's completely turned you adrift, and more than that, you've put her in possession of the

property by your wrongheadedness, without doing any good to either of us."

"I acted according to your own instructions," replied Dick Hatherden; "but recrimination between us is of no use. She has the money, and now I mean to have her."

"That's right," said Ordin; "but there's one difficulty in the way."

"What is that?"

"She has already refused you."

"Yes."

"How, then, are you going to make her change her mind?"

Dick smiled grimly.

"You don't understand. I'm going to punish her this time."

"How?"

"In a very simple way. Before this I have begged, and pleaded, and fawned to her. Now I shall adopt a different plan. I'll force her—but there—I am getting weak—I'll say more in the morning. It'll be many days before I'm able to do anything towards the accomplishment of my object."

He turned over savagely, almost, towards the wall.

And in a short time, despite his golden visions, he was asleep.

Exhausted nature, in fact, overcame mental excitement.

And all through the night Ordin kept faithful watch over him.

Why?

Did he so love Dick Hatherden?

Was there such a bond of brotherly feeling between them that he disliked to see him suffer?

No.

The truth was that, as we have seen, he had now ascertained the amount of gold that Dick Hatherden had secured.

And then—

He knew not, as yet, where it had been secreted away.

Had he but known where to lay his hand on it, he would have robbed his companion without compunction.

As it was he had to wait and watch.

So—cunning and treacherous fox that he was—he pretended the utmost friendship, and tended his wounded companion with a pretence of assiduous kindness.

On the following morning, after a visit from the doctor, Dick Hatherden felt better able to speak.

Then he unfolded to Ordin his plans.

"I tell you what, in the first place, Ordin," he said; "after all that has happened, England's no place for me. I'm off to America."

"To America!"

"Aye; convulsed as it may be, it's a better place than this, and besides, there's less likelihood of being discovered. I know a man whose ship will sail in a week from this, and on board his vessel I'll start."

"But Aurora Halsted?"

"She will go with me, of course. I shall force myself into Hallwyn House and carry her off.

She'll be insensible until we're far out at sea, and then she'll be glad enough to become my wife. I'll punish her now, for what to her can be a greater punishment and degradation than being compelled to become the wife of one whom she hates."

Ordin laughed.

"Well," he said, "it's a curious change. You once seemed to worship her."

"So I do now," said Dick, fiercely; "else why do I swear she shall be mine?"

"Because she is rich."

"Madman! if I carry her off will one penny of hers be mine?" answered he, angrily. "No, no; I depend solely on my own thousand pounds. With that I must make my way in the new country, and she must be content to live as I do. But say, will you aid me?"

"With all my heart," said Ordin; "yet there is one thing."

"What is that?"

"I should like to go with you."

The treacherous hound!

He thought there might just be a chance of his being unable to rob his fellow-thief in this country.

On the voyage or in America there would be every chance of the contrary.

Out in the wild backwoods, too, he might not only secure the treasure but his pretty bride.

"Certainly," replied Dick Hatherden, who had not the slightest notion of his friend's forgetfulness of the maxim of "honour among thieves;" "certainly, two in a place like that can get on far better."

"Then I'll go, and together we'll make a fortune," cried Ordin, with apparent enthusiasm. "In the meantime, if we're going to break into Hallwyn House we want materials."

"Yes."

"Well, and to get them we want money."

Dick made a petulant gesture.

"You know I have plenty," he said. "I don't keep it here because it is not safe, but to-morrow night or the next, if I have recovered sufficiently, we will go to the place where I have hidden it, and then we'll bring it away!"

Ordin's wicked heart leaped within him.

He turned away his face to hide his satisfaction.

"All right," he said; "don't get nasty about it, for there's no reason. It's nothing to me where you keep it, only, of course, I shall be glad to get some. I'll tell you one thing, though."

"What is that?"

"It will be folly to bring it all away—to carry about such a sum with you until you've made sure of the girl."

"Well, perhaps you're right," said Dick; "I had better only bring away a part."

This was exactly what Ordin desired.

Once he discovered the spot where Dick Hatherden had deposited his treasure, then—

Why, Dick might shift for himself, and he would fly the country instead of him.

CHAPTER XV.

THE TREASURE.

It was quite three days before Dick Hatherden was able to move about.

Even then he acted somewhat against the doctor's orders.

His wounds had been severe.

A general bodily weakness had resulted, and it was prophesied that any superabundant bodily exertion would result in a relapse.

However, Dick was in far too great a fever of excitement to care for this.

He was well aware that he was marked by the police, and he desired as quick as possible to quit England.

In the second place he was eager to have his revenge on Aurora Halsted.

A strange revenge, truly.

A revenge tinged with love.

The evening soon came, and Ordin and Dick started on their expedition.

Their way lay for a long time along the lighter thoroughfares of the city.

Then, suddenly, Dick slunk off through some dark and narrow alleys and reached the old ruins, where, our readers will remember, the first fight took place between Dick and Guy the Foundling in the commencement of my tale.

He led the way in through the same door, and crossed over the broken and rugged ground until he reached the opposite side.

Here he halted.

"Now," he said, in a low tone, "we must observe a little caution. I have chosen the best place, but nevertheless there are windows where people may overlook us."

However, no one seemed on the alert.

In fact, most of the inhabitants of the vicinity had retired to rest.

Having ascertained this fact, Dick Hatherden led the way down some rugged steps, or, rather, some natural projections in a kind of hollow, where the débris of a house had been dug out, and at the bottom of this he turned into what had once been a cellar.

Here he halted.

It was a very well selected place for safety.

No light could be observed above.

In fact, it was quite twenty feet below the surface of the ground above.

"This isn't half a bad place for hiding a treasure in," said Dick, as he groped about in a corner, and with the light of the lantern he had turned on began displacing some bricks from the wall.

"No," said Ordin, coming near and eyeing him covetously.

Dick's suspicions were for the first time roused by the look in his companion's face.

So he raised himself up.

"Look here," he said, "we don't want two people to do a little job like this. Go to the door and keep watch. How do we know how many people are wandering about here."

"A guilty conscience," says the old saying, "requires no accusing."

Ordin knew at once that he was suspected.

Gladly would he at this moment have tried an issue of strength with Dick.

But there was that in Hatherden's eye—a kind of feverish madness—that really seemed to alarm him.

"All right," he said, "I'll go outside and watch."

Full as his mind was of the thirst for gold, he yet managed to say these words in so steady and measured a voice that he quite disarmed Dick Hatherden of all suspicion.

And, indeed, as regarded his life actually he had no more cause to fear.

It had only been a thought of the moment.

Ordin, when he left the cellar, was quite content to wait and rob.

Within the space of a few moments Dick reappeared.

"I've brought away fifty pounds," he said, "and left the rest. When all's square, and she's on board, you and I can come hither and take away the remainder. What I've got here'll be plenty for us for two days."

"Aye, abundance," said the other, who had no wish that the treasure should be squandered. "And now will you take my advice?"

"If it's good."

"It is this simply, then. In the first place, you are far from strong."

"Well?"

"Then you're not going to be so mad, I hope, as to attempt anything at Hallwyn House to-night?"

"Certainly not."

"Very well, then;" continued Ordin, "we don't know what traitor we may have had round us at those lodgings—don't let us go back there at all, but let us hurry on a little part of the way, and put up at some little country inn, where we shall not be known. There we shall be in safety, and there we can rest till to-morrow night."

"I agree with you," said Dick; "and the more so that I never intended to go back to-night, or, in fact, ever again to my old lodgings. We will hire horses at the Wheatsheaf, close by here, and after we've had supper we'll push on to Alstone, a distance of six miles hence, and about three from Hallwyn House. There we can put up."

"Very good," said Ordin, who by no means liked the tone of his companion's remarks, showing, as they did, an absence of absolute trust; "I will leave it all to you. It's your affair, and you know best what you want to do."

In a few minutes they had quitted the ruins and made their way to the Wheatsheaf.

Here they ordered horses to be prepared for them in half an hour, and then proceeded to supper.

Ordin's plan was now a settled one.

He would ply Dick Hatherden with drink both here and at the inn at Alstone, and then, in the middle of the night, ride back to London and secure the treasure.

So he was in high spirits.

He kept filling and refilling Dick's glass.

He forgot, or, rather, did not observe that he was filling his own also.

So that when they started they were almost on an equality as regarded drink.

Their horses were fresh and the distance short, and in a very short space of time they reached the inn at Alstone.

Here they partook of more drink, and at a comparatively early hour retired to rest.

Or, rather, Dick retired to rest.

Ordin retired to his room to watch, taking with him as a companion a bottle of strong spirit.

Time passed rapidly.

But very slow it seemed to him.

It appeared to him as if the people of the tavern had a conspiracy against him, and would never go to bed.

And as he chafed and paced his room he kept sustaining his courage with small nips of spirit.

At length, one by one, the noises died away.

The guests ceased roaring below. The voices of those who *would* sing going home lapsed with the distance, and then the bars and locks were seen to, and the heavy tread of the landlord was heard coming up the stairs.

A few moments more and all was still.

Now Ordin waited patiently.

It was no use being too precipitate.

So—with the treasure already, mentally, in his grasp—he waited for another half hour.

Then he carefully undid his door.

All was quiet without as he put out his head and listened.

Then, stealthily, he undid his dark lantern, and half turning it on, proceeded by its feeble light to descend the stairs.

Everything seemed to favour him.

All in the house, in fact, appeared to have gone off into a deep sleep, while a heavy wind which had arisen was moaning so loudly among the trees and in and out the chimney pots, that his footsteps, even had they been louder, would have been heard by no one.

It was not long, in fact, before he had emerged from the inn, and was making his way towards the stables.

Now everything was ready to his hand.

Used as he was to the forcing of doors and the picking of locks he found no difficulty in making his way into the stable.

Here he took the freshest horse, and having saddled it, was soon on his road.

He intended to act upon a very cool and methodical principle.

He had locked the inn on the outside, in the first place.

He reckoned, in fact, that he would not be more than an hour and a half altogether on his journey, and that he would be able to return and be found in his bedroom the next morning as if nothing had happened.

In this way Dick Hatherden's suspicions would not be aroused until he returned to London and found the treasure absolutely lost.

On arriving outside the ruins he, of course, found everything as dark as pitch.

The night, in fact, was an unusually gloomy one.

Not a glimpse of moonlight or starlight was visible.

But Ordin felt no fear.

The greed for gold was too great to permit of its presence.

So, tying his horse up to a post, he made his way into the dark waste ground.

He knew nothing of his way except what feeble reminiscences of it he had from his walk to the spot with Dick.

In fact, had he known it well it would have been a matter of no ordinary difficulty to reach the place.

But he groped on.

His dark lantern, of course, aided him.

But its confined rays did not prevent his stumbling hither and thither over the rugged stones and mounds of rough earth.

On he went recklessly.

On, with the glitter of the gold, as it were, in his eyes, obscuring all else.

Then, suddenly, there came a dull pain—a stumble—a long, long fall—and a horrid crash of bones upon the jagged stones twenty feet below.

He had struck against a piece of timber, and in avoiding it had stepped over the edge of the hole before he had known he was anywhere near it.

The agony of the fall was something terrible.

Yet, after a moment, there came a numbness over him and the pain went.

That is to say, enormously abated.

"Ah! I am not so badly hurt, after all," he groaned.

And he essayed to move.

It was in vain.

He was as if he were glued to the earth.

He had, in fact, so injured his back that to raise himself was impossible.

He tried to raise his voice and cry for help.

In vain, too.

His tongue refused to utter more than a feeble cry.

Then the awful truth stole over him.

He should lie there and die, unless——

Ah! there was one hope——

Unless some one saw his horse tied to the post—should suspect the presence of the owner near at hand, and make a search.

He would not have indulged this hope had he known that already a thief had found his horse and ridden away with it.

So there he lay helpless.

There, within a few yards of the much-coveted treasure.

Presently a flash of lightning dashed across the dark heavens.

Then a boom of thunder shook the earth, and a few large drops fell.

Grateful, indeed, was the parched wretch for these.

But yet there was no hope.

He felt he *must* die.

Another hour, and his agony was less, but his weakness was rapidly increasing.

The storm increased in violence.

The thunder rolled terribly over the old ruins, and stones, displaced from the edge of the hole, began to fall on the wretched man's head.

Ordin looked up despairingly.

THE RIVAL APPRENTICES

A TALE OF THE RIOTS OF 1780.

AURORA'S ATTEMPT TO ESCAPE.

But he could move no way.

As he had fallen, there he lay still, gazing with burning eyes up at the sky.

Presently there was a more terrible flash—a more fearful crash—than the one before, and a huge boulder came toppling over the edge.

He saw it coming, but he could not avoid it, and in another moment it had fallen on his head, and all was over.

The treasure-seeker lay dead within arm's length of the gold.

CHAPTER XVI.

JEALOUSY AND HATE.

WHEN, on the following morning, the flight of Ordin was discovered, Dick Hatherden at once guessed whither he had gone.

Of course, he never for a moment guessed the terrible catastrophe that had happened,

Full, therefore, of fear for the loss of his treasure, he hastily paid his score at the inn, and hurried away on horseback towards London.

We need not waste time in explaining the ghastly sight that awaited him at the ruins.

The crushed and mangled body of Ordin was enough to tell him that his treasure was safe.

However, he hurried towards the place where he had concealed it, and in spite of the danger attending the carrying about of so large a sum of money, he placed it in his pocket, and hurried away from the ruins quicker than he had come.

On returning to the inn at Alstone, he wisely made no remark respecting the death of his treacherous comrade, but quietly waited for the evening.

On his way to the inn he had left word at a place of low resort where he had once been a good customer, and he expected, therefore, the assistance of one or two of his most desperate companions.

Had Ordin remained faithful, he would have attempted the abduction of Aurora Halsted without the assistance of anyone else.

Now, however, he had determined to speak of no large rewards, and he would merely speak of the matter as one of ordinary importance.

The men, however, knew enough of Dick Hatherden to be aware that he would not ask them to join in any enterprise without any prospect of reward, and, accordingly, about nine o'clock at night saw the arrival at the inn of two fellows whose appearance in itself was enough to hang them.

These men had been amongst the most brutal rioters during the last sad days, and although with money in their pockets, were always ready to accept any work which promised reward.

The plan which Dick Hatherden had decided upon following was soon explained, and after he had plied them well with drink, they all set forward on horseback in the direction of Hallwyn House.

The night was all they could have desired.

Not a star was visible, and, in fact, as they approached their destination it was difficult to tell the house from the immense trees that surrounded it.

Dick Hatherden knew well the ruins where Alexis Rainsford and his Catholic friends had been confined by Simon Grandley.

Here, therefore, he descended with his friends, and, leading them into the subterraneous passage by which Alexis had escaped, left them to commence the breaking open of the door, while he went up to the house to reconnoitre.

He had no sooner left the plantation and approached the house than he saw that, late as the hour was, the inmates had not retired to rest.

There were lights particularly brilliant in the drawing-room.

Here, of course, Dick naturally anticipated that he should see Aurora Halsted, and he at once resolved to mount the terrace which ran round the building, and ascertain what was going on within.

This was easily accomplished.

A kind of spiral staircase ran from it to the grounds.

This he at once mounted, and in a few moments was at the window of the drawing-room.

There a sight met his eyes which frightfully exasperated him.

Aurora Halsted was seated on a sofa in all the glory of her youthful beauty, a low-necked dress displaying all the glories of her splendid bosom, over which her dark brown hair coiled luxuriantly.

By her side sat Alexis Rainsford, with one of her hands in his, while his other arm encircled her glowing waist.

Her eyes were gazing up into his with a look of confidence, if not of love.

What could it mean?

Had Aurora, then, found a new love?

Or was she playing some false game?

Such were Dick Hatherden's thoughts.

He preferred to suppose the latter.

He would not think that she really loved another.

In his vanity he would not give in that she had entirely discarded him.

He preferred to think that even after her insults she was only coquetting with him.

Yet the sight maddened him.

He alone should have pressed that warm and glowing form to his heart.

He alone should have evoked the swelling emotions of that glowing bosom.

He alone should have pressed that hand and have felt that plump arm encircling his neck.

He alone should have culled the nectar from those dewy lips.

Yet—even as he gazed—Alexis's lips met hers in a long, thrilling kiss.

A curse long and deep escaped from the clenched teeth of Dick Hatherden.

If there was one thing more resolute than another in his feelings it was his passion for this girl.

To see her toying with another, to see their lips meeting in passionate kisses, to know that those feelings which *he* desired to rouse in her were being roused in her by another was madness to him, and it was only by dint of an almost superhuman effort that he contrived to keep himself from dashing into the room and tearing them asunder.

However, he remained quiet.

He stood there watching their amorous dalliance—such as had never been permitted to him—every loving look and gesture only increasing his fury, and determining him the more to succeed in his scheme for carrying her off.

It would be a greater revenge than he had hoped

for to take her from the arms of a new love and make her his own.

Presently, after a low whispering, the lovers rose, and Aurora, having suffered Alexis to give her a tender embrace, quitted the room.

Alexis stroked his silky moustache and looked complacently happy.

"Ah! ha! my fine fellow," muttered Dick Hatherden, "be not so satisfied. You will change before morning."

Then he withdrew to the outer edge of the balcony, where he could command a view of the bedroom windows.

There he stood very quiet in the soft moonlight.

Presently he saw a light and the reflection of a figure on a blind.

He knew the form at once.

It was that of Aurora Halsted.

Having ascertained, accordingly, in what room Aurora Halsted had retired to rest, Dick Hatherden went down from the terrace and hastened towards the place where he had left his companions.

Had he been about to engage in an ordinary burglary he would not have made so many preparations. He would simply have broken into the place in the way usual to burglars.

In that case, of course, he could have fled immediately upon discovery.

But in this case it was different.

His assault on the house would be futile unless he carried Aurora away; and with her in his arms, how could they make good their escape from the place?

So they had to go the longest way to work.

However, the men had lost no time.

In fact, when he reached the subterranean passage he found that they had displaced a great quantity of earth so as to loosen the bolts.

Within a few minutes the door was open and the way clear.

"It is by this way that we must quit the house," said Dick, "so leave the door wide open, that we may be able to make our way quickly through in case of pursuit."

They hurried along until they reached the vaults beneath the house of Mr. Hallwyn.

Here they turned the light of their lanterns round hither and thither until they discovered the ladder leading to the trapdoor through which Aurora and the old housekeeper had descended to the aid of Mr. Hallwyn and his friends.

This trapdoor, of course, was fastened on the upper side.

But this was not at all disheartening to such men as these.

They knew well how to get over a difficulty of this kind.

By means of a small saw of the finest workmanship they cut a hole completely round the place where the bolts were fixed, and in an incredibly short space of time they had pushed the trap-door open and ascended into the room above.

This, as will be remembered by my readers, was a disused one.

It communicated, however, by an open door with the passage of the house.

Dick's evil heart beat high.

His scheme prospered.

Nothing better, in fact, could be desired.

He made first for the drawing-room.

Then, having found this, he looked for the staircase and made his calculations.

He thus easily ascertained in which room Aurora had retired to rest.

"Now," he said, in a whisper, to his companions, "you can go into that room and secure what you please, but be ready on the instant if I give the alarm. I will secure the girl myself."

So saying, he left them to go on their errand of plunder, and passed on tiptoe up the stairs.

Instinct led him at once to the room of Aurora Halsted.

The door was ajar.

The night, in fact, was close and oppressive.

In Dick stole, like a thief as he was.

All was dark.

He closed the door and locked it.

He had resolved on desperate measures.

She should either accompany him, or——

It gave him a savage pleasure to think it—

She should die!

Yes; sooner than she should become the wife of another man he would kill her.

When he approached her bed, he could tell by her regular breathing that—lulled by dreams of love—the young girl was already asleep.

He gently threw the light of the dark lantern upon her.

There she lay, looking very beautiful in her slumber; her coral lips slightly open, showing her pearly teeth; her cheeks flushed by the sweet visions which were floating through her brain, her shoulders bare, and her breast—only hidden by a gauzy covering—heaving regularly its globes of snow.

Dick set his teeth savagely as he gazed down upon her.

"And she was to have been mine willingly," he muttered: "but no, Alexis Rainsford shall never possess her; not even if she escapes me now, and I have to shoot them down at the altar!"

Leaning over her, he shook her gently by the shoulder.

It was some moments before she awoke.

Then she raised her snowy arm, and pressed her hand over her eyes, as if to avoid the glare of light.

"Surely it is not morning yet, Lizette," she murmured.

She fancied day had come, and her maid was arousing her.

"No," said Dick, leaning over her, and speaking in a quick, hoarse voice: "no, it is not daylight, and it is not Lizette who is rousing you. It is I, Dick Hatherden, and if you cry out I will kill you."

He then put the light of the lantern full on, and allowed her to see his face.

A ghastly change took place in her looks.

A livid pallor overspread her face and neck.

Her eyes glared with an unnatural brilliance.

In fact, her whole soul recoiled from the fate she saw before her.

She saw by the look upon his face that he meant all he threatened.

Death was hard for her to contemplate now.

For the first time in her life she had awakened to a dream of love.

Alexis Rainsford had touched a chord in her heart that no man had ever had the power to touch before.

She loved him.

We need say no more.

That tells everything.

She resolved, consequently, to temporise.

"What want you with me?" she said.

He knew by her look and her voice how much terror there was in her heart.

It softened him a little.

Just by chance.

It might have had an opposite effect.

"Aurora," he said, "I desire not to harm you. But you must quit this place with me to-night."

"Oh! Heaven protect me!"

"I tell you I mean you no harm," he continued, sternly. "I was a witness this very night to an interview between you and Alexis Rainsford that nearly drove me mad. And yet I love you still. I come to take you away from here—to carry you away from this country and make you my wife. Nay, tremble not; this man, this Alexis Rainsford, is an impostor. You will lose nothing in losing him. But come, time presses. I will light your lamp and retire to the window. If you attempt to give the slightest alarm I shall kill you, for I have sworn you shall never be another's.

There was nothing for it but to obey.

He lit the lamp, half drew the curtains, and then retired to the window, where, although he did not look round, he watched eagerly for every sound.

After a very few minutes a voice said—

"I am ready."

Dick turned hastily, and hurried towards her.

The time of waiting had seemed an age.

She was fully attired, ready for a journey.

She had resolved, in fact, upon a course of action.

To resist now would be to court immediate death.

She would go away with him now, therefore, and watch eagerly for a chance of escape before she quitted English soil.

"Before we go," said Dick, "I must impose one thing upon you. Shall I gag you to prevent you from yielding to a temptation to cry out, or will you prefer remaining as you are, and run the risk of my vengeance if you break faith with me?"

"Vengeance comes strangely side by side with the word 'love,'" said Aurora; "but be assured I will make no sound—utter no cry for help. Life is still dear to me, and I wish, therefore, to live."

Having obtained from her this assurance, Dick Hatherden unlocked the door.

"Whither are we going?" she asked, in a whisper.

"By the trap-door and through the subterranean way," said Dick. "There are two friends of mine in the room below; let them not alarm you."

With these words he gently intimated that he desired her to go on first.

Aurora knew well her way towards the room where she had descended to the assistance of Alexis Rainsford.

She hurried down, therefore, as fast as she could; and passing by the two thieves, who were waiting in the passage, led the way to the secret room.

She was, in fact, the first to descend the ladder.

But in the darkness at the bottom she halted.

One wild thought had entered her brain—

"Shall I escape now?"

But the evil face of Dick Hatherden as he threatened death restrained her.

"Don't let her see what you have with you, or suspect what you are," whispered Dick to his two friends ere they descended; "it would ruin me."

"Never fear," replied one of them; "we didn't come here to sell you. Lead on and we'll behave like respectable gentlemen."

Out in the grounds and no pursuit!

So it was in a few moments.

Then a deadly sense of helplessness came over Aurora.

Still more so when she heard Dick say—

"Here, Bob; here's the money I promised you. Now go to the inn and hire a close carriage. Bring it round to the cross roads. I'll be there before you."

"But the coachman?"

Dick leaned forward and whispered.

What it was she did not hear.

But she felt that it was something evil.

And yet she dared not interfere—dared not question her abductor.

"All right," said Bob, in reply to Dick's whispered word, and in a moment he and his companion hurried away.

"Now, Aurora," said Dick, drawing her arm in his, "let us hasten away. The vicinity of your uncle's house has no charms for me, as you may imagine."

Aurora stood still, and struggled to release herself.

"I have promised," she said, "to go quietly away with you; but if you have left within your breast any manly feelings, do not subject me to unnecessary insult."

"Insult!" cried Dick; "what mean you? I proffered none. I simply, as the way is rough and long, asked you to take my arm."

"That is enough insult to me," replied Aurora. "Remember, there is one question between you and me that remains still unanswered. What do you know of my father's death?"

Dick almost cursed aloud.

"This is no time to talk of that," he said, angrily; "let us hasten."

He led the way at once through the tangled brushwood into the high road, and in a short time they had reached the spot which he had mentioned to Bob as the cross roads.

CHAPTER XVII.

AWAY FROM LOVE—TO MISERY!

THERE was a faint hope in the mind of Aurora

Halsted that going along the road they might fall in with people in sufficient number to enable her to make a sudden rush from the side of Dick Hatherden and seek protection from them.

But this hope soon faded away.

The road itself was gloomy enough.

The cross roads were worse.

In fact, the spot was gloomy—sepulchral—dark—suggestive of murder.

Not a soul besides themselves seemed to care to be out.

They met only one man during their journey.

On reaching the cross roads the chill at the heart of the young girl was so great that she stooped to entreaty.

She clutched Dick by the arm.

"Oh! hear me," she cried; "have pity on me!"

"Pity!" he exclaimed; "yes, I *have* pity for you. What do you wish for?"

"Ah! let me go, Dick!" she exclaimed, passionately. "See, I call you by the name I used once, when I thought you loved me. I am rich; you shall have all—all, if only——"

"If only," repeated Dick, with a sneer; "if only I will allow you to spend the rest of your life in the arms of Alexis Rainsford. No, no, Aurora; you are mine. You promised yourself to me: I have won you fairly now, and I will not part with you."

As he spoke, the faint sound of carriage-wheels was heard in the distance.

There was no hope, then.

At any rate, at present.

She was hopelessly in his power.

Pretended submission, therefore, was her proper *rôle* to play.

Nearer came the carriage.

Then the idea came to her mind—

What had become of the coachman?

Had he been murdered?

And on her account.

The idea was horrible.

She could keep silent no longer.

"Dick Hatherden," she said, "one question more. Answer me truly."

"Well?"

"When the coachman of yonder carriage was mentioned, you whispered some words to your companions. What did they imply?"

Dick laughed.

"You thought I meant to harm him."

"I still think so."

"Then you are wrong. If my instructions have been faithfully carried out by my men, he has been seized a few hundred yards from the inn, gagged and bound, and placed far out of harm's way on the side of the road. No, no; I may be bad, but murder does not lie on my soul."

He said this with such an air of apparent truth that the hope sprang up in the breast of Aurora Halsted that, after all, he was right.

That he had been maligned—falsified.

Not that she experienced in the slightest degree any of the softening influences of love towards him, but simply she experienced a certain pleasure in believing that, perhaps, after all, she was not in the power of her father's murderer.

The carriage in a few moments drew up.

Bob and his companion were on the box.

Now was the time to realise her position.

Dick opened the door, helped her in, and sprang in himself.

Then they drove off rapidly.

Aurora burst into tears.

Dick took no notice of this.

"Mine, mine, now," he murmured, and clasped her passionately in his arms, raining kisses on her unwilling lips, and breathing hot words of passion.

"Unmanly ruffian," said Aurora, faintly; "oh! may heaven punish you for all these insults."

"Insults!" cried Dick, kissing her again and again on her mouth, and then releasing her. "Is it an insult to tell you how I love you! that I live but for you? You are mine now; in a few hours you will be my wife, and then you will learn to love me."

Aurora shuddered.

"Love you!" she cried; "that will only increase my hate!"

Dick ground his teeth with rage.

He had seen how the endearments of Alexis Rainsford had affected her; how much, in fact, she had responded to his amorous dalliance.

The result of his own toying was only to produce a feeling of loathing.

"Aurora," he said, bending his face close to her, and holding her hand tightly clenched in his, "do you remember old times? do you remember how once your eyes looked love into mine? do you remember how your whole being thrilled when I held you in my arms? do you remember those stolen meetings, when for an hour at a time you have lain in rapture on my breast? And can you now talk of hate?"

"Richard Hatherden," answered Aurora, "there was not then a river of blood between us."

The words were said so solemnly that even Dick Hatherden, hardened as he was, could not avoid feeling the force of them.

A cold shiver ran through his frame.

He knew well how true her words were.

A river of blood!

Had he not seen it?

Had he not in his dreams beheld the red stream flowing in horrid brilliance before him?

Had he not seen the spirits of the murdered hovering over its hideous tide?

"You speak in such terrible terms that you alarm me," cried he.

"Alarm you," she said, sneeringly.

"Aye, alarm me; but not as you imagine. I am alarmed: not for myself."

"For what then?"

"Your reason."

"For my reason!" replied Aurora, with a bitter laugh; "you think of that somewhat late, sir, I am thinking. Is it not enough to craze the wisest mind to be snatched from your friends by a man whom you hate—by a man who has the power to remind you of scenes which it makes you blush to recall; to be dragged, in fact, from a dream of love to a reality of misery?"

Dick saw that it was useless to pursue the matter further.

At any rate for the time.

He clung still to the hope that time would soften her.

"Be it so, think as you please now," he said; "but time will change you. I know it—I feel it. If not, if you *do* refuse to behave to me with kindness, you shall live such a life with me as my wife that you will curse the hour you were born."

"I should curse it now," answered Aurora, "did I not hope to escape."

No more was said.

Dick was too angry to speak.

His love, even, was for the moment quenched in anger.

"But no matter," thought he. "I will have a deadly vengeance, one full of terrors for her. If she is not my willing wife she shall be my slave."

The carriage rolled rapidly on.

On through the streets of London.

A few people were moving about.

Oh! how Aurora longed for an opportunity of appealing to them.

But such a chance was not to be given her.

The watch was heard approaching.

Aurora made a slight movement.

Dick at once detected it, and, bending down, gazed in her face.

He caught a gleam of joy in her eye.

"Ah!" he muttered, "you think of crying for help to the watch. Nay, do not deny it. I know well what were your thoughts. But, remember, it is the same with them as with others. If you rouse them to attack this carriage I will not hesitate an instant. I am desperate, and will plunge this knife into your bosom."

He produced a knife as he spoke, and held it up so that it glittered in the moonlight.

Aurora shuddered.

"You are a demon," she said, "and yet you dare to talk to me of love."

"It *is* love," cried Dick Hatherden, fiercely; "it is love which makes me utter these words. I would kill you, because then I should be certain that no one else could enjoy you."

The young girl only shuddered at this.

She could make no reply.

So on they went in silence.

At length, after a short lapse of time, they emerged from the denser part of the town, and passed along a long lane of houses running along the river bank.

Here at length they stopped, and Bob, descending from the carriage-box, opened the door after knocking at that of the house.

The aspect of the place struck terror into the heart of Aurora Halsted.

She gave one frightened look up and down the dark and narrow street, cast one glance up at the gloomy building, and then fainted away into the arms of Dick Hatherden.

"So much the better," muttered Dick, as he raised her, and prepared to bear her into the house; "it saves a world of trouble."

He carried her in, gave Bob some more money, and directed them what to do with the carrriage, and bade them go to the old haunts until they received further orders from him.

Then the old woman who had opened the door to them closed it again, and conducted Dick Hatherden to a bedroom on the second story, where he laid his senseless burden on a bed.

"See to her," he said, after he had kissed her white lips, "and be sure she is locked carefully in. There are no means of escape, I trust. Let me see, where does this window lead to?"

He approached the casement and looked out.

There was a deep fall—one of at least twenty feet—upon stone flags.

"Good," he said; "she is safe here. Ah! she is arousing from her swoon. I will not let her see me again, for my presence is to-night distasteful to her. I will go to my own room, and, meanwhile, do all you can to soothe her. Above all, however, see when you leave her that the door is locked and bolted with care."

So saying, he quitted the chamber.

CHAPTER XVIII.
HOPE AND DESPAIR.

WHEN Aurora awoke from her sleep on the following morning she gazed in wonder about her.

Not that she now saw the room for the first time.

When Dick, on the previous night, had quitted the room, the old woman had, with some rude show of kindness, undressed her and put her to bed, and while she was administering to her certain necessary refreshments, Aurora had time to look about her.

In spite of her grief and anger, however, her fatigue caused her to go to sleep soon after the old woman had quitted the room.

When morning came, therefore, as I have said, she gazed at first confusedly round her.

Then the dreadful truth broke in all its horror on her mind.

She sprang out of bed and rushed to the door.

There was a strong bolt on the inside.

This she shot at once, and then approached the window and looked out.

No hope there.

The fall was far too great.

Then she hurried to the bed to dress herself.

But as she did so she started in wonderment.

Her clothes were gone!

And in their stead was a suit of men's clothes.

A smile broke over her face.

"Good," thought she; "good. The very thing which, for some reason or another, he thinks will turn out for his good, may prove my safety."

Hastily, therefore, she dressed herself; and had just completed her toilet when a knock came at the door.

"Who is there?" she asked.

"Only me," said the voice of the old woman.

Aurora unbarred the door.

The old woman stood without—alone.

"You can come down to my room for breakfast," she said, expressing no surprise at the appearance of Aurora in her strange garb; "it's lonesome up here."

A bright idea struck Aurora.

She might bribe the old woman to let her escape.

The dame did not look particularly hard or villanous; though there was something about the mouth which spoke of the greed for money.

So she gladly followed the woman to the room, where she found a breakfast provided.

"Where is he?—where is the man who brought me here?" she asked.

"He went out early."

"Are you alone, then?"

A fresh idea leaped into Aurora's breast.

She was young and active.

She might overpower the feeble old woman and escape.

But this hope was soon dissipated.

"No, I am not alone," replied her companion; "my son is below."

She at once had comprehended Aurora's ideas and provided against them.

Eagerly, then, while they discussed breakfast, did Aurora pour into the old woman's ear the story of all her wrongs.

The woman listened with every attention.

When, however, Aurora began speaking of her own riches she pricked up her ears most sharply.

She knew at once what Aurora was driving at.

She was about to promise a reward.

And a reward she did promise.

One that fairly made the old woman turn pale.

A hundred pounds!

"Well," she said, "I've heard Dick Hatherden say as how you was a rich lady. But he didn't say you was a generous one like that."

"I will gladly give it."

"Well, you see, there's two things to be said."

"What are they?"

"In the first place, how am I to know that you will pay me right?"

"I will give you an order on my uncle for the amount. When I tell him what you have done for me he'll gladly pay it."

"Well, and in the second place, if Dick Hatherden were to know that I helped you to escape he'd murder me. He's awful set on having you; and if he doesn't get you, and I'm the one to help you, I'll be murdered."

"Is there not some method by which he can be prevented from knowing it?" said Aurora, hope springing up in her breast as she found the old woman beginning to yield. "Surely, for such a bribe, you can contrive in some way."

"Stop," said the old woman; "you have noticed your window?"

"Yes."

"And the depth of the yard beneath it?"

"Yes."

"Have you courage to descend from it by a rope ladder alone?"

"Yes, yes; anything rather than remain in this place."

"Very good, then; I can manage it. But first write me out the order on your uncle for the hundred pounds."

She hurried to the sideboard, and with trembling hands placed before the young girl the materials for writing.

With eager hands, then, Aurora wrote as follows—

"DEAR UNCLE,—Please pay to Mrs. Absolom (so the old woman said she was named) the sum of one hundred pounds on my account. The money is not to be paid unless at the time of receiving this I am safe at home.

"Your affectionate niece,
"AURORA HALSTED.

"To Mr. Robert Hallwyn,
"Hallwyn House,
"Royston."

"Is that sufficient? asked Aurora.

The old woman read it eagerly.

"Yes, yes," she cried; "quite right—quite right. Now listen to me, for he'll be back soon. I will supply you with rope, and you must make the ladder yourself. My son is hand and glove with Dick Hatherden, and I can't trust him, or he'd make it stronger. Before you get out of the window you must bolt your door on the inside, to show that no one's been helping you, and I'll manage the rest."

"Oh! I am so grateful," cried Aurora. "May Heaven bless you!"

"Well, well," said Mrs. Absolom, who, now she had secured the promise of so rich a reward, was inclined to boast a little of her virtue; "you see, I always like to do anyone a good turn, and you are not the sort of girl to mate with such a fellow as Dick Hatherden. But come, I'll get the rope."

In a few minutes she returned with a full armful.

This they carried up into the bedroom.

"Keep it well concealed under the bedclothes," said Mrs. Absolom when she left her; "and be sure and keep your door bolted. If he saw this he'd murder all the lot of us."

And with these words of cheer Mrs. Absolom departed.

As may well be imagined, Aurora Halsted lost no time.

She at once bolted the door, and sitting down on the bed began her task.

How she did it she never knew.

She had about as much experience in the making of rope ladders as she had in the command of a vessel.

But somehow or another the work came ready to her hand.

She had seen many a wooden ladder, and she accordingly formed hers by imitating, as far as possible, the formation of that.

It was a long—a wearisome—a hard and heavy task, as can be imagined.

But she went on with untiring zeal.

Hours passed.

Then she was summoned to her dinner.

She would gladly have dispensed with that.

But the old woman would not hear of such a thing.

"No," she said, "it will excite his suspicion: make him, perhaps, come up into your room, which he does not seem inclined to do."

"But how will he know?"

"He is here now."

However, he made no appearance at dinner.

For some reason or another he was disposed to keep away from her.

This, according to his own plans, however, was not for long.

That very night, at midnight, was the time chosen to carry her off.

So Mrs. Absolom informed Aurora, and all the more vigorously she worked, therefore, when she returned to her task.

At length night came.

Once more Mrs. Absolom came in and brought her some refreshment.

Then, without a word, she went out; and Aurora, even more carefully than before, saw to the fastenings of the door.

Anon, with renewed ardour, she set to her task, taking care to leave open the window, that she might hear the striking of the clock of the neighbouring church.

On, on, she worked.

The clock struck eleven.

There were still yards to complete it.

It was growing too late to do so.

Her hope of escape had roused up within her almost a manly courage.

So, instead of so completing the rope ladder that it would reach to the ground, she fastened a single rope to the end.

Thus, at the dangerous part of the descent she would have the use of the ladder, while at the bottom she could without fear run down it.

At a quarter past eleven all was ready.

She glanced out.

All was still.

Her heart beat violently, but carefully and slowly she fastened the end of the rope ladder to the heavy bedstead.

Then, after one more look out, she breathed a prayer and began the descent.

"No one will see me," she thought, as she put her foot on the first part of the ladder; "and if they do they will think I am a man."

But here she was wrong.

No one would have thought that that beautifully rounded leg belonged to a man.

Bravely she descended.

All was still.

But she had forgotten one thing.

The ladder crossed the lower window.

As she approached it she caught sight of a man's face.

The face of Dick Hatherden.

A loud curse escaped his lips as he leaned out and saw her descending.

"Ten thousand devils!" he shouted; "she is escaping!"

And with the words he sprang out and began the descent also.

A cry of despair escaped the young girl's lips.

But still she kept bravely on!

CHAPTER XIX.

ANOTHER VILLAIN.

WE must return now to the point where Will Lightmore rescued the young girl from the hands of Giles Roper.

We have met him since, during the riots, but we must now go back to explain how he fared, and what happened to the man whom Guy the Foundling had discovered in the grounds insulting Betty the servant maid.

Will never drew rein until he reached the country retreat of Mrs. Grandley.

Betty opened the door, and was not a little surprised and shocked at seeing Will holding in his arms such a pretty piece of goods as the young girl he had rescued.

A toss of the head explained to Will Lightmore the state of her mind.

But a few words told all, and reconciled her to the situation.

Betty was full of kindness, and at once took charge of the newcomer, while Will Lightmore went up to Mrs. Grandley to explain.

It is almost unnecessary to state that that worthy lady, on hearing of Alice's forlorn condition, at once undertook the care of her.

Alexis Rainsford was not known, of course, to know anything of her.

Nor did they for one moment imagine that any connection existed between her and Guy the Foundling.

Still the fact that she was friendless and in trouble was enough.

Will was furious when he heard of the conduct of the prisoner.

He insisted at once upon visiting him.

He found him in the cellar sullenly devouring some food which had been given him.

He glared up at Will with a half insolent, half angry look.

"Who are you?" he cried; "and what do you want?"

"Have a care, and keep a civil tongue in your head," cried Will Lightmore, "or you may find that I'll show you who I am in a way you won't like."

The man growled out something, but made no definite answer.

"You will find it far better," said Will Lightmore, seating himself on the edge of a table, "to make a clean breast of it. Who sent you here?"

The man laughed.

He seemed pretty secure in the notion that he would not be murdered.

"Do you think I'm fool enough to tell?" he said.

"No; perhaps you're not a fool," said Will, "and perhaps you are. 'There are more things in heaven and earth, Horatio, than are dreamt of in our philosophy,' and perhaps your philosophy has not taught you to tell the truth. However, I will teach you the way. You will remain here without food until you do tell; and I warn you that if, before a few hours, you do not make up your mind, I shall have left the house, and the women will know nothing of it. Be quick and decide."

The man only laughed.

He apparently knew his game.

Will Lightmore was irritated.

What could the fellow mean?

It was evident to him that he had some plan in view.

Yet what?

THE RIVAL APPRENTICES

A TALE OF THE RIOTS OF 1780.

THE EXPLOSION AT THE SMUGGLER'S CAVE.

There he was in an underground cell, away from all communication with mankind, and utterly unable, as it truly seemed, to move hand or foot to aid himself.

Yet he was thus insolent.

"You seem merry, my friend," said he. "Perhaps you will change your tune before many hours are over your head."

"Surely I may laugh," said the strange prisoner.

"Yes; but I should like to know why you laugh."

"That is my business; for the same reason, perhaps, that you keep me here."

"I keep you here because my master and my fellow apprentice placed you here, and until I know from them their reason I shall not release you. So I will depart. Remain here if you like, and be as stolidly obstinate as you like; but this one thing is certain, until you confess for whom you are acting as a spy you do not leave this place."

So saying he rose abruptly.

In a moment the prisoner was alone.

But Will Lightmore's words only sufficed to elicit a smile.

A smile as he went.

A loud laugh as the man was once more alone.

"Ha, ha!" he cried, when he knew himself to be in security; "ha, ha! you will find, my fine fellow, that your prisoner will soon break out of this, and take away with him your pretty bird that you prize so much."

As he said this he went to a corner of the cell, and removed some bricks.

They were quite loose, and he very easily moved them.

Evidently he had long been at work.

In a few minutes he had removed enough to make a large hole in the wall.

Then he drew from a dark corner some small pieces of iron and began working again.

A cheery song escaped his lips as he did so.

He was a daring villain.

And yet had Will Lightmore known all he would have been aware that Betty's honour was at his mercy.

All through that night he worked.

When once he had got through the bricks he had only earth to work through.

So his progress was quick.

The more so because he had a kind of feeling of revenge.

On the next day Will Lightmore came again.

Still the prisoner would say nothing.

So his food was stopped.

He only smiled.

He had his vengeance ready.

On the next night he worked still harder.

He seemed to know which way to take.

He had no desire to reach the outside of the house.

His goal was Betty's chamber.

The spot where he could take revenge for the insult he had sustained in the grounds.

An hour's work and the implement he was using went through into empty air.

The villain's heart bounded.

He was near freedom.

And revenge too.

He had more brutal ideas in his abduction of Betty than Dick Hatherden in the kidnapping of Aurora Halsted.

Dick Hatherden really intended and wished for marriage.

This fellow, however, only wished to obtain possession of the poor girl's person and then send her adrift, to return in shame and misery to her lover.

A few more powerful blows, and the fellow was in one of the cellars.

It was a long disused wine cellar, and the door was open.

He had now the free range of the house.

He could open any door and be at liberty to depart.

But this thought never entered his head.

Revenge was his first thought.

"I'll have a breath of fresh air," he muttered, as in stocking feet he ascended to the kitchen; "then I'll have a good supper, and then—the girl's mine, or my name is not Jabez Oldridge."

Cautiously he opened the back door and peered out.

It was a calm and lovely night.

A balmy and exquisite breeze was blowing from the river.

The stars and moon shed a bright lustre over all things.

Jabez gazed lazily round him, inhaled a little of the fresh air of which he had long been deprived, and then, setting the door ajar, went into the pantry, and, having struck a light, set to work at the eatables and drinkables of all kinds, until he had had his fill.

Then he prepared for his villainous enterprise.

He had no conception in what room Betty slept.

But this difficulty he resolved to get over by looking into each chamber as he came to them.

This was a dangerous method.

But, as luck would have it, he obtained means to prosecute his adventure safely, at any rate, with proper means of defence.

On the table of the first room into which he pryed were a purse and a loaded pistol.

Both these he appropriated with a grin.

"These are both loaded," said he, as he placed the one in his pocket and grasped the other in his hand tightly. "One will enable me to get quickly away from this, the other will take me safely through this night's work."

One by one, with the noiselessness and stealthiness which are the peculiar accomplishments of a thief, he opened the door of the rooms and peered in by the light of the lamp he carried.

At length he saw the head of Betty reclining in peaceful slumber on the pillow.

But, oh! horror to him!

By her side slept Alice!

This was a startling discovery.

He could not successfully compete with both.

However, he had with him an all powerful agent, which he had not intended to bring into requisition.

It was a dangerous experiment.

But he must try it.

He crept in on his hands and knees, and carefully closed and locked the door behind him.

Then, approaching the bed, he shaded the lamp so as not to awaken the sleepers, and then, taking

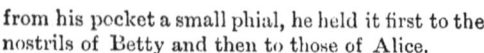

from his pocket a small phial, he held it first to the nostrils of Betty and then to those of Alice.

One look of alarm the girl gave as the movement of the bed awoke her.

Then she lapsed into insensibility.

With a gratified glance at their senseless forms the ruffian then turned and made a bundle of some female clothes that were on a chair at the side of the bed.

Then he took Betty from the bed, and, after imprinting a kiss upon her resistless lips, wrapped her in a blanket and bore her from the room.

No one was moving, and without any hindrance, therefore, he made his way into the open country, and carried his prize with rapid strides across the fields.

At length he reached a barn-like building at some distance from the house of Simon Grandley.

Into this he made his way, and laid Betty gently down in a corner.

Then he took from his pocket a bottle of brandy, which he had purloiled from the pantry, and took a long, deep draught.

The carrying of a fine plump girl across such an extent of rugged country, without any aid from herself, was no easy task, and, wearied out as he consequently was, he indulged so heavily that he presently fell into a deep sleep.

When Betty woke in the morning she was astounded to find herself in such a place, lying undressed, wrapped in a blanket, her clothes beside her, and the man who had been confined in the cellar lying asleep not far from her.

She hurriedly dressed herself, and then glanced out of the little barn window.

All out there was open country.

But where was she, and how came she there?

Neither of these questions could she answer.

However, of this one thing she was determined: she would slip out unperceived, and trust herself rather to an unknown part of the country than to the tender mercies of a villain, whose mercy to her hitherto, when she had been in his power all the night through, was a mystery she was unable to solve.

So at length, having dressed, she slipped by and made for the door.

But she had miscalculated here.

He had found the door open.

But he had not left it so.

He had forced a huge piece of wood wedge-like into the ground, so as to prevent anyone departing without exerting their strength to the utmost.

As it was, the noise she made in endeavouring to remove it awoke Jabez.

With a savage howl he at once sprang up and rushed towards her.

"Ah!" he cried, "you think to escape then?"

Betty trembled.

"Oh! why, why am I here?" she cried.

He laughed savagely.

"Why are you here? Ha, ha! Do you forget me?" he cried; "how you spurned me, and had me confined in a vault? I am going to have my revenge, for you shall be mine now."

CHAPTER XX.

CAUGHT.

IT was a wild and maddening thought that inspired Aurora Halsted as she still hurried down the rope, in spite of the pursuit of Dick Hatherden.

There was no doubt that if he chose he could soon overtake her.

But then a cry for help, even in that wild and infamous neighbourhood, might rouse some one to her aid.

So she hastened onwards, and as she reached the single part of the rope, she coiled her limbs round it, and slid down it.

She was now in a narrow court, from which, however, she soon saw a mode of egress into an adjoining street.

Without waiting an instant to think whither this would lead her, she dashed at full speed along this passage just as a heavy thud on the ground told her that her foe had also landed.

The noise of his pursuing feet was soon heard, and with a heart fainting with terror the young girl sped along.

He was gaining on her.

Yet she would not give in.

A horrid thought seized her.

The river was not far off.

What if she fled thither, and ended her life and her persecution in its dark waters?

Only the madness produced by the despair at her failure made her conceive this idea.

If she had reasoned a moment—if the thought of Alexis Rainsford and her new-born love for him had entered her mind—she would never have dreamed of death.

But as she heard the nearer approach of her enemy, she felt as if she were rapidly losing her senses.

She glanced behind her.

Dick Hatherden was not many yards off.

Then a wild and piercing scream escaped from her lips.

At this moment Dick stumbled and fell.

Here was a chance again.

She redoubled her efforts, and flew like the wind.

But she was not destined to escape.

Fate, indeed, seemed against her.

Just as she reached a corner, and was about to rush along a second street, a man in sailor's garb caught her in his arms.

He thought at first that it was a thief or a murderer running from justice.

He seized her, therefore, firmly in his arms, crying—

"Where away, where away, my hearty? Ah!" he added, as he felt the softness of her form; "a woman, by all that's wonderful, and in disguise, too."

"Oh! sir, I am in trouble," she cried; "I am pursued by a villain who seeks my destruction. Save me—save me from him!"

"Hold her tight, hold her tight," shouted the voice of Dick Hatherden; "she is mad."

And in a few moments he was at the side of Aurora Halsted, who now faint, weary, panting, was unable to resist longer.

There was a lamp swinging across the street at this point, and as the two men met there passed between them a look of recognition.

"Why, Hatherden, this is well met," cried the man in the sailor's dress; "I was just coming up to the crib."

A look of pleasure overspread Dick's face.

"Why, Hardy, this is indeed well met," cried he. "This is the one whom I spoke to you about. Is the boat ready?"

"Yes; come quickly this way," replied Hardy.

And he led the way towards a narrow passage, leading down to the river.

Aurora saw now there was no hope.

This fellow was, of course, the one with whom Dick was in league for her abduction.

One more piercing shriek she gave.

This deprived her of her last chance.

In an instant Dick seized her, and despite her incessant struggles, gagged her.

Then he raised her in his arms and carried her, still struggling, away.

It was not long before they reached the margin of the Thames.

Here a boat was waiting at the bottom of a wooden staircase.

Into this Aurora was quickly placed, and with a feeling of horror which we cannot express felt herself being rowed rapidly away.

The river was so still, and so entirely divested of all human life, that even had she been ungagged she could have succeeded in securing no help.

So along they went, through the arches of old London Bridge, and at length reached the ship's side.

Here, at a signal given by Hardy, a ladder was let down, and Aurora was soon aboard.

Then the gag was removed from her lips, and she was conducted to the cabin destined for her reception.

Here she was bolted in and left alone with her thoughts.

CHAPTER XXI.

THE JOURNEY—THE MULATTO GIRL.

ON the next morning, Aurora, on looking out of the little porthole which formed her only window, saw that she was out on the open sea.

She had found a lock and key inside her cabin, left there probably to give her confidence.

This she had accordingly fastened, and, wearied as she was by the continued excitements of the day, she flung herself on the bed, and slept heavily until morning.

In vain she glanced round the wide expanse of ocean.

Scarcely a sail was to be seen anywhere.

And certainly not one following in their track.

In fact, how could she expect it?

No one knew or could suspect whither she had gone.

Mr. Hallwyn had probably learned of her cap-

tivity from Mrs. Absalom, who had, of course, been quite unaware that Dick had discovered and prevented her escape.

But how could he know whether she had fled or been taken?

She felt herself, accordingly, utterly at the mercy of her destroyer, and looking back upon the ruin of all her hopes, she found herself wishing that the ship would go down at sea, and carry her to the peaceful arms of death with her enemies.

About eleven in the morning, when Aurora had begun to feel faint and sick, a knock came at the door.

Then the outside bolts were unfastened, and the lock tried.

"Who is there?" asked Aurora.

"Only me," said a female voice.

"Who are you?"

"Your servant."

Aurora hesitated a moment.

"Is anyone with you?" she said.

"No one."

Aurora thought an instant, and then unlocked the door.

On the threshold stood a young girl, whose dark skin proclaimed her a mulatto.

She entered the room, bearing a tray with breakfast, and then closed the door behind her.

Then she sat down at the table, and before saying a word tasted everything on the tray.

Aurora watched her with amusement.

"Why do you do that?" she asked.

"That you may know you can eat with safety," replied the girl, with a smile. "You might have thought they were poisoned. Eat and drink, then, for you have presently a trial to go through."

Aurora paled.

"What mean you?" she asked.

"Your marriage," replied the girl.

Aurora shuddered.

"What marriage can legally take place here?" she cried. "No clergyman would perform such a ceremony, nor is it likely that one would be found among such a set of vagabonds."

The girl lowered her voice.

"Yes, yes," she said, "it will be a marriage, for the one who intends you to be his wife is resolved that the tie shall be as binding as possible. It is for the sake of property, I think, or to prevent another having you. I was treated in the same way."

She said this with a sigh.

"Who, then, are you?" asked Aurora.

"I am the wife of Hardy," she said; "I was married by the same priest who is to marry you. Your intended husband has taken advantage of the fact of your being a Roman Catholic to bribe this man, whose habits and doings, if they were known, would cause him to be kicked out of the church. However, he is a member of it now, and those who are married by him are legally so."

A desperate resolve entered Aurora's mind.

She would obtain as large a supply of provisions as she could from the mulatto girl.

Then she would barricade herself in the room, and stand a siege until they arrived in some port.

It was a wild and almost hopeless idea, but she clung to it as they say a drowning man would catch at a straw.

The mulatto girl had a good-natured face, and she had proved herself a friend by the way in which she had spoken in regard to the marriage.

The girl readily assented.

It seemed that the wedding was to take place in the afternoon, so that there was some hours for preparation.

It was arranged, accordingly, that, under pretence of bring Aurora Halsted an early dinner, she should procure for her enough provisions to last for three days.

She was as good as her word, and ere one o'clock in the day had supplied her with everything she wanted.

The girl then quitted the room, and Aurora, having locked the door, at once proceeded to pile against it every bit of available furniture in the room.

It was not long before she had formed a strong barricade.

Then she sat down near the little loophole, which, as I have said, was her only window, and looked out upon the vast and monotonous expanse of sea, waiting for the arrival of her enemies.

The time passed very slowly for Aurora.

At length, however, she heard footsteps descending the companion ladder.

Her heart beat violently, and she sprang up as if to prepare for an attack.

The bolts were withdrawn, and the door pushed violently.

But it resisted well, as she had hoped.

Hardy, the captain, burst into a loud laugh, as he glanced at the angry face of Dick Hatherden.

"Your bird likes her cage, and has barricaded herself in," he said. "What is to be done now?"

"Burst in the door," said Dick.

"That's exactly what we can't do," said Hardy, "without destroying the whole of the cabin wall. You are not in such a deuce of a hurry; we shall soon be at the cave in the rocks, and you can be married there."

"It is all very well for you," said he, "but delay is always dangerous. Can't we enter by the windows?"

"There is only one," said Hardy, "and that is so small you could not possibly enter it. No, no, you must have patience; we shall not be many hours reaching our destination."

Despite his eagerness, Dick Hatherden had to submit, and with a sullen air he took his way to the deck.

Towards evening they came in view of a rocky coast, on the face of which were visible several large caves.

Towards this the vessel began to run quickly, and as darkness came on a number of flickering lights were visible on the beach below the cliffs.

As the ship came closer in shore, its crew could see a small bay into which they could run safely, and conceal themselves entirely from observation, and it was not long before they were riding safely at anchor in deep water.

CHAPTER XXII.

THE MARRIAGE.

THE men whom Hardy commanded were some of the most daring smugglers in the channel.

For years they had successfully evaded the law, and their home was the repository of every imaginable kind of merchandise, from a Dutch cheese to a diamond.

For, be it said, it was not all contraband goods that were seized by these men.

They were pickers-up of unconsidered trifles everywhere.

They were, in fact, river thieves, pirates, and smugglers combined.

Their home was comfortable enough, considering everything.

In fact, in some parts of the cavern they had fitted up rooms, so that not even the bare rocks could be seen.

One of these was destined by Dick Hatherden to be the home of Aurora.

As soon, therefore, as they had come to anchor, and the vessel was riding, as I have said, in deep still water, a consultation was held to ascertain how Aurora was to be got out of her room.

There was no doubt in the minds of any of them that Aurora had made the desperate resolve to suffer death rather than submit to the fate that threatened her.

Out at sea there was more danger of destroying the cabin wall by breaking in; but now it was decided to do something of the kind.

The only way in which they could make an entrance into the cabin was by sawing a hole through one of the partitions, and this they at once proceeded to do.

It was not without much persuasion that Captain Hardy consented to do this, for, villain as he was, he was a true sailor, and looked upon his ship as some men do upon their sweethearts.

But, as we have said, Dick Hatherden, had plenty of money with him.

This is the best of persuaders, and the offer of a good round sum in gold soon wrought a change in Captain Hardy's ideas.

Aurora, of course, had not even dreamed of such an emergency as this.

If she had thought of it she could have done but little.

The whole of the furniture in the room had been placed against the door, which she regarded of course, as the most vulnerable point of the fortress.

So now she was completely at their mercy.

She had gained delay.

But of what avail was that?

Not a single vessel was in sight.

In fact, in the black darkness of that miserable night it was impossible to discern any object.

In the course of a few minutes the aperture had been made, and Dick Hatherden and Hardy entered.

Aurora was standing in the middle of the room— still, of course, in her male attire— pale and angry.

"Well, Aurora," said Dick, with a malignant smile, "you have enjoyed your privacy till we reached port, but now, since we have arrived at our rendezvous, you must follow us."

Resistance, she saw, was useless.

She had no weapon at hand to defend herself, and no means of escape.

As to one thing, however, she was determined.

Rather than be possessed by Dick Hatherden, whom she now detested as greatly as she had formerly loved him, she would die, no matter by what fearful death.

"I am helpless," she said, "and so I follow you."

With a look of triumph, Dick led the way up to the deck.

From this she was borne down into a boat, and in a few moments she found herself one of a circle of uncouth and fantastically-garbed men in the huge cave.

In vain she gazed from one to the other.

There was not a face among them that spoke of sympathy.

She would find no one there to aid her.

"Now," whispered Dick Hatherden to the priest, "let us settle this ceremony at once. Then she can be locked up in one of the inner rooms, and I will do my best to aid you."

"Very well," said Hardy with a laugh; "you're in a mighty hurry to be tied up. So come this way. Here, Nalda."

This last was addressed to the mulatto girl, his wife.

Then they proceeded towards the inner room.

"Now," said Dick, "let the ceremony proceed."

Aurora looked at the priest.

She fancied that she saw in his sleek and oily countenance some slight trace of good nature and pity.

Flinging herself on her knees, therefore, before him, she clasped her hands, and cried wildly—

"Oh, sir, let me entreat you not to perform this unholy ceremony. This is a marriage which will be hateful in the sight of heaven. This man is a villain—my father's murderer—whom it would be a crime to unite to me in wedlock. Oh, sir, pity me, and refuse to proceed further."

The priest, it must be said, felt some degree of compunction in his heart, but the reward which had been promised him by Dick Hatherden was too much for his morality.

There were plenty of ways of persuading himself that things would turn out for the best.

Aurora might yield at last.

She might get used to her husband, and even love him when they was married.

And so he said, with affected solemnity—

"My child, my word is pledged; and besides," he added, bending over her, "my life depends upon compliance."

There was no hope.

So Aurora sprang up.

"The curse of heaven will be upon you all," she cried. "Proceed with the ceremony, but you cannot force me to reply to any one question."

The ceremony then proceeded.

Dick Hatherden gave all the responses, but Aurora, as she had said, uttered not a word.

In a few minutes Dick Hatherden and Aurora Halsted were, as far as mere ceremony was concerned, man and wife.

As the priest closed the book, Dick leaned over and whispered in her ear—

"I have to leave you for awhile, wife of my heart; but I will return in an hour."

A shudder was her only answer.

"Death first," was the response of her heart.

But Dick paid no heed to her.

He desired to hurry over the duty he had to perform; and in a few moments he had quitted the room, and she was once more alone.

CHAPTER XXIII.

THE REPRISAL.

WE need not occupy our space in describing the service in which Dick Hatherden had promised to aid the smugglers, because the service was never performed.

Suffice it to say that the boats had been got out and manned, and were ready to start on their errand, when out from the darkness flashed two muskets, and then several rockets ascended fizzing into the air.

Then there was a rush of several boats, and Hardy's men found themselves intercepted.

The boats dashed against one another, and ere the smugglers could seize their arms, the enemy, whoever they were, had leaped into the water, and were wading towards shore, holding their pistols high over their heads.

When they reached the dry land some rushed into the cave, and bringing forth some inflammable bales of merchandise, set fire to them on the shingle.

They could thus see the scene around them.

The beach on which they stood was surmounted by rocks full one hundred and fifty feet in height.

On neither side was there any mode of escape from the tide, except by the stone steps leading to the smugglers' cave, which was always above the level of high water.

The daring foes which had so suddenly attacked Hardy and his men were, of course, now between two fires.

But they had evidently prepared themselves for some desperate enterprise, and were resolved not even to attempt to retreat until they had effected their object.

In spite of the confusion which the sudden inroad of the boats had made, Hardy and his men soon recovered themselves, and dashed back towards the spot where already a severe fight was going on by the light of the blazing bonfire.

The bold invaders had the disadvantage in numbers.

But they were not long left unassisted.

The whole of the little bay was aglow with a red light, and into the circle of it soon came two more swift boats laden with armed men.

These at once joined their companions on the beach, the first man who leapt out crying in a loud voice—

"Alexis, where are you?"

It was Robert Hallwyn who said this.

Here there was a mystery.

Who had given them such information that they were enabled to follow the kidnappers across the seas?

We cannot pause here to explain.

We must hurry on to finish the combat.

The smugglers were as resolute as those who had so suddenly and so mysteriously attacked their secret home.

But there were brave men among the invaders—men who had seen adventures of every kind, and among them were many well known faces.

Simon Grandley was there, and Guy the Foundling, and brave Will Lightmore, whom, in spite of old differences, Alexis seemed to have rallied round him for the purpose of rescuing Aurora or punishing her betrayer.

Gradually the followers of Alexis drove the smugglers into the sea, at the same time drawing from their place of concealment those who were in the cave.

In order to do this they fought in bouble ranks —one facing the rocks, the other facing the sea.

Captain Hardy, at last, seeing his men falling around him so quickly, and not dreaming that his enemies were any other than revenue officers, he expected naturally to be taken prisoner.

Capture in those days meant to a smuggler nothing less than death.

It may be supposed, therefore, that in the expectation of being arrested no second thoughts came into the captain's mind.

"We are outnumbered; save himself who can," he shouted.

Then, with a sudden dash, he made for the boats.

Alexis Rainsford had no desire to pursue them.

All his wishes were centred in the release of Aurora Halsted from the hands of her enemies.

As soon, therefore, as Hardy and his followers had made their escape, he turned round upon the second band of ruffians, and began forcing his way towards the cave.

He had little difficulty in doing this.

The numbers opposed to him were small, and the men, besides, were disheartened by the flight of their leader, in spite of the efforts of Dick Hatherden to rally them.

Seeing, however, that all his endeavours were in vain, Dick suddenly dashed up the stone steps into the cave.

He returned in a few moments bearing a small cask in his hands, and as his enemies rushed up the stairs he concealed himself in the shadow of the rocks.

Alexis had nothing by which he could be guided in the search for Aurora.

He knew, however, she was there, and that a thorough search in all the chambers of the cave would be certain to result in her discovery.

Patiently, therefore, he went from room to room, and at length they came to a door that was locked.

This they had no difficulty in bursting open, although no sound came from within to make them believe anyone was within.

Alexis, of course, knew nothing of the fact that Aurora was in male attire, and seeing some one standing in the middle of the room dressed in semi-nautical costume, he, for a moment, in the dim light, did not know who it was.

The figure, however, sprang forward with a joyful cry, and in a moment Aurora was clasped in her lover's arms.

"Let us leave this horrid place at once," cried she; "there is nothing but death and ruin here."

"We have nothing to delay for," said Alexis; "come, let us hasten away at once."

He would have paused yet had he known the awful peril that awaited them.

They had scarcely reached the middle of the staircase leading to the beach when a terrific explosion was heard, fragments of rocks and bodies of men went flying upwards into the air, and then, after the one terrific blaze of light, all was darkness.

Dick Hatherden had thrown the powder keg into the centre of the blazing bonfire, risking destruction for himself rather than Aurora should escape with the one he hated.

Alexis saw something flash near them; then, with a cry of pain, Aurora sank into his arms helpless and lifeless, while a wild shout of gratified revenge rose on the night air.

CHAPTER XXIV.
THE CLUE TO THE MYSTERY.

WE need not waste much time in detailing the mysterious manner in which Alexis heard of the abduction of Aurora.

But we must, nevertheless, do something in the way of explanation.

When on the next day after her kidnapping by Dick Hatherden, her absence was discovered, it was a matter of utter bewilderment both to Mr. Hallwyn and Alexis Rainsford.

There was not the slightest sign in her bedroom of any struggle or any secret departure.

What then could be the meaning of her absence?

She was used to take long and solitary rambles.

But she never stopped out a whole day.

So, late in the evening, they resolved to proceed in search of her.

Asking accidentally at the tavern on the way to the cross-roads, they learned that the landlord had seen a rough-looking man driving a carriage, which, he felt sure, belonged to the landlord at Alstone.

He said he knew the carriage by its peculiar build, and he felt sure that the man on the box was not a regular driver.

"It would be better," he suggested, "to inquire at the tavern."

Robert Hallwyn and Alexis Rainsford were not slow in taking this advice.

They at once started off in the direction of the place, where, having told the landlord of their enterprise, they were introduced to the driver of the coach.

The man, although gagged and violently thrown on the roadside, had still enough sense left in him to watch the proceedings of those who had attacked him

Of course there was in his heart a resolution to take vengeance if he could.

He saw the men take the direction of the house of Mr. Hallwyn, and they did not return.

They must, therefore, have gone on by the cross-roads.

This was all he could say.

But though this little was apparently uninportant, it proved by no means so.

From the cross-roads no carriage but one had passed on that night.

This was proved by men at the turnpikes, of which there were four.

The carriage had passed through one and taken the left hand road.

This road, by a somewhat circuitous route, led to London.

Of course, as the day progressed, the carriage was less noticeable, for even at that hour of the night many vehicles were about.

However, one incident helped them.

They had, I omitted to state, hired horses at the inn at Alstone.

One of these, when not many streets off the house of Mrs. Absalom, dropped his shoe, and they had to pull up at a blacksmith's.

Full of their enterprise they became communicative, and while the man was doing the job told him of the business which had brought him up to the metropolis.

The man, like all people, liked mysteries.

So he asked numerous questions.

Their replies made him more attentive, and presently he cried, slapping his leg, and hitting the horse instead of the shoe as he sprang up—

"Hang me if you ain't come to the very right one after all."

"Why, what do you mean?" exclaimed both Mr. Hallwyn and Alexis Rainsford at once. "What do you know of her?"

"Why, see here," said the man, "do you know a fellow called Dick Hatherden?"

"Dick Hatherden!" cried Alexis; "aye, the veriest villain that ever lived. He has been her persecutor for many a day."

"Do you suspect he's taken her?"

"That is very likely," said Mr. Hallwyn, "but at present we suspect no one, for we have no clue whatever."

"Well, then, all I can say is that I believe he's the one you want. On that night you speak of I was over at the tavern yonder, when a carriage drove up. The man on the box leaped down, and went to the door.

"'Dick,' said he, 'I'm frightful dry, and I'm going to have a drain. Shall I bring yer out a drop?'

"'Yes. I don't suppose the old woman will have anything in,' answered the voice of Dick Hatherden.

"And the lady, will she take anything?' said the man.

"'The lady doesn't want any,' said Dick. 'Be quick.'

"'The lady,' thinks I. 'I wonder what sort of wench Dick Hatherden has got in there that this chap calls a lady.'

"And with that I goes a little nearer and tries to have a peep.

"But it wasn't no good.

"There was a kind of scuffle in the carriage as if the girl was a-trying to get out, and Dick Hatherden was a-keeping of her back.

"Then the chap comes out with the drink, which they disposed of quick, and then hurried down the street yonder.

"I didn't watch any more, because it didn't concern me.

"And that's all I've got to tell, though it's very puzzling to my mind if that there lady wasn't your niece that you're a-looking for."

"I think as you do," replied Hallwyn, "and a very simple chain of circumstances as led us up to this point. If we are quick we shall now be in time."

He then pressed a gold piece into the hand of the delighted blacksmith, and with Alexis hurried away.

"Well—well," said the blacksmith as he returned to his forge, "honesty's the best policy after all; and, besides, I owe that cursed devil's imp, Dick Hatherden, a grudge."

So he satisfactorily adjusted his conscience in two respects.

Of course, when Mr. Hallwyn and Alexis turned down the street indicated there were no further indications to guide them.

No one knew anything about any particular carriage.

And so, after having searched and searched in vain, they took down the name of the narrow thoroughfare, "Earl's Row," and went heavy-hearted away.

They pursued their search to the very evening of Aurora's attempted escape.

Early the following morning Mrs. Absalom presented herself at Hallwyn House, and having to a certain extent confided her business to the butler, the latter at once requested her to accompany him to London to the Crown Tavern, where he knew his master always put up.

The old woman was alarmed enough when she found that Aurora had not escaped.

Mr. Hallwyn was at first disinclined to believe any of her story, and suspected that Aurora had been the victim of foul play.

But the evidently real alarm of the old woman at length convinced him; and he proceeded to act upon her words.

More than this, too.

As Aurora had been seized by Dick Hatherden, he, of course, had left England.

She had nothing, therefore, to fear from him.

"If," she said, hesitatingly, "if I thought he could not find out and come back and murder me—"

Mr. Hallwyn interrupted her.

"Fear nothing," he said; "if you act in this as a friend to me and my unfortunate niece, I will see that you come to no harm. I will give you money, and you can, if you like, leave this neighbourhood for ever. But do not, for Heaven's sake, keep back anything that would enable me to save my child."

Under these circumstances the old woman told her whole story unreservedly.

RIVAL APPRENTICES

A TALE OF THE RIOTS OF 1780.

THE WOMAN WAS LEANING OVER HIM AND LISTENING INTENTLY.

"And now," she said, "I'll tell you where he is. He's gone in the 'Firefly' with Captain Hardy to a smuggling place on the coast of Germany, that I've often heard him speak of. You'll find all about him if you go the 'Three Stumps,' down in Thaver Street, and I've no doubt with a little money you could bribe one of his companions to tell the exact spot where they have gone.

Mr. Hallwyn and Alexis Rainsford were not slow in taking advantage of this advice.

They at once made their way to the "Three Stumps," and on inquiring for Dick Hatherden and Captain Hardy were accosted by a rough-looking sailor.

"What do you want with Hardy?" he asked, suspiciously.

He knew Hardy's character.

And naturally, therefore, he regarded them as revenue officers.

"I want to see him," said Alexis.

The sailor laughed.

"Ah! I know your game," he said.

"I'd stake my life you don't," cried Alexis; "but come—you take us for revenue officers. We are not, but, if you like to earn a hundred pounds, tell us where we can have a little talk with you in private."

"A hundred pounds!"

Don't reckon it by your own ideas, reader, you who have plenty.

Reckon it as a poor man would.

A man struggling for existence.

A hundred pounds!

To be earned, perhaps, in a moment.

And without any hard work.

This was an important item.

Working men will work; and that hard and willingly.

But give them something to do which will relieve them from their incessant toil, and they greet it like a small slice of Paradise.

"A hundred pounds!" he said; "that's a large sum—I'm almost a mind to think that you're making game of me, gentlemen."

Mr. Hallwyn put his hand in his pocket and pulled out a sovereign.

"See here," he said, "people don't give away even sovereigns for nothing. You've told us nothing, but take this in earnest of future money."

The man took it, spit on it, and put it in his pocket.

"Come with me this way," he said.

He led the way into a little room adjoining the drinking-room, after speaking a few words to the landlord.

"You took away my breath, gentlemen," he said, "so I ordered some drink, and now if you'll be good enough I should be glad to hear as soon as possible how I'm to earn all this money. A hundred pounds is a deal to a man like me, remember."

"I dare say it is," replied Alexis Rainsford; "but this I can promise, that directly you give us real information you shall have fifty pounds, and the other fifty when our object is achieved."

The man's eyes glistened.

"Question me," he said; "you'll find I'll answer to the point."

Quickly Alexis told the story of Aurora's disappearance.

"Well," he said, "and I suppose you want me to help you to get back the girl."

"Yes; and to do that we must know the whereabouts of Hardy."

"Of course; but as you ain't revenue officers it don't matter where the exact spot is, so long as you get the girl back."

"Of course not. All we wish is to assure her safety."

"Well, then, this very night we'll start after them," said the man; "that is, if money don't stand in the way."

"I will spare no trouble or expense," said Mr. Hallwyn. "Let no consideration of money stop you. Simply name what it is necessary to do and I will pay the expense."

"A good thing for my friend Abraham Holler," thought the man who rejoiced in the name of Isaac Oliver—all the men in the vicinity appearing to rejoice in some connection with the Jewish fraternity.

"Well," he said, "I have a friend named Abraham Holler, who has about the swiftest craft that ever sailed out of the mouth of the Thames. He's in the house now—in fact, he only reached this place last night, and hasn't even thought yet of taking in any cargo for the return voyage. He's a Dutchman; but he's not like the rest of his breed. His vessel is a regular fly-away, and will catch up the "Firefly" within a few hours if we start soon. But he'll want a tidy sum for his craft, I can tell you."

"As I said before," returned Mr. Hallwyn, "that matters not. I wish only to arrange matters at once."

"In that case I'll go and fetch him," said Oliver. "I'll just simply explain to him what you want, and that will save you the trouble."

So saying he rose from his seat and hurried away.

He was not gone long.

He returned, in fact, after a few minutes with a tall, bronzed, weather-beaten man, the very reverse of the kind of fellow whom the friends would have imagined to be on good terms with such a suspicious character as Isaac Oliver.

In fact, he was a sailor and nothing more.

A dare-devil, courageous seaman, perhaps capable of doing a little smuggling now and then, but nothing worse.

He at once fell in with the plans of Mr. Hallwyn and Alexis.

In fact they pleased him.

Independently of the money entirely.

A sailor always loves the idea of a chase, more especially if it is likely to show off the superiority of his own craft.

So, at what seemed a moderate sum to the eager pursuers of Aurora, a bargain was quickly struck, a little refreshment was taken, and Mr. Hallwyn and Alexis were soon being rowed down the river by Holler and Oliver—the latter with fifty pounds in his pocket.

How they chased the villains, and how they attacked them at the smuggler's cave, we already know.

We must turn to another point in our narrative, which is now drawing fast to a close.

We must, in fact, return to the abode of that villain among villains, Giles Roper.

CHAPTER XXV.

IN WHICH GILES ROPER HAS A STRANGE VISITOR
—A NEW COMPLICATION.

GILES ROPER, after the escape of the young girl
whom Alexis Rainsford, under the name of "Turner," had left in his charge, felt really as if his
life were not safe.

He knew nothing, of course, of Guy the Foundling or Alexis by name.

Nor did he know of any connection between Guy
and Alice, and being unaware that Alexis and the
Foundling knew one another he naturally concluded
that when "Turner" should return and ask from
him his charge he would be unable to say whither
she had gone, and would be suspected of another
dastardly attempt upon her honour and her life.

So he hit upon an ingenious plan of assuring his
safety.

He apparently sold his business.

But it was only apparently.

Giles Roper certainly disappeared, and in his
stead came a man of about the same height, but
of stouter build, with large whiskers, and beard of
the same hue as his carroty shock head.

But those who knew best about it, and more
especially his wife, knew it to be Giles Roper in
disguise.

He had succeeded in his time in accomplishing
many villainies, and in these he had used great
tact and astuteness.

But he never succeeded so well as he did now.

He even disguised his voice so successfully that
not one of his customers knew him.

There are some, however, who can penetrate all
disguises.

And so at length it proved with Giles Roper.

Sitting one evening as usual in his bar, surrounded
by some of those parasites who always cling round
a new landlord, he was descanting on the goodness
of his ales, when a tall stranger entered the bar.

He was a spare, weather-beaten man, who had
evidently seen a deal of travel, and yet whose hair
was not silvered but iron-grey.

He glanced round him a strange wistful glance,
as if the aspect of the place brought to mind scenes
and events long gone by, and then advanced politely to the bar.

He seemed for a moment puzzled at the aspect
of the new landlord.

"Where is Giles Roper?" he said. "I wish a
word with him."

The disguised landlord rose and approached the
new-comer politely.

"Giles Roper is gone, sir," he said. "He has
been gone some time."

The stranger glanced at him for a moment inquiringly.

Then he said, leaning over the bar—

"I think a few words with yourself will answer
the same purpose. Can I have a private interview
with you?"

Giles Roper suspected nothing.

How should he?

"Certainly," he said; "these gentlemen will
excuse me—come this way, sir."

In a few moments they were closeted in a little
room.

"Sir," said the stranger, "by what name shall
I call you?"

"Eggar."

"Very well, Mr. Eggar," pursued the other,
"do you know a person of the name of Alexis
Rainsford?"

"I do not."

"He sometimes goes by the name of Turner.
Now do you recognise him?"

Giles Roper began to feel queer.

"Yes, I do know a person of the name of Turner.
What do you desire of him? I only know him by
hearsay. Before Giles Roper quitted the business
he told me he was the plague of his life."

"Very likely," returned the other, drily, as he
leaned over towards his companion, "but shall I
tell you one thing?"

"If you like."

"I have discovered your secret."

"What secret?" cried the landlord, nervously.

"You are Giles Roper!"

Giles started in fear and nervousness.

"You are mad," he said.

The stranger laughed.

"No," he said, "I am not mad, and you know
it. However, it is not worth while to argue. I
never saw you in my life before, but I know you
are Giles Roper. You were agitated when I first
asked for him—you looked as if I had made a discovery, and I had.

"I knew you at first; but understand, I came to
do you no injury, so do not imagine so—do not attempt to deny anything, or it will be useless to
talk at all. I come to ask of you a service for
which I will pay you well; so quit all absurd disguises, and speak as yourself."

Giles Roper was not even now sure that this
was not some emissary of "Turner's" come to
molest him.

"Well," he said, "I am not the man you take
me for; but it matters not. I know a great deal
of his affairs, and if I——"

The stranger rose.

"Very well," he said, "since you are obstinate,
and you in your own character can alone aid me,
why I will go."

Giles Roper saw the promised reward melting
from his grasp.

Should he risk all?

Personally he was no coward; and they were
but man to man.

"Well," he said, "I will tell the truth. I am
Giles Roper; what is it you want with me?"

The stranger smiled, and at once resumed his
seat.

"I knew it would come to this, and you might
just as well have given in at once. Now, in the
first place, you had for some time in your charge a
young girl entrusted to you by this Turner, or,
rather, Alexis Rainsford, had you not?"

Giles Roper turned pale and trembled from head
to foot.

Here was the very thing, after all, against which he had been fighting, cropping up to annoy him.

And after he had confessed his identity to a stranger !

But there was no use in attempting to draw back now.

"Yes," he said, "I had a young girl in my care ; "but she was more than I could manage. She was fearfully self-willed, and when I remonstrated with her she repaid me by running away. I am in continual dread lest he should demand her of me. I can tell him nothing as to where she has gone, and he will most certainly say I have killed her."

The stranger smiled.

"He has no great opinion of your virtue, then," he said. "However, I am in no way interested by his charge ; it is he whom I wish to discover. Have you no means of discovering him ?"

"Discovering him," thought Giles Roper; "no; and if I had, I'd take good care I'd not disturb him, wherever he might be."

He said, however, aloud—

"No ; I have no conception where he is. He came mysteriously at first, and he goes and comes mysteriously now. He goes by a false name, as you have seen, and he never dreams of giving me anything like an address. He may call here, however, and then I will say you called if you will give me a name."

The stranger sighed.

"My name," he said, "is Grandley."

"What, Simon Grandley the carpenter ?"

He had never seen Simon.

But he had heard enough of him in connection with the riots.

"No ; but a relation," cried the other, excitedly. "It is he I desire to find. Where does he live ?"

Giles Roper quickly gave the address.

"Tell Alexis Rainsford, if he comes, that I have gone thither," said the stranger, "and bid him come after me. Here is your reward."

And so saying, he placed five pounds in the hand of the tavern-keeper.

The stranger then, without stopping to take any refreshment, quitted the inn, and took his way rapidly in the direction which had been pointed out to him by Giles Roper.

CHAPTER XXVI.

THE REUNION.

DURING the riots, Simon Grandley had been singularly fortunate.

Not because he had been a favourite of the rioters.

This, as we have seen, was of no avail as a security against pillage and murder.

It simply happened that there was nothing worth robbing the carpenter of, and his house, therefore, was passed by as not offering any chance of plunder.

Mrs. Grandley and her family had not, as we have seen, returned yet from their country abode, but Simon himself had reopened his shop, and began business once more as if nothing had happened to alter the course of events.

When, however, the stranger who had called himself Grandley, and stated himself to be a relative of the carpenter's, arrived at the house, he found no one there but a servant.

Simon Grandley and his two apprentices, as we have seen, had accompanied Alexis Rainsford and Mr. Hallwyn on their expedition against the kidnappers of Aurora Halsted.

The servant, of course, could give no information as to where they had gone, or how long they would be absent.

Warned by former events, she was far from being disposed to disclose to a stranger, of whom she knew nothing, the situation of the country house which Simon Grandley had taken as a kind of hiding-place for his family.

From her, therefore, the stranger saw it would be useless to attempt to obtain information.

"I will depart," he said, with some sternness, "but tell your master when he returns that someone has called to see him, after many years' sojourn abroad, and he will come again, when he will expect a better welcome."

On leaving the house of the carpenter he did not proceed to any distance.

There was an inn not far from Grandley's house. There he ensconced himself in a room, from the window of which he could command a view of every one who entered the carpenter's house.

He had not very long to wait.

On the evening of the second day he saw Simon approach.

A glow overspread his face as he saw him.

"Many, many years have elapsed since we met," he murmured, as he prepared to descend from his room, "but I know well his face, although his form is changed. I wonder if the recognition will be mutual."

He was at the carpenter's door ere Simon had passed in.

"Simon Grandley," he said, "I wish you good night."

The carpenter turned and eyed the speaker without speaking.

There was something in his voice, in his manner, in his appearance, which made him tremble, which seemed like the echo of some far off time.

"Who are you, sir?" he asked. "I do not know you."

Yet his voice belied him.

He seemed to imply—

"One word from you will tell me all."

"I left a message with your servant," said the other, "which would have explained all. I said I had returned to England after for many years being incarcerated in a prison. Simon, don't you know me ?"

Simon Grandley started forward and seized the stranger by both his hands.

"Is it possible," he cried, earnestly, and with a trembling of the voice, and then repeated again, "is it possible that you are my father ?"

Whatever speeches the stranger had made up his mind to deliver, and whatever trials he had meant to subject Simon Grandley to, were all forgotten now.

He opened his arms to the great stalwart car-

penter as if he had been a little child, and pressed him with fond emotion to his breast.

We have no time now that our story is drawing to a close to describe at length the scene between father and son.

When the first emotion had passed away Simon insisted upon his father accompanying him to the house in the country, where he was introduced to his family and apprentices by the delighted carpenter.

How Grandley and his friends had fared after the explosion at the smuggler's cave we must describe hereafter, and remain for the moment at the quiet fireside of Simon.

"I will explain at another time," said the elder Grandley, when, at the request of all, he commenced his story, "the reasons why I left England, never hoping to return, and why you have not until lately heard from me for so many years.

"I had resolved at length to risk a return to this country.

"Most of the enemies whom I feared are dead, and I thought, naturally enough, that after so many years' absence, a disguise would effectually prevent my being recognised by any whose interest it would be to injure me.

"I had made all my arrangements; I had banked all my money, and was only waiting for a few minor details to be completed, when an event happened which entirely overthrew all my plans.

"I was walking along one of the streets of Vienna, when a shrill, loud cry for help smote my ear.

"I stopped and listened.

"But all remained still.

"I had concluded to proceed onwards without taking notice of the incident, since I had nothing to guide me, when in the semi-darkness of an archway, nearly opposite to me, a scene presented itself which at once arrested my attention.

"A man, evidently insensible from the effects of a blow, was lying upon his back, and a woman was kneeling near him.

"She was bending over him, with one hand resting on his knee, while with the other she was feeling in his pockets.

"She had evidently knocked him down with a stick, which lay beneath his legs, and was now proceeding to rob him.

"The natural impulse of any man, under such circumstances, would be to rush forward and assist the victim.

"I had forgotten that I was in a foreign country.

"I had forgotten that I was in a city where justice had no place.

"In fact, I had forgotten everything except that a man was in deadly peril, and that it was my duty to aid him.

"I dashed forward, therefore, and in the German language shouted, 'What are you doing to that man? Let him rise at once.'

"The woman eyed me with the ferocity of a tigress.

"'He is my husband!' she cried, savagely, 'he has fallen down because he is drunk. It's no business of yours.'

"I felt certain that she was lying, and felt it, therefore, no sin to stretch the truth a little to discover her villainy.

"'It is not true,' I said. 'You struck him with that stick there that is even now all over blood, and you were robbing him when I came up.'

"She knew not, of course, whether what I said was true or not, but, knowing her own guilt, she thought it no use to attempt denial.

"She sprang to her feet, and seized the heavy bludgeon with which she dealt the unfortunate man the blow which had rendered him insensible. She was evidently going to attack me, and though a woman, she was of that powerful build that it would have needed all my exertions to defend myself.

"I drew my sword. Fortunately I was spared the contest.

"At the moment she was about to rush at me like an infuriated demon there was the tramp of feet, and a patrol came suddenly upon us round the corner of an adjoining street.

"A devilish idea at once sprang into the woman's brain.

"'Quick, quick,' she cried, 'here is a thief—a murderer. Secure him.'

"Certainly my appearance with a drawn sword in my hand, and a man apparently dead at my feet, was against me.

"Quickly, however, I explained to the chief of the patrol the circumstances of the affair.

"'I am an Englishman,' I added, 'and I can prove that I have no motive whatever for such a crime as that which this woman would fix upon me.'

"The woman burst into a hoarse laugh.

"'The villain!' she cried, 'he attacked my husband with the stick that lies yonder, and was about to murder me when you came up.'

"She then whispered a few words in the patrol's ear, and I was at once seized and marched off.

"It was in vain that I protested, in vain that I declared that searching my lodgings would prove the truth of my words.

"I was refused any explanation, and thrust into a dark dungeon.

"I was evidently imprisoned there under the notion that I was an escaped prisoner, but I have never till this day received any explanation.

"It is not worth while to say any more on this part of my adventure.

"Days rolled rapidly by, and weeks, and months, and years, and in spite of the narrowness and misery of a cell not ten feet square I lived, aye, and kept my health.

"At length, finding that I was quiet—that, in fact, I had discovered the folly of making any attempts at obtaining release I was allowed a little liberty.

"By liberty I mean that I was permitted to walk in a kind of yard where one other prisoner besides myself was in the habit of walking.

"We became fast friends.

"Who, under the circumstances, would not do the same?

"Men of utterly different temperaments would in such a position at once become as brothers.

"But it was not so with us.

"We were exactly of the same temperament, though not of the same age, and we wandered to and fro in the prison yard during our brief interval of liberty, living over again our youth, and comparing the events of our eventful lives.

"I found that he was an English nobleman.

"His name was Guy Riverdale, Baron of Riverdale, in the county of Yorkshire.

"He had a brother who from his earliest youth was his enemy.

"This brother was a year younger, but was resolved, no matter what villainy it required, to accomplish the ruin of his brother and obtain the title and estates.

"He succeeded in driving him from England by accusing him of a fearful crime and bringing an array of bribed false witnesses to prove it.

"Then, in France, he contrived that he should be arrested as a spy, and condemned to eternal imprisonment in a dungeon.

"But this was not the matter that weighed most heavily on him.

"He had married very early in life a young and beautiful girl.

"Of this girl his brother had been secretly enamoured, and her marriage with Guy Riverdale only increased his fury.

"By some infernal means, which my friend has never been able to discover, this unnatural ruffian compassed her death.

"This did not occur until a year had passed, and a little child—a boy—had been born to them.

"It was of this boy that my friend was always thinking.

"He told me a strangely romantic story in regard to him.

"He said that being afraid to trust him in any position where his uncle could get at him, he left him on the doorstep of some worthy man—he named a name like yours, and said he was a carpenter—begging them not to desert him, but to bring him up as their own.

"He told only the name of Guy, and left to the future the discovery of the fact that he was heir to the noble house of Riverdale.

"However, there are certain indications which will satisfactorily prove his identity, and, moreover, papers were left with him, which can at any moment be explained."

It may easily be imagined with what intense anxiety Simon Grandley and those gathered round him listened to this recital.

Minnie Grandley and Guy the Foundling sat hand in hand, without uttering a syllable, scarcely, indeed, able to believe their senses.

Could there be a doubt that it was Guy the Foundling—the waif and stray of that winter's night—to whom the elder Grandley alluded?

But then——

Was he indeed the heir of a noble house?

Simon Grandley once or twice glanced over at him and at his wife.

But he did not interrupt the narrative of his father.

Even now, when he paused to take a draught of home-brewed ale, Simon would not think of interrupting him.

In fact, he hoped to hear more.

Was Alexis Rainsford a deceiver?

Was that sum of five hundred pounds really intended for the release of his father?

That was the problem now about to be solved satisfactorily.

"Well," continued Hugh Grandley, "he often spoke of this child with emotion, and even wept at the knowledge that, cooped up as he was in prison, he could send him no money.

"Even if he had been able to send a word of kindness and remembrance to him he would have been satisfied.

"But the laws of the prison were rigid.

"Under the disguise of a private letter to a son might be concealed a secret danger against the Government.

"So year after year rolled by, and he was unable even to send a word of kindness to his child.

"'Ah!' he would say, 'if he is still alive he must be a fine lad now, but he will curse the memory of his father.'"

"Never!" cried Guy, impetuously.

Hugh Grandley gazed at him in surprise.

"What said you, young man?" he asked.

Guy flushed crimson.

"I did but say that a good son would never curse his father."

Had the elder Grandley suspected for one moment that Guy the Foundling had been left a waif and stray on the doorstep of his son's house, he would, of course, have stopped in the middle of his narrative to inundate the apprentice with questions, and elucidate the mystery.

But he was far too much interested in his story to notice the interruption further than regarding it as the very natural impulse of a noble-minded youth.

"You are right in that," he said. "But to resume. I and my newly-made friend at length began to deal so extensively in reminiscences that our blood began to warm with the enthusiasm of youth, and we thought for the first time of escape.

"When I say for the first time, I do not mislead you.

"We had hoped and dreamed often.

"But we had never really had an idea of attempting it.

"The fortress was too large, too utterly isolated, standing as it did in the centre of a wild and desolate country.

"Besides, our courtyard—our 'pleasure-ground,' as we facetiously called it—was on the summit of the first range of battlements.

"We could contemplate truly a splendid range of country.

"But then——

"It taught us also to contemplate the utter uselessness of hope.

"However, so stirred were we in our hearts at the thoughts of home—renewed by speech—that we began really to consider if we were not living in a state of absurd inaction.

"We must plot and scheme.

"At any rate, even if we failed, it would be a source of excitement.

"And excitement was indeed a necessary of life in such a place.

"The first thing was to measure the depth of the walls.

"These were stupendous.

"It was useless to think of making our escape that way.

"Then how?

"It must be done by bribery.

"Then, again—money.

"Where was that to come from?

"This seemed suddenly to be placed within our reach.

"An old friend of my worthy friend Lord Riverdale had died, leaving to his son as a legacy the duty of discovering and aiding him.

"So one day, when we had almost began to despair, a visitor was announced.

"By strange courtesy he was permitted to see us in the courtyard, and accordingly we were able to talk unreservedly.

"The authorities were too firmly convinced of the strength of their fortress to be alarmed at the idea of our interview.

"When he approached us we imagined him to be an inspector of prisons.

"More especially as he came alone, and was bowed into the courtyard.

"So we received him stiffly.

"We had been annoyed enough by visits of inspection before.

"But we were soon undeceived.

"Pleasantly enough.

"The sound of the English language, spoken purely by a native, was sufficient to rouse in our hearts the most delicious emotions.

"He knew nothing of me, of course.

"He had come to see Lord Riverdale.

"'My lord,' he said, advancing to him, and bowing respectfully, 'I have come from England specially to see you. You do not know me, but you know my name well, I believe. It is Rainsford.'

"Lord Riverdale flushed.

"'Are you, then, the son of my dear old friend, Howard Rainsford?' he asked.

"'I am,' replied the stranger, 'and I have been left by him the heritage of rescuing you from this gloomy prison. I am told by all here that you are the bosom friend of Hans Offler here, and you will excuse me therefore for speaking thus openly before him.'

"In spite of our wretched condition we both smiled.

"Hans Offler!

"Such then was my name!

"The mistake was soon explained, and heartily, in the prospect of an attempt at escape, did we laugh over it.

"But the question came, who was to be bribed, and with what money

"Alexis had been left by his father the heritage of release.

"But alas!

"With the exception of a small income he possessed nothing.

"All the wealth which should have been his was hopelessly involved in lawsuits, through Mr. Rainsford's will being lost.

"I at once thought of you, Simon.

"Lord Riverdale was helpless.

"He, as you know, had been got out of the way by his younger brother, who was in full and undisputed possession of the property, and would rather have paid even to murder him than to aid his escape.

"But I sent to you.

"You know as well as I do how nobly you responded.

"I received your five hundred pounds."

(Mrs. Grandley, who knew nothing of this money, glanced at her husband in surprise, but Simon only nodded, as much as to say, "Wait a bit, and I will explain all.")

"I received your five hundred pounds, and we at once commenced operations.

"Alexis Rainsford proceeded to England himself, as you know, to obtain the money.

"When he returned he found we had not been idle.

"The gaoler had been taken ill, and had been absent from duty.

"He was an old Austrian, surly, wedded to the prison, believing implicitly in the right of the Emperor and his Government.

"To bribe him it would have been useless to attempt.

"His successor for the time was a different kind of man.

"He was a young, gay, flighty sort of fellow—just the opposite of the old fellow who had so long and for so many monotonous, interminable years been our gaoler.

"Fritz, as he was called, thought more of his gay uniform, of his lager beer, and of his sweethearts, than he did of the duties of the prison.

"He never dreamt of the possibility of any one escaping from such a colossal fortress.

"In fact, with the exception of the two Englishmen, there was no one in the prison who was sentenced to more than a short term of imprisonment, and he knew, therefore, that it would not be worth their while to risk the sudden death that would be the result of capture.

"As for the Englishmen, if he had been asked he would have shrugged his shoulders and said—

"'Oh, as for them, they have been here so long that they are used to it; they will not attempt escape now.'

"Both Lord Riverdale and myself, seeing what kind of man he was, set ourselves to work to make ourselves as agreeable to him as possible.

"Until Alexis Rainsford returned we had no means of doing this save by kind words, and so on.

"But when he once more made his appearance, we altered our tactics.

"Money is all powerful in England.

"It is worshipped in Austria—because, perhaps, it is so scarce.

"Fritz had, as I have said, had a sweetheart.

"She was young, pretty, and had expensive tastes.

"He was young, handsome, and had no money.

"Consequently, when she asked him to make her a present, he had to put her off with a variety of excuses, and talk vaguely about a future day which would put him in possession of some little patrimony, a little farm of a few acres, situated in some outlandish place, the name of which she had never heard.

"It was, of course, a difficult matter for either of us to approach. With all his love of money and his desire to appear grand before his sweetheart, he might yet have sufficient patriotism left in him to prevent him from allowing those who were said to be the enemies of his country to escape.

"When, however, Fritz saw displayed before him a seemingly unlimited quantity of English gold, it was easy to perceive, by the glisten of his eye, that he would do almost anything to obtain it.

"'Fritz,' I said to him one day, 'we have nothing to amuse ourselves in this dull place, and want to try some experiments.'

"'Very well, gentlemen,' he said, 'you are at liberty to do as you please.'

"'Very likely,' I said, 'but in order to succeed in this experiment we must have a rope.'

"Fritz was no fool; few Germans are.

"He started and looked intently at us. 'You are joking, gentlemen,' he said. 'Indeed no,' I replied, 'I am not joking; but we have made bets in regard to the depth of these walls, and without a rope we cannot tell who is in the right.'

"'You will probably have to go to the bottom, one of you to make the experiment complete.'

"'Just so, Fritz,' I replied; 'in fact we intend to escape.'

"Fritz turned pale.

"'You are jesting, I hope, gentlemen,' he said. 'If you were to escape you would ruin me.'

"'Of course, we are jesting,' I said; 'but, seriously speaking, tell me what you would lose if it were known that you were aiding us in escaping.'

"Fritz looked very doleful at this.

"'Well,' he said, 'first of all, I should lose my situation; and then, if I did not prove very satisfactorily that I had no hand in the matter, I should lose my head.'

"'Your situation is worth about a pound a week to you,' I said.

"'Quite that,' he said, seriously.

"'So that it would take you ten years to get five hundred pounds.'

"Fritz nodded, as though he did not quite understand our meaning.

"'Well, to be plain,' I added, 'we will save you the trouble of waiting all that interminable long time.'

"'We want this rope, as we have said—a good stout rope, that will bear our weight down yonder immense depth, and we will give you five hundred pounds for it.'

"Fritz looked incredulous.

"Well he might, considering how much that sum of money was to him in his poverty, and how little it was to us in comparison with liberty.

"We soon, however, convinced him that we meant what we said.

"We took from our pockets handsful of English gold, and showed it to him, at the same time handing him one or two pieces for himself.

"'I will see what I can do,' he said, pocketing the money with a grunt of satisfaction.

"On the following day, as he made no reference, however, to our idea of escape, we ventured to remind him that, however easy he might be on the subject, we were in a state of terrible anxiety.

"He shrugged his shoulders.

"'I am going to do all I can,' he said, 'but you must not be impatient. The idea of the rope is absurd; it must be done some other way. The depth from these ramparts to the moat is one hundred and twenty feet. If I were to attempt to bring into the prison sufficient to enable you to escape, I should certainly be discovered, unless, indeed, I was to bring it in small quantities. If I were to do that I might succeed just by the time the old gaoler had recovered and returned.'

"It was in vain to question him on the new plan that had entered his head.

"He merely said we should see.

"When we parted for the day we began to fear that the stolid German would not be satisfied by the small amount of money he had received from us, and would put us off now with promises.

"But we had entirely mistaken his character.

"On the evening of that very day he entered my cell suddenly.

"So suddenly and quiet, in fact, that I never even heard his feet along the stone corridor.

"What surprised me most of all was the fact that, in spite of the rules of the prison, he had brought Lord Riverdale with him.

"He entered, and carefully locked the door behind him.

"'Gentlemen,' he said, 'an opportunity has occurred such as will seldom occur again. If you are brave and are willing to fall in with my plans, escape for one of you is immediate and certain.'

"'For one of us!' we exclaimed in a breath; 'why not for both?'

"Fritz shrugged his shoulders in his usual way.

"'I cannot do impossibilities,' he said. 'If one of you escape, he can assist in the escape of the other. What I propose is this—that you should draw lots for escape, and the one who wins can be freed within an hour. I shall then only want half the money.'

"There was not much time for thought.

"Fritz evidently meant business.

"And so, without any further delay, and without any foolish attempts at magnanimity which we could not have felt, we proceeded to draw lots.

"A minute decided it.

"I was the winner.

"Lord Riverdale acted nobly. The slightest shade of disappointment crossed his features.

"But it vanished in a moment.

"'I congratulate you, my friend,' he said, giving me a hearty shake of the hand. 'And now, friend Fritz, tell us what is your plan?'

"'It is one,' replied the German, 'that, as I have said before, requires some courage; but that, of course, will be no impediment.

"'This morning one of the prisoners died. He

THE RIVAL APPRENTICES

A TALE OF THE RIOTS OF 1780.

A STRANGE DUEL.

was very near the time of his release, and would not, of course, be buried in the prison if his friends claimed the body.

"'It happens, however, that this poor unfortunate had no friends, and he would have been buried in the prison yard had not the bright idea occurred to me.

"'My Gretchen, of course, is in my secret, as in a few days I shall fly for ever from this part of the country.

"'I induced her, therefore, to come this morning and represent herself as the sister of the dead man, and claim his body.

"'This evening the coffin will leave the prison, but instead of the dead body it must contain this brave gentleman, who has won the lot.'

"The proposition was at once agreed upon.

"We followed Fritz, and quietly and noiselessly we made our way along the corridor to the dead-house.

"Fritz advanced boldly, opened the door, and without any ceremony showed us the body lying there in still and solemn state.

"'Now,' he said, 'we must dispose of him first.'

"'What are we going to do with him?' I asked.

"'We must take him out of the coffin," replied the gaoler, 'and carry him to the top of the battlements, whence we must hurl him into the moat.'

"'But the body will be found.'

"'Fear not,' returned Fritz. 'I will accompany Gretchen and her "brother," and together we will dig his grave.'

"'Well, then,' said I, all impatience, 'let us begin at once.'

"We soon took the unfortunate convict out of his narrow bed.

"Then we carried him as noiselessly as we could up the staircase.

"In a few moments we stood on the ramparts.

"Then a few heaves, and the body was launched into mid-air.

"A few instants of stillness.

"Then a loud, dull thud.

"The body had fallen on the earth beyond the moat.

"Nothing could have happened better.

"If it had fallen into the moat, perhaps the loud splash would have roused some of the sentinels.

"We descended to the dead-house once more, and here I thought it high time to pay my reckoning before entering the coffin.

"So into the trembling hands of Fritz I paid the two hundred and fifty pounds in gold and Bank of England notes.

"Then they helped me into the wooden box, and after Fritz had made some holes in the side to enable me to breathe, the lid was screwed down.

"It was an awful time for me.

"Perfectly helpless as I was, a torrent of ideas rushed into my brain.

"What if this man played me false?

"What if, now he had got the money, he were to resolve to save himself by destroying me?

"This was an agonising thought.

"But it was of no use complaining, even to myself.

"There I was, and I must abide by the consequences.

"Besides, after all, would not death be preferable to a lengthening of my term of imprisonment?

"So I remained perfectly still.

"Half an hour I waited there, thinking it was an age.

"Then I heard the tramp of men's feet, and presently a number of men entered the dead-house.

"They hoisted me up on their shoulders and carried me jolting and carelessly along the stone corridor— so carelessly, indeed, that every moment I expected they would let me fall on the pavement.

"However, we reached the front door in safety, and there I heard the soft voice of a girl, saying—

"'Is this he?'

"'Yes,' said Fritz. 'Have you the cart here?'

"'Yes.'

"'Very well, then, I'll drive it round for you,' he added, carelessly. 'Here, Hans, see to the gate till I return.'

"In a few minutes we were jolting away along the rough country road, and we were not long before we reached the spot where had been thrown the dead body from the ramparts.

"Here Fritz stopped the cart, and unscrewed the coffin lid.

"And as soon as I quitted my uncomfortable bed, we descended from the cart, and placed the dead prisoner in his proper receptacle.

"Then we started off at a rapid trot towards the cottage of Gretchen.

"In spite of my joy at my own deliverance, my thoughts soon reverted to my friend, whom I had left behind without a companion in the gloomy fortress.

"I was bound by my oath to save him; and I resolved that, as soon as I succeeded in reaching the spot where Alexis Rainsford was, I would commence operations.

"My reflections were abruptly terminated by the cart stopping at a little cottage.

"Gretchen got down and at once opened the door.

"We quickly followed, and to my surprise and delight I was met by Alexis Rainsford.

"Fritz, who since my starting him in life, as he said, had become my firm and fast friend, had prepared this little surprise for me.

"'It is scarcely safe to stay long,' said Alexis; 'but, at any rate, you have time to rest yourself and take a little refreshment here. They will not discover your flight until the morning.'

"'No; and I do not wish to go too far away,' I answered; 'for I am sworn to aid my companion to escape.'

"'Yes, yes,' replied Alexis; 'and I shall never feel happy in quitting Austria without him.'

"For hours we sat there trying to invent plans to assist Guy Riverdale.

"But in vain.

"On the following morning Fritz took us to a wild, deserted place among the hills.

"Here, in a long unoccupied shepherd's hut, he left us, while he returned to the prison to see how the land lay.

"He returned in less than three hours, pale and terrified.

"Gretchen was with him.

"He had not been to the prison, for when he approached it he met one of the warders, who had informed him that the supreme governor of the

State prison had arrived the night before, and had discovered my escape.

"The warder was an old friend of Fritz.

"'If you have anything to do with this escape,' he said, 'you had better fly at once.'

"'We must escape while we have time,' said Fritz, when he had told his story, 'for very likely before another hour the country will be scoured in search of me.'

"We started off, and rapidly passed through a village, where he obtained a quantity of provisions, and then made for another hut high up the mountains, where Fritz declared we could remain for a long time concealed.

"We were not pursued to our mountain retreat.

"However, we found not the slightest chance of effecting the escape of Lord Riverdale, and we at last resolved to come to England and organise a party of adventurers for his deliverance."

As soon as Hugh Grandley had finished his story there was silence for a few minutes.

Then, after a few whispered words to his wife, Simon asked his father to quit the room with him.

They returned after an absence of a quarter of an hour, and Hugh Grandley, with much emotion, approached Guy, saying—

"Allow me to be the first to congratulate you, Mr. Guy Riverdale, on the acquisition of a name and a father. You shall be leader of the band which we will organise to wrest him from the power of a cruel tyrant."

We will not linger over this scene.

Suffice it to say that the proofs which Hugh Grandley had seen were all-sufficient to prove that Guy the Foundling had a name at last, and that instead of being a friendless waif and stray, he was now the Honourable Guy Riverdale, and heir to a splendid barony.

CHAPTER XXVII.

THE FIRST ATTEMPT AT ESCAPE.

A FEW words are enough to explain to our readers what happened at the smugglers' cave after the terrible explosion.

When Aurora fell into the arms of Alexis Rainsford, she had but fainted from the effects of the shock; and though she remained some time insensible, she had not suffered any real injury.

They did not stop to see what havoc they had made, or what injury had been caused among the smugglers by the explosion.

Immediately entering their boats they made off to their ship, and, without any opposition, they passed on board and made for England, with the loss of only three men, and of these were none of our hero's friends.

There appeared no necessity for the assistance of Simon Grandley or any of his friends in the affair of the Grandley estate.

Hugh Grandley, therefore, quitted them for a few days, bidding his son look out for some brave fellows who would assist him in the adventure in the strange land.

At the end of six days he returned.

The estates had been formally delivered over to him, and he was now in possession of plenty of money.

Simon Grandley and his friends had not been idle.

Six of the stoutest young fellows known to the carpenter and his apprentices (among whom, by-the-bye, Guy must no longer be reckoned), had offered to join them as much for the love of adventure as the promise of reward.

With Simon and his father, Guy Riverdale, Will Lightmore, Alexis Rainsford, and Robert Hallwyn, the band of deliverers numbered twelve.

After many adieus, and kisses and embraces, the little band set forth.

They arrived in Vienna safe and sound.

Arms and ammunition were there seen to, and having borrowed horses at an inn, they started by night for the mountains.

It would, indeed have been a gain to them had they but been able to obtain a knowledge of the whereabouts of Fritz.

But this, of course, was impossible.

Fritz had, no doubt, fled across the frontier into France or into Prussia, and with his Gretchen had probably settled down on a little farm or in a business under another name.

Hugh Grandley succeeded in leading his little band under the very shadow of the fortress.

Here an unexpected piece of good fortune awaited them.

The little cottage of Gretchen stood there empty.

The door was open, and there was no reason why they should not take possession of it as a temporary sleeping place.

So securing the door, they lay down in their clothes on the floor and slept till morning.

Their plan of operations was simple.

But yet it was one which offered a fair chance of success.

They resolved to appear in parties of twos and threes, and pass to and fro beneath the walls during the time which Hugh Grandley knew to be the exercise time of Lord Riverdale.

If he saw and recognised them an air gun was to be discharged in the direction of the ramparts, containing a small ball of lead which was attached at the end of a long piece of silk.

To this silk would be attached a long string, and to the string a rope, which was to be drawn up at dusk and put in use at once.

They walked accordingly to and fro.

At length, to their no small joy, they saw the prisoner leaning over the parapet.

On seeing the forms of men crossing and recrossing, and casting evidently eager glances up at the prison, he at once sprang erect.

Hope long dead leaped once more into his heart.

"By heavens! they are friends," he murmured, exultingly, as he saw them making signs, "and if I mistake not that tall and noble form belongs to none other than Hugh Grandley. What do they mean?"

They were waving him to go back, and as soon as he understood what they meant he retired to the back of the yard.

Then, without any report, the bullet came whizzing through the air and fell at his feet.

Round it was wrapped a piece of paper, and he could see at once as he picked it up the thin silk attached.

On the paper were directions and congratulations, while at the bottom were the words—

"Be careful, be courageous; I have found your son, and he is here to aid in your escape."

Who shall tell the torrent of emotion that swelled the breast of Lord Riverdale as he read the letter?

But he kept down his feelings.

He must work, and that carefully.

How was he to draw up the rope without attracting the notice of the sentinel on the rampart just above him?

At any rate he must make the trial; so, fixing the bullet as well as he could in a niche of the old wall, he re-entered his gloomy cell and brought out a book.

With this he seated himself at one end of the battlements, and began to pretend to read.

While seated here he slowly and cautiously drew up the silk until the end of the string came to his hand.

Then he broke off the silk and flung it over, and began hauling up the rope.

At length the end of the rope touched his hand and sent a thrill through his frame.

It seemed the first step towards freedom.

But now came the question to what part of the battlements could he safely secure the end of the rope?

He was just cogitating upon this when he heard a slight noise, and saw the sentinel making his way from the upper ramparts.

Something seemed to tell him that his movements had been observed.

What was to be done?

He had but a moment to think.

To be found with a rope in his hand would be to court close imprisonment morning, noon, and night in his solitary cell.

So he formed the brave resolution of dropping it.

Not without a pause did he determine upon this, for it seemed like wilfully throwing his liberty from him.

But from the man's manner he saw something was certainly wrong, and so, letting the heavy rope run, he felt the last of the twine rush through his fingers just as the man approached him.

"You are busy to-day," said the man.

"Busy reading — yes," replied Lord Riverdale.

He knew well that the sentry could see nothing in the moat below.

"No, I do not allude to reading," said the man, who hoped to obtain money from the governor by his discovery; "I allude to what you were drawing up from below."

As he said this, there came a sinister, unpleasant grin upon his features.

Lord Riverdale sprang up with well-assumed indignation.

"I insist upon being searched," he cried, "now

at once, and in the morning I shall bring your conduct before the governor of this prison."

The man, seeing him so confident, hesitated.

But Lord Riverdale was determined now, and making the man enter the cell, he caused a thorough search of his person to be made.

Of course, nothing was found.

"Now," he said, "perhaps this will teach you civility. To-morrow, perhaps, will see you removed.

The sentinel was profuse in his apologies, and went away.

But he remained unconvinced.

"If I did not see him hauling up something from below, then I'm a blind man."

However, there was but little more time for the prisoner's promenade that evening, so he walked up and down once more, never even observing his prisoner.

Lord Riverdale, as may be supposed, took immediate advantage of this.

The rope was gone beyond his reach.

But he had with him a pencil, and on the fly-leaf of the book he wrote—

"Discovered at the last moment. I therefore have dropped the rope into the moat. Recover it before morning."

He waited patiently, and presently one of the "peasants," an unusual quantity of whom seemed to have passed to and fro, went by at a quick pace, casting a hurried glance up at the battlements.

Then, when the back of the sentinel was turned, he flung it over.

The "peasant" watched the fluttering note as it descended, and, having seen the spot where it fell, hastened away.

Consternation was general in the minds of all when they read the missive of Lord Riverdale.

But still they were not discouraged.

On the next day, however, they kept very close, only sending one of their number at a time to watch the prison.

Towards evening, a second letter fell.

It was longer than the first, and explained in full the whole occurrence.

The idea of again attempting to effect the escape of Lord Riverdale by means of a rope was at once abandoned as useless.

The sentinel who had discovered him in the first instance would undoubtedly keep watch upon the prisoner more earnestly than ever.

After a long and earnest discussion, therefore, it was resolved to adopt a new system of tactics altogether; a more daring one, too.

Where stratagem had failed, force might prevail.

On the morning following their deliberations, two of their number were deputed to watch for the appearance of the prisoner on the ramparts of the old fort.

As soon as he made his appearance an air-gun was pointed towards him, and in another moment a bullet fell at his feet as before.

He picked it up eagerly, after a glance round him to see that no one was near.

Then, opening it, he read as follows—

"Drop a letter to-day into the moat. Tell us the number of men in the prison; state what time the last rounds are; and whether the governor of the fort is at his post. Keep up your courage. Your escape may appear slow, but it will be certain. We shall remain here till you are free."

Lord Riverdale carefully jotted down, as far as lay in his power, the strength of the garrison of the State prison, and the other details they desired.

This letter he wrapped round the bullet, and flung far away towards the high road.

During the night, dark as it was, Guy the Foundling contrived to find it.

"Twenty men only," cried he, enthusiastically, as he read the letter; "why there will be no difficulty whatever in overcoming them. Let us go on at once and attack the place. I am on fire while my father is still in the power of these villains."

"Patience," said Hugh Grandley; "it would be of no avail to proceed further now. Do you not see by your father's own letter that the warders have already gone their last round? We must defer our attempt until to-morrow night."

Before dawn Hugh Grandley started upon a secret mission.

Making his way along the high road for about a mile, he came to a tavern.

The object of Hugh Grandley in visiting this inn, was to ascertain as far as he could the character of Herr Hoffman, the governor of the gaol.

He hoped, in fact, to discover, some peculiar prejudice or idiosyncracy by which he could approach him without the necessity of using force.

The disguise he had assumed was that of a Hungarian farmer, and he had so bespattered himself with mud on his short journey that he looked as if he had come hundreds of miles.

When he entered the public room he found himself in the presence of a number of Austrian peasants of the better class, with whom he soon put himself on good terms by ordering and paying for an immense quantity of the famous lager.

"You seem to have come a long journey," said one of the farmers, as they seated themselves round the comfortable fire.

"Yes," replied Hugh Grandley, speaking with an accent which they took to be Hungarian; "I have come some hundreds of miles, and the end of my voyage is to be a prison."

"Why, what do you mean?" said one of the peasants.

"Well, to tell you the truth," said Hugh Grandley, "I have come to visit the governor; I bring him glad news from Hungary. A relation of his there has just died and left him a lot of money."

"It is to be hoped that he has left him the guardianship of a pretty daughter as well," said one of the farmers; "that's more in his line."

Hugh Grandley pricked up his ears. He had accidentally hit upon a peculiarity of the governor at last.

"Is he fond of the ladies, then?" he said.

The men laughed in chorus.

Then they looked at one another, and again burst into a loud laugh, in which Hugh Grandley could not refrain from joining.

"Are you a friend of his?" asked one.

"Not I; I never saw him."

"Never saw the little rat! the little baboon! Why he's a perfect oddity—a regular sensualist, and worshipper of the fair sex, and yet as ugly as sin, and not more than four feet and a half high. He thinks all the women are in love with him, and is mad for girls about seventeen or eighteen, who only refrain from laughing at the old imbecile because they want his money."

This and a good deal more to the same effect escaped from the lips of the Austrian peasants, and, while laughing with them and enjoying the joke, Hugh Grandley digested a plan.

He then quitted the inn, declining any more refreshment, and made his way with all possible speed back towards his friends.

CHAPTER XXVIII.

HERR HOFFMAN HAS A YOUNG LADY VISITOR.

HERR HOFFMAN was in appearance about the last man you would have thought fit for the governorship of a State prison.

Although not, perhaps, quite so diminutive as he was said to be by the Austrian peasants, he was, nevertheless, certainly under five feet.

In spite of his diminutive size, however, he ruled the prison with a rod of iron, and the men obeyed without a murmur.

On the evening of the day on which Hugh Grandley paid his visit to the tavern, Herr Hoffman was seated in his study when a knock came at the door, and a man servant entered bearing a letter.

This was an unusual thing, and Herr Hoffman took it with undisguised eagerness.

His face was suffused with pleasure as he gazed on the superscription.

It was in a female hand.

"Ha, ha!" said the little baboon to himself, as he tore the missive open, "there is here perhaps a pleasurable surprise for me."

His pleasure seemed to turn to annoyance as he began perusing the note, but was soon again succeeded by a smile.

The letter ran as follows—

"DEAR FRIEND HOFFMAN,

"You have not, I am certain, forgotten your cousin Gertrude."

"Not likely," growled Hoffman; "as ugly as sin and without a penny. But let me see")—

"She has just died, and left me here friendless and alone. I am not without money, but, though my neighbours are very kind to me, I do not care to remain here among comparative strangers. Although I was but four years old when I saw you, I still remember your face, and my mother often spoke to me of your kindness."

The letter went on to say how much she wished to see him again, and that she was on her way then to the prison.

"In fact," said the writer, "I shall very likely reach the castle almost as soon as my letter."

"Well, that's what I call deuced cool," said the governor of the prison, as he threw himself back in his chair ; "but still, if she is good-looking and likes to make herself agreeable, I shall let her stop."

The words were scarcely out of his mouth when the door opened, and the man servant who had before entered said—

"Herr Hoffman, there is a young lady below who desires to speak to you."

The eyes of the little baboon-like German glittered with pleasure.

"Bring her up at once," said he, "and say that I have been expecting her."

In a few minutes the man returned, and ushered into the room a tall young lady, of a handsome, although a bold, cast of features.

"My darling cousin !" she said, and rushing forward she caught the little governor in her arms and hugged him in such an embrace that when at last he was released he fell half-suffocated into his chair.

"Der Teuffel !" he muttered to himself, "these young women from the provinces are very strong. She has nearly killed me. But she is a handsome wench, and I will not let her see that I am at all astonished by her reception of me.

"There, sit down there, Annette," he said, "and tell me about your mother's death ; and you, Hans, bring in some supper and some wine."

When Hans brought in the meal the governor and his handsome visitor were sitting very cosily together by the fire.

So things went on for three days.

On the evening of the third day, however, there was such a commotion in the governor's room as had never been heard before.

The smash of a lot of glass had plainly been heard, and then the unmistakable clashing of swords.

Hans and another of the men made for the room, where, on opening the door, they found the governor and his fair guest standing in the centre of the room with crossed swords, and evidently in the middle of a fierce conflict.

CHAPTER XXIX.

THE EXPLANATION OF A MYSTERY.

The morning following her arrival Annette breakfasted early with the governor.

It was then arranged, at her special request, that she should be shown over the prison.

This was put in practice directly after breakfast.

Annette seemed highly delighted.

Presently they neared the prison yard, and looked out upon it from the door.

"Who is that tall, noble-looking man ?" she asked, pointing to Lord Riverdale, who was pacing to and fro.

"Oh !" said Herr Hoffman, "he belongs to a different class of prisoners from those ruffians you have just seen. He is a political prisoner."

"Oh !" returned Annette ; "he is a gentleman, then ?"

"Yes."

"Oh ! do let us speak to him," cried Annette. "It will be a pleasure for him."

"True," said Herr Hoffman. "Come with me, and I will introduce you to him."

Lord Riverdale bowed low as they approached.

He spoke very little, however, though he could not avoid the belief that the young lady was trying to catch his eye.

She succeeded at last.

Then she put her finger to her lip, in token that he was to restrain his feelings, and said—

"You have friends in Austria, have you not ?"

"I have reason to believe so."

"Then be assured they will not much longer leave you here."

Then, turning to Herr Hoffman, she added—

"Can you believe they will leave him here all his life ?"

"I hope, indeed, it will not be so," he said ; "but, at any rate, you see I am not responsible. But come, Annette, see what a view Lord Riverdale has from his exercise ground."

And he led her to the ramparts.

Leaning over here, Annette, who stood next to Lord Riverdale, drew something from her pocket.

It was a short, narrow parcel wrapped in paper.

The conversation now became rapid and general, and Annette's laughter was loud and her gestures full of animation.

During this time she contrived to pass the parcel to Lord Riverdale.

He did not pause to look at it then.

He quickly transferred it to his pocket, but when presently in his cell he looked at it, he found it to be a loaded pistol.

Annette, then, was an emissary of his friends !

That day and the next passed.

And so came the evening of the third day of Annette's visit.

On this occasion Annette expressed a desire to sup early.

During the meal Hoffman was particularly loving.

"Do you know, Annette," he said at length, edging his chair up close to her, "do you know, Annette, that you're a deucedly handsome girl ?"

"Am I ?" said the girl, complacently.

"Yes ; and I've half a mind to fall in love with you."

Annette burst into a loud laugh.

"Oh ! that would be funny," she cried.

Herr Hoffman did not exactly see the joke.

But he dissembled his feelings.

"Yes," he continued, "you see you're not at all rich—you've not much chance of making a good match. In fact, as you will not be going into society at all, you won't have the chance of making any. Now I'm rich—I've no one to love or to leave my money to. Suppose you stop with me altogether, and—and—be my own little Annette —my own—eh ! what ?"

He had been on the point of sealing the bargain with a kiss.

But Annette drew a line at kissing.

She pushed him against the table, and down he went, supper, glasses, and all, in one heap on the floor.

The little wretch rose to his feet, smeared with wine and jellies, and, choking with rage, he drew his sword, shrieking—

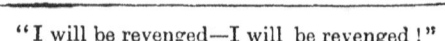

"I will be revenged—I will be revenged!"

Seeing this, Annette, who was convulsed with laughter, seized a sword from the place where it hung over the chimney-piece.

With mouth foaming with rage, and his little goggle eyes starting from his head, Hoffman attacked furiously the girl who had dared thus to beard him in his den.

It was in the middle of this ludicrous scene that the door was burst open and two of the domestics entered.

Herr Hoffman, finding himself decidedly getting the worst of it, shouted out at the top of his voice, as he retreated rapidly—

"Take off this mad woman. She will be the death of me."

Annette, however, seemed to be in no way desirous of following up her victory.

Being assured that Herr Hoffman was no longer able to do any harm, she subsided into a chair and indulged in a most unfeminine burst of laughter.

"Take him away—take this little wretch away," she cried, "or I shall really die with laughter."

This was too much for the risible faculties of the maid servant and her companion.

They fairly roared with laughter, and Herr Hoffman, having in vain endeavoured to awe them into subjection by a look (which only made him look more ridiculous), stalked off to his room.

"Pray," said Annette, as soon as she had in some measure recovered from her exuberant gaiety, "pray bring me some wine. You see, Herr Hoffman has emptied all the bottles, and this scene has made me quite faint."

The serving-maid at once quitted the room.

As soon as she was gone Annette underwent a complete transformation.

Her female habiliments were thrown off in a twinkling, and there she stood before the eyes of the astonished man-servant a young man dressed in plain Austrian civil costume.

The amazement of the young girl when she returned and saw Annette's transformation was comical to see, and the peals of laughter which resounded once more through the room reached the ears of the wretched little governor, and set him pacing to and fro foaming with rage.

"I'll put that fellow in irons, and as for Annette and that cursed maid, I'll have them publicly flogged!" he spluttered forth.

He would have sworn more had he but known that Annette was none other than our versatile, comedy-loving, courageous friend Will Lightmore.

The idea had been put into his head when Hugh Grandley had narrated his interview with the Austrian farmers.

He at once proposed to take advantage of the peculiar love of Herr Hoffman for the fair sex, and use it as a means of bringing about Lord Riverdale's release.

He bought some ladies' finery at the neighbouring town, and primed himself well with the story of Gertrude, Herr Hoffman's cousin, of whom Hugh Grandley had heard from the farmers.

So far so good.

But now came a still more difficult part of the task.

This was the release of Lord Riverdale.

However, he had with him the means of making this easy.

Carefully he contrived to pour some powder into two glasses.

Then he poured out some wine.

"Drink some of the old fellow's best Rhenish," he said, and handed a glass to each of the two servants.

They drank with him, nothing loth, and were soon wrapped in the heavy sleep of insensibility.

The man who acted as personal servant to Herr Hoffman was also the keeper of the keys, and Will at once proceeded to search him.

Finding the keys, he quitted the room, and crept along the dark corridor.

He soon reached Lord Riverdale's cell, and throwing it open entered.

It was in total darkness.

"Who is there?" asked the prisoner.

"Hush!" said Will Lightmore. "It is I—a friend."

Rapidly Will explained who he was, and the ruse he had employed.

"And now," said Riverdale, "what is your next move?"

"We must go on the ramparts and strike a light. It will tell our friends that we are waiting for them. They will then come round to the front gate, where they can aid us in the attack.

"Then we must let loose all the prisoners, and give them their liberty, on condition that they assist us in the attack upon the warders."

No time was lost.

They issued forth at once into the exercise yard.

On reaching the ramparts, Will drew from his pocket a small firework, and setting a light to it, flung it up into the air, where it burst into flame without noise.

Then they made their way towards the first row of cells.

There were about four and twenty prisoners in the gaol, who, on being told that their escape depended upon overcoming the warders at the gate, needed no further incitement to exertion.

Before any one of the guardians of the prison was aware than anything unusual had happened, the six men in the guard-room found themselves surrounded by the prisoners.

They knew well that all the men before them wanted was liberty, and without attempting any resistance they advanced to the gate, at which a loud knocking was already to be heard.

The ponderous, iron-bound portal was soon swung open, and the prisoners passed out into the night.

All Lord Riverdale's friends were mounted, and two horses were there in readiness for Will Lightmore and the rescued captive.

As for the other prisoners, they were, of course, to go whither they liked, and having bade them good night, and counselled them to be off as quick as possible to the mountains, our party of friends galloped off towards Vienna, and arrived after a tedious journey safely in London.

————

CHAPTER XXX.
CONCLUSION.

WHEN Dick Hatherden threw the keg of powder into the bonfire his firm resolution had been to destroy himself and Aurora Halsted.

However, as his good luck or ill luck would have it, he was spared.

Stunned and bleeding he lay for some time.

But that was all.

He recovered to find the morning sun streaming on his face, and the place deserted.

He resolved to remain there during the day.

When evening at length came round he was in wondrous good humour with himself.

He had eaten well, and had, moreover, imbibed an immense quantity of the spirits which were stored in the cave below.

There he sat then that evening beside a large fire he had made up, ignorant of the fact that a face was peering in at him from the window.

"Yes," he said to himself, rubbing his hands, "there's no doubt now that I'm in a queer way. Somehow or another I've lost all that cursed money I had saved up, and I must get some more. I don't much care how. I heard old Hardy say that the Government had offered a large reward for the capture and breaking up of the smuggler band. That's my game. I'll go and split on the lot, get the money, and be off to America."

As he spoke there was a knock at the door.

He started up, expecting naturally that it was some emissary of the revenue officers.

In a moment or two the door swung open.

Those who entered, Dick Hatherden with a kind of guilty conscience recognised at once.

They were Hardy, the captain, and the rest of the smugglers.

"Well, you're a long time opening the door," cried Hardy, gruffly, as they closed and barred the door behind them. "What made you so long?"

"I took you for revenue officers."

"Ah! I dare say," said Hardy, with a quiet irony that somewhat alarmed Dick. "Here, let's have some of that grog ; you seem to be making yourself comfortable. Here, you fellows," he added, turning to his men, "here, take a swig, and then go down and bring up that barrel of powder."

With a grim smile the men drank the proffered grog, and then descended into the cavern.

Dick Hatherden began to feel uncomfortable.

"What are you going to do with that powder?" he said, with a sickly smile. "Are you going to blow up the Dutchmen in their beds?"

"Well, that's just it," said Hardy; "there is going to be a blow up. Here they come. Easy there—don't burst it. Stand it there on its end. So—that's right—now then, seize him."

In an instant Dick Hatherden found himself seized without the chance of helping himself; and before he well knew what they meant he was seated on top of the barrel of gunpowder, bound and helpless.

Terror was piteously delineated in every feature.

"Why, what does this mean?" he cried. "Have you all taken leave of your senses?"

Hardy smiled.

"No," he said, "but I fancy you have. Do you see that window with the broken pane?"

"Yes."

"Well, you see we can hear exactly what is said in here and we heard all you said. I won't advise you not to do so again, because you won't have the chance. We heard all your plans for making a market of your treachery to us—selling us to the Government and bolting with the money. But you won't get the chance. Wherever you're going, you'll go by a swift journey ; so, if you've prayers to say, say them quickly."

So saying, the resolute smuggler, who had never before taken a man's life except in self-defence, knocked in the bung of the cask and let a quantity of the powder run out on the ground.

Then he made a long train, and bade his men leave the place and stand at a long distance off.

At the end of ten minutes the smuggler, who had been waiting for a poker to become red hot, took it from the fire, and holding the door half-open fired the train.

One last despairing yell rose from the throat of the maddened victim.

Then, with the speed of a hare, Hardy dashed away.

He had not time to regain his comrades; but after going a sufficient distance to escape danger he flung himself on his face.

Then a terrific explosion rent the air and fairly made the earth tremble.

Amid the debris of the shattered hut it was impossible to distinguish the body of Dick Hatherden, and when they searched the spot not an atom of it could be seen!

Such was the end of a wicked and useless life.

* * * * * *

We have now little more to add.

Our hero and his friends arrived safely in England, and within a week the whole party was assembled at the lovely country seat of Lord Riverdale.

In a fortnight after this the bells of the village church rang out a merry peal, and at the altar there stood three of the handsomest and happiest couples that ever were gathered together for the ceremony of marriage.

Need we say that these were Guy Riverdale (no longer the Foundling) and sweet Minnie Grandley, Alexis Rainsford and Aurora Halsted, and last, not least, Betty and Will Lightmore, for whom a pretty but small estate had been bought in the neighbourhood by Lord Riverdale and Hugh Grandley.

THE END.